no second chance

Also by Harlan Coben

HARLAN COBEN

no second chance

DOUBLEDAY LARGE PRINT HOME LIBRARY EDITION

DUTTON

This Large Print Edition, prepared especially for Doubleday Large Print Home Library, contains the complete, unabridged text of the original Publisher's Edition.

DUTTON
Published by Penguin Group (USA) Inc., 375 Hudson Street, New York, New York 10014, U.S.A.
Penguin Books Ltd, 80 Strand, London WC2R 0RL, England
Penguin Books Australia Ltd, 250 Camberwell Road, Camberwell, Victoria 3124, Australia
Penguin Books Canada Ltd, 10 Alcorn Avenue, Toronto, Ontario, Canada M4V 3B2
Penguin Books (N.Z.) Ltd, Cnr Rosedale and Airborne Roads, Albany, Auckland 1310, New Zealand

Penguin Books Ltd, Registered Offices: Harmondsworth, Middlesex, England

Published by Dutton, a member of Penguin Group (USA) Inc.

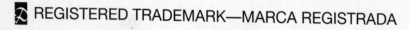 REGISTERED TRADEMARK—MARCA REGISTRADA

ISBN 0-7394-3470-5

Printed in the United States of America

This Large Print Book carries the
Seal of Approval of N.A.V.H.

In loving memory of my mother-in-law,
Nancy Armstrong

And in celebration of her grandchildren:

Thomas, Katharine, McCallum, Reilly, Charlotte,
Dovey, Benjamin, Will, Ana, Eve, Mary, Sam,
Caleb, and Annie

no second chance

chapter 1

When the first bullet hit my chest, I thought of my daughter.

At least, that is what I want to believe. I lost consciousness pretty fast. And, if you want to get technical about it, I don't even remember being shot. I know that I lost a lot of blood. I know that a second bullet skimmed the top of my head, though I was probably already out by then. I know that my heart stopped. But I still like to think that as I lay dying, I thought of Tara.

FYI: I saw no bright light or tunnel. Or if I did, I don't remember that either.

Tara, my daughter, is only six months old. She was lying in her crib. I wonder if the gunfire frightened her. It must have. She probably began to cry. I wonder if the familiar albeit grating sound of her cries somehow sliced through my haze, if on some level I actually heard her. But again I have no memory of it.

What I do remember, however, was the moment Tara was born. I remember Monica—that's Tara's mother—bearing down for one last push. I remember the head appearing. I was the first to see my daughter. We all know about life's forks in the road. We all know about opening one door and closing another, life cycles, the changes in seasons. But the moment your child is born . . . it's beyond surreal. You have walked through a *Star Trek*–like portal, a full-fledged reality transformer. Everything is different. You are different, a simple element hit with a startling catalyst and metamorphosed into one far more complex. Your world is gone; it shrinks down to the dimensions of—in this case, anyway—a six-pound fifteen-ounce mass.

Fatherhood confuses me. Yes, I know that with only six months on the job, I am an amateur. My best friend, Lenny, has four kids. A girl and three boys. His oldest, Marianne, is ten, his youngest just turned one. With his face permanently set on happily harried and the floor of his SUV permanently stained with congealed fast food, Lenny reminds me that I know nothing yet. I agree. But when I get seriously lost or afraid in the realm of raising a child, I look at the helpless bundle in the crib and she looks up at me and I wonder what I would not do to protect her. I would lay down my life in a second. And truth be told, if push came to shove, I would lay down yours too.

So I like to think that as the two bullets pierced my body, as I collapsed onto the linoleum of my kitchen floor with a half-eaten granola bar clutched in my hand, as I lay immobile in a spreading puddle of my own blood, and yes, even as my heart stopped beating, that I still tried to do something to protect my daughter.

I came to in the dark.

I had no idea where I was at first, but then I heard the beeping coming from my right. A familiar sound. I did not move. I merely listened to the beeps. My brain felt as if it'd been marinated in molasses. The first impulse to break through was a primitive one: thirst. I craved water. I had never known a throat could feel so dry. I tried to call out, but my tongue had been dry-caked to the bottom of my mouth.

A figure entered the room. When I tried to sit up, hot pain ripped like a knife down my neck. My head fell back. And again, there was darkness.

When I awoke again, it was daytime. Harsh streaks of sunlight slashed through the venetian blinds. I blinked through them. Part of me wanted to raise my hand and block the rays, but exhaustion would not let the command travel. My throat was still impossibly parched.

I heard a movement and suddenly there was someone standing over me. I looked up and saw a nurse. The perspective, so different from the one I was used to, threw me. Nothing felt right. I was supposed to be the one standing looking down, not the other way around. A white hat—one of those small, harshly triangular numbers—sat like a bird's nest on the nurse's head. I've spent a great deal of my life working in a wide variety of hospitals, but I'm not sure I've ever seen a hat like that outside of TV or the movies. The nurse was heavyset and black.

"Dr. Seidman?"

Her voice was warm maple syrup. I managed a very slight nod.

The nurse must have read minds because she already had a cup of water in her hand. She put the straw between my lips and I sucked greedily.

"Slow down," she said gently.

I was going to ask where I was, but that seemed pretty obvious. I opened my mouth to find out what had happened, but again she was one step ahead of me.

"I'll go get the doctor," she said, heading for the door. "You just relax now."

I croaked, "My family . . ."

"I'll be right back. Try not to worry."

I let my eyes wander about the room. My vision had that medicated, shower-curtain haze. Still, there were enough stimuli getting through to make certain deductions. I was in a typical hospital room. That much was obvious. There was a drip bag and IV pump on my left, the tube snaking down to my arm. The fluorescent bulbs buzzed almost, but not quite, imperceptibly. A small TV on a swinging arm jutted out from the upper right-hand corner.

A few feet past the foot of the bed, there

was a large glass window. I squinted but could not see through it. Still, I was probably being monitored. That meant I was in an ICU. That meant that whatever was wrong with me was something pretty bad.

The top of my skull itched, and I could feel a pull at my hair. Bandaged, I bet. I tried to check myself out, but my head really did not want to cooperate. Dull pain quietly boomed inside me, though I couldn't tell from where it originated. My limbs felt heavy, my chest encased in lead.

"Dr. Seidman?"

I flicked my eyes toward the door. A tiny woman in surgical scrubs complete with the shower cap stepped into the room. The top of the mask was untied and dangled down her neck. I am thirty-four years old. She looked about the same.

"I'm Dr. Heller," she said, stepping closer. "Ruth Heller." Giving me her first name. Professional courtesy, no doubt. Ruth Heller gave me a probing stare. I tried to focus. My brain was still sluggish, but I could feel it sputtering to life. "You are at St. Elizabeth Hospital," she said in a properly grave voice.

The door behind her opened and a man

stepped inside. It was hard to see him clearly through the shower-curtain haze, but I don't think I knew him. The man crossed his arms and leaned against the wall with practiced casualness. Not a doctor, I thought. You work with them long enough, you can tell.

Dr. Heller gave the man a cursory glance and then she turned her full attention back to me.

"What happened?" I asked.

"You were shot," she said. Then added: "Twice."

She let that hang for a moment. I glanced toward the man against the wall. He hadn't moved. I opened my mouth to say something, but Ruth Heller pressed on. "One bullet grazed the top of your head. The bullet literally scraped off your scalp, which, as you probably know, is incredibly rich with blood."

Yes, I knew. Serious scalp wounds bled like beheadings. Okay, I thought, that explained the itch on top of my head. When Ruth Heller hesitated, I prompted her. "And the second bullet?"

Heller let out a breath. "That one was a bit more complicated."

I waited.

"The bullet entered your chest and nicked the pericardial sac. That caused a large supply of blood to leak into the space between your heart and the sac. The EMTs had trouble locating your vital signs. We had to crack your chest—"

"Doc?" the leaning man interrupted—and for a moment, I thought he was talking to me. Ruth Heller stopped, clearly annoyed. The man peeled himself off the wall. "Can you do the details later? Time is of the essence here."

She gave him a scowl, but there wasn't much behind it. "I'll stay here and observe," she said to the man, "if that's not a problem."

Dr. Heller faded back and now the man loomed over me. His head was too big for his shoulders so that you feared his neck would collapse from the weight of it. His hair was crew cut all around, except in the front, where it hung down in a Caesar line above his eyes. A soul patch, an ugly smear of growth, sat on his chin like a burrowing insect. All in all, he looked like a member of a boy band gone to serious seed. He smiled down at me, but there was no warmth behind it. "I'm Detective Bob Regan of the Kasselton Police Department," he said. "I know you're confused right now."

"My family—" I began.

"I'll get to that," he interrupted. "But right now, I need to ask you some questions, okay? Before we get into the details of what happened."

He waited for a response. I tried my best to clear the cobwebs and said, "Okay."

"What's the last thing you remember?"

I scanned my memory banks. I remembered waking up that morning, getting dressed. I remembered looking in on Tara. I remembered turning the knob on her black-n-white mobile, a gift from a colleague who insisted it would help stimulate a baby's brain or something. The mobile hadn't moved or bleated out its tinny song. The batteries were dead. I'd made a mental note to put in new ones. I headed downstairs after that.

"Eating a granola bar," I said.

Regan nodded as if he'd expected this answer. "You were in the kitchen?"

"Yes. By the sink."

"And then?"

I tried harder, but nothing came. I shook

my head. "I woke up once before. At night. I was here, I think."

"Nothing else?"

I reached out again but to no avail. "No, nothing."

Regan flipped out a pad. "Like the doc here told you, you were shot twice. You have no recollection of seeing a gun or hearing a shot or anything like that?"

"No."

"That's understandable, I guess. You were in a bad way, Marc. The EMTs thought you were a goner."

My throat felt dry again. "Where are Tara and Monica?"

"Stay with me, Marc." Regan was staring down at the pad, not at me. I felt the dread begin to press down on my chest. "Did you hear a window break?"

I felt groggy. I tried to read the label on the drip bag to see what they were numbing me with. No go. Pain medication, at the very least. Probably morphine in the IV pump. I tried to fight through the effects. "No," I said.

"You're sure? We found a broken window near the rear of the house. It may have been how the perpetrator gained entry."

"I don't remember a window breaking," I said. "Do you know who—"

Regan cut me off. "Not yet, no. That's why I'm here asking these questions. To find out who did this." He looked up from his pad. "Do you have any enemies?"

Did he really just ask me that? I tried to sit up, tried to gain some sort of angle on him, but there was no way that was going to happen. I did not like being the patient, on the wrong end of the bed, if you will. They say doctors make the worst patients. This sudden role reversal is probably why.

"I want to know about my wife and daughter."

"I understand that," Regan said, and something in his tone ran a cold finger across my heart. "But you can't afford the distraction, Marc. Not right yet. You want to be helpful, right? Then you need to stay with me here." He went back to the pad. "Now, what about enemies?"

Arguing with him any further seemed futile or even harmful, so I grudgingly acquiesced. "Someone who would shoot me?"

"Yes."

"No, no one."

"And your wife?" His eyes settled hard on

me. A favorite image of Monica—her face lighting up when we first saw Raymondkill Falls, the way she threw her arms around me in mock fear as the water crashed around us—rose like an apparition. "Did she have enemies?"

I looked at him. "Monica?"

Ruth Heller stepped forward. "I think that might be enough for now."

"What happened to Monica?" I asked.

Dr. Heller met up with Detective Regan, standing shoulder to shoulder. Both looked at me. Heller started to protest again, but I stopped her.

"Don't give me this protect-the-patient crap," I tried to shout, fear and fury battling against whatever had put my brain in this fuzz. "Tell me what happened to my wife."

"She's dead," Detective Regan said. Just like that. Dead. My wife. Monica. It was as if I hadn't heard him. The word couldn't reach me.

"When the police broke into your home, you had both been shot. They were able to save you. But it was too late for your wife. I'm sorry."

There was another quick flash now—Monica at Martha's Vineyard, on the beach, tan bathing suit, that black hair whipping across those cheekbones, giving me the razor-sharp smile. I blinked it away. "And Tara?"

"Your daughter," Regan began with a quick throat-clear. He looked at his pad again, but I don't think he planned on writing anything down. "She was home that morning, correct? I mean, at the time of the incident?"

"Yes, of course. Where is she?"

Regan closed the pad with a snap. "She was not at the scene when we arrived."

My lungs turned to stone. "I don't understand."

"We originally hoped that maybe she was in the care of a family member or friend. A baby-sitter even, but . . ." His voice faded.

"Are you telling me you don't know where Tara is?"

There was no hesitation this time. "Yes, that's correct."

It felt as if a giant hand were pushing down on my chest. I squeezed my eyes shut and fell back. "How long?" I asked.

"Has she been missing?"

"Yes."

Dr. Heller started speaking too quickly.

"You have to understand. You were very seriously injured. We were not optimistic you would survive. You were on a respirator. A lung collapsed. You also contracted sepsis. You're a doctor, so I know I don't have to explain to you how serious that is. We tried to slow down the meds, help you wake up—"

"How long?" I asked again.

She and Regan exchanged another glance, and then Heller said something that ripped the air out of me all over again. "You've been out for twelve days."

chapter 2

"We're doing all we can," Regan said in a voice that sounded too rehearsed, as if he'd been standing over my bed while I was unconscious, working on his delivery. "As I told you, we were not sure we had a missing child at first. We lost valuable time there, but we've recovered now. Tara's photo has been sent out to every police station, airport, tollbooth plaza, bus and train station—anything like that within a hundred-mile radius. We've run background profiles on similar abduction cases, see if we can find a pattern or a suspect."

"Twelve days," I repeated.

"We have a trace on your various phones—home, business, cell—"

"Why?"

"In case someone calls in a ransom demand," he said.

"Have there been any calls?"

"Not yet, no."

My head dropped back to the pillow. Twelve days. I'd been lying in this bed for twelve days while my baby girl was . . . I pushed the thought away.

Regan scratched at his beard. "Do you remember what Tara was wearing that morning?"

I did. I had developed something of a morning routine—wake up early, tiptoe toward Tara's crib, stare down. A baby is not all joy. I know that. I know that there are moments of mind-numbing boredom. I know that there are nights when her screams work on my nerve endings like a cheese grater. I don't want to glorify life with an infant. But I liked my new morning routine. Looking down at Tara's tiny form fortified me somehow. More than that, this act was, I guess, a form of rapture. Some people find rapture in a house of worship. Me—and yeah, I know how corny this sounds—I found rapture in that crib.

"A pink one-piece with black penguins," I said. "Monica got it at Baby Gap."

He jotted it down. "And Monica?"

"What about her?"

His face was back in the pad. "What was she wearing?"

"Jeans," I said, remembering the way they slid over Monica's hips, "and a red blouse."

Regan jotted some more.

I said, "Are there—I mean, do you have any leads?"

"We're still investigating all avenues."

"That's not what I asked."

Regan just looked at me. There was too much weight in that stare.

My daughter. Out there. Alone. For twelve days. I thought of her eyes, the warm light only a parent sees, and I said something stupid. "She's alive."

Regan tilted his head like a puppy hearing a new sound.

"Don't give up," I said.

"We won't." He continued with the curious look.

"It's just that . . . are you a parent, Detective Regan?"

"Two girls," he said.

"It's stupid, but I'd know." The same way I knew the world would never be the same when Tara was born. "I'd know," I said again.

He did not reply. I realized that what I was saying—especially coming from a man who scoffs at notions of ESP or the supernatural—was ridiculous. I knew that this "sense" merely came from want. You want to believe so badly that your brain rearranges what it sees. But I clung to it anyway. Right or wrong, it felt like a lifeline.

"We'll need some more information from you," Regan said. "About you, your wife, friends, finances—"

"Later." It was Dr. Heller again. She moved forward as if to block me from his gaze. Her voice was firm. "He needs to rest."

"No, now," I said to her, upping the firm-o-meter a notch past hers. "We need to find my daughter."

Monica had been buried at the Portman family plot on her father's estate. I missed her funeral, of course. I don't know how I felt about that, but then again, my feelings for my wife, in those stark moments when I was honest with myself, have always been muddled. Monica had that beauty of privilege, what with the too-fine cheekbones, straight silk-black hair, and that country-club lockjaw that both annoyed and aroused. Our marriage was an old-fashioned one—shotgun. Okay, that's an exaggeration. Monica was pregnant. I was fence-sitting. The upcoming arrival tilted me into the matrimonial pasture.

I heard the funeral details from Carson Portman, Monica's uncle and the only member of her family who kept in touch with us. Monica had loved him dearly. Carson sat at my hospital bedside with his hands folded in his lap. He looked very much like your favorite college professor—the thick-lensed spectacles, the nearly shedding tweed coat, and the overgrown shock of Albert Einstein-meets-Don King hair. But his brown eyes glistened as he told me in his sad baritone that Edgar, Monica's father, had made sure that my wife's funeral was a "small, tasteful affair."

Of that, I had no doubt. The small part, at least.

Over the next few days I had my share of visitors at the hospital. My mother—everyone called her Honey—exploded into my room every morning as if fuel propelled. She wore Reebok sneakers of pure white. Her sweatsuit was blue with gold trim, as if she coached the St. Louis Rams. Her hair, though neatly coifed, had the brittle of too many colorings, and there was the whiff of a last cigarette about her. Mom's makeup did little to disguise the anguish of losing her only grandchild. She had amazing energy, staying by my bedside day after day and managing to exude a steady stream of hysteria. This was good. It was as though she was, in part, being hysterical for me, and thus, in a strange way, her eruptions kept me calm.

Despite the room's nearly supernova heat—and my constant protestations—Mom would put an extra blanket over me when I was asleep. I woke up one time—my body drenched in sweat, naturally—to hear my mother telling the black nurse with the formal hat about my previous stay at St. Elizabeth's when I was only seven.

"He had salmonella," Honey stated in a conspiratorial whisper that was only slightly louder than a bullhorn. "You never smelled diarrhea like that. It was just pouring out of him. His stench practically seeped into the wallpaper."

"He ain't all roses now either," the nurse replied.

The two women shared a laugh.

On Day Two of my recovery, Mom was standing over my bed when I awoke.

"Remember this?" she said.

She was holding a stuffed Oscar the Grouch someone had given me during that salmonella stay. The green had faded to a light mint. She looked at the nurse. "This is Marc's Oscar," she explained.

"Mom," I said.

She turned her attention back to me. The mascara was a little too heavy today, crinkling into the wrinkle lines. "Oscar kept you company back then, remember? He helped you get better."

I rolled and then closed my eyes. A memory came to me. I had gotten the salmonella from raw eggs. My father used to add them into milkshakes for the protein. I remember the way pure terror had gripped me when I'd first learned that I would have to stay in the hospital overnight. My father, who had recently ruptured his Achilles tendon playing tennis, was in a cast and constant pain. But he saw my fear and as always, he made the sacrifice. He worked all that day at the plant and spent all night in a chair by my hospital bed. I stayed at St. Elizabeth's for ten days. My father slept in that chair every night of them.

Mom suddenly turned away, and I could see she was remembering the same thing. The nurse quickly excused herself. I put a hand on my mother's back. She didn't move, but I could feel her shudder. She stared down at the faded Oscar in her hands. I slowly took it from her.

"Thank you," I said.

Mom wiped her eyes. Dad, I knew, would not come to the hospital this time, and while I am sure my mother had told him what had happened, there was no way to know if he even understood. My father had had his first stroke when he was forty-one years old— one year after staying those nights with me at the hospital. I was eight at the time.

I also have a younger sister, Stacy, who is either a "substance abuser" (for the more politically correct) or "crack-head" (for the more accurate). I sometimes look at old pictures from before my dad's stroke, the ones with the young, confident family of four and the shaggy dog and the well-groomed lawn and the basketball hoop and the coal-overloaded, lighter fluid–saturated barbecue. I look for hints of the future in my sister's front-teeth-missing smile, her shadow self perhaps, a sense of foreboding. But I see none. We still have the house, but it's like a sagging movie prop. Dad is still alive, but when he fell, everything shattered Humpty-Dumpty style. Especially Stacy.

Stacy had not visited or even called, but nothing she does surprises me anymore.

My mother finally turned to face me. I gripped the faded Oscar a little tighter as a thought struck me anew: It was just us again. Dad was pretty much a vegetable. Stacy was hollowed out, gone. I reached out and took Mom's hand, feeling both the warmth and the more recent thickening of her skin. We stayed like that until the door opened. The same nurse leaned into the room.

Mom straightened up and said, "Marc also played with dolls."

"Action figures," I said, quick on the correction. "They were action figures, not dolls."

My best friend, Lenny, and his wife, Cheryl, also stopped by the hospital every day. Lenny Marcus is a big-time trial lawyer, though he also handles my small-time stuff like the time I fought a speeding ticket and the closing on our house. When he graduated and began working for the county prosecutor, friends and opponents quickly dubbed Lenny "the Bulldog" because of his aggressive courtroom behavior. Somewhere along the line, it was decided that the name was too mild for Lenny, so now they called him "Cujo." I've known Lenny since elementary school. I'm the godfather of his son Kevin. And Lenny is Tara's godfather.

I haven't slept much. I lie at night and stare at the ceiling and count the beeps and listen to the hospital night sounds and try very much not to let my mind wander to my little daughter and the endless array of possibilities. I am not always successful. The mind, I have learned, is indeed a dark, snake-infested pit.

Detective Regan visited later with a possible lead.

"Tell me about your sister," he began.

"Why?" I said too quickly. Before he could elaborate, I held up my hand to stop him. I understood. My sister was an addict. Where drugs roamed, so too did a certain criminal element. "Were we robbed?" I asked.

"We don't think so. Nothing seems to be missing, but the place was tossed."

"Tossed?"

"Someone made a mess. Any thoughts on why?"

"No."

"So tell me about your sister."

"You have Stacy's record?" I asked.

"We do."

"I'm not sure what I can add."

"You two are estranged, correct?"

Estranged. Did that apply to Stacy and me? "I love her," I said slowly.

"And when was the last time you saw her?"

"Six months ago."

"When Tara was born?"

"Yes."

"Where?"

"Where did I see her?"

"Yes."

"Stacy came to the hospital," I said.

"To see her niece?"

"Yes."

"What happened during that visit?"

"Stacy was high. She wanted to hold the baby."

"You refused?"

"That's right."

"Did she get angry?"

"She barely reacted. My sister is pretty flat when she's stoned."

"But you threw her out?"

"I told her she couldn't be a part of Tara's life until she was clean."

"I see," he said. "You were hoping that would force her back into rehab?"

I might have chuckled. "No, not really."

"I'm not sure I understand."

I wondered how to put this. I thought of the smile in the family photo, the one without the front teeth. "We've threatened Stacy with worse," I said. "The truth is that my sister won't quit. The drugs are part of her."

"So you hold out no hope for recovery?"

There was no way I was about to voice that. "I didn't trust her with my daughter," I said. "Let's leave it at that."

Regan headed over to the window and looked out. "When did you move into your current residence?"

"Monica and I bought the house four months ago."

"Not far from where you both grew up, no?"

"That's right."

"Had you two known each other long?"

I was puzzled by the line of questioning. "No."

"Even though you grew up in the same town?"

"We traveled in different circles."

"I see," he said. "And just so I have it straight, you bought your house four months ago and you hadn't seen your sister in six months, correct?"

"Correct."

"So your sister has never visited you at your current residence?"

"That's right."

Regan turned to me. "We found a set of Stacy's fingerprints at your house."

I said nothing.

"You don't seem surprised, Marc."

"Stacy is an addict. I don't think she's capable of shooting me and kidnapping my daughter, but I've underestimated how low she could sink before. Did you check her apartment?"

"No one has seen her since you were shot," he said.

I closed my eyes.

"We don't think your sister could pull off something like this by herself," he went on. "She might have had an accomplice—a boyfriend, a dealer, someone who knew your wife was from a wealthy family. Do you have any thoughts?"

"No," I said. "So, what, you think this whole thing was a kidnapping plot?"

Regan started clawing at his soul patch again. Then he gave a small shrug.

"But they tried to kill us both," I went on. "How do you collect ransom from dead parents?"

"They could have been so doped up that they made a mistake," he said. "Or maybe they thought they could extort money from Tara's grandfather."

"So why haven't they yet?"

Regan did not reply. But I knew the answer. The heat, especially after the shooting, would be too much for crack-heads. Crack-heads don't handle conflict well. It is one of the reasons they snort or shoot themselves up in the first place—to escape, to fade away, to avoid, to dive down into the white. The media would be all over this case. The police would be making inquiries. Crack-heads would freak under that kind of pressure. They would flee, abandon everything.

And they would get rid of all the evidence.

But the ransom demand came two days later.

Now that I had regained consciousness, my recovery from the gunshot wounds was proceeding with surprising smoothness. It could be that I was focused on getting better or that lying in a quasi-catatonic state for twelve days had given my injuries time to heal. Or it could be that I was suffering from a pain way beyond what the physical could inflict. I would think of Tara and the fear of the unknown would stop my breath. I would think of Monica, of her lying dead, and steel claws would shred me from within.

I wanted out.

My body still ached, but I pressed Ruth Heller to release me. Noting that I was proving the adage about doctors making the worst patients, she reluctantly gave me the okay to go home. We agreed that a physical therapist would come by every day. A nurse would pop by periodically, just to be on the safe side.

On the morning of my departure from St.

Elizabeth, my mother was at the house—the former crime scene—getting it "ready" for me, whatever that meant. Oddly enough, I wasn't afraid to go back there. A house is mortar and brick. I didn't think the sight of it alone would move me, but maybe I was just blocking.

Lenny helped me pack and get dressed. He is tall and wiry with a face darkened by a Homer Simpson five-o'clock shadow that pops up six minutes after he shaves. As a child Lenny wore Coke-bottle glasses and too-thick corduroy, even in the summer. His curly hair had a habit of getting outgrown to the point where he'd start resembling a stray poodle. Now he keeps the curls religiously close cropped. He had laser eye surgery two years ago, so the glasses are gone. His suits lean toward the upscale side.

"You sure you won't stay with us?" Lenny said.

"You have four kids," I reminded him.

"Oh yeah, right." He paused. "Can I stay with you?"

I tried to smile.

"Seriously," Lenny said, "you shouldn't be alone in that house."

"I'll be fine."

"Cheryl cooked you some dinners. She put them in the freezer."

"That was nice of her."

"She's still the world's most godawful cook," Lenny said.

"I didn't say I was going to eat them."

Lenny looked away, busying himself with the already packed bag. I watched him. We have known each other a long time, since Mrs. Roberts's first-grade class, so it probably did not surprise him when I said, "You want to tell me what's up?"

He'd been waiting for the opening and thus quickly exploited it. "Look, I'm your lawyer, right?"

"Right."

"So I want to give you some legal advice."

"I'm listening."

"I should have said something earlier. But I knew you wouldn't listen. Now, well, now it's a different story, I think."

"Lenny?"

"Yeah?'

"What are you talking about?"

Despite his physical enhancements, I still saw Lenny as a kid. It made it hard to take his advice too seriously. Don't get me

wrong. I knew that he was smart. I had cel-
ebrated with him when he got his accept-
ance to Princeton and then Columbia Law.
We took the SATs together and were in the
same AP chemistry class our junior year.
But the Lenny I saw was the one I desperately cruised with on muggy Friday and
Saturday nights. We used his dad's wood-
paneled station wagon—not exactly a
"babe trawler"—and tried to hit the parties.
We were always let in but never really welcome, members of that high school major-
ity I call the Great Unseen. We would stand
in corners, holding a beer, bopping our
heads to the music, trying hard to be noticed. We never were. Most nights we
ended up eating a grilled cheese at the Her-
itage Diner or, better, at the soccer field behind Benjamin Franklin Middle School, lying
on our backs, checking out the stars. It was
easier to talk, even with your best friend,
when you were looking at the stars.

"Okay," Lenny said, overgesturing as was
his custom, "it's like this: I don't want you
talking to the cops anymore without my being present."

I frowned. "For real?"

"Maybe it's nothing, but I've seen cases

like this. Not *like* this, but you know what I mean. The first suspect is always family."

"Meaning my sister."

"No, meaning close family. Or clos*er* family, if possible."

"Are you saying the police suspect me?"

"I don't know, I really don't." He paused but not for very long. "Okay, yeah, probably."

"But I was shot, remember? My kid was the one taken."

"Right, and that cuts both ways."

"How do you figure that?"

"As the days pass, they're going to start suspecting you more and more."

"Why?" I asked.

"I don't know. That's just how it works. Look, the FBI handles kidnappings. You know that, right? Once a child is gone twenty-four hours, they assume it's interstate and the case is theirs."

"So?"

"So for the first, what, ten days or so, they had a ton of agents here. They monitored your phones and waited for the ransom call, that kinda thing. But the other day, they pretty much pulled up stakes. That's normal, of course. They can't wait indefinitely, so they scale back to an agent or two. And their thinking shifted too. Tara became less a possible kidnapping-for-ransom and more a straight-on abduction. But my guess is, they still have the taps on the phones. I haven't asked yet, but I will. They'll claim they're leaving them there in case a ransom demand is eventually made. But they'll also be hoping to hear you say something in-criminating."

"So?"

"So be careful," Lenny said. "Remember that your phones—home, biz, cell—are probably tapped."

"And again I ask: So? I didn't do any-thing."

"Didn't do . . . ?" Lenny waved his hands as if preparing to take flight. "Look, just be careful is all. This might be hard for you to believe, but—and try not to gasp when I say this—the police have been known to twist and distort evidence."

"You're confusing me. Are you saying I'm a suspect simply because I'm the father and husband?"

"Yes," Lenny said. "And no."

"Well, okay, thanks, that clears it up."

A phone next to my bed rang. I was on

the wrong side of the room. "You mind?" I said.

Lenny picked it up. "Dr. Seidman's room." His face clouded over as he listened. He spat out the words "Hold on," and handed the phone to me, as if it might have germs. I gave him a puzzled look and said, "Hello?"

"Hello, Marc. This is Edgar Portman."

Monica's father. That explained Lenny's reaction. Edgar's voice was, as always, way too formal. Some people weigh their words. A select few, like my father-in-law, take each one and put it on a scale before letting it leave their mouths.

I was momentarily taken aback. "Hello, Edgar," I said stupidly. "How are you?"

"I'm fine, thank you. I feel remiss, of course, for not having called you earlier. I understood from Carson that you were busy recuperating from your wounds. I felt it best if I let you be."

"Thoughtful," I said with nary a whiff of sarcasm.

"Yes, well, I understand you're being released today."

"That's right."

Edgar cleared his throat, which seemed

out of character for him. "I was wondering if perhaps you could stop by the house."

The house. Meaning his. "Today?"

"As soon as possible, yes. And alone please."

There was silence. Lenny gave me a puzzled look.

"Is something wrong, Edgar?" I asked.

"I have a car waiting downstairs, Marc. We'll talk more when you arrive."

And then, before I could say another word, he was gone.

The car, a black Lincoln Town Car, was indeed waiting.

Lenny wheeled me outside. I was familiar with this area, of course. I had grown up scant miles from St. Elizabeth. When I was five years old, my father had rushed me to the emergency room here (twelve stitches) and when I was seven, well, you already know too much about my salmonella visit. I'd gone to medical school and did my residency at what was then called Columbia Presbyterian in New York, but I returned to St. Elizabeth for a fellowship in ophthalmology for reconstruction.

Yes, I am a plastic surgeon, but not in the

way you think. I do the occasional nose job, but you won't find me working with sacks of silicone or any of that. Not that I'm judging. It just isn't what I do.

I work in pediatric reconstructive surgery with my former medical school classmate, a fireball from the Bronx named Zia Leroux. We work for a group called One World WrapAid. Actually, Zia and I founded it. We take care of children, mostly overseas, who suffer deformities either through birth, poverty, or conflict. We travel a lot. I have worked on facial smashes in Sierra Leone, on cleft palates in Upper Mongolia, on Crouzon's in Cambodia, on burn victims in the Bronx. Like most people in my field, I've done extensive training. I've studied ENT—ears, nose, and throat—with a year of reconstructive, plastics, oral, and, as I mentioned above, ophthalmology. Zia's training history is similar, though she's stronger with the maxillofacial.

You may think of us as do-gooders. You'd be wrong. I had a choice. I could do boob jobs or tuck back the skin of those who were already too beautiful—or I could help wounded, poverty-stricken children. I chose the latter, not so much to help the disadvantaged, but alas, because that is where the cool cases lie. Most reconstructive surgeons are, at heart, puzzle lovers. We're weird. We get jazzed on circus-sideshow congenital anomalies and huge tumors. You know those medical textbooks that have hideous facial deformities that you have to dare yourself to look at? Zia and I love that stuff. We get off on repairing it—taking what's shattered and making it whole— even more.

The fresh air tickled my lungs. The sun shone as if it were the first day, mocking my gloom. I tilted my face toward the warmth and let it soothe me. Monica used to like to do that. She claimed that it "destressed" her. The lines in her face would disappear as if the rays were gentle masseurs. I kept my eyes closed. Lenny waited in silence, giving me the time.

I have always thought of myself as an overly sensitive man. I cry too easily at dumb movies. My emotions are easily manipulated. But with my father, I never cried. And now, with this terrible blow, I felt—I don't know—beyond tears. A classic defense mechanism, I assumed. I had to push forward. It's not so different from my business: When cracks appear, I patch them up before they become full-fledged fissures.

Lenny was still fuming from the phone call. "Any idea what that old bastard wants?"

"Not a one."

He was quiet a moment. I know what he was thinking. Lenny blamed Edgar for his father's death. His old man had been a middle manager at ProNess Foods, one of Edgar's holdings. He had slaved for the company twenty-six years and had just turned fifty-two years old when Edgar orchestrated a major merger. Lenny's father lost his job. I remember seeing Mr. Marcus sitting slump shouldered at the kitchen table, meticulously stuffing his résumé into envelopes. He never found work and died two years later of a heart attack. Nothing could convince Lenny that the two events were unrelated.

He said, "You sure you don't want me to come?"

"Nah, I'll be all right."

"Got your cell?"

I showed it to him.

"Call me if you need anything."

I thanked him and let him walk away. The

driver opened the door. I winced my way in. The drive was not far. Kasselton, New Jersey. My hometown. We passed the split-levels of the sixties, the expanded ranches of the seventies, the aluminum sidings of the eighties, the McMansions of the nineties. Eventually the trees grew denser. The houses sat farther back from the road, protected by the lush, away from the great unwashed who might happen by. We were nearing old wealth now, that exclusive land that always smelled of autumn and woodsmoke.

The Portman family had first settled in this thicket immediately following the Civil War. Like most of suburban Jersey, this had been farmland. Great-great-grandfather Portman slowly sold off acreage and made a fortune. They still had sixteen acres, making their lot one of the largest in the area. As we climbed the drive, my eyes drifted left—toward the family burial plot.

I could see a small mound of fresh dirt.

"Stop the car," I said.

"Sorry, Dr. Seidman," the driver replied, "but I was told to bring you right up to the main house."

I was about to protest but thought better

of it. I waited until the car stopped by the front door. I got out and headed back down the drive. I heard the driver say, "Dr. Seidman?" I kept going. He called after me again. I ignored him. Despite the lack of rain, the grass was a green usually reserved for rain forests. The rose garden was in full bloom, an explosion of color.

I tried to hurry on, but my skin still felt as if it might rip. I slowed. This was only my third visit inside the Portman family estate—I had seen it from the outside dozens of times in my youth—and I had never visited the family plot. In fact, like most rational people, I did my best to avoid it. The idea of burying your kin in your backyard like a family pet . . . it was one of those things that rich people do that we regular folk could never quite grasp. Or would want to.

The fence around the plot was maybe two feet high and blindingly white. I wondered if it'd been freshly painted for the occasion. I stepped over the superfluous gate and walked past the modest gravestones, keeping my eye on the dirt mound. When I reached the spot, a shudder tore through me. I looked down.

Yep, a recently dug grave. No stone yet.

The marker on it, printed up in wedding-invitation calligraphy, read simply: OUR MONICA.

I stood there and blinked. Monica. My wild-eyed beauty. Our relationship had been turbulent—a classic case of too much passion in the beginning and not enough near the end. I don't know why that happens. Monica was different, no question. At first that crackle, that excitement, had been a draw. Later, the mood swings simply made me weary. I didn't have the patience to dig deeper.

As I looked down at the pile of dirt, a painful memory jabbed at me. Two nights before the attack, Monica had been crying when I came to the bedroom. It was not the first time. Not even close. Playing my part in the stage show that was our lives, I asked her what was wrong, but my heart was not in it. I used to ask with more concern. Monica never replied. I would try to hold her. She would go rigid. After a while the nonresponsiveness got tiresome, taking on a boy-who-cried-wolf aspect that eventually frosts the heart. Living with a depressive is like that. You can't care all the time. At some point, you have to start to resent.

At least, that was what I told myself.

But this time, there was something different: Monica did indeed reply to me. Not a long reply. One line, actually. "You don't love me," she said. That was it. There was no pity in her voice. "You don't love me." And while I managed to utter the necessary protestations, I wondered if maybe she was right.

I closed my eyes and let it all wash over me. Things had been bad, but for the past six months anyway, there had been an escape for us, a calm and warm center in our daughter. I glanced at the sky now, blinked again, and then looked back down at the dirt that covered my volatile wife. "Monica," I said out loud. And then I made my wife one last vow.

I swore on her grave that I would find Tara.

A servant or butler or associate or whatever the current term was led me down the corridor and into the library. The décor was understated though unequivocally rich—finished dark floors with simple oriental carpets, old-Americana furniture that was solid rather than ornate. Despite his wealth and large plot of land Edgar was not one for show wealth. The term *nouveau riche* was to him profane, unspeakable.

Dressed in a blue cashmere blazer, Edgar rose from behind his expansive oak desk. There was a feather quill pen on the top— his great-grandfather's, if I recall—and two bronze busts, one of Washington and one of Jefferson. I was surprised to see Uncle Carson sitting there too. When he'd visited me in the hospital, I had been too frail to embrace. Carson made up for that now. He pulled me close. I held on to him in silence. He, too, smelled of autumn and woodsmoke.

There were no photographs in the room— no family-vacation snapshots, no school portraits, no shot of the man and his missus decked out at a charity formal. In fact, I do not think I had ever seen a photograph anywhere in the house.

Carson said, "How are you feeling, Marc?"

I told him that I was as well as could be expected and turned toward my father-in-law. Edgar did not come around the desk. We did not embrace. We did not, in fact, even shake hands. He gestured toward the chair in front of the desk.

I did not know Edgar very well. We had only met three times. I do not know how much money he has, but even out of these dwellings, even on a city street or at a bus depot, hell, even naked, you could tell that the Portmans were from money. Monica had the bearing too, the one ingrained over generations, the one that cannot be taught, the one that may literally be genetic. Monica's choice to live in our relatively modest dwelling was probably a form of rebellion.

She had hated her father.

I was not a big fan of his either, probably because I had met his type before. Edgar thinks himself a pull-up-by-the-bootstraps sort, but he himself earned his money the old-fashioned way: He inherited it. I don't know many superwealthy people, but I noticed that the more things were handed to you on a silver platter, the more you complain about welfare mothers and government handouts. It is bizarre. Edgar belongs to that unique class of the entitled who have deluded themselves into believing that they somehow earned their status through hard work. We all live with self-justification, of course, and if you have never fended for yourself, if you live in luxury and have done nothing to deserve it, well, that is going to compound your insecurities, I guess. But it shouldn't make you such a prig, to boot.

I sat. Edgar followed suit. Carson remained standing. I stared at Edgar. He had the plump of the well fed. His face was all soft edges. The normal ruddy on his cheeks, so far from anything rawbone, was gone now. He laced his fingers and rested them on his paunch. He looked, I was somewhat surprised to see, devastated, drawn, and sapless.

I say *surprised*, because Edgar always struck me as pure id, a person whose own pain and pleasure trumped all others', who believed those who inhabited the space around him were little more than window dressing for his own bemusement. Edgar had now lost two children. His son, Eddie the Fourth, had died while speeding under the influence ten years ago. According to Monica, Eddie veered across the double yellow line and plowed into the semi on purpose. For some reason, she blamed her father. She blamed him for a lot of things.

There is also Monica's mother. She

"rests" a lot. She takes "extended vacations." In short, she is in and out of institutions. Both times we met, my mother-in-law was propped up for some social affair, well dressed and powdered, lovely and too pale, a vacancy in her eyes, a slur in her speech, a sway in her stance.

Except for Uncle Carson, Monica had been estranged from her family. As you might imagine, I hardly minded.

"You wanted to see me?" I said.

"Yes, Marc. Yes, I did."

I waited.

Edgar put his hands on his desk. "Did you love my daughter?"

I was caught off guard, but I still said, "Very much," with no hesitation.

He seemed to see the lie. I worked hard to keep my gaze steady. "She still wasn't happy, you know."

"I'm not sure you can blame me for that," I said.

He nodded slowly. "Fair point."

But my own pass-the-buck defense didn't really work on me. Edgar's words were a fresh body blow. The guilt came roaring back.

"Did you know that she was seeing a psychiatrist?" Edgar asked.

I turned toward Carson first, then back to Edgar. "No."

"She didn't want anyone to know."

"How did you find out?"

Edgar did not reply. He stared down at his hands. Then he said: "I want to show you something."

I sneaked another look at Uncle Carson. His jaw was set. I thought I saw a tremble. I turned back to Edgar. "Okay."

Edgar opened his desk drawer, reached in, and pulled out a plastic bag. He raised it into view, gripping the bag at the corner between his forefinger and thumb. It took a moment, but when I realized what I was looking at, my eyes went wide.

Edgar saw my reaction. "You recognize it then?"

I couldn't speak at first. I glanced over at Carson. His eyes were red. I looked back at Edgar and nodded numbly. Inside the plastic bag was a small swatch of clothing, maybe three inches by three inches. The pattern was one I had seen two weeks ago, moments before being shot.

Pink with black penguins.

My voice was barely a hush. "Where did you get this?"

Edgar handed me a large brown envelope, the kind with bubble wrap on the inside. This, too, was protected in plastic. I turned it around. Edgar's name and address had been printed on a white label. There was no return address. The postmark read New York City.

"It came in today's mail," Edgar said. He gestured to the swatch. "Is it Tara's?"

I think I said yes.

"There's more," Edgar said. He reached into the drawer again. "I took the liberty of putting everything in plastic bags. In case the authorities need to test it."

Again he handed me what looked like a Ziploc bag. Smaller this time. There were hairs inside. Little wisps of hair. With mounting dread, I realized what I was looking at. My breath stopped.

Baby hair.

From far away, I heard Edgar ask, "Are they hers?"

I closed my eyes and tried to picture Tara in the crib. The image of my daughter, I was horrified to realize, was already fading in the mind's eye. How could that be? I could no longer tell if I was seeing memory or something I conjured up to replace what I was already forgetting. Damn it. Tears pressed against my eyelids. I tried to bring back the feel of my daughter's soft scalp, the way my finger would trace the top.

"Marc?"

"They could be," I said, opening my eyes. "There's no way for me to know for sure."

"Something else," Edgar said. He handed me another plastic bag. Gingerly, I put down the bag with her hair on the desk. I took the new bag. There was a sheet of white paper in it. A note from some kind of laser printer.

If you contact the authorities, we disappear. You will never know what happened to her. We will be watching. We will know. We have a man on the inside. Your calls are being monitored. Do not discuss this over the phone. We know that you, Grandpa, are rich. We want two million dollars. We want you, Daddy, to deliver the ransom. You, Grandpa, will get the money ready. We are enclosing a cell phone. It is untraceable. But if you dial out or use it in any way, we will know. We will disappear and you will never see the child again. Get the money ready. Give it to Daddy. Daddy, keep the money and phone near you. Go home and wait. We will call and tell you what to do. Deviate from what we ask, and you will never see your daughter again. There will be no second chance.

The syntax was odd, to put it mildly. I read the note three times and then I looked up at Edgar and Carson. A funny calm spread over me. Yes, this was terrifying, but receiving this note . . . it was also a relief. Something had finally happened. We could act now. We could get Tara back. There was hope.

Edgar stood and headed toward the corner of the room. He opened a closet door and pulled out a gym bag with a Nike logo on it. Without preamble, he said, "It's all here."

He dropped the bag onto my lap. I stared down at it. "Two million dollars?"

"The bills are not sequential, but we have a list of all the serial numbers, just in case."

I looked at Carson and then back at Edgar. "You don't think we should contact the FBI?"

"Not really, no." Edgar perched himself on the lid of the desk, folding his arms across his chest. He smelled of barbershop bay rum, but I could sense something more primitive, more rancid, that lay just beneath. Up close, his eyes had the dark rings of exhaustion. "It's your decision, Marc. You're the father. We'll respect whatever you do. But as you know, I have had some dealings with the federal authorities. Perhaps my views are colored by my own sense of their incompetence, or perhaps I am biased because I've witnessed the degree to which they are ruled by personal agendas. If it were my daughter, I'd rather trust my own judgment than theirs."

I was not sure what to say or do. Edgar took care of that. He clapped his hands once and then gestured toward the door.

"The note says that you should go home and wait. I think it's best if we obey."

chapter 3

The same driver was there. I slid into the backseat, the Nike bag pressed against my chest. My emotions rocketed between abject fear and the strangest tinge of elation. I could get my daughter back. I could blow it all.

But first things first: Should I tell the police?

I tried to calm myself, to look at it coldly, at a distance, weigh the pros and cons. That was impossible, of course. I am a doctor. I have made life-altering decisions before. I know that the best way to do that is to remove the baggage, the ardent excess, from the equation. But my daughter's life was at stake. My own daughter. To echo what I said in the beginning: my world.

The house Monica and I bought is literally

around the corner from the house I grew up in and where my parents still reside. I am ambivalent about that. I really don't like living so close to my parents, but I dislike the guilt of abandoning them even more. My compromise: Live near them and then travel a lot.

Lenny and Cheryl live four blocks away, near the Kasselton Mall, in the house where Cheryl's parents had raised her. Cheryl's parents moved to Florida six years ago. They keep a condo up here in neighboring Roseland so they can visit their grandchildren and escape the molten-lava summers of the Sunshine State.

I don't particularly like living in Kasselton. The town has changed very little over the past thirty years. In our youth, we scoffed at our parents, their materialism, their seemingly aimless values. Now we are our parents. We have simply replaced them, pushed Mom and Dad into whatever retirement village would have them. And our children have replaced us. But Maury's Luncheonette is still on Kasselton Avenue. The fire department is still mostly volunteer. The Little League still plays at Northland Field. The high-tension wires are still too close to

my old elementary school. The woods behind the Brenners' house on Rockmont Terrace is still a place where kids hang out and
smoke. The high school still gets between
five and eight national merit finalists a year,
though when I was younger the list was
more Jewish while today it tilts toward the
Asian community.

We turned right on Monroe Avenue and
drove past the split-level where I was
raised. With its white paint and black shut-
ters, with its kitchen, living room, and dining room up three steps on the left and
its den and garage entrance two steps
down on the right, our house, though a bit
more threadbare than most, was pretty
much indistinguishable from the other
cookie-cutters on the block. What did make
it stand out, the only thing really, was the
wheelchair ramp. We put it in after my dad's
third stroke when I was twelve years old. My
friends and I liked to skateboard down it.
We built a jump out of plywood and cinder
blocks and put it at the bottom.

The nurse's car was in the driveway. She
comes in during the days. We don't have
someone full time. My father has been con-
fined to a wheelchair for more than two

decades now. He cannot speak. His mouth has an ugly down-hook curve on the left side of it. Half his body is totally paralyzed and the other half is not that much better.

When the driver made the turn at Darby Terrace, I saw that my house—our house—looked the same as it had a few weeks before. I didn't know what I'd expected. Yellow crime-scene tape maybe. Or a big bloodstain. But there was nothing hinting at what had occurred two weeks earlier.

When I'd bought the house, it'd been in foreclosure. For thirty-six years the Levinsky family had lived there, but no one really knew them. Mrs. Levinsky had been a seemingly sweet woman with a facial tic. Mr. Levinsky was an ogre who always yelled at her out on the lawn. He scared us. One time, we saw Mrs. Levinsky run out of the house in a nightgown, Mr. Levinsky chasing her with a shovel. Kids cut through every yard but theirs. When I was fresh out of college, rumors surfaced that he had abused his daughter Dina, a sad-eyed, stringy-haired waif I'd gone to school with since the first grade. Looking back on it, I must have been in a dozen classes with Dina Levinsky and I don't remember ever hearing her speak above a whisper and only then when forced to by well-meaning teachers. I never reached out to Dina. I don't know what I could have done, but I still wished that I'd tried.

Sometime during that year out of college, when the rumors of Dina's abuse began to take root, the Levinskys had upped and moved away. No one knew where. The bank took over the house and began to rent it out. Monica and I made an offer a few weeks before Tara was born.

Months later, when we first settled in, I'd stay awake at night and listen for—I don't know—sounds of some sort, for signs of the house's past, of the unhappiness within. I would try to figure out which bedroom had been Dina's and try to imagine what it'd been like for her, what it was like now, but there were no clues here. As I said earlier, a house is mortar and brick. Nothing more.

Two strange cars were parked in front of my house. My mother was standing by the front door. When I got out, she rushed me like those newscasts of returning POWs. She hugged me hard, and I got a whiff of too much perfume. I was still holding the

Nike bag with the money, so it was hard for me to reciprocate.

Over my mother's shoulder, Detective Bob Regan stepped out of my house. Next to him stood a large black man with a gleaming shaved head and designer sunglasses. My mother whispered, "They've been waiting for you."

I nodded and moved toward them. Regan cupped a hand over his eyes, but only for effect. The sun was not that strong. The black man remained stonelike.

"Where have you been?" Regan asked. When I didn't reply right away, he added, "You left the hospital more than an hour ago."

I thought about the cell phone in my pocket. I thought about the bag of money in my hand. For now, I'd go for the semitruth. "I visited my wife's grave," I said.

"We need to talk, Marc."

"Step inside," I said.

We all moved back into the house. I stopped in the foyer. Monica's body had been found less than ten feet from where I now stood. Still in the entranceway, my eyes scanned the walls, looking for any telltale sign of violence. There was only one. I found it fairly quickly. Above the Behrens lithograph near the stairwell, a bullet hole— one created from the only bullet that had not hit either Monica or me—had been spackled over. The spackle was too white for the wall. It would need a coat of paint.

I stared at it for a long moment. I heard a throat being cleared. It snapped me out of it. My mother rubbed my back and then headed to the kitchen. I showed Regan and his buddy to the living room. They took the two chairs. I took the couch. Monica and I hadn't truly decorated yet. The chairs dated back to my college dorm and looked it. The couch had come from Monica's apartment, a too-formal hand-me-down that looked like something kept in storage at Versailles. It was heavy and stiff and, even in its hey- day, had had very little padding.

"This is Special Agent Lloyd Tickner," Re- gan began, motioning toward the black man. "He's with the FBI."

Tickner nodded. I nodded back.

Regan tried to smile at me. "Good to see you're feeling better," he began.

"I'm not," I said.

He looked puzzled.

"I won't be better until I have my daughter back."

"Right, of course. About that. We have a few follow-up questions, if you don't mind."

I let them know I didn't.

Regan coughed into his fist, buying himself time. "You have to understand something. We need to ask these questions. I don't necessarily like it. I'm sure you don't either, but these questions need to be asked. You understand?"

I didn't really, but this was no time to encourage elaboration. "Go ahead," I said.

"What can you can tell us about your marriage?"

A warning light flashed across my cortex. "What does my marriage have to do with anything?"

Regan shrugged. Tickner remained still. "We're just trying to put some pieces together, that's all."

"My marriage has nothing to do with any of this."

"I'm sure you're right, but look, Marc, the truth is, the trail is getting cold here. Every day that passes hurts us. We need to explore every avenue."

"The only avenue I'm interested in is the one that leads to my daughter."

"We understand that. That's the main focus of our investigation. Finding out what happened to your daughter. And you too. Let's not forget that someone tried to kill you too, am I right?"

"I guess."

"But, see, we can't just ignore these other issues."

"What other issues?"

"Your marriage, for example."

"What about it?"

"When you got married, Monica was already pregnant, right?"

"What does that . . . ?" I stopped myself. I wanted to attack with both barrels, but Lenny's words roared back at me. Don't talk to the cops without him present. I should call him. I knew that. But something about their tone and posture . . . if I stopped now and said I wanted to call my lawyer, it would make me look guilty. I had nothing to hide. Why feed into their suspicions? It would only distract them. Of course, I also knew that this was how they worked, how the police played the game, but I'm a doctor. Worse, a surgeon. We often make the mistake of thinking we're smarter than everyone else.

I went with honesty. "Yes, she was pregnant. So?"

"You're a plastic surgeon, correct?"

The change of subjects threw me. "That's right."

"You and your partner travel overseas and repair cleft palates, serious facial trauma, burns, that kind of thing?"

"Something like that, yes."

"You travel a lot then?"

"A fair amount," I said.

"In fact," Regan said, "in the two years before your marriage, isn't it fair to say that you were probably out of the country more than you were in it?"

"Possibly," I said. I squirmed against the padless cushion. "Could you tell me what the relevance of any of this is?"

Regan gave me his most disarming smile. "We're just trying to get a complete picture here."

"Picture of what?"

"Your work partner"—he checked his notes—"a Ms. Zia Leroux."

"Dr. Leroux," I corrected.

"Dr. Leroux, yes, thank you. Where is she now?"

"Cambodia."

"She's performing surgery on deformed children over there?"

"Yes."

Regan tilted his head, feigning confusion. "Weren't you originally scheduled to take that trip?"

"A long time ago."

"How long ago?"

"I'm not sure I follow."

"How long ago did you take yourself off the schedule?"

"I don't know," I said. "Eight, nine months ago maybe."

"And so Dr. Leroux went instead, correct?"

"Yes, that's correct. And the point of that is . . . ?"

He wouldn't bite. "You like your job, don't you, Marc?"

"Yes."

"You like traveling overseas? Doing this commendable work?"

"Sure."

Regan scratched his head too dramatically, pretending in the most obvious way to be bewildered. "So if you like the traveling, why did you cancel and let Dr. Leroux go in your place?"

Now I saw where he was heading. "I was cutting back," I said.

"On travel, you mean."

"Yes."

"Why?"

"Because I had other obligations."

"Those obligations being a wife and daughter, am I correct?"

I sat up and met his eye. "Point," I said. "Is there a point to all this?"

Regan settled back. The silent Tickner did likewise. "Just trying to get a complete picture, that's all."

"You said that already."

"Yeah, hold on, give me a second here." Regan flipped through the pages of his notebook. "Jeans and a red blouse."

"What?"

"Your wife." He pointed at his notes. "You said that she was wearing jeans and a red blouse that morning."

More images of Monica flooded me. I tried to stem the tide. "So?"

"When we found her body," Regan said, "she was naked."

The tremors began in my heart. They spread down my arms, tingling my fingers.

"You didn't know?"

I swallowed. "Was she . . . ?" My voice died in my throat.

"No," Regan said. "Not a mark on her, other than the bullet holes." He did that help-me-understand head-tilt again. "We found her dead in this very room. Did she often parade in here with no clothes on?"

"I told you." Overload. I tried to process this new data, keep up with him. "She was wearing jeans and a red blouse."

"So she was dressed already?"

I remembered the sound of the shower. I remembered her coming out, throwing her hair back, lying on the bed, working the jeans over the hips. "Yes."

"Definitely?"

"Definitely."

"We've been through the whole house. We can't find a red blouse. Jeans, sure. She had several pairs. But no red blouse. Don't you think that's odd?"

"Wait a second," I said. "Her clothes weren't near her body?"

"Nope."

This made no sense. "I'll look in her closet, then," I said.

"We already did that, but sure, go ahead. Of course, I'd still like to know how clothes she was wearing ended up back in her closet, wouldn't you?"

I had no answer.

"Do you own a gun, Dr. Seidman?"

Another subject shift. I tried to keep up, but my head was spinning. "Yes."

"What kind?"

"A Smith and Wesson thirty-eight. It belonged to my father."

"Where do you keep it?"

"There's a compartment in the bedroom closet. It's on the top shelf in a lockbox."

Regan reached behind him and pulled out the metal lockbox. "This it?"

"Yes."

"Open it."

He tossed it to me. I caught it. The gray-blue metal was cold. But more than that, it felt shockingly light. I moved the wheels to the right combination and flipped it open. I poked through the legal documents—the car title, the deed on the house, the property survey—but that was just to get my bearings. I knew right away. The gun was gone.

"You and your wife were both shot with a thirty-eight," Regan said. "And yours seems to be missing."

I kept my eyes on the box, as if I expected the weapon to suddenly materialize in it. I tried to put it together, but nothing was coming to me.

"Any idea where the gun is?"

I shook my head.

"And something else strange," Regan said.

I looked up at him.

"You and Monica were shot with *different* thirty-eights."

"Excuse me?"

He nodded. "Yeah, I found it hard to believe too. I made ballistics check it twice. You and your wife were shot with two different guns, both thirty-eights—and yours seems to be missing." Regan shrugged theatrically. "Help me understand, Marc."

I looked at their faces. I didn't like what I saw. Lenny's warning came back to me again, firmer this time. "I want to call my lawyer," I said.

"You sure?"

"Yes."

"Go ahead."

My mother had been standing by the kitchen door, wringing her hands. How much had she heard? Judging by her face, too much. Mom looked at me expectantly. I nodded, and she went to call Lenny. I folded my arms, but that didn't feel right. I tapped my foot. Tickner took off the sunglasses. He met my eye and spoke for the first time.

"What's in the bag?" he asked me.

I just looked at him.

"That gym bag you been groping." Tickner's voice, belying his tough looks, had a nerdy cadence to it, a quasi-whine quality. "What's in it?"

This had all been a mistake. I should have listened to Lenny. I should have called him right away. Now I was not sure how to reply. In the background, I heard my mother urging Lenny to hurry. I was sifting through a response that might work as a semitruthful stall—none were convincing—when a sound ripped my attention away.

The cell phone, the one the kidnappers had sent to my father-in-law, began to ring.

chapter 4

Tickner and Regan waited for me to answer.

I excused myself, rising before they had a chance to react. My hand fumbled with the phone as I hurried outside. The sun hit me full in the face. I blinked and looked down at the keypad. The phone's answer button was located in a different spot from mine. Across the street, two girls donning brightly hued helmets were riding neon bikes. Ribbon strips of pink cascaded out of the handlebars of one.

When I was little, this neighborhood sheltered more than a dozen kids my age. We used to meet up after school. I don't remember what games we played—we were never organized enough for, say, a real game of baseball or anything like that—but they all involved hiding and chasing and some form of feigned (or borderline-real) violence. Childhood in suburbia is purportedly a time of innocence, but how many of those days ended in tears for at least one kid? We would argue, shift alliances, make declarations of friendship and war, and like some short-term memory case, it was all forgotten the next day. A clean slate every afternoon. New coalitions forged. A new kid running home in tears.

My thumb finally touched down on the right button. I pressed it and brought the phone to my ear, all in one move. My heart thumped against my rib cage. I cleared my throat and, feeling like a total idiot, I simply said, "Hello?"

"Answer yes or no." The voice had the robotic hum of one of those customer-care phone systems, the ones that tell you to press one for service, press two to check the status of an order. "Do you have the money?"

"Yes."

"You know the Garden State Plaza?"

"In Paramus," I said.

"In exactly two hours from now, I want you parked at the north lot. That's near

Nordstrom's. Section Nine. Someone will approach your car."

"But—"

"If you're not alone, we disappear. If you're being followed, we disappear. If I smell a cop, we disappear. There will be no second chances. Do you understand?"

"Yes, but when—"

Click.

I let my hand drop to my side. Numbness seeped in. I did not fight it. The little girls across the street were quarreling now. I couldn't hear the specifics, but the word *my* popped up a lot, that simple syllable accentuated and drawn out. An SUV sped around the corner. I watched it as though from above. The brakes shrieked. The driver-side door was open before the car had come to a complete stop.

It was Lenny. He took one look at me and picked up his pace. "Marc?"

"You were right." I nodded toward the house. Regan was standing by the door now. "They think I'm involved."

Lenny's face darkened. His eyes narrowed, his pupils shrinking to pinpoints. In sports, you call it putting on your "game face." Lenny was becoming Cujo. He stared at Regan as if deciding which limb to chew off. "You talked to them?"

"A little."

Lenny jerked his gaze toward me. "Didn't you tell them you wanted counsel?"

"Not at first."

"Damn it, Marc, I told you—"

"I got a ransom demand."

That made Lenny pull up. I checked my watch. Paramus was a forty-minute ride. With traffic, it could take as much as an hour. I had time, but not much. I started filling him in. Lenny gave Regan another glare and led me farther away from the house. We stopped at the curb, those familiar cloud-gray stones that lie on property lines like sets of teeth, and then, like two children, we squatted deep and sat on them. Our knees were at our chins. I could see Lenny's skin between the argyle sock and tapered cuff. Squatting like this was uncomfortable as hell. The sun was in our eyes. We both looked off rather than at each other, again just like in our youths. It made it easier to spill it all out.

I spoke quickly. Midway through my recap, Regan began to move toward us.

Lenny turned to him and shouted, "Your balls."

Regan stopped. "What?"

"Are you arresting my client?"

"No."

Lenny pointed toward Regan's crotch. "Then I'm going to have them bronzed and hanging from my rearview mirror, if you take another step."

Regan straightened his spine. "We have some questions for your client."

"Tough. Go abuse the rights of someone with a lesser lawyer."

Lenny made a dismissive gesture and nodded at me to continue. Regan did not look happy, but he took two steps back. I glanced at my watch again. Only five minutes had passed since the ransom call. I finished up while Lenny kept the laser glare aimed at Regan.

"You want my opinion?" he said.

"Yes."

Still glaring. "I think you should tell them."

"You sure?"

"Hell, no."

"Would you?" I said. "I mean, if it was one of your kids?"

Lenny gave it a few seconds. "I can't put

myself in your place, if that's what you mean. But yeah, I think I would. I play the odds. The odds are better when you tell the cops. Doesn't mean it works out every time, but they're experts at this. We're not." Lenny put his elbows on his knees and rested his chin in his hands—a pose from his youth. "That's the opinion of Lenny the Friend," he went on. "Lenny the Friend would encourage you to tell them."

"And Lenny the Lawyer?" I asked.

"He would be more insistent. He would strongly urge you to come forward."

"Why?"

"If you go off with two million dollars and it vanishes—even if you get Tara back—their suspicions will be, to put it mildly, aroused."

"I don't care about that. I just want Tara back."

"Understood. Or should I say, Lenny the Friend understands."

Now it was Lenny's turn to check his watch. My insides felt hollow, scooped out canoe-style. I could almost hear the tick-tick. It was maddening. I tried again to do the rational thing, to list the pros on the right, the cons on the left, and then add them up. But the tick-tick would not stop.

Lenny had talked about playing the odds. I don't gamble. I'm not a risk taker. Across the street one of the little girls shouted, "I'm telling!" She stormed down the street. The other girl laughed at her and got back on her bike. I felt my eyes well up. I wished like hell Monica were here. I shouldn't be making this decision alone. She should be in on this, too.

I looked back at the front door. Regan and Tickner were both outside now. Regan had his arms folded across his chest, bouncing on the balls of his feet. Tickner did not move, his face the same placid pool. Were these men I could trust with my daughter's life? Would they put Tara first, or as Edgar had suggested, would they follow some unseen agenda?

The tick-tick grew louder, more insistent.

Someone had murdered my wife. Someone had taken my child. For the past few days, I had asked myself why—why us?—trying again to stay rational and not allowing myself extended forays in the deep end of the pity pool. But no answer came. I could see no motive and maybe that was most

frightening of all. Maybe there was no reason. Maybe it was just pure bad luck.

Lenny stared straight ahead and waited.
Tick, tick, tick.

"Let's tell them," I said.

Their reaction surprised me. They panicked.

Regan and Tickner tried to hide it, of
course, but their body language was suddenly all wrong—the flutter in the eyes, the
tightness at the corners of their mouths, the
unduly modulated, FM-soft-rock timbre in
their tones. The time frame was simply too
close for them. Tickner quickly dialed up the
FBI specialist on kidnapping negotiations to
enlist his help. He cupped his hand around
the mouthpiece while he spoke into it. Regan got hold of his police colleagues in
Paramus.

When Tickner hung up, he said to me,
"We'll get people to cover the mall. Dis-
creetly, of course. We're going to try to get
men in cars near every exit and on Route
Seventeen in both directions. We'll have
people inside the mall by all the entrances.
But I want you to listen to me closely, Dr.
Seidman. Our expert tells us that we should

try to stall him. Maybe we can get the kidnapper to postpone—"

"No," I said.

"They won't just run away," Tickner said. "They want the money."

"My daughter has been with them for almost three weeks," I said. "I'm not putting this off."

He nodded, not liking it, trying to keep up with the placid. "Then I want to put a man in the car with you."

"No."

"He can duck down in the back."

"No," I said again.

Tickner tried another avenue. "Or better yet—we've done this before—we tell the kidnapper that you can't drive. Hell, you're just out of the hospital. We have one of our men drive instead. We say it's your cousin."

I frowned and looked at Regan. "Didn't you say you thought my sister might be involved?"

"It's possible, yes."

"Don't you think she'd know if this guy was a cousin or not?"

Tickner and Regan both hesitated and then nodded in unison. "Good point," Regan said.

Lenny and I exchanged a glance. These were the professionals I was trusting with Tara's life. The thought was not comforting. I started for the door.

Tickner put a hand on my shoulder. "Where are you going?"

"Where the hell do you think?"

"Sit down, Dr. Seidman."

"No time," I countered. "I have to start heading up there. There could be traffic."

"We can clear the traffic."

"Oh, and that won't look suspicious," I said.

"I highly doubt he's going to follow you from here."

I spun on him. "And you'd be willing to risk your child's life on that?"

He paused just long enough.

"You don't get it," I went on, in his face now. "I don't care about the money or if they get away. I just want my daughter back."

"We understand that," Tickner said, "but there is something you're forgetting."

"What?"

"Please," he said. "Sit down."

"Look, do me a favor, okay? Just let me stand. I'm a doctor. I know the delivering-bad-news drill as well as anyone. Don't try to play me."

Tickner held his palms up and said, "Fair enough." He proceeded to take a long, lingering breath. Stall tactic. I was not in the mood.

"So what is it?" I said.

"Whoever did this," he began, "they shot you. They killed your wife."

"I understand that."

"No, I don't think you do. Think about it a second. We can't just let you go in on your own. Whoever did this tried to end your life. They shot you twice and left you for dead."

"Marc," Regan said, moving closer, "we threw some wild theories at you before. The problem is, that's all they are. Theories. We don't know what these guys are really after. Maybe this is just a simple kidnapping, but if it is, it's not like any we've seen before." His interrogation face was gone now, replaced with an aw-shucks, eyebrow-raised attempt at openness. "What we do know with certainty is that they tried to kill you. You don't try to kill the parents, if you're just after ransom."

"Maybe they planned on getting the money from my father-in-law," I said.

"Then why did they wait so long?"

I had no answer.

"Maybe," Tickner went on, "this isn't about kidnapping at all. At least, not at first. Maybe that's become a sideline. Maybe you and your wife were the targets all along. And maybe they want to finish the job."

"You think this is a setup?"

"It's a strong possibility, yes."

"So what are you advising?"

Tickner took that one. "Don't go alone. Buy us some time so we can prepare properly. Let them call you back."

I looked at Lenny. He saw it and nodded. "That's not possible," Lenny said.

Tickner turned at him hard. "With all due respect, your client is in grave danger here."

"So is my daughter," I said. Simple words. This decision was a no-brainer when you kept it simple. I pulled away and started toward my car. "Keep your people at a distance."

chapter 5

There was no traffic, so I made it to the mall with plenty of time to spare. I turned the engine off and sat back. I glanced around. I figured that the feds and cops were probably still on me, but I couldn't see them. That was a good thing, I guess.

Now what?

No idea. I waited some more. I fiddled with the radio, but nothing caught my attention. I turned on the CD player/tape deck. When Donald Fagan of Steely Dan began singing "Black Cow," I felt a slight jerk. I had not listened to this particular tape since, what, my college days. Why did Monica have it? And then, with a renewed pang, I realized that Monica had been the last to use this car, that this may have been the last song she ever heard.

I watched the shoppers prepare for mall entry. I concentrated on the young mothers; the way they flipped open the back door of the minivan; the way they unfolded the baby strollers midair with a magician's flourish; the way they struggled to release their off-spring from safety seats that reminded me of Buzz Aldrin's on *Apollo 11*; the way the mothers skirted forward, heads high, smartly pressing the remote control that slid the minivan door to a close.

The mothers, all of them, looked so blasé. Their children were with them. Their safety, what with the five-star side-collision rating and NASA-sleek car seats, was a given. And here I sat with a bag of ransom money, hoping to get my daughter back. The thin line. I wanted to roll down the window and shout out a warning.

We were getting close to drop time. The sun beat down on my windshield. I reached for my sunglasses but then thought better of it. I don't know why. Would putting on my sunglasses somehow make the kidnapper uneasy? No, I don't think so. Or maybe it would. Better to just leave them off. Take no chances.

My shoulders bunched up. I kept trying to

look around without, for some odd reason, looking conspicuous about it. Whenever someone parked near me or walked any-where in the vicinity of my car, my stomach tightened and I wondered:

Was Tara nearby?

We were at the two-hour mark now. I wanted this over. The next few minutes would decide everything. I knew that. Calm. I needed to stay calm. Tickner's warning re-verberated in my head. Would someone simply walk up to my car and blow my brains out?

It was, I realized, a very real possibility.

When the cell phone rang, I started for-ward. I brought it to my ear and barked a too-quick hello.

The robotic voice said, "Pull out by the west exit."

I was confused. "Which way is west?"

"Follow the signs for Route Four. Take the overpass. We're watching. If someone fol-lows, we disappear. Keep the phone near your ear."

I obeyed with gusto; my right hand pressed the phone against my ear to the point where I started losing circulation. My left hand gripped the wheel as if preparing to tear it off.

"Get on Route Four heading west."

I took the right turn and jug-handled onto the highway. I looked in my rearview mirror to see if anyone was following me. Hard to tell.

The robotic voice said, "You'll see a strip mall."

"There's a million strip malls," I said.

"It's on the right, next to a store selling baby cribs. In front of the Paramus Road exit."

I saw it. "Okay."

"Pull in there. You'll see a driveway on the left. Take it to the back and kill the engine. Have the money ready for me."

I understood immediately why the kidnapper had picked this spot. There was only one way in. The stores were all for rent, except for the baby-crib place. That was on the far right. In other words, it was self-contained and directly off a highway. There was no way anyone could come around back or even slow down without being noticed.

I hope the feds understood that.

When I reached the back of the building, I saw a man standing by a van. He wore a red-and-black flannel shirt with black jeans, dark sunglasses, and a Yankee baseball cap. I tried to find something distinct, but the word that came to mind was *average*. Average height, average build. The only thing was his nose. Even from this distance I could see it was misshapen, like an ex-boxer's. But was that real or some kind of disguise? I didn't know.

I checked out the van. There was a sign for "B & T Electricians" of Ridgewood, New Jersey. No phone number or address. The license plate was from New Jersey. I mem-orized it.

The man raised a cell phone to his lips walkie-talkie style, and I heard the mechan-ical voice say, "I'm going to approach. Pass the money through the window. Do not get out of the car. Do not say a word to me. When we're safely away with the money, I'll call and tell you where to pick up your daughter."

The man in red flannel and black jeans lowered the phone and approached. His shirt was untucked. Did he have a gun? I couldn't tell. And even if he did, what could I do about it now? I hit the button to open the windows. They didn't budge. The key needed to be turned. The man was getting closer. The Yankee cap was pulled down until the brim touched the sunglasses. I reached for the key and gave it a tiny twist. The lights on the dashboard sprung to life. I pressed the button again. The window slid down.

Again I tried to find something about the man that was distinct. His walk was slightly off balance, as though maybe he'd had a drink or two, but he didn't look nervous. His face was unshaven and patchy. His hands were dirty. His black jeans were ripped in the right knee. His sneakers, canvas high-tops from Converse, had seen better days.

When the man was only two steps from the car, I pushed the bag up to the window and braced myself. I held my breath. Without breaking stride, the man took the money and swirled toward the van. He hurried his step now. The van's back doors opened and he leapt in, the door immediately closing behind him. It was as if the van had swallowed him whole.

The driver gunned the engine. The van sped off and now, for the first time, I realized that there was a back entrance onto a side road. The van shot down it and was gone.

I was alone.

I stayed where I was and waited for the cell phone to ring. My heart pounded. My shirt was drenched in sweat. No other car traveled back here. The pavement was cracked. Cardboard boxes jutted out of the garbage Dumpster. Broken bottles littered the ground. My eyes stared hard at the ground, trying to make out the words on faded beer labels.

Fifteen minutes passed.

I kept picturing my reunion with my daughter, how I would find her and pick her up and cradle her and hush her with gentle sounds. The cell phone. The cell phone was supposed to ring. That was part of what I was picturing. The phone ringing, the robotic voice giving me instructions. Those were parts one and two. Why wasn't the damn phone cooperating?

A Buick Le Sabre pulled into the lot, keeping a decent distance away from me. I did not recognize the driver, but Tickner was in the passenger seat. Our eyes met. I tried to read something in his expression, but he was still pure stoic.

I stared now at the cell phone, not daring

to look away. The tick-tick was back, this time slow and thudding.

Ten more minutes passed before the phone grudgingly issued its tinny song. I had it to my ear before the sound had a chance to travel.

"Hello?" I said.

Nothing.

Tickner watched me closely. He gave me a slight nod, though I had no idea why. His driver still had both hands on the wheel at ten and two o'clock.

"Hello?" I tried again.

The robotic voice said, "I warned you about contacting the cops."

Ice flooded my veins.

"No second chance."

And then the phone went dead.

chapter 6

There was no escape.

I longed for the numb. I longed for the comatose state of the hospital. I longed for that IV bag and the free flow of anesthetics. My skin had been torn off. My nerve endings were exposed now. I could feel everything.

Fear and helplessness overwhelmed me. The fear locked me in a room, while the helplessness—the awful knowing that I had blown it and could do nothing to alleviate my child's pain—wrapped me in a straitjacket and turned out the lights. I may very well have been losing my mind.

Days passed in a syrupy haze. Most of the time I sat by the phone—by several phones, actually. My home phone, my cell phone, and the kidnapper's cell phone. I bought a charger for the kidnapper's cell, so I could keep it working. I stayed on the couch. The phones sat on my right. I tried to look away, to watch television even, because I remembered that old saying about a watched kettle never boiling. I still stole glances at those damn phones, fearing that they might somehow flee, willing them to ring.

I tried to mine that supernatural father-daughter connection again, the one that had insisted earlier that Tara was still alive. The pulse was still there, I thought (or at least, made myself believe), beating faintly, the connection now tenuous at best.

"No second chance . . ."

To add to my guilt, I had dreamt last night of a woman other than Monica—my old love, Rachel. It was one of those time-and-reality warp dreams, the ones where the world is totally alien and even contradictory and yet you don't question any of it. Rachel and I were together. We had never broken up yet we had been apart all these years. I was still thirty-four, but she hadn't aged since the day she left me. Tara was still my daughter in the dream—she had, in fact, never been kidnapped—but somehow she was also Rachel's, though Rachel wasn't the mother. You've probably had dreams like this. Nothing really makes sense, but you don't challenge what you see. When I woke up, the dream faded into smoke the way dreams always do. I was left with an aftertaste and a longing that pulled with unexpected force.

My mother hung around too much. She had just plopped another tray of food in front of me. I ignored it and for the millionth time, Mom repeated her mantra: "You have to keep up your strength for Tara."

"Right, Mom, strength is the key here. Maybe if I do enough bench presses, that'll bring her back."

Mom shook her head, refusing to rise to the bait. It was a cruel thing to say. She was hurting too. Her granddaughter was missing and her son was in horrific shape. I watched her sigh and head back to the kitchen. I didn't apologize.

Tickner and Regan visited frequently. They reminded me of Shakespeare's sound and fury signifying nothing. They told me about all the technological wonders that were being utilized in the quest to find Tara—stuff involving DNA and latent prints and security cameras and airports and toll-booths and train stations and tracers and surveillance and labs. They trotted out the tried-and-true cop clichés like "no stone un-turned" and "every possible avenue." I nod-ded at them. They had me look at mug shots, but the bagman in flannel was not in any of the books.

"We ran a trace on B and T Electricians," Regan told me that first night. "The com-pany exists, but they use magnetic signs, the kind you can just peel off a truck. Some-one stole one two months ago. They never thought it was worth reporting."

"What about the license plate?" I asked.

"The number you gave us doesn't exist."

"How can that be?"

"They used two old license plates," Re-gan explained. "See, what they do is, they cut the license plates in half and then they weld the left half of one with the right half of the other."

I just stared at him.

"There is something of a bright side to that," Regan added.

"Oh?"

"It means we're dealing with profession-als. They knew that if you contacted us, we'd be set up at the mall. They found a drop spot that we couldn't get to without being seen. They have us tracking down useless leads with the fake sign and welded license plates. Like I said, they're pros."

"And that's good because . . . ?"

"Pros usually aren't bloodthirsty."

"So what are they doing?"

"Our theory," Regan said, "is that they're softening you up, so they can ask for more money."

Softening me up. It was working.

My father-in-law called after the ransom fiasco. I could hear the disappointment in Edgar's voice. I don't want to sound unkind here—Edgar was the one who provided the money and made it clear he would do so again—but the disappointment sounded more aimed at me, at the fact that I had not taken his advice about not contacting the police, than at the final outcome.

Of course, he was right about that. I had messed up big time.

I tried to participate in the investigation, but the police were far from encouraging. In the movies the authorities cooperate and share information with the victim. I naturally asked Tickner and Regan a lot of questions about the case. They didn't answer. They never discussed specifics with me. They treated my interrogatories with near disdain. I wanted to know, for example, more about how my wife was found, about why she'd been naked. They stonewalled.

Lenny was at the house a lot. He had trouble meeting my eye because he, too, blamed himself for encouraging me to come forward. The faces of Regan and Tickner fluctuated between guilt because everything had gone so wrong and guilt of another kind, like maybe I, the grieving husband and father, had been behind this from the get-go. They wanted to know about my shaky marriage to Monica. They wanted to know about my missing gun. It was exactly as Lenny had predicted. The more time passed, the more the authorities aimed their sights on the only available suspect.

Yours truly.

After we hit the one-week mark, the police and FBI presence started fading. Tickner and Regan no longer came by very much. They checked their watches more often. They excused themselves for phone calls involving other cases. I understood that, of course. There had been no new leads. Things were quieting down. Part of me welcomed the respite.

And then, on the ninth day, everything changed.

At ten o'clock, I began to get undressed and ready for bed. I was alone. I love my family and friends, but they began to realize that I needed some time by myself. They had all left before dinner. I ordered delivery from Hunan Garden and, per Mom's earlier instructions, ate for strength.

I looked at the bedside alarm clock. That's how I knew that the time was exactly 10:18 P.M. I glanced at the window, just a casual land sweep. In the dark, I almost missed it—nothing consciously registered anyway—but something snagged my gaze. I stopped and looked again.

There, standing on my walk like a stone, staring at my house, was a woman. I assume that she was staring. I did not know for certain. Her face was lost in the shadows. She had long hair—that much I could see in the silhouette—and she wore a long coat. Her hands were jammed into her pockets.

She just stood there.

I was not sure what to make of it. We were in the news, of course. Reporters stopped by at all hours. I looked up and down the street. No cars, no news vans, nothing. She had come on foot. Again that was not unusual. I live in a suburban neighborhood. People take walks all the time, usually with a dog or spouse or both, but it was hardly earth shattering for a woman to be walking alone.

Then why had she stopped?

Morbid curiosity, I figured.

She looked tall from here, but that was pretty much a guess. I wondered what to do. An uneasy feeling slithered up my back. I grabbed my sweatshirt and threw it over my pajama top. Ditto with a pair of sweatpants and the bottoms. I looked out the window again. The woman stiffened.

She had seen me.

The woman turned and began to hurry away. My chest felt tight. I tried to open the window. It was stuck. I hit the sides to loosen it and tried again. It grudgingly gave me an inch. I lowered my mouth to the opening.

"Wait!"

She picked up the pace.

"Please, hold up a second."

She broke into a run. Damn. I turned away and sprinted after her toward the door. I had no idea where my slippers were and there was no time for shoes. I ran outside. The grass tickled my feet. I sprinted in the direction she had gone. I tried to follow, but I lost her.

When I got back inside my house, I called Regan and told him what had happened. It sounded stupid even as I said it. A woman had been standing in front of my house. Big deal. Regan, too, sounded thoroughly unimpressed. I convinced myself that it was nothing, just a nosy neighbor. I climbed back into bed, flipped the television, and eventually I closed my eyes.

The night, however, was not over.

It was four in the morning when my phone rang. I was in the state I now refer to as sleep. I never fall into true slumber anymore. I hang above it with my eyes shut. The nights struggle by like the days. The separation between the two is the flimsiest of curtains. At night, my body manages to rest, but my mind refuses to shut down.

With my eyes closed, I was replaying the morning of the attack for the umpteenth time, hoping to stir a new memory. I started where I am now: in the bedroom. I remembered my alarm clock going off. Lenny and I were going to play racquetball that morning. We'd started playing every Wednesday about a year before, and so far, we had progressed to the point where our games had improved from "pitiful" to "almost remedial." Monica was awake and in the shower. I was scheduled for surgery at 11:00 A.M. I got up and looked in on Tara. I headed back to the bedroom. Monica was out of the shower now and putting on her jeans. I went down to the kitchen, still in my pajamas, opened the cabinet to the right of the Westinghouse refrigerator, chose the raspberry granola bar over the blueberry (I had actually told this detail to Regan recently, as if it might be relevant), and bent over the sink while I ate. . . .

Bam, that was it. Nothing until the hospital.

The phone rang a second time. My eyes opened.

My hand found the phone. I picked it up and said, "Hello?"

"It's Detective Regan. I'm with Agent Tickner. We'll be over in two minutes."

I swallowed. "What is it?"

"Two minutes."

He hung up.

I got out of bed. I glanced out the window, half expecting to see that woman again. No one was there. My jeans from yesterday were crumpled on the floor. I slid them on. I pulled a sweatshirt over my head and made my way down the stairs. I opened the front door and peered out. A police car turned the corner. Regan was driving. Tickner was in the passenger seat. I don't think that I had ever seen them arrive in the same vehicle.

This, I knew, would not be good news.

The two men stepped out of the car. Nausea swept over me. I had prepared myself for this visit since the ransom had gone wrong. I'd even gone so far as to rehearse in my mind how it would all happen—how they would deliver the hammer blow and how I would nod and thank them and excuse myself. I practiced my reaction. I knew precisely how it would all go down.

But now, as I watched Regan and Tickner head toward me, those defenses fled. Panic set in. My body began to shiver. I could barely stand. My knees wobbled, and I leaned against the door frame. The two men moved in step. I was reminded of an old war movie, the scene where the officers come to the mother's house with solemn faces. I shook my head, wishing them away.

When they reached the door, the two men pushed inside.

"We have something to show you," Regan said.

I turned and followed. Regan flicked on a lamp, but it didn't provide much light. Tickner moved to the couch. He opened his laptop computer. The monitor sprang to life, bathing him in an LCD-blue.

"We had a break," Regan explained.

I moved closer.

"Your father-in-law gave us a list of the serial numbers on the ransom bills, remember?"

"Yes."

"One of those bills was used at a bank yesterday afternoon. Agent Tickner is bringing up a video feed right now."

"From the bank?" I asked.

"Yes. We downloaded the video onto his laptop. Twelve hours ago, someone brought a hundred-dollar bill to this bank in order to get smaller notes. We want you to take a look at the video."

I sat next to Tickner. He pressed a button. The video started up immediately. I expected black-and-white or poor, grainy quality. This feed had neither. The angle was shot from above in almost too-brilliant color. A bald man was talking to a teller. There was no sound.

"I don't recognize him," I said.

"Wait."

The bald man said something to the teller. They appeared to be sharing a good-natured chuckle. He picked up a slip of paper and waved a good-bye. The teller gave a small wave back. The next person in line approached the booth. I heard myself groan.

It was my sister, Stacy.

The numb I had longed for suddenly flooded me. I don't know why. Perhaps because two polar emotions pulled at me simultaneously. One, dread. My own sister had done this. My own sister, whom I loved dearly, had betrayed me. But, two, hope—we now had hope. We had a lead. And if it was Stacy, I could not believe that she would harm Tara.

"Is that your sister?" Regan asked, pointing his finger at her image.

"Yes." I looked at him. "Where was this taken?"

"The Catskills," he said. "A town called—"

"Montague," I finished for him.

Tickner and Regan looked at each other. "How do you know that?"

But I was already heading for the door. "I know where she is."

chapter 7

My grandfather had loved to hunt. I always found this strange because he was such a gentle, soft-spoken soul. He never talked about his passion. He didn't hang deer heads over the fireplace mantel. He did not keep trophy pictures or souvenir antlers or whatever else hunters liked to do with carcasses. He did not hunt with friends or family members. Hunting was a solitary activity for my grandfather; he did not explain, defend, or share it with others.

In 1956, Grandpa purchased a small cabin in the hunting woods of Montague, New York. The cost, or so I am told, was under three thousand dollars. I doubt that it would fetch much more today. There was only one bedroom. The structure managed to be rustic without any of the charm associated with that term. It was almost impossible to find—the dirt road stopped two hundred yards before the cabin. You had to hike along a root-infested trail the rest of the way.

When he died four years ago, my grandmother inherited it. At least, that is what I assumed. No one really thought about it much. My grandparents had retired to Florida almost a decade before. My grandmother was in the murky throes of Alzheimer's now. The old cabin, I guessed, was part of her estate. In terms of taxes and whatever expenses, it was probably deep in arrears.

When we were children, my sister and I spent one weekend each summer with our grandparents at the cabin. I did not like it. Nature to me was boredom occasionally broken up by an onslaught of mosquito bites. There was no TV. We went to bed too early and in too much darkness. During the day, the deep silence was too often shattered by the charming echo of shotgun blasts. We spent most of our time taking walks, an activity I find tedious to this very day. One year, my mother packed me only khaki-colored clothes. I spent two days terrified that a hunter would mistake me for a deer.

Stacy, on the other hand, found solace out there. Even as a young child, she seemed to revel in the escape from our suburban rat-maze of school and extracurricular activities, of sport teams and popularity. She would wander for hours. She would pick leaves off the trees and collect inchworms in a jar. She would shuffle her feet across carpets of fallen pine needles.

I explained about the cabin to Tickner and Regan as we sped up Route 87. Tickner radioed the police department in Montague. I still remembered how to find the cabin, but describing it was harder. I did my best. Regan kept his foot on the gas pedal. It was four-thirty in the morning. There was no traffic and no need for the siren. We reached Exit 16 on the New York Thruway and sped past the Woodbury Common Outlet Center.

The woods were a blur. We were not far now. I told him where to turn off. The car wound up and down back roads that had not changed one iota in the past three decades.

Fifteen minutes later, we were there.

*   *   *

Stacy.

My sister had never been very attractive. That may have been part of her problem. Yes, that sounds like nonsense. It is silly, really. But I lay it out for you anyway. No one asked Stacy to any prom. Boys never called. She had very few friends. Of course, there are many adolescents with such hardships. Adolescence is always a war; no one gets out unscathed. And yes, my father's illness was a tremendous burden on us. But that doesn't explain it.

In the end, after all the theories and psychoanalyzing, after all the combing through her childhood traumas, I think what went wrong with my sister was more basic. She had some kind of chemical imbalance in her brain. Too much of one compound flowing here, not enough of another flowing there. We did not recognize the warning signs soon enough. Stacy was depressed in an era when such behavior was mistaken for sullen. Or maybe, yet again, I use this sort of convoluted rationale to justify my own indifference to her. Stacy was just my weird younger sister. I had my own problems, thank you very much. I had the selfishness of a teenager, a truly redundant description if ever I've heard one.

Either way, be the origins of my sister's unhappiness physiological, psychological, or the deluxe combo plan, Stacy's destructive journey was over.

My little sister was dead.

We found her on the floor, curled up in a tight fetal position. That was how she had slept when she was a child, her knees up to her chest, her chin tucked. But even though there was not a mark on her, I could see that she was not sleeping. I bent down. Stacy's eyes were open. She stared straight at me, unblinking, questioning. She still looked so very lost. That wasn't supposed to be. Death was supposed to bring solitude. Death was supposed to bring the peace she had found so elusive in life. Why, I wondered, did Stacy still look so damn lost?

A hypodermic needle lay on the floor by her side, her companion in death as in life. Drugs, of course. Intentional or otherwise, I did not yet know. I had no time to dwell on it either. The police fanned out. I wrested my eyes away from her.

Tara.

The place was a mess. Raccoons had

found their way in and made a little home for themselves. The couch where my grandfather had taken his naps, always with his arms folded, was torn up. The stuffing had bled onto the floor. Springs popped up looking for someone to stab. The entire place smelled like urine and dead animals.

I stopped and listened for the sound of a crying baby. There was none. Nothing in here. Only one other room. I dived into the bedroom behind a policeman. The room was dark. I hit the light switch. Nothing happened. Flashlights sliced through the black like saber swords. My eyes scanned the room. When I saw it, I nearly cried out.

There was a playpen.

It was one of those modern Pack 'N Plays with the mesh sides that fold up for easy transport. Monica and I have one. I don't know anyone with a baby who doesn't. The product tag dangled off the side. It had to be new.

Tears came to my eyes. The flashlight cut past the Pack 'N Play, giving it a strobe-light effect. It appeared to be empty. My heart sank. I ran over anyway, in case the light had caused an optical illusion, in case Tara was nestled so sweetly that she—I don't know—barely made a bump.

But there was only a blanket inside.

A soft voice—a voice from a whispery, inescapable nightmare—floated across the room: "Oh Christ."

I swiveled my head toward the sound. The voice came again, weaker this time. "In here," a policeman said. "In the closet."

Tickner and Regan were already there. They both looked inside. Even in the dim glow, I saw their faces lose color.

My feet stumbled forward. I crossed the room, nearly falling, grabbing the closet doorknob at the last moment to regain my balance. I looked through the doorway and saw it. And then, as I looked down at the frayed fabric, I could actually feel my insides implode and crumble into ash.

There, lying on the floor, torn and discarded, was a pink one-piece outfit with black penguins.

eighteen months later

chapter 8

Lydia saw the widow sitting alone at Starbucks.

The widow was on a stool seat, gazing absently at the gentle trickle of pedestrians. Her coffee was near the window, the steam forming a circle on the glass. Lydia watched her for a moment. The devastation was still there—the battle-scarred, thousand-yard stare, the posture of the defeated, the hair with no sheen, the shake in the hands.

Lydia ordered a grande skim latte with an extra shot of espresso. The *barista*, a too-skinny black-clad youth with a goatee, gave her the shot "on the house." Men, even ones this young, did stuff like that for Lydia. She lowered her sunglasses and thanked him. He nearly wet himself.

Lydia moved toward the condiment table,

knowing he was checking out her ass. Again she was used to it. She added a packet of Equal to her drink. The Starbucks was fairly empty—there were plenty of seats—but Lydia slid up on the stool immediately next to the widow. Sensing her, the widow startled out of her reverie.

"Wendy?" Lydia said.

Wendy Burnet, the widow, turned toward the soft voice.

"I'm very sorry for your loss," Lydia said.

Lydia smiled at her. She had, she knew, a warm smile. She wore a tailored gray suit on her petite, tight frame. The skirt was slit fairly high. Business sexy. Her eyes had that shiny-wet thing going, her nose small and slightly upturned. Her hair was auburn ringlets, but she could—and often did—change that.

Wendy Burnet stared just long enough for Lydia to wonder if she'd been recognized. Lydia had seen that stare plenty of times before, that unsure I-know-you-from-somewhere expression, even though she had not been on TV since she turned thirteen. Some people would even comment, "Hey, you know who you look like?" but Lydia—she had been billed as Larissa Dane back then—would shrug it away.

But alas, this hesitation was not like that. Wendy Burnet was still shell-shocked from the horrible death of her beloved. It simply took her a while to register and assimilate unfamiliar data. She was probably wondering how to react, if she should pretend she knew Lydia or not.

After another few seconds, Wendy Burnet went for the noncommittal. "Thank you."

"Poor Jimmy," Lydia followed up. "Such an awful way to go."

Wendy fumbled for the paper coffee cup and downed a healthy sip. Lydia checked out the little boxes on the side of the cup and saw that the Widow Wendy had ordered a grande latte too, though she'd chosen half decaf and soy milk. Lydia slid a little closer to her.

"You don't know who I am, do you?"

Wendy gave her a weak got-me smile. "I'm sorry."

"No need to be. I don't think we ever met."

Wendy waited for Lydia to introduce herself. When she didn't, Wendy said, "You knew my husband then?"

"Oh yes."

"Are you in the insurance business too?"

"No, I'm afraid not."

Wendy frowned. Lydia sipped her beverage. The awkwardness grew, at least for Wendy. Lydia was fine with it. When it became too much, Wendy rose to leave.

"Well," she said, "it was nice meeting you."

"I . . ." Lydia began, hesitating until she was sure that she had Wendy's full attention, "I was the last person to see Jimmy alive."

Wendy froze. Lydia took another sip and closed her eyes. "Nice and strong," she said, gesturing toward the cup. "I love the coffee here, don't you?"

"Did you say . . . ?"

"Please," Lydia said with a small sweep of her arm. "Have a seat so I can explain properly."

Wendy glanced over at the *baristas*. They were busy gesticulating and whining about what they thought was the great world conspiracy that kept them from the most amazing of lives. Wendy slid back onto the stool. For a few moments, Lydia just stared at her. Wendy tried to hold her gaze.

"You see," Lydia began, offering up a fresh, warm smile and tilting her head to the side, "I'm the one who killed your husband."

Wendy's face went pale. "That isn't funny."

"True, yes, I'd have to agree with you on that, Wendy. But then again humor was not really my aim. Would you like to hear a joke instead? I'm on one of those joke e-mail lists. Most are duds, but every once in a while, they send a howler."

Wendy sat stunned. "Who the hell are you?"

"Calm down a second, Wendy."

"I want to know—"

"Shhh." Lydia put her finger to Wendy's lip with too much tenderness. "Let me explain, okay?"

Wendy's lips trembled. Lydia kept her finger there for a few more seconds.

"You're confused. I understand that. Let me clarify a few things for you. First off, yes, I'm the one who put the bullet in Jimmy's head. But Heshy"—Lydia pointed out the window in the direction of an enormous man with a misshapen head—"he did the earlier damage. Personally, by the time I shot Jimmy, well, I think I might have been doing him a favor."

Wendy just stared.

"You want to know why, am I right? Of course, you do. But deep down inside, Wendy, I think you know. We're women of the world, aren't we? We know our men."

Wendy said nothing.

"Wendy, do you know what I'm talking about?"

"No."

"Sure you do, but I'll say it anyway. Jimmy, your dearly departed husband, owed a great deal of money to some very unpleasant people. As of today, the amount is just under two hundred thousand dollars." Lydia smiled. "Wendy, you're not going to pretend you know nothing about your husband's gambling woes, are you?"

Wendy had trouble forming the words in her mouth. "I don't understand. . . ."

"I hope your confusion has nothing to do with my gender."

"What?"

"That would be really narrow and sexist on your part, don't you think? This is the twenty-first century. Women can be whatever they want."

"You"—Wendy stopped, tried again—"you murdered my husband?"

"Do you watch much television, Wendy?"

"What?"

"Television. You see, on television, whenever someone like your husband owes money to someone like me, well, what happens?"

Lydia stopped as if she really expected her to answer. Wendy finally said, "I don't know."

"Sure you do, but again I'll answer for you. The someone-like-me—okay, usually the *male* someone-like-me—is sent to threaten him. Then maybe my cohort Heshy out there would beat him up or break his legs, something like that. But they never kill the guy. That's one of those TV-bad-guy rules. 'You can't collect from a dead man.' You've heard that, haven't you, Wendy?"

She waited. Wendy finally said, "I guess."

"But, see, that's wrong. Let's take Jimmy, for example. Your husband had a disease. Gambling. Am I right? It cost you everything, didn't it? The insurance business. That had been your father's. Jimmy took it over for him. It's gone now. Wiped out. The bank was ready to foreclose on your house.

You and the kids barely had enough money for groceries. And still Jimmy didn't stop." Lydia shook her head. "Men. Am I right?"

There were tears in Wendy's eyes. Her voice, when she was able to speak, was so weak. "So you killed him?"

Lydia looked up, shaking her head gently. "I'm really not explaining this well, am I?" She lowered her gaze and tried again. "Have you ever heard the expression that you can't squeeze blood from a stone?"

Again Lydia waited for an answer. Wendy finally nodded. Lydia seemed pleased.

"Well, that's the case here. With Jimmy, I mean. I could have Heshy out there work him over—Heshy is good at that—but what good would that do? Jimmy didn't have the money. He would never be able to get his hands on that kind of cash." Lydia sat a little straighter and put out her hands. "Now, Wendy, I want you to think like a businessman—check that, a business*person*. We don't have to be raving feminists, but I think we should at least keep ourselves on equal footing."

Lydia gave Wendy another smile. Wendy cringed.

"Okay, so what am I—as a wise business*person*—what am I supposed to do? I can't let the debt go unpaid, of course. In my line of work, that's professional suicide. Someone owes my employer money, they have to pay. No way around that. The problem here is, Jimmy doesn't have a cent to his name but"—Lydia stopped and widened her smile—"but he does have a wife and three kids. And he used to be in the insurance business. Do you see where I'm going with this, Wendy?"

Wendy was afraid to breathe.

"Oh, I think you do, but again I'll say it for you. Insurance. More specifically, *life* insurance. Jimmy had a policy. He didn't admit it right away, but eventually, well, Heshy can be persuasive." Wendy's eyes drifted toward the window. Lydia saw the shiver and hid a smile. "Jimmy told us he had two policies, in fact, with a total payout of nearly a million dollars."

"So you"—Wendy was struggling to comprehend—"you killed Jimmy for the insurance money?"

Lydia snapped her fingers. "You go, girlfriend."

Wendy opened her mouth but nothing came out.

"And, Wendy? Let me make this crystal clear. Jimmy's debts don't die with him. We both know that. The bank still wants you to pay the mortgage, am I right? The credit-card companies don't stop mounting the interest." Lydia shrugged her small shoulders, palms to the sky. "Why should my employer be any different?"

"You can't be serious."

"Your first insurance check should come in about a week. By that time, your husband's debt will be two hundred eighty thousand dollars. I'll expect a check for that amount on that day."

"But the bills he left alone—"

"Shhh." Again Lydia silenced her with a finger to her lips. Her voice dropped to an intimate whisper. "That doesn't really concern me, Wendy. I have given you the rare opportunity to get out from under. Declare bankruptcy, if you must. You live in a ritzy area. Move out. Have Jack—that's your eleven-year-old, correct?"

Wendy jolted at the sound of her son's name.

"Well, no summer camp for Jack this year. Have him get a job after school. Whatever. None of that concerns me. You, Wendy, will pay what you owe, and that will be the end of this. You will never see or hear from me again. If you don't pay, however, well, take a good look at Heshy over there." She paused, letting Wendy do just that. It had the desired effect.

"We'll kill little Jack first. Then, two days later, we'll kill Lila. If you report this conversation to the police, we'll kill Jack and Lila and Darlene. All three, in age order. And then, after you bury your children—please listen, Wendy, because this is key—I'll still make you pay."

Wendy couldn't speak.

Lydia followed up a deep, caffeinated sip with an "Ahh" of satisfaction. "Dee-lightful," she said, rising from her seat. "I really enjoyed our little girl chat, Wendy. We should get together again soon. Say, your house at noon on Friday the sixteenth?"

Wendy kept her head down.

"Do you understand?"

"Yes."

"What are you going to do?"

"I'm going to pay the debt," Wendy said.

Lydia smiled at her. "Again, my sincerest condolences."

Lydia headed outside and breathed in the

fresh air. She looked behind her. Wendy Burnet had not moved. Lydia waved good-bye and met up with Heshy. He was nearly six six. She was five one. He weighed 275 pounds. She was 105. He had a head like a misshapen pumpkin. Her features seemed to have been made in the Orient out of porcelain.

"Problems?" Heshy asked.

"Please," she said with a dismissive wave. "On to more profitable ventures. Did you find our man?"

"Yes."

"And the package is already out?"

"Sure, Lydia."

"Very good." She frowned, felt a gnawing.

"What's wrong?" he asked.

"I have a funny feeling, that's all."

"You want to back out?"

Lydia smiled at him. "Not on your life, Pooh Bear."

"Then what do you want to do?"

She thought about it. "Let's just see how Dr. Seidman reacts."

chapter 9

"Don't drink any more apple juice," Cheryl told her two-year-old, Conner.

I stood on the sidelines with my arms folded. It was a bit nippy, the frosty, damp chill of late New Jersey autumn, so I pulled the hood of my sweatshirt over my Yankee cap. I also had on a pair of Ray-Bans. Sunglasses and hood. I looked very much like the police sketch of the Unabomber.

We were at a soccer game for eight-year-old boys. Lenny was the head coach. He needed an assistant and recruited me because, I assume, I am the only one who knows even less about soccer than he does. Still our team was winning. I think the score was about eighty-three to two, but I am not certain.

"Why can't I have more juice?" Conner asked.

"Because," Cheryl answered with the patience of a mother, "apple juice gives you diarrhea."

"It does?"

"Yes."

To my right, Lenny drowned the kids in a steady stream of encouragement. "You're the best, Ricky." "Way to go, Petey." "Now *that's* what I call hustle, Davey." He always added a *y* to the end of their names. And yes, it is annoying. Once, in a pitch of overexcitement, he called me Marky. Once.

"Uncle Marc?"

I feel a tug at my leg. I look down at Conner, who is twenty-six months old. "What's up, pal?"

"Apple juice gives me a diarrhea."

"Good to know," I said.

"Uncle Marc?"

"Yeah?"

Conner gave me his gravest look. "Diarrhea," he said, "is not my friend."

I glanced at Cheryl. She smothered a smile, but I saw the concern there too. I looked back at Conner. "Words to live by, kid."

Conner nodded, pleased by my response. I love him. He breaks my heart and brings me joy in equal measure and at exactly the same time. Twenty-six months old. Two months older than Tara. I watch his development with awe and a longing that could heat a furnace.

He turned back to his mother. Littered about Cheryl was the product of her mommy-as-pack-mule harvest. There were Minute Maid juice boxes and Nutri-Grain bars. There were Pampers Baby-Dry diapers (as opposed to Baby-Wet?) and Huggies wipes containing aloe vera for the discriminating buttock. There were angled baby bottles from Evenflo. There were cinnamon Teddy Grahams and well-scrubbed baby carrots and sectioned oranges and cut-up grapes (sliced the long way so as to make them chokeproof) and cubes of what I hoped was cheese, all hermetically sealed in their own Ziploc bags.

Lenny, the head coach, was yelling out key, game-winning strategy to our players. When we are on offense, he tells them to "Score!" When we are on defense, he advises them to "Stop him!" And then sometimes, like right now, he offers keen insight into the subtleties of the game:

"Kick the ball!"

Lenny glanced at me after he'd shouted that for the fourth time in a row. I gave him a thumbs-up and way-to-go nod. He wanted to give me the finger, but there were too many underage witnesses. I refolded my arms and squinted at the field. The kids were geared up like the pros. They wore cleats. Their socks were pulled up over their shin guards. Most wore that black grease under their eyes, even though there was nary a hint of sunshine. Two even had those breathing strip-bandages across their noses. I watched Kevin, my godson, try, per his father's instructions, to kick the ball. And then it hit me like a body blow.

I staggered back.

That was how it always happened. I will be watching the game or I'll be having dinner with friends or I'll be working on a patient or listening to a song on the radio. I'll be doing something normal, average, feeling pretty decent, and then, wham, I get blindsided.

My eyes welled up. That never used to happen to me before the murder and kidnapping. I am a doctor. I know how to play poised in both my professional and personal life. But now I wear sunglasses all the time like some self-important B movie star. Cheryl looked up at me and again I saw the concern. I straightened and forced a smile. Cheryl was becoming beautiful. That happened sometimes. Motherhood agreed with certain women. It gave their physical appearance a wonder and richness that borders on the celestial.

I don't want to give you the wrong impression. I don't spend every day crying. I still live my life. I am bereaved, sure, but not all the time. I am not paralyzed. I work, though I haven't yet had the courage to travel overseas. I keep thinking that I need to stay close by, in case there is a new development. That kind of thinking is, I know, not rational and perhaps even delusional. But I am still not ready.

What gets me—what gives me that surprise wham—is the way grief seems to relish in catching you unawares. Grief, when spotted, can be, if not handled, somewhat manipulated, finessed, concealed. But grief likes to hide behind bushes. It enjoys leaping out of nowhere, startling you, mocking

you, stripping away your pretense of normalcy. Grief lulls you to sleep, thus making
that blindside hit all the more jarring.

"Uncle Marc?"

It was Conner again. He talked pretty well
for a kid his age. I wondered what Tara's
voice would have sounded like, and behind
my sunglasses, my eyes closed. Sensing
something, Cheryl reached out to pull him
away. I shook her off. "What is it, pal?"

"What about poop?"

"What about it?"

He looked up and closed one eye in concentration. "Is poop my friend?"

Hell of a question. "I don't know, pal.
What do you think?"

Conner considered his own query so hard
it appeared as if he might explode. Finally
he replied, "It's more my friend than diarrhea."

I nodded sagely. Our team scored
another goal. Lenny shot his fists into the air
and shouted, "Yes!" He nearly cartwheeled
out to congratulate Craig (or should I say
Craigy), the goal scorer. The players followed him. There was much high-fiving. I
didn't join in. My job, I figured, was to be the
quiet partner to Lenny's histrionics, the

Tonto to his Lone Ranger, the Abbott to his Costello, the Rowan to his Martin, the Captain to his Tennille. Balance.

I watched the parents on the sidelines. The mothers became clusters. They talked about their kids, about their child's achievements and extracurricular activities, and no one listened much because other people's children are boring. The fathers offered more variety. Some videotaped. Some yelled encouragement. Some rode their kids in a way that borders on the unhealthy. Some gabbed on cell phones and constantly fiddled with handheld electronics of one kind or another, experiencing a bit of the bends after spending all week immersed in their work.

Why did I go to the police?

I have been told countless times since that terrible day that I am not to blame for what happened. On one level, I realize that my actions may have changed nothing. In all likelihood, they had never intended to let Tara come home. She might even have been dead before the first ransom call. Her death may have been accidental. Maybe they just panicked or were strung out. Who knows? I certainly don't.

And, ah, there's the rub.

I cannot, of course, be certain that I am not responsible. Basic science: For every action, there is a reaction.

I do not dream about Tara—or if I do, the gods are generous enough to not let me remember. That is probably giving them too much credit. Let me rephrase. I may not dream about Tara specifically, but I do dream about the white van with the mix-and-match license plate and the stolen magnetic sign. In the dreams I hear a noise, muffled, but I'm pretty sure it is the sound of a baby crying. Tara, I know now, was in the van, but in my dream, I don't go toward the sound. My legs are buried deep in that nightmare muck. I can't move. When I finally wake up, I cannot help but ponder the obvious. Was Tara that close to me? And more important: Had I been a little braver, could I have saved her then and there?

The referee, a lanky high-school boy with a good-natured grin, blew the whistle and waved his hands over his head. Game over. Lenny shouted, "Woo, yeah!" The eight-year-olds stared at one another, confused. One asked a teammate, "Who won?" and the teammate shrugged. They lined up,

Stanley Cup hockey style, for the postgame handshakes.

Cheryl stood up and put a hand on my back. "Great win, Coach."

"Yeah, I carry this team," I said.

She smiled. The boys started rambling back toward us. I congratulated them with my stoic nod. Craig's mother had brought a fifty-pack of Dunkin' Donuts Munchkins in a box with a Halloween design. Dave's mom had boxes of something called Yoo-hoo, a perverse excuse for chocolate milk that tastes like chalk. I popped a Munchkin in my mouth and skipped the washdown. Cheryl asked, "What flavor was that?"

I shrugged. "They come in different flavors?" I watched the parents interact with their children and felt tremendously out of place. Lenny came toward me.

"Great win, wasn't it?"

"Yeah," I said. "We're the balls."

He gestured for us to step away. I complied. When we were out of earshot, Lenny said, "Monica's estate is almost wrapped up. It shouldn't be too much longer now."

I said, "Uh-huh," because I didn't really care.

"I also have your will drawn up. You need to sign it."

Neither Monica nor I had made up a will. For years, Lenny had warned me about that. You need to put in writing who gets your money, he'd remind me, who is going to raise your daughter, who is going to care for your parents, yadda, yadda, yadda. But we didn't listen. We were going to live forever. Last wills and testaments were for, well, the dead.

Lenny changed subjects on the fly. "You want to come back to the house for a game of foosball?"

Foosball, for those of you who lack a basic education, is that tabletop bar game with the soccer-type men skewered on sticks. "I'm already champion of the world," I reminded him.

"That was yesterday."

"Can't a man revel in his title for a little while? I'm not yet ready to let go of the feeling."

"Understood." Lenny headed back to his family. I watched his daughter, Marianne, corner him. She was gesturing like mad. Lenny slumped his shoulders, took out his wallet, peeled out a bill. Marianne took it, kissed him on the cheek, ran off. Lenny watched her disappear, shaking his head. There was a smile on his face. I turned away.

The worst part—or should I say the best part—was that I have hope.

Here was what we found that night at Grandpa's cabin: my sister's corpse, hairs belonging to Tara in the Pack 'N Play (DNA confirmed), and a pink one-piece with black penguins that matched Tara's.

Here was what we did not find and, in fact, still have not found: the ransom money, the identity, if any, of Stacy's accomplices—and Tara.

That's right. We never found my daughter.

The forest is big and sprawling, I know. The grave would be small and easily hidden. There could be rocks over it. An animal might have found it and dragged the contents deeper into the thicket. The contents could be miles from my grandfather's cabin. They could be somewhere else entirely.

Or—though I keep this thought to myself—maybe there is no grave at all.

So you see, the hope is there. Like grief, hope hides and pounces and taunts and never leaves. I am not sure which of the two is the crueler mistress.

The police and FBI theorize that my sister acted in conjunction with some very bad people. While no one is quite sure if their original intention was kidnapping or robbery, most everyone agrees that someone panicked. Maybe they thought that Monica and I would not be home. Maybe they thought that they would just have to contend with a baby-sitter. Whatever, they saw us, and acting in some drugged or crazed state, someone fired a shot. Then someone else fired a shot, ergo the ballistic tests showing Monica and I were shot by different .38's. They then kidnapped the baby. Eventually they double-crossed Stacy and killed her with an overdose of heroin.

I keep saying "they" because the authorities also believe that Stacy had at least two accomplices. One would be the professional, the cool head who knew how to work the drop and weld the license plates and disappear without a trace. The other accomplice would be the "panicker," if you will, the one who shot us and probably caused the death of Tara.

Some, of course, don't buy that theory.

Some believe that there was only one accomplice—the cool professional—and that
the one who panicked was Stacy. She, this
theory goes, was the one who fired the first
bullet, probably at me since I don't remember any shots, and then the professional
killed Monica to cover the mistake. This theory is backed up by one of the few leads we
had following that night in the cabin: a drug
dealer who, in some bizarre plea bargain on
another charge, told authorities that Stacy
had purchased a gun from him, a .38, a
week before the murder-kidnapping. This
theory is further backed up by the fact that
the only unexplained hairs and fingerprints
found at the murder scene were Stacy's.
While the cool pro would know to wear
gloves and be careful, a drugged-out accomplice would probably not.

Still others do not embrace that theory either, which is why certain members of the
police department and FBI cling to and support a more obvious third scenario:

I was the mastermind.

The theory goes something like this: first
caveat, the husband is always suspect
number one. Second, my Smith & Wesson
.38 is still missing. They press me on this

question all the time. I wish I had an answer. Third, I never wanted a child. Tara's birth forced me into a loveless marriage. They believe that they have evidence that I was considering divorce (something that yes, I did indeed contemplate) and so I planned the whole thing, top to bottom. I invited my sister over to my house and perhaps enlisted her help so that she would take the fall. I have the ransom money hidden away. I killed and buried my own daughter.

Awful, yes, but I am past anger. I am past exhaustion. I am not sure where I am anymore.

The main problem with their hypothesis is, of course, that it is hard to finesse my being left for dead. Did I kill Stacy? Did she shoot me? Or—drum roll here—is there a third possibility out there, a blending of the two different theories into one? Some believe that yes, I was behind it, but I had another accomplice besides Stacy. That accomplice killed Stacy, perhaps against my wishes, perhaps as part of my grand scheme to deflect my guilt and avenge my own shooting. Or something like that.

And round and round we go.

In sum, when you cut through it all, they—

and I—have nothing. No ransom money. No idea who did it. No idea why. And most important: no small corpse.

That is where we are today—a year and a half after the abduction. The file is still technically open, but Regan and Tickner have moved on to new cases. I haven't heard a word from either in nearly six months. The media gnawed on us for a few weeks, but with nothing new to feed on, they too, slithered toward juicier troughs.

The Dunkin' Donuts Munchkins were gone. Everyone started heading to a parking lot overloaded with minivans. After the game we coaches take our budding athletes to Schrafft's Ice Cream Parlor, a tradition in our town. Every coach in every other league in every other age group follows the same tradition. The place was packed. Nothing like an ice cream cone in the autumn frost to burrow the chill into the bone.

I stood with my Cookies-n-Cream cone and surveyed the scene. Children and fathers. It was getting to be too much for me. I checked my watch. Time for me to leave anyway. I met Lenny's eye and motioned that I was going. He mouthed the words *Your will* at me. In case I didn't get the drift, he even made a signing motion with his hand. I waved that I understood. I got back into my car and flipped on the radio.

For a long while, I sat there and watched the flow of families. I kept my eyes on the fathers mostly. I gauged their reactions to this most domestic of activities, hoping to see a flicker of doubt, something in the eyes that might comfort me. But I didn't.

I'm not sure how long I stayed like that. Not more than ten minutes, I suppose. An old favorite by James Taylor came on the radio. It brought me back. I smiled, started up the car, and made my way toward the hospital.

An hour later, I was scrubbing up to perform surgery on an eight-year-old boy with—to use terminology familiar to both layman and professional—a facial smash. Zia Leroux, my medical partner, was there.

I'm not sure why I first chose to be a plastic surgeon. It was neither the siren song of easy dollars nor the ideal of helping my fellowman. I had wanted to be a surgeon pretty much from the get-go, but I saw myself more in the vascular or cardiac fields. Life's turns come in funny ways though.

During my second year of residency, the cardiac surgeon who ran our rotation was—what's the phrase?—a total prick. On the other hand, the doctor in charge of the cosmetic surgery, Liam Reese, was incredible. Dr. Reese had that enviable have-it-all feel to him, that combination of good looks, calm confidence, and internal warmth that naturally drew people. You wanted to please him. You wanted to be like him.

Dr. Reese became my mentor. He showed how reconstructive surgery was creative, a Humpty-Dumpty process that forced you to find new ways to put back together what had been destroyed. The bones in the face and skull are the most complex stretch of skeletal landscape in the human body. We who repair them are artists. We are jazz musicians. If you talk to orthopedic or thoracic surgeons, they can be pretty specific about their procedures. Our work—reconstruction—is never exactly the same. We improvise. Dr. Reese taught me that. He appealed to my inner techno-weenie with talk of microsurgery and bone grafts and synthetic skin. I remember visiting him in Scarsdale. His wife was long legged and beautiful. His daughter was school valedictorian. His son was captain of the basketball team and the nicest kid I've ever met. At the age of forty-nine Dr. Reese was killed in a car crash on Route 684 heading to Connecticut. Somebody might find something poignant in that, but that person wouldn't be me.

When I was finishing up residency, I landed a one-year fellowship to train in oral surgery overseas. I didn't apply to be a do-gooder; I applied because it sounded pretty cool. This trip would be, I hoped, my version of backpacking through Europe. It was not. Things went wrong right away. We got caught up in a civil war in Sierra Leone. I handled wounds so horrible, so unfathomable, that it was hard to believe the human mind could conjure up the necessary cruelty to inflict them. But even in the midst of this destruction, I felt a strange exhilaration. I don't try to figure out why. Like I said before, this stuff gets me jazzed. Maybe part of it was the satisfaction of helping people truly in need. Or maybe I was drawn to this work the same way some are drawn to extreme sports, who need the risk of death to feel whole.

When I came back, Zia and I set up One

World, and we were on our way. I love what I do. Perhaps our work is like an extreme sport, but it also has a very—pardon the pun—human face. I like that. I love my patients and yet I love the calculating distance, the necessary coldness, of what I do. I care about my patients so much, but then they are gone—intense love mixed with fleeting commitment.

Today's patient presented us with a rather complicated challenge. My patron saint—the patron saint of many in reconstructive surgery—is the French researcher René LeFort. LeFort tossed cadavers off a tavern roof onto their skulls to see the natural pattern of fracture lines in the face. I bet this impressed the ladies. Today we name certain fractures for him—more specifically, LeFort type I, LeFort type II, LeFort type III. Zia and I checked the films again. The Water view gave us the best look, but the Caldwell and lateral backed it up.

Simply put, the fracture line on this eight-year-old was a LeFort type III, causing a complete separation of the facial bones and the cranium. I could pretty much rip off the boy's face like a mask if I wanted to.

"Car accident?" I asked.

Zia nodded. "Father was drunk."

"Don't tell me. He's fine, right?"

"He even remembered to put on his own seat belt."

"But not his son's."

"Too much trouble. What with him being tired from raising a glass so many times."

Zia and I started our life's journey in two very different places. Like the Story's classic seventies song "Brother Louie," Zia is black as the night while I am whiter than white (my skin tone, as described by Zia: "underwater fish belly"). I was born at Beth Israel Hospital in Newark and grew up on the suburban streets of Kasselton, New Jersey. Zia was born in a mud hut in a village outside of Port-au-Prince, Haiti. Sometime during the reign of Papa Doc, her parents became political prisoners. No one knows too many details. Her father was executed. Her mother, when released, was damaged goods. She grabbed her daughter and escaped on what might liberally be dubbed a raft. Three passengers died on the journey. Zia and her mother survived. They made their way to the Bronx where they took up residence in the basement of a beauty parlor. The two spent their days quietly sweeping hair. The hair, it seemed to Zia, was inescapable. It was on her clothes, clinging to her skin, in her throat, in her lungs. She lived forever with that feeling that a stray strand was in her mouth and she couldn't quite pull it out. To this day, when Zia gets nervous, her fingers play with her tongue, as though trying to pluck out a memento of her past.

When the surgery was over, Zia and I collapsed onto a bench. Zia untied her surgical mask and let it fall to her chest.

"Piece of cake," she said.

"Amen," I agreed. "How did your date go last night?"

"It sucked," she said. "And I don't mean that literally."

"Sorry."

"Men are such scum."

"Don't I know it."

"I'm getting so desperate," she said, "I'm thinking of sleeping with you again."

"Gasp," I said. "Woman, have you no standards?"

Her smile was blinding, the bright white against the dark skin. She was a shade under six feet tall with smooth muscles and cheekbones so high and sharp you feared they might pierce her skin. "When are you going to start dating?" she asked.

"I date."

"I mean, long enough to have a sexual encounter."

"Not all women are easy as you, Zia."

"Sad," she said, giving my arm a playful punch.

Zia and I slept together once—and we both knew that it would never happen again. It was how we met. We hooked up during my first year of medical school. Yep, a one-night stand. I have had my fair share of one-night stands, but only two have been memorable. The first led to disaster. The second—this one—led to a relationship I will cherish forever.

It was eight o'clock at night by the time we got out of our scrubs. We took Zia's car, a tiny thing called a BMW Mini, to the Stop & Shop on Northwood Avenue and picked up some groceries. Zia chatted without letup as we wheeled carts down the aisles. I liked when Zia talked. It gave me energy. At the deli counter Zia pulled a call number. She looked at the specials board and frowned.

"What?" I said.

"Boar's Head ham on sale."

"What about it?"

"Boar's Head," she repeated. "What marketing genius came up with that name? 'Say, I have an idea. Let's name our premium cold cuts after the most disgusting animal imaginable. No, check that. Let's name it after its head.' "

"You always order it," I said.

She thought about it. "Yeah, I guess."

We moved to the checkout line. Zia put her stuff up front. I placed the divider down and unloaded my cart. A portly cashier began to ring up her items.

"You hungry?" she asked me.

I shrugged. "Guess I could go for a couple of slices at Garbo's."

"Let's do it." Zia's eyes drifted over my shoulder and then jerked to a stop. She squinted and something crossed her face. "Marc?"

"Yeah."

She waved it off. "Nah, can't be."

"What?"

Still staring over my shoulder, Zia gestured with her chin. I turned slowly and when I saw her, I felt it in my chest.

"I've only seen her in pictures," Zia said, "but isn't that . . . ?"

I managed a nod.

It was Rachel.

The world closed in around me. It shouldn't feel this way. I knew that. We had broken up years ago. Now, after all this time, I should be smiling. I should feel something wistful, a passing nostalgia, a poignant remembrance of a time when I was young and naïve. But no, that was not what was going on here. Rachel stood ten yards away and it all flooded back. What I felt was a still-too-powerful yearning, a longing that tore through me, that made both the love and heartbreak feel fresh and alive.

"You okay?" Zia said.

Another nod.

Are you one of those who believe that we all have one true soul mate—one and only one preordained love? There, across three Stop & Shop checkout lanes and under a sign reading EXPRESS LANE—15 ITEMS OR LESS, stood mine.

Zia said, "I thought she got married."

"She did," I said.

"No ring." Then Zia punched my arm. "Oooh, this is exciting, isn't it?"

"Yeah," I said. "Exhilaration city."

Zia snapped her fingers. "Hey, you know what this is like? That crappy old album you used to play. The song about meeting the old lover in the grocery store. What's the name of it?"

The first time I'd seen Rachel, when I was a lad of nineteen years, the effect was relatively gentle. There was no big boom. I'm not even sure that I found her overly attractive. But as I'd soon learn, I like a woman whose looks grow on you. You start off thinking, Okay, she's pretty decent looking, and then, a few days later, maybe it's something she says or the way she tilts her head when she says it, but then, wham, it's like getting hit by a bus.

It felt like that again now. Rachel had changed but not by much. The years had made that sneaky beauty harden maybe, more brittle and angled. She was thinner. Her dark blue-black hair was pulled back and tied into a ponytail. Most men like the hair down. I've always liked it tied back, the openness and exposure of it, I guess, especially with Rachel's cheekbones and neck.

She wore jeans and a gray blouse. Her hazel eyes were down, her head bent in that pose of concentration I knew so well. She had not seen me yet.

" 'Same Old Lang Syne,' " Zia said.

"What?"

"The song about the lovers in the grocery store. By Dan Somebody. That's the title. 'Same Old Lang Syne.' " Then she added: "I think that's the title."

Rachel reached into her wallet and plucked out a twenty. She began to hand it to the cashier. Her gaze lifted—and that was when she saw me.

I can't say exactly what crossed her face. She did not look surprised. Our eyes met, but I did not see joy there. Fear, perhaps. Maybe resignation. I don't know. I also don't know how long we both stood there like that.

"Maybe I should move away from you," Zia whispered.

"Huh?"

"If she thinks you're with a chick this hot, she'll conclude that she has no chance."

I think I smiled.

"Marc?"

"Yeah."

"Better," she said.

"Come here often?"

"Good. Now say, 'Haven't we met before?' "

"Nah." I arched an eyebrow. "No way I'd forget meeting a foxy lady like you."

We both laughed. We were both trying oo hard. We both knew it.

"You look good," I said.

"So do you."

Brief silence.

"Okay," I said, "I'm out of uncomfortable clichés and forced banter."

"Whew," Rachel said.

"Why are you here?"

"I'm buying food."

"No, I mean—"

"I know what you meant," she interrupted. "My mother moved into a condo development in West Orange."

A few of the strands had escaped her ponytail and fell across her face. It took all my willpower to stop from pushing them away.

Rachel glanced away and then back at me. "I heard about your wife and daughter," she said. "I'm sorry."

"Thank you."

"The way you're standing like tha
ing like a total whack job. It's a little

"Thanks."

I felt her hand push on my back. "G
and say hello."

My feet started moving, though I dc
member the brain issuing any comm
Rachel let the cashier bag her groc
She stepped toward me and tried to s
Her smile had always been spectacula
kind that makes you think of poetry
spring showers, a dazzler that can ch
your day. This smile, however, was no
that. It was tighter. It was pained. A
wondered if she was holding back or if
could no longer smile like she used t
something had dimmed the wattage peri
nently.

We stopped a yard away from each oth
neither sure if the proper protocol called
a hug, a kiss, a handshake. So we did no
of the above. I stood there and felt the h
everywhere.

"Hi," I said.

"Good to see you still have all the smoo
lines, " Rachel replied.

I feigned a rakish grin. "Hey, baby, what'
your sign?"

"I wanted to call or write but . . ."

"I heard you got married," I said.

She wiggled the fingers on her left hand. "Not anymore."

"And that you were an agent with the FBI."

Rachel put her hand back down. "Also not anymore."

More silence. Again I don't know how long we stood there. The cashier had moved on to the next shopper. Zia came up behind us. She cleared her throat and jammed her hand toward Rachel. "Hi, I'm Zia Leroux," she said.

"Rachel Mills."

"Good to meet you, Rachel. I'm Marc's practice partner." Then, thinking about it, she added: "We're just friends."

"Zia," I said.

"Oh, right, sorry. Look, Rachel, I'd love to stay and chat, but I have to run." She jerked her thumb toward the exit to emphasize the point. "You two talk. Marc, I'll meet you back here later. Great meeting you, Rachel."

"Same here."

Zia rushed off. I shrugged. "She's a great doctor."

"I bet she is." Rachel took hold of her

cart. "I have someone waiting in the car, Marc. It was good seeing you."

"You too." But surely, with all I'd lost, I must have learned something, right? I couldn't just let her go. I cleared my throat and said, "Maybe we should get together."

"I'm still living in Washington. I head back tomorrow."

Silence. My insides turned to jelly. My breathing was shallow.

"Good-bye, Marc," Rachel said. But those hazel eyes were wet.

"Don't go yet."

I tried to keep the pleading out of my voice, but I don't think I was successful. Rachel looked at me, and she saw everything. "What do you want me to say here, Marc?"

"That you want to get together too."

"That's all?"

I shook my head. "You know that's not all."

"I'm not twenty-one anymore."

"Neither am I."

"The girl you loved is dead and gone."

"No," I said. "She's right in front of me."

"You don't know me anymore."

"So let's get reacquainted. I'm not in a rush."

"Just like that?"

I tried to smile. "Yeah."

"I live in Washington. You live in New Jersey."

"So I'll move," I said.

But even before the impetuous words came out, even before Rachel made that face, I could recognize my own false bravado. I couldn't just leave my parents or dump my business with Zia or—or abandon my ghosts. Somewhere between my lips and her ears the sentiment crashed and burned.

Rachel turned to leave then. She did not say good-bye again. I watched her push the cart toward the door. I saw it automatically swing open with an electric grunt. I saw Rachel, the love of my life, disappear again without so much as a backward glance. I stayed still. I did not follow her. I felt my heart tumble and shatter, but I did nothing to stop her.

Maybe I hadn't learned anything, after all.

chapter 10

I drank.

I am not a big drinker—pot had been my elixir of choice during my younger days—but I found an old bottle of gin in a cabinet over the sink. There was tonic in the fridge. I have an automatic icemaker in the freezer. You do the math.

I still lived in the old Levinsky house. It is much too big for me, but I don't have the heart to let it go. It feels like a portal now, a lifeline (albeit a fragile one) to my daughter. Yes, I know how that sounds, but selling it now would be like closing a door on her. I can't do that.

Zia wanted to stay with me, but I begged off. She did not push it. I thought about the corny Dan Fogelberg (not Dan Somebody) song where the old lovers talk until their tongues get tired. I thought about Bogie questioning the gods who would allow Ingrid Bergman into his, of all possible, gin joints. Bogie drank after she left. It seemed to help him. Maybe it would help me too.

The fact that Rachel could still pack this kind of wallop annoyed the hell out of me. It was stupid and childish really. Rachel and I had first met during summer break between my sophomore and junior years of college. She was from Middlebury, Vermont, and supposedly a distant cousin of Lenny's wife, Cheryl, though no one could ascertain the exact relationship. That summer—the summer of all summers—Rachel stayed with Cheryl's family because Rachel's folks were going through a nasty divorce. We were introduced, and like I said before, it took some time for the bus to smack into me. Maybe that's what made it all the more potent when it did.

We began to date. We doubled a lot with Lenny and Cheryl. The four of us spent every weekend at Lenny's summer house on the Jersey shore. It was indeed a glorious summer, the kind of summer everyone should experience at least once in a lifetime.

If this were a movie, we'd be cueing up the montage music. I went to Tufts University while Rachel was starting out at Boston College. First scene of the montage, well, they'd probably have us on a boat on the Charles, me paddling, Rachel holding a parasol, her smile tentative then mocking. She'd splash me and then I'd splash her and then the boat would tip. It never happened, but you get the point. Next maybe there would be a picnic scene on campus, a shot of us studying in the library, our bodies entwined on a couch, me staring mesmerized as Rachel reads from her textbook, her glasses on, absentmindedly tucking a hair behind her ear. The montage would probably close on two bodies tussling under a white satin sheet, even though no college student uses satin sheets. Still, I'm thinking cinematic here.

I was in love.

During one Christmas break, we visited Rachel's grandmother, a card-carrying yenta from the old school, in a nursing home. The old woman took both our hands in hers and declared us *beshert* which is a Yiddish word that means predestined or fated.

So what happened?

Our ending was not an uncommon one. We were young, I guess. During my senior year, Rachel decided that she wanted to spend a semester in Florence. I was twenty-two. I got pissed off and while she was away, I slept with another woman—a one-night stand with a featureless coed from Babson. It meant absolutely nothing. I understand that makes it no better, but maybe it should. I don't know.

Anyway, someone at the party told someone else and eventually it got back to Rachel. She called me from Italy and broke it off, just like that, which I saw as something of an overreaction. Like I said, we were young. At first, I was too proud (read: too stupid) to beg and then, when I started soaking in the repercussions, I called and wrote letters and sent flowers. Rachel never responded. It was over. We were done.

I stood and stumbled to my desk. I fished out the key I had taped under the credenza and unlocked the bottom drawer. I lifted off the files and found my secret stash underneath. No, not drugs. The past. Rachel things. I found the familiar photo and pulled it into view. Lenny and Cheryl still have this picture in their den, which had, understandably enough, angered Monica to no end. It was a photograph of the four of us—Lenny, Cheryl, Rachel, and I—at a formal during my senior year. Rachel is wearing a spaghetti-strap black dress and the thought of the way it clung to her shoulders still takes my breath away.

A long time ago.

I've moved on, of course. Per my life plan, I went to medical school. I always knew that I wanted to be a doctor. Most doctors I know will tell you the same. It is rarely a decision you come to late.

And I dated too. I even had other one-night stands (remember Zia?), but—and this is going to sound pitiful—even after all these years, I never go through a day without thinking, at least fleetingly, about Rachel. Yes, I know that I've romanticized the romance, if you will, completely out of proportion. Had I not made that stupid blunder, I would probably not be living in some blissful alternative universe, still entwined on the couch with my beloved. As Lenny once pointed out in a moment of naked honesty, if my relationship with Rachel had been that great, it surely could have survived this most hackneyed of speed bumps.

Am I saying that I never loved my wife? No. At least, I think the answer is no. Monica was beautiful—right-away beautiful, nothing slow about the way her looks hit you—and passionate and surprising. She was also wealthy and glamorous. I tried not to compare—that is a terrible way to live your life—but I could not help but love Monica in my smaller, less bright, post-Rachel world. Given time, the same might have happened had I stayed with Rachel, but that's using logic and in matters of the heart, logic need not apply.

Over the years, Cheryl grudgingly kept me informed on what Rachel was up to. Rachel, I'd learned, had gone into law enforcement and become a federal agent in Washington. I can't say I was totally surprised. Three years ago, Cheryl told me that Rachel had gotten married to an older guy, a senior fed. Even after all this time—Rachel and I had been broken up eleven years by then—I felt my insides cave in. I realized with a heavy thud just how badly I'd messed up. I'd always assumed somehow that Rachel and I were biding our time, living in some sort of suspended animation, until we inevitably came to our senses and got back together. Now she had married someone else.

Cheryl saw my face and has never again spoken to me about Rachel.

I stared at the picture and heard the familiar SUV pull up. No surprise there. I did not bother walking to the door. Lenny had a key. He never knocked anyway. He'd know where I was. I put away the photograph as Lenny entered the room carrying two enormous, brightly clad paper cups.

Lenny held up the Slurpees from 7-Eleven. "Cherry or cola?"

"Cherry."

He handed it to me. I waited.

"Zia called Cheryl," he said in way of explanation.

I had figured that. "I don't want to talk about it," I said.

Lenny hopped onto the couch. "Me neither." He reached into his pocket and took out a thick sheaf of papers. "The will and the final stuff on Monica's estate. Read it whenever." He picked up the remote control and began to flip. "Don't you have any porno?"

"No, sorry."

Lenny shrugged and settled on a college

basketball game on ESPN. We watched a few minutes in silence. I broke it.

"Why didn't you tell me Rachel was divorced?"

Lenny grimaced in pain and raised his palm as if stopping traffic.

"What?" I said.

"Brain freeze." He rode it out. "I always drink these things too fast."

"Why didn't you tell me?"

"I thought we weren't going to talk about it."

I looked at him.

"It's not that simple, Marc."

"What's not?"

"Rachel has been through some tough times."

"So have I," I said.

Lenny watched the game a little too closely.

"What happened to her, Lenny?"

"It's not my place." He shook his head. "You haven't even seen her in, what, fifteen years?"

Fourteen actually. "Something like that."

His eyes scanned the room and rested on a photograph of Monica and Tara. He looked away and sipped his Slurpee. "Have to stop living in the past, my friend."

We both settled back and pretended to watch the game. Stop living in the past, he'd said. I looked at the photograph of Tara and wondered if Lenny was talking about more than Rachel.

Edgar Portman picked up the leather dog leash. He jingled the end. Bruno, his champion bull mastiff, clattered toward the sound at full speed. Bruno had won a Best in Breed at the Westminster Dog Show six years ago. Many believed that he had what it took to earn Best in Show. Edgar chose instead to retire Bruno. A show dog is never home. Edgar wanted Bruno with him.

People disappointed Edgar. Dogs never.

Bruno stuck out his tongue and wagged his tail. Edgar clipped the leash onto the collar. They would go for an hour. Edgar looked down at his desk. There, on the shiny veneer, sat a cardboard package, identical to the one he had received eighteen months earlier. Bruno whimpered. Edgar wondered if it was a whimper of impatience or if he could sense his master's dread. Maybe both.

Either way, Edgar needed air.

The package from eighteen months ago had undergone every possible forensic test. The police had learned nothing. Edgar was relatively certain, based on that past experience, that the incompetents in law enforcement would find nothing again. Eighteen months ago, Marc had not listened to him. That mistake, Edgar hoped, would not be repeated.

He started for the door. Bruno led the way. The air felt good. He stepped outside and sucked in a deep breath. It did not change his outlook, but it helped. Edgar and Bruno started down the familiar route, but something made Edgar veer to the right. The family plot. He saw it every day, so often that he no longer saw it, so to speak. He never visited the stones. But today, suddenly, he felt drawn. Bruno, surprised by the deviation in his routine, grudgingly followed.

Edgar stepped over the small fence. His leg throbbed. Old age. These walks were getting more difficult. He had begun using a walking stick a lot of the time—he had purchased one purportedly used by Dashiell Hammet during a TB stint—but for some reason, Edgar never took it with him when he was with Bruno. It felt wrong somehow.

Bruno hesitated and then leapt the fence. They both stood in front of the two most recent headstones. Edgar tried not to ponder about life and death, about wealth and its relativity to happiness. That sort of lint picking was best left to others. He realized now that he had probably not been a very good father. He had learned, however, from his father, who learned from his. And in the end, perhaps his aloofness had saved him. Had he loved his children fully, had he been deeply involved in their lives, he doubted that he could have survived their deaths.

The dog began to whimper again. Edgar looked down at his companion, deep into his eyes. "Time to go, boy," he said softly. The front door of the house opened. Edgar turned and spotted his brother Carson, rushing toward him. Edgar saw the look on his brother's face.

"My God," Carson called out.

"I assume you saw the package."

"Yes, of course. Did you call Marc?"

"No."

"Good," Carson said. "It's a hoax. It has to be."

Edgar did not reply.

"You don't agree?" Carson said.

"I don't know."

"You can't possibly think that she's still alive."

Edgar gave the leash a gentle tug. "Best to wait for the tests to come back," he said. "Then we'll know for certain."

I like to work night hours. I always have. I am lucky in my career choice. I love my job. It is never a chore or drudgery or something I do simply to put food on the table. I disappear into my work. Like a troubled athlete, I forget everything when I'm playing my game. I enter the zone. I am at my best.

This night, however—three nights after seeing Rachel—I was off duty. I sat alone in my den and flipped stations. I, like most males of our species, hit the remote too frequently. I can watch several hours of nothing. Last year, Lenny and Cheryl got me a DVD player, explaining to me that my VCR was heading the way of the eight-track. I checked the clock on it now. A few minutes after nine. I could pop in a DVD and still get to bed by eleven.

I had just removed the rental DVD from its

box and was about to stick it into the machine—they do not have a remote that does that yet—when I heard a dog bark. I rose. A new family had moved in two houses down. They had four or five young kids, something like that. Hard to say when a family has that many. They seem to blur into one another. I had not introduced myself yet, but I had seen in their yard an Irish wolfhound, who was approximately the size of a Ford Explorer. The bark, I believed, was his.

I pushed the curtain aside. I looked out the window, and for some reason—a reason I cannot properly articulate—I was not surprised by what I saw.

The woman stood in the exact same spot where I had seen her eighteen months earlier. The long coat, the long hair, the hands in the pockets—all the same.

I was afraid to let her out of my sight, but then again, I did not want her to see me. I dropped to my knees and slid to the side of the window, super-sleuth-style. With my back and cheek pressed against the wall, I considered my options.

First off, I was now not watching her. That meant she could leave and I wouldn't notice. Hmm, not good. I had to risk a look. That was the first thing.

I turned my head and sneaked a peek. Still there. The woman was still out front, but she had moved a few steps closer to my front door. I had no idea what that meant exactly. So now what? How about going to the door and confronting her? That seemed a pretty good move. If she ran, well, I guess that I would pursue.

I risked another glimpse, just a quick head turn, and when I did, I realized that the woman was staring directly at my window. I fell back. Damn. She'd seen me. No way around it. My hands grabbed the bottom of the window, readying to open it, but she had already started hurrying up the block.

Oh no, not this time.

I was wearing surgical scrubs—every doctor I know has a few pairs for lounge-wear use—and I was barefoot. I sprinted to the door and threw it open. The woman was almost to the top of the block. When she saw me at the door, she stopped the hurry-walk and broke into an all-out run.

I gave chase. To hell with my feet. Part of me felt ridiculous. I am not the fastest fellow on two legs. I am probably not even the fastest on one leg—and here I was running down a strange woman because she was standing in front of my house. I don't know what I hoped to find here. The woman was probably taking a walk, and I had spooked her. She would probably call the police. I could see their reaction. Bad enough I killed my own family and got away with it. Now I was chasing strange women around my neighborhood.

I did not stop.

The woman turned right onto Phelps Road. She had a big lead. I pumped my arms and willed my legs to pick up the pace. The pebbles on the sidewalk dug into the soles of my feet. I tried to stay on grass. She was out of view now, and I was out of shape. I had gone maybe a hundred yards and I could already hear the wheeze in my breath. My nose started running.

I reached the end of my street and made the right.

But there was no one.

The road was long and straight and well enough lit. In other words, she should still be visible. For some dumb reason I looked the other way too, behind me. But the woman was not there either. I ran the route she'd taken. I looked down Morningside Drive, but there was no sign of her.

The woman was gone.

But how?

She could not have been that fast. Carl Lewis was not that fast. I stopped, put my hands on my knees, sucked in some very necessary oxygen. Think. Okay, could she live in one of these houses? Perhaps. And if she did, so what? That meant that she was taking a walk in her own neighborhood. She had seen something that had struck her as curious. She stopped to take a look.

Like she did eighteen months ago?

Okay, first off, we don't know if it was the same woman.

So two women stopped in front of your house in the exact same spot and stood like statues?

It was possible. Or maybe it was the same woman. Maybe she liked looking at houses. Maybe she was into architecture or something.

Oh yes, the ever-desirable architecture of the seventies suburban split-level. And if her visit was totally innocent, why did she run away?

I don't know, Marc, but maybe—and this

is just a stab in the dark—maybe because some lunatic chased her?

I shook the voice away and started running again, looking for I-don't-know-what. But when I passed the Zuckers' house, I came to a halt.

Was that possible?

The woman had simply disappeared. I had checked both exit roads. She was not on either one of them. So that meant, A, she lived in one of the houses, B, she was hiding.

Or C, she had taken the Zucker path in the woods.

When I was a kid, we sometimes used to cut through the Zuckers' backyard. There was a path to the middle-school fields. It was not easy to find, and Old Lady Zucker really didn't like us going through her lawn. She would never say anything, but she would stand by the window, her beehive hair glazed like a Krispy Kreme, and glare us down. After a while, we stopped using the path and took the long way.

I looked left and right. No sign of her.

Could the woman know about the path?

I sprinted into the blackness of the Zuckers' backyard. I half expected Old Lady

Zucker to be at her kitchen window, glaring at me, but she had moved out to Scottsdale years ago. I don't know who lived here anymore. I didn't even know if the path was still there.

It was black-hole dark in the yard. No lights were on in the house. I tried to remember where exactly the path was. Actually, that took no time. You remember stuff like that. It's automatic. I ran toward it and something whacked me in the head. I felt the thud and fell on my back.

My head swam. I looked up. In the faint moonlight, I could see a swing set. One of those fancy wooden ones. It hadn't been there in my childhood, and in the dark, I hadn't seen it. I felt woozy, but time was key here. I leapt to my feet with too much bravado, reeling back.

The path was still there.

I headed along it as fast as I could. Branches whipped my face. I did not care. I stumbled on a root. I did not care. The Zucker path was not long, maybe forty, fifty feet. It opened into a big clearing of soccer fields and baseball diamonds. I was still making good enough time. If she had taken this route, I would be able to spot her in the recreational expanse.

I could see the smoky haze from the fluorescent lights drifting down from the field's parking lots. I burst out into the opening and quickly scanned my surroundings. I saw several sets of soccer posts and one chain-link backstop.

But no woman.

Damn.

I had lost her. Again. My heart fell. I don't know. I mean, when you thought about it, what was the point? This whole thing was stupid, really. I looked down at my feet. They hurt like hell. I felt a trickle of what was probably blood on my right sole. I felt like an idiot. A defeated idiot, at that. I started to turn away. . . .

Hold the phone.

In the distance, under the lights of the parking lot, there was a car. One solitary car, all by its lonesome. I nodded to myself and followed my thoughts. Let's say that the car belonged to the woman. Why not? If it doesn't, well, nothing lost, nothing gained. But if it did, if she had parked here, it made sense. She parks, she goes through the woods, she stands in front of my house.

Why she would do any of this, I had no idea. But for right now, I decided to go with it.

Okay, if that was the case—if that was her car—then I could conclude that she had not yet departed. No flies on me. So what had happened here? She's spotted, she runs, she starts heading down the path. . . .

. . . and she realizes that I might follow.

I almost snapped my fingers. The mystery woman would know that I had grown up in this neighborhood and thus might remember the path. And if I did, if I somehow put together (as I had) that she would use the path, then I would spot her in the opening. So what would she do?

I thought about it and the answer came pretty quickly.

She would hide in the woods along the path.

The mystery woman was probably watching me at this very moment.

Yes, I know that this argument barely reached the level of flimsy conjecture. But it felt right. Very right. So what to do? I gave a heavy sigh and said out loud, "Damn." I slumped my shoulders as though deflated, trying hard not to oversell this, and started trudging back through the path to the

Zucker place. I lowered my head, my eyes swerving left and right. I walked delicately, my ears alert, straining to hear a rustle of some sort.

The night remained silent.

I reached the end of the path and kept walking as if I were heading home. When I was deep in the thicket of darkness, I dropped to the ground. I commando-crawled back under the swing set toward the path's opening. I stopped and waited.

I don't know how long I stayed there. Probably not more than two or three minutes. I was about to give up when I heard the noise. I was still on my stomach, my head raised. The silhouette rose and started down the path.

I scrambled to my feet, trying to stay quiet, but that was a major no-go. The woman spun toward the sound, spotting me.

"Wait," I shouted. "I just want to talk to you."

But she had already darted back into the woods. Off the path, the woods were thick and yep, it was plenty dark. I could lose her easily. I was not about to risk that. Not again. Maybe I couldn't *see* her, but I could still *hear* her.

I jumped into the thicket and almost immediately hit a tree. I saw stars. Man, that had been a dumb move. I stopped now and listened.

Silence.

She had stopped. She was hiding again. So now what?

She had to be nearby. I considered my options and then thought, Ah, the hell with it. Remembering where I had last heard a noise, I leapt at the spot, spread-eagle, my hands and legs stretched to the max so that my body would cover as much territory as possible. I landed on a shrub.

But my left hand touched something else.

She tried to crawl away, but my fingers closed tight around her ankle. She kicked at me with her free leg. I held on like a dog digging his teeth in.

"Let go of me!" she shouted.

I did not recognize the voice. I did not let go of her ankle.

"What the—let go of me!"

No. I got some leverage and pulled her toward me. It was still too dark, but my eyes were beginning to adjust. I gave another tug. She rolled onto her back. We were close enough now. I was finally able to see her face.

It took a few moments to register. The memory was an old one, for one thing. The face, or what I could see of it, had changed. She looked different. What gave it away, what helped me recognize her, was the way her hair had fallen in front of her face during our tussle. That was almost more familiar than the features—the vulnerability of the pose, the way she now avoided eye contact. And of course, living in that house, that house I had always so closely associated with her, had kept her image in the forefront of my memory banks.

The woman pushed her hair to the side and looked up at me. I fell back to school days, the brick building barely two hundred yards from where we now lay. Now maybe it made some sort of sense. The mystery woman had been standing in front of the house where she used to live.

The mystery woman was Dina Levinsky.

chapter 11

We sat at the kitchen table. I made tea, a Tazo blend of Chinese green I'd bought at Starbucks. It was supposed to soothe. We'd see. I handed Dina a cup.

"Thank you, Marc."

I nodded and sat across from her. I had known Dina my whole life. I knew her in the way only a kid can know another kid, the way only elementary-school classmates know each other, even—bear with me here—even though I don't think we ever really spoke to one another.

We all have a Dina Levinsky in our past. She was the class victim, the girl so much an outcast, so often teased and abused, you wonder how she stayed sane. I never picked on her, but I stood on the sidelines plenty of times. Even if I didn't reside in her childhood home, Dina Levinsky would still live in me. She lives in you too. Quick: Who was the most picked-on kid in your elementary school? Right, exactly, you remember. You remember their first and last name and what they looked like. You remember watching them walk home alone or sitting in the cafeteria in silence. Whatever, you remember. Dina Levinsky stays with you.

"I hear you're a doctor now," Dina said to me.

"Yes. And you?"

"A graphic designer and artist. I have a show in the Village next month."

"Paintings?"

She hesitated. "Yes."

"You were always a good artist," I said.

She cocked her head, surprised. "You noticed?"

There was a brief pause. Then I found myself saying, "I should have done something."

Dina smiled. "No, I should have."

She looked good. No, she had not grown into a beauty like those ugly-duckling-swans you see in the movies. First off, Dina had never been ugly. She had been plain. Maybe she still was. Her features were still too narrow, but they worked better on an adult face. Her hair, so drippy in her youth, had body now.

"Do you remember Cindy McGovern?" she asked me.

"Sure."

"She tortured me more than anyone."

"I remember."

"Well, this is funny. I had an exhibit a few years back at a gallery in midtown—and Cindy shows up. She comes up to me and gives me a big hug and kiss. She wants to talk about old times, you know, like 'Remember how dorky Mr. Lewis was?' She's all smiles and I swear, Marc, she didn't remember what she'd been like. She wasn't pretending either. She just totally blocked out how she'd treated me. I find that sometimes."

"Find what?"

Dina raised the cup with two hands. "No one remembers being the bully." She hunched over, her eyes darted about the room. I wondered about my own remembrance. Had I just been on the sidelines—or was that, too, some sort of revisionist history?

"This is so messed up," Dina said.

"Being back in this house?"

"Yeah." She put down the cup. "I guess you want an explanation."

I waited.

Her eyes started darting again. "You want to hear something bizarre?"

"Sure."

"This is where I used to sit. I mean, when I was a kid. We had a rectangular table too. I always sat in the same spot. When I came in here now, I don't know, I just naturally gravitated to this chair. I guess—I guess that's part of the reason why I was here tonight."

"I'm not sure I understand."

"This house," she said. "It still has a pull on me. A hold." She leaned forward. Her eyes met mine for the first time. "You've heard the rumors, haven't you? About my father and what happened here."

"Yes."

"They're true," she said.

I forced myself not to wince. I had no idea what to say. I thought about the hell of school. I tried to add on to that the hell of this house. It was unfathomable.

"He's dead now. My father, I mean. He died six years ago."

I blinked and looked away.

"I'm okay, Marc. Really. I was in therapy—well, I mean, I still am. Do you know Dr. Radio?"

"No."

"That's his real name. Stanley Radio. He's pretty famous for the Radio Technique. I've been with him for years. I'm much better. I'm over the self-destructive tendencies. I'm past feeling worthless. It's funny though. I got over it. No, I mean it. Most victims of abuse have commitment and sex issues. I never did. I'm able to be intimate, no problem. I'm married now. My husband is a great guy. It's not happily-ever-after, but it's pretty damn good."

"I'm glad," I said, because I had no idea what else to say.

She smiled again. "Are you superstitious, Marc?"

"No."

"Me neither. Except, I don't know, when I read about your wife and daughter, I started to wonder. About this house. Bad karma and all that. Your wife was so lovely."

"You knew Monica?"

"We'd met."

"When?"

Dina did not reply right away. "Are you familiar with the term *trigger*?"

I remembered it from my medical school rotations. "You mean, in terms of psychiatry?"

"Yes. You see, when I read about what happened here, it was a trigger. Like with an alcoholic or anorexic. You're never fully cured. Something happens—a trigger—and you fall back into bad patterns. I started biting my nails. I started doing physical harm to myself. It was like—it was like I had to face down this house. I had to confront the past in order to defeat it."

"And that's what you were doing tonight?"

"Yes."

"And when I spotted you eighteen months ago?"

"Same thing."

I sat back. "How often do you stop by?"

"Once every couple of months, I guess. I park at the school lot and come through the Zucker path. But there's more to it than that."

"More to what?"

"My visits. See, this house still holds my secrets. I mean that literally."

"I'm not following."

"I keep trying to work up the courage to knock on the door again, but I can't do it. And now I'm inside, in this kitchen, and I'm okay." She tried to smile, as if to prove the point. "But I still don't know if I can do it."

"Do what?" I asked.

"I'm babbling." Dina started scratching the back of her hand, hard and fast, digging her nails in and nearly breaking skin. I wanted to reach out to her, but it felt too forced. "I wrote it all down. In a journal. What happened to me. It's still here."

"In the house?"

She nodded. "I hid it."

"The police went through here after the murder. They searched this place pretty good."

"They didn't find it," she said. "I'm sure of it. And even if they did, it's just an old journal. There'd be no reason for them to disturb it. Part of me wants it to stay put. It's over and done with it, you know what I mean? Let sleeping dogs lie. But another part wants to let it out into the light. Like it's a vampire and the sunshine will kill it."

"Where is it?" I asked.

"In the basement. You have to stand on the dryer to get to it. It's behind one of the ducts in the crawl space." She glanced at the clock. She looked at me and hugged herself. "It's getting late."

"Are you okay?"

The eyes were darting again. Her breathing was suddenly uneven. "I don't know how much longer I can stay here."

"Do you want to look for your journal?"

"I don't know."

"Do you want me to get it for you?"

She shook her head hard. "No." She stood, gulping air now. "I better go now."

"You can always come back, Dina. Anytime you want."

But she wasn't listening. She was in full panic mode and heading for the door.

"Dina?"

She suddenly spun toward me. "Did you love her?"

"What?"

"Monica. Did you love her? Or was there someone else?"

"What are you talking about?"

Her face drained of color. She stared at me now, backing away, petrified. "You know who shot you, don't you, Marc?"

I opened my mouth, but nothing came out. By the time I found my voice, Dina had turned away.

"I'm sorry, I have to go."

"Wait."

She flung the door open and ran out. I stood by the window and watched her scurry back up toward Phelps Road. This time, I chose not to follow.

Instead, I turned and with her words— *"You know who shot you, don't you, Marc?"*—still reverberating in my ears, I sprinted to the basement door.

All right, let me explain something here. I was not going down into the dingy, unfinished subdwelling to invade Dina's privacy. I did not pretend to know what was best for her, what might salve her horrendous pain. Many of my psychiatry colleagues would disagree, but sometimes I wonder if the past is better left buried. I don't have the answer, of course, and as my psychiatry colleagues would remind me, I don't ask them for their take on the best way to handle a cleft palate. So in the end, all I know for certain is that it is not my place to decide for Dina.

And I was not going in the basement out of curiosity about her past either. I had no interest in reading the details of Dina's torment. In fact, I actively did not want to know them. To speak selfishly, I was creeped out plenty just knowing such horrors had occurred in the place I call home. It was already enough in my face, thank you very much. I needed to hear or read no more.

So what exactly was I after?

I hit the light switch. A bare bulb came on. I was putting the pieces together even as I started to descend. Dina had said several curious things. Putting aside the most dramatic for a moment, I was starting to pick up on the more subtle ones. It was a night of spontaneous behavior on my part. I decided to let the trend continue.

First off, I remembered how Dina, when she was still the mystery woman on the sidewalk, had taken a step toward the door. I know now, as Dina herself had told me, that she'd been "trying to work up the courage to knock on the door again."

Again.

Knock on the door *again.*

The obvious implication was that Dina

had, on at least one other occasion, worked up the courage to knock on my door.

Second, Dina had told me that she had "met" Monica. I could not imagine how. Yes, Monica, too, had grown up in this town, but from all I knew of her, she might as well have grown up in a different, more opulent era. The Portman estate was on the opposite end of our rather sprawling suburb. Monica had started boarding school at a young age. No one in town knew her. I remember seeing her once at the Colony movie theater over the summer of my sophomore year in high school. I had stared. She had studiously ignored me. Monica had that whole remote-beauty thing down pat by then. When I met her years later—she actually coming on to me—the flattery turned my head. Monica had seemed so fabulous at a distance.

So how, I wondered now, had my wealthy, remote, beautiful wife met poor, drab Dina Levinsky? The most likely answer, when you consider the "again" comment, was that Dina had knocked on the door and Monica had answered. They met then. They probably talked. Dina probably told Monica about the hidden journal.

"You know who shot you, don't you, Marc?"

No, Dina. But I plan on finding out.

I had reached the cement floor. Boxes that I would never throw away and never open were piled everywhere. I noticed, perhaps for the first time, that there were paint splatters on the floor. A large variety of hues. They'd probably been here since Dina's time, a reminder of her sole escape.

The washer and dryer were in the corner on the left. I moved slowly toward them in the shadowy light. I tiptoed, actually, as though I were afraid of waking Dina's sleeping dogs. Stupid really. As I said before, I am not superstitious and even if I were, even if I believed in evil spirits and the like, there was no reason to fear angering them. My wife was dead and my daughter was missing—what else could they do to me? In fact, I should disturb them, make them act, hope they let me know what really happened to my family, to Tara.

There it was again. Tara. Everything circled back to her eventually. I don't know how she fitted into all this. I don't know how her kidnapping was connected to Dina

Levinsky. It probably wasn't. But I was not turning back.

You see, Monica never mentioned meeting Dina Levinsky.

I found that odd. True, I am building this ridiculous theory on pure foam. But if Dina had indeed knocked on the door, if Monica had indeed opened it, you would think that my wife would have mentioned it to me at some point. She knew that Dina Levinsky had gone to school with me. Why keep her visit—or the fact that they had met—a secret?

I hopped up on the dryer. I had to both crouch and look above me. Dust city. Spider webs were everywhere. I saw the duct and reached up. I felt around. It was difficult. There was a web of pipes, and my arm was having trouble fitting between them. It would have been much easier for a young girl with thin arms.

Eventually I worked my hand through the copper. I slid my fingertips to the right and pushed up. Nothing. My hand crawled a few more inches over and pushed again. Something gave way.

I pulled up my sleeve and twisted my arm in another inch or two. Two pipes pressed against my skin, but they gave enough. I was able to reach into the crawl space. I felt around, found something, pulled it into view.

The journal.

It was a classic school notebook with the familiar black marble cover. I opened and paged through it. The handwriting was minuscule. It reminded me of that guy in the mall who writes names on a grain of rice. Dina's immaculate penmanship—belying, no doubt, the content—started at the very top of the sheet and ran all the way to the bottom. There were no left or right margins. Dina had used both sides of every sheet.

I did not read it. Again that was not what I had come down for. I reached back up and put the journal back in its place. I don't know how this would set me with the gods—if just touching it would unleash a King Tut–like curse—but again I didn't care very much either.

I felt around again. I knew. I don't know how, but I just knew. Eventually my hand hit something else. My heart thumped. It felt smooth. Leather. I pulled it into view. Some dust followed. I blinked the particles out of my eyes.

It was Monica's DayRunner.

I remembered when she bought it at some chic boutique in New York. Something to organize her life, she'd told me. It'd had the customary calendar and datebook. When had we bought it? I wasn't sure. Maybe eight, nine months before she died. I tried to remember the last time I'd seen it. Nothing came to me.

I jammed the leather planner between my knees and put the ceiling panel back in place. I grabbed the datebook and climbed down from the dryer. I considered waiting until I got upstairs into better light, but, uh-uh, no way. The datebook had a zipper. Despite the dust it opened smoothly.

A CD fell out and landed on the floor.

It glittered in the low light like a jewel. I picked it up by the edges. There was no label on it. Memorex had manufactured it. "CD-R," it said, "80 Minutes."

What the hell is this?

One way to find out. I hurried upstairs and booted up my computer.

chapter 12

When I put the disk into the CD drive, the following screen appeared:

Password: _ _ _ _ _ _
MVD
Newark, NJ

Six-digit password. I typed in her birthday. No go. I tried Tara's birthday. No go. I put in our anniversary and then my birthday. I tried the code for our ATM. Nothing worked.

I sat back. So now what?

I debated calling Detective Regan. By now it was closing in on midnight, and even if I could reach him, what exactly would I say? "Hi, I found a CD hidden in my basement, rush over"? No. Hysterics would not work here. Better to show calm, to feign rationality. Patience was key. Think it through. I could call Regan in the morning. Nothing he could or would do tonight anyway. Sleep on it.

Fine, but I was not about to give up quite yet. I logged on to the Internet and brought up a search engine. I typed in MVD in Newark. A listing popped up.

"MVD—Most Valuable Detection."

Detection?

There was a link to a Web site. I clicked it, and the MVD Web site came up. My eyes did a quick scan. MVD was a "group of professional private investigators" who "provided confidential services." They offered online background checks for less than a hundred dollars. Their ads exclaimed, "Find out if that new boyfriend has a criminal record!" and "Where is your old sweetheart? Maybe she's still pining for you!" Stuff like that. They also did more "intense, discreet investigations" for those who required such things. They were, per the top banner, a "full-service investigative entity."

So, I asked myself, what had Monica needed investigated?

I picked up the phone and dialed MVD's

800 number. A machine picked up—no surprise considering the hour—and told me
how much they appreciated my call and
that their office opened at nine in the morning. Okay. I'd call back then.

I hung up the phone and pressed the e:
drive's eject button. The CD slid into view. I
lifted up by the edges and checked for, I
don't know, clues, I guess. Nothing new.
Time to think here. It seemed pretty clear
that Monica had hired MVD to investigate
something and that this CD contained
whatever it was she wanted investigated.
Not exactly a brilliant deduction on my part,
but it was a start.

Let's go back then. Fact is, I had no idea
what Monica wanted investigated or why or
any of that. But if I was right, if this CD did
indeed belong to Monica, if she had hired a
private investigator for whatever reason, it
would naturally follow that she would have
had to pay MVD for said services.

I nodded. Okay, a better start.

But—and here is where confusion immediately set in—the police had thoroughly
combed through our bank accounts and financial records. They had scrutinized every

transaction, every Visa purchase, every written check, every ATM withdrawal. Had they seen one to MVD? If so, they decided not to tell me. Of course, I had not been a potted plant here. My daughter was gone. I, too, had examined those financial statements. There was nothing to any detective agency nor were there any cash withdrawals out of the ordinary.

So what did that mean?

Maybe this CD was old.

That was a possibility. I don't think any of us checked transactions going back more than six months before the attack. Maybe her relationship with Most Valuable Detection predated that. I could probably check through the old statements.

But I wasn't buying it.

This CD was not old. I was fairly certain of that. And it didn't matter much anyway. Time frame, when I thought about it, was irrelevant. Recent or otherwise, the key questions remained: Why would Monica hire a private investigator? What was password protected on that damn CD? Why had she hidden it in that creepy space in the basement? What, if anything, did Dina Levinsky have to do with any of this? And most important, did it have anything to do with the attack—or was this all a big exercise in wishful thinking on my part?

I looked out the window. The street was clear and silent. Suburbia sleeps. No more answers would come tonight. In the morning, I would take my father for our weekly walk and then I would call MVD and maybe even Regan.

I climbed into bed and waited for sleep.

The phone next to Edgar Portman's bed rang at four-thirty in the morning. Edgar jerked awake, pulled out in middream, and fumbled with the phone.

"What?" he barked.

"You said to call as soon as I knew."

Edgar rubbed his face. "You have the results."

"I do."

"And?"

"It's a match."

Edgar closed his eyes. "How certain are you?"

"It's preliminary. If I were taking it to court, I'd need a few more weeks to line up all the arrows. But that would just be following proper protocol."

Edgar could not stop shaking. He thanked the man, put the phone back in its cradle, and began to prepare.

chapter 13

At six the next morning, I left my house and walked down the block. Using a key I've had since college, I unlocked the door and slipped into my childhood home.

The years had not been a friend to this dwelling, but then again, it hadn't been featured in *House and Garden* (except maybe as one of their "before" photos) to begin with. We'd replaced the shag carpet four years ago—the blue-white speck had been so faded and threadbare, it practically replaced itself—and went with close-cropped office-gray so that my father's wheelchair could move with ease. Other than that, nothing had been changed. The overvarnished side tables still held Lladró porcelain knickknacks from a long-ago trip to Spain. Holiday Inn–like oils of violins and fruit—

none of us are the least bit musical or, uh, fruity—still adorned the white-painted wood paneling.

There were photos on the fireplace mantel. I always stopped and looked at the ones of my sister, Stacy. I don't know what I was looking for. Or maybe I do. I was searching for clues, for foreshadowing. I was searching for any hint that this young, fragile, damaged woman would one day buy a gun off the street, shoot me, harm my daughter.

"Marc?" It was Mom. She knew what I was doing. "Come help me, okay?"

I nodded and headed toward the back bedroom. Dad slept on the ground floor now—easier than trying to get up the stairs with a wheelchair. We dressed him, which was a bit like dressing wet sand. My father lolls from side to side. His weight has a tendency toward sudden shifts. My mother and I were used to that, but it doesn't make the task less arduous.

When my mother kissed me good-bye, the faint and familiar whiff of breath mint and cigarette smoke came off her. I had urged her to quit. She kept promising, but I knew that it would never happen. I noticed how loose the skin on her neck was getting, her gold chains almost embedded in their folds. She leaned down and kissed my father on the cheek, holding her lips to him a few seconds too long.

"Be careful," she told us. Then again, that was what she always told us.

We began our journey. I pushed Dad past the train station. We live in a commuter town. Mostly men but yes, women, too, were lined up in long coats, briefcase in one hand, coffee cup in the other. This might sound odd, but even before 9/11, these people were heroes to me. They board that damn train five times a week. They take it to Hoboken and switch to the PATH. That train takes them into New York City. Some will head up to Thirty-third Street and change to hit midtown. Others will take it to the financial center, now that it's opened up again. They make the everyday sacrifice, stifling their own wants and dreams in order to provide for those they love.

I could be doing cosmetic plastic surgery and making a mint. My parents would be able to afford better care for my dad. They could move someplace nice, get that full-time nurse, find a place that could cater more to their needs. But I don't do that. I don't help them by taking the more traveled route because, frankly, working such a job would bore me. So I choose to do something more exciting, something I love to do. For that, people think I'm the heroic one, that I am the one making the sacrifice. Here's the truth. The person who works with the poor? They are usually more selfish. We are not willing to sacrifice our needs. Working a job that provides for our families is not enough for us. Supporting those we love is secondary. We need personal satisfaction, even if our own family is made to do without. Those suits I now watch numbingly board the NJ Transit train? They often hate where they are going and what they are doing, but they do it anyway. They do it to take care of their families, to provide a better life for their spouses, their children, and maybe, just maybe, their aging and ill parents.

So, really, which one of us is to be admired?

Dad and I followed the same route every Thursday. We took the path around the park behind the library. The park was chockful—and you'll notice a suburban theme here—of soccer fields. How much quality real estate was tied up in this supposedly second-tier foreign sport? My father seemed comforted by the playground, by the sights and sounds of children at play. We stopped and took deep breaths. I glanced to my left. Several healthy women jogged by clad in your finest, sheer-clingy Lycra. Dad seemed very still. I smiled. Maybe Dad's liking this spot had nothing to do with soccer.

I no longer remember what my father used to be like. When I try to think back that far, my memories are snapshots, flashes—a man's deep laugh, a little boy clinging to his bicep, dangling off the ground. That was pretty much it. I remember that I loved him deeply, and I guess that has always been enough.

After his second stroke sixteen years ago, Dad's speech became extremely labored. He'd get stuck midsentence. He'd drop words. He'd go silent for hours and sometimes days. You'd forget that he was there. No one really knew for sure if he understood, if he had classic "expressive aphasia"—you understand but you can't really communicate—or something even more sinister.

But on a hot June day during my senior year of high school, my father suddenly reached out and grabbed hold of my sleeve with an eagle-talon grip. I'd been heading out to a party at the time. Lenny was waiting for me by the door. My father's surprisingly strong grasp stopped me cold. I looked down. His face was pure white, the tendons of his neck taut, and more than anything, what I saw was naked fear. That look on his face haunted my sleep for years afterward. I slid into the chair next to him, his hand still clutching my arm.

"Dad?"

"I understand," he pleaded. His grip on my sleeve tightened. "Please." Every word was a struggle. "I still understand."

That was all he said. But it was enough. What I took it to mean was this: "Even though I can't speak or respond, I comprehend. Please don't shut me out." For a while, the doctors agreed. He had expressive aphasia. Then he had another stroke, and the doctors became less sure of what he did and did not understand. I don't know if I apply my own version of Pascal's Wager here—if he understands me, then I should talk to him, if he doesn't, what's the harm?—but I figure that I owe him that. So I talk to him. I tell him everything. And right now, I was telling him about Dina Levinsky's visit—"Do you remember her, Dad?"—and the hidden CD.

Dad's face was locked, immobile, the left side of his mouth turned down in an angry slash-hook. I often wished that he and I never had that "I understand" conversation. I don't know which is worse: to be beyond comprehension, or to understand how trapped you really are. Or maybe I do know.

I was making the second turn, the one by the new skateboard run, when I spotted my former father-in-law. Edgar Portman sat on a bench, splendid in his casual best, his legs crossed, his pants crease sharp enough to slice tomatoes. After the shootings, Edgar and I tried to keep up a relationship that had never existed when his daughter was alive. We had hired a detective agency together—Edgar, of course, knew the best—but they came up with nothing. After a while, Edgar and I both grew weary of the pretense. The only bond between us was one that conjured up the worst moment of my life.

Edgar's being here could, of course, have been a coincidence. We live in the same town. It would only be natural to bump into one another from time to time. But that wasn't the case. I knew that. Edgar was not one for casual park visits. He was here for me.

Our eyes met, and I wasn't sure I liked what I saw. I wheeled the chair toward the bench. Edgar kept his eyes on me, never glancing down at my father. I might as well have been pushing a shopping cart.

"Your mother told me I'd find you here," Edgar said.

I stopped a few feet away from him. "What's up?"

"Sit with me."

I set my father's chair on my left. I lowered the brake. My father stared straight out. His head lolled toward his right shoulder, the way it does when he gets tired. I turned and faced Edgar. He uncrossed his legs.

"I've been wondering how to tell you this," he began.

I gave him a little space. He looked off. "Edgar?"

"Hmm."

"Just tell me."

He nodded, appreciating my directness. Edgar was that kind of man. Without pre-

amble, he said, "I got another ransom demand."

I reeled back. I don't know what I had expected to hear—maybe that Tara had been
found dead—but what he was saying . . . I
couldn't quite comprehend it. I was about to
ask a follow-up question when I saw that he
now had a satchel in his lap. He opened it
and pulled something into view. It was in a
plastic bag—just like the last time we went
through this. I squinted. He handed it to me.
Something ballooned in my chest. I blinked
and looked at the bag.

Hairs. There were hairs inside it.

"This is their proof," Edgar said.

I could not speak. I just looked at the
hairs. I laid the bag gently on my lap.

"They understood that we would be
skeptical," Edgar said.

"Who understood?"

"The kidnappers. They said they'd give us
a few days. I immediately brought the hairs
to a DNA laboratory."

I looked up at him and then back at the
hairs.

"The preliminary results came in two
hours ago," Edgar said. "Nothing they could
use in court, but it's still pretty conclusive.

The hairs match the ones sent to us a year and a half ago." He stopped and swallowed. "The hairs belong to Tara."

I heard the words. I didn't understand them. For some reason, I shook my head no. "Maybe they just saved them from before. . . ."

"No. They have aging tests too. Those hairs came from a child around two years old."

I guess that I knew that already. I could look and see that these were not my daughter's wispy baby hairs. She wouldn't have them anymore. Her hair would have darkened and thickened. . . .

Edgar handed me a note. Still in a fog, I took it from him. The font was the same as from the note we'd gotten eighteen months before. The top line over the fold said:

WANT ONE LAST CHANCE?

I felt the thud deep in my chest. Edgar's voice seemed suddenly far away. "I probably should have told you immediately, but it seemed an obvious hoax. Carson and I didn't want to get your hopes up unnecessarily. I have friends. They were able to rush through the DNA results. We still had hairs from the last mailing." He put a hand on my shoulder. I did not move.

"She's alive, Marc. I don't know how or where, but Tara is alive."

My eyes stayed on the hairs. Tara. They belonged to Tara. The sheen, that golden-wheat hue. I petted them through the plastic. I wanted to reach inside the bag, to touch my daughter, but I thought my heart would burst.

"They want another two million dollars. The note warns us again about calling the police—they claim to have an inside source. They sent another cell phone for you. I have the money in the car. We have another twenty-four hours maybe. That was the window they gave us for the DNA testing. You'll have to be ready."

I finally read the note. Then I looked over at my father in his wheelchair. He still stared straight ahead.

Edgar said, "I know you think I'm rich. I am, I guess. But not like you'd think. I'm leveraged and . . ."

I turned toward him. His eyes were wide. His hands shook.

"What I mean to say is that I don't really

have that many liquid assets left. I'm not made of money. This is it."

"I'm surprised you're doing this at all," I said.

The words, I could see immediately, wounded him. I wanted to take them back, but for some reason I didn't. I let my eyes drift back toward my father. Dad's face remained frozen, but—I looked closer—there was a tear on his cheek. That didn't mean anything. Dad has teared up before, usually with no apparent provocation. I did not take this as any kind of sign.

And then, I don't know why, I followed his gaze. I looked across the soccer field, past the goalposts, past two women with Baby Joggers, all the way to the street nearly a hundred yards away. My stomach dropped. There, standing on the sidewalk, looking back at me with his hands in his pockets, was a man wearing a flannel shirt and black jeans and a Yankee cap.

I couldn't say for sure that it was the same man from the ransom drop. Red-and-black flannel is hardly an uncommon pattern. And maybe it was my imagination—I was pretty far away—but I think he was smiling at me. I felt my whole body jerk.

Edgar said, "Marc?"

I barely heard him. I rose and kept my eyes up. At first, the man in the flannel stayed perfectly still. I ran toward him.

"Marc?"

But I knew that it was no mistake. You don't forget. You close your eyes and you still see him. He never leaves you. You wish for moments like this. I knew that. And I knew what wishes could bring. But I ran straight toward him. Because there was no mistake. I knew who it was.

When I was still a good distance away, the man lifted his hand and waved to me. I kept moving, but I could already see that it was futile. I was only halfway across the park when a white van drove up. The man in flannel snapped a salute in my direction before disappearing into the back.

The van was out of sight before I reached the street.

chapter 14

Time started playing games with me. Going in and out. Speeding up and slowing down. In focus and suddenly blurred. But that did not last long. I let the surgeon side of me take over. He, Marc the Doctor, knew how to compartmentalize. I have always found this easier to do at work than in my personal life. The skill—to partition, to separate, to detach—has never translated. At work, I am able to take my emotional excess and channel it, allow it to converge into a constructive focus. I have never been successful at doing this at home.

But this crisis had forced a change. Compartmentalizing wasn't a question of desire as much as survival. To get emotional, to allow myself to wallow in doubt or consider the implications of a child missing for eighteen months . . . it would paralyze me. That was probably what the kidnappers wanted. They wanted me to come apart. But I work well under pressure. I am at my best. I know that. I had to do that now. The walls came up. I could look at the situation rationally.

First thing: No, I would not contact the police this time.

But that did not mean I had to wait around helplessly.

By the time Edgar handed me the duffel bag stuffed with money, I had an idea.

I called Cheryl and Lenny's house. There was no answer. I checked my watch. Eight-fifteen in the morning. I didn't have Cheryl's cell phone, but it would be better to do this in person anyway.

I drove over to Willard Elementary School and arrived at eight twenty-five. I parked behind a line of SUVs and minivans and got out. This elementary school, like so many others, has the bricks, the cement back steps, the one level, the architectural design made shapeless by the many additions. Some additions try to blend in, but then there are the others, usually built between 1968 and 1975, that were faux-sleek with blue glass and odd tiling. They looked like post-apocalyptic greenhouses.

Kids scrambled around the playground as they always do. The difference was, the parents now stayed and watched. They chatted with one another and when the bell rang, they made sure that their charges were safely ensconced inside the brick or sleek blue glass before departing. I hated to see the fear in the eyes of the parents. But I understood it. The day you become a parent, fear becomes your constant companion. It never lets you go. My life was Exhibit A in the why.

Cheryl's blue Chevy Suburban pulled into the drop-off line. I started toward her. She was unharnessing Justin from his car seat when she spotted me. Justin gave her a dutiful kiss, an act he takes for granted which, I guess, is how it should be, and then he ran off. Cheryl watched him as though afraid he could vanish on the short concrete trek. Kids can never understand that fear, but that's okay. Hard enough to be a kid without having that weight on you.

"Hey," Cheryl said to me.

I said hi back. Then: "I need something."

"What?"

"Rachel's phone number."

Cheryl was already back at the driver-side door. "Get in."

"My car is parked over there."

"I'll bring you back. Swim practice ran late. I've got to get Marianne to school."

She had already started the car. I hopped up into the front passenger seat. I turned and smiled at Marianne. She wore headphones and quick-fingered her Game Boy Advance. She gave me an absentminded wave, barely glancing up. Her hair was still wet. Conner was in the child seat next to her. The car reeked of chlorine, but I found the smell oddly comforting. Lenny, I know, cleans out the car religiously, but you can't possibly keep up. There were French fries in the crevice between the seats. Crumbs of unknown origin clung to the upholstery. On the floor by my feet lay a potpourri of school notices and children's artwork that had been subjected to onslaughts of rain boots. I sat on a small action figure, the kind that McDonald's gives away with their Happy Meals. A CD case reading NOW THAT'S WHAT I CALL MUSIC 14 sat between us, providing listeners with the latest from Britney and Christina and Generic Boy Band. The windows in the back were smeared with greasy fingerprints.

The kids were only allowed to play with the Game Boy in the car, never in the house. They were never, under any circumstance, allowed to watch a PG-13 movie. I asked Lenny about how he and Cheryl went about deciding such matters and he responded, "It's not the rules themselves, but the fact that there are rules." I think I know what he meant.

Cheryl kept her eyes on the road. "It's not my nature to pry."

"But you want to know my intentions."

"I guess."

"And if I don't want to tell you?"

"Maybe," she said, "it's better if you don't."

"Trust me here, Cheryl. I need the number."

She flipped on her signal light. "Rachel is still my closest friend."

"Okay."

"It took her a long time to get over you." She hesitated.

"And vice versa."

"Exactly. Look, I'm not saying this right.

It's just . . . there are some things you need to know."

"Like?"

She kept her eyes on the road, two hands on the wheel. "You asked Lenny why we never told you she got divorced."

"Yes."

Cheryl glanced in the rearview mirror, not at the road, but at her daughter. Marianne seemed wrapped up in her game. "She didn't get divorced. Her husband is dead."

Cheryl glided to a stop in front of the middle school. Marianne took off the headphones and slid out. She did not bother with the dutiful kiss, but she did say goodbye. Cheryl put the car back in drive.

"I'm sorry to hear that," I said, because that was what people said under these circumstances. I almost added, because the mind works in very strange and even macabre ways: Hey, Rachel and I have something else in common.

And then, as if Cheryl could read these thoughts, she said, "He was shot."

This eerie parallel sat between us for several seconds. I stayed quiet.

"I don't know the details," she quickly added. "He was with the FBI too. Rachel was one of the highest-ranking women in the bureau at the time. She resigned after he died. She stopped taking my calls. It hasn't been good for her since." Cheryl pulled up to my car and stopped. "I'm telling you this because I want you to understand. A lot of years have passed since college. Rachel isn't the same person you loved all those years ago."

I kept my tone steady. "I just need her phone number."

Without another word, Cheryl grabbed a pen from the visor, uncapped it with her teeth, and jotted the number on a Dunkin' Donuts napkin.

"Thanks," I said.

She barely nodded as I got out.

I did not hesitate. I had my cell phone. I slipped into my car and dialed the number. Rachel answered with a tentative hello. My words were simple enough.

"I need your help."

chapter 15

Five hours later, Rachel's train pulled into Newark Station.

I couldn't help but think of all those old movies where trains separate lovers, steam billowing from beneath, the conductor calling a last warning, the whistle sounding, the chug-chug as the wheels begin to move, one lover hanging out and waving, the other running along the platform. I don't know why I thought of this. The Newark train station is about as romantic as a pile of hippo dung with head lice. The train approached with nary a whisper and nothing you'd want to see or smell wafted in the air.

But when Rachel stepped off, I still felt the hum in my chest. She was dressed in faded blue jeans and a red turtleneck. Her overnight bag dangled from one shoulder, and she hoisted it up as she stepped down. For a moment, I just stared. I'd just turned thirty-six years old. Rachel was thirty-five. We had not been together since our very early twenties. We had lived our entire adult lives apart. Odd when you think of it that way. I told you before about our breakup. I try to unearth the whys, but maybe it is that simple. We were kids. Kids do dumb things. Kids don't understand repercussions, don't think long term. Kids don't understand that the hum may never really leave your chest.

Yet today, when I realized that I needed help, I thought first of Rachel. And she had come.

She moved toward me with no hesitation. "You okay?"

"Fine."

"Did they call?"

"Not yet."

She nodded and started walking down the platform. Her tone was no nonsense. She, too, had slipped into her role as a professional. "Tell me more about the DNA test."

"I don't know anything else."

"So it's not definitive?"

"Not court-evidence definitive, no, but they seem pretty sure."

Rachel shifted her bag from her right shoulder to her left. I tried to keep up with her pace. "We have to make some tough decisions, Marc. You ready for that?"

"Yes."

"First off, are you certain that you don't want to contact the cops or FBI?"

"The note said they had an inside source."

"That's probably bull," she said.

We walked a few more steps.

"I contacted the authorities last time," I said.

"Doesn't mean it was the wrong move."

"But it certainly wasn't the right one."

She made a yes-no gesture with her head. "You don't know what happened last time. Maybe they spotted the tail. Maybe they watched your house. But most likely, they never intended to give her back. You understand that?"

"Yes."

"But you still want them left out."

"It's why I called you."

She nodded and finally stopped, waiting for me to signal which way. I pointed to the right. She started up again. "Another thing," she said.

"What?"

"We can't let them dictate the tempo this time. We have to insist on assurances that Tara is alive."

"They'll say the hairs prove it."

"And we'll say the tests were inconclusive."

"You think they'll buy that?"

"I don't know. Probably not." She kept walking, the cut of her jaw held high. "But this is what I mean by tough decisions. That flannel-shirt guy in the park? That's about head games. They want to intimidate and weaken you. They want you to follow blindly again. Tara is your child. If you want to just hand over the money again, that's up to you. But I wouldn't advise it. They vanished before. There's no reason to think they won't again."

We entered the parking garage. I handed the attendant my ticket. "So what do you suggest?" I asked her.

"A few things. First, we have to demand an exchange. No 'Here's the money, call us later.' We get your daughter when they get the money."

"And if they don't agree?"

She looked at me with those eyes. "Tough decisions. You understand?"

I nodded.

"I also want a total electronic surveillance hookup, so I can stay with you. I want to strap on a fiber-optic camera and see what this guy looks like, if possible. We don't have manpower, but there are still things we can do."

"Suppose they catch on?"

"Suppose they run away again?" she countered. "We're taking chances here no matter what we do. I'm trying to learn from what happened the first time. There are no guarantees. I'm simply trying to improve our odds."

The car arrived. We slid in and started up McCarter Highway. Rachel suddenly grew very quiet. The years again melted away. I knew this posture. I had seen it before.

"What else?" I said.

"Nothing."

"Rachel."

Something in my tone made her look away. "There are some things you should know."

I waited.

"I called Cheryl," she said. "I know she filled you in on most of it. You understand that I'm not a fed anymore."

"Yes."

"There's a limit to what I can do."

"I understand that." She sat back. The posture was still there. "What else?"

"You need a reality check here, Marc."

We pulled to a red light. I turned and looked at her—really looked at her—for the first time. The eyes still had that hazel with gold flakes. I know the years had been tough, but it didn't show in the eyes.

"The odds that Tara is still alive are minuscule," she said.

"But the DNA test," I countered.

"I'll handle that later."

"Handle it?"

"Later," she said again.

"What the hell does that mean? It's a match. Edgar said the final confirmation is a formality."

"Later," she repeated with steel in her voice. "Right now we might as well assume that she's alive. We should go through with the ransom drop-off as if there is a healthy child on the other end. But somewhere along the line, I need you to understand that this could be an elaborate con."

"How do you figure?"

"That's not relevant."

"Like hell it isn't. Are you saying, what, they faked a DNA test?"

"I doubt it." Then she added, "But it's a possibility."

"How? There was a match between the two sets of hairs."

"The hairs matched each other."

"Yes."

"But," she said, "how do you know the first set of hairs—the ones you got a year and a half ago—belonged to Tara?"

It took a few moments for the meaning to reach me.

"Did you ever run a test on the first set, see if the DNA matched yours?" she asked.

"Why would we?"

"So for all you know, the original kidnappers sent you the hairs of another kid."

I tried to shake my head clear. "But they had a snippet of her clothes," I said. "The pink with black penguins. How do you explain that?"

"You don't think the Gap sold more than one of those? Look, I don't know what the story is yet, so let's not get bogged down in hypotheticals. Let's just concentrate on what we can do here and now."

I sat back. We fell into silence. I wondered if I had made the right move by calling her. There was so much excess baggage here. But at the end of the day, I trusted her. We needed to maintain the professional, to keep compartmentalizing.

"I just want my daughter back," I said.

Rachel nodded, opened her mouth as if to say something, and then grew silent again. And that was when the ransom call came in.

chapter 16

Lydia liked to stare at old photographs.

She did not know why. They offered her little comfort. The nostalgia factor was, at best, limited. Heshy never looked back. For reasons that she could never properly articulate, Lydia did.

This particular photograph had been taken when Lydia was eight years old. It was a black-and-white still from the beloved classic TV sitcom *Family Laughs*. The show ran for seven years—in Lydia's case, from the age of six until just near her thirteenth birthday. *Family Laughs* starred ex–movie hunk Clive Wilkins as the widowed father of three adorable children: twin boys, Tod and Rod, who were eleven when the series began, and an adorable pixie of a little sister named, cutely enough, Trixie, played by the irrepressible Larissa Dane. Yes, the show was at least three steps beyond precious. Old repeats of *Family Laughs* still run on TV Land.

Every once in a while, the *E! True Hollywood Story* runs a piece on the old cast of *Family Laughs*. Clive Wilkins died from pancreatic cancer two years after the show ended. The narrator would note that Clive was "just like a father on the set," which, Lydia knew, was a load of crap. The guy drank and smelled liked tobacco. When she hugged him for the cameras, it took all her considerable young acting skills not to gag from the stench.

Jarad and Stan Frank, the real-life identical twins who played Tod and Rod, had been trying to get a music career going since the show's cancellation. On *Family Laughs*, they had a groovy garage band with a repertoire of songs written by others, instruments played by others, and voices so echoed and distorted by synthesizers that even Jarad and Stan, who could not hold a key if it was tattooed into their palms, started to believe that they were genuine musical artistes. The twins were both nearing forty now, both clearly clients of the Hair

Club, both deluding themselves that, even though they claimed to be "tired of the fame," they were one break away from the return to stardom.

But the true draw here, the gripping enigma of the *Family Laughs* saga, involved the fate of the adorable "Pixie named Trixie," Larissa Dane. Here is what is known about her: During the show's final season, Larissa's parents got divorced and fought bitterly over her earnings. Her dad ended up blowing his brains out. Her mother remarried a con artist who disappeared with the money. Like most child actors, Larissa Dane became an immediate has-been. Rumors of promiscuity and drug abuse swirled, though—this being before the nostalgia craze—no one really cared enough to be interested. She overdosed and nearly died when she was just fifteen. She was sent to a sanitarium of some sort and seemingly dropped off the face of the earth. No one really knows what became of her. Many believe that she died from a second drug overdose.

But of course, she had not.

Heshy said, "You ready to make the call, Lydia?"

She did not answer right away. Lydia moved to the next photograph. Another shot from *Family Laughs*, this time Season Five, Episode 112. Little Trixie wore a cast on her arm. Tod wanted to draw a guitar on it. Father didn't really approve. Tod protested, "But, Dad, I promise only to draw it, not play it!" The laugh track howled. Young Larissa didn't understand the joke. Grown-up Lydia didn't either. What she did remember, however, was how she had broken her arm that day. Typical kid stuff really. She was horsing around and fell down the stairs. The pain was tremendous, but they needed to get this show in the can. With that in mind, the studio doctor shot her up with Lord-knows-what and two hack screenwriters incorporated the injury into the script. She was barely conscious when they filmed.

But please, do not start up the violins.

Lydia had read Danny Partridge's book. She had listened to the whining of Willis on *Diff'rent Strokes*. She had heard all about the plight of the child star, the abuse, the stolen money, the long hours. She had seen all the talk shows, heard all the complaints, seen all the crocodile tears from her colleagues—and their dishonesty sickened her.

Here was the truth about the child star dilemma. No, it's not the abuse, though when Lydia was young and foolish enough to believe a shrink could help, he kept telling her how she must be "blocking," that she had in all likelihood been molested by one of the show's producers. And no, don't blame parental neglect for what child stars become. Or, in reverse, parental pushing. It's not the lack of friends, the long hours, the poor socialization skills, the stream of studio tutors. No, it is none of that.

It is, quite simply, the loss of the spotlight. Period. The rest are excuses because no one wants to admit that they are that shallow. Lydia began working on the show when she was six. She had few memories that dated back before then. All she remembers, thus, is being a star. A star is special. A star is royalty. A star is the closest thing on earth to a god. And for Lydia, there had never been anything else. We teach our children that they are special, but Lydia lived it. Everyone thought she was adorable. Everyone thought she was the perfect daughter, loving and kind and yet properly sassy. People stared at her with a bizarre longing. People wanted to be near her, to know about her life, spend time with her, touch the hem of her cloak.

And then, one day, poof—all gone.

Fame is more addictive than crack. Adults who lose fame—one-hit wonders, for example—usually tailspin into depression, though they try to act like they're above it. They don't want to admit the truth. Their whole life is a lie, a desperate scramble for another dose of that most potent of drugs. Fame.

Those adults had a mere sip of the nectar before it was snatched away. But for a child star, that nectar is mother's milk. It's all they've ever known. They can't comprehend that it's fleeting, that it won't last. You can't explain that to a child. You can't prepare them for the inevitable. Lydia had never known anything but adulation. And then, pretty much overnight, the spotlight went out. She was, for the first time in her life, alone in the dark.

That was what screws you up.

Lydia recognized that now. Heshy had helped her. He had gotten her off the junk once and for all. She had hurt herself, had been a slut, had snorted and shot up more narcotics than one could imagine. She did none of these things to escape. She did them to lash out, to hurt something or someone. Her mistake, she realized in rehab after a truly horrific and violent incident, was that she was hurting *herself*. Fame raises you up. It makes others lesser. So why on earth was she hurting the one who should be on top? Instead, why not hurt the pitiful masses, those who had worshiped her, who had given her such heady power, who had turned on her? Why harm the superior species, the one who'd been worthy of all this praise?

"Lydia?"

"Hmm."

"I think we should call now."

She turned to Heshy. They had met in the loony bin, and right away, it was as if their mutual misery could reach out and embrace. Heshy had rescued her when two orderlies had pinned her down. At the time, he had merely pushed them off her. The orderlies threatened them, and they both promised not to say anything. But Heshy understood how to bide his time. He waited. Two weeks later, he ran over one of the goons with a stolen car. While the goon lay wounded, Heshy backed up over his head and then, positioning the tire near the base of the neck, hit the accelerator. A month later, the second goon—the lead orderly—was found in his home. Four of his fingers had been ripped off. Not cut or sliced, but twisted. The ME could tell by the rotation tears. The fingers had been rotated around and around until the tendons and bone finally snapped. Lydia still had one of the fingers somewhere in the basement.

Ten years ago, they ran off together and changed their names. They altered their appearances just enough. They both started over, avenging angels, damaged but superior, above the riffraff. She didn't hurt anymore. Or at least, when she did, she found an outlet.

They had three residences. Heshy purportedly lived in the Bronx. She had a place in Queens. They both had working addresses and working phones. But that was all for show. Business offices, if you will. Neither of them wanted anyone to know that they were, in fact, a team, connected, lovers. Lydia, using an alias, had bought this bright yellow house four years ago. It had two bedrooms and one and a half baths. The kitchen, where Heshy now sat, was airy and happy. They were on a lake in the tippy north corner of Morris County, New Jersey. It was peaceful here. They loved the sunsets.

Lydia kept staring at the pictures of "Pixie Trixie." She tried to remember what she'd felt like back then. The memories were pretty much gone. Heshy stood behind her now and waited with his usual patience. There were those who would claim that she and Heshy were cold-blooded killers. That, Lydia quickly realized, was pretty much a misnomer, another Hollywood creation. Like the wonderfulness of Pixie Trixie. No one enters this violent business merely because it is profitable. There are easier ways to make a living. You may act like a professional. You may keep your emotions in check. You may even delude yourself into thinking it's just another day at the office, but when you look at it honestly, the reason you walk on this wrong side of the line is because you enjoy it. Lydia understood that. Hurting someone, killing someone, fading or turning out the light in a person's eyes . . .

no, she did not need that. She did not crave it as she had the spotlight. But yes, no question, there was that pleasant jolt, that unmistakable thrill, a lessening of her own pain.

"Lydia?"

"I'm on it, Pooh Bear." She picked up the cell phone with the stolen number and the scramble. She turned and faced Heshy. He was hideous, but she didn't see that. He nodded at her. She flipped on the voice changer and dialed the number.

When Lydia heard Marc Seidman's voice, she said, "Shall we try this again?"

chapter 17

Before I answered the phone, Rachel put her hand over mine. "This is a negotiation," she said. "Fear and intimidation are tools in that. You have to stay strong. If they intend to let her go, they will be flexible."

I swallowed and flicked on the phone. I said hello.

"Shall we try this again?"

The voice had the same robotic hum. I felt a tick in my blood. I closed my eyes and said, "No."

"Pardon me?"

"I want assurances that Tara is alive."

"You received hair samples, did you not?"

"Yes."

"And?"

I looked over at Rachel. She nodded. "The match was inconclusive."

"Fine," the voice said. "I might as well hang up now."

"Wait," I said.

"Yes?"

"You drove off last time."

"So we did."

"How do I know you won't do that again?"

"Did you call the police this time?"

"No."

"Then you have nothing to worry about. Here is what I want you to do."

"It's not going to work like that," I said.

"What?"

I could feel my body begin to quake. "We make a swap. You don't get the money until I get my daughter."

"You're not in any position to bargain."

"I get my daughter," I said, my words coming out slowly, dead weights. "You get your money."

"It's not going to work like that."

"Yes," I said, trying to force bravado into my voice. "This ends here and now. I don't want you running away again and then coming back for more. So we make an exchange and end this."

"Dr. Seidman?"

"I'm here."

"I want you to listen to me carefully."

The silence was too long, straining my nerves.

"If I hang up now, I won't call back for another eighteen months."

I closed my eyes and hung on.

"Think about the repercussions for a moment. Aren't you wondering where your daughter has been? Aren't you wondering what will become of her? If I hang up, you won't know anything for another eighteen months."

It felt like a steel belt was being tightened around my chest. I couldn't breathe. I looked at Rachel. She stared back steadily, urging me to stay strong.

"How old would she be then, Dr. Seidman? I mean, if we keep her alive."

"Please."

"Are you ready to listen?"

I squeezed my eyes shut. "I'm just asking for assurances."

"We sent you the hair samples."

"I bring the money. You bring my daughter. You get the money when I see her."

"Are you trying to dictate terms, Dr. Seidman?"

The robotic voice had a funny lilt now.

"I don't care who you are," I said. "I don't care why you did any of this. I just want my daughter back."

"Then you'll make the drop exactly as I tell you."

"No," I said. "Not without assurances."

"Dr. Seidman?"

"Yes."

"Good-bye."

And then the phone went dead.

chapter 18

Sanity is a thin string. Mine snapped.

No, I did not scream. Just the opposite. I grew impossibly calm. I pulled the phone away from my ear and looked it as if it'd just materialized there and I had no idea what it was.

"Marc?"

I looked at Rachel. "They hung up."

"They'll call back," she said.

I shook my head. "They said not for another eighteen months."

Rachel studied my face. "Marc?"

"Yes?"

"I need you to listen to me closely."

I waited.

"You did the right thing here."

"Thanks. Now I feel better."

"I've had experience with this. If Tara is

still alive and if they have any intention of giving her back, they'll give on this issue. The only reason not to make this exchange is because they don't want to—or can't."

Can't. The tiny part of my brain that remained rational understood that. I reminded myself of my training. Compartmentalize. "So now what?"

"We get ready just as we planned before. I have enough equipment with me. We'll wire you up. If they call back, we'll be ready."

I nodded dumbly. "Okay."

"Meanwhile, is there anything else we can do here? Did you recognize the voice at all? Do you remember anything new about the man in flannel, about the van, anything?"

"No," I said.

"On the phone, you mentioned finding a CD in your basement."

"Yes." I quickly told her the story about the disk and the label reading MVD. She took out a pad and jotted down notes.

"Do you have the disk with you?"

"No."

"Doesn't matter," she said. "We're in Newark now. We might as well see what we can learn from this MVD."

chapter 19

Lydia lifted the Sig-Sauer P226 into the air.

"I don't like how that went," she said.

"You made the right move," Heshy said. "We cut out now. This is over."

She stared at the weapon. She wanted very much to pull the trigger.

"Lydia?"

"I heard you."

"We were doing this because it was simple."

"Simple?"

"Yes. We thought that it would be easy money."

"Lots of money."

"True," he said.

"We can't just walk away."

Heshy saw the wetness in her eyes. This

was not about the money. He knew that. "He's tortured either way," he said.

"I know."

"Think about what you just did to him," Heshy said. "If he never hears from us again, he will spend the rest of his life wondering, blaming himself."

She smiled. "Are you trying to turn me on?"

Lydia moved onto Heshy's lap, curled into him like a kitten. He wrapped his giant arms around her and for a moment, Lydia calmed. She felt safe and quiet. She closed her eyes. She loved the feeling. And she knew—as did he—that it would never last. That it would never be enough.

"Heshy?"

"Yes."

"I want to get that money."

"I know you do."

"And then, I think, it would be best if he died."

Heshy pulled her close. "Then that's what will happen."

chapter 20

I don't know what I expected from the offices of Most Valuable Detection. A pebbled-glass door à la Sam Spade or Philip Marlowe maybe. A soiled building of faded brick. A walk-up, for sure. A buxom secretary with a bad dye job.

But the office of Most Valuable Detection had none of that. The building was shiny and bright, part of the "urban renewal" program of Newark. I keep hearing about Newark's renaissance, but I don't see it. Yes, there are several beautiful office buildings—like this one—and a stunning Performing Arts Center conveniently located so that those who can afford to attend (read: those who don't live in Newark) can get to it without, well, driving through the city. But these sleek edifices are flowers among the weeds, scant stars in an otherwise black sky. They do not change the basic color. They do not blend or bleed. They remain removed. Their sterile beauty is not contagious.

We stepped off the elevator. I still held the bag with two million dollars in it. It felt weird in my hand. There were three headphone-clad receptionists behind a wall of glass. Their desk was high. We stated our names into an intercom. Rachel showed an ID that listed her as a retired FBI agent. We were buzzed in.

Rachel pushed open the door. I trailed behind her. I felt empty, but I was functioning. The horror of what had happened—the hang-up—was so great that I had pushed beyond paralysis to a strange state of focus. Again I compare all this to the surgery room. I enter that room, I cross that gateway, and I shed the world. I had a patient once, a six-year-old boy, who was getting a fairly routine cleft palate repair. While on the table, his vitals dropped suddenly. His heart stopped. I didn't panic. I fell into a state of focus, not unlike this one. The boy pulled through.

Still flashing the ID, Rachel explained that

we wanted to see someone in charge. The receptionist smiled and nodded in that way people do when they aren't listening. She never took off the headphones. Her fingers pressed some buttons. Another woman appeared. She led us down the corridor and into a private office.

For a moment, I couldn't tell if we were in the presence of a man or a woman. The bronze nameplate on the desk read Conrad Dorfman. Conclusion: a man. He rose theatrically. He was too slim in a blue suit with *Guys and Dolls*–wide pinstripes, tapered at the waist so that the bottom of the jacket flared out almost enough to be mistaken for a skirt. His fingers were thin like a pianist's, his hair slicked down like Julie Andrews's in *Victor/Victoria*, and his face had a blotchy smoothness I usually associate with a cosmetic foundation.

"Please," he said in a voice with too much affect. "My name is Conrad Dorfman. I'm the executive vice president of MVD." We shook his hand. He held our hands a second too long, putting the free hand over the shake and peering intently into our eyes. Conrad invited us to sit. We did. He asked us if we'd enjoy a cup of tea. Rachel, taking the lead, said that we would.

There were a few more minutes of chitchat. Conrad asked Rachel questions about her time with the FBI. Rachel was vague. She implied that she, too, worked in the private detection biz and was thus his colleague and worthy of professional courtesy. I said nothing, letting her work. There was a knock on the door. The woman who had escorted us down the corridor opened the door and wheeled in a silver teacart. Conrad began to pour. Rachel got to the point.

"We were hoping you could help us," Rachel said. "Dr. Seidman's wife was a client of yours."

Conrad Dorfman concentrated on the tea. He used one of those screen-door sifters that seemed all the rage nowadays. He shook out some leaves and slowly poured.

"You folks provided her with a CD that's password protected. We need to get into it."

Conrad handed a cup of tea to Rachel first, then me. He settled back and took a deep sip. "I'm sorry," he said. "I can't help you. The password is set by the client on their own."

"The client is dead."

Conrad Dorfman did not blink. "That really doesn't change anything."

"Her husband here is next of kin. That makes the CD his."

"I wouldn't know," Conrad said. "I don't practice estate law. But we have no control over any of that. As I said before, the client sets the password. We may have given her the CD—I really can't confirm or deny that at this stage—but we would have no idea what numbers or letters she programmed in for the password."

Rachel waited a beat. She stared at Conrad Dorfman. He stared back but dropped his eyes first. He picked up his tea and took another sip. "Can we find out why she came to you in the first place?"

"Without a court order? No, I don't think so."

"Your CD," she said. "There's a back entry."

"Excuse me?"

"Every company has one," Rachel said. "The info isn't lost forever. Your company programs in its own password so that you folks can get on the CD."

"I don't know what you're talking about."

"I used to be an FBI agent, Mr. Dorfman."

"So?"

"So I know these things. Please don't insult my intelligence."

"That was not my intent, Ms. Mills. But I simply can't help."

I looked at Rachel. She seemed to be weighing her options. "I still have friends, Mr. Dorfman. In the department. We can ask questions. We can poke around. The feds don't much like private eyes. You know that. I don't want trouble. I just want to know what's on the CD."

Dorfman put down his cup. He strummed his fingers. There was a knock, and the same woman opened the door. She beckoned Conrad Dorfman. He rose, again too theatrically, and practically leapt across the floor. "Excuse me a moment."

When he left the office, I looked at Rachel. She wouldn't turn toward me. "Rachel?"

"Let's just see how it plays out, Marc."

But there really wasn't much more to play. Conrad came back into the office. He crossed the room and stood over Rachel, waiting for her to look up. She wouldn't give him the satisfaction.

"Our president, Malcolm Deward, is a former federal agent himself. Did you know that?"

Rachel said nothing.

"He made some calls while we chatted." Conrad waited. "Ms. Mills?" Rachel finally looked up. "Your threats are impotent. You have no friends at the agency. Mr. Deward, alas, does. Get out of my office. Now."

chapter 21

I said, "What the hell was that all about?"

"I told you before. I'm not an agent anymore."

"What happened, Rachel?"

She kept her eyes forward. "You haven't been a part of my life in a long time."

There was nothing to add. Rachel drove now. I held on to the cell phone, again willing it to ring. When we arrived back at my house, dusk had settled in. We went inside. I debated calling Tickner or Regan, but what good would that do now?

"We need to get that DNA checked," Rachel said. "My theory might sound implausible, but does the idea of your daughter being held all this time sound any more so?"

So I called Edgar. I told him that I wanted

to run some additional tests on the hair. He said that would be fine. I hung up without telling him that I had already endangered the drop by enlisting the help of a former FBI agent. The less said on that, the better. Rachel called someone she knew to pick up the samples from Edgar, as well as a blood sample from me. He ran a private lab, she said. We would know something within twenty-four to forty-eight hours, which would probably be, in terms of a ransom demand, too late.

I settled into a chair in the den. Rachel sat on the floor. She opened her bag and pulled out wires and electronic contraptions of all sorts. Being a surgeon makes me pretty good with my hands, but when it comes to high-tech gizmos, I'm totally lost. She carefully spread the contents of the bag across the carpet, giving this action her full attention. Again I was reminded of the way she'd do the same thing with textbooks when we were in college. She reached into the bag and pulled out a razor.

"The bag of money?" she said.

I handed it to her. "What are you going to do?"

She opened it. The money was in packs

of hundred-dollar bills. She grabbed a wad and slowly slipped the money out, not breaking the band around it. She cut the bills like they were a deck of cards.

"What are you doing?" I asked.

"I'm going to cut a hole."

"In the actual currency?"

"Yup."

She did it with the straight razor. She dug out a circle about the perimeter of a silver dollar, maybe a quarter inch thick. She scanned the floor, found a black device that was about the same size, fit it into the bills. Then she put the wrapping back on it. The device was totally hidden in the middle of the money wad.

"A Q-Logger," she said in way of explanation. "It's a GPS device."

"You say so."

"GPS stands for Global Positioning System. Put simply, it will track the money. I'll put one in the lining of the bag too, but most criminals know about that. They usually dump the cash into a bag of their own. But with all this money, they won't have time right away to search through every pack."

"How small do those things come?"

"The Q-Loggers?"

"Yes."

"They can make them even thinner, but the problem is the power source. You need a battery. That's where we lose out. I need something that can travel at least eight miles. This will do it."

"And where does it go to?"

"You mean where do I keep track of the movements?"

"Yes."

"Most of the time it goes to a laptop, but this is state of the art." Rachel lifted a device into the air, one I see too often in the world of medicine. In fact, I think I'm the only doctor on the planet without one.

"A Palm Pilot?"

"Designed with a special tracking screen. I'll have it on me if I have to move." She went back to work.

"What's all the other stuff?" I asked.

"Surveillance equipment. I don't know how much I'll be able to use, but I'd like to put a Q-Logger in your shoe. I want to get a camera on the car. I'd like to see if I can hook up some fiber-optics on you, but that could be riskier." She started to organize her equipment, lost in the activity. Her eyes were down when she spoke again. "Something else I want to explain to you."

I leaned forward.

"Do you remember when my parents got divorced?" she asked.

"Yeah, sure." It had been when we first met.

"Close as we were, we never talked about it."

"I always got the impression you didn't want to."

"I didn't," she said too quickly.

And, I thought, neither had I. I was selfish. We were supposedly in love for two years—and yet I never so much as nudged her to open up about her parents' divorce. It was more than an "impression" that made me hold my tongue. I knew something dark and unhappy lay there. I did not want to poke at it, disturb it, have it possibly turn its attention in my direction.

"It was my father's fault."

I almost said something really stupid like "It's never anyone's fault" or "There are two sides to every story," but a flyby of good sense kept my tongue in check. Rachel still hadn't looked up. "My father destroyed my mother. Crushed her soul. Do you know how?"

"No."

"He cheated on her."

She lifted her head and held my gaze. I did not look away. "It was a destructive cycle," she said. "He'd cheat, he'd get caught, he'd swear he'd never do it again. But he always did. It wormed into my mother, ate away at her." Rachel swallowed, turned back to her high-tech toys. "So when I was away in Italy and I heard you'd been with someone else . . ."

I thought of a million different things to say, but they were all meaningless. Frankly so was what she was telling me. It explained a lot, I guess, but it was the ultimate too-little-too-late. I stayed where I was, not moving from the chair.

"I overreacted," she said.

"We were young."

"I just wanted . . . I should have told you about this back then."

She was reaching out. I started to say something, but I pulled up short. Too much. Just all too much. It had been six hours since the ransom call. The seconds tick-

ticked, a deep, painful pounding in the well of my chest.

I jumped when the phone rang, but it was my regular line, not the kidnapper's cell. I picked it up. It was Lenny.

"What's wrong?" he said without preamble.

I looked at Rachel. She shook her head. I nodded back that I understood. "Nothing," I said.

"Your mom told me you saw Edgar in the park."

"Don't worry."

"That old bastard will screw you, you know that."

There was no reasoning with Lenny when it came to Edgar Portman. He also might be right. "I know."

There was brief silence.

"You called Rachel," he said.

"Yes."

"Why?"

"Nothing important."

There was another pause. Then Lenny said, "You're lying to me, right?"

"Like a Vegas toupee."

"Yeah, okay. Hey, we still on for racquetball tomorrow morning?"

"I better cancel."

"No problem. Marc?"

"Yeah."

"If you need me . . ."

"Thanks, Lenny."

I hung up. Rachel was busy with her electronic gizmos. The words she had said were gone now, dissipated smoke. She looked up and saw something in my face.

"Marc?"

I didn't speak.

"If your daughter is alive, we'll bring her home. I promise."

And for the first time, I was not sure that I believed her.

chapter 22

Special Agent Tickner stared down at the report.

The Seidman murder-kidnapping had been beyond back-burner. The FBI had realigned its priorities in recent years. Terrorism was number one on the most wanted list. Numbers two through ten were, well, terrorism. The Seidman case had only involved him when it became a kidnapping issue. Despite what you see on television, the local police are usually anxious to have the FBI involved. The feds have the resources and the know-how. Calling them too late can cost a life. Regan had been smart enough not to wait.

But once the kidnapping issue was—and he hated to use this term for it—"resolved," Tickner's job (unofficially at least) was to back off and leave it to the locals. He still thought about it a lot—you don't forget the sight of a baby's clothing in a cabin like that—but in his mind, the case had been in-active.

Until five minutes ago.

He read the brief report for the third time. He wasn't trying to put it together. Not yet. This was too weird for that. What he was trying to do, what he hoped to accomplish, was to find some kind of angle, some sort of handle he could grip. Nothing came to him.

Rachel Mills. How the hell did she fit into this?

A young subordinate—Tickner couldn't remember if his name was Kelly or Fitzger-ald, something Irish like that—stood in front of the desk, hands not sure what to do. Tickner leaned back in the chair and crossed his legs. He tapped the pen against his lower lip.

"There has to be a connection between them," he told Sean or Patrick.

"She claimed to be a private detective."

"Is she licensed?"

"No, sir."

Tickner shook his head. "There's more to it than that. Check phone records, find some friends, whatever. Trace it down for me."

"Yes, sir."

"Call that detective agency. The MVD. Tell them I'm on my way."

"Yes, sir."

The Irish kid left. Tickner stared off. He and Rachel had gone through training together at Quantico. They'd both had the same mentor. Tickner thought about what to do here. While he didn't always trust the locals, he liked Regan. The guy was just off enough to be an asset. He picked up the phone and dialed Regan's cell.

"Detective Regan."

"Long time, no speak."

"Ah, Federal Agent Tickner. You still wearing the sunglasses?"

"You still stroking that soul patch—uh, among other things?"

"Yes. And maybe."

Tickner could hear sitar music in the background. "You busy?"

"Not at all. I was just meditating."

"Like Phil Jackson?"

"Exactly. Except I don't have all those pesky championship rings. You should join me sometime."

"Yeah, I'll put that on my list of must-dos."

"It would relax you, Agent Tickner. I hear tremendous strain in your voice." Then: "I assume that there was a reason for this call?"

"Remember our favorite case?"

There was a funny pause. "Yes."

"How long has it been since we had something new?"

"I don't think we ever had anything new."

"Well, we may now."

"I'm listening."

"We just got a strange call from an ex–FBI agent. Guy named Deward. He's a private dick in Newark now."

"So?"

"It seems our friend Dr. Seidman paid his office a visit today. And he had someone very special with him."

Lydia dyed her hair black—the better to blend in with the night.

The plan, as it were, was simple.

"We confirm that he has the money," she told Heshy. "Then I kill him."

"You sure?"

"Positive. And the beauty of it is, the murder will automatically get tied to the original shooting." Lydia smiled at him. "Even if something goes wrong, nothing ties back to us."

"Lydia?"

"Something the matter?"

Heshy shrugged his giant shoulders. "Don't you think it would be better if I kill him?"

"I'm the better shot, Pooh Bear."

"But"—he hesitated, shrugged again—"I don't need a weapon."

"You're trying to protect me," she said.

He said nothing.

"That's sweet." And it was. But one of the reasons she wanted to do it herself was to protect Heshy. He was the vulnerable one here. Lydia never worried about getting caught. Part of it was classic overconfidence. Dumb people get caught, not those who were careful. But more than that, she knew if she did get nabbed, they'd never convict her. Forget her still girl-next-door looks, though that would undoubtedly be an asset. What no prosecutor would ever overcome would be the weepy Oprahization of her case. Lydia would remind them of her "tragic" past. She would claim abuses in many forms. She would cry on the talk shows. She would talk about the plight of the child star, of the calamity of being forced into the world of Pixie Trixie. She would look adorably victimized and innocent. And the public—not to mention the jury—would lap it up.

"I think it's best this way," she told him. "If he sees you approach, well, he is apt to run. But if he catches sight of lil' ol' me . . ." Lydia let her voice die out with a small shrug.

Heshy nodded. She was right. This should be cake. She stroked his face and handed him the car keys.

"Does Pavel understand his part?" Lydia asked.

"He does. He'll meet us there. And yes, he'll be wearing the flannel shirt."

"Then we might as well start on our way," she said. "I'll call Dr. Seidman."

Heshy used the remote to unlock the car doors.

"Oh," she said, "I have to check something before we go."

Lydia opened the back door. The child was fast asleep in the car seat. She checked the straps and made sure that they were secure. "I better sit in the back, Pooh Bear," she said. "Just in case a little some-one wakes up."

Heshy angled his way into the driver's seat. Lydia took out the phone and voice changer and dialed the number.

chapter 23

We ordered a pizza, which I think was a mistake. Late-night pizzas are college. It was yet another not-so-subtle reminder of the past. I kept staring at the mobile phone, wishing it to ring. Rachel was quiet, but that was okay. We had always been good with silence. That, too, was weird. In many ways, we were falling back, picking up where we'd left off. But in many more ways, we were strangers with a tenuous, awkward connection.

What was odd was that my memories were suddenly hazy. I'd thought that once I saw her again, they'd head straight to the surface. But few specifics came to me. It was more a feeling, an emotion, like the way I remembered the ruddy cold of New England. I don't know why I couldn't remember. And I wasn't sure what it meant.

Rachel's brow creased as she toyed with the electronic equipment. She took a bite of pizza and said, "Not as good as Tony's."

"That place was awful."

"A little greasy," she agreed.

"A little? Didn't the large come with a coupon for a free angioplasty?"

"Well, there was that sludge-through-the-veins feel to it."

We looked at each other.

"Rachel?"

"Yeah."

"Suppose they don't call."

"Then they don't have her, Marc."

I let that settle in. I thought about Lenny's son, Conner, the things he could say and do, and I tried to apply it to the baby I'd last laid eyes on in her crib. It wouldn't compute, but that didn't mean anything. There was hope. I held on to that. If my daughter was dead, if that phone never rang again, the hope would, I know, kill me. But I didn't care. Better to go down this way than try to go the distance.

So I had hope. And I, the cynic, let myself believe the best.

When the cell phone finally did ring, it was nearly ten. I did not even glance over to Rachel and wait for her nod. My finger was on the answer button before the first chirp could die off.

"Hello?"

"Okay," the robotic voice said, "you'll get to see her."

I couldn't breathe. Rachel moved over closer and put her ear near mine.

"Good," I said.

"You have the money?"

"Yes."

"All of it?"

"Yes."

"Then listen closely. Deviate from what I tell you and we disappear. Do you understand?"

"Yes."

"We checked with our police sources. So far, so good. It appears that you haven't contacted the authorities. But we need to make sure. You will drive alone toward the George Washington Bridge. Once there, we will be in range. Use the two-way radio feature on the phone. I will tell you where to go and what to do. You will be searched. If we

find any weapons or wires, we will disappear. Do you understand?"

I could feel Rachel's breath quicken.

"When do I see my daughter?"

"When we meet."

"How do I know you won't just take the
money?"

"How do you know I'm not going to hang
up on you now?"

"I'm on my way," I said. Then I quickly
added, "But I won't hand over the money
until I see Tara."

"Then we are in agreement. You have an
hour. Signal me then."

chapter 24

Conrad Dorfman did not appear happy to be dragged back into the MVD office this late. Tickner didn't care. If Seidman had come here alone, that would be an important lead, no doubt about it. But the fact that Rachel Mills had been here, too, that she was somehow involved, well, let's just say that Tickner's curiosity was more than piqued.

"Did Ms. Mills show you an ID?" he asked.

"Yes," Dorfman replied. "But it was stamped 'Retired.' "

"And she was with Dr. Seidman?"

"Yes."

"They arrived together."

"I think so. I mean, yes, when they came in here, they were together."

Tickner nodded. "What did they want?"

"A password. For a CD-ROM."

"I'm not sure I follow."

"They claimed that they had a CD-ROM we provided to a client. Our CDs are password protected. They wanted us to give them the password."

"Did you?"

Dorfman looked properly shocked. "Of course not. We had a call put in to your agency. They explained to us . . . well, they never quite explained to us anything really. They just stressed that we should not cooperate with Agent Mills in any way."

"*Ex*-agent," Tickner said.

How? Tickner wondered. How the hell had Rachel Mills hooked up with Seidman? He had tried to give her the benefit of the doubt. Unlike his fellow agents, he had known her, had seen her in action. She'd been a good agent, maybe even a great one. But now he wondered. He wondered about the timing. He wondered about her being here. He wondered about her flashing her badge and trying to apply pressure.

"Did they tell you how they came by this CD-ROM?"

"They claimed that it belonged to Dr. Seidman's wife."

"Does it?"

"I believe so, yes."

"Are you aware that his wife died more than a year and a half ago, Mr. Dorfman?"

"I know that now."

"But you didn't when they were here?"

"Right."

"Why did Seidman wait eighteen months to ask for the password?"

"He didn't say."

"Did you ask?"

Dorfman shifted in his seat. "No."

Tickner smiled, buddy-to-buddy. "No reason you should," he said, faux-genteel. "Did you give them any information at all?"

"None."

"You didn't tell them why Mrs. Seidman hired your agency in the first place?"

"That's correct."

"Okay, very good." Tickner leaned forward, his elbows on his knees now. He was about to ask another question when his cell phone rang. "Excuse me," he said, reaching into his pocket.

"Is this going to take much longer?" Dorfman asked. "I have plans."

He didn't even bother responding. Rising, he put the phone to his ear. "Tickner."

"It's Agent O'Malley," the young kid said.

"Did you find anything?"

"Oh yeah."

"I'm listening."

"We checked the phone records going back three years. Seidman never called her—at least, not from his house or office—until today."

"Am I about to hear a *but*?"

"You are. But Rachel Mills called him—once."

"When?"

"June two years ago."

Tickner did the math. That would have been about three months before the murder and kidnapping. "Anything else?"

"Something big, I think. I had one of our agents check Rachel's apartment in Falls Church. He's still poking around, but guess what he found in her night-table drawer?"

"Does this look like a quiz show, O'Ryan?"

"O'Malley."

Tickner rubbed the bridge of his nose. "What did the agent find?"

"A prom photo."

"What?"

"I mean, I don't know if it's from the prom exactly. It's some kind of old formal. Photo gotta be fifteen, twenty years old. She's wearing her hair in some flip-style and she's got one of those flower bands on her arm. What do you call those?"

"A corsage?"

"Right."

"What the hell does this have to do with—"

"The guy in the picture."

"What about him?"

"Our agent is sure. The guy she's with—her date, I mean—is our own Dr. Seidman."

Tickner felt the thrum rush through him. "Keep digging," he said. "Call me when you get more."

"On it."

He hung up the phone. Rachel and Seidman went to a prom together? What the hell was going on? She was from Vermont, if he remembered correctly. Seidman lived in New Jersey. They didn't go to high school together. How about college? They'd have to look into it.

"Something wrong?"

Tickner turned. It was Dorfman. "Let me

see if I have this straight, Mr. Dorfman. This CD-ROM belonged to Monica Seidman?"

"That's what we were told, yes."

"Yes or no, Mr. Dorfman."

He cleared his throat. "We believe the answer is yes."

"So she was a client here?"

"Yes, that we've been able to confirm."

"So to sum up, a murder victim was a client of yours."

Silence.

"Her name was in every paper in the state," Tickner went on, giving him the hard stare. "How come you never came forward?"

"We didn't know."

Tickner kept with the hard stare.

"The guy who handled that case is no longer employed by us," he added quickly. "See, he was gone by the time Mrs. Seidman was killed. So no one here put the pieces together."

Defensive. Tickner liked that. He believed him, but he didn't show it. Make the guy anxious to please.

"What was on the CD?"

"Photographs, we think."

"Think?"

"That's usually the case. Not always. We use the CD to store photographs, but there could be some scanned documents too. I really couldn't tell you."

"Why the hell not?"

He put up both hands. "Don't worry. We have a backup. But any file more than a year old is stored in the basement. The office was closed, but when I heard you were interested, I got someone to come in. He's running off the material on the backup CD right now."

"Where?"

"He's on the lower level." Dorfman checked his watch. "He should be done or just about by now. Do you want to go down and see?"

Tickner stood. "Let's rumble."

chapter 25

"There are still things we can do," Rachel said. "This stuff is state of the art. Even if they pat you down, we can get away with it. I have a bulletproof vest that has a pinhole camera right in the center."

"And you don't think they'll find that with a pat-down?"

"Yeah, okay, look, I know you're worried about them finding out, but let's be realistic here. There's an excellent chance this is all a setup. Don't give up the money until you see Tara. Don't get yourself stuck some-where alone. Don't worry about the Q-Log-ger—if they're being up front, we'll have Tara before they can search the stacks of money. I know this isn't an easy decision, Marc."

"No, you're right. I played it safe last time.

I think we need to take some chances. But the vest is out."

"Okay, here's what we're going to do. I'm going to be in the trunk. They may check the backseat to see if someone is lying there. The trunk will be a safer bet. I'll disconnect the wires back there so when the trunk opens, no lights will come on. I'll try to keep up with you, but I have to stay at a safe distance. Make no mistake here. I'm not Wonder Woman. I might lose you, but remember: Don't look for me. Not even casually. These guys are probably pretty good. They'll spot that."

"I understand." She was dressed totally in black. I said, "You look like you're going to do a reading in the Village."

"Kumbaya, my Lord. You ready?"

We both heard the car pull up. I looked out the window and felt my panic needle jump. "Damn," I said.

"What?"

"That's Regan, the cop on the case. I haven't seen him in more than a month." I looked at her. Her face was stark white against the black outfit. "Coincidence?"

"No coincidence," she said.

"How the hell did he find out about the ransom?"

She moved back from the window. "He's probably not here for that."

"Then what?"

"My guess would be that they got word of my involvement from MVD."

I frowned. "So?"

"No time to explain. Look, I'm going to go out to the garage and hide. He's going to ask about me. Tell him I went back to D.C. If he presses, tell him I'm an old friend and leave it at that. He's going to want to interrogate you."

"Why?"

But she was already moving away from me. "Just be firm and get him out of there. I'll wait for you by the car."

I didn't like it, but now was not the time. "Okay."

Rachel headed to the garage via the door in the den. I waited until she was out of sight. When Regan hit my front walkway, I opened the door, trying to cut him off at the pass.

Regan smiled. "Were you expecting me?" he asked.

"I heard your car."

He nodded as if I'd said something that required serious analysis. "Do you have a few moments, Dr. Seidman?"

"Actually, it's a bad time."

"Oh." Regan did not break stride. He slid past me and into my front foyer, his eyes taking in everything. "Heading out, are we?"

"What do you want, Detective?"

"Some new information has come to our attention."

I waited for him to say more.

"Don't you want to know what it is?"

"Of course."

Regan had a strange, almost serene look on his face. He looked up at the ceiling, as if he were considering what color to paint it. "Where have you been today?"

"Get out, please."

His eyes were still on the ceiling. "Your hostility surprises me." But he did not look surprised.

"You said you had some new information. If you do, say it. If not, get out. I'm not in the mood to be questioned."

He made a well-well face. "We hear that you visited a private detective agency in Newark today."

"So?"

"So what were you doing there?"

"Tell you what, Detective. I'm going to ask you to leave because I know answering your questions will bring me no closer to finding my daughter."

He looked at me. "You sure about that?"

"Kindly get the hell out of my house. Now."

"Suit yourself." Regan started for the door. When we reached it, he asked, "Where's Rachel Mills?"

"Don't know."

"She's not here?"

"Nope."

"No idea at all where she could be?"

"I think she's on her way back to Washington."

"Hmm. How do you two know each other?"

"Good night, Detective."

"Okay, sure. But one last question."

I stifled a sigh. "You've watched too many episodes of *Columbo*, Detective."

"Indeed I have." He smiled. "But let me ask it anyway."

I spread my hands for him to go ahead.

"Do you know how her husband died?"

"He was shot," I said too quickly, and

immediately regretted it. He leaned a little more into my space and kept on me.

"And do you know who shot him?"

I stood without moving.

"Do you, Marc?"

"Good night, Detective."

"She killed him, Marc. A bullet to the head at close range."

"That," I said, "is a load of bull."

"Is it? I mean, are you sure?"

"If she killed him, why isn't she in jail?"

"Good question," Regan said, backing down the walkway. When he reached the end of the walkway, he added, "Maybe you should ask her."

chapter 26

Rachel was in the garage. She looked up at me. She suddenly looked small, I thought. And I saw fear in her face. The car trunk was open. I moved toward the driver-side door.

"What did he want?" she asked.

"What you said."

"He knew about the CD?"

"He knew we'd been at MVD. He didn't say anything about the CD."

I slid into the car. She let it drop. Now was not the time to raise any new issues. We both knew that. But again I questioned my judgment here. My wife had been murdered. So had my sister. Someone had tried very hard to kill me. Stripping it bare, I was trusting a woman I really didn't know. I was trusting her not only with my life, but with my daughter's. How stupid when you think about it. Lenny had been right. It was not so simple. In truth, I had no idea who she was or what she'd become. I had deluded myself into making her something she might not be, and now I wondered what it might cost me.

Her voice cut through my haze. "Marc?"

"What?"

"I still think you should wear the bullet-proof vest."

"No."

My tone was firmer than I'd wanted. Or maybe not. Rachel climbed into the trunk and closed it. I put the duffel bag with the money on the seat next to me. I hit the garage-door opener under the sun-visor and started the car.

We were on our way.

When Tickner was nine years old, his mother bought him a book of optical illusions. You'd look at a drawing of, say, an old lady with a big nose. You'd look a little longer and then, poof, it appeared now to be a young woman with her head turned. Tickner had loved the book. When he got a little older, he moved on to those Magic Eyes, staring for however long it took for the horsey or whatever to appear in the swirling colors. Sometimes it would take a long time. You'd even start to wonder if there was anything there at all. And then, suddenly, the image surfaced.

That was what was happening here.

There were moments in a case, Tickner knew, that altered everything—just like those old optical illusions. You are viewing one reality and then, with a gentle tilt, reality changes. Nothing is as it appeared.

He had never really bought the conventional theories on the Seidman murder-kidnapping. They all felt too much like reading a book with missing pages.

Over the years, Tickner had not dealt with that many murders. They were, for the most part, left to the local cops. But he knew plenty of homicide investigators. The best ones were always off center, overly theatrical, ridiculously imaginative. Tickner had heard them talk about a point in the case where the victim "reaches out" from the grave. The victim "talks" to them somehow, pointing them toward the killer. Tickner would listen to this nonsense and nod politely. It always sounded like a load of hyperbole, just one of those meaningless things cops say because the general public laps it up.

The printer still whirred. Tickner had seen twelve photos already.

"How many more?" he asked.

Dorfman looked at the computer screen. "Six more."

"Same as these?"

"Pretty much, yeah. I mean, same person."

Tickner stared down at the photographs. Yes, the same person was featured in all of them. They were all in black and white, all taken without the subject knowing, probably from a distance with a zoom lens.

The reach-from-the-grave stuff—it no longer sounded so silly. Monica Seidman had been dead for eighteen months. Her murderer had gone free. And now, with all hope lost, she seemed to have risen from the dead to point a finger. Tickner looked again and tried to understand.

The subject of the pictures, the person Monica Seidman was pointing at, was Rachel Mills.

When you take the eastern spur of the New Jersey Turnpike north, the night skyline of Manhattan beckons. Like most people who see it nearly every day, I used to take it for granted. No more. For a while afterward, I thought I could still see the Towers. It was as though they were bright lights I'd stared at for a long time, so that even when I closed my eyes, their images were still there, imbedded. But like any sunspot, the images eventually began to fade. It is different now. When I drive this route, I still make myself look for them. Even tonight. But sometimes I forget precisely where those towers stood. And that angers me more than I can express.

Out of habit, I took the lower level of the George Washington Bridge. There was no traffic at this hour. I drove through the E-ZPass. I had managed to keep myself distracted. I flipped stations between two talk radio shows. One was a sports station where lots of guys named Vinny from Bayside called up and complained about inept coaches and how much better they'd be at the job. The other station featured two beyond-puerile Howard Stern rip-offs who thought it was funny for a college freshman to call his mother and tell her he had testicular cancer. Both were, if not entertaining, mildly distracting.

Rachel was in the trunk, which was totally weird if I thought about it. I reached for the cell phone and flipped on the two-way radio feature. My finger pressed down on the call button and almost instantly I heard the robotic voice say, "Take the Henry Hudson north."

I put the phone to mouth, walkie-talkie style. "Okay."

"Tell me the moment you get on the Hudson."

"Right."

I got into the left lane. I knew the way. This area was familiar to me. I had done a fellowship at New York Presbyterian, which resided about ten blocks south. Zia and I had roomed with a cardiac resident named Lester in an Art Deco building at the tail end of Fort Washington Avenue in upper, upper Manhattan. When I lived here, this section of the city was known as the far northern point of Washington Heights. Now I had noticed several realtors redubbing it "Hudson Heights" so as to differentiate it, in both substance and cost, from its lower-class roots.

"Okay, I'm on the Hudson," I said.

"Take your next exit."

"Fort Tryon Park?"

"Yes."

Again I knew it. Fort Tryon floats cloudlike high above the Hudson River. It is a quiet and restful jagged cliff, New Jersey on its west, Riverdale-Bronx on its east. The park is a mishmash of terrains—walkways of harsh stone, fauna from a bygone era, terraces of stone, nooks and crannies of cement and brick, thick brush, rocky slopes, open grass. I had spent plenty of summer days on her green lawns, adorned in shorts and T-shirt, Zia and unread medical books my companions. My favorite time here: summer, right before dark. The orange glow bathing the park in something almost ethereal.

I put on my blinker and glided onto the exit ramp. There were no cars and few lights. The park was closed at night, but the roadway stayed open for through traffic. My car chugged up the steep road and entered what felt like a medieval fortress. The Cloisters, a former quasi-French monastery that was now part of the Metropolitan Museum of Art, held middle ground. It houses a fabulous collection of medieval artifacts. Or so I'm told. I've been in this park a hundred times. I've never been inside the Cloisters.

It was, I thought, a smart place for a ransom drop—dark, quiet, filled with serpentine trails, stone cliffs, sudden drops, thick woods, paved and unpaved walks. You could get lost here. You could hide here for a very long time and never be found.

The robotic voice asked, "Are you there yet?"

"I'm in Fort Tryon, yes."

"Park near the café. Get out and walk up to the circle."

Riding in the trunk was noisy and jarring. Rachel had brought a padded blanket, but there was not much she could do about the noise. A flashlight stayed in her satchel. She had no interest in turning it on. Rachel had never minded the dark.

Sight could be distracting. The dark was a good place to think.

She tried to keep her body loose, riding bumps, and wondered about Marc's behavior right before they left. The cop at the house had, no doubt, said something that shook him. About her? Probably. She wondered what exactly he had said and how she should react.

Didn't matter now. They were on their way. She had to concentrate on the task at hand.

Rachel was falling back into a familiar role. There was a pang here. She missed being with the FBI. She had loved her job. Yes, perhaps it was all she had. It was more than her escape—it was the only thing she really enjoyed doing. Some people pushed through the nine-to-five so they could go home and live their lives. For Rachel, it was the opposite.

After all these years apart, here was something that she and Marc had in common: They'd both found careers they loved. She wondered about that. She wondered if there was a connection, if their careers had become some kind of true-love substitute. Or was that looking at it too deeply?

Marc still had his job. She did not. Did that make her more desperate?

No. His child was gone. Game, set, match.

In the darkness of the trunk, she smeared her face with black make-up, enough to take the shine away. The car started climbing upward. Her gear was packed and ready.

She thought about Hugh Reilly, the son of a bitch.

Her breakup with Marc—and everything after—was his fault. Hugh had been her dearest friend in college. That was what he wanted, he told her. Just to be her friend. No pressure. He understood that she had a boyfriend. Had Rachel been naïve or purposefully naïve? Men who want to "just be friends" do so because they hope to be next in line, as though friendship were an on-deck circle, a good place for practice swings before heading to the plate. Hugh had called her in Italy that night with nothing but the best of intentions. "I just think you should know," he said, "as your friend." Right. And then he told her what Marc had done at some stupid frat party.

Yes, enough blaming herself. Enough blaming Marc. Hugh Reilly. If that son of a bitch had just minded his own business, what would her life be like right now? She couldn't say. Ah, but what had her life become? That was easier to answer. She drank too much. She had a bad temper. Her stomach bothered her more than it should.

She spent too much time reading *TV Guide*. And let's not forget the pièce de résistance: She had gotten herself ensnared in a self-destructive relationship—and gotten herself out of it in the worst way possible.

The car veered and climbed upward, forcing Rachel to roll back. A moment or two later, the car stopped. Rachel lifted her head. The cruel musings fled.

It was game time.

From the old fort's lookout tower, some two hundred fifty feet above the Hudson River, Heshy had one of the most stunning views of the Jersey Palisades, stretching from the Tappan Zee Bridge on the right to the George Washington Bridge on his left. He actually took the time to appreciate it before he got to the matter at hand.

As though on cue, Seidman took the exit off the Henry Hudson Parkway. No one followed. Heshy kept his eyes on the road. No car slowed. No car sped up. No one was trying to make it look as though they weren't following.

He spun around, lost sight of the car for a brief moment, then spotted it again as it came back into view. He could see Seidman in the driver's seat. No one else was visible. That didn't mean much—someone could be ducking down in the back—but it was a start.

Seidman parked the car. He turned off the engine and opened the door. Heshy lifted the microphone to his mouth.

"Pavel, you ready?"

"Yes."

"He's alone," he said, speaking now for Lydia's benefit. "Proceed."

"Park near the café. Get out and walk up to the circle."

The circle, I knew, was Margaret Corbin Circle. When I reached the clearing, the first thing I spotted, even in the dark, was the bright colors of the children's playground near Fort Washington Avenue at 190th Street. The colors still leapt out. I'd always liked this playground, but tonight the yellows and blues taunted me. I thought of myself as a city boy. When I lived near here, I'd imagined staying in this neighborhood— too sophisticated was I for the vanilla suburbs—and of course, that meant that I would bring my children to this very park.

I took that as an omen, but I didn't know of what.

The phone squawked. "There's a subway station on the left."

"Okay."

"Take the stairs down toward the elevator."

I might have suspected this. He would put me on the elevator and then on the A train. It would be difficult, if not impossible, for Rachel to follow me.

"Are you on the stairs?"

"Yes."

"At the bottom, you'll see a gate on the right."

I knew where it was. It led to a smaller park and was locked except for weekends. It had been set aside as something of a small picnic area. There were Ping-Pong tables, though you had to bring your own net and paddles to play. There were benches and eating areas. Kids used it for birthday parties.

The wrought-iron gate, I remember, was always locked.

"I'm there," I said.

"Make sure no one sees you. Push open the gate. Slip through and quickly close it."

I peered inside. The park was black. Distant streetlights reached out and gave the area no more than a dull glow. The duffel bag felt heavy. I adjusted it up my shoulder. I looked behind me now. No one. I looked to my left. The subway elevators were still. I put my hand on the gate door. The padlock had been cut. I gave the area one more quick glance because that was what the robotic voice had told me to do.

No sign of Rachel.

The gate creaked when I pushed it open. The echo ripped through the still night. I slipped through the opening and let the dark swallow me whole.

Rachel felt the car rock as Marc got out.

She made herself wait a full minute, which felt like two hours. When she thought that it was probably safe, Rachel lifted the trunk an inch and peeked out.

She saw no one.

Rachel had a gun with her, a fed-issue Glock .22 40-caliber semiautomatic, and she carried her night-vision goggles, Rigel 3501 military-grade Gen. 2+. The Palm Pilot that could read the Q-Logger transmitter was in her pocket.

She doubted that anyone would see her, but she still only opened the trunk wide enough so she could roll out. She huddled down low. Her hand reached back and grabbed the semiautomatic and night-vision goggles. Then she quietly closed the trunk.

Field operations had always been her favorite—or at least, the training for them. There had been very few missions that required this sort of cloak-and-dagger reconnaissance. For the most part, stakeouts were high-tech. You had vans and spy planes and fiber-optics. You rarely found yourself crawling through the night in black clothes and greasepaint.

She made herself small against the back tire. In the distance, she saw Marc heading up the drive. She put the gun in its holster and strapped the night-vision goggles to her belt. Keeping low, Rachel moved up the grass to higher ground. There was still enough light. She didn't need the goggles yet.

A sliver of moon sliced through the sky. There were no stars tonight. Up ahead, she could see that Marc had the cell phone near his ear. The duffel bag was on his shoulder.

Rachel looked around, saw no one. Would the drop take place here? It wasn't a bad place, if you had a planned escape route. She started to think about the possibilities.

Fort Tryon was hilly. The secret would be to try to get higher. She started climbing and was just about to settle in when Marc exited the park.

Damn. She'd have to move again.

Rachel commando-crawled down the hill. The grass was prickly and smelled like hay, the cause being, she assumed, the recent water shortage. She tried to keep her eyes on Marc, but she lost him when he left the park grounds. She took a risk and moved quicker. At the park gate, she ducked behind a stone pillar.

Marc was there. But not for very long.

With the phone back to his ear, Marc veered to the left and vanished down the steps leading to the A train.

Up ahead, Rachel saw a man and a woman walking a dog. They could be part of this—or they could be a man and a woman walking a dog. Marc was still out of sight. No time for debate now. She ducked low at a stone wall.

Leaning her back against it, Rachel made her way toward the stairs.

Tickner thought that Edgar Portman looked like something out of a Noël Coward production. He wore silk pajamas under a red robe that appeared to have been tied with great care. There were velvet slippers on his feet. His brother, Carson, on the other hand, looked properly ruffled. His pajamas were askew. His hair was all over the place. His eyes were bloodshot.

Neither Portman could take his eyes off the photographs from the CD.

"Edgar," Carson said, "let's not jump to conclusions."

"Not jump . . . ?" Edgar turned to Tickner. "I gave him money."

"Yes, sir," Tickner said. "A year and a half ago. We know about that."

"No." Edgar tried to make the word snap with impatience, but he didn't have the strength. "I mean, recently. Today, in fact."

Tickner sat up. "How much?"

"Two million dollars. There was another ransom demand."

"Why didn't you contact us?"

"Oh sure." Edgar made a sound that was

half chortle, half sneer. "You all did such a wonderful job last time."

Tickner felt the tick in his blood. "Are you saying that you gave your son-in-law an additional two million dollars?"

"That is precisely what I'm saying."

Carson Portman was still staring at the photographs. Edgar glanced at his brother, then back at Tickner. "Did Marc Seidman kill my daughter?"

Carson stood up. "You know better."

"I'm not asking you, Carson."

Both men looked at Tickner now. Tickner was not having any of it. "You said you met with your son-in-law today?"

If Edgar was upset about his question being ignored, he did not show it. "Early this morning," he said. "At Memorial Park."

"That woman in the pictures." Tickner gestured toward them. "Was she with him?"

"No."

"Has either of you ever seen her before?"

Both Carson and Edgar answered in the negative. Edgar picked up one of the photographs. "My daughter hired a private investigator to take these?"

"Yes."

"I don't understand. Who is she?"

Tickner again ignored his question. "The ransom note came to you, like last time?"

"Yes."

"I'm not sure I follow. How did you know that it wasn't a hoax? How did you know that you were dealing with the real kidnappers?"

Carson took that one. "We did think it was a hoax," he said. "At first, I mean."

"So what changed your mind?"

"They sent hairs again." Carson quickly explained about the tests and about Dr. Seidman's request for additional tests.

"You gave him all the hairs, then?"

"We did, yes," Carson said.

Edgar seemed lost in the photographs again. "This woman," he spat. "Was Seidman involved with her?"

"I can't answer that."

"Why else would my daughter want these pictures taken?"

A mobile phone rang. Tickner excused himself and put the receiver to his ear.

"Bingo," O'Malley said.

"What?"

"We got a hit on Seidman's E-ZPass. He

crossed the George Washington Bridge five minutes ago."

The robotic voice told me, "Walk down the path."

There was still enough light to see the first few steps. I started down them. The darkness gathered around, closed in. I started to use my foot to feel my way, like a blind man swinging a cane. I didn't like this. I didn't like this at all. I wondered again about Rachel. Was she near here? I tried to follow the path. It curved to the left. I stumbled on the cobblestone.

"Okay," the voice said. "Stop."

I did so. I could see nothing in front of me. Behind me, the street was a faded glow. On my right was a steep incline. The air had that city-park smell to it, a swirling potpourri of fresh and stale. I listened for some sort of clue, but there was nothing other than the distant humming swish of traffic.

"Put down the money."

"No," I said. "I want to see my daughter."

"Put down the money."

"We had a deal. You show me my daughter, I show you the money."

There was no reply. I could hear the blood

roaring in my ears. The fear was crippling. No, I did not like this. I was too exposed. I checked the path behind me. I could still break into a run and scream like a psycho. This neighborhood was tighter than most in Manhattan. Someone might call the police or try to help.

"Dr. Seidman?"

"Yes?"

And then a flashlight hit my face. I blinked and raised a hand to block my eyes. I squinted, trying to see past it. Someone lowered the flashlight beam. My eyes quickly adjusted, but there was no need. The beam was cut off by a silhouette. There was no mistake. I could see immediately what was being highlighted.

There was a man. I may have even seen flannel, I'm not sure. As I said, it was in silhouette. I couldn't really make out features or colors or design. So that part could have been my imagination. But not the rest. I saw the shapes and outlines clear enough to know.

Standing next to the man, gripping his leg just above the knee, was a small child.

chapter 27

Lydia wished that there was more light. She would very much like to see the look on Dr. Seidman's face right now. Her desire to see his expression had nothing to do with the cruelty that was about to come down. It was curiosity. It was deeper than the slow-to-see-the-car-accident aspect of human nature. Imagine. This man had had his child taken away. For a year and a half, he had been left to wonder about her fate, tossing through sleepless nights, conjuring up horrors best left in the dark abyss of our subconscious.

Now he had seen her.

It would be unnatural *not* to want to see the expression on his face.

Seconds ticked away. She wanted that. She wanted to stretch the tension, pull him beyond what a man could handle, soften him for the final blow.

Lydia took out her Sig-Sauer. She held it to her side. Peering out from behind the bush she judged the distance between her and Seidman at thirty, maybe forty feet. She put the voice changer and phone back to her mouth. She whispered into it. Whisper or scream, it made no difference. The voice changer made it all sound the same.

"Open the money bag."

From her perch, she watched him move like a man in a trance. He did what she asked—now without question. This time, she was the one using the flashlight. She shone it at his face and then dropped the beam to the bag.

Money. She could see the stacks. She nodded to herself. They were good to go.

"Okay," she said. "Leave the money on the ground. Walk slowly down the path. Tara will be waiting for you."

She watched Dr. Seidman drop the bag. He was squinting at the spot where he believed his daughter would be waiting. His movements were stiff, but then again his vision had probably been affected by the lights in his eyes. That again would make it easier.

Lydia wanted a close shot. Two quick bullets to the head, in case he was wearing a flap jacket. She was a good shot. She could probably hit him in the head from here. But she wanted the sure thing. No mistakes. No chance to run.

Seidman moved toward her. He was twenty feet away. Then fifteen. When he was only ten feet away, Lydia raised the pistol and took aim.

If Marc took the subway, Rachel knew that it'd be near impossible to follow him without being spotted.

Rachel hurried toward the stairwell. When she got there, she looked down into the dark. Marc was gone. Damn. She scanned the surroundings. There was a sign for elevators leading down to the A train. On the right was a closed wrought-iron gate. Nothing else.

He had to be in an elevator heading down to the subway.

Now what?

She heard footsteps behind her. With her right hand, Rachel quickly wiped the greasepaint, hoping to make herself look at least semi-presentable. With her left hand, she slid the goggles behind her and out of sight.

Two men trotted down the stairs. One caught her eye and smiled. She wiped her face again and smiled back. The men jogged the rest of the way down the steps and turned toward the elevator bank.

Rachel quickly considered her options. Those two men could be her cover. She could follow them down, get into the same elevator, get off with them, maybe even engage them in conversation. Who'd suspect her then? Hopefully Marc's subway car hadn't left yet. If it had . . . well, no use in thinking negative.

Rachel started toward the men when something made her stop. The wrought-iron gate. The one she had seen on her right. It was closed. The sign on it read: OPEN ON WEEKENDS AND MAJOR HOLIDAYS ONLY.

But through the thicket, Rachel saw the beam of a flashlight.

She pulled up. She tried to peer through the fence, but all she could see was the light beam. The brush was too thick. On her left, she heard the ding of an elevator. The doors slid open. The men stepped inside. No time to pull out the Palm Pilot and check the GPS. Besides, the elevator and beam of flashlight were too close. It would be hard to pinpoint the difference.

The man who had smiled at her put his hand against the side, keeping the door open. She wondered what to do.

The flashlight beam went out.

"Are you coming?" the man asked.

She waited for the flashlight beam to come back on. It didn't. She shook her head. "No, thank you."

Rachel quickly broke back up the stairs, trying to find a dark spot. It had to be dark for the goggles to work. The Rigels came with a built-in overlight sensor system to protect from bright lights, but Rachel still found that the fewer artificial lights, the better. Street level looked down over the park. Okay, the positioning was pretty good, but there was still too much light from the street.

She moved to the side of the stone hut that housed the elevators. On the left, there was a spot that—if she pressed herself against the wall—would give her total darkness. Perfect. The trees and bushes were still too heavy to get a clear view. But it would have to do.

Her goggles were supposedly lightweight but they still felt bulky. She should have bought a model you could just hold up to your face, binocular style. Most have that feature. This model didn't. You could not just hold it to up your eyes. You had to strap it on as a mask. The advantage, however, was obvious: If you attached it like a mask, you could keep your hands free.

As she pulled them over her head, the flashlight beam appeared again. Rachel tried to follow it, see where it was coming from. It seemed to her that it was a different spot this time. Over on the right now. Closer.

And then, before she could pinpoint it, the beam was gone.

Her eyes locked on the spot where she thought the beam had come from. Dark. Very dark now. Still keeping her eyes looking there, she finished getting the night-vision goggles in place. Night-vision goggles are not magic. They don't really see in the dark. Night-vision optics work by intensifying existing light, even very small amounts. But here, there was pretty much nothing. That used to be a problem, but now most brands came with an infrared illuminator standard. The illuminator cast a beam of infrared light that was not visible to the human eye.

But it was visible to the night-vision goggles.

Rachel flipped on the illuminator. The night lit up in full green. She was looking not through a lens, but at a phosphor screen, not unlike the one on your TV set. The eyepiece magnified the picture—you were looking at a picture, not the actual site—and the picture was green because the human eye can differentiate more shades of green than any other phosphor color. Rachel stared.

Got something.

The view was hazy, but it looked to Rachel like a small woman. The woman seemed to be hiding behind a bush. She held something up to her mouth. A phone maybe. Peripheral vision is nearly nonexistent with these goggles, though these claimed to give you a thirty-seven-degree angle. She had to swivel her head to the right, and there, putting down the duffel bag with the two million dollars in it, was Marc.

Marc started walking toward the woman. His steps were short, probably because he was on cobblestones in the dark.

Rachel swiveled her head from the woman, to Marc, back to the woman. Marc was approaching, getting closer. The woman was still crouched in hiding. There was no way Marc could see her. Rachel frowned and wondered what the hell was going on.

Then the woman swung her arm up.

It was hard to see clearly—there were trees and branches in the way—but the woman seemed to be pointing her finger at Marc. They were not far apart anymore. Rachel squinted at the screen attached to her face. And it was then that she realized that the woman was not pointing a finger. The image was too big for a hand.

It was a gun. The woman was pointing a gun at Marc's head.

A shadow crossed over Rachel's vision. She started back, opening her mouth to call out a warning, when a hand like a baseball glove covered her mouth and smothered all sound away.

*   *   *

Tickner and Regan hooked up on the New Jersey Turnpike. Tickner drove. Regan sat next to him and stroked his face.

Tickner shook his head. "Can't believe you still have that soul patch."

"You don't like it?"

"You think you're Enrique Iglesias?"

"Who?"

"Exactly."

"What's wrong with the soul patch?"

"It's like wearing a T-shirt that says, 'I Had a Middle-Age Crisis in 1998.' "

Regan thought about it. "Yeah, okay, fair point. By the way, those sunglasses you always wear. I was wondering if they were FBI issue."

Tickner grinned. "Helps me land the chicks."

"Yeah, those and your stun gun." Regan shifted in the chair. "Lloyd?"

"Uh-huh."

"I'm not sure I get it."

They weren't talking about eyewear or facial hair anymore.

"We don't have all the pieces," Tickner said.

"But we're getting close?"

"Oh yeah."

"Let's go through it then, cool?"

Tickner nodded. "First off, if the DNA lab Edgar Portman used is correct, the child is still alive."

"Which is weird."

"Very. But it explains a lot. Who would be most likely to keep a kidnapped child alive?"

"Her father," Regan said.

"And whose gun mysteriously vanished from the murder scene?"

"Her father's."

Tickner made a gun with his forefinger and thumb, aimed it at Regan, dropped the hammer. "Righto."

"So where has the kid been all this time?" Regan asked.

"Hidden."

"Well, gee, that helps."

"No, think about it. We've been looking at Seidman. We've looked closely. He knows that. So who would be the best person to hide his kid?"

Regan saw where he was going. "The girlfriend we didn't know about."

"More than that, a girlfriend who used to work for the feds. A girlfriend who would know how we work. How to do a ransom drop. How to hide a child. Someone who would know Seidman's sister, Stacy, and be able to enlist her help."

Regan thought about it. "Okay, let's assume I believe all that. They commit this crime. They get two million dollars and the kid. But then what? They bide their time for eighteen months? They decide they need more cash? What?"

"They need to wait to avoid suspicion. Maybe they wanted the wife's estate to clear. Maybe they need another two million dollars to run away, I don't know."

Regan frowned. "We're still trying to finesse away the same point."

"What's that?"

"If Seidman was behind this, how come he was nearly killed? This was no wound-me-so-it-looks-good injury. He was flatlined. The paramedics were sure they had a goner when they first got there. Hell, we quietly called it a double homicide for almost ten days."

Tickner nodded. "It's a problem."

"And more than that, where the hell is he going right now? I mean, crossing the George Washington Bridge. Do you think he decided now was the time to flee with the two million dollars?"

"Could be."

"If you were fleeing, would you use your E-ZPass to pay the toll?"

"No, but he might not know how easy it is to trace."

"Hey, everyone knows how easy it is to trace. You get the bill in the mail. It tells you what time you hit what tollbooth. And even if he was dumb enough to forget that, your federal agent Rachel Whatshername isn't."

"Rachel Mills." Tickner nodded slowly. "Good point, though."

"Thank you."

"So what conclusions can we draw?"

"That we still don't have a clue what the hell is going on," Regan said.

Tickner smiled. "Nice to be in familiar territory."

The cell phone rang. Tickner picked it up. It was O'Malley. "Where are you?" O'Malley asked.

"A mile from the George Washington Bridge," Tickner said.

"Hit the accelerator."

"Why? What's up?"

"NYPD just spotted Seidman's car,"

O'Malley said. "It's parked at Fort Tryon Park—a mile, maybe mile and a half, from the bridge."

"Know it," Tickner said. "We'll be there in less than five."

Heshy had thought that it was all going a little too smoothly.

He'd watched Dr. Seidman leave his car. He waited. No one else had come out. He'd started down from the old fort's tower.

That was when he spotted the woman.

He paused, watching her head down toward the subway elevators. Two guys were with her. Nothing suspicious in that. But then, when the woman sprinted back up alone, well, that was when things had changed.

He kept a close eye from then on. When she moved into the darkness, Heshy started creeping toward her.

Heshy knew that his appearance was intimidating. He also knew that much of the circuitry inside of his brain was not wired normally. He didn't much care, which, he assumed, was part of the wiring problem. There were those who would tell you that Heshy was pure evil. He had killed sixteen people in his life, fourteen of them slowly. He had left six men alive who still wished that he hadn't.

Supposedly, people like Heshy did not understand what they were doing. Other people's pain did not reach them. That was not true. His victims' pain was not something distant to him. He knew what pain was like. And he understood love. He loved Lydia. He loved her in ways most people could never fathom. He would kill for her. He would die for her. Many people say that about their loved ones, of course—but how many are willing to put it to the test?

The woman in the dark had binoculars strapped onto her head. Night-vision goggles. Heshy had seen them on the news. Soldiers in battle wore them. Having them did not necessarily mean she was a cop. Most weaponry and military gizmos were available online to anyone with the proper dollars. Heshy watched her. Either way, cop or no cop, if the goggles worked, this woman would be a witness to Lydia committing murder.

So she had to be silenced.

He closed in slowly. He wanted to hear if she was talking to anyone, if she had some kind of radio control to other units. But the woman was silent. Good. Maybe she was indeed on her own.

He was about two yards away from her when her body stiffened. The woman gave a little gasp. And Heshy knew that it was time to close her down.

He hurried over, moving with a grace that defied his bulk. He snaked one hand around her face and clasped it over her mouth. His hand was big enough to cover her nose too. Cut off the air supply. With his free hand, he cupped the back of her skull. He pushed his hands together.

And then, with both hands firmly placed on the woman's head, Heshy lifted her all the way off the ground.

chapter 28

A sound made me stop. I turned to my right. I thought that maybe I heard something up there, near the street level. I tried to see, but my eyes were still suffering from the onslaught of the flashlight. The trees also helped cut off my view. I waited, seeing if I heard a follow-up. Nothing. The sound was gone now. It wasn't important anyway. Tara should be waiting for me at the end of this path. Whatever else might go on, that was all that counted.

Focus, I thought again. Tara, end of the path. All else was extraneous.

I started up again, not even glancing behind me to check on the fate of the duffel bag with the two million dollars in it. It, too, was, like everything else but Tara, irrelevant. I tried to conjure up the shadowy image again, the silhouette made by the flashlight. I trudged on. My daughter. She could be right here, scant steps from where I now walked. I had been given a second chance to rescue her. Focus on that. Compartmentalize. Let nothing stop me.

I continued down the path.

While with the Federal Bureau of Investigation, Rachel had been well trained in weapons and hand-to-hand combat. She had learned much during her four months at Quantico. She knew that true fighting was nothing like you saw on TV. You would never, for example, mess around with a high kick to the face. You would never try anything involving turning your back on an opponent, spinning, leaping—none of that.

Successful hand-to-hand combat could be broken down pretty simply. You aimed for the vulnerable spots on the body. The nose was good—it usually made your opponent's eyes well up with tears. The eyes, of course. The throat was good too—anyone who has ever been struck there knew how it could shut down your will to fight. The groin, well, obvious. You always hear that. The groin, however, is a difficult target, probably because a man is prone to defend it. It's usually better as a decoy move. Fake there and then go to one of the other more exposed, vulnerable spots.

There were other areas—the solar plexus, the instep, the knee. But there was also a problem with all these techniques. In the movies, a smaller opponent might beat a larger one. In reality, yes, that can happen, but when the woman is as small as Rachel and the man as large as her current attacker, the odds of her coming out on the winning end are very small. If the attacker knows what he is doing, very small becomes pretty close to nonexistent.

The other problem for a woman is that fights never go as they do in the movies. Think about any physical altercation you may have seen in a bar or at a sporting event or even on a playground. The battle almost always ends up in a grapple on the floor. On TV or in a boxing ring, sure, people stand and hit each other. In real life, one or the other ducks down and grabs the opponent and they go down to the ground and wrestle. It didn't matter how much training you had. If the fight reached that stage,

Rachel would never defeat an opponent this large.

Lastly, while Rachel had practiced and trained and been in simulated dangerous situations—Quantico went so far as to have a "mock town" for these purposes—she had never been involved in a real physical altercation before. She was not ready for the pure panic, the tingly, unpleasant numbness in the legs, the way adrenaline mixed with fear saps your strength.

Rachel could not breathe. She felt the hand on her mouth and, out of her element, reacted wrong. Instead of immediately kicking behind her—trying to take out his knee or stomping down on the instep—Rachel worked on instinct and used both her hands to pry her mouth free. It did not work.

Within seconds, the man had his other hand on the base of her head, holding her skull in a viselike grip. She could feel his fingers dig into her gums, push in her teeth. His hands seemed so powerful that Rachel was sure he could crush her skull like an eggshell. He didn't. Instead he wrenched up. Her neck took the brunt of it. It felt as if her head was being torn off. The hand against her mouth and nostrils effectively cut off her air supply. He lifted more. Her feet fully left the ground. She took hold of his wrists and tried to pull up, tried to lessen the strain on her neck.

But she still could not breathe.

There was a roaring in her ears. Her lungs burned. Her feet kicked out. They landed on him, blows so tiny and impotent he didn't bother to block them. His face was close to her now. She could feel the spit in his breath. Her night-vision goggles had been knocked askew but not all the way off. They blocked her sight.

The pressure in her head was pounding. Trying to remember her training, Rachel dug her nails into the pressure point on his hand beneath the thumb. No effect. She kicked harder. Nothing. She needed a breath. She felt like a fish on the line, flailing, dying. Panic took hold.

Her gun.

She could reach for it. If she could just control herself long enough, to have the courage to release her hand, she could go for her pocket, pull out the weapon, and fire it. It was her only chance. Her brain was going groggy. Consciousness was starting to ebb away.

With her skull seconds away from exploding, Rachel dropped her left hand away. Her neck stretched so taut, she was sure it would snap like a rubber band. Her hand found her holster. Her fingers touched the gun.

But the man saw what she was doing. With Rachel still dangling in the air like a rag doll, he kneed her hard in the kidney. Pain exploded in a flash of red. Her eyes rolled back. But Rachel did not give in. She kept going for the gun. The man had no choice. He put her down.

Air.

Her breathing passage was finally opened. She tried not to gulp it down, but her lungs had other ideas. She couldn't stop.

Her relief, however, was short lived. With one hand, the man stopped her from pulling out her gun. With the other, he delivered a dartlike blow to her throat. Rachel gagged and went down. The man took hold of her weapon and tossed it away. He dropped hard on top of her. The little wind she had managed to gather was gone now. He straddled her chest and moved his hands toward her throat.

That was when the police car sped past.

The man suddenly sat up. She tried to take advantage, but he was simply too big. He grabbed a cell phone from his pocket and put it to his mouth. In a harsh whisper, he said, "Abort! Cops!"

Rachel tried to move, tried to do something. But there was nothing left. She looked up in time to see the man cock his fist. It started toward her. She tried to turn away. But there was no place to go.

The blow jarred her head back against the cobblestone. And then darkness flooded in.

When Marc walked past her, Lydia stepped out of the bush from behind him with the gun up. She was aiming at the back of the head and had her finger on the trigger. The "Abort! Cops!" call in her earpiece startled her so, she almost pulled the trigger. But her mind worked fast. Seidman was still heading down the path. Lydia saw everything. Saw it clearly. She dumped the gun. No gun on her, no proof of any wrongdoing. The weapon could never be tied to her as long as it was not in her possession. Like most weapons, it was untraceable. She wore gloves, of course, so there would be no fingerprints.

But—her mind was still working fast here—what was there to prevent her from taking the money?

She was just Miss Citizen taking a stroll through the park. She could spot the duffel bag, right? If she was caught with it, well, she was just being a good Samaritan. Given the chance, she would have brought the bag to the police. No crime there. No risk.

Not when you consider that two million dollars was inside it.

Her mind quickly ran through the pros and cons. Simple when you think about it. Take the money. If they caught her with it, so what? There was absolutely nothing to tie her to this crime. She had dumped the gun. She had dumped the cell phone. Sure, someone might find it. But it would not lead to either her or Heshy.

She heard a noise. Marc Seidman, who'd been about fifteen feet in front of her, broke into a sprint. Fine, no problem. Lydia started toward the money. Heshy appeared around the corner. She continued toward him. Without hesitation, Lydia scooped up the bag.

Then Lydia and Heshy headed down the path, fading into the night.

I continued to stumble forward. My eyes were beginning to adjust, but they were still several minutes from being particularly useful. The path slid downward. There were small cobblestones. I tried not to trip. The route grew steeper now, and I let the momentum carry me so that I could move faster without appearing to be running.

On my right, I could see the abrupt slope that overlooked the Bronx. Lights twinkled from way below.

I heard a child's yelp.

I stopped. It was not loud, but the sound was unmistakably that of a small child. I heard rustling. The child yelped again. It was farther away now. The rustling sound was gone, but I could hear the steady slap of footsteps on the pavement. Someone was running. Running with a child. Away from me.

No.

I broke into a sprint. The faraway lights provided enough illumination so that I could stay on the path. Up ahead, I saw the chain-link fence. It had always been locked. When

I reached it, I saw that someone had used a bolt cutter on it. I pushed through and was back on the path now. I looked to my left, which led back up to the park.

No one.

Damn, what the hell had gone wrong? I tried to think rationally. Focus. Okay, if I were the one running away, which way would I go? Simple. I would veer to the right. The paths were confusing, dark, windy. You could easily hide in the shrubs. That would be the way to go if one were a kidnapper. I stopped for only an instant, hoping to pick up the sounds of a child. I didn't. But I did hear someone say, "Hey!" with what sounded like genuine surprise.

I cocked my head. The sound had indeed come from my right. Good. I sprinted again, searching the horizon for a flannel shirt. Nothing. I continued down the hill. I lost my footing and almost tumbled down the hill. From my time living in this area, I knew the homeless found sanctuary on the off-path inclines too steep for the casual trekker. They made shelter out of branches and caves. Every once in a while, you could hear a rustling too loud for a squirrel. Sometimes a homeless guy would emerge out of seemingly nowhere—long haired, matted beard, the stench coming off him in waves. There was a spot not far from here where the male street prostitutes plied their trade to the businessmen getting off the A train. I used to jog by that area during the quiet of the day. Condom wrappers often littered the walkway.

I kept running, trying to keep my ears open. I hit a fork in the path. Damn. Again I asked, What way was the more twisty? I didn't know. I was about to veer right again when I heard a sound.

Rustling in the bush.

Without thinking, I dived in. There were two men. One in a business suit. Another, much younger and dressed in jeans, was on his knees. The business suit yelled an expletive. I did not back away. Because I had heard the man's voice before. Seconds ago.

He had been the one who yelled "Hey."

"Did you see a man and a little girl go by here?"

"Get the hell out—"

I crossed over and slapped him in the face. "Did you see them?"

He looked far more shocked than hurt. He

pointed to the left. "They went up that way. He was carrying the kid."

I jumped back on the path. Okay, right. They were heading back up toward the green. If they stayed that route, they would come out not far from where I'd parked. I started running again, pumping my arms. I ran past the male prostitutes sitting on the wall. One of them caught my eye—he had a blue kerchief on his head—nodded, and pointed to stay on the path. I nodded a thanks back. I kept running. In the distance, I could see the lights of the park. And there, crossing in front of the lamppost, I caught a fleeting glimpse of the man in the flannel shirt carrying Tara.

"Stop!" I shouted. "Someone stop him!"

But they were gone.

I swallowed and started up the path, still shouting for help. No one reacted or shouted back. When I reached the outpost where lovers often gazed at the eastern view, I again spotted the flannel shirt. He was jumping over the wall into the woods. I started to follow but when I turned the corner, I heard someone yell, "Freeze!"

I looked behind me. It was a cop. He had his gun drawn.

"Freeze!"

"He has my kid! This way!"

"Dr. Seidman?"

The familiar voice came to my right. It was Regan.

What the . . . ? "Look, just follow me."

"Where's the money, Dr. Seidman?"

"You don't understand," I said. "They just jumped over that wall."

"Who did?"

I saw where this was going. Two cops had their guns pointed. Regan was staring at me with his arms crossed. Tickner appeared behind him.

"Let's talk about this, okay?"

Not okay. They wouldn't shoot. Or if they did, I didn't much care. So I started running. They took chase. The cops were younger and no doubt in better shape. But I had something going for me. I was crazed. I jumped the fence and fell down the incline. The cops pursued, but they were moving more gingerly, with normal human care.

"Freeze!" the cop yelled again.

I was breathing too fast to try to yell out more explanation. I wanted them to stay with me—I just didn't want them to catch up.

I curled up my body and rolled down the hill. Dried glass clung to me and got caught up in my hair. The dust kicked up. I stifled a cough. Just as I was picking up speed, my rib cage slammed into the trunk of tree. I could hear the hollow thud. I gasped, the wind almost knocked out of me, but I hung on. Sliding to the side, I reached the path. The cops' flashlights pursued. They were within sight but far enough behind. Fine.

On the path, my eyes swerved right, then left. No sign of the flannel shirt or Tara. I tried again to figure out which way he might run. Nothing came to me. I stopped. The police were coming closer.

"Freeze!" the cop yelled yet again.

Fifty-fifty chance.

I was about to break to my left, to head back into the darkness, when I saw the young man with the blue kerchief, the one who had nodded at me earlier. He shook his head this time and pointed in the direction behind me. "Thank you," I said.

He might have said something in return, but I was already on my way. I cut back up and headed through the same chain-link fence I had pushed through earlier. I heard footsteps, but they were too far away. I looked up and again spotted the flannel shirt. He was standing near the lights of the subway steps. He seemed to be trying to catch his breath.

I ran faster.

So did he.

There was probably fifty yards that separated us. But he had to carry a child. I should be able to close in on him. I started running. The same cop yelled "Halt!" this time, I guess for the sake of variety. I hoped like hell they didn't decide to shoot.

"He's back on the street!" I shouted. "He has my daughter."

I don't know if they were listening or not. I reached the steps and took them three at a time. I was out of the park again, back on Fort Washington Avenue at Margaret Corbin Circle. I looked ahead at the playground. No movement. I glanced down Fort Washington Avenue and spotted someone running near Mother Cabrini High School, near the chapel.

The mind flashes to odd things. Cabrini Chapel was one of the most surreal stops in all of Manhattan. Zia had dragged me to Mass there once to see without telling why the chapel was something of a tourist spot.

I immediately understood the draw. Mother Cabrini died in 1901, but her embalmed body is kept in what looks like a lucite block. That's the altar. The priests conduct mass over her body/table. No, I'm not making that up. The same guy who preserved Lenin in Russia worked on Mother Cabrini. The chapel is open to the public. It even has a gift shop.

My legs felt heavy, but I kept moving. I no longer heard the police. I quickly glanced behind me. The flashlights were far away.

"Over here!" I shouted. "Near Cabrini High!"

I started sprinting again. I reached the entrance to the chapel. It was locked. There was no sign of flannel shirt anywhere. I looked around, eyes wide, panicked. I had lost them. They were gone.

"This way!" I shouted, hoping that either (or both) the police and Rachel would hear me.

But my heart sank. My chance. My daughter was gone again. I felt the weight on my chest. And that was when I heard the car start up.

My head jerked to the right. I scanned the street and started running. A car started moving. It was about ten yards in front of me. A Honda Accord. I memorized the license plate, even as I knew that would be futile. The driver was still trying to maneuver out of a parking spot. I couldn't see who it was. But I wasn't about to take any chances.

The Honda had just cleared the bumper of the car in front of it and was about start up when I grabbed the driver's side door handle. Lucky break finally—he hadn't locked the door. No time, I assumed, because he'd been in a rush.

Several things happened in a very short period of time. As I started pulling the door open, I was able to see through the window. It was indeed the flannel-shirt man. He reacted quickly. He grabbed the door and tried to hold it closed. I pulled harder. The door opened a crack. He hit the accelerator.

I tried to run with the car, like you see in the movies. The problem is, cars move faster than people. But I would not let go. You hear those stories about people gaining extraordinary strength in certain circumstances, about average men being able to lift cars off the ground to rescue trapped loved ones. I scoff at those stories. You probably do too.

I am not saying that I lifted a car. But I held on. I wedged my fingers in and wrapped them around the divide between the front door and back. I used both hands and willed my fingers into vises. I would not let go. No matter what.

If I hold on, my daughter lives. If I let go, my daughter dies.

Forget focus. Forget compartmentalizing. This thought, this equation, was as simple as breathing.

The man in the flannel shirt pushed down on the gas. The car was picking up speed now. I kicked my legs off the ground, but there was no place to perch them. They slid down the back door and landed with a clunk. I felt the skin of my ankles being scraped off on the pavement. I tried to regain my footing. No go. The pain was tremendous but inconsequential. I held on.

The status quo, I knew, was working against me. I couldn't hang on much longer, no matter how much I willed it. I had to make a move. I tried to pull myself into the car, but I wasn't strong enough. I hung on and let my arms go straight. I tried hopping up again. My body was horizontal now, parallel to the ground. I extended my body. My right leg reached up and curled around something. The antenna on the top of the car. Would that hold me? I didn't think so. My face was pressed against the backseat window. I saw the little car seat.

It was empty.

Panic seized me again. I felt my hands slipping. We had only driven maybe a twenty, thirty yards. With my face against the glass, my nose bouncing against the window, my body and face scraped and battered, I looked at the child in the front seat and a crushing truth pried my hands off the car window.

Again the mind works in odd ways. My first thought was classically doctor: The child should be sitting in the back. The Honda Accord has a passenger-side airbag. No child under the age of twelve should ever sit in the front. Also, small children should be in a proper car seat. That was, in fact, the law. Riding out of a car seat and in the front . . . that was doubly unsafe.

Ridiculous thought. Or maybe natural. Either way, that was not the thought that ripped the fight out of me.

The flannel-shirted man yanked the steering wheel to the right. I heard the tires squeak. The car jerked, and my fingers slipped away. My grip was gone now. I went airborne. My body landed hard, skidding across the pavement like a stone. I could hear the police sirens behind me. They would, I thought, follow the Honda Accord. But it wouldn't matter. I had only gotten a brief glimpse. But it had been enough to know the truth.

The child in the car was not my daughter.

chapter 29

Again I was in a hospital, this time New York Presbyterian—my old stomping grounds. They hadn't yet run X rays, but I was pretty sure they'd find a cracked rib. Nothing you could really do about it other than shoot yourself up with painkillers. It would hurt. That was okay. I was pretty scraped up. There was a gash on my right leg that looked like the work of a shark attack. Skin had been ripped off both elbows. None of that mattered.

Lenny arrived in record time. I wanted him here because I was not really sure how to handle this. At first, I almost convinced myself that I had made a mistake. A child changes, right? I had not seen Tara since she was six months old. A lot of growth occurs in that period. She'd have matured from wee infancy to an older toddler. I'd been hanging on to a moving car, for crying out loud. I had only gotten the briefest of glimpses.

But I knew.

The child in the front seat of the car looked to be a boy. He was probably closer to three years old than two. His skin, his coloring, was simply too pale.

It was not Tara.

I knew that Tickner and Regan had questions. I wanted to cooperate. I also wanted to know how the hell they had found out about the ransom drop. I hadn't seen Rachel yet either. I wondered if she were in the building. I also wondered about the fate of the ransom money, the Honda Accord, the man in the flannel shirt. Had they caught him? Had he kidnapped my daughter originally—or had that first ransom drop been a con job too? If so, how had my sister, Stacy, fitted into it?

In short, I was confused. Enter Lenny aka Cujo.

He burst through the door dressed in baggy khakis and a pink Lacoste shirt. His eyes had that scared, wild look that again brought back memories of our childhood.

He pushed past a nurse and approached my bed.

"What the hell happened?"

I was about to give Lenny an overview when he stopped me with a raised finger. He turned to the nurse and asked her to leave. When we were alone he nodded for me to go ahead again. Starting with seeing Edgar in the park, I ran through calling Rachel, her arrival, her preparation with all the electronic gizmos, the ransom calls, the drop, my dive on the car. I backtracked and told him about the CD. Lenny interrupted— he always interrupted—but not as often as usual. I saw something cross his face, and maybe—I don't want to read too much into it here—but maybe he was hurt that I hadn't confided in him. The look didn't last long. Lenny gathered himself a piece at a time.

"Any chance that Edgar has been playing you?" he asked.

"To what end? He's the one who's lost four million dollars."

"Not if he's the one who set it up."

I made a face. "That doesn't make any sense."

Lenny didn't like it, but he didn't have a response either. "So where is Rachel now?"

"She's not here?"

"I don't think so."

"I don't know, then."

We both went quiet a second.

"Maybe she went back to my house," I said.

"Yeah," Lenny said. "Maybe."

There was nary a trace particle of conviction in his voice.

Tickner pushed open the door. His sunglasses sat atop his shaved head, a look I found disconcerting; if he bent his neck and drew a mouth on the lower part of his pate, it would look like a second face. Regan followed in a sort of hip-hop step, or maybe the soul patch was affecting the way I viewed him. Tickner took the lead.

"We know about the ransom demand," he said. "We know your father-in-law gave you another two million dollars. We know that you visited a private detective agency today called MVD and asked about the password to a CD-ROM owned by your late wife. We know that Rachel Mills was with you and that she did not, as you told Detective Regan earlier, return to the Washington, D.C., area. So we can skip all that."

Tickner moved closer. Lenny watched

him, ready to pounce. Regan folded his arms and leaned against the wall. "So let's start with the ransom money," Tickner said. "Where is it?"

"I don't know."

"Did someone take it?"

"I don't know."

"What do you mean, you don't know?"

"He told me to put it down."

"Who is 'he'?"

"The kidnapper. Whoever was on the cell phone."

"Where did you put it down?"

"In the park. On the path."

"And then what?"

"He said to start walking forward."

"Did you?"

"Yes."

"And then?"

"That's when I heard a child cry and someone start running. Everything went crazy after that."

"And the money?"

"I told you. I don't know what happened to the money."

"How about Rachel Mills?" Tickner asked. "Where is she?"

"I don't know."

I looked at Lenny, but he was studying Tickner's face now. I waited.

"You lied to us about her returning to Washington, D.C., isn't that correct?" Tickner asked.

Lenny put a hand on my shoulder. "Let's not start by mischaracterizing my client's statements."

Tickner made a face as if Lenny were a turd that had plopped down from the ceiling. Lenny stared back, unfazed. "You told Detective Regan that Ms. Mills was on her way back to Washington, did you not?"

"I said I didn't know where she was," I corrected him. "I said she *might* have gone back."

"And where was she at the time?"

Lenny said, "Don't answer."

I let him know that it was okay. "She was in the garage."

"Why didn't you tell Detective Regan that?"

"Because we were getting ready for the ransom drop. We didn't want anything slowing us down."

Tickner folded his arms. "I'm not sure I understand."

"Then ask another question," Lenny snapped.

"Why would Rachel Mills be involved in the ransom drop?"

"She's an old friend," I said. "And I knew she'd been a special agent with the FBI."

"Ah," Tickner said. "So you thought maybe her experience could help you here?"

"Yes."

"You didn't call Detective Regan or myself?"

"That's correct."

"Because?"

Lenny took that one. "You know damn well why."

"They told me no cops," I said. "Like last time. I didn't want to risk it again. So I called Rachel."

"I see." Tickner looked back at Regan. Regan looked off as if trying to follow a stray thought. "You chose her because she used to be a federal agent?"

"Yes."

"And because you two were"—Tickner made vague hand gestures—"close."

"A long time ago," I said.

"Not anymore?"

"No. Not anymore."

"Hmm, not anymore," Tickner repeated. "And yet you chose to call her in a matter involving your child's life. Interesting."

"Glad you think so," Lenny said. "By the way, is there a point to any of this?"

Tickner ignored him. "Before today, when was the last time you saw Rachel Mills?"

"What difference does that make?" Lenny said.

"Please just answer my question."

"Not until we know—"

But my hand was on Lenny's arm now. I knew what he was doing. He had automatically snapped into his adversarial pose. I appreciated it, but I wanted to get past this as quickly as possible.

"About a month ago," I said.

"Under what circumstances?"

"I bumped into her at the Stop & Shop on Northwood Avenue."

"Bumped into her?"

"Yes."

"You mean, as in a coincidence? As in not knowing the other was going to be there, out of the blue?"

"Yes."

Tickner turned around and looked at

Regan again. Regan kept perfectly still. He wasn't even toying with the soul patch.

"And before that?"

"What before that?"

"Before you 'bumped' "—Tickner's sarcasm spit the word across the room—"into Ms. Mills at the Stop & Shop, when was the last time you'd seen her?"

"Not since college," I said.

Again Tickner spun toward Regan, his face lit up with incredulity. When he turned back, the glasses dropped down to his eyes. He pushed them back up onto his forehead. "Are you telling us, Dr. Seidman, that the only time you've seen Rachel Mills between your college days and today was just that one time at the supermarket?"

"That's exactly what I'm telling you."

For a moment, Tickner seemed at a loss. Lenny looked as if he might have something to add, but he kept himself in check.

"Have you two spoken on the phone?" Tickner asked.

"Before today?"

"Yes."

"No."

"Not ever? You never talked to her on the

phone before today? Not even when you were dating?"

Lenny said, "Jesus Christ, what kind of question is that?"

Tickner snapped his head toward Lenny. "You have a problem?"

"Yeah, your questions are moronic."

They started again with the death stares. I broke the silence. "I hadn't spoken to Rachel on the phone since college."

Tickner turned to me. His expression was openly skeptical now. I glanced behind him at Regan. Regan was nodding to himself. While they both looked off balance, I tried to press it. "Did you find the man and child in the Honda Accord?" I asked.

Tickner considered the question a moment. He looked back at Regan, who shrugged a why-not. "We found the car abandoned on Broadway near 145th Street. It'd been stolen a few hours earlier." Tickner took out his notebook but didn't look at it. "When we spotted you at the park, you began yelling about your daughter. Do you believe that she was the child in the car?"

"I thought so at the time."

"But not anymore?"

"No," I said. "It wasn't Tara."

"What made you change your mind?"

"I saw him. The child, I mean."

"It was a he?"

"I think so."

"When did you see him?"

"When I jumped on the car."

Tickner spread his hands. "Why don't you start at the beginning and tell us exactly what happened?"

I told them the same story I'd told Lenny. Regan never moved from the wall. He still hadn't said a word. I found that odd. As I spoke, Tickner seemed to be growing more and more agitated. The skin on his cleanly shaven head tightened, making the sunglasses, which still sat perched on the top of his skull, start sliding forward. He kept readjusting them. I saw the pulse near his temples flutter. His jaw was locked.

When I was done, Tickner said, "You're lying."

Lenny slid between Tickner and my bed. For a moment, I thought that they might come to blows, which, let's face it, would not be good for Lenny. But Lenny never gave an inch. It reminded me of the time in third grade when Tony Merullo picked a fight with me. Lenny had stepped between us then, faced Tony bravely, and gotten clobbered.

Lenny stayed nose-to-nose with the larger man. "What the hell is wrong with you, Agent Tickner?"

"Your client is a liar."

"Gentlemen, this interview is over. Get out."

Tickner bent his neck so that his forehead pressed against Lenny's. "We have proof he's lying."

"Let's see it," Lenny said. Then, "No, wait, forget it. I don't want to see it. Are you arresting my client?"

"No."

"Then get your sorry butt out of this hospital room."

I said, "Lenny."

With one more glare at Tickner to show he wasn't intimidated, Lenny looked back at me.

"Let's finish this now," I said.

"He's trying to hang you for this."

I shrugged because I didn't really care. I think Lenny saw that. He slid away. I nodded for Tickner to do his worst.

"You've seen Rachel before today."

"I told you—"

"If you hadn't seen or spoken to Rachel Mills, how did you know she'd been a federal agent?"

Lenny started to laugh.

Tickner quickly spun toward him. "What are you laughing at?"

"Because, numb-nuts, my wife is friends with Rachel Mills."

That confused him. "What?"

"My wife and I talk to Rachel all the time. We introduced them." Lenny laughed again. "That's your proof?"

"No, that's not my proof," Tickner snapped, defensive now. "Your story about getting this ransom call, about reaching out to an old girlfriend like that. You expect that to fly?"

"Why," I said, "what do you think happened?"

Tickner said nothing.

"You think I did it, right? That this was yet another elaborate scheme to, what, get another two million from my ex–father-in-law?"

Lenny tried to slow me down. "Marc . . ."

"No, let me just say something here." I tried to get Regan into it, but he still looked off, so I locked eyes with Tickner. "Do you really think I staged all this? Why go through all the machinations of having this meeting in the park? How did I know you'd track me down there—hell, I still don't know how you did that. Why would I bother leaping on a car like that? Why wouldn't I have just taken the money and hidden it and come up with a story for Edgar? If I was just running a scam, did I hire this guy with the flannel shirt? Why? Why involve another person or a stolen car? I mean, come on. It makes no sense."

I looked at Regan, who still wasn't biting. "Detective Regan?"

But all he said was "You're not being straight with us, Marc."

"How?" I asked. "How am I not being straight with you?"

"You claim that before today you and Ms. Mills haven't spoken on the phone since college."

"Yes."

"We have phone records, Marc. Three months before your wife was murdered, there was a call from Rachel's house to yours. Do you want to explain that?"

I turned to Lenny for help, but he was staring down at me. This made no sense.

"Look," I said, "I have Rachel's cell phone number. Let's call her and find out where she is."

"Do that," Tickner said.

Lenny picked up the hospital phone next to my bed. I gave him the number. I watched him dial it, all the while trying to put it together. The phone rang six times before I heard Rachel's voice tell me she could not answer her phone and that I should leave a message. I did so.

Regan finally peeled himself off the wall. He pulled a chair to the side of my bed and sat. "Marc, what do you know about Rachel Mills?"

"Enough."

"You dated in college?"

"Yes."

"How long?"

"Two years."

Regan spread his arms, all open and wide eyed. "See, Agent Tickner and I still aren't sure why you called her. I mean, okay, you dated a long time ago. But if you haven't been in touch at all"—he shrugged—"why her?"

I thought about how to put this and chose the direct route. "There's still a connection."

Regan nodded as if that explained a lot. "You were aware that she got married?"

"Cheryl—that's Lenny's wife—she told me."

"And you knew her husband was shot?"

"I learned about it today." Then, realizing that it had to be after midnight, "I mean, yesterday."

"Rachel told you?"

"Cheryl told me." Regan's words from his late-night visit to my abode came back to me. "And then you said Rachel shot him."

Regan looked back at Tickner. Tickner said, "Did Ms. Mills mention that to you?"

"What, that she shot her husband?"

"Yes."

"You're kidding, right?"

"You don't believe it, do you?"

Lenny said, "What's the difference what he believes?"

"She confessed," Tickner said.

I looked at Lenny. Lenny looked away. I tried to sit up a little more. "Then why isn't she in jail?"

Something dark crossed Tickner's face. His hands clenched into fists. "She claimed the shooting was accidental."

"And you don't believe that?"

"Her husband was shot in the head at point-blank range."

"So again I ask: Why isn't she in jail?"

"I'm not privy to all the details," Tickner said.

"What does that mean?"

"The local cops handled the case, not us," Tickner explained. "They decided not to pursue it."

I am neither a cop nor a great student of psychology, but even I could see that Tickner was holding something back. I looked at Lenny. His face was emotionless, which, of course, is not at all like Lenny. Tickner took a step away from the bed. Regan filled the void.

"You said you still felt a connection with Rachel?" Regan began.

"Asked and answered," Lenny said.

"Did you still love her?"

Lenny couldn't let that one go without comment. "Are you Ann Landers now, Detective Regan? What the hell does any of this have to do with my client's daughter?"

"Bear with me."

"No, Detective, I will not bear with you. Your questions are nonsense." Again I put my hand on Lenny's shoulder. He turned to me. "They want you to say yes, Marc."

"I know that."

"They're hoping to use Rachel as a motive for killing your wife."

"I know that too," I said. I looked at Regan. I remembered the feeling when I first saw Rachel at the Stop & Shop.

"You still think about her?" Regan asked.

"Yes."

"Does she still think about you?"

Lenny was not about to surrender. "How the hell would he know that?"

"Bob?" I said. It was the first time I had used Regan's first name.

"Yes."

"What are you trying to get at here?"

Regan's voice was low, almost conspiratorial. "Let me ask you one more time: Before the incident at the Stop & Shop, had you seen Rachel Mills since you broke up in college?"

"Jesus Christ," Lenny said.

"No."

"You're sure?"

"Yes."

"No communication at all?"

"They didn't even pass notes during

study hall," Lenny said. "I mean, get on with it."

Regan leaned away. "You went to a private detective agency in Newark to ask about a CD-ROM."

"Yes."

"Why today?"

"I'm not sure I understand."

"Your wife has been dead for a year and a half. Why the sudden interest in the CD?"

"I'd just found it."

"When?"

"The day before yesterday. It was hidden in the basement."

"So you had no idea that Monica had hired a private detective?"

It took me a moment to answer. I thought about what I had learned since my beautiful wife's death. She had been seeing a psychiatrist. She had hired a private detective. She had hidden his findings in our basement. I hadn't known about any of it. I thought about my life, my love of work, my wanting to keep traveling. Sure, I loved my daughter. I cooed on command and marveled at the wonder of her. I would die—and kill—to protect her, but in my honest moments, I knew that I had not accepted all the changes and sacrifices she'd brought to my life.

What kind of husband had I been? What kind of father?

"Marc?"

"No," I said softly. "I had no idea she had hired a private investigator."

"Do you have any idea why she did?"

I shook my head. Regan faded back. Tickner pulled out a manila folder.

"What's that?" Lenny said.

"The contents of the CD." Tickner looked at me one more time. "You never saw Rachel, right? Just that time in the super-market."

I did not bother answering.

Without fanfare, Tickner withdrew a photograph and handed it to me. Lenny snapped on his half-moon reading glasses and stood over my shoulder. He did that thing where you tilt your head up to look down. The photograph was black and white. It was a shot of Valley Hospital in Ridgewood. There was a date stamped on the bottom. The photograph had been taken two months before the shooting.

Lenny frowned. "The lighting is pretty

good, but I'm not sure about the overall composition."

Tickner ignored the sarcasm. "That's where you work, is it not, Dr. Seidman?"

"We have an office there, yes."

"We?"

"My partner and I. Zia Leroux."

Tickner nodded. "There's a date stamped on the bottom."

"I can see that."

"Were you in the office on that day?"

"I really don't know. I'd have to check my calendar."

Regan pointed to near the hospital entrance. "Do you see that figure over there?"

I looked harder, but I couldn't make much out. "No, not really."

"Just notice the length of the coat, okay?"

"Okay."

Then Tickner handed me a second glossy. The photographer had used the zoom lens on this one. Same angle. You could see the person in the coat clearly now. She wore sunglasses, but there was no mistake. It was Rachel.

I looked up at Lenny. I saw the surprise on his face too. Tickner pulled out another photo. Then another. They were all taken in front of Valley Hospital. In the eighth one, Rachel entered the building. In the ninth one, taken one hour later, I exited alone. In the tenth, taken six minutes after that, Rachel went out the same doors.

At first, my mind could simply not soak in the implications. I was one big, swirling "Huh?" of bewilderment. There was no time to process. Lenny seemed stunned too, but he recovered first.

"Get out," Lenny said.

"You don't want to explain these photographs first?"

I wanted to argue, but I was too dazed.

"Get out," Lenny said again, more forcefully this time. "Get out now."

chapter 30

I sat up in the bed. "Lenny?"

He made sure the door was closed. "Yes," he said. "They think you did it. Check that, they think you and Rachel did it together. You two were having an affair. She killed her husband—I don't know if they think you were involved with that or not—and then you both killed Monica, did who-knows-what with Tara, and came up with this scheme to rip off her father."

"That makes no sense," I said.

Lenny kept quiet.

"I was shot, remember?"

"I know."

"So what, they think I shot myself?"

"I don't know. But you can't talk to them anymore. They have evidence now. You can deny a relationship with Rachel to the skies, but Monica was suspicious enough to hire a private detective. Then, Jesus, think about it. The private detective delivers. He takes those photographs and gives them to Monica. Next thing you know, your wife is dead, your kid is gone, and her father is out two million bucks. Skip ahead a year and a half. Her father is out another two million and you and Rachel are lying about being with one another."

"We're not lying."

Lenny would not look at me.

"What about all I was saying," I tried, "about how no one would go through all this? I could have just taken the ransom money, right? I didn't have to hire that guy with the car and the kid. And what about my sister? Do they think I murdered her too?"

"Those pictures," Lenny said softly.

"I never knew about them."

He could barely look at me, but that didn't stop him from reverting to our youth. "Well, duh."

"No, I mean I don't know anything about them."

"You really haven't seen her except for that time at the supermarket?"

"Of course not. You know all this. I wouldn't hide it from you."

He weighed that statement for too long. "You might hide it from Lenny the Friend."

"No, I wouldn't. But even if I would, there's no way I could keep it from Lenny the Lawyer."

His voice was soft. "You didn't tell either one of us about this ransom drop."

So there it was. "We wanted to keep it contained, Lenny."

"I see." But he didn't. I couldn't blame him. "Another thing. How did you find that CD in the basement?"

"Dina Levinsky came by the house."

"Dina the fruitcake?"

"She's had it rough," I said. "You have no idea."

Lenny waved off my sympathy. "I don't understand. What was she doing at your house?" I filled him on the story. Lenny started making a face. When I finished, I was the one who said, "What?"

"She told you she was better now? That she was married?"

"Yes."

"That's bull."

I stopped. "How do you know that?"

"I do some legal work for her aunt. Dina Levinsky has been in and out of asylums since she was eighteen. She even served time for aggravated assault a few years back. She's never been married. And I doubt she's ever had an art exhibit."

I did not know what to make of that. I remembered Dina's haunting face, the way the color ebbed away when she said, *"You know who shot you, don't you, Marc?"*

What the hell had she meant by that anyway?

"We need to think this through," Lenny said, rubbing his chin. "I'm going to check with some of my sources, see what I can learn. Call me if anything comes up, okay?"

"Yeah, okay."

"And promise me you won't say another word to them. There is an excellent chance they'll arrest you." He raised a hand before I could protest. "They have enough for an arrest and maybe even an indictment. True, the *t*'s aren't all crossed and the *i*'s aren't all dotted. But think about that Skakel case. They had less there and they convicted him. So if they come back in here, promise me you won't say a word."

I promised because, yet again, the authorities were on the wrong track. Cooperating with them would not help find my daughter. That was the bottom line. Lenny left me alone. I asked him to shut off the lights. He did. But the room did not grow dark. Hospital rooms never get totally dark.

I tried to understand what was happening. Tickner had taken those strange photographs with him. I wished he hadn't. I wanted to take another look because no matter how I laid it out, those pictures of Rachel at the hospital made no sense. Were they for real? Trick photography was a strong possibility, especially in this digital day and age. Could that be the explanation? Were they phonies, a simple cut-and-paste job? My thoughts veered toward Dina Levinsky again. What had her bizarre visit really been about? Why had she asked if I loved Monica? Why did she think I knew who shot me? I was considering all of this when the door opened.

"Is this the room belonging to the Stud in Scrubs?"

It was Zia. "Hey."

She entered, gestured at my supine position with a sweep of her hand. "This supposed to be your excuse for missing work?"

"I was on call last night, wasn't I?"

"Yep."

"Sorry."

"They woke my ass up instead, interrupting, I might add, a rather erotic dream." Zia pointed with her thumb toward the door. "That big black man down the hall."

"The one with the sunglasses on top of a shaved head?"

"That's him. He a cop?"

"An FBI agent."

"Any chance you can introduce us? Might make up for interrupting my dream."

"I'll try to do that," I said, "before he arrests me."

"After is okay too."

I smiled. Zia sat on the edge of the bed. I told her what had happened. She didn't offer a theory. She didn't throw up a question. She just listened, and I loved her for it.

I was just getting to the part about being a serious suspect when my cell phone started ringing. Both of us, because of our training, were surprised. Cell phones in the hospital were a no-no. I reached it for quickly and brought it to my ear.

"Marc?"

It was Rachel. "Where are you?"

"Following the money."

"What?"

"They did exactly what I thought," she said. "They dumped the bag, but they haven't spotted the Q-Logger in the pack of bills. I'm heading up the Harlem River Drive right now. They're maybe a mile ahead of me."

"We need to talk," I said.

"Did you find Tara?"

"It was a hoax. I saw the kid they had with them. It wasn't my daughter."

There was a pause.

"Rachel?"

"I'm not doing so good, Marc."

"What do you mean?"

"I took a beating. At the park. I'm okay, but I need your help."

"Wait a second. My car is still at the scene. How are you following them?"

"Did you notice a Parks Department van on the circle?"

"Yes."

"I stole it. It's an old van, easy to hot-wire. I figured it wouldn't be missed until the morning."

"They think we did it, Rachel. That we were having an affair or something. They found photos on that CD. You in front of where I work."

Cell-phone-static silence.

"Rachel?"

"Where are you?" she asked.

"I'm at New York Presbyterian Hospital."

"Are you okay?"

"Banged up. But I'm fine, yeah."

"The cops there?"

"The feds too. A guy named Tickner. You know him?"

Her voice was soft. "Yes." Then, "How do you want to play it?"

"What do you mean?"

"Do you want to keep following them? Or do you want to turn it over to Tickner and Regan?"

I wanted her back here. I wanted to ask her about those photos and the phone call to my house. "I'm not sure it matters," I said. "You were right from the beginning. It was a con job. They must have used someone else's hair."

More static.

"What?" I said.

"You know anything about DNA?" she asked me.

"Not much," I said.

"I don't have time to explain it, but a DNA test goes layer by layer. You start seeing things match up. It takes at least twenty-four hours before we can really say with any degree of certainty that there's a match."

"So?"

"So I just spoke to my lab guy. We've only had about eight hours. But so far, that second set of hairs that Edgar got?"

"What about them?"

"They match yours." I wasn't sure I heard correctly. Rachel made a sound that might have been a sigh. "In other words, he hasn't ruled out that you're the father. Just the opposite, in fact."

I nearly dropped the phone. Zia saw it and moved closer. Again I focused and compartmentalized. Process. Rebuild. I considered my options. Tickner and Regan would never believe me. They would not allow me to go. They'd probably arrest us. At the same time, if I told them, I might be able to prove our innocence. On the other hand, proving my innocence was irrelevant.

Was there a chance my daughter was still alive?

That was the only question here. If she was, then I had to resort to our original plan.

Confiding in the authorities, especially with their fresh suspicions, would not work. Suppose there was, as the ransom note said, a mole? Right now, whoever had picked up that bag of money had no idea that Rachel was onto them. But what would happen if the cops and feds got involved? Would the kidnappers run, panic, do something rash?

There was something else here that I should be considering: Did I still trust Rachel? Those photographs had shaken my faith. I didn't know what to believe anymore. But in the end, I had no choice but to treat those doubts as a distraction. I needed to focus on one goal. Tara. What would give me the best chance of finding out what really happened to her?

"How badly hurt are you?" I asked.

"We can do this, Marc."

"I'm on my way, then."

I hung up and looked at Zia.

"You have to help me get out of here."

Tickner and Regan sat in the doctors' lounge down the hall. A lounge seemed a strange name for this threadbare dwelling with too much light and a rabbit-ear TV set. There was a minifridge in the corner. Tickner had opened it. There were two brown-bag lunches in it, both with names written on them. It reminded him of elementary school.

Tickner collapsed on a couch with absolutely no springs. "I think we should arrest him now."

Regan said nothing.

"You were awfully quiet in there, Bob. Something on your mind?"

Regan started scratching the soul patch. "What Seidman said."

"What about it?"

"Don't you think he had a point?"

"You mean that stuff about him being innocent?"

"Yes."

"No, not really. You buy it?"

"I don't know," Regan said. "I mean, why would he go through all this with the money? He couldn't have known we'd learn about that CD and decide to track him with E-ZPass and find him at Fort Tryon Park. And even if he had, why go through all that? Why jump on a moving car? Christ, he's lucky he wasn't killed. Again. Which brings us back to the original shooting and our original problem. If he and Rachel Mills did this together, why was he nearly killed?"

Regan shook his head. "There are too many holes."

"Which we are filling in one by one," Tickner said.

Regan made a yes-no with a head tilt.

"Look at how many we plugged today by learning about Rachel Mills's involvement," Tickner said. "We just need to get her in here and sweat them both."

Regan looked off again.

Tickner shook his head. "What now?"

"The broken window."

"The one at the crime scene?"

"Yeah."

"What about it?"

Regan sat up. "Play along with me, okay? Let's go back to the original murder-kidnapping."

"At the Seidman house?"

"Right."

"Okay, go."

"The window was broken from the outside," Regan said. "That could be how the perp gained entry to the house."

"Or," Tickner added, "Dr. Seidman broke the window to throw us off."

"Or he had an accomplice do it."

"Right."

"But either way, Dr. Seidman would have been in on the broken window, right? If he was involved, I mean."

"Where are you going with this?"

"Just stay with me, Lloyd. We think Seidman was involved. Ergo, Seidman knew that the window had been broken to make it look like, I don't know, a random break-in. Agreed?"

"I guess."

Regan smiled. "Then how come he never mentioned the broken window?"

"What?"

"Read his statement. He remembers eating a granola bar and then—bam—nothing. No sound. No one sneaking up on him. Nothing." Regan spread his hands. "Why doesn't he remember hearing the window break?"

"Because he broke it himself to make it look like an intruder."

"But see, if that's the case, he would have kept the broken window in his story. Think about it. He breaks the window to convince us the perp broke in and shot him. So what would you say if you were him?"

Now Tickner saw where he was heading.

"I'd say, 'I heard the window break, I turned and bam, the bullets hit me.' "

"Exactly. But Seidman did none of that. Why?"

Tickner shrugged. "Maybe he forgot. He was seriously injured."

"Or maybe—just stay with me—maybe he's telling the truth."

The door opened. An exhausted-looking kid in scrubs looked in. He saw the two cops, rolled his eyes, left them alone. Tickner turned back toward Regan. "But wait a second, you've caught yourself in a Catch-22."

"How so?"

"If Seidman didn't do it—if it really was a perp who broke the window—why didn't Seidman hear it?"

"Maybe he doesn't remember. We've seen this a million times. A guy getting shot and hurt that seriously loses some time." Regan smiled, warming up to this theory. "Especially if he saw something that totally shocked him—something he wouldn't want to remember."

"Like his wife being stripped down and killed?"

"Like that," Regan said. "Or maybe something worse."

"What's worse?"

A beeping sound came from the corridor. They could hear the nearby nurse's station. Someone was bitching about a shift time or schedule change.

"We said we're missing something," Regan said slowly. "We've been saying that from the beginning. But maybe it's just the opposite. We've been *adding* something."

Tickner frowned.

"We keep adding Dr. Seidman. Look, we both know the score. In cases like this, the husband is always involved. Not nine times out of ten—ninety-nine times out of a hundred. Every scenario we've devised includes Seidman."

Tickner said, "And you think that's wrong?"

"Listen to me a second. We've had Seidman in our sights from the get-go. His marriage was not idyllic. He got married because his wife was pregnant. We seized on all that. But if their marriage had been friggin' *Ozzie and Harriet*, we'd still say, 'Nah, no one is that happy,' and leap on that. So whatever we've stumbled across, we've tried to fit it into that reality: Seidman had to be involved. So for just a second, let's take him out of the equation. Let's pretend he's innocent."

Tickner shrugged. "Okay, so?"

"Seidman talked about a connection with Rachel Mills. One that's lasted all these years."

"Right."

"He sounded a little obsessed with her."

"A little?"

Regan smiled. "Suppose the feeling was mutual. Check that. Suppose it was more than mutual."

"Okay."

"Now remember. We're assuming Seidman didn't do it. That means he's telling us the truth. About everything. About when he last saw Rachel Mills. About those photographs. You saw his face, Lloyd. Seidman isn't that great an actor. Those pictures shocked him. He didn't know about them."

Tickner frowned. "Hard to say."

"Well, there was something else I noticed about those pictures."

"What?"

"How come that private eye didn't get any pictures of the two of them together?

We have her outside the hospital. We have him coming out. We have her going out. But none of them together."

"They were careful."

"How careful? She was hanging outside his place of work. If you're being careful, you don't do that."

"So what's your theory?"

Regan smiled. "Think about it. Rachel had to know Seidman was inside the building. But did he have to know she was outside?"

"Wait a second," Tickner said. A smile started coming to his face. "You think she was stalking him?"

"Maybe."

Tickner nodded. "And—whoa—we're not talking about just any woman here. We're talking about a well-trained federal agent."

"So one, she would know how to run a professional kidnapping operation," Regan added, raising a finger. He raised another. "Two, she would know how to kill someone and get away with it. Three, she would know how to cover her tracks. Four, she would know Marc's sister, Stacy. Five"—the thumb now—"she'd be able to use her old contacts to find and set the sister up."

"Holy Christ." Tickner looked up. "And what you said before. About seeing something so horrible Seidman doesn't remember."

"How about seeing the love of your life shooting you? Or your wife. Or . . ."

They both stopped.

"Tara," Tickner said. "How does the little girl fit into all this?"

"A way of extorting money?"

Neither one of them liked that. But whatever other answers they came up with, they liked those even less.

"We can add something else," Tickner said.

"What?"

"Seidman's missing thirty-eight."

"What about it?"

"His gun was in a lockbox in his closet," Tickner said. "Only someone close to him would know where it was hidden."

"Or," Regan added, seeing something else now, "maybe Rachel Mills brought her own thirty-eight. Remember that two were used."

"But that raises another question: Why would she need two guns?"

Both men frowned, ran a few new theories through their heads, and came up with a solid conclusion. "We're still missing something," Regan said.

"Yep."

"We need to go back and get some answers."

"Like?"

"Like why did Rachel skate on the murder of her first husband?"

"I can ask around," Tickner said.

"Do that. And let's get a man on Seidman. She has four million dollars now. She might want to eliminate the only guy who can still tie her to this."

chapter 31

Zia found my clothes in the closet. Blood-stains darkened my jeans, so we decided to go with surgical scrubs. She ran down the hall and found me a pair. Wincing from the cracked ribs, I slipped them on and tied the string waist. It would be a slow go. Zia checked to see if the coast was clear. She had a backup plan in case the feds were still watching. Her friend, Dr. David Beck, had been involved in a major federal case a few years ago. He knew Tickner from that. Beck was on call. If it came to it, he was waiting at the end of the hall and would try to slow them down with some sort of reminiscence.

In the end, we didn't need Beck. We simply walked out. No one questioned us. We made our way through the Harkness Pavilion and out into the courtyard north of Fort

Washington Avenue. Zia's car was parked in the lot on 165th and Fort Washington. I moved gingerly. I felt sore as hell, but basically all right. Marathon running and heavy lifting would be out, but the pain was controllable and I had full range of motion. Zia had slipped me a bottle of Vioxx, the fifty-milligram big-boys. They'd be good because they worked without making you drowsy.

"If anyone asks," she said, "I'll tell them I took public transportation and that my car is home. You should be okay for a while."

"Thanks," I said. "Actually, can I also trade cell phones?"

"Sure, why?"

"They might try, I don't know, to track me down using mine."

"They can do that?"

"Beats the hell out of me."

She shrugged and dug out her cell. It was a tiny thing, the size of a compact mirror. "You really think Tara is alive?"

"I don't know."

We hurried up the parking garage's cement steps. The stairwell stank, as always, of urine.

"This is insane," she said. "You know that, right?"

"Yeah."

"I got my pager. You need me, you page me."

"I will."

We stopped at the car. Zia handed me the keys.

"What?" I said to her.

"You got a pretty big ego, Marc."

"This your idea of a pep talk?"

"Just don't let it get you hurt or anything," Zia said. "I need you."

I hugged her and slipped into the driver's seat. I started north on the Henry Hudson, dialing Rachel's number. The night was clear and still. The lights from the bridge made the dark water look like a star-filled sky. I heard two rings and then Rachel picked up. She didn't say anything and then I realized why. She probably had Caller ID and didn't recognize the number.

"It's me," I said. "I'm using Zia's phone."

Rachel asked, "Where are you?"

"About to get on the Hudson."

"Keep going north to the Tappan Zee. Cross it and start heading west."

"Where are you now?"

"By that huge Palisades Mall."

"In Nyack," I said.

"Right. Keep in phone touch. We'll find a place to hook up."

"I'm on my way."

Tickner was on his mobile phone, filling in O'Malley. Regan hurried back into the lounge. "Seidman's not in his room."

Tickner looked annoyed. "What do you mean, he's not in his room?"

"How many different ways are there to interpret that, Lloyd?"

"Did he go down to X ray or something?"

"Not according to the nurse," Regan said.

"Damn. The hospital has security cameras, right?"

"Not on every room."

"But they have to cover the exits."

"They must have a dozen exits here. By the time we get the tapes and review them—"

"Yeah, yeah, yeah." Tickner thought about it. He put the phone back to his ear. "O'Malley?"

"I'm here."

"You heard?"

"Yup."

"How long will it take you to get phone logs from both Seidman's hospital room and cell phone?" Tickner asked.

"Immediate calls?"

"It would have to have been in the past fifteen minutes, yeah."

"Give me five."

Tickner pressed the "end" button. "Where's Seidman's lawyer?"

"I don't know. I think he said he was leaving."

"Maybe we should give him a ring."

"He didn't hit me as the helpful type," Regan said.

"That was before, when we thought his client was a wife-and-baby killer. We're now theorizing that an innocent man's life is in danger." Tickner handed Regan the business card Lenny had given him.

"Worth a shot," Regan said, and began dialing.

I caught up with Rachel just over the north New Jersey–south New York border town of Ramsey. Using our phones we managed to hook up in the parking lot of the Fair Motel on Route 17 in Ramsey, New Jersey. The motel was a no-tell, complete with a sign proudly reading COLOR TV! (as if most motels were still using black and white) where all the letters (and the exclamation point) are a different color, in case you don't know what the word *color* means. I always liked the name. The Fair Motel. We're not great, we're not terrible. We're, well, Fair. Honesty in advertising.

I pulled into the lot. I was scared. I had a million questions for Rachel, but in the end, it all boiled down to different variations of the same thing. I wanted to know about her husband's death, sure, but more than that, I wanted to know about those damn private-eye pictures.

The lot was dark, most of the light coming off the highway. The stolen Parks Department van sat by a Pepsi machine on the far right side. I pulled next to it. I never saw Rachel leave the van, but the next thing I knew she had slid into the passenger seat next to me.

"Start moving," she said.

I turned to confront her, but her face made me pull up short. "Jesus, are you all right?"

"I'm fine."

Her right eye was swollen over like a

boxer's who had gone the distance. There were yellow-purple bruises around her neck. Her face had a giant red mark across both cheeks. I could see scarlet indentations from where her attacker had dug in his fingers. The fingernails had even broken the skin. I wondered if there was deeper trauma to her face, if whatever blow she took to the eye had been powerful enough to break a bone. I doubted it. A break like that would normally knock someone out of commission. Then again, best-case scenario and these were only surface wounds: It was amazing she was still upright.

"What the hell happened?" I asked.

She had her Palm Pilot out. The screen was dazzlingly bright in the dark of the car. She looked down at it and said, "Take Seventeen south. Hurry, I don't want to get too far behind."

I put the car in reverse, backed up, started down the highway. I reached into my pocket and pulled out the bottle of Vioxx. "These should help deaden the pain."

She pulled off the top. "How many should I take?"

"One."

Her index finger scooped it out. Her eyes

never left the Palm Pilot's screen. She swallowed it down and said thanks.

"Tell me what happened," I said.

"You first."

I filled her in as best I could. We stayed on Route 17. We passed the Allendale and Ridgewood exits. The streets were empty. The shops—and, man, there were lots of them, the entire highway pretty much one continuous strip mall—were all closed up. Rachel listened without interrupting. I glanced at her as I drove. She looked in pain.

When I finished, she asked, "Are you sure it wasn't Tara in the car?"

"Yes."

"I called my DNA guy again. The layers are still matching up. I don't get that."

Neither did I. "What happened to you?"

"Somebody jumped me. I was watching you through the night-vision goggles. I saw you put down the money bag and start walking. There was a woman in the bushes. Did you see her?"

"No."

"She had a gun. I think she planned on killing you."

"A woman?"

"Yes."

I wasn't sure how to react to that. "Did you get a good look at her?"

"No. I was about to call out a warning when this monster grabbed me from behind. Strong as hell. He lifted me off my feet by my head. I thought he was going to rip my skull off."

"Jesus."

"Anyway, a cop car drove by. The big guy panicked. He punched me here"—she pointed to the swollen eye—"and it was lights-out. I don't know how long I was lying on the pavement. When I woke up, the cops were all over the place. I was huddled in a corner in the dark. I guess they didn't see me or figured I was a homeless guy sleeping one off. Anyway, I checked the Palm Pilot. I saw the money was on the move."

"Which direction?"

"South, walking near 168th Street. Then suddenly they went still. See, this thing"—she gestured to the screen—"works two ways. I zoom in, I can get as close as a quarter mile. I go out a little farther, like right now, I get more an idea than an exact address. Right now, based on the speed, I figure they're driving about six miles ahead of us still on Route Seventeen."

"But when you first spotted them, they were on 168th Street?"

"Right. Then they start heading downtown fast."

I thought about it. "The subway," I said. "They took the A train from the 168th Street stop."

"That's what I figured. Anyway, I stole the van. I started downtown. I was near the seventies when all of a sudden they started going east. This time it was more stop and go."

"They were stopping for lights. They had a car now."

Rachel nodded. "They sped up on the FDR and Harlem River Drive. I tried to cut across town, but that took too long. I fell behind by five, six miles. Anyway, you know the rest."

We slowed for night construction near the Route 4 interchange. Three lanes became one. I looked at her, at the bruises and the swelling, at the giant handprint on her skin. She looked back at me and didn't say a word. My fingers reached out and caressed her face as gently as I knew how. She closed her eyes, the tenderness seemingly too much, and even in the midst of all this we both knew that it felt right. A stirring, an old one, a dormant one, started deep inside of me. I kept my eyes on that lovely, perfect face. I pushed back her hair. A tear escaped her eye and ran down her cheek. She put her hand on my wrist. I felt the warmth start there and spread.

Part of me—and, yes, I know how this will sound—wanted to forget this quest. The kidnapping had been a hoax. My daughter was gone. My wife was dead. Someone was trying to kill me. It was time to start again, a new chance, a way, this time, to get it right. I wanted to turn the car around and start heading in the other direction. I wanted to drive—keep driving—and never ask about her dead husband and those pictures on the CD. I could forget all that, I knew I could. My life was filled with surgical procedures that altered the surface, that helped people begin anew, that improved what was visible and thus what was not. That could be what would happen here. A simple face-lift. I would make my first incision the day before that damn frat party, pull the four-teen-year-old folds across time, close the suture at now. Stick the two moments to-gether. Nip and tuck. Make those fourteen years disappear, as though they'd never happened.

Rachel opened her eyes now and I could see that she was thinking pretty much the same thing, hoping I'd call it off and turn around. But of course, that could not be. We blinked. The construction cleared. Her hand left my forearm. I risked another glance at Rachel. No, we were not twenty-one years old anymore, but that didn't matter. I saw that now. I still loved her. Irrational, wrong, stupid, naïve, whatever. I still loved her. Over the years, I might have convinced my-self otherwise, but I had never stopped. She was still so damn beautiful, so damn per-fect, and when I thought of how close she'd just come to death, those giant hands smothering away her breath, those niggling doubts began to soften. They wouldn't go away. Not until I knew the truth. But no mat-ter what the answers were, they would not consume me.

"Rachel?"

But she suddenly sat up, her eyes back on the Palm Pilot.

"What is it?" I asked.

"They've stopped," Rachel said. "We'll be on them in two miles."

chapter 32

Steven Bacard replaced the phone's receiver.

You slip-slide into evil, he thought. You cross the line for just one moment. You cross back. You feel safe. You change things, you believe, for the better. The line is still there. It's still intact. Okay, maybe there's a smudge there now, but you can still see it clearly. And next time you cross, maybe that line smudges a little more. But you have your bearings. No matter what happens to that line, you remember where it is.

Don't you?

There was a mirror above the fully stocked bar in Steven Bacard's office. His interior decorator had insisted that all people of prestige had to have a place to toast their successes. So he had one. He didn't even drink. Steven Bacard stared at his reflection and thought, not for the first time in his life: Average. He had always been average. His grades in school, his SAT and LSAT scores, his law-school ranking, his bar score (he passed it on the third attempt). If life were a game where children choose sides for kickball, he'd be picked in the middle of the pack, after the good athletes and before the really bad ones—in that cusp for those who leave no mark.

Bacard became a lawyer because he believed that being a JD would give him a level of prestige. It didn't. No one hired him. He opened up his own pitiful office near the Paterson courthouse, sharing space with a bail bondsman. He ambulance-chased, but even as a member of this small-time pack, he couldn't distinguish himself. He managed to marry a woman slightly above his station, though she reminded him of that as often as she could.

Where Bacard had indeed been below average—*way* below average—was in sperm count. Try as he might—and Dawn, his wife, didn't really like him to try—he could not impregnate his wife. After four years, they tried to adopt. Again, Steven Bacard fit into the abyss of the great unspectacular, which made finding a white baby—something Dawn truly craved—nearly impossible. He and Dawn traveled to Romania, but the only children available were too old or born drug addled.

But it was there, overseas in that god-deserted place, that Steven Bacard finally came up with an idea that, after thirty-eight years, made him rise above the crowd.

"Problem, Steven?"

The voice startled him. He turned away from his reflection. Lydia stood in the shadows.

"Staring in the mirror like that," Lydia said, adding a tsk-tsk at the end. "Wasn't that Narcissus's downfall?"

Bacard could not help it. He began to tremble. It wasn't just Lydia, though, in truth, she often had that effect on him. The phone call had set him on edge. Lydia popping up like that—that was the clincher. He had no idea how she'd gotten in or how long she'd been standing there. He wanted to ask what had happened tonight. He wanted details. But there was no time.

"We do indeed have a problem," Bacard said.

"Tell me."

Her eyes chilled him. They were big and luminous and beautiful and yet you sensed nothing behind them, only a cold chasm, windows to a house long abandoned.

What Bacard had discovered while in Romania—what had finally helped him rise above the pack—was a way to beat the system. Suddenly, for the first time in his life, Bacard was on a roll. He stopped chasing ambulances. People started looking up to him. He was invited to fund-raisers. He became a sought-after speaker. His wife, Dawn, started to smile at him again and ask him about his day. He even appeared on News 12 New Jersey when the cable station needed a certain kind of legal expert. He stopped, however, when a colleague overseas reminded him of the danger of too much publicity. Besides, he no longer needed to attract clients. They found him, these parents searching for a miracle. The desperate have always done that, like plants stretching through the dark for any sliver of sunlight. And he, Steven Bacard, was that sunlight.

He pointed to the phone. "I just got a call."

"And?"

"The ransom money is bugged," he said.

"We switched bags."

"Not just the bags. There's some kind of device in the money. Between the bills or something."

Lydia's face clouded over. "Your source didn't know about this before?"

"My source didn't know about any of it until just now."

"So what you're telling me," she said slowly, "is that while we stand here the police know exactly where we are?"

"Not the police," he said. "The bug wasn't planted by the cops or the feds."

That seemed to surprise her. Then Lydia nodded. "Dr. Seidman."

"Not exactly. He has a woman named Rachel Mills helping him. She used to be a fed."

Lydia smiled as if this explained something. "And this Rachel Mills—this ex-fed—she's the one who bugged the money?"

"Yes."

"Is she following us right now?"

"No one knows where she is," Bacard

said. "No one knows where Seidman is either."

"Hmm," she said.

"The police think this Rachel woman is involved."

Lydia lifted her chin. "Involved in the original kidnapping?"

"And the murder of Monica Seidman."

Lydia liked that. She smiled and Bacard felt a fresh shiver slink down his back. "Was she, Steven?"

He teetered. "I wouldn't know."

"Ignorance is bliss, that it?"

Bacard chose to say nothing.

Lydia said, "Do you have the gun?"

He stiffened. "What?"

"Seidman's gun. Do you have it?"

Bacard did not like this. He felt as if he were sinking. He considered lying, but then he saw those eyes. "Yes."

"Get it," she said. "How about Pavel? Have you heard from him?"

"He's not happy with any of this. He wants to know what's going on."

"We'll call him in the car."

"We?"

"Yes. Now let's hurry, Steven."

"I'm coming with you?"

"Indeed."

"What are you going to do?"

Lydia put her fingers to her lips. "Shh," she said. "I have a plan."

Rachel said, "They're on the move again."

"How long did they stop?" I asked.

"Maybe five minutes. They could have met up with someone and transferred the money. Or maybe they were just getting gas. Turn right here."

We pulled up on Centuro Road off Route 3. Giants Stadium loomed in the distance. About a mile up, Rachel pointed out the window. "They were somewhere over there."

The sign read METROVISTA and the parking lot appeared to be a never-ending expanse, disappearing in the distant marsh. Metro-Vista was a classic New Jersey office complex, built during the great expanse of the eighties. Hundreds of offices, all cold and impersonal, sleek and robotic, with too many tinted windows not letting in enough sunlight. The vapor lights buzzed and you could imagine, if not actually hear, the drone of worker bees.

"They weren't stopping for gas," Rachel muttered.

"So what do we do?"

"Only thing we can," she said. "Let's keep following the money."

Heshy and Lydia headed west toward the Garden State Parkway. Steven Bacard followed in the car behind them. Lydia ripped open the wads of bills. It took her ten minutes to find the tracking device. She dug it out from the money crevice.

She held it up, so Heshy could see it. "Clever," she said.

"Or we're slipping."

"We've never been perfect, Pooh Bear."

Heshy did not reply. Lydia opened the car window. She stuck her hand out and signaled for Bacard to follow them. He waved back that he understood. When they slowed for the toll, Lydia quickly pecked Heshy's cheek and got out of the car. She took the money with her. Heshy was now left alone with just the tracking device. If this Rachel woman still had any juice or if the police got wind of what was happening, they would pull Heshy over. He would toss the tracking device into the street. They would find the device, sure, but they wouldn't be able to prove it had come from his car. And even if they could, so what? They would search Heshy and his car and find nothing. No kid, no ransom note, no ransom money. He was clean.

Lydia hurried over to Steven Bacard's car and slipped into the passenger's side. "You got Pavel on the line?" she asked.

"Yes."

She took the phone. Pavel started screaming in whatever the hell language was native to him. She waited and then told him the meeting place. When Bacard heard the address, his head snapped toward her. She smiled. Pavel, of course, didn't understand the significance of the location, but then again, why should he? He ranted a little more, but eventually Pavel calmed enough to say he'd be there. She hung up the phone.

"You can't be serious," Bacard said to her.

"Shh."

Her plan was simple enough. Lydia and Bacard would race ahead to the meeting spot while Heshy, who had the tracker on him, would stall. When Lydia was set up and fully prepared, she would call Heshy on the cell phone. Then and only then would Heshy go to the meeting spot. He would have the tracking device with him. The woman, this Rachel Mills, would hopefully follow.

She and Bacard arrived in twenty minutes. Lydia spotted a car parked up the block. Pavel's, she figured. A stolen Toyota Celica. Lydia didn't like that. Strange cars parked on streets like these were noticed. She glanced over at Steven Bacard. His face was moon pale. It almost seemed detached, floating. The scent of fear came off him in waves. His fingers gripped the wheel, tense. Bacard didn't have the stomach for this. That would be a liability.

"You can just drop me off," she said.

"I want to know," he began, "what you plan on doing here."

She just looked at him.

"My God."

"Spare me the indignant act."

"No one was supposed to be hurt."

"You mean like Monica Seidman?"

"We had nothing to do with that."

Lydia shook her head. "And the sister, what was her name, Stacy Seidman?"

Bacard opened his mouth as though he might counter. Then he lowered his head. She knew what he had planned on saying. Stacy Seidman had been a drug addict. She was expendable, a waste, a danger, heading for death, whatever justification floated his boat. Men like Bacard needed justification. In his mind, he wasn't selling babies. He really believed that he was helping. And if he made money—lots of money—from it and broke the law, well, he was taking tremendous risk to better lives. Shouldn't he be well compensated?

But Lydia had no interest in digging into his psyche nor comforting it. She had counted the money in the car. He had hired her. Her take was a million dollars. Bacard got the other million. She shouldered the duffel bag with her—and Heshy's—money. She stepped out of the car. Steven Bacard stared straight ahead. He did not refuse the money. He did not call her back and say that he wanted to wash his hands of this. There was a million dollars sitting in the seat next to him. Bacard wanted it. His family had a big house in Alpine now. His kids went to private school. So no, Bacard did not back off. He simply stared ahead and put the car in drive.

When he was gone, Lydia called Pavel with the two-way radio portion of the cell phone. Pavel was hiding behind some shrubs up the block. He still wore the flannel shirt. His walk was a labored lumber. His teeth had suffered under a lifetime of cigarettes and ill care. He had a squashed-from-too-many-fights nose. He was Balkan rough trade. He had seen a lot in his life. Didn't matter, though. When you don't know what's happening, you are in over your head.

"You," he said, spitting the word. "You no tell me."

Pavel was right. She no tell him. In other words, he'd known nothing. His English was beyond broken, which was why he had been the perfect front man for this crime. He'd come over from Kosovo two years ago with a pregnant woman. During the first ransom drop, Pavel had been given specific instructions. He'd been told to wait for a certain car to pull into the lot, to approach the car without speaking to the man, to take a bag from him, to get into the van. Oh, and to confuse matters a little more, they told

Pavel to keep a phone in front of his mouth and pretend to talk into it.

That was it.

Pavel had no idea who Marc Seidman was. He had no idea about what was in the bag, about a kidnapping, about a ransom, nothing. He didn't wear his gloves—his fingerprints were not on file in the United States—and he didn't carry ID.

They paid him two thousand dollars and sent him back to Kosovo. Based on Seidman's rather specific description, the police circulated a sketch of a man who, for all practical purposes, was impossible to find. When they decided to rerun the ransom drop, Pavel was the natural go-to guy. He would dress the same, look the same, play with Seidman's head in case he decided to fight back this time.

Still, Pavel was a realist. He would adapt. He had spent time selling women in Kosovo. White slavery in the guise of strip clubs was a big market over there, though Bacard had come up with another way of using those women. Pavel, no stranger to sudden change, would do what needed to be done. He gave Lydia some attitude, but once she handed him a wad of bills adding up to five thousand dollars, he grew quiet. The fight was out of him. It was only a question of how.

She handed Pavel a gun. He knew how to use it.

Pavel set up near the driveway, keeping his two-way radio channel open. Lydia called Heshy and told them they were ready. Fifteen minutes later, Heshy drove past them. He tossed the tracking device out the car window. Lydia caught it and threw back a kiss. Heshy kept driving. Lydia brought the tracking device into the backyard. She took out her gun and waited.

The night air was starting to give way to the morning dew. That tingle was there, lighting up her veins. Heshy, she knew, was not far away. He wanted to join in, but this was her game. The street was silent. It was 4:00 A.M.

Five minutes later, she heard the car pull up.

chapter 33

Something was very wrong here.

The roads were becoming so familiar I barely noticed them. I was wired, jazzed, the pain in my ribs barely noticeable. Rachel was absorbed in her Palm Pilot. She'd click screens with her little wand, tilt her head, change viewing angles. She dug through the backseat and found Zia's road atlas. With the cap of the Flair pen in her mouth, Rachel started marking up the route, trying to discern a pattern, I guess. Or maybe she was just stalling, so I wouldn't ask the inevitable.

I called her name softly. She flicked her eyes at me and then back to the screen.

"Did you know about that CD-ROM before you got here?" I said.

"No."

"There were photos of you in front of the hospital where I work."

"So you told me."

She clicked the screen again.

"Are the photos real?" I asked.

"Real?"

"I mean, were they digitally altered or something—or were you really in front of my office two years ago?"

Rachel kept her head down, but out of the corner of my eye, I could see her shoulders slump. "Make a right," she said. "Up here."

We were on Glen Avenue now. This was getting creepy. My old high school was up on the left. They'd refurbished it four years ago, adding a weight room, a swimming pool, and a second gymnasium. The façade had been intentionally scuffed up and aged with ivy, giving the place a proper collegiate feel, reminding the youth of Kasselton what was expected of them.

"Rachel?"

"The pictures are real, Marc."

I nodded to myself. I don't know why. Maybe I was trying to buy myself some time. I was heading into something worse than unchartered waters here. I knew that the answers would alter everything again, make it all go topsy-turvy, just when I hoped to set the world right. "I think I'm owed an explanation," I said.

"You are." She kept her head down on the screen. "But not right now."

"Yeah, right now."

"We need to concentrate on what we're doing."

"Don't hand me that crap. We're just driving here. I can handle two things at the same time."

"Maybe," she said softly, "I can't."

"Rachel, what were you doing in front of that hospital?"

"Whoa."

"Whoa what?"

We were approaching the traffic lights at Kasselton Avenue. Because of the hour, they were blinking yellow and red. I frowned and turned to her. "Which way?"

"Right."

My heart iced. "I don't understand."

"The car has stopped again."

"Where?"

"Unless I'm reading this wrong," Rachel said, and finally she looked up and met my gaze, "they're at your house."

* * *

I made the right turn. Rachel no longer needed to direct me. She kept her eyes on the screen. We were less than a mile away now. My parents had taken this route to the hospital on the day I was born. I wondered how many times I'd been on this road since. Weird thought, but the mind goes where it must.

I made the right on Monroe. My parents' house was on the left. The lights were off except, of course, for the lamp downstairs. We had it on a timer. It stayed on from 7:00 P.M. to 5:00 A.M. every day. I'd put in one of those long-life, energy-saving light bulbs that look like soft-ice-cream swirls. Mom bragged about how long it lasted. She'd read somewhere that keeping a radio on was also a good way to scare away burglars, so she had an old AM radio constantly tuned into a talk station. The problem was, the sound of the radio kept her up at night, so now Mom put the volume so low that a burglar would have to press his ear against it to be warded off.

I started making the turn onto my road, onto Darby Terrace, when Rachel said, "Slow down."

"They moving?"

"No. The signal is still coming from your house."

I looked up the block. I started thinking about it. "They didn't exactly take a direct route here."

She nodded. "I know."

"Maybe they found your Q-Logger," I said.

"That's exactly what I was thinking."

The car inched forward. We were in front of the Citrons' house now, two away from mine. No lights were on—not even a timer lamp. Rachel chewed on her lower lip. We were at the Kadisons' house now, nearing my driveway. It was one of those situations people describe as "too quiet," as if the world had frozen, as if all you saw, even animate objects, were trying to stay still.

"This has to be a setup," she said.

I was just about to ask her what we should do—pull back, park and walk, call the cops for help?—when the first bullet shattered the front windshield. Shards of glass smacked my face. I heard a short scream. Without conscious thought, I ducked my head and raised my forearm. I looked down and saw blood.

"Rachel!"

The second shot zinged so close to my head that I felt it in my hair. The impact hit my seat with a sound like a pillowy wallop. Instincts took over again. But this time it had a mission, a direction of sorts. I hit the accelerator. The car lurched forward.

The human brain is an amazing instrument. No computer can duplicate it. It can process millions of stimuli in hundredths of a second. That was, I guess, what was going on now. I was hunched over in the driver's seat. Someone was taking shots at me. The base part of my brain wanted to flee, but something farther along the evolutionary path realized that there might be a better way.

The thought process took—and this is just a rough estimate—less than a tenth of a second. I had my foot on the accelerator. The tires shrieked. I thought about my house, the familiar setup of it, the direction the bullets had come from. Yes, I know how that sounds. Maybe panic speeds up those brain functions, I don't know, but I realized that if I were the one doing the shooting, if I had been lying in wait for this car to approach, I'd have hidden behind the three shrubs that divide my property from the Christies' next door. The shrubs were big and bushy and right on our driveway. If I had pulled all the way in, bam, you could have blown us away from the passenger side. When I hesitated, when the shooter had seen that we might back away, he was still in position, though not as good, to take us from the front.

So I looked up, turned the wheel, and aimed the car for those bushes.

A third bullet rang out. It hit something metal, probably the front grill, with a *ka-ping*. I sneaked a glance at Rachel long enough to take a visual snapshot: her head was down, her hand pressed against the side of her head, blood seeping through the fingers. My stomach fell, but my foot stayed on the pedal. I moved my head back and forth, as if that might throw off the shooter's aim.

My headlights illuminated the bushes.

I saw flannel.

Something happened to me. I talked before about sanity being a thin string and that mine had snapped. In that case, I went quiet. This time, a mix of rage and dread roared through my body. I pressed the pedal harder, almost through the floor. I heard a yell of surprise. The man in the flannel shirt tried to leap to the right.

But I was ready.

I turned the steering wheel toward him like we were playing bumper cars. There was a crash, a dull thud. I heard a scream. The bushes were caught up in the bumper. I looked for the man in the flannel. Nothing. I had my hand on the door handle, about to open it and go after him, when Rachel said, "No!"

I stopped. She was alive!

Her hand reached up and shifted the car into reverse. "Go back!"

I listened. I don't know what I'd been thinking. The man was armed. I wasn't. Despite the impact, I didn't know if he was dead or injured or what.

I started back. I noticed that my dark suburban street was lit up now. Shots and shrieking tires are not common noises here on Darby Terrace. People had woken up and turned on the lights. They'd be dialing 911.

Rachel sat up. Relief flooded me. She had a gun in one hand. The other was still over her wound. "It's my ear," she said, and again, the mind working in funny ways, I had already started thinking about what procedure I would use to repair the damage.

"There!" she shouted.

I turned. The man in the flannel was hobbling down the driveway. I turned the wheel and aimed the car lights in his direction. He disappeared around back. I looked over at Rachel.

"Back up," she said. "I'm not sure he's alone."

I did. "Now what?"

Rachel had her gun out, her free hand on the door handle. "You stay."

"Are you out of your mind?"

"You keep revving the engine and moving a little. Let them think we're still in the car. I'll sneak up on them."

Before I could protest any further, she rolled out. With blood still flowing down her side, she darted away. I, per her instructions, revving the engine and feeling like a total dweeb, shifted the car into drive, moved forward, shifted the car into reverse, went back.

A few seconds later, I lost sight of Rachel.

A few seconds after that, I heard two more shots.

Lydia had watched it all from her spot in the backyard.

Pavel had shot too early. It was a mistake on his part. From her vantage point behind a wall of firewood, Lydia could not see who was in the car. But she'd been impressed. The driver had not only flushed Pavel out but wounded him as well.

Pavel limped into view. Lydia's eyes adjusted enough to see the blood on his face. She raised her arm and waved him toward her. Pavel fell and then started crawling. Lydia kept her eyes on the routes to the backyard. They would have to come from the front. There was a fence behind her. She was near the back neighbor's gate in case she needed to escape.

Pavel kept crawling. Lydia urged him on while keeping watch. She wondered how this ex-fed would play it. The neighbors were awake now. Lights were going on. The cops would be on their way.

Lydia would have to hurry.

Pavel made it to the pile of firewood and rolled next to her. For a moment, he stayed on his back. His breathing was wheezy and wet. Then he forced himself up. He knelt next to Lydia and looked out into the yard. He winced and said, "Leg broken."

"We'll take care of it," she said. "Where's your gun?"

"Dropped."

Untraceable, she thought. Not a problem. "I have another weapon you can use," she told him. "Keep a lookout."

Pavel nodded. He squinted into the dark.

"What?" Lydia said. She moved a little closer to him.

"Not sure."

As Pavel stared out, Lydia pressed the barrel of her gun against the hollow spot behind his left ear. She squeezed the trigger, firing two shots into his head. Pavel dropped to the ground like a marionette with his strings cut.

Lydia looked down at him. In the end, this might be best. Plan B was probably better than Plan A anyway. Had Pavel killed the woman—an ex–FBI agent—that would not have ended it. They'd probably search even harder for the mysterious man in flannel. The investigation would have continued. There wouldn't be closure. This way, with

Pavel dead—dead by the gun used at the original Seidman crime scene—the police would conclude that either Seidman or this Rachel (or both) was behind it. They'd be arrested. The charges might not stick, but no matter. The police would stop looking for anyone else. They could disappear with the money now.

Case closed.

Lydia suddenly heard the shriek of tire wheels. She tossed the weapon into the neighbor's yard. She didn't want it in plain sight. That would be too obvious. She quickly checked Pavel's pockets. There was money, of course, the wad of bills she'd just given him. She'd let him keep that. One more thing to tie it all up nice and neat.

There was nothing else in his pockets— no wallet, no slip of paper, no identification or anything that could trace back to any- thing. Pavel had been good about that. More lights in windows now. Not much time. Lydia rose.

"Federal agent! Drop your weapon!"

Damn! A woman's voice. Lydia fired toward where she thought the voice had originated from and ducked back behind the firewood. Shots came back in her direction. She was pinned down. What now? Still behind the firewood, Lydia stretched up behind her and released the gate hatch.

"All right!" Lydia shouted. "I'm surrendering!"

Then she jumped up with the semiautomatic already going. She pulled the trigger as fast as she could. Bullets flew, the sound ringing in her ears. She didn't know if the shots were being returned or not. She didn't think so. There was no hesitation, though. The gate was open. She darted through it.

Lydia ran hard. A hundred yards away, Heshy was waiting in a neighbor's yard. They met up. Keeping low, they followed a trail of recently pruned shrubs. Heshy was good. He always tried to prepare for the worst. His car was hidden in a cul-de-sac two blocks down.

When they were safely on their way, Heshy asked, "You okay?"

"Fine, Pooh Bear." She took a deep breath, closed her eyes, and settled back. "Just fine."

It wasn't until they were near the highway that Lydia wondered what had happened to Pavel's cell phone.

*   *   *

My first reaction, naturally enough, was panic.

I opened the car door to give chase, but my brain finally kicked in and made me pull up. It was one thing to be brave or even foolhardy. It was another to be suicidal. I did not have a gun. Both Rachel and her assailant did. Rushing to her aid unarmed would be, at best, fruitless.

But I couldn't just stay here.

I closed the car door. Once again, my foot stamped down on the accelerator. The car bolted forward. I spun the wheel and veered across my front lawn. The shots had come from the back of the house. I aimed the car there. I tore through the flower beds and shrubs. They had been here so long that I almost cared.

My headlights danced through the dark. I started toward the right, hoping that I could work around the big elm. No go. The tree was too close to the house. The car wouldn't fit. I floored it in reverse. The tires ripped into dewy lawn, taking a second or two to catch. I headed toward the Christies' property line. I took out their new gazebo. Bill Christie would be pissed.

I was in the backyard now. The headlights

slipped along the Grossmans' stockade fence. I swung the steering wheel toward the right. And then I saw her. I hit the brake. Rachel stood by the pile of firewood. The wood had been there when we bought the house. We hadn't used any. It was probably rotten and bug infested. The Grossmans had complained that it was so close to their fence that the bugs would start eating into it. I had promised to get rid of it, but I hadn't yet gotten around to it.

Rachel had her gun drawn and pointing down. The man in the flannel was lying at her feet like yesterday's refuse. I didn't have to roll down a window. The windshield was gone from the earlier gunshots. I heard nothing. Rachel lifted her hand. She waved to me, signaling that it was okay. I hurried out of the car.

"You shot him?" I asked, almost rhetorically.

"No," she said.

The man was dead. You didn't have to be a doctor to see that. The back of his skull had been blown off. Brain matter, congealed and pink-white, clung to the firewood. I am not on expert on ballistics but the damage was severe. It was either a very large bullet or from very close range.

"Someone was with him," Rachel said. "They shot him and escaped through that gate."

I stared down at him. The rage boiled up again. "Who is he?"

"I checked his pockets. He has a wad of bills but no ID."

I wanted to kick him. I wanted to shake him and ask what he had done with my daughter. I looked at his face, damaged yet handsome, and wondered what had led him here, why our life paths had crossed. And that was when I noticed something odd.

I tilted my head to the side.

"Marc?"

I dropped to my knees. Brain matter did not bother me. Bone splinters and bloody tissue did not faze me in the least. I had seen worse trauma. I examined his nose. It was practically putty. I remembered that from last time. A boxer, I'd thought. Either that or he'd lived some rough years. His head lolled back at a funny angle. His mouth was open. That was what had drawn my eye.

I put my fingers on his jaw and palate and pulled his mouth farther open.

"What the hell are you doing?" Rachel asked.

"Do you have a flashlight?"

"No."

Didn't matter. I lifted his head up and aimed his mouth toward the car. The headlights did the trick. I could see clearly now.

"Marc?"

"It always bothered me that he let me see his face." I lowered my head toward his mouth, trying to do so without casting too much of a shadow. "They were so careful about everything else. The altered voice, the stolen van sign, the welding together of license plates. Yet he lets me see his face."

"What are you talking about?"

"I thought maybe he'd worn an elaborate disguise the first time I'd seen him. That would make sense. But now we know that's not the case. So why would he let me see him?"

She seemed taken aback that I was asserting myself, but that didn't last long. She joined in. "Because he had no record."

"Maybe. Or . . ."

"Or what? Marc, we don't have time for this."

"His dental work."

"What about it?"

"Look at his crowns. They're tin cans."

"They're what?"

I lifted my head. "On his upper right molar and upper left cuspid. See, our crowns used to be made of gold, though most are now porcelain. Your dentist makes a mold so you can get an exact fitting. But this is just an aluminum, ready-made cap. You put it over the teeth and squeeze it on with pliers. I did two oral rotations overseas, mostly dealing with reconstruction, but I saw lots of mouths with these things in them. They call them tin cans. And they don't do it here in the USA, except maybe as a temporary."

She took a knee next to me. "He's foreign?"

I nodded. "I'd bet he's from the old Soviet bloc, something like that. The Balkans, maybe."

"That would make sense," she said. "Whatever prints they'd find they'd send down to NCIC. Same with any sort of face ID. Our files and computers wouldn't pick him up. Hell, it'll take the police forever to ID him unless someone comes forward."

"Which probably won't happen."

"My God, that's why they killed him. They know that we won't be able to trace him back."

The sirens sounded. Our eyes locked.

"You got a choice to make here, Marc. We stay, we're going to jail. They'll think he was part of our plot and we killed him. My guess is, the kidnappers knew that. Your neighbors will claim it was quiet until we drove up. Suddenly there's shrieking tires and gunfire. I'm not saying that we won't be able to explain it eventually."

"But it will take time," I said.

"Yes."

"And whatever opening we have here, it will close. The cops will pursue it their own way. Even if they can help, even if they believe us, they'll make a lot of noise."

"One more thing," she said.

"What?"

"The kidnappers set us up. They knew about the Q-Logger."

"We figured that out already."

"But now I'm wondering, Marc. How did they find it?"

I looked up, remembering the warning in the ransom note. "A leak?"

"I wouldn't rule it out anymore."

We both started toward the car. I put my hand on her arm. She was still bleeding. Her eye was almost swollen shut now. I looked at her, and again something primitive took over: I wanted to protect her. "If we run, it'll make us look guilty," I said. "I don't mind that—I don't have anything to lose here—but what about you?"

Her voice was soft. "I don't have anything to lose either."

"You need a doctor," I said.

Rachel almost smiled. "Aren't you one?"

"True enough."

There was no time to discuss the pros and cons. We had to act. We got into Zia's car. I swerved it around and headed out the back way, the Woodland Road exit. Thoughts—rational, clear thoughts—were starting to filter in now. When I really considered where we were and what we were doing, the truth nearly crushed me. I almost pulled over. Rachel saw it.

"What?" she said.

"Why are we running?"

"I don't understand."

"We hoped to find my daughter or at least who did this to her. We said there was a small opening."

"Yes."

"But don't you see? The opening, if there ever really was one, is gone. That guy back there is dead. We know he's foreign, but so what? We don't know who he is. We've reached a dead end. We don't have any other clues."

There was suddenly a trace of mischief on Rachel's face. She reached into her pocket and pulled something into a view. A cell phone. It wasn't mine. It wasn't hers. "Maybe," she said, "we do."

chapter 34

"First thing," Rachel said, "we need to get rid of this car."

"The car," I said, shaking my head at the damage. "If this search doesn't kill me, Zia will."

Rachel managed another smile. We were in the zone now, so deep in, so far past scared that we had found a little quiet. I debated where we should go, but really there was only one alternative.

"Lenny and Cheryl," I said.

"What about them?"

"They live four blocks from here."

It was five in the morning. Dark had begun to surrender to the inevitable. I dialed Lenny's home number and hoped that he hadn't gone back to the hospital. He answered on the first ring and barked a hello.

"I got a problem," I said.

"I hear sirens."

"That would be part of the problem."

"The police called me," he said. "After you took off."

"I need your help."

"Is Rachel with you?" he asked.

"Yes."

There was an awkward silence. Rachel fiddled with the dead man's cell phone. I had no idea what she was looking for. Then Lenny said, "What are you trying to do here, Marc?"

"Find Tara. Are you going to help me or not?"

Now there was no hesitation. "What do you need?"

"To hide the car we're using and borrow another."

"And then what are you going to do?"

I turned the car to the right. "We'll be there in a minute. I'll try to explain it to you then."

Lenny wore a pair of old gray sweatpants, the kind with the tie waist, a pair of slippers, and a Big Dog T-shirt. He pressed a button and the garage door slid to a smooth close as soon as we entered. Lenny looked exhausted, but then again, I don't think Rachel and I were ready for our close-ups either.

When Lenny saw the blood on Rachel, he took a step back. "What the hell happened?"

"Do you have any bandages?" I asked.

"Cabinet over the kitchen sink."

Rachel still had the cell phone in her hand. "I need to get on the Internet," she said.

"Look," Lenny said, "we have to discuss this."

"Discuss it with him," Rachel said. "I need Web access."

"In my office. You know where it is."

Rachel hurried inside. I followed, staying in the kitchen. She continued on to the den. We both knew this house well. Lenny stayed with me. They had recently renovated the kitchen into something French Farmesque and added a second refrigerator because four kids ate like four kids. The fronts of both fridges were overloaded with artwork and family photos and a brightly colored alphabet. The new one had one of those magnetic poetry sets. The words I STAND ALONE AROUND THE SEA ran down the handle.

I started going through the cabinet over the sink.

"You want to tell me what's going on?"

I found Cheryl's first aid kit and pulled it out. "There was a shooting at our house."

I gave him the bare bones, opening the first aid kit and checking the supplies. There'd be enough in here for now. I finally glanced at him. Lenny just gaped at me. "You ran away from a murder scene?"

"If I stayed, what would have happened?"

"The police would have picked you up."

"Exactly."

He shook his head and kept his voice low. "They don't think you did it anymore."

"What do you mean?"

"They think it was Rachel."

I blinked, not sure how to react.

"Has she explained those photos to you?"

"Not yet," I said. Then, "I don't understand. How did they figure it was Rachel?"

Lenny rapidly outlined a theory involving jealousy and rage and my forgetting key moments before the shooting. I stood there too stunned to respond. When I did, I said, "That's nuts."

Lenny did not reply.

"That guy with the flannel shirt just tried to kill us."

"And what ended up happening to him?"

"I told you. Someone else was with him. He was shot."

"You saw someone else?"

"No. Rachel . . ." I saw where he was going. "Come on, Lenny. You know better."

"I want to know about those photos on the CD, Marc."

"Fine, let's go ask her."

When we left the kitchen, I spotted Cheryl on the stairwell. She looked down at me, arms crossed. I don't think I had ever seen that look on her face before. It made me pause. There was some blood on the carpet, probably from Rachel. On the wall was one of those studio photos of all four kids, trying to look casual in matching white turtlenecks against a white background. Children and all that white.

"I'll take care of it," Lenny told her. "You stay upstairs."

We hurried through the den. A DVD case from the latest Disney movie lay splayed on top of the television. I nearly tripped over a Wiffle Ball and plastic bat. A game of Monopoly featuring Pokemon characters was spread across the floor in midgame clutter. Someone, one of the kids I assumed, had scrawled DO NOT TOUCH A THING! on a piece of paper and laid it over the board. As we passed the fireplace mantel, I noticed that they'd recently updated the photographs. The kids were older now, in those images as in real life. But the oldest photograph, the "formal dance" image of the four of us, was gone. I don't know what that meant. Probably nothing. Or maybe Lenny and Cheryl were taking their own advice: It was time to move on.

Rachel sat at Lenny's desk, hovering over the keyboard. The blood had dried down the left side of her neck. Her ear was a mess. She glanced up when she saw us and then went back to typing. I examined her ear. Severe damage. The bullet had scraped along the upper region. It had skimmed the side of her head too. Another inch—hell, another quarter inch—and she'd probably be dead. Rachel ignored me, even when I applied the Bactine and threw on a bandage. It would be good enough for now. I'd fix it for real when we had the chance.

"Bang," Rachel said suddenly. She smiled and hit a key. The printer began to

whir. Lenny nodded toward me. I put the finishing touches on the bandage and said,
"Rachel?"

She looked up at me.

"We need to talk," I said.

"No," she countered, "we need to get out
of here. I just found us a major lead."

Lenny stayed where he was. Cheryl
slipped into the room now, her arms still
folded. "What lead?" I asked.

"I checked the logs on the cell phone,"
Rachel said.

"You can do that?"

"They're in plain view, Marc," she said,
and I could hear the impatience. "The dialed
and received call logs. It's pretty much standard on every phone."

"Right."

"The dial log didn't help. No numbers
were listed, which means, if the guy did dial
out, it was to a blocked number."

I was trying to stay with her. "Okay."

"But the received log is another story.
There was only one incoming call on the list.
According to the internal timer, it came in at
midnight. I just checked the phone number
in the reverse directory at Switchboard dot-

com. It's a residence. One Verne Dayton in Huntersville, New Jersey."

Neither the name nor the city rang any bells. "Where is Huntersville?"

"I MapQuested it. It's near the Pennsylvania border. I zoomed in to within a few hundred yards. The house is all by itself out there. Acres of land in the heart of Nowheresville."

The chill started in my center and spread. I turned to Lenny. "I need to borrow your car."

"Hold up a second," Lenny said. "What we need here are some answers."

Rachel stood. "You want to know about the photos on the CD."

"For starters, yes."

"It's me in the pictures. Yes, I was there. The rest is none of your business. I owe Marc an explanation, not you. What else?"

For once, Lenny didn't know what to say.

"You also want to know if I killed my husband, right?" She looked at Cheryl. "Do you think I killed Jerry?"

"I don't know what to think anymore," Cheryl said. "But I want you both out of here."

"Cheryl," Lenny said.

She shot him a look that could have downed a charging rhino. "They shouldn't have brought this to our doorstep."

"He's our best friend. He's the godfather of our son."

"Which makes it that much worse. He drags this danger into our home? Into the lives of our children?"

"Come on, Cheryl. You're exaggerating."

"No," I said. "She's right. We should get out of here now. Let me have the keys."

Rachel grabbed the sheet out of the printer. "Directions," she explained.

I nodded and looked at Lenny. His head was down. His feet rocked back and forth. Again, I thought of our childhood. "Shouldn't we call Tickner and Regan?" he said.

"And tell them what?"

"I can explain it to them," Lenny said. "If Tara is at this place"—he stopped, shook his head as if he suddenly saw how ridiculous the thought was—"they'll be better equipped to go in."

I moved right up next to him. "They found out about Rachel's tracking device."

"What?"

"The kidnappers. We don't know how.

But they found it. Add it up, Lenny. The ransom note warned us that they had an inside source. First time out, they knew I'd told the cops. Second time out, they learn about the tracking device."

"That doesn't prove anything."

"Do you think I have time to look for proof?"

Lenny's face sank.

"You know I can't risk that."

"Yeah," he said. "I know."

Lenny reached into his pocket and handed me the keys. We were off.

chapter 35

When Regan and Tickner got the call about the shooting at the Seidman residence, both men leapt to their feet. They were nearing the elevator when Tickner's cell phone rang.

A stiff, overly formal female voice said, "Special Agent Tickner?"

"Speaking."

"This is Special Agent Claudia Fisher."

Tickner knew the name. He may have even met her once or twice. "What's up?" he asked.

"Where are you right now?" she asked.

"New York Presbyterian Hospital, but I'm heading out to New Jersey."

"No," she said. "Please come down to One Federal Plaza immediately."

Tickner checked the time. It was only five in the morning. "Now?"

"That is what immediately means, yes."

"May I ask what this is about?"

"Assistant Director in Charge Joseph Pistillo would like to see you."

Pistillo? That made him pause. Pistillo was the top agent on the East Coast. He was the boss of Tickner's boss's boss. "But I'm on the way to a crime scene."

"This isn't a request," Fisher said. "Assistant Director Pistillo is waiting. He expects you here within the half hour."

The phone went dead. Tickner lowered his hand.

"What the hell was that about?" Regan asked.

"I gotta go," Tickner said, heading down the corridor.

"Where?"

"My boss wants to see me."

"Now?"

"Right now." Tickner was already halfway down the hall. "Call me when you know something."

"This isn't easy to talk about," Rachel said.

I drove. The unanswered questions had started to gather, weighing us both down, sapping our energy. I kept my eyes on the road and waited.

"Was Lenny with you when you saw the photos?" she asked.

"Yes."

"Was he surprised by them?"

"Looked that way to me."

She settled back. "Cheryl probably wouldn't have been."

"Why's that?"

"When you asked for my number, she called to warn me."

"About what?" I asked.

"About us."

No further explanation required. "She warned me too," I said.

"When Jerry died—that was my husband's name, Jerry Camp—when he died, let's just say it was a very hard time for me."

"I understand."

"No," she said. "Not like that. Jerry and I, we hadn't worked in a very long time. I don't know if we ever did. When I went for training at Quantico, Jerry was one of my instructors. More than that, he was a legend.

One of the best agents ever. You remember that KillRoy case a few years back?"

"He was a serial killer, right?"

Rachel nodded. "That capture was mostly due to Jerry. He had one of the most distinguished records in the bureau. With me . . . I don't know how it happened exactly. Or maybe I do. He was older. Something of a father figure maybe. I loved the FBI. It was my life. Jerry had a crush on me. I was flattered. But I don't know if I ever really loved him."

She stopped. I could feel her eyes on me. I kept mine on the road.

"Did you love Monica?" she asked. "I mean, really love her?"

The muscles in my shoulder bunched. "What the hell kind of a question is that?"

She was still. Then she said, "I'm sorry. That was out of line."

The silence grew. I tried to slow my breathing. "You were telling me about the photos?"

"Yes." Rachel started fidgeting. She only wore one ring. Now she twisted and tugged at it. "When Jerry died—"

"Was shot," I interjected.

Again I could feel her eyes on me. "Was shot, yes."

"Did you shoot him?"

"This isn't good, Marc."

"What isn't?"

"You're already angry."

"I just want to know if you shot your husband."

"Let me tell it my way, okay?"

There was a touch of steel in her voice now. I backed down, gave her a suit-yourself shrug. "When he died, I pretty much lost it. I was forced to resign. Everything I had—my friends, my work, hell, my life—was wrapped in the bureau. Now it was gone. I started drinking. I sank deeper into a funk. I hit bottom. And when you hit bottom, you look for a way to bounce back up. You look for anything. You get desperate."

We slowed at an interchange.

"I'm not saying this right," she said.

I surprised myself then. I reached through the red and put my hand on hers. "Just tell me, okay?"

She nodded, keeping her gaze down, staring at my hand on hers. I kept it there. "One night, when I had too much to drink, I dialed your number."

I remembered what Regan had told me about the phone records. "When was this?"

"A few months before the attack."

"Did Monica answer?" I asked.

"No. Your machine picked up. I—I know how stupid this sounds—I left a message for you."

I slowly took my hand back. "What did you say exactly?"

"I don't remember. I was drunk. I was crying. I think I said that I missed you and hoped you'd call back. I don't think I went further than that."

"I never got the message," I said.

"I realize that now."

Something clicked. "That means," I said, "that Monica listened to it."

A few months before the attack, I thought. When Monica was feeling her most insecure. When we were starting to have serious problems. I remembered other things too. I remembered how often Monica had cried at night. I remembered how Edgar had told me that she'd started seeing a psychiatrist. And there I was, in my oblivious little world, taking her to Lenny and Cheryl's house, subjecting her to that picture with my old lover in it—my old lover who had called our house late at night and said she missed me.

"My God," I said. "No wonder she hired a private investigator. She wanted to know if I was cheating on her. She probably told him about your call, about our past."

She said nothing.

"You still haven't answered the question, Rachel. What were you doing in front of the hospital?"

"I came to New Jersey to see my mother," she began. There was a hitch in her voice now. "I told you that she has a condo now in West Orange."

"So? Are you trying me to tell me she was a patient there?"

"No." She went quiet again. I drove. I almost flipped on the radio, just out of habit, just to do something. "Do I really have to say this?"

"I think so, yeah," I said. But I knew. I understood exactly.

Her voice was stripped of all passion. "My husband is dead. My job is gone. I've lost everything. I'd been talking to Cheryl a lot. I could tell from what she said that you and your wife were having problems." She turned to me full. "Come on, Marc. You know we never got over each other. So that day I went to the hospital to face you. I don't know what I expected. Was I really naïve enough to think you'd sweep me into your arms? Maybe, I don't know. So I hung around and tried to work up the courage. I even went up to your floor. But in the end, I couldn't go through with it—not because of Monica or Tara. I wish I could say I was that noble. I wasn't."

"So why then?"

"I walked away because I thought you'd reject me and I wasn't sure I could handle that."

We fell into silence then. I had no idea what to say. I don't even know how I felt.

"You're angry," she said.

"I don't know."

We drove some more. I wanted so very much to do the right thing. I thought about it. We both stared straight ahead. The tension pressed against the windows. Finally I said, "It doesn't matter anymore. All that matters is finding Tara."

I glanced at Rachel. I saw a tear on her cheek. The sign was up ahead now—small, discreet, nearly indiscernible. It read simply:

HUNTERSVILLE. Rachel brushed the tear away and sat up. "Then let's concentrate on that."

Assistant Director in Charge Joseph Pistillo was at his desk, writing. He was large, barrel chested, big shouldered, and bald, the sort of old-timer that makes you think of dock workers and city-saloon fights—power without the show muscle. Pistillo was probably on the wrong side of sixty. Rumor had it that he'd be retiring soon.

Special Agent Claudia Fisher showed Tickner into the office and closed the door as she left. Tickner took his sunglasses off. He stood with his hands behind his back. He was not invited to sit. There was no greeting, no handshake, no salute, or anything such.

Without looking up, Pistillo said, "I understand you've been asking about the tragic death of Special Agent Jerry Camp."

Alarm bells rang in Tickner's head. Whoa, that was fast. He'd only started his inquiries a few hours ago. "Yes, sir."

More scribbling. "He taught you at Quantico, isn't that right?"

"Yes, sir."

"He was a great teacher."

"One of the best, sir."

"*The* best, Agent."

"Yes, sir."

"Your inquiries into his death," Pistillo went on, "do they have anything to do with your past relationship with Special Agent Camp?"

"No, sir."

Pistillo stopped writing. He put down the pen and folded his rock-breaking hands on his desk. "Then why are you asking about it?"

Tickner looked for the traps and pitfalls he knew lurked in his answer. "His wife's name has arisen in another case I'm working on."

"That would be the Seidman murder-kidnapping case?"

"Yes, sir."

Pistillo frowned. His forehead crinkled. "You think there's a connection between the accidental shooting death of Jerry Camp and the Tara Seidman kidnapping?"

Careful, Tickner thought. Careful. "It's an avenue I need to explore."

"No, Agent Tickner, it is not."

Tickner stayed still.

"If you can tie Rachel Mills to the Seidman murder-kidnapping, do it. Find evidence that connects her to the case. But you don't need Camp's death to do that."

"They could be related," Tickner said.

"No," Pistillo said in a voice that left little room for doubt, "they're not."

"But I need to look—"

"Agent Tickner?"

"Yes, sir."

"I've looked into the file already," Pistillo said. "More than that, I helped investigate the death of Jerry Camp personally. He was my friend. Do you understand?"

Tickner did not reply.

"I am completely satisfied that his shooting was a tragic accident. That means you, Agent Tickner"—Pistillo pointed a meaty finger at Tickner's chest—"are completely satisfied too. Do I make myself clear?"

The two men stared at each other. Tickner was not a foolish man. He liked working for the bureau. He wanted to rise up the ladder. It would not pay to upset someone as powerful as Pistillo. So in the end, Tickner was the first to look away.

"Yes, sir."

Pistillo relaxed. He picked up his pen. "Tara Seidman has been missing for over a year now. Is there any proof she is still alive?"

"No, sir."

"Then the case doesn't belong to us anymore." He started writing now, making no bones about the fact that this was a dismissal. "Let the locals handle it."

New Jersey is our most densely populated state. That doesn't surprise people. New Jersey has cities, suburbs, and plenty of industry. That doesn't surprise people either. New Jersey is called the Garden State and has plenty of rural areas. That surprises people.

Even before we hit the border of Huntersville, signs of life—human life, that is—had already started fading away. There were few houses. We had passed one general store straight out of *Mayberry RFD*, but that was boarded up. During the next three miles we hit six different roads. I saw no houses. I passed no cars.

We were in the thick of the woods. I made my final turn and the car climbed up the side of a mountain. A deer—the fourth I'd seen by my count—sprinted out of the road, far enough up so I wasn't in any danger of hitting it. I was beginning to suspect that the name Huntersville was to be taken literally.

"It'll be on the left," Rachel said.

A few seconds later, I could see the mail-box. I began to slow, searching for a house or building of some kind. I saw nothing but trees.

"Keep driving," Rachel said.

I understood. We couldn't just pull into the driveway and announce ourselves. I found a small indentation off the road about a quarter of a mile up. I parked and turned off the engine. My heart started to trip-hammer. It was six in the morning. Dawn was here.

"Do you know how to use a gun?" Rachel asked me.

"I used to fire my dad's at the range."

She jammed a weapon into my hand. I stared down at it as if I'd just discovered an extra finger. Rachel had her gun out too. "Where did you get this?" I asked.

"At your house. Off the dead guy."

"Jesus."

She shrugged as if to say, *Hey, you never know.* I looked at the gun again and suddenly a thought hit me: Was this the weapon used to shoot me? To kill Monica?

I stopped there. There was no time for this squeamish nonsense. Rachel was already out the door. I followed. We started into the woods. There was no path. We made our own. Rachel took the lead. She tucked her weapon into the back of her pants. For some reason, I didn't do the same. I wanted to hold the gun. Faded orange signs tacked to trees warned trespassers to stay away. They had the word NO in giant font and a surprising amount of finer print, over-explaining what seemed to me to be pretty obvious.

We angled closer to where we thought the driveway was. When we spotted it, we had our guiding star. We stayed near the un-paved stretch and continued on our way. A few minutes later, Rachel stopped. I nearly bumped into her. She pointed ahead.

A structure.

It looked like a barn of some sort. We were more careful now. We kept low. We darted from tree to tree and tried to stay out of sight. We did not speak. After a bit, I started hearing music. Country, I think, but I'm no expert. Up ahead, I spotted a clear-ing. There was indeed a barn that appeared to be in mid-demolition. There was another structure too—a ranch or maybe extended trailer.

We moved a little closer, right to the end of the woods. We pressed ourselves against trees and peeked out. There was a tractor in the yard. I saw an old Trans Am up on cement blocks. Directly in front of the ranch was a white, overly sporty car—some might call it a "hot rod," I guess—with a thick black stripe up the hood. It looked like a Camaro.

The woods had ended, but we were still at least fifty feet from the ranch house. The grass was high, knee level. Rachel took out her gun. I still held mine. She dropped to the ground and began to commando-crawl. I did the same. On television commando-crawling looks pretty easy. You simply crawl with your butt down. And for about ten feet, it is pretty easy. Then it gets a lot harder. My elbows ached. The grass kept getting caught up in my nose and mouth. I do not suffer from hay fever or allergies, but we were kicking up something. Gnats and the like rose vengefully as we disturbed their slumber. The music was louder now. The singer—a man hitting nary a note—complained about his poor, poor heart.

Rachel stopped. I crawled to her right and pulled up even. "You okay?" she whispered.

I nodded, but I was panting.

"We may have to do something once we get there," she said. "I can't have you exhausted. We can slow down if you need to."

I shook her off and started moving. I was not going to slow down. Slowing down was simply not on the menu. We were getting closer. I could see the Camaro more clearly now. There were black mud flaps with the silver silhouette of a shapely girl behind the rear tires. There were bumper stickers on the back. One read: GUNS DON'T KILL PEOPLE, BUT THEY SURE MAKE IT EASIER.

Rachel and I were near the end of the grass, almost exposed, when the dog started barking. We both froze.

There are several varieties of dog barks. The yap of an annoying toy dog. The call of a friendly golden retriever. The warning of a basically harmless pet. And then there is that guttural, junkyard, rip-out-the-thorax bark that makes the blood thin.

This bark fit into the last category.

I was not particularly scared of the dog. I had a gun. It'd be easier, I guess, to use it on a dog than a human being. What did frighten me, of course, was that the barking would be heard by the ranch's occupant. So we waited. A minute or two later, the dog stopped. We kept our eyes on the ranch door. I was not sure what we would do if someone came out. Suppose we were spotted. We couldn't shoot. We still didn't know anything. The fact that a call had been made from the residence of Verne Dayton to the cell phone of a dead man did not add up to much. We didn't know if my daughter was here or not.

We knew, in fact, nothing.

There were hubcaps in the yard. The rising sun gleamed off them. I spotted a bunch of green boxes. And something about them held my gaze. Forgetting caution, I started moving closer.

"Wait," Rachel whispered.

But I couldn't. I needed to get a better look at those boxes. Something about them . . . but I couldn't put my finger on it. I crawled to the tractor and then hid behind it. I peered out toward the boxes again. Now I saw it. The boxes were indeed green. They also had a graphic featuring a smiling baby.

Diapers.

Rachel was next to me now. I swallowed. A big box of diapers. The kind you buy in bulk at a price club. Rachel saw it too. She put her hand on my arm, warning me to stay calm. We got back down on the ground. She signaled that we were going to make our way to a side window. I nodded that I understood. There was a long fiddle solo blaring from the stereo now.

We were both on our stomachs when I felt something cold against the back of my neck. I slid my eyes toward Rachel. There was a rifle barrel there too, pressed against the base of her skull.

A voice said, "Drop your weapons!"

It was a man. Rachel's right hand was bent in front of her face. The gun was in it. She let it go. A work boot stepped forward and kicked it away. I tried to discern the odds. One man. I could see that now. One man with two rifles. I could conceivably make a move here. No way I'd make it in time, but it might free up Rachel. I met her eyes and saw panic in them. She knew what I was thinking. The rifle suddenly dug deeper into my skull, pushing my face into the dirt.

"Don't try it, Chief. I can splatter two sets of brains as easy as one."

My mind scurried, but it kept hitting dead ends. So I let the gun drop from my hand and watched this man kick away our hope.

chapter 36

"Stay on your stomachs!"

"I'm an agent with the Federal Bureau of Investigation," Rachel said.

"Shut the hell up."

With our faces still in the dirt, he had us both put our hands on top of our head, fingers laced. He put a knee in my spine. I grimaced. Using his body for leverage, the man pulled my arms back, nearly popping my shoulders out of their sockets. My wrists were expertly bound together with nylon flex cuffs. They felt like those ridiculously complicated plastic ties they use to package toys so they can't be shoplifted.

"Put your feet together."

Another cuff fastened my ankles together. He pushed down on my back to get up. Then he moved over to Rachel. I was going to say something stupidly chivalric like *Leave her alone!* but I knew that this would be, at best, futile. I kept still.

"I'm a federal agent," Rachel said.

"I heard you the first time."

He put a knee in her back and pulled her hands together. She grunted in pain.

"Hey," I said.

The man ignored me. I turned and took my first real look at him, and it was like I'd been dropped into a time warp. No doubt about it—the Camaro belonged to him. His hair was eighties-hockey-player long, maybe permed, the color a strange offshoot of orange-blond, tucked back behind his ears and styled into the kind of mullet cut I hadn't seen since a Night Ranger music video. He had a cheesy blond mustache that could have been a milk stain. His T-shirt read UNIVERSITY OF SMITH AND WESSON. His jeans were unnaturally dark blue and looked stiff.

After he bound Rachel's hands, he said, "Get up, missy. You and me are taking a walk."

Rachel tried to make her voice stern. "You're not listening," she said, her hair falling down over her eyes. "I'm Rachel Mills—"

"And I'm Verne Dayton. So what?"

"I'm a federal agent."

"Your ID says retired." Verne Dayton smiled. He wasn't toothless, but he wasn't exactly an orthodontic poster boy either. His right incisor was totally turned in like a door off its hinge. "Kinda young to be retired, don't you think?"

"I still work special cases. They know I'm here."

"Really? Don't tell me. There's a bunch of agents waiting down yonder and if they don't hear from you in three minutes, they're all gonna come storming in. That about it, Rachel?"

She stopped. He had read her bluff. She had nowhere else to go.

"Get up," he said again, this time pulling on her arms.

Rachel stumbled to her feet.

"Where are you taking her?" I asked.

He did not reply. They started walking toward the barn. "Hey!" I called out, my voice booming with impotence. "Hey, come back!" But they kept walking. Rachel struggled, but her hands were tied behind her back. Every time she moved too much, he lifted the hands up, forcing her to bend forward. Eventually she complied and just walked.

Fear lit my nerves. In a frenzy, I looked for something, anything, that would get me free. Our guns? No, he had picked them up already. And even if he hadn't, what would I do? Fire with my teeth? I debated rolling over onto my back, but I wasn't sure how that would help yet. So now what? I started moving inchworm-style toward the tractor. I looked for a blade or anything that I might use to cut myself free.

In the distance, I heard the barn door creak open. My head swerved in time to see them disappear inside. The door closed behind them. The sound echoed into silence. The music—it must have been a CD or tape—had stopped. It was quiet now. And Rachel was gone from sight.

I had to get my hands free.

I started crawling forward, lifting my butt, pushing off with my legs. I made it to the tractor. I searched for some kind of blade or sharp edge. Nothing. My eyes darted to the barn.

"Rachel!" I shouted.

My voice echoed through the stillness. That was the only reply. My heart started doing flip-flops.

Oh God, now what?

I rolled onto my back and sat up. Pushing with my legs, I pressed against the tractor. I had a clear view of the barn. I don't know what the hell that did for me. There was still no movement, no sound. My eyes darted all over the place, desperately hunting for something that could bring salvation. But there was nothing.

I thought about going for the Camaro. A gun nut like this probably had two, three concealed weapons on him at all times. There might be something in there. But again, even if I managed to get there in time, how would I open the door? How would I search for a gun? How would I fire it when I found one?

No, I had to get this cuff off me first.

I looked on the ground for . . . I don't even know. A sharp rock. A broken beer bottle. Something. I wondered how much time had passed since they disappeared. I wondered what he was doing to Rachel. My throat felt as if it might close up.

"Rachel!"

I heard the desperation in the echo. It scared me. But again there was no reply.

What was going on in there?

I looked again for some kind of edge on the tractor, something I could use to break free. There was rust. Lots of rust. Would that work? If I rubbed the cuff against a rusty corner, would it eventually cut through? I doubted it, but there was nothing else.

I managed to get on my knees. I leaned my wrists against the rusted corner and moved up and down like a bear using a tree to scratch his back. My arms slipped. The rust bit into my skin, and the sting ran up my arm. I looked back over at the barn, listened hard, still heard nothing.

I kept going.

The problem was, I was doing this by feel. I turned my head as far as I could, but I couldn't see my wrists. Was this having any effect at all? I had no idea. But it was all I had to work with. So I continued moving up and down, trying to break free by pulling my arms apart like Hercules in a B movie.

I don't know how long I kept it up. Probably no more than two or three minutes, though it felt like a lot longer. The cuff did not break or even loosen. What finally made me stop was a sound. The barn door had opened. For a moment, I saw nothing. Then the Hick with the Hair came out. Alone. He started walking toward me.

"Where is she?"

Without speaking, Verne Dayton bent down and checked my cuffs. I could smell him now. He smelled of dried grass and work sweat. He was studying my hands. I glanced back. There was blood on the ground. My blood, no doubt. An idea suddenly came to me.

I reared back and aimed a head butt in his direction.

I know how devastating a proper head-butt can be. I had performed surgeries on faces crushed by such blows.

This would not be the case here.

My body position was awkward. My hands and feet were both bound. I was on my knees. I was twisting behind me. My skull didn't land on the nose or softer part of his face. It caught him on the forehead. There was a hollow *klunk* like something out of a Three Stooges soundtrack. Verne Dayton rolled back, cursing. I was totally off balance now, in free fall with nothing but my face to cushion my landing. My right cheek took the brunt of it, rattling my teeth. But I was beyond pain. I slid my eyes in his direction. He sat shaking out the cobwebs. There was a small laceration on his forehead.

Now or never.

Still tied up, I flailed toward him. But I was too slow.

Verne Dayton leaned back and raised a work boot. When I was close enough, he stomped my face as if he were beating back a brushfire. I fell back. He backpedaled to a safe distance and grabbed the rifle.

"Don't move!" His fingers checked the gash on his head. He looked at the blood in disbelief. "You out of your mind?"

I was flat on my back, my breaths coming in deep heaves. I didn't think anything was broken, but then again, I wasn't sure it was going to matter. He walked over to me and kicked me hard in the ribs. I rolled over. He grabbed my arms and started dragging me. I tried to get my feet under me. He was strong as hell. The steps to the trailer didn't slow him down. He pulled me up them, shouldered the door open, and tossed me in like bag of peat moss.

I landed with a thud. Verne Dayton

stepped inside and closed the door. My eyes took in the room. It was half what you'd expect, half not. The expected: There were guns mounted on the wall, antique muskets, hunter's rifle. There was the obligatory deer head, a framed NRA membership made out to Verne Dayton, a quilted American flag. The unexpected: The place was spotless and what some might call tastefully furnished. I spotted a playpen in the corner, but it wasn't cluttered. The toys were in one of those fiberglass chests with different color drawers. The drawers were categorized and labeled.

He sat down and looked at me. I was still on my stomach. Verne Dayton toyed with his hair a little, pushing back the strands, tucking the long sides behind his ears. His face was thin. Everything about him screamed yokel.

"You the one beat her up?" he said.

For a moment I didn't know what he was talking about. Then I remembered that he'd seen Rachel's injuries. "No."

"That get you off, huh? Beating up a woman?"

"What did you do with her?"

He took out a revolver, opened the chamber, slid a bullet into it. He spun it to a close and pointed it at my knee. "Who sent you?"

"No one."

"You want to get capped?"

I'd had enough. I rolled onto my back, waiting to hear him pull the trigger. But he didn't shoot. He let me move, keeping the gun on me. I sat up and stared him down. That seemed to confuse him. He took a step back.

"Where's my daughter?" I said.

"Huh?" He tilted his head. "You trying to be funny?"

I looked into his eyes and I saw it. This was no act. He had no idea what I was talking about.

"You come here with guns," he said, his face reddening. "You want to kill me? My wife? My kids?" Verne raised the gun to my face. "Give me one good reason I don't blow you both away and bury you in the woods?"

Kids. He said kids. Something about this whole setup suddenly wasn't making sense. I decided to take a chance. "Listen to me," I said. "My name is Marc Seidman. Eighteen months ago, my wife was murdered and my daughter abducted."

"What are you babbling about?"

"Please, just let me explain."

"Wait a second." Verne's eyes narrowed. He rubbed his chin. "I remember you. From the television. You were shot too, right?"

"Yes."

"So why do you want to steal my guns?"

I closed my eyes. "I'm not here to steal your guns," I said. "I'm here"—I wasn't sure how to say this—"I'm here to find my daughter."

It took this a second to register. Then his mouth dropped open. "You think I had something to do with that?"

"I don't know."

"You better start explaining."

So I did. I told him all of it. The story sounded insane in my ears, but Verne listened. He gave me his full attention. Toward the end, I said, "The man who did this. Or was somehow involved. I don't know anymore. We got his cell phone. He only had one incoming call. It came from here."

Verne thought about it. "This man. What's his name?"

"We don't know."

"I call a lot of people, Marc."

"We know the call was made sometime last night."

Verne shook his head. "Nope, no way."

"What do you mean?"

"I wasn't home last night. I was on the road, making a delivery. I only got home about half an hour before you got here. Spotted you when Munch—that's my dog—started the low growl. The bark, that don't mean much. It's the low growl tells me someone's there."

"Wait a second. No one was here last night?"

He shrugged. "Well, my wife and boys. But the boys are six and three. I don't think they were calling anyone. And I know Kat. She wouldn't be making any calls that late either."

"Kat?" I said.

"My wife. Kat. It's short for Katarina. She's from Serbia."

"Get you a beer, Marc?"

I surprised myself by saying, "That would be nice, Verne."

Verne Dayton had cut off the plastic cuffs. I rubbed my wrists. Rachel was next to me. He hadn't harmed her. He'd just wanted us separated, in part, he said, because he thought that I'd beaten her up and forced her to help me. Verne had a valuable gun collection—many of them still in working condition—and people were a little too interested in them. He'd figured that was the case with us.

"A Bud, okay?"

"Sure."

"You, Rachel?"

"No thanks."

"Soft drink? Some ice water maybe?"

"Water would be great, thanks."

Verne smiled, which wasn't the most pleasant sight. "No problem." I rubbed my wrists again. He spotted it and grinned. "We used those in the Gulf War. Kept them Iraqis under control, I can tell you."

He disappeared into the kitchen. I looked at Rachel. She shrugged. Verne came back with two Buds and a glass of water. He passed out the drinks. He raised the bottle for us to clink. I did. He sat down.

"I got two kids of my own. Boys. Verne Junior and Perry. If something ever happened to them . . ." Verne whistled low and shook his head. "I don't know how you even get out of bed in the morning."

"I think about finding her," I said.

Verne nodded hard at that. "I can relate, I guess. Long as a man ain't fooling himself, you know what I mean?" He looked over at Rachel. "You absolutely sure the phone number is mine?"

Rachel took out the cell phone. She pressed some digits and then showed him the small screen. Using his mouth, Verne extracted a Winston from the pack. He shook his head. "I don't understand it."

"We're hoping your wife can help."

He nodded slowly. "She wrote a note, says she went food shopping. Kat likes to do that early in the morning. At the twenty-four-hour A and P." He stopped. I think Verne was torn here. He wanted to be able to help, but he didn't want to hear that his wife had called a strange man at midnight. He raised his head. "Rachel, how about I get you some fresh bandages?"

"I'm fine."

"You sure?"

"Really, thank you." She held the glass of water with both hands. "Verne, do you mind if I ask you how you and Katarina met?"

"Online," he said. "You know, one of those Web sites for foreign brides. Cherry

Orchid, it's called. They used to call it mail order. I don't think they do that anymore. Anyway, you go to the site. You look at these pictures of women from all over— Eastern Europe, Russia, the Philippines, wherever. They list measurements, a little bio, likes and dislikes, that kinda thing. You see one that strikes your fancy, you can buy her address. They got package deals too, if you want to write to more than one."

Rachel and I gave each other a quick glance. "How long ago was this?"

"Seven years ago. We started sending each other e-mails and stuff. Kat was living on a farm in Serbia. Her parents had nothing. She used to walk four miles to get computer access. I wanted to call too, you know, talk on the phone. But they didn't even have one. She had to call me. Then one day, she says she's coming over. To meet me."

Verne put his hands up, as if to silence an interruption. "Now see, this is where the girls usually hit you up for some money, you know, dollars to buy a plane ticket and stuff. So I was ready for that. But Kat didn't. She came over on her own. I drove up to New York City. We met. We were married three weeks later. Verne Junior came in a year. Perry three years after that."

He took a deep sip of his beer. I did the same. The coldness felt wonderful sliding down my throat.

"Look, I know what you're thinking," Verne said. "But it ain't like that. Kat and me, we're real happy. I was married before to a grade-A American ball-buster. All she did was whine and complain. I wasn't making enough money for her. She wanted to stay at home and do nothing. Ask her to do a load of laundry, she'd go all ballistic on me with that feminazi crap. Always tearing me down, telling me I'm a loser. With Kat, it ain't like that. Do I like the fact that she makes a nice house and home? Sure, okay, that's important to me. If I'm working outside and it's hot, Kat'll fetch me a beer without giving me a *Ms.* magazine lecture. Is there anything wrong with that?"

Neither of us replied.

"Look, I want you to think about it, okay? Why are any two people attracted to each other? Looks maybe? Money? Because you have an important job? We all join up because we want to get something out of it. Give and take, am I right? I wanted a loving wife who'd help me raise children and take care of a home. I wanted a partner too, someone, I don't know, who'd just be nice to me. I get that. Kat, she wanted out of a terrible life. I mean, they were so poor, dirt was a luxury. She and me, we got it good here. In January, we took the kids and went down to Disney World. We like hiking and canoeing. Verne Junior and Perry, they're good kids. Hey, maybe I'm simple. Hell, I'm *definitely* simple. I like my guns, my hunting and fishing—and most of all, my family."

Verne lowered his head. His mullet hair dropped like a curtain blocking his face. He started ripping the label off the beer. "Some places—probably most, I don't know—marriages are arranged. That's the way it's always been. The parents decide. They force them. Well, no one forced Kat and me. She could walk away anytime. Me too. But it's been seven years now. I'm happy. So is she."

Then he shrugged his shoulders. "At least, I thought she was."

We drank in silence.

"Verne?" I said.

"Yeah?"

"You're an interesting man."

He laughed, but I could see the fear. He took a swig of beer to hide it. He'd carved out a life for himself. A nice life. It's funny. I am not a very good judge of people. My initial impressions are usually wrong. I see this gun-toting redneck with his hair and his bumper stickers and his monster-truck-rally 'tude. I hear he has a mail-order bride from Serbia. How can you not judge? But the more I listened to him, the more I liked him. I must be at least as alien to him. I'd crept up on his house with a gun. Yet as soon as I had started telling my story, Verne had acted. He knew that we were telling the truth.

We heard the car pull up. Verne moved to the window and looked out. There was a small, sad smile on his face. His family was pulling into the drive. He cherished them. Intruders had come to his home with guns, and he had done what he could to protect it. And now, maybe, in my attempt to bring my family together, I might tear apart his.

"Look! Daddy's home!"

That had to be Katarina. The accent was unmistakably foreign, something in the Balkan–East European–Russian family. I am not linguist enough to know which. I heard the happy squeals of little children. Verne's smile widened a bit. He stepped out onto the porch. Rachel and I stayed where we were. We could hear running feet on the steps. The greeting lasted a minute or two. I stared at my hands. I heard Verne say something about presents in the truck. The kids sprinted for them.

The door opened. Verne entered with his arm around his wife.

"Marc, Rachel, this here's my wife, Kat."

She was lovely. She wore her long hair straight down. Her yellow sundress left her shoulders exposed. Her skin was pure white, her eyes blue ice. She had that certain bearing so that I could have told, even if I hadn't known, that she was foreign. Or maybe I was projecting. I tried to guess her age. She could pass for mid-twenties, but the age lines around the eyes told me I was probably a decade off.

"Hi," I said.

We both stood and shook her hand. It was dainty, but there was steel in the grip. Katarina held on to the hostess smile, but it wasn't easy. Her eyes stayed on Rachel, on the wounds. The sight, I guess, was rather shocking. I was almost getting used to it.

Still smiling, Katarina turned to Verne as if to ask a question. He said, "I'm trying to help them out."

"Help them?" she repeated.

The children had located the presents and were hooting and hollering. Verne and Katarina didn't seem to hear. They were looking at each other. He held her hand. "That man over there"—he gestured with his chin toward me—"somebody murdered his wife and took away his little girl."

She put a hand to her mouth.

"They're here trying to find his daughter."

Katarina did not move. Verne turned to Rachel and nodded a go-ahead.

"Mrs. Dayton," Rachel began, "did you make a phone call last night?"

Katarina's head jerked as though she'd just been startled. She looked at me first, as if I were some kind of circus oddity. Then she turned her attention to Rachel. "I don't understand."

"We have a phone record," Rachel said. "Last night at midnight, someone placed a call from this house to a certain cell phone. We assume it was you."

"No, that's not possible." Katarina's eyes started shifting as if seeking out an escape route. Verne still held her hand. He tried to meet her gaze, but she kept avoiding it. "Oh wait," she said. "Maybe I know."

We waited.

"Last night, when I was sleeping, the phone rang." She tried the smile again, but it was having trouble staying anchored. "I don't know what time it was. Very late. I thought maybe it was you, Verne." She looked at him and now the smile held. He smiled back. "But when I answered it, there was no one there. So I remembered something I saw on the television. Star, six, nine. You hit those numbers and it dials the number. So I did that. A man answered. It wasn't Verne, so I hung up."

She looked at us expectantly. Rachel and I exchanged a glance. Verne was still smiling, but I saw his shoulders drop. He let go of her hand and half collapsed onto the couch.

Katarina started toward the kitchen. "You need another beer, Verne?"

"No, darling, I don't. I want you to sit here next to me."

She was hesitant but she listened. She sat with her spine still ramrod. Verne, too, sat up tall and again took her hand.

"I want you to listen to me, okay?"

She nodded. The children were wailing with delight outside. Corny to say, but there are few sounds like the unimpeded laughter of children. Katarina looked at Verne with an intensity that almost made me turn away.

"You know how much we love our boys, right?"

She nodded.

"Imagine if someone took them away from us. Imagine if that happened more than a year ago. Think about it. Imagine if someone stole, say, Perry and for more than a year, we didn't know where he was." He pointed to me. "That man over there. He doesn't know what happened to his little girl."

Her eyes were brimming with tears.

"We have to help him, Kat. Whatever you know. Whatever you done. I don't care. If there are secrets, you tell them now. We wipe the slate clean. I can forgive just about anything. But I don't think I can forgive if you don't help that man and his little girl."

She lowered her head and said nothing.

Rachel ratcheted up a notch. "If you're trying to protect the man you called, don't bother. He's dead. Someone shot him a few hours after you called."

Katarina's head stayed down. I rose and started pacing. From outside, there was another squeal of laughter. I walked over to the window and looked out. Verne Junior—the boy looked to be about six—shouted, "Ready or not, here I come!" It wouldn't be too hard to find him. I couldn't see Perry, but the hiding child's laughter was clearly coming from behind the Camaro. Verne Junior pretended to look elsewhere but not for very long. He sneaked up on the Camaro and yelled, "Boo!"

Perry popped out still laughing and ran. When I saw the boy's face, I felt my world, already teetering, take another hit. See, I recognized Perry.

He was the little boy I'd seen in the car last night.

chapter 37

Tickner parked in front of the Seidman house. They hadn't put up the yellow crime-scene tape yet, but he counted six squad cars and two news vans. He wondered if it'd be a good idea to approach, what with the cameras rolling. Pistillo, his boss's boss, had made it pretty clear where he stood. In the end, Tickner figured that it was safe enough to stay. If he was caught on camera, he could always opt for the truth: He had come to let the locals know that he was off the case.

Tickner found Regan in the backyard with the body. "Who is he?"

"No ID," Regan said. "We'll send in the prints, see what we come up with."

They both looked down.

"He matches that sketch Seidman gave us last year," Tickner said.

"Yup."

"So what does that mean?"

Regan shrugged.

"What have you learned so far?"

"Neighbors heard shots first. That was followed by screeching tires. They saw a BMW Mini driving across the grass. More shots. They spotted Seidman. One neighbor said he might have seen a woman with him."

"Probably Rachel Mills," Tickner said. He looked up in the morning sky. "So what does it mean?"

"Maybe the victim worked for Rachel. She silenced him."

"In front of Seidman?"

Regan shrugged. "The BMW Mini struck a chord though. I remembered that Seidman's partner had one. Zia Leroux."

"That would be who helped him get out of the hospital."

"We have an APB on the car."

"I'm sure they switched vehicles."

"Yeah, probably." Then Regan stopped. "Uh-oh."

"What?"

He pointed at Tickner's face. "You're not wearing your sunglasses."

Tickner smiled. "Bad omen?"

"The way this case is going? Maybe it's a good one."

"I came to tell you I'm off the case. Not just me. The bureau. If you can prove the girl is still alive—"

"—which we both know she ain't—"

"—or that she was transported across state lines, I can probably get back in. But this case is no longer a priority."

"Back to terrorism, Lloyd?"

Tickner nodded. He looked back up in the sky. It felt weird without the sunglasses.

"What did your boss want, anyway?"

"To tell me what I just told you."

"Uh-huh. Anything else?"

Tickner shrugged. "The shooting of Federal Agent Jerry Camp was accidental."

"Your big boss called you into his office before six in the morning to tell you that?"

"Yep."

"Yowza."

"Not only that, he investigated the case personally. He and the victim were friends."

Regan shook his head. "Does this mean Rachel Mills has powerful friends?"

"Not at all. If you can nail her for the Seidman murder or kidnapping, go to it."

"Just don't involve the death of Jerry Camp."

"There you go."

Someone called out. They looked over. A gun had been found in the neighbor's yard. A quick sniff told them that it had been fired recently.

"Convenient," Regan added.

"Yup."

"Any thoughts?"

"Nope." Tickner turned to him. "It's your case, Bob. Always was. Good luck."

"Thanks."

Tickner walked away.

"Hey, Lloyd?" Regan called out.

Tickner stopped. The gun had been bagged. Regan stared at it, then at the body by his feet.

"We still don't know what's going on here, do we?"

Tickner continued toward his car. "Not a clue," he said.

Katarina had her hands in her lap. "Is he really dead?"

"Yes," Rachel said.

Verne stood, fuming, his arms folded over his chest. He had been that way since I told him that Perry had been the child I saw in the Honda Accord.

"His name is Pavel. He was my brother."

We waited for her to say more.

"He was not a good man. I always knew that. He could be cruel. Kosovo makes you that way. But kidnapping a small child?" She shook her head.

"What happened?" Rachel asked.

But her eyes were on her husband. "Verne?"

He would not look at her.

"I lied to you, Verne. I lied to you about so much."

He tucked his hair behind his ears and blinked. I saw him wet his lip with his tongue. But he would still not look at her.

"I didn't come from a farm," she said. "My father died when I was three. My mother took any job she could. But we couldn't get by. We were too poor. We'd steal rinds out of the garbage. Pavel, he stayed on the streets, begging and stealing. I started working in sex clubs when I was fourteen. You can't imagine what it was like, but there is no way out of that life in Kosovo. I wanted to kill myself, I can't tell you how many times."

She raised her head toward her husband, but Verne still wouldn't meet her gaze. "Look at me," she said to him. When he didn't she leaned forward, "Verne?"

"This ain't about us," he said. "Just tell them what they need to know."

Katarina put her hands in her lap. "After a while, when you live like that, you don't think about escape. You don't think about pretty things or happiness or any of that. You become like an animal. You just hunt and survive. And I don't even know why you do that. But one day, Pavel came to me. He told me he knew a way out."

Katarina stopped. Rachel moved closer to her. I let her handle this. She had experience with interrogation and at the risk of sounding sexist, I thought that Katarina would have an easier time being drawn out by a fellow female.

"What was the way out?" Rachel asked.

"My brother said he could get us some money—and to America—if I could get pregnant."

I thought—check that: I hoped—I'd heard wrong. Verne whipped his head toward her.

This time Katarina was ready. She looked at him steadily.

"I don't understand," Verne said.

"I'm worth something as a prostitute. But a baby is worth more. If I get pregnant, someone can get us to America. They will pay us money."

The room went silent. I could still hear the children outside, but the sound suddenly seemed far away, a distant echo. I was the one who spoke next, reaching through the numb. "They pay you," I said, hearing the horror and disbelief in my own voice, "for the baby?"

"Yes."

Verne said, "Sweet Jesus."

"You can't understand."

"Oh, I understand," Verne said. "Did you go through with it?"

"Yes."

Verne turned away as if he'd been slapped. His hand reached up and took hold of the curtain. He stared out at his own children.

"In my country, if you have a baby, they put it in a horrible orphanage. American parents, they want so much to adopt. But it's hard. It takes a long time. More than a year sometimes. Meanwhile, the baby lives in squalor. The parents, they must pay government officials. The system is so corrupt."

"I see," Verne said. "You were doing it for the good of mankind?"

"No, I did it for me. For me only, okay?"

Verne winced. Rachel put her hand on Katarina's knee. "So you flew over here?"

"Yes. Pavel and I."

"Then what?"

"We stayed at a motel. I would visit a woman with white hair. She would check on me, make sure I was eating okay. She gave me money to buy food and supplies."

Rachel nodded, encouraging. "Where did you have the baby?"

"I don't know. A van with no windows came. The woman with white hair, she was there. She delivered the baby. I remember hearing it cry. Then they took it away. I don't even know if it was a boy or a girl. They drove us back to the motel. The woman with the white hair, she gave us our money."

Katarina shrugged.

It felt as if my circulation had stopped. I tried to think this through, get past the horror. I looked at Rachel and started to ask how, but she shook her head. Now was not the time to make deductions. Now was the time to gather information.

"I loved it here," Katarina said after some time had passed. "You think you have a wonderful country. But you really have no idea. I wanted so much to stay. But the money started running low. I looked for ways. I met a woman who told me about the Web site. You put your name and men write you. They wouldn't want a whore, she told me. So I made up a biography with a farm. When men asked, I gave them an e-mail address. I met Verne three months later."

Verne's face fell even farther. "You mean the whole time we were writing . . . ?"

"I was in America, yes."

He shook his head. "Was anything you told me the truth?"

"Everything that mattered."

Verne made a scoffing sound.

"What about Pavel?" Rachel asked, trying to get us back on topic. "Where did he go?"

"I don't know. He went back home sometimes, I know. He would recruit other girls to bring over. For the finder's fee. Time to time, he would contact me. If he needed a few dollars, I'd give it to him. It was really no big deal. Until yesterday."

Katarina looked up at Verne. "The children, they will be hungry."

"They can wait."

"What happened yesterday?" Rachel asked.

"Pavel called late in the afternoon. He says he needs to see me right away. I don't like that. I ask him what he wants. He says he'll tell me when he gets here, not to worry. I don't know what to say."

"How about no?" Verne snapped.

"I couldn't say no."

"Why not?"

She didn't answer.

"Oh, I see. You were afraid he'd tell me the truth. Isn't that it?"

"I don't know."

"What the hell's that supposed to mean?"

"Yes, I was terrified he'd tell you the truth." Again she looked up at her husband. "And I prayed he would."

Rachel tried to get us back on course. "What happened when your brother got here?"

She started welling up.

"Katarina?"

"He said he needed to take Perry with him."

Verne's eyes widened.

Katarina's chest started hitching, as if it was hard to get air. "I said to him no. I said I wouldn't let him touch my children. He threatened me. He said he'd tell Verne everything. I said I didn't care. I wasn't going to let him take Perry. Then he punched me in the stomach. I fell down. He promised me he'd bring Perry back in a few hours. He promised me no one would get hurt unless I said something. If I called Verne or the police, he'd kill Perry."

Verne's hands were balled into tight fists. His face was scarlet.

"I tried to stop him. I tried to stand up, but Pavel pushed me back down. And then"— her voice caught—"then he drove away. With Perry. The next six hours were the longest of my life." She sneaked a guilty glance in my direction. I knew what she was thinking. She had experienced this terror for six hours. I'd been living with it for a year and half.

"I didn't know what to do. My brother is a bad man. I know that. But I couldn't believe he'd ever hurt my children. He was their uncle."

I thought about Stacy then, my sister, my words of sibling defense echoing in hers.

"For hours, I stayed by the window. I couldn't stand it. Finally, at midnight, I called his cell phone. He told me he was on his way back. Perry was fine, he said. Nothing had happened. He tried to sound light, but there was something in his voice. I asked him where he was. He told me he was on Route Eighty near Paterson. I couldn't just sit in the house and wait. I told him I'd meet him halfway. I packed Verne Junior and we went. When we got to the gas station by the Sparta exit. . . ." She looked at Verne. "He was fine. Perry. I felt such relief, you can't imagine."

Verne was tugging on his bottom lip with his thumb and index finger. He looked away again.

"Before I left, Pavel grabbed my arm hard. He pulled me close to him. I could see how scared he was. He said no matter what, never tell anybody about what happened. That if they found out about me—if they knew he had a sister—they would kill us all."

"Who is they?" Rachel asked.

"I don't know. Whoever he was working for. The people who bought the babies, I think. He said they were crazy."

"What did you do then?"

Katarina opened her mouth, closed it, tried again. "I went to the supermarket," she said with a sound that might have even been a laugh. "I bought the kids juice boxes. I let them drink while we shopped. I just wanted to do something normal. To, I don't know, to put it all behind me."

Katarina looked up at Verne then. I followed her gaze. I again studied this man with the long hair and the bad teeth. After a moment, he turned to her.

"It's all right," Verne said in the gentlest voice I'd ever heard. "You were scared. You've been scared your whole life."

Katarina started sobbing.

"I don't want you to be scared anymore, okay?"

He moved toward her. He took her in his arms. She settled enough to say, "He said they'd come after us. The whole family."

"Then I'll protect us," Verne said simply. He looked at me over her shoulder. "They took my kid. They threatened my family. You hear what I'm saying?"

I nodded.

"I'm in this now. I'm with you till it's over."

Rachel sat back. I saw her grimace. Her eyes closed. I didn't know how much longer she could go. I moved toward her. She held up her palm. "Katarina, we need you to help us here. Where was your brother staying?"

"I don't know."

"Think. Do you have any of his possessions, something that can lead us to who he worked for?"

She let go of her husband. Verne stroked her hair with a blend of tenderness and strength I envied. I turned to Rachel. I wondered if I had the courage to do the same.

"Pavel just arrived from Kosovo," Katarina said. "And he would not come here empty handed."

Rachel nodded. "You think he brought a pregnant woman with him?"

"He always did before."

"Do you know where she's staying?"

"The women always stay at the same place—the same place I stayed. It's in Union City." Katarina looked up. "You'll want this woman to help you, right?"

"Yes."

"Then I'll have to go with you. She most likely won't speak English."

I looked at Verne. He nodded. "I'll watch the kids."

No one moved for several moments. We needed to gather our strength, adjust as if we'd entered a no-gravity zone. I used the time to step outside and call Zia. She answered on the first ring and started right in.

"The cops might be listening in, so let's not stay on the line too long," Zia said.

"Okay."

"Our friend Detective Regan came to my house. He told me that he thought you used my car to leave the hospital. I called Lenny. Lenny told me to neither confirm nor deny any allegation. You can probably guess the rest."

"Thanks."

"You being careful?"

"Always."

"Sure. By the way, the cops aren't stupid. They figure that if you used one friend's car, maybe they would look for another."

I got her meaning—don't use Lenny's car.

"Better hang up now," she said. "Love you."

The phone went dead. I moved back inside. Verne had unlocked his gun cabinet using a key. He was checking weapons. On the other side of the room, he had a safe with ammunition. It opened by combination. I looked over his shoulder. Verne wiggled his eyebrows at me. He had enough firepower to overthrow a European country.

I told them about my conversation with Zia. Verne did not hesitate. He slapped my back and said, "I have just the vehicle for you."

Ten minutes later, Katarina, Rachel, and I drove off in a white Camaro.

chapter 38

We found the pregnant girl right away.

Before we vroomed off in Verne's ride, Rachel jumped in the shower to rinse off the blood and grime. I quickly changed her bandage. Katarina loaned her a summer dress with a flower print, the kind that fits loose but clings just right. Rachel's hair was wet and kinky, still dripping when we reached the car. Forget the bruises and swelling—I am not sure that I ever saw a more beautiful woman in my life.

We started driving. Katarina insisted on taking the fold-down seat in the back. That left Rachel and me in the front. For a few minutes, nobody spoke. We were, I think, decompressing.

"What Verne said," Rachel began. "About

getting the secrets out of the way and wiping the slate clean."

I kept driving.

"I didn't kill my husband, Marc."

She didn't seem to care that Katarina was in the car. Neither did I. "The official word is that it was an accident," I said.

"The official word is a lie." She let out a long breath. She needed time to gather herself. I gave it to her.

"It was Jerry's second marriage. He had two kids from his first. His son, Derrick, has cerebral palsy. The expenses are ridiculous. Jerry was never good with finances or anything like that, but he did his best there. He even set up a large life-insurance policy in case something happened to him."

In my peripheral vision, I could see her hands. They didn't move or tighten into fists. They just sat primly in her lap.

"Our marriage fell apart. There were a lot of reasons. I mentioned some before. I really didn't love him. I think he sensed that. But most of all, Jerry was a manic depressive. When he stopped taking his medication, it got worse. So I finally filed for divorce."

I peeked over at her. She was biting her lip and blinking.

"On the day they served him papers, Jerry shot himself in the head. I was the one who found him slumped over our kitchen table. There was an envelope with my name on it. I recognized Jerry's handwriting right away. I opened it up. There was just a single sheet of paper with one word written on it. 'Bitch.' "

Katarina put a comforting hand on Rachel's shoulder. I concentrated hard on the road.

"I think Jerry did it like that on purpose," she said, "because he knew what I'd have to do."

"What was that?" I asked

"A suicide would mean that the life insurance wouldn't pay. Derrick would be financially devastated. I couldn't let that happen. I called one of my old bosses, a friend of Jerry's named Joseph Pistillo. He's a big deal in the FBI. He brought down a few of his men, and we made it look like an accident. The official line was, I mistook him for a burglar. The local cops and the insurance company were both pressured into signing off on it." She shrugged.

"So why did you leave the bureau?" I asked.

"Because the rank-and-file never bought it. They all thought that I must be sleeping with someone powerful. Pistillo couldn't protect me. It would look bad. I couldn't defend myself, for that matter. I tried to tough it out, but the FBI is not a place for the unwanted."

Her head dropped back against the pad. She looked out the passenger window. I didn't know what to make of the story. I didn't know what to make of any of this yet. I wished that I could say something comforting. I couldn't. I just kept driving until we mercifully arrived at the motel in Union City.

Katarina approached the check-in desk, pretending to speak only Serbian, gesturing like mad, until the clerk, figuring that it was the only way to settle her down, told her the room number of the only other person on the premises who seemed to speak that language. We were in business.

The pregnant girl's room was more a low-end efficiency unit than something you'd find in a normal highway motel. I refer to her as a pregnant "girl" because Tatiana—that was what she said her name was—claimed to be sixteen. I suspected that she was younger. Tatiana had the sunken eyes of a child who'd just stepped out of a war newsreel, which in this situation, may have literally been the case.

I stayed back, almost out of the room. So did Rachel. Tatiana did not speak English. We let Katarina handle it. The two of them talked for about ten minutes. After that, there was a brief silence. Tatiana sighed, opened the drawer under the phone, and gave Katarina a piece of paper. Katarina kissed her cheek and then came over to us.

"She's scared," Katarina said. "She only knew Pavel. He left her yesterday and said not to leave the room under any circumstances."

I glanced over at Tatiana. I tried to give her a reassuring smile. It fell, I'm certain, way short.

"What did she say?" Rachel asked.

"She doesn't know anything, of course. Like me. She only knows that her baby will find a good home."

"What was that piece of paper she gave you?"

Katarina lifted the slip of paper into view. "It's a phone number. If there is an emergency, she's supposed to call and dial in four nines."

"A beeper," I said.

"Yes, I believe so."

I looked at Rachel. "Can we trace it?"

"I doubt it will lead anywhere. It's easy to get beepers using a phony name."

"So let's call it," I said. I turned to Katarina. "Has Tatiana met anyone else besides your brother?"

"No."

"Then you make the call," I said to her. "You say you're Tatiana. You tell whoever answers that you're bleeding or in pain or something."

"Whoa," Rachel said. "Slow down a second."

"We need to get someone here," I said.

"And then what?"

"What do you mean, then what? You interrogate them. Isn't that what you do, Rachel?"

"I'm not a fed anymore. And even if I was, we can't just bulldoze them over like that. Pretend you're one of them for a second. You show up and I confront you. What would you do if you were involved in something like this?"

"Cut a deal."

"Maybe. Or maybe you'd just clam up and ask for a lawyer. Then where would we be?"

I thought about that. "If the person asks for a lawyer," I said, "you leave them alone with me."

Rachel stared at me. "Are you serious?"

"We're talking about my daughter's life."

"We're talking about a lot of children now, Marc. These people buy babies. We need to put them out of business."

"So what are you suggesting?"

"We page them. Like you said. But Tatiana will have to do the talking. She'll have to say whatever to get them here. They'll examine her. We check their license plate. We follow them when they leave. We find out who they are."

"I don't understand," I said. "Why can't Katarina make the call?"

"Because whoever comes will want to examine the person they talked to on the phone. Katarina and Tatiana don't sound alike. They'll know what we're up to."

"But why do we need to go through all that? We'll have them here. Why risk following them home?"

Rachel closed her eyes, then opened them again. "Marc, think. If they find out we're on to them, how will they react?"

I stopped.

"And I want to be clear about something else. This isn't about just Tara anymore. We need to bring these guys down."

"And if we just jump them here," I said, seeing her true point now, "they'll be fore-warned."

"That's right."

I wasn't sure how much I cared about that. Tara was my priority. If the FBI or cops want to build a legal case against these people, I was all for it. But that sat way off my personal radar.

Katarina talked to Tatiana about our plan. I could see it wasn't taking. The young girl was petrified. She kept shaking her head no. Time passed—time we really didn't have. I snapped and decided to do some-thing fairly stupid. I picked up the phone, dialed the beeper number, and pressed the nine button four times. Tatiana went still.

"You'll do it," I said.

Katarina translated.

No one spoke for the next two minutes. We all just stared at Tatiana. When the phone rang, I did not like what I saw in the young girl's eyes. Katarina said something, her tone urgent. Tatiana shook her head and crossed her arms. The phone rang a third time. Then a fourth.

I took out my gun.

Rachel said, "Marc."

I kept the gun at my side. "Does she know we're talking about my daughter's life?"

Katarina burst off something in Serbian. I looked Tatiana hard in the eyes. There was no reaction. I raised the gun and fired. The lamp exploded, the sound reverberating too loudly in the room. Everyone jumped. Another stupid move. I knew that. I just wasn't sure I cared.

"Marc!"

Rachel put her hand on my arm. I shook it off. I looked at Katarina. "Tell her if the caller hangs up . . ."

I never finished the thought. Katarina started talking quickly. I gripped the gun, but it was back at my side now. Tatiana still had her eyes on me. Sweat popped up on my forehead. I felt my body shake. As Tatiana watched me, something in her face began to soften.

"Please," I said.

On the sixth ring Tatiana snatched up the receiver and started talking.

I glanced over at Katarina. She listened to the conversation and then she nodded at me. I moved back to the other side of the room. I still had the gun in my hand. Rachel stared at me. But I stared back.

Rachel blinked first.

We parked the Camaro in a restaurant lot next door and waited.

There was not a lot of chitchat. The three of us looked everywhere but at each other, as if we were all strangers on an elevator. I wasn't sure what to say. I wasn't sure what I felt. I had fired a gun and come pretty close to threatening a teenage girl. Worse, I don't think I cared very much. The repercussions, if there were any, seemed far away, storm clouds that might gather and then again might disperse.

I flipped on the radio and dialed into the local news station. I half expected someone to say, "We interrupt this program with this special bulletin," and then announce our names and give out descriptions and maybe warn that we were armed and dangerous. But there were no stories on a shooting in Kasselton or a police search for us.

Rachel and I were still in the front while Katarina lay across the fold-down seat in the back. Rachel had her Palm Pilot out. The stylus was in her hand, poised to tap. I debated calling Lenny, but I remembered Zia's warning. They'd be listening in. I had nothing much to report anyway—just that I had threatened a pregnant sixteen-year-old girl with an illegal handgun taken off the corpse of a man who'd been murdered in my backyard. Lenny the Lawyer would certainly not relish the details.

"Do you think she'll cooperate?" I said.

Rachel shrugged.

Tatiana had promised that she was now with us. I didn't know if we could believe her or not. To be on the safe side, I unplugged her phone and took the cord with me. I searched the room for papers and writing material, so she couldn't sneak her visitor a note. I found nothing. Rachel also put her cell phone on the window ledge to be used as a listening device. Katarina had the phone to her ear now. Again she would translate.

Half an hour later, a gold-toned Lexus SC 430 roared into the lot. I whistled low. A colleague at the hospital had just bought the same car. It put him back sixty grand. The woman who emerged sported a short, spiky shock of white hair. She wore a too-tight, hair-matching white shirt and, keeping with the theme, white pants so tight they seemed to be hovering below skin level. Her arms were toned and tan. The woman had that look. You know the one. She brought on memories of the hot mother strutting around the tennis club.

Rachel and I both turned to Katarina. Katarina nodded solemnly. "That's her. That's the woman who delivered my baby."

I saw Rachel begin working her Palm Pilot. "What are you doing?" I asked.

"Putting in the license plate and make. We should know who the car is registered to in a matter of minutes."

"How do you do that?"

"It's not hard," Rachel said. "Every law enforcement officer makes connections. And if you don't, you pay off someone at the DMV. Five hundred bucks usually."

"Are you online or something?"

She nodded. "Wireless modem. A friend

of mine named Harold Fisher, he's a tech geek who works freelance. He didn't like how the feds pushed me out."

"So he helps you now?"

"Yes."

The white-haired woman leaned back in and pulled out what might have been a medical bag. She threw on a pair of designer sunglasses and hurried toward Tatiana's room. The woman knocked, the door opened, Tatiana let her in.

I turned around in my seat and watched Katarina. She had the phone on mute. "Tatiana is telling her that she feels better now. The woman is annoyed she called for nothing." She paused.

"Have you heard a name yet?"

Katarina shook her head. "The woman is going to examine her."

Rachel stared at her tiny Palm Pilot screen as if it were a magic eight ball. "Bang."

"What?"

"Denise Vanech, Forty-seven Riverview Avenue, Ridgewood, New Jersey. Forty-six years of age. No outstanding parking violations."

"You got it that fast?"

She shrugged. "All Harold has to do is type the license plate. He's going to see what he can dig up on her." Her stylus started up again. "Meanwhile I'm going to plug the name into Google."

"The search engine?"

"Yup. You'd be surprised what you can find."

I knew about that, actually. I once put my own name in. I don't remember why. Zia and I were drunk and did it for fun. She calls it "ego surfing."

"Not much speaking now." Katarina's face was a mask of concentration. "Maybe she's examining her?"

I looked over at Rachel. "Two hits on Google," she said. "The first is a Web site for the Bergen County planning board. She requested a variance to subdivide her lot. It was rejected. The second, however, is more interesting. It's an alumni site. It lists past graduates that they're trying to locate."

"What school?" I asked.

"University of Philadelphia Family Nurse and Midwifery."

That fit.

Katarina said, "They're done."

"Fast," I said.

"Very."

Katarina listened some more. "The woman is telling Tatiana to take care of herself. That she should eat better, for the baby. That she should call if she feels any further discomfort."

I turned to Rachel. "Sounds more pleasant than when she arrived."

Rachel nodded. The woman we assumed was Denise Vanech came out. She walked with her head high, her rear end twitching in that cocky way. The stretched white shirt was ribbed and, I couldn't help but notice, rather see-through. She got in her car and took off.

I started up the Camaro, the engine roaring like a lifetime smoker with a hacking cough. I followed at a safe distance. I wasn't too worried about losing her. We knew where she lived now.

"I still don't understand," I said to Rachel. "How do they get away with buying babies?"

"They find desperate women. They lure them here with promises of money and a stable, comfortable home for their child."

"But in order to adopt," I said, "there's a whole procedure you have to go through.

It's a pain in the ass. I know some children overseas—physically deformed children—people tried to bring over. You can't believe the paperwork. It's impossible."

"I don't have the answer to that, Marc."

Denise Vanech veered onto the New Jersey Turnpike north. That would be the way back to Ridgewood. I let the Camaro drop back another twenty, thirty feet. The right blinker came on, and the Lexus turned off at the Vince Lombardi rest stop. Denise Vanech parked and headed inside. I pulled the car to the side of the ramp and looked at Rachel. She was biting her lip.

"Could be she's using the bathroom," I said.

"She washed up after examining Tatiana. Why didn't she go then?"

"Maybe she's hungry?"

"Does she look like she eats much Burger King to you, Marc?"

"So what do we do?"

There was little hesitation. Rachel gripped the door handle. "Drop me off by the door."

Denise Vanech was pretty sure that Tatiana was faking.

The girl had claimed to be hemorrhaging.

Denise checked the sheets. They hadn't been changed, yet there was no blood on them. The tiles on the bathroom floor were clean. The toilet seat was clean. There was no blood anywhere.

That alone, of course, wouldn't mean all that much. There was a chance the girl had cleaned up. But there were other things. The gynecological examination showed no signs of distress. Nothing. Not the slightest red tint. Her vaginal hairs, too, had no traces of blood. Denise checked the shower when she finished up. Dry as bone. The girl had called less than an hour before. She claimed to be bleeding heavily.

It didn't add up.

Lastly, the girl's demeanor was wrong. The girls are always scared. That goes without saying. Denise had moved out of Yugoslavia when she was nine, during Tito's reign of relative peace, and she knew what a hellhole it was. To this girl, from where she had come, the United States must seem like Mars. But her fear had a different quality to it. Usually the girls stare at Denise as if she were some kind of parent or savior, looking up to her with a mix of trepidation and hope. But this girl averted her gaze. She fidgeted too much. And there was something else. Tatiana had been brought in by Pavel. He was usually good about watching them. But he hadn't been there. Denise was about to ask about that, but she decided to wait and play it out. If nothing was wrong, the girl would certainly raise Pavel's name.

She hadn't.

Yes, something was definitely wrong.

Denise did not want to raise suspicion. She finished the exam and hurried out. Behind her sunglasses, she checked for possible surveillance vans. There were none. She looked for obvious unmarked police cars. Again nothing. Of course, she was no expert. Though she had been working with Steven Bacard for nearly a decade, there had never been any complications. Perhaps that was why she'd let her guard down.

As soon as she got back into her car, Denise reached for her cell phone. She wanted to call Bacard. But no. If they were somehow on to them, they'd be able to trace that back. Denise debated using a pay phone at the nearest gas station. But they'd be expecting that too. When she saw the sign for the rest stop, she remembered that they had a huge bank of pay phones. She could call from there. If she moved fast enough, they wouldn't see her or know what phone she used.

But was that safe either?

She quickly sorted through the possibilities. Suppose she was indeed being followed. Driving to Bacard's office would definitely be the wrong move. She could wait and call him when she got home. But they might have a tap on her phone. This—calling from the large bank of pay phones—seemed the least risky.

Denise grabbed a napkin and used it to keep her fingerprints off the receiver. She was careful not to wipe it off. There were probably dozens of fingerprints already on it. Why make their job any easier?

Steven Bacard picked up. "Hello?"

The obvious strain in his voice made her heart sink. "Where is Pavel?" she asked.

"Denise?"

"Yes."

"Why are you asking?"

"I just visited his girl. Something isn't right."

"Oh God," he moaned. "What happened?"

"The girl called the emergency number.

She said she was hemorrhaging, but I think she was lying."

There was silence.

"Steve?"

"Go home. Don't talk to anyone."

"Okay." Denise saw the white Camaro pull up. She frowned. Hadn't she seen it before?

"Are there any records in your house?" Bacard asked.

"No, of course not."

"You're sure?"

"Positive."

"Okay, good."

A woman was getting out of the Camaro. Even from this distance, Denise could see the bandage on the woman's ear.

"Go home," Bacard said.

Before the woman could turn around, Denise hung up the phone and slipped into the bathroom.

Steven Bacard had loved the old *Batman* TV show as a kid. Every episode, he remembered, started out pretty much the same way. A crime would be committed. They would flash to Commissioner Gordon and Chief O'Hara. The two law-enforcement buffoons would be grim faced. They would discuss the situation and realize that there was only one way out. Commissioner Gordon would then pick up the red Batphone. Batman would answer, promise to save the day, turn to Robin and say, "To the Batpoles!"

He stared at the phone with that creepy feeling in the pit of his stomach. This was no hero he was calling. Just the opposite, in fact. But in the end, survival was what mattered. Pretty words and justification were great during times of peace. In times of war, in times of life and death, it was simpler: Us or Them. He picked up the phone and dialed the number.

Lydia answered sweetly. "Hello, Steven."

"I need you again."

"Bad?"

"Very."

"We're on our way," she said.

chapter 39

"When I got in there," Rachel said, "she was in the bathroom. But I have a feeling she made a call first."

"Why?"

"There was a line in the bathroom. She was only three people ahead of me. She should have been more."

"Any way of figuring out who she called?"

"Not in the near future, no. Every phone in that place is taken. Even if I had full FBI access, it would take some time."

"So we keep following."

"Yes." She turned behind her. "Do you have an atlas in the car?"

Katarina smiled. "Many. Verne likes maps. World, country, state?"

"State."

She dug into the pocket behind my seat

and handed Rachel the atlas. Rachel uncapped a pen and started marking it up.

"What are you doing?" I asked.

"I'm not sure."

The cell phone rang. I picked it up.

"You guys all right?"

"Yeah, Verne, we're fine."

"Got my sister to watch the kids for me.
I'm in the pickup heading east. What's your
ten-forty?"

I told him we were heading to Ridgewood. He knew the town.

"I'm about twenty minutes away," he
said. "I'll meet you at the Ridgewood Coffee
Company on Wilsey Square."

"We may be at this midwife's house," I
said.

"I'll wait."

"Okay."

"Hey, Marc," Verne said, "not to get sen-
timental or anything, but if somebody needs
shooting—"

"I'll let you know."

The Lexus turned off at Linwood Avenue.
We dropped farther back. Rachel kept her
head down, alternating between the stylus
on the Palm Pilot and the marker on the at-

las. We hit the suburbs. Denise Vanech turned left on Waltherly Road.

"She's definitely heading home," Rachel said. "Let her go. We need to think this through."

I couldn't believe what she was suggesting. "What do you mean, think this through? We need to approach her."

"Not yet. I'm working on something."

"What?"

"Just give me a few minutes."

I slowed my speed and turned down Van Dien, right near Valley Hospital. I looked back at Katarina. She gave me a small smile. Rachel kept working at whatever. I checked the dashboard clock. Time to meet Verne. I took North Maple to Ridgewood Avenue. A parking spot opened in front of a store named Duxiana. I grabbed it. Verne's pickup truck was parked across the street. It had mag wheels and two bumper stickers, one reading, CHARLTON HESTON FOR PRESIDENT and the other: DO I LOOK LIKE A HEMORRHOID? THEN GET OFF MY ASS.

Ridgewood's town center was a blend of turn-of-the-century picture-postcard splendor and modern-day extravagant food-court mall. Most of the old mom-n-pop shops were gone now. Sure, the independent bookstore still thrived. There was an upscale mattress store, a cute place that sold sixties paraphernalia, a smattering of boutiques, beauty parlors, and jewelry stores. And, yes, a few of the chains—Gap, Williams-Sonoma, the prerequisite Starbucks—had gobbled up space. But more than anything, the town center had become a veritable smorgasbord, a potpourri of eateries for too many tastes and budgets. Name a country, they had a bistro here. Throw a stone, even pathetically, in any direction, you would hit three such eateries.

Rachel took the atlas and Palm Pilot with her. She worked as we walked. Verne was already inside the coffee shop, chatting up the burly guy behind the counter. Verne wore a Deere baseball cap with a T-shirt that read: MOOSEHEAD: A GREAT BEER AND A NEW EXPERIENCE FOR A MOOSE.

We grabbed a table.

"So what's the deal?" Verne said.

I let Katarina fill him in. I was watching Rachel. Every time I started to speak, she held up a finger to silence me. I told Verne that he should take Katarina home. We didn't need their help anymore. They should be with their children. Verne was reluctant.

The time was sneaking up on 10:00 A.M. I wasn't really tired. Lack of sleep—even for reasons far less adrenaline generating than this—does not bother me. I credit my medical residency and the many nights on call for that.

"Bang," Rachel said again.

"What?"

With her eyes still on the Palm Pilot, Rachel put out her hand. "Let me use your phone."

"What is it?"

"Just give it to me, okay?"

I handed her the cell phone. She dialed and moved to the corner of the café. Katarina excused herself to use the bathroom. Verne poked me with his elbow and pointed at Rachel.

"You two in love?"

"It's complicated," I said.

"Only if you're a dumb-ass."

I may have shrugged.

"You either love her or you don't," Verne said. "The rest? That's for dumb-asses."

"Is that how you dealt with what you heard this morning?"

He thought about that. "What Kat said. What she did in the past. It don't matter much. There's a core. I've slept with that woman for eight years. I know the core."

"I don't know Rachel that well."

"Yeah, you do. Look at her." I did. And I felt something airy and light travel all the way through me. "She got beaten up. She got shot, for Chrissake." He paused. I wasn't looking, but I bet he shook his mane in disgust. "You let that go, you know what you are?"

"A dumb-ass."

"A *professional* dumb-ass. You give up your amateur status."

Rachel hung up the phone and hurried back over. Maybe it was something Verne said, but I could swear that I saw a bit of fire back in her eyes. In that dress, with her hair mussed, with the confident lick-the-world smile, I was transported back. It didn't last long. No more than a moment or two. But maybe it was enough.

"Bang?" I asked.

"Cannon-fire, Fourth-of-July bang." She starting tapping with the stylus again. "I just need to do one more thing. In the meantime, look at this atlas."

I pulled it over. Verne looked over my shoulder. He smelled like motor oil. There were all kinds of markings on the atlas—little stars, crosses, but the thickest line was a circuitous route. I recognized enough of it.

"That's the route the kidnappers took last night," I said. "When we were following them."

"Right."

"What's with all the stars and stuff?"

"Okay, first thing. Look at the actual route they took. Up north over the Tappan Zee. Then west. Then south. Then west again. Then back east and north."

"They were stalling," I said.

"Right. It's like we said. They were setting up that trap for us at your house. But think about it a second. Our theory is that someone from law enforcement warned them about the Q-Logger, right?"

"So?"

"So no one knew about the Q-Logger until you were at the hospital. That means, for at least part of the journey, they wouldn't have known I was tailing them."

I wasn't sure I followed, but I said, "Okay."

"Do you pay your phone bill online?" she asked.

The subject change threw me for a moment. "Yes," I said.

"So you get a statement, right? You click on the link, you sign in, you can see all your calls. It probably has a reverse directory link too—so you can click on the number and see who you called."

I nodded. It did.

"Well, I got Denise Vanech's last phone bill." She held up a hand. "Don't worry about how. Again it's fairly easy. Harold could probably do it by hacking, if he had more time, but having a connection or giving a bribe is easier. Now with the Internet billing, it's easier than ever."

"Harold sent you her bill online?"

"Yep. Anyway, Ms. Vanech makes a fair amount of calls. That's what took me so long. We've been sorting through them, finding the names, then the addresses."

"And a name popped out?"

"No, an address did. I wanted to see if she called anybody on the kidnapper's route."

Now I saw where she was going. "And I assume the answer is yes?"

"Better than yes. Remember when they stopped at the MetroVista office complex?"

"Sure."

"Over the past month, Denise Vanech placed six calls to the law office of a Steven Bacard." Rachel pointed to the star she'd drawn on the map. "At MetroVista."

"A lawyer?"

"Harold is going to see what he can dig up, but again I just used Google. The name Steven Bacard pops up frequently."

"In what context?"

Rachel smiled again. "His expertise is adoption."

Verne said, "Sweet mother of God."

I sat back and tried to digest it all. Warning lights flashed, but I wasn't sure what they meant. Katarina came back to the table. Verne told her what we'd found. We were getting close. I knew that. But I felt adrift. My cell phone—or should I say, Zia's—rang. I looked down at the Caller ID. It was Lenny. I debated not answering, remembering what Zia had said. But of course, Lenny would know about the possibility of a tap. He had been the one who warned Zia.

I hit the answer button.

"Let me talk first," Lenny said before I could even utter a hello. "For the record, if this is being taped, this conversation is between an attorney and his client. It is thus protected. Marc, don't tell me where you are. Don't tell me anything that would force me to lie. You understand?"

"Yes."

"Did your trip bear fruit?" he asked.

"Not the fruit we wanted. Not yet anyway. But we're getting very close."

"Any way I can help?"

"I don't think so." Then, "Wait." I remembered that Lenny had handled my sister's arrests. He had been her main legal advisor. "Did Stacy ever say anything to you about adoption?"

"I'm not following."

"Did she ever think about giving up a baby for adoption, or in any way mention adoption to you?"

"No. Is this somehow connected with the kidnapping?"

"Could be."

"I don't remember anything like that. Look, they might be taping us, so let me tell you why I called. They found a dead body at your house—a man shot twice in the head."

Lenny knew that I was already aware of this. I assumed that he was saying this for the benefit of whoever might be eavesdropping. "They haven't made an ID, but they did locate the murder weapon in the Christies' backyard."

I was not surprised. Rachel had figured that they'd plant the gun somewhere.

"The thing is, Marc, the murder weapon is your old gun, the one that's been missing since the shooting at your house. They already ran a ballistics test. You and Monica were shot with two different thirty-eights, remember?"

"Yes."

"Well, that gun—*your* gun—was one of the two used that morning."

I closed my eyes. Rachel mouthed a "what?" at me.

"I better go," Lenny said. "I'll look into Stacy and an adoption angle, if you want. See what I can dig up."

"Thanks."

"Stay safe."

He hung up. I turned to Rachel and told her about the gun discovery and the ballistics test. She leaned back and bit down on her lower lip, another familiar habit from our dating days. "So that means," she said, "that Pavel and the rest of these people are definitely linked to the first attack."

"You still had doubts?"

"A few hours ago, we thought it was a total hoax, remember? We thought that maybe these guys knew enough to fake like they had Tara, just to con some ransom money out of your father-in-law. But now we know different. These people were there that morning. They were part of the original abduction."

It made sense, but something about it still felt wrong. "Where do we go from here?" I asked.

"The logical step is to visit this lawyer, Steven Bacard," Rachel said. "The problem is, we don't know if he's the boss or just another employee. For all we know, Denise Vanech is the mastermind and he works for her. Or they both work for a third party. And if we go busting in there, Bacard is just going to clam up. He's a lawyer. He's too smart to talk to us."

"So what do you suggest?"

"I'm not sure," she said. "It might be time to call in the feds. Maybe they can raid his office."

I shook my head. "That'll take too long."

"We might be able to get them to move fast."

"Assuming they believe us—which is a big assumption—how fast?"

"I don't know, Marc."

I didn't like it. "Suppose Denise Vanech was suspicious back there. Suppose Tatiana gets scared and calls her again. Suppose there is indeed a leak. There are too many variables here, Rachel."

"So what do you think we should do?"

"A two-prong attack," I said, the words coming out without much thought. There was a problem. I suddenly had a solution. "You take Denise Vanech. I take Steven Bacard. We coordinate it so that we hit them at the same time."

"Marc, he's a lawyer. He's not going to open up to you."

I looked at her. She saw it. Verne sat up a little and made a small *woo-ee* noise.

"You're going to threaten him?" Rachel asked.

"We're talking about my child's life."

"And you're talking about taking the law into your own hands." Then she added, "Again."

"So?"

"You threatened a teenage girl with a gun."

"I was trying to intimidate, that's all. I would have never really hurt her."

"The law—"

"The law hasn't done squat to help my daughter," I said, trying not to shout. In the corner of my eye, I saw Verne nodding along with my outrage. "They're too busy wasting time on you."

That made her straighten up. "Me?"

"Lenny told me at the house. They think you did it. Without me. That you were obsessed with having me back or something."

"What?"

I rose from the table. "Look, I'm going to see this Bacard guy. I don't plan on hurting anyone, but if he knows something about my daughter, I'm going to find out what it is."

Verne raised his fist. "Right on."

I asked Verne if I could keep borrowing the Camaro. He reminded me that he was behind me all the way. I expected Rachel to argue some more. She didn't. Maybe she knew that I would not change my mind. Maybe she knew I was right. Or maybe—

perhaps most likely—she had been stunned to learn that her old colleagues had zeroed in on her as the sole serious suspect.

"I'll come with you," Rachel said.

"No." My voice left no wiggle room. I had no idea what I would do when I got there, but I knew that I was capable of plenty. "What I said before makes sense." I could hear my familiar surgeon-tone taking over. "I'll call you when I get to Bacard's office. We hit him and Denise Vanech at the same time."

I didn't wait for a response. I got back in the Camaro and started toward the Metro-Vista office complex.

chapter 40

Lydia checked her surroundings. She was a little more in the open than she liked to be, but that couldn't be helped. She had on the spiky blond wig—the one not unlike Steven Bacard's description of Denise Vanech. She knocked on the door of the efficiency.

The curtain next to the door moved. Lydia smiled. "Tatiana?"

No reply.

She had been warned that Tatiana spoke very little English. Lydia had debated how to play this. Time was critical. Everything and everyone needed to be shut down. When someone who dislikes blood as much as Bacard says that, you immediately understand the ramifications. Lydia and Heshy had split up. She had come down here. They would meet up afterward.

"It's okay, Tatiana," she said through the door. "I'm here to help."

There was no movement.

"I'm a friend of Pavel's," she tried. "You know Pavel?"

The curtain moved. A young woman's face appeared for a brief moment, gaunt and childlike. Lydia nodded at her. The woman still did not open the door. Lydia scanned her surroundings. Nobody looking, but she still felt too exposed. This had to end fast.

"Wait," Lydia said. Then, looking at the curtain, she reached into her purse. She pulled out a piece of paper and pen. She wrote something down, making sure that if someone was still at the window, they would see exactly what she was doing. She capped the pen and stepped close to the window. Lydia held the piece of paper up to the pane of glass so Tatiana could read it.

It was like drawing a scared cat out from under the sofa. Tatiana moved slowly. She came toward the window. Lydia stayed still, so as not to startle her. Tatiana leaned closer. Here, kitty, kitty. Lydia could see the girl's face now. She was squinting, trying to see what was on the piece of paper.

When Tatiana came close enough, Lydia pressed the barrel of the gun against the glass and aimed between the young girl's eyes. At the last second, Tatiana tried to veer away. Too little, too late. The bullet went clean through the glass and into Tatiana's right eye. Blood appeared. Lydia fired again, automatically tilting the gun downward. It caught the falling Tatiana in the top of the forehead. But the second bullet had been superfluous. The first shot, the one in the eye, had ripped into the brain and killed the young girl instantly.

Lydia hurried away. She risked a glance behind her. No one. When she reached the neighboring mall, she dumped the wig and the white coat. She found her car in a lot another half mile away.

I called Rachel when I arrived at Metro-Vista. She was parked down the street from Denise Vanech's house. We were both ready to go.

I'm not sure what I expected to happen here. I guess I figured that I would explode into Bacard's office, stick my gun in his face, and demand answers. What I hadn't foreseen was a regular, state-of-the-state office setup—that is, Steven Bacard had a well-appointed reception area. There were two people waiting—a married couple, by all appearances. The husband had his face stuck in a waiting-room-laminated *Sports Illustrated*. The wife looked to be in pain. She tried to smile at me, but it was as if the effort would wound her.

I realized how shoddy I must look. I was still in my hospital scrubs. I was unshaven. My eyes were undoubtedly red from lack of sleep. My hair, I imagined, was probably sticking up in a textbook case of bedhead.

The receptionist was behind one of those sliding glass windows I usually associate with a dental practice. The woman—a small nameplate read AGNES WEISS—smiled at me sweetly.

"May I help you?"

"I'm here to see Mr. Bacard."

"Do you have an appointment?" She kept the tone sweet, but there was a rhetorical twang there too. She already knew the answer.

"This is an emergency," I said.

"I see. Are you a client of ours, Mr. . . . ?"

"Doctor," I snapped back automatically. "Tell him Dr. Marc Seidman needs to see him immediately. Tell him it's an emergency."

The young couple was watching us now. The receptionist's sweet smile began to falter. "Mr. Bacard's schedule is very full today." She opened her appointment ledger. "Let me see when we have something available, okay?"

"Agnes, look at me."

She did.

I gave her my gravest, you-might-die-if-I-don't-operate-right-away expression. "Tell him Dr. Seidman is here. Tell him it's an emergency. Tell him if he doesn't see me now, I will go to the police."

The young couple exchanged a glance.

Agnes adjusted herself in the chair. "If you'll just have a seat—"

"Tell him."

"Sir, if you don't step back, I'll call security."

So I stepped back. I could always step forward again. Agnes did not pick up the phone. I moved to a nonthreatening distance. She slid the little window closed. The couple looked at me. The husband said, "She's covering for him."

The wife said, "Jack!"

Jack ignored her. "Bacard ran out of here half an hour ago. That receptionist keeps telling us he'll be right back."

I noticed a wall of photographs. Now I took a closer look. The same man was in all of them with a potpourri of politicos, quasi celebrities, gone-to-flab athletes. Steven Bacard, I assumed. I stared at the man's face—pudgy, weak chinned, country-club shiny.

I thanked the man named Jack and started for the door. Bacard's office was on the first floor, so I decided to wait by the entrance. This way, I could catch him unawares on neutral ground and before Agnes had a chance to warn him. Five minutes passed. Several suits came and went, all harried from their days of printer toner and paperweights, dragged down by briefcases the size of car trunks. I paced the corridor.

Another couple entered. I could tell right away by their tentative steps and shattered eyes that they, too, were heading for Bacard's office. I watched them and wondered what path they had taken here. I saw them getting married, holding hands, kissing freely, making love in the morning. I saw their careers begin to thrive. I saw them feel the pang and segue toward the initial attempts at conceiving, the wait-till-next-month shrug when the home tests were negative, the slowly blossoming worry. A year passes. Still nothing. Their friends are starting to have children now and talk about them incessantly. Their parents are wondering when they'll have grandkids. I see them visiting the doctor—"a specialist"—the endless probing for the woman, the humiliation of masturbating into a beaker for the man, the personal questions, the blood and urine samples. More years pass. Their friends drift away. Making love is now strictly about procreation. It is calculated. It is always tinged with sadness. He stops holding her hand. She rolls over at night unless it's the right time in her cycle. I see the drugs, the Pergonal, the ridiculously expensive in-vitro fertilization, the time off from work, the checking of calendars, the same home tests, the crushing disappointments.

And now they were here.

No, I didn't know if any of this was really the case. But somehow I suspected that I was close. How far, I wondered, would they go to end this pain? How much would they pay?

"Oh my God! Oh my God!"

I jerked my head toward the scream. A man banged through the door.

"Call nine-one-one!"

I ran toward him. "What is it?"

I heard another scream. I ran through the door and outside. Yet another scream, this one more high pitched. I turned to my right. Two women were running out of the lower-level parking garage. I sprinted down the ramp. I slipped past the gate where you pick up your parking ticket. Someone else was calling for help, begging people to call 911.

Up ahead, I saw a security guard shouting into a walkie-talkie of some sort. He broke into a full gallop too. I followed him. When we turned the corner, the security guard pulled up. There was a woman next to him. She had her hands on her cheeks and was screaming. I ran next to them and looked down.

The body was jammed between two cars. His eyes stared open at nothing. His face was still pudgy, weak chinned, country-club shiny. The blood flowed from the wound in his head. The world teetered again.

Steven Bacard, maybe my last hope, was dead.

chapter 41

Rachel rang the doorbell. Denise Vanech had one of those pretentious chimes that ring up and then down the scale. The sun was all the way up now. The sky was blue and clear. On the street, two women power-walked carrying tiny mauve dumbbells. They nodded at Rachel, never missing a step. Rachel nodded back.

The intercom sounded. "Yes?"

"Denise Vanech?"

"Who is this please?"

"My name is Rachel Mills. I used to work with the FBI."

"Did you say, used to?"

"Yes."

"What do you want?"

"We need to talk, Ms. Vanech."

"About what?"

Rachel sighed. "Could you please just open the door?"

"Not until I know what this is about."

"The young girl you just visited in Union City. It's about her. For starters."

"I'm sorry. I don't discuss my patients."

"I said, for starters."

"Why would a former FBI agent be interested in any of this anyway?"

"Would you prefer I call a current agent?"

"I don't care what you do, Ms. Mills. I have nothing else to say to you. If the FBI has questions, they can call my lawyer."

"I see," Rachel said. "And would your lawyer be Steven Bacard?"

There was a brief silence. Rachel glanced back at the car.

"Ms. Vanech?"

"I don't have to talk to you."

"No, that's true. I'll start going door-to-door maybe. Talk to your neighbors."

"And say what?"

"I'll ask them if they know anything about a baby-smuggling operation that runs out of this house."

The door opened quickly. Denise Vanech with her tan skin and white hair pushed her head through the door. "I'll sue you for libel."

"Slander," Rachel said.

"What?"

"Slander. Libel is for the printed word. Slander is for the spoken. You mean slander. But either way, you'd have to prove what I'm saying is untrue. And we both know better."

"You have no evidence I've done anything wrong."

"Sure I do."

"I was treating a woman who claimed to be ill. That's all."

Rachel pointed up the lawn. Katarina stepped out of the car. "And what about this former patient?"

Denise Vanech put a hand to her mouth.

"She'll testify that you paid her money for her baby."

"No, she won't. They'll arrest her."

"Oh sure, right, the FBI would much rather crack down on a poor Serbian woman than break up a baby-smuggling ring. That's rich."

When Denise Vanech paused, Rachel pushed open the door. "Mind if I come in?"

"You have it wrong," she said quietly.

"Cool." Rachel was inside now. "You can correct me on all my misgivings."

Denise Vanech seemed suddenly unsure what to do. With one more look at Katarina, she slowly closed the front door. Rachel was already heading into the den. It was white. Totally white. White sectional couches against a white carpet. White porcelain statues of naked women riding horses. White coffee table, white side tables, and two of those white ergonomic-looking chairs with no backs. Denise followed her in. Her white clothes blended into the background, camouflagelike, making it look like her head and arms were floating.

"What do you want?"

"I'm looking for a specific child."

Denise let her eyes wander toward the door. "Hers?"

She was talking about Katarina.

"No."

"It wouldn't matter. I don't know anything about placement."

"You're a midwife, correct?"

She folded the smooth, muscular arms under her bosom. "I'm not answering any of your questions."

"See, Denise, I know most of it. I just

need you to fill in a few blanks." Rachel sat on the vinyl couch. Denise Vanech didn't move. "You have people in a foreign country. Maybe more than one country, I don't know. But I know about Serbia. So let's start there. You have people there who recruit girls. The girls come over pregnant, but they don't mention that at customs. You deliver the baby. Maybe here, maybe you have another spot, I don't know."

"You don't know a lot."

Rachel smiled. "I know enough."

Denise put her hands on her hips now. Her poses all seemed unnatural, as if she practiced them in front of a mirror.

"Anyway, the women have the babies. You pay them. You turn the baby over to Steven Bacard. He works for desperate couples who might be willing to bend the rules. They adopt the child."

"That's a nice story."

"Are you saying it's fiction?"

Denise grinned. "Total fiction."

"Cool, fine." She took out her cell phone. "Then let me call the feds. I'll introduce them to Katarina. They can go down to Union City and grill Tatiana. They can start going through your phone records, your finances—"

Denise started waving her hands. "Okay, okay, tell me what you want. I mean, you said you're not an FBI agent anymore. So what do you want with me?"

"I want to know how it works."

"You trying to cut yourself in?"

"No."

Denise waited a beat. "You said before that you're looking for a specific kid."

"Yes."

"You're working for someone, then?"

Rachel shook her head. "Look, Denise, you don't have a lot of options here. You either tell me the truth or you do serious jail time."

"And if I do tell you what I know?"

"Then I'll leave you out of it," Rachel said. It was a lie. But it was an easy one. This woman was involved in baby selling. There was no way Rachel was just going to let that go.

Denise sat. The tan seemed to be leaving her face. She looked suddenly older. The lines around her mouth and eyes deepened. "It's not what you think," she began.

Rachel waited.

"We aren't hurting anyone. The truth is, we're helping."

Denise Vanech picked up her purse—white, of course—and dug out a cigarette. She offered one to Rachel. Rachel shook her off.

"Do you know anything about orphanages in poor countries?" Denise asked.

"Just what I see on PBS documentaries."

Denise lit the cigarette and drew a deep breath. "They are beyond awful. They may house forty babies to one nurse. The nurse is uneducated. The job is often a political favor. Some of the children are abused. Many are born drug dependent. The medical care—"

"I get the picture," Rachel said. "It's bad."

"Yes."

"And?"

"And we've found a way to save some of these children."

Rachel sat back and crossed her legs. She could see where this was going. "You pay pregnant women to fly over and sell you their babies?"

"That's hyperbole," she said.

Rachel shrugged. "How would you put it?"

"Put yourself in their position. You are a poor woman—and I mean poor—maybe a prostitute or somehow involved in white slavery. You are dirt. You have nothing. Some man knocks you up. You can abort or, if your religion forbids that, you can stick the kid in a godforsaken orphanage."

"Or," Rachel added, "if they're lucky, they end up with you?"

"Yes. We will give them adequate medical care. We will offer financial restitution. And most importantly, we will make sure that their baby is placed in a loving home with caring, financially stable parents."

"Financially stable," Rachel repeated. "As in wealthy?"

"The service is expensive," she admitted. "But let me ask you something now. Take your friend out there. Katarina you said her name was?"

Rachel kept still.

"What would her life be like right now if we hadn't brought her here? What would her child's life be like?"

"I don't know. I don't know what you did with her child."

Denise smiled. "Fine, be argumentative. But you know what I mean. Do you think the baby would be better off with a dirt-poor prostitute in a war-torn hellhole—or with a caring family here in the United States?"

"I see," Rachel said, trying not to squirm. "So you're sort of like the world's most wonderful social worker. This is charity work you're doing?"

Denise chuckled. "Look around you. I have expensive taste. I live in a ritzy neighborhood. I have a kid in college. I like to vacation in Europe. We have a house in the Hamptons. I do this because it's incredibly profitable. But so what? Who cares about my motives? My motives don't change the conditions in those orphanages."

"I still don't understand," Rachel said. "The women sell you their babies."

"They give us their babies," she corrected. "In return, we offer financial restitution—"

"Yeah, yeah, whatever. You get the baby. They get money. But then what? There has to be paperwork on the child, otherwise the government would step in. They wouldn't just let Bacard keep running adoptions like this."

"True."

"So how do you work it?"

She smiled. "You plan on busting me, don't you?"

"I don't know what I'm going to do."

She was still smiling. "You'll remember I cooperated, right?"

"Yes."

Denise Vanech pressed her palms together and closed her eyes. It looked as if she might be praying. "We hire American mothers."

Rachel made a face. "Excuse me?"

"For example, let's say Tatiana is about to have the baby. We might hire you, Rachel, to pose as the mother. You'd go to vital records at your town hall. You'd tell them you're pregnant and going to have a home birth, so there won't be a hospital record. They give you forms to fill out. They never check to see if you're really pregnant. How would they? It's not like they can give you a gynecological exam."

Rachel sat back. "Jesus."

"It's pretty simple when you think about it. There is no record that Tatiana is going to have a baby. There is a record that you are. I deliver the baby. I sign as the attending witness to your child being born. You become the mother. Bacard has you fill in the paperwork for adoption. . . ." She shrugged.

"So the adopting parents never learn the truth?"

"No, but they don't look too hard either. They're desperate. They don't want to know."

Rachel suddenly felt drained.

"And before you turn us in," Denise went on, "consider something else. We've been doing this for almost ten years now. That means there are children who've been happily placed with families that long. Dozens. All of those adoptions will be considered null and void. The birth mothers can come over here and demand their children back. Or take a payoff. You'd be ripping apart a lot of lives."

Rachel shook her head. It was too much to consider right now. Another time. She was getting off track. Had to keep her eye on the prize. She turned and squared her shoulders. She looked Denise deep in the eye.

"So how does Tara Seidman fit into all this?"

"Who?"

"Tara Seidman."

Now it was Denise's turn to look confused. "Wait a second. Wasn't that the little girl kidnapped in Kasselton?"

Rachel's cell phone rang. She checked the Caller ID and saw it was Marc. She was just about to press the answer button when a man stepped into view. Her breath stopped. Sensing something, Denise turned around. She jumped back at the sight.

It was the man from the park.

His hands were huge, making the gun he now pointed at Rachel look like a child's toy. He wiggled his fingers in her direction. "Give me the phone."

Rachel handed it to him, trying her best to avoid his touch. The man put the barrel of the gun against her head. "Now give me your gun."

Rachel reached into her handbag. He told her to lift it into view with two fingers. She complied. The phone rang for the fourth time.

The man hit the answer button and said, "Dr. Seidman?"

Even Rachel could hear the reply. "Who is this?"

"We're all at Denise Vanech's house now.

You will come here unarmed and alone. I will tell you all about your daughter then."

"Where's Rachel?"

"She's right here. You have thirty minutes. I will tell you what you need to know. You have a tendency to try to be cute in these situations. But not this time or your friend Ms. Mills dies first. Do you understand?"

"I understand."

The man hung up the phone. He looked down at Rachel. His eyes were brown with a gold center. They looked almost gentle, the eyes of a doe. Then the big man swung his gaze toward Denise Vanech. She flinched. A smile came to the man's lips.

Rachel saw what he was about to do.

She shouted, "No!" as the big man aimed the gun at Denise Vanech's chest and fired three shots. All three hit dead center. Denise's body went slack. She slid off the couch and onto the floor. Rachel started to stand, but now the gun was pointed at her.

"Stay put."

Rachel obeyed. Denise Vanech was clearly dead. Her eyes were open. Her blood streamed down, the color startlingly red against a sea of white.

chapter 42

Now what do I do?

I had been calling to tell Rachel about the shooting death of Steven Bacard. Now this man was holding her hostage. Okay, so what's my next step? I tried to think it through, to analyze the data carefully, but there was not enough time. The man on the phone had been right. I had been "cute" in the past. During the first ransom drop, I had let the police and FBI in on it. During the second, I'd enlisted the aid of an ex–federal agent. For a long time, I blamed the first drop-gone-wrong on my decision. Not anymore. I had played the odds both times, but now I think the game was fixed from the get-go. They had never intended to give me back my daughter. Not eighteen months ago. Not last night.

And not now.

Maybe I had been on a search for an answer that I knew all along. Verne had understood my quest with one caveat: "Long as a man ain't fooling himself." But maybe I had been. Even now, even as we were uncovering this baby-smuggling scam, I had allowed myself fresh hope. Perhaps my daughter was alive. Perhaps she had gotten ensnared in this adoption con. Would that be horrible? Yes. But the obvious alternative—that Tara is dead—was a hell of a lot worse.

I no longer knew what to believe.

I checked my watch. Twenty minutes had passed. I wondered about how to play it. First things first. I called Lenny on the private line at his office.

"A man named Steven Bacard was just murdered in East Rutherford," I said.

"Bacard the lawyer?"

"You know him?"

"I worked a case with him a few years ago," Lenny said. Then: "Oh damn."

"What?"

"You asked before about Stacy and an adoption. I didn't see a connection. But now that you say Bacard's name . . . Stacy asked me about him, what, three, four years ago."

"What about him?"

"I don't remember anymore. Something about being a mother."

"What does that mean?"

"I don't know. I really didn't pay that much attention. I just told her not to sign anything without showing it to me." Then Lenny asked, "How do you know he's been murdered?"

"I just saw his body."

"Whoa, don't say anything else. This line might not be secure."

"I need your help. Call the cops. They need to get Bacard's records. He ran an adoption scam. There's a possibility that he had something to do with Tara's kidnapping."

"How?"

"I don't have time to explain."

"Yeah, okay, I'll call Tickner and Regan. Regan's been searching for you pretty much nonstop, you know."

"I figured."

I hung up before he could ask more. I am not really sure what I expected them to find. I couldn't make myself believe that the answer to Tara's fate lay in some file cabinet in a law office. But maybe. And if something went wrong here—and there was certainly a decent chance of that happening—I wanted someone to be able to follow up.

I was in Ridgewood now. I did not believe for a second that the man on the phone was telling the truth. They were not in the trade-information business. They were here to clean house. Rachel and I knew too much. They were drawing me there so that they could kill us.

So what do I do?

There was very little time. If I stalled—if it took me much longer than a half an hour—the man on the phone would start getting antsy. That would be bad. I thought again about calling the police, but I remembered his warning about being "cute" and I still worried about a leak. I had a gun. I knew how to use it. I was a pretty good shot, but that was at a range. Shooting at people would, I assumed, be different. Or maybe not. I no longer had qualms about killing these people. I'm not sure I ever had.

A block away from Denise Vanech's house, I parked the car, grabbed the gun, and started down the street.

*   *   *

He called her Lydia. She called him Heshy.

The woman had arrived five minutes ago. She was petite and pretty, her baby-doll eyes wide with excitement. She stood in front of Denise Vanech's corpse and watched the blood still trickling out. Rachel sat still. Her hands had been bound behind her back with duct tape. The woman named Lydia turned to Rachel.

"That stain is going to be a bitch to get out."

Rachel stared at her. Lydia smiled.

"You don't think that's funny?"

"Inside," Rachel said. "Inside I'm cracking up."

"You visited a young girl named Tatiana today, yes?"

Rachel said nothing. The big man named Heshy began to pull down the shades.

"She's dead. Just thought you'd like to know." Lydia sat next to Rachel. "Do you remember the TV show *Family Laughs*?"

Rachel wondered how to play this. This Lydia was insane, no doubt about it. Tentatively she said, "Yes."

"Were you a fan?"

"The show was puerile nonsense."

Lydia threw back her head and laughed. "I played Trixie."

She smiled at Rachel. Rachel said, "You must be very proud."

"Oh I am. I am." Lydia stopped, tilted her face, moved it closer to Rachel's. "You know, of course, that you're going to die soon."

Rachel did not blink. "Then how about telling me what you did with Tara Seidman?"

"Oh please." Lydia stood. "I was an actress, remember? I was on television. So, what, is this the part of the show where we tell all so that the audience can catch up and your hero can sneak up on us? Sorry, sweetie." She turned to Heshy. "Gag her, Pooh Bear."

Heshy used the duct tape and wrapped it around Rachel's mouth and the back of her head. He moved back toward the window. Lydia bent close to Rachel's ear. Rachel could feel the woman's breath.

"I will tell you this," she whispered, "because it's funny." Lydia bent in a little closer. "I have no idea what happened to Tara Seidman."

*   *   *

Okay, I wasn't about to drive up and knock on the door.

Let's face it. They were out to kill us. My only chance was to surprise them. I didn't know the layout of the house, but I figured that I could find a side window and try to sneak in. I was armed. I was confident I could shoot without hesitation. I really wished that I had a better plan, but even if I had more time, I doubt that I'd come up with anything.

Zia had mentioned my surgeon's ego. I admit that it scared me. I actually felt confident that I could pull this off. I was smart. I knew how to be careful. I would look for an opening. If I didn't see one, I would offer them a trade—me for Rachel. I would not be sucked in by talk of Tara. Yes, I wanted to believe that she was still alive. Yes, I wanted to believe that they knew where she was. But I would no longer risk Rachel's life for a pipe dream. My life? Sure. But not Rachel's.

I moved closer to Denise Vanech's house, trying to duck behind trees while not looking conspicuous. In an upscale suburban neighborhood, this was impossible. People don't skulk. I imagined the neighbors watching me from behind the blinds, their fingers on the auto-911 dial button. I couldn't worry about it. Whatever was going to happen, one way or the other, would happen before any police could get here.

When my cell phone rang, I nearly jumped out my skin. I was three houses away now. I cursed under my breath. Dr. Cool—Dr. Confident—had forgotten to put his phone on vibrate. I realized with a sinking certainty that I was deluding myself. I was out of my element here. Suppose, for example, the phone had rung when I was right up against the house. What then?

I leapt behind a shrub and answered it with a snap of my wrist.

"You got a lot to learn about sneaking up on places," Verne whispered. "I mean, you're godawful at it."

"Where are you?"

"Check out the second-floor window, far back."

I peeked out at Denise Vanech's house. Verne was in the window. He waved to me.

"Back door was unlocked," Verne whispered. "I let myself in."

"What's going on in there?"

"Stone-cold killing. I heard them say they

killed that girl at the motel. They blew away that Denise woman. She's lying dead not three feet from Rachel."

I closed my eyes.

"This is a trap, Marc."

"Yeah, I figured that."

"There's two of them—one man, one woman. I want you to hustle back to your car. I want you to drive and park on the street. You'll be far enough away so that they won't get a clear shot at you. Stay there. Don't get any closer. I just want you to draw their attention, you got me?"

"Yes."

"I'll try to keep one alive, but I can't make any promises."

He hung up. I hurried back to the car and did as he said. I could feel my heart pounding against my chest. But there was hope now. Verne was there. He was inside the house and armed. I pulled up to the front of Denise Vanech's house. The blinds and curtains were drawn. I took a deep breath. I opened the car door and stood.

Silence.

I expected to hear shots. But that was not what came first. The first sound was shattering glass. And then I saw Rachel fall out the window.

"His car just pulled up," Heshy said.

Rachel's hands were still bound behind her back, the duct tape over her mouth. She knew that this was it. Marc would come to the door. They would let him in, this mutant version of Bonnie and Clyde, and then they would shoot them both.

Tatiana was already dead. Denise Vanech was already dead. There was no other way to play this. Heshy and Lydia could not let them survive. Rachel had hoped that Marc would realize this and go to the police. She hoped that he wouldn't show up, but of course, that would not be an option for him. So he was here. He would probably try something foolhardy or maybe he was still so blinded by hope that he would simply walk into the trap.

Either way, Rachel had to stop him.

Her only chance was to surprise them. Even then, even if everything fell into place, the best she could realistically hope for was to save Marc. The rest was fool's gold.

Time to act.

They hadn't bothered to tie her feet. With

her hands behind her back and her mouth taped shut, what harm could she do? Trying to run at them would be suicide. She'd make an easy target.

And that was what she was counting on.

Rachel got to her feet. Lydia turned around and pointed the gun at her. "Sit down."

She didn't. And now Lydia had a dilemma. If she fired the gun, Marc would hear it. He would know something was wrong. A stalemate. But it wouldn't last. An idea—a pretty lame idea—came to Rachel. She broke into a run. Lydia would either have to shoot or give chase or . . .

The window.

Lydia saw what Rachel was doing, but there was no way to stop her. Rachel lowered her head like a battering ram and dived straight toward the picture window. Lydia raised her gun to shoot. Rachel braced herself. She knew that this would hurt. The glass broke with surprising ease. Rachel flew through it, but what she hadn't counted on was how far off the ground she was. Her hands were still tied behind her back. There was no way to break the fall.

She turned to the side and took the

impact on her shoulder. Something popped. She felt a stabbing pain run down her leg. A shard of glass stuck out of her thigh. The sound would warn Marc, no question about it. He could be saved. But as Rachel rolled over, dread—deep, heavy dread—hit her next. Yes, she had warned Marc. He had seen her fall out the window.

But now, without thinking of the danger, Marc was running toward her.

Verne was crouched on the stairs.

He'd been about to make his move when Rachel suddenly stood up. Was she crazy? But no, he realized, she was just a brave lady. After all, she had no idea that he was hiding upstairs. She couldn't just sit there and let Marc walk in on this setup. She wasn't built that way.

"Sit down."

The woman's voice. The pert thing named Lydia. She started to swing her gun up. Verne panicked. He wasn't in position yet. He wouldn't have a clear shot. But Lydia didn't pull the trigger. Verne watched in amazement as Rachel ran and jumped through the window.

Talk about a distraction.

Verne moved now. He had heard countless times about how time stands still in moments of extreme violence, that brief seconds can drag so that you can see everything clearly. In reality, that was total bull. When you looked back, when you ran it through your mind in safety and comfort, that's when you imagine it went by slowly. But in the heat of the moment, when he and three buddies had gotten into a firefight with some of Saddam's "elite" soldiers, time had actually sped up. That was what was happening here.

Verne spun around the corner. "Drop it!"

The big man had his gun aimed at the window where Rachel had fallen out. There was no time to call out another warning. Verne fired twice. Heshy went down. Lydia screamed. Verne ducked into a roll and disappeared behind the couch. Lydia screamed again.

"Heshy!"

Verne peered out, expecting to see Lydia aiming the gun at him. But that wasn't the case. She ditched the weapon. Still crying out, Lydia dropped to her knees and gently cradled Heshy's head.

"No! Don't die. Please, Heshy, please don't leave me!"

Verne kicked her gun away. He kept his pointed at Lydia.

Her voice was low now, soft and motherly. "Please, Heshy. Please don't die. Oh God, please don't leave me."

Heshy said, "I never will."

Lydia looked at Verne, her eyes pleading. He didn't bother calling 911. He could hear the sirens now. Heshy grabbed Lydia's hand. "You know what you have to do," he said.

"No," she said, her voice small.

"Lydia, we planned for this."

"You're not going to die."

Heshy closed his eyes. His breathing was labored.

"The world will think you were a monster," she said.

"I only care what you think. Promise me, Lydia."

"You're going to be fine."

"Promise me."

Lydia shook her head. The tears were flowing freely now. "I can't do it."

"You can." Heshy managed a final smile. "You're a great actress, remember?"

"I love you," she said.

But his eyes were closed. Lydia kept sobbing. She kept pleading with him not to leave her. The sirens came closer. Verne stepped back. The police arrived. When they came inside, they stood around her in a circle. Lydia suddenly lifted her head off Heshy's chest.

"Thank God," she said to them—and the tears started rolling again. "My nightmare is finally over."

Rachel was rushed to the hospital. I wanted to follow, but the police had other ideas. I spoke to Zia. I asked her to look in on Rachel for me.

The police questioned us for hours. They questioned Verne, Katarina, and me separately and then together. I think they believed us. Lenny was there. Regan and Tickner showed up, but it took some time. They'd been going through Bacard's files per Lenny's phone call.

Regan took the lead with me. "Long day, huh, Marc?"

I sat across from him. "Do I look in the mood for chitchat, Detective?"

"The woman goes by the name Lydia Davis. Her real name is Larissa Dane."

I made a face. "Why does that name sound familiar?"

"She was a child actor."

"Trixie," I said, remembering. "On *Family Laughs*."

"Yep, that's her. Or at least, that's what she says. Anyway, she claims this guy—we only know him as Heshy—kept her locked up and abused her. She said he forced her to do things. Your friend Verne thinks it's all a scam. But that's not important right now. She claims that she doesn't know anything about your daughter."

"How can that be?"

"She says they were just hired hands. That Bacard came to Heshy with this scheme about asking for ransom for a kid they hadn't kidnapped. Heshy loved the idea. Lot of money—and since they didn't really have the kid, there was almost no risk."

"She says they had nothing to do with the shooting at my house?"

"That's right."

I looked at Lenny. He saw the problem

too. "But they had my gun. The one they used on Katarina's brother."

"Yeah, we know. She claims that Bacard gave it to Heshy. To set you up. Heshy shot Pavel and planted the gun so you and Rachel would take the fall."

"How did they get Tara's hair for the ransom drop? How did they get her clothes?"

"According to Ms. Dane, Bacard provided them."

I shook my head. "So Bacard was the one who kidnapped Tara?"

"She claims not to know."

"How about my sister? How did she get involved?"

"Again she claims it was Bacard. He gave them Stacy's name as a fall guy. Heshy gave Stacy the money and told her to cash it at a bank. Then he killed her."

I looked over at Tickner, then back at Regan. "It doesn't add up."

"We're still working on it."

Lenny said, "I have a question. Why did they come back after a year and a half and try it again?"

"Ms. Dane claims not to know for sure, but she suspects it was simple greed. She says Bacard called and asked if Heshy would want to make another million. He said yes. Going through Bacard's records, he was clearly in financial trouble. We think she's right. Bacard simply decided to take another bite of the apple."

I rubbed my face. My ribs began to ache. "Did you find Bacard's adoption records?"

Regan glanced at Tickner. "Not yet."

"How can that be?"

"Look, we just got on this. We'll find them. We're going to check every adoption he's ever made, especially anything involving a female eighteen months ago. If Bacard had Tara adopted, we'll find out."

I shook my head again.

"What is it, Marc?"

"That doesn't make any sense. The guy has a decent thing going with this adoption scam. Why shoot me and Monica and up the ante to kidnapping and murder?"

"We don't know," Regan said. "I think we can all agree that there's more to the story. But the truth is, the most likely scenario right now is that your sister and an accomplice shot you and Monica and took the baby. She then brought it to Bacard."

I closed my eyes and replayed it in my head. Could Stacy have really done that?

Could she have broken into my house and shot me? I still couldn't make myself believe. And then I thought of something.

Why hadn't I heard the window break?

More than that, before I was shot, why hadn't I heard *anything*? A window break, a doorbell, heck, a door opening. Why hadn't I heard any of that? The answer, according to Regan, had been that I was blocking. But now I saw that wasn't it.

"The granola bar," I said.

"Pardon me?"

I turned to him. "Your theory is that I'm forgetting something, right? Stacy and her accomplice either broke the window or, I don't know, rang the doorbell. I would have heard either one of those. But I didn't. I remember eating my granola bar and then going down."

"Right."

"But see, I was pretty specific. I had the granola bar in my hand. When you found me, it was on the floor. How much had been eaten?"

"Maybe a bite or two," Tickner said.

"Then your amnesia theory is wrong. I was standing over the sink eating the granola bar. I remember that. When you found me, that's what I was doing. There is no time unaccounted for. And if it was my sister, why would she strip Monica, for Chrissake . . . ?" I stopped.

Lenny said, "Marc?"

Did you love her?

I stared straight ahead.

You know who shot you, don't you, Marc?

Dina Levinsky. I thought about her bizarre visits to the house she'd grown up in. I thought about the two guns—one being mine. I thought about the CD-ROM hidden in the basement, in the spot Dina had told me about. I thought about those pictures taken in front of the hospital. I thought about what Edgar said about Monica seeing a psychiatrist.

And then an awful thought, one so terrible I might indeed have suppressed it, began to surface.

chapter 43

I feigned illness and excused myself. I went to the bathroom and dialed Edgar's phone number. My father-in-law himself answered. "Hello?"

"You said Monica was seeing a psychiatrist?"

"Marc? Is that you?" Edgar cleared his throat. "I just heard from the police. Those pissant fools had me convinced that you were behind all this—"

"I don't have time for that now. I'm still trying to find Tara."

"What do you need?" Edgar asked.

"Did you ever find out the name of her psychiatrist?"

"No."

I thought about it. "Is Carson there?"

"Yes."

"Put him on."

There was a brief pause. I tapped my foot. Uncle Carson's rich voice came over the line. "Marc?"

"You knew about those pictures, didn't you?"

He didn't reply.

"I checked our accounts. The money didn't come from us. You paid for the private detective."

"It had nothing to do with the shooting or kidnapping," Carson said.

"I think it did. Monica told you the name of her psychiatrist, didn't she? What was it?"

Again he did not reply.

"I'm trying to find out what happened to Tara."

"She only saw him twice," Carson said. "How can he help you?"

"He can't. His name can."

"What?"

"Just tell me, yes or no. Was his name Stanley Radio?"

I could hear him breathing.

"Carson?"

"I already spoke to him. He knows noth-ing—"

But I had already hung up. Carson wouldn't say any more.

But Dina Levinsky might.

I asked Regan and Tickner if I was under arrest. They said no. I asked Verne if I could still borrow the Camaro.

"No problemo," Verne said. Then squinting, he added, "Do you need my help?"

I shook my head. "You and Katarina are out of this now. It's over for you."

"I'm still here, if you need me."

"I don't. Go home, Verne."

He surprised me with a big hug then. Katarina kissed my cheek. I let go and watched them drive off in the pickup. I headed toward the city. There was heavy traffic at the Lincoln Tunnel. It took me over an hour to get through the tolls. That gave me time to make some phone calls. I learned that Dina Levinsky shared an apartment in Greenwich Village with a friend.

Twenty minutes later, I knocked on her door.

When Eleanor Russell returned from lunch, there was a plain manila envelope on her chair. It was addressed to her boss,

Lenny Marcus, and marked PERSONAL AND CONFIDENTIAL.

Eleanor had worked with Lenny for eight years. She loved him dearly. Having no family of her own—she and her husband, Saul, who had died three years before, had never been blessed with children—she had become something of a surrogate grandmother to the Marcuses. Eleanor even had photographs of Lenny's wife, Cheryl, and their four children on her desk.

She studied the envelope and frowned. How had it gotten here? She peeked into Lenny's office. He looked so harried. That was because Lenny had just returned from a homicide scene. The case involving his best friend, Dr. Marc Seidman, had exploded back into the headlines. Normally Eleanor would not bother Lenny at a time like this. But the return address . . . well, she thought he should see it for himself.

Lenny was on the phone. He saw her enter and put his hand over the receiver. "I'm kinda busy," he said.

"This came for you."

Eleanor handed him the envelope. Lenny almost ignored it. Then Eleanor watched as he spotted the return address. He turned it over, then back again.

The return address simply read, *From a friend of Stacy Seidman.*

Lenny put down the phone and tore open the envelope.

I don't think Dina Levinsky was surprised to see me.

She let me in without a word. The walls were blanketed with her paintings, many hung at odd angles. The effect was dizzying, giving the entire apartment a Salvador Dalí feel. We sat in the kitchen. Dina offered to make tea. I said no. She put her hands on the table. I could see that her fingernails were bitten down past the cuticle. Had they been that way at my house? She seemed different now, sadder somehow. Her hair was straighter. Her eyes were downcast. It was as if she was transforming back to the pitiful girl I had known in elementary school.

"You found the pictures?" she asked.

"Yes."

Dina closed her eyes. "I should have never led you to them."

"Why did you?"

"I lied to you before."

I nodded.

"I'm not married. I don't enjoy sex. I do have troubles with relationships." She shrugged. "I even have problems with telling the truth."

Dina tried to smile. I tried to smile back.

"In therapy we're taught to confront our fears. The only way to do that is to let the truth in, no matter how much it hurts. But see, I wasn't even sure what the truth was. So I tried to lead you there."

"You were back in the house before the night I saw you, weren't you?"

She nodded.

"And that's how you met Monica?"

"Yes."

I kept going. "You two became friends?"

"We had something in common."

"That being?"

Dina looked up at me, and I saw the pain.

"Abuse?" I said.

She nodded.

"Edgar sexually abused her?"

"No, not Edgar. Her mother. And it wasn't sexual. It was more physical and emotional. The woman was very ill. You knew that, right?"

"I guess I did," I said.

"Monica needed help."

"So you introduced her to your thera-pist?"

"I tried. I mean, I set up an appointment for her with Dr. Radio. But it didn't work out."

"How come?"

"Monica was not the sort of woman who believed in therapy. She thought that she could best handle her own problems."

I nodded. I knew. "At the house," I said, "you asked me if I loved Monica."

"Yes."

"Why?"

"She thought you didn't." Dina put her finger in her mouth, searching for a sliver of nail to bite. There was none. "Of course, she thought herself unworthy of love. Like me. But there was a difference."

"What was that?"

"Monica felt that there was one person who could love her forever."

I knew the answer here. "Tara."

"Yes. She trapped you, Marc. You proba-bly realize that. It wasn't an accident. She wanted to get pregnant."

Sadly, I was not surprised. Again I tried, as in surgery, to put the pieces together.

"So Monica believed that I no longer loved her. She was afraid I wanted a divorce. She was troubled. She was crying at night." I paused. I was saying this as much for my benefit as Dina's. I didn't want to keep following this train of thought, but there was no way to stop me. "She's fragile. Her mind is frayed. And then she hears that phone message from Rachel."

"That's your ex-girlfriend?"

"Yes."

"You still keep her picture in your desk drawer. Monica knew about that too. You keep mementos of her."

I closed my eyes, remembering the Steely Dan CD in Monica's car. College music. Music I had listened to with Rachel. I said, "So she hired a private detective to see if I was having an affair. He took those photographs."

Dina nodded.

"So now she has proof. I'm going to leave her for another woman. I'm going to claim she's unstable. I'll say she's an unfit mother. I'm a well-respected doctor, and Rachel has connections with law enforcement. We'd end up with custody of the only thing that really mattered to Monica. Tara."

Dina rose from the table. She washed out a glass in the sink and then filled it with water. I thought again about what had happened that morning. Why hadn't I heard the window break? Why hadn't I heard the doorbell ring? Why hadn't I heard the intruder enter?

Simple. Because there was no intruder.

Tears filled my eyes. "So what did she do, Dina?"

"You know, Marc."

I squeezed my eyes shut.

"I didn't think she'd really do it," Dina said. "I thought she was just acting out, you know? Monica was so despondent. When she asked me if I knew how to get a gun, I thought she wanted to kill herself. I never thought . . ."

"She would shoot me?"

The air was suddenly heavy. Exhaustion overwhelmed me. I was too tired to cry anymore. But there was still more to unearth here. "You said she asked you to help her get a gun?"

Dina wiped her eyes and nodded.

"Did you?"

"No. I wouldn't know how to get one. She said you had a gun at home, but she didn't want something that could trace back. So she went to the only person she knew with seedy enough contacts to help."

I saw it now. "My sister."

"Yes."

"Did Stacy get her a gun?"

"No, I don't think so."

"What makes you say that?"

"The morning you were both shot, Stacy came to see me. See, Monica and I had come up with the idea of going to Stacy together. So Monica mentioned me to her. She came and asked what Monica needed a gun for. I didn't tell her because, well, I really wasn't all that sure. Stacy ran out. I was in a panic. I wanted to ask Dr. Radio what to do, but my next session was that afternoon. I figured it could wait."

"And then?"

"I still don't know what happened, Marc. That's the truth. But I know Monica shot you."

"How?"

"I got scared. So I called your house. Monica answered. She was crying. She told me you were dead. She kept saying, 'What have I done, what have I done?' And then suddenly she hung up. I called back. But no one answered. I really didn't know what to do. Then the TV had the story. When they said your daughter was missing . . . I didn't understand. I thought they'd find her right away. But they never did. And I never heard anything about those pictures either. I hoped, I don't know, I hoped leading you to those photographs might shed some light on what really happened. Not so much for the two of you. But for your daughter."

"Why did you wait so long?"

Her eyes closed and for a moment, I thought that she might be praying. "I had a bad spell, Marc. Two weeks after you were shot, I was hospitalized with a breakdown. The truth is, I was so far gone I forgot about it. Or maybe I wanted to forget, I don't know."

My cell phone rang. It was Lenny. I picked it up.

"Where are you?" he asked.

"With Dina Levinsky."

"Get over to Newark Airport. Terminal C. Now."

"What's going on?"

"I think," Lenny said. Then he slowed down, caught his breath. "I think I may know where we can find Tara."

chapter 44

By the time I arrived at Terminal C, Lenny was already standing by the Continental check-in desk. It was six o'clock at night now. The airport was jammed with the weary. He handed me the anonymous note that had been found in his office. It read:

Abe and Lorraine Tansmore
26 Marsh Lane
Hanley Hills, MO

That was it. Just the name and address. Nothing else.

"It's a suburb near St. Louis," Lenny explained. "I did some research already."

I just kept staring down at the name and address.

"Marc?"

I looked up at him.

"The Tansmores adopted a daughter eighteen months ago. She was six months old when they got her."

Behind him, a Continental service rep said, "Next please." A woman pushed past me. She might have said, "Excuse me," but I'm not sure.

"I have us booked on the next flight to St. Louis. We're leaving in an hour."

When we reached the departure gate, I told him about my meeting with Dina Levinsky. We sat, as we often do, next to each other, facing out. When I finished, he said, "You have a theory now."

"I do."

We watched a plane take off. An old couple sitting across from us shared a tin of Pringles. "I'm a cynic. I know that. I hold no illusions about drug addicts. If anything, I overestimate their depravity. And that, I think, is what I did here."

"How do you figure?"

"Stacy wouldn't shoot me. And she would never hurt her niece. She was an addict. But she still loved me."

"I think," Lenny said, "that you're right."

"I look back. I was so wrapped up in my own world that I never saw . . ." I shook my head. Now was not the time for this. "Monica was desperate," I said. "She couldn't get a gun and maybe, she decided, she didn't have to."

"She used yours," Lenny said.

"Yes."

"And then?"

"Stacy must have guessed what was up. She ran to the house. She saw what Monica had done. I don't know how it played exactly. Maybe Monica tried to shoot her too—that could explain the bullet hole near the stairs. Or maybe Stacy just reacted. She loved me. I was lying there. She probably thought I was dead. So I don't know, but either way Stacy came armed. And she shot Monica."

The gate attendant announced that the flight would soon be boarding but those with special needs or One Pass Gold and Platinum members could board now.

"You said on the phone that Stacy knew Bacard?"

Lenny nodded. "She mentioned him, yeah."

"Again I'm not sure how it played exactly.

But think about it. I'm dead. Monica is dead. And Stacy is probably freaking out. Tara is crying. Stacy can't just leave her. So she takes Tara with her. Later she realizes that she can't raise a kid on her own. She's too messed up. So she turns her over to Bacard and tells him to find her a good family. Or, if I want to be cynical, maybe she gives Tara over for the money. We'll never know."

Lenny was nodding.

"From there, well, we just follow what we already learned. Bacard decides to rake in extra money by pretending it was a kidnapping. He hires those two lunatics. Bacard would be able to get hair samples, for example. He double-crossed Stacy. He set her up to take the fall."

I saw something cross Lenny's face.

"What?"

"Nothing," he said.

They called our row.

Lenny stood. "Let's board."

The flight was delayed. We didn't arrive in St. Louis until past midnight local time. It was too late to do anything tonight. Lenny booked us a room at the Airport Marriott. I bought clothes at their all-night boutique.

When we got to the room, I took a very long, very hot shower. We settled in and stared at the ceiling.

In the morning, I called the hospital to check on Rachel. She was still sleeping. Zia was in her room. She assured me that Rachel was doing fine. Lenny and I tried to eat the hotel's buffet breakfast. Nothing would stay down. Our rental car was waiting for us. Lenny had gotten directions to Hanley Hills from the desk clerk.

I don't remember what we saw on the drive. Aside from the Arch in the distance, there was nothing distinct. The United States has a strip-mall sameness about it now. It's easy to criticize that—I often do—but maybe the appeal is that we all like what we already know. We claim to embrace change. But in the end, especially in these times, what truly draws us is the familiar.

When we reached the town limits, I felt a tingling in my legs. "What do we do here, Lenny?"

He had no answer.

"Do I just knock on the door and say, 'Excuse me, I think that's my daughter?' "

"We could call the police," he said. "Let them handle it."

But I didn't know how that would play out. We were so close now. I told him to keep on driving. We made a right onto Marsh Lane. I was shaking now. Lenny tried to give me a buck-up look, but his face was pale too. The street was more modest than I'd expected. I had assumed that all of Bacard's clients were wealthy. That was clearly not the case with this couple.

"Abe Tansmore works as a school-teacher," Lenny said, reading my thoughts as usual. "Sixth grade. Lorraine Tansmore works for a day-care center three days a week. They're both thirty-nine years old. They've been married for seventeen years."

Up ahead, I saw a house with a cherry-wood sign that read 26—THE TANSMORES. It was a small, one-level, what I think they called "bungalow" style. The rest of the houses on the block seemed tired. This one did not. The paint glistened like a smile. There were lots of clusters of color, of flowers and shrubs, all trimly laid out and perfectly pruned. I could see a welcome mat. A low picket fence encircled the front yard. A station wagon, a Volvo model from several years back, sat in the driveway. There was a tricycle, too, and one of those bright-hued plastic Big Wheels.

And there was a woman outside.

Lenny pulled over in front of an empty lot. I barely noticed. The woman was in the flower beds, on her knees. She was working a small digging spade. Her hair was tied back with a red bandanna. Every few digs she would wipe her forehead with her sleeve.

"You say she works at a day-care center?"

"Three days a week. The daughter goes with her."

"What do they call the daughter?"

"Natasha."

I nodded. I don't know why. We waited. The woman, this Lorraine, worked hard, but I could see she enjoyed it. There was a serenity about her. I opened the car window. I could hear her whistling to herself. I don't know how many minutes passed. A neighbor walked by. Lorraine rose and greeted her. The neighbor gestured toward the garden. Lorraine smiled. She wasn't a beautiful woman, but she had a great smile. The neighbor left. Lorraine waved good-bye and turned back to her garden.

The front door opened.

I saw Abe. He was a tall man, thin and wiry, slightly balding. He had a neatly trimmed beard. Lorraine stood and looked over at him. She gave him a small wave.

And then Tara ran outside.

The air around us stopped. I felt my insides shut down. Next to me, Lenny stiffened and muttered, "Oh my God."

For the last eighteen months, I had never really believed that this moment was possible. What I had done instead was convince myself—no, trick myself—into believing that maybe, somehow, Tara was still alive and okay. But my subconscious knew it was only a self-delusion. It winked at me. It nudged me in my sleep. It whispered the obvious truth: that I would never see my daughter again.

But it was my daughter. She was alive.

I was surprised at how little Tara had changed. Oh she'd grown, of course. She was able to stand. She was even able, as I now saw, to run. But her face . . . there was no mistake. No being blinded by hope. It was Tara. It was my little girl.

With a huge smile, Tara ran with total abandon toward Lorraine. Lorraine bent low, her face lighting up in that celestial way only a mother's can. She swept my child into her arms. Now I could hear the melodious sound of Tara's laughter. The sound pierced my heart. Tears streamed down my face. Lenny put a hand on my arm. I could hear him sniffling. I saw the husband, this Abe, walk toward them. He was smiling too.

For several hours, I watched them in their small, perfect yard. I saw Lorraine patiently point out the flowers, explaining what each one was. I saw Abe give her a horsey ride on his back. I saw Lorraine teach her how to pat the dirt down with her hand. Another couple dropped by. They had a little girl about Tara's age. Abe and the other father pushed the girls on the metal swing-set in the backyard. Their giggles pounded in my ears. Eventually they all went inside. Abe and Lorraine were the last to disappear. They walked through the door with their arms around each other.

Lenny turned to me. I let my head drop back. I had hoped that today would be the end of my journey. But it wasn't.

After a while, I said, "Let's go."

chapter 45

When we got back to the Airport Marriott, I told Lenny to go home. He said he would stay. I told him that I could handle this on my own—that I *wanted* to handle this on my own. He reluctantly agreed.

I called Rachel. She was doing well. I told her what had happened. "Call Harold Fisher," I said. "Ask him to do a thorough background check on Abe and Lorraine Tansmore. I want to know if there's something there."

"Okay," she said softly. "I wish I could be there."

"Me too."

I sat on my bed. My head dropped into my hands. I don't think I cried. I don't know what I felt anymore. It was over. I had learned as much as I would. When Rachel called back two hours later, nothing she told me was a surprise. Abe and Lorraine were solid citizens. Abe was the first person in his family to graduate college. He had two younger sisters who lived in the area. Both had three children. He had met Lorraine during their freshman year at Washington University in St. Louis.

Night fell. I stood and looked in the mirror. My wife had tried to kill me. Yes, she was unstable. I knew that now. Hell, I probably knew it then. I didn't much care, I guess. When a child's face breaks, I put it back together. I can do miracles in the surgical room. But my own family fell apart and I did nothing but watch.

I thought now about what it meant to be a father. I loved my daughter. I know that. But when I saw Abe today, when I see Lenny coaching soccer, I wonder. I wonder about my fitness. I wonder about my commitment. And I wonder if I am worthy.

Or do I already know the answer?

I wanted so badly to have my little girl back with me. I also wanted so badly for this not to be about me or my wants.

Tara had looked so damn happy.

It was midnight now. I looked at myself in

the mirror again. What if leaving this alone—letting her stay with Abe and Lorraine—was the right thing? Was I really brave enough, strong enough, to walk away? I kept staring in the mirror, challenging myself. Was I?

I lay back. I think I fell asleep. A knock on the door startled me awake. I glanced at the digital clock next to my bed. It read 5:19 A.M.

"I'm sleeping," I said.

"Dr. Seidman?"

It was a male voice.

"Dr. Seidman, my name is Abe Tansmore."

I opened the door. He was handsome up close, in a sort of James Taylor way. He wore jeans and a tan shirt. I looked at his eyes. They were blue but tinged with red. So, I knew, were mine. For a long time, we just stared at one another. I tried to speak, but I couldn't. I stepped back and let him in.

"Your lawyer stopped by. He"—Abe stopped, swallowed hard—"he told us the whole story. Lorraine and I stayed up all night. We talked it out. We cried a lot. But I think we knew right from the get-go that there was only one decision here." Abe Tansmore was trying to hold on, but he was losing it now. He closed his eyes. "We have to give you your daughter back."

I didn't know what to say. I shook my head. "We have to do what's best for her."

"That's what I'm doing, Dr. Seidman."

"Call me Marc. Please." It was a dumb thing to say. I know that. But I wasn't ready for this. "If you're worried about a long, drawn-out court case, Lenny shouldn't have—"

"No, that's not it."

We stood there a little longer. I pointed toward the chair in the room. He shook his head. Then he looked at me. "All night, I've been trying to imagine your pain. I don't think I can. I think there are places a man just can't get to without experience. Maybe this is one of them. But your pain, awful as it must be, that's not why Lorraine and I came to this decision. And it's not because we blame ourselves either. In hindsight, maybe we should have wondered what was going on. We went to Mr. Bacard. But the fees would have added up to over a hundred thousand dollars. I'm not a rich man. I couldn't afford that. Then a few weeks later, Mr. Bacard calls us. He said he had a baby that needed immediate placing. She wasn't a newborn, he said. The mother had just abandoned her. We knew something was not quite right, but he said that if we wanted this, we'd have to go in no questions asked."

He looked off then. I watched his face. "I think deep down, maybe we always knew. We just couldn't face it. But that's not the reason we came to this decision either."

I swallowed. "What then?"

His eyes drifted toward mine. "You can't do the wrong thing for the right reason." I must have looked confused. "If Lorraine and I don't do this, we're not fit to raise her. We want Natasha to be happy. We want her to be a good person."

"You might be the best ones to make that happen."

He shook his head. "That's not how it works. We don't give children to whatever parents would be best to raise them. You and I can't make that judgment. You don't know how hard this is for us. Or maybe you do."

I turned away. I caught my reflection in the mirror. Just for a second. Less maybe. But it was enough. I saw the man I was. I saw the man I wanted to be. I turned to him and said, "I want us both to raise her."

He was stunned. So was I. "I'm not sure I understand," he said.

"Neither do I. But that's what we're going to do."

"How?"

"I don't know."

Abe shook his head. "It can't work. You know that."

"No, Abe, I don't know that. I came here to bring my daughter home—and I find that maybe she already is. Is it right for me to rip her away from that? I want you both in her life. I'm not saying it'll be easy. But kids are raised by single parents, by stepparents, in foster homes. There are divorces and separations and who-knows-what. We all love this little girl. We'll make it work."

I saw the hope return to the man's thin face. He couldn't speak for a few seconds. Then he said, "Lorraine is in the lobby. Can I go talk to her?"

"Of course."

They didn't take long. There was a knock on my door. When I opened it, Lorraine threw her arms around me. I hugged her back, this woman I had never met. Her hair smelled of strawberry. Behind her, Abe came into the room. Tara was sleeping in his arms. Lorraine let go of me and moved away. Abe stepped closer. He handed me my daughter carefully. I held her, and my heart burst into flame. Tara began to stir. She started to fuss. I still held her. I rocked her back and forth and made shushing sounds.

And soon she settled on me and fell back to sleep.

chapter 46

It started to all go wrong again when I looked at the calendar.

The human brain is amazing. It is a curious mix of electricity and chemicals. It is, in effect, pure science. We understand more about the workings of the great cosmos than we do about the curious circuitry of the cerebrum, cerebellum, hypothalamus, medulla oblongata, and all the rest. And like any tricky compound, we are never sure how it will react to a certain catalyst.

There were several things that gave me reason to pause. There was the question of leaks. Rachel and I had thought that someone in either the FBI or police department had told Bacard and his people what was happening. But that never fit in with my theory about Stacy shooting Monica. There was the fact that Monica was found with no clothes on. I think I understood why now, but the thing is, Stacy wouldn't have.

But the main catalyst occurred, I think, when I looked at the calendar and realized that today was Wednesday.

The shootings and original abduction had taken place on a Wednesday. Of course, there had been plenty of Wednesdays in the past eighteen months. The day of the week was a pretty innocuous thing. But this time, after we had learned so much, after my brain had digested all the fresh data, something meshed. All those little questions and doubts, all those idiosyncrasies, all those moments I took for granted and never really examined . . . they all shifted a little. And what I saw was even worse than what I had originally imagined.

I was back in Kasselton now—at my house where it had all started. I called Tickner for confirmation.

I said, "My wife and I were shot with thirty-eights, right?"

"Yes."

"And you're sure they were two different guns?"

"Positive."

"And my Smith and Wesson was one of them?"

"You know all this, Marc."

"Did you get all the ballistic reports back yet?"

"Most of them."

I licked my lips and readied myself. I hoped to hell that I was wrong. "Who was shot with my gun—me or Monica?"

He turned coy on me. "Why are you asking me this now?"

"Curiosity."

"Yeah, right. Hold on a second." I could hear him shuffling papers. I felt my throat constrict. I almost hung up. "Your wife was."

When I heard the car pull up outside, I put the receiver back in the cradle. Lenny turned the knob and opened the door. He didn't knock. After all, Lenny never knocked, right?

I was sitting on the couch. The house was still, all the ghosts sleeping now. He had a Slurpee in either hand and a broad smile. I wondered how many times I had seen that smile. I remembered it more crooked. I remembered it jammed to overflowing with braces. I remembered it bleeding after he hit a tree when we went sledding down the Gorets' backyard. I thought again about when big Tony Merruno picked a fight with me in third grade, how Lenny jumped on his back. I remembered now that Tony Merruno broke Lenny's glasses. I don't think Lenny cared.

I knew him so well. Or maybe I hadn't known him at all.

When Lenny saw my face, his smile faded away.

"We were supposed to play racquetball that morning, Lenny. Remember?"

He lowered the cups and put them on the end table.

"You never knock. You always just open the door. Like today. So what happened, Lenny? You came to pick me up. You opened the door."

He started shaking his head, but I knew now.

"The two guns, Lenny. That's what gave it away."

"I don't know what you're talking about." But there was no conviction in his voice.

"We figured that Stacy didn't get Monica a gun—that Monica used mine. But you see, she didn't. I just checked with ballistics. It's funny. You never told me that Monica was shot with my gun. I was shot with the other weapon."

"So?" Lenny said, suddenly the attorney again. "That doesn't mean anything. Maybe Stacy got her a gun, after all."

"She did," I said.

"So fine, okay, it still adds up."

"Tell me how."

He shifted his feet. "Maybe Stacy helped Monica get a gun. Monica shot you with it. When Stacy arrived a few minutes later, Monica tried to shoot her." Lenny moved over to the staircase as if to demonstrate. "Stacy ran upstairs. Monica fired—that would explain the bullet hole." He pointed to the spackled area by the stairs. "Stacy grabbed your gun out of the bedroom, came downstairs, and shot Monica."

I looked at him. "Is that how it happened, Lenny?"

"I don't know. I mean, it could be."

I waited a beat. He turned away. "One problem," I said.

"What?"

"Stacy didn't know where I hid the gun. She didn't know the lockbox's combination either." I took a step closer. "But you did, Lenny. I kept all my legal documents there.

I trusted you with everything. So now I want the truth. Monica shot me. You came in. You saw me lying on the floor. Did you think I was dead?"

Lenny closed his eyes.

"Make me understand, Lenny."

He shook his head slowly. "You think you love your daughter," he said. "But you have no idea. What you feel, it grows every day. The longer you have a child, the more attached you get. The other night I came home from work. Marianne was crying because some girls were teasing her in school. I went to bed feeling sick, and I realized something. I can only be as happy as my saddest child. Do you understand what I'm saying?"

"Tell me what happened," I said.

"You have it pretty much right. I came to your house that morning. I opened the door. Monica was on the phone. She was still holding the gun in her hand. I ran over to you. I couldn't believe it. I felt for a pulse but . . ." He shook his head. "Monica started screaming at me, about how she wouldn't let anyone take away her baby. She pointed the gun at me. I mean, Jesus Christ. I thought for sure I was going to die.

I rolled away and then I ran for the stairs. I remembered you had a gun up there. She fired at me." He pointed again. "That's the bullet hole."

He stopped. He took a few breaths. I waited.

"I grabbed your gun."

"Did Monica follow you up the stairs?"

His voice was soft. "No." He started blinking. "Maybe I should have tried to use the phone. Maybe I should have sneaked out. I don't know. I've gone through it hundreds of times. I try to imagine how I should have played it. But you were lying there, my best friend, dead. That crazy bitch was shouting about running away with your daughter—my godchild. She had already taken a shot at me. I didn't know what she would do next."

He looked away.

"Lenny?"

"I don't know what happened, Marc. I really don't. I sneaked back down the stairs. She still had the gun. . . ." His voice tailed.

"So you shot her."

He nodded. "I didn't mean to kill her. At least, I don't think I did. But suddenly you were both lying there, dead. I was going to call the police. But now I wasn't sure how it would look. I had shot Monica at a funny angle. They could claim her back was turned."

"You thought maybe they'd arrest you?"

"Of course. The cops hate me. I'm a successful defense attorney. What do you think would have happened?"

I didn't reply. "You broke the window?"

"From the outside," he said. "So it would look like an intruder."

"And you took Monica's clothes off?"

"Yes."

"Same reason?"

"I knew that there would be gunpowder residue on the clothes. They'd realize she fired a gun. I was trying to make it look like a random attacker. So I got rid of her clothes. I used a baby wipe to clean off her hand."

That was another thing that had bothered me. Monica being stripped down. There had been the possibility that Stacy would have done it to throw off the police, but I couldn't imagine her thinking of that. Lenny was the defense attorney—him I could see.

We were getting to the heart of it now. We

both knew that. I crossed my arms. "Tell me about Tara."

"She was my godchild. It was my job to protect her."

"I don't understand."

Lenny spread his hands. "How many times did I beg you to write a will?"

I was confused. "What does that have to do with anything?"

"Think it through for a second. During all this, when you were in trouble, you resorted to your surgical training, right?"

"I guess."

"I'm an attorney, Marc. I did the same. You were both dead. Tara was wailing in the other room. And I, Lenny the Lawyer, realized instantly what would happen."

"What?"

"You hadn't made out a will. You hadn't named guardians. Don't you see? That meant Edgar would get your daughter."

I looked at his face. I hadn't thought of that.

"Your mother might contest, but she wouldn't stand a chance against his finances. She had your father to worry about. She had a drunk driving conviction six years ago. Edgar would get custody."

I saw it now. "And you couldn't allow that."

"I'm Tara's godfather. It was my job to protect her."

"And you hated Edgar."

He shook his head. "Was I clouded by what he did to my dad? Yeah, maybe subconsciously, a little. But Edgar Portman is evil. You know that. Look at how Monica turned out. I couldn't let him destroy your daughter like he did his own."

"So you took her."

He nodded.

"You brought her to Bacard."

"He had been a client. I knew some of what he did, though not to what extent. I also knew that he would keep it confidential. I told him I wanted the best family he had. Forget money, forget power. I wanted good people."

"So he placed her with the Tansmores."

"Yes. You have to understand. I thought you were dead. Everyone did. And then it looked like you might end up a vegetable. By the time you were okay, it was too late. I couldn't tell anybody. I would go to prison for sure. Do you know what that would do to my family?"

"Gee, I can't imagine," I said.

"That's not fair, Marc."

"I don't have to be fair here."

"Hey, I didn't ask for any of this." He was shouting now. "I walked in on a terrible situation. I did what I thought best—for your daughter. But you can't expect me to sacrifice my family."

"Better to sacrifice mine?"

"The truth? Yes, of course. I'd give up anything to protect my children. Anything. Wouldn't you?"

Now I was the one who stayed silent. I had said it before: I would lay down my life in a second for my daughter. And truth be told, if push came to shove, I would lay down yours too.

"Believe it or not, I tried to think through this coldly," Lenny said. "A cost-benefit analysis. If I come forward with the truth, I destroy my wife and four children and you take your daughter from a loving home. If I keep quiet . . ." He shrugged. "Yeah, you suffered. I didn't want to do that. It hurt me to watch you. But what would you have done?"

I didn't want to think about it. "You're leaving something out," I said.

He closed his eyes and muttered something unintelligible.

"What happened to Stacy?"

"She wasn't supposed to be hurt. It was like you said. She had sold Monica the gun and when she realized why, she rushed to stop her."

"But she arrived too late?"

"Yes."

"She saw you?"

He nodded. "Look, I told her everything. She wanted to help, Marc. She wanted to do the right thing. But in the end, the habit was too strong."

"She blackmailed you?"

"She asked for money. I gave it to her. That wasn't important. But she was there. And when I went to Bacard, I told him everything that had happened. You have to understand. I thought you were going to die. When you didn't, I knew that you'd go nuts without closure. Your daughter was gone. I talked to Bacard about it. He came up with the idea of a fake kidnapping. We'd all make a lot of money."

"You took money for this?"

Lenny leaned back as if I'd just slapped him. "Of course not. I put my share into a trust fund for Tara's college. But the idea of this fake kidnapping appealed to me. They'd set it up so in the end, it would look like Tara was dead. You'd have closure. We'd also be taking money from Edgar and funneling at least some of it to Tara. It seemed like a win-win."

"Except?"

"Except when they heard about Stacy, they decided that they couldn't depend on a drug addict to keep quiet. The rest you know. They lured her with money. They made sure she got caught on tape. And then, without telling me, they killed her."

I thought about that. I thought about Stacy's last minutes in the cabin. Did she know that she was going to die? Or did she just drift off, thinking she was merely getting yet another fix?

"You were the leak, weren't you?"

He didn't reply.

"You told them about the police being involved."

"Don't you see? It made no difference. They never intended to give Tara back. She was already with the Tansmores. After the ransom drop, I thought it was over. We all tried to move on."

"So what happened?"

"Bacard decided to run the ransom again."

"Were you in on it?" I asked.

"No, he kept me out of the loop."

"When did you learn about it?"

"When you told me in the hospital. I was furious. I called him. He told me to relax, that there was no way it could be traced back to us."

"But we did it trace it back."

He nodded.

"And you knew that I was getting close to Bacard. I told you on the phone."

"Yes."

"Wait a minute." A fresh chill ran up my neck. "In the end, Bacard wanted to clean house. He called those two lunatics. The woman, that Lydia, she went out and killed Tatiana. Heshy was sent to take care of Denise Vanech. But"—I thought it through— "but when I saw Steven Bacard, he had just been shot. He was still bleeding. There was no way either of them could have done it."

I looked up. "You killed him, Lenny."

Rage seeped into his voice. "You think I wanted to?"

"Then why?"

"What do you mean, why? I was Bacard's get-out-of-jail-free card. When it all started to go wrong, he said he would turn state's evidence against me. He'd claim I shot you and Monica and brought him Tara. Like I said before, the cops hate me. I've gotten too many bad guys off. They'd go for the deal in a second."

"You'd have gone to jail?"

Lenny looked near tears.

"Your kids would have suffered?"

He nodded.

"So you killed a man in cold blood."

"What else could I do? You're looking at me like that, but deep down, you know the truth. This was your mess. I got stuck cleaning it up. Because I cared about you. I wanted to help your child." He stopped, closed his eyes, and added, "And I knew that if I killed Bacard, maybe I could save you too."

"Me?"

"Another cost-benefit analysis, Marc."

"What are you talking about?"

"It was over. Once Bacard was dead, he could take the fall. For everything. I was in the clear." Lenny came over and stood in front of me. For a moment I thought he was going to try to hug me. But he just stood there.

"I wanted you to have peace, Marc. But that would never be. I knew that now. Not until you found your daughter. With Bacard dead, my family was safe. I could let you know the truth."

"So you wrote up that anonymous note and left it on Eleanor's desk."

"Yes."

I nodded and Abe's words came back to me. "You did the wrong thing for the right reason."

"Put yourself in my place. What would you have done?"

"I don't know," I said.

"I did it for you."

And the saddest part was, he was telling the truth. I looked at him.

"You were the best friend I ever had, Lenny. I love you. I love your wife. I love your children."

"What are you going to do?"

"If I say I'm going to talk, will you kill me too?"

"Never," he said.

But I wasn't sure, much as I loved him, much as he loved me, that I believed him.

epilogue

A year has passed.

During the first two months, I racked up the frequent flier miles coming out to St. Louis every week, trying to figure out with Abe and Lorraine what we were going to do. We started slowly. For the first few visits, I asked Abe and Lorraine to stay in the room. Eventually, Tara and I started going places alone—the park, the zoo, the merry-go-round at the mall—but she looked over her shoulder a lot. It took some time for my daughter to get comfortable with me. I understood that.

My father passed away in his sleep ten months ago. After his funeral, I bought a house on Marsh Lane, two down from Abe and Lorraine, and moved out here permanently. Abe and Lorraine are remarkable people. Get this: We call "our" daughter Tasha. Think about it. It's short for Natasha and close to Tara. The reconstructive surgeon in me likes that. I keep waiting for things to go wrong. They haven't. It's weird, but I don't question it much.

My mother bought a condo and moved out here too. With Dad gone, there was no reason for her to stay in Kasselton anymore. After all the tragedies—my father's poor health, Stacy, Monica, the attack, the abduction—we both needed a second act. I'm glad she's near us. Mom has a new boyfriend, a guy named Cy. She's happy. I like him, and not just because he has season tickets to the Rams. They laugh a lot. I almost forgot how hard my mom could laugh.

I talk to Verne a fair amount. He and Katarina brought Verne Junior and Perry out in an RV during the spring. We had a great week together. Verne took me fishing, a first for me. I liked it. Next time he wants to hunt. I told him no way, but Verne can be pretty persuasive.

I don't talk much to Edgar Portman. He sends presents on Tasha's birthday. He's called twice. I'm hoping he'll come out and see his granddaughter soon. But there is simply too much guilt there for both of us. It's like I said before. Maybe Monica was unstable. Maybe it was just a chemical thing. I know that a great deal of psychiatry problems stem more from the physical, from hormonal imbalances, than life experiences. Chances are there was nothing we could have done. But in the end, whatever may have been the origin, we both let Monica down.

Zia was initially hit hard by my leaving, but then she saw it as an opportunity. She has a new doctor in the practice. I hear he's pretty good. I've opened up a One World WrapAid branch office in St. Louis. So far, it seems to be going well.

Lydia—or Larissa Dane, if you prefer—is going to get off. She did a double-flip off a murder rap and stuck the "I was abused" landing with both feet. She is a celebrity again, what with the mysterious return of the Pixie named Trixie. Lydia appeared on *Oprah*, crying on cue about the years of torment at the hands of Heshy. They flashed his picture up on the screen. The audience gasped. Heshy is hideous. Lydia is beautiful. So the world believes. Rumor has it she is set to appear in a TV movie based on her life story.

As for the baby-smuggling case, the FBI decided to "enforce the law," which meant bringing the bad guys to justice. Steven Bacard and Denise Vanech were the bad guys here. They're both dead. Officially, authorities are still searching for the records, but nobody wants to look too closely at what child ended up where. I think that's best.

Rachel fully recovered from her injuries. I ended up doing the reconstructive work on her ear myself. Her bravery got major play in the press. She received credit for smashing the baby-smuggling ring. The FBI rehired her. She requested and received a post in St. Louis. We live together. I love her. I love her more than you can imagine. But if you are expecting a totally happy ending, I'm not sure I can give you one.

As of now, Rachel and I are still together. I cannot imagine living without her. I think about losing her and it makes me physically ill. Yet I'm not sure that's enough. There is a lot of baggage here. It confuses things. I understand about her making that late-night call and showing up outside the hospital—

and yet, I know those acts eventually led to death and destruction. I don't blame Rachel, of course. But there is something there. Monica's death has given our relationship a second chance. That feels strange. I tried explaining all of this to Verne when he visited. He told me that I'm a dumb-ass. I think he's probably right.

The doorbell rings. There is a tug on my leg. Yes, it's Tasha. She is fully acclimated to having me in her life now. Children, after all, adapt better than adults. Across the room, Rachel is on the couch. She is sitting with her legs curled under her. I look at her, then at Tasha, and I feel the wondrous blend of bliss and fear. They—bliss and fear—are constant companions. Rarely does one venture out without the other.

"One second, pumpkin," I say to her. "Let's go answer the door, okay?"

"Okay."

The UPS man is there. He has packages. I bring them inside. When I look at the return address, I feel the familiar ache. The little sticker tells me that they are from Lenny and Cheryl Marcus of Kasselton, New Jersey.

Tasha looks up at me. "My present?"

I never told the police about Lenny. There was no evidence anyway—only his confession to me. That wouldn't stand up in court. But that's not why I decided not to say anything.

I suspect Cheryl knows the truth. I think maybe she knew from the beginning. I flash back to her face on the stairs, the way she snapped when Rachel and I arrived at their house that night, and now I wonder if it was out of anger or fear. I suspect the latter.

The fact is, Lenny was right. He did do it for me. What would have happened if he had just left the house? I don't know. It might have been even worse. Lenny asked me if I would have done the same in his place. Back then, probably not. Because maybe I wasn't that good a man. Verne, I bet, would have. Lenny was trying to protect my daughter without sacrificing his own family. He just messed up.

But man, I miss him. I think about how big a part of my life he was. There are times I reach for the phone and begin dialing his number. But I never finish the call. I won't speak to Lenny again. Not ever. I know that. And it hurts like hell.

But I also think about little Conner's inquisitive face at the soccer game. I think about Kevin playing soccer and Marianne's hair smelling of chlorine from her morning swim practice. I think about how beautiful Cheryl had become since she had the children.

I look down at my daughter now, safe and with me. Tasha is still gazing up. It is indeed a present for her from her godfather. I remember the first time I met Abe, that strange day at the Airport Marriott. He told me that you shouldn't do the wrong thing for the right reason. I thought about that a lot before deciding what to do about Lenny.

In the end, well, chalk it up as "too close to call."

I mix it up sometimes. Is it the wrong thing for the right reason or the right thing for the wrong reason? Or are they same? Monica needed to feel love, so she deceived me and got pregnant. That was how it all started. But if she hadn't done that, I wouldn't be staring down at the most wonderful creation I would ever know. Right reason? Wrong reason? Who's to say?

Tasha tilts her head and twitches her nose at me. "Daddy?"

"It's nothing, sweetheart," I say softly.

Tasha gives me a big, elaborate kid shrug. Rachel looks up. I see the concern on her face. I take the package and place it high up in the closet. Then I close that door and pick up my daughter.

acknowledgments

The author—man, I love referring to myself in the third person—would like to thank the following for their technical expertise: Steven Miller, M.D., Director of Pediatric Emergency Medicine, Children's Hospital of New York Presbyterian, Columbia University; Christopher J. Christie, United States Attorney for the state of New Jersey; Anne Armstrong-Coben, M.D., Medical Director of Covenant House Newark; Lois Foster Hirt, R.D.H.; Jeffrey Bedford, FBI; Gene Riehl, FBI (retired); Andrew McDade, brother-in-law extraordinaire and renaissance man. Any mistakes are theirs and theirs alone. After all, they're the experts, right? Why should I take the heat?

I also want to acknowledge Carole Baron, Mitch Hoffman, Lisa Johnson, and everyone at Dutton and Penguin Group (USA); Jon Wood, Susan Lamb, Malcolm Edwards, Anthony Cheetham, Juliet Ewers, Emily Furniss, and everyone at Orion; and the always reliable Aaron Priest, Lisa Erbach Vance, Maggie Griffin, and Linda Fairstein.

Oh, and of course, a big thanks to Katharine Foote and Rachel Cooke for freeing me up so I could get over that final hurdle.

about the author

Harlan Coben is the winner of the Edgar, Shamus, and Anthony Awards, the first writer to win all three. He is the author of nine previous novels, including *Tell No One*, an international bestseller, as well as the recent blockbuster *Gone for Good*, a main selection of the Book-of-the-Month Club. He lives with his family in New Jersey.

MAN OF MY DREAMS

Further Titles by Johanna Lindsey from Severn House

A HEART SO WILD
LOVE ONLY ONCE
SAVAGE THUNDER
WHEN LOVE AWAITS

MAN OF MY DREAMS

Johanna Lindsey

SEVERN
SH
HOUSE

This title first published in Great Britain 1998 by
SEVERN HOUSE PUBLISHERS LTD of
9–15 High Street, Sutton, Surrey SM1 1DF.
This first hardcover edition published 1998 in the USA by
SEVERN HOUSE PUBLISHERS INC of
595 Madison Avenue, New York, N.Y. 10022,
by arrangement with Avon Books,
a division of the Hearst Corporation.

British Library Cataloguing in Publication Data

Lindsey,   Johanna

   Man of my dreams
   1.   Love stories
   I.   Title
   813.5'4 [F]

ISBN 0 7278 2214 4

Printed and bound in Great Britain by
MPG Books Ltd, Bodmin, Cornwall.

For Lee Ann and Harry
When true love happens, it endures

Chapter 1

England, 1878

"Just *what* do you think you're staring at, Tyler Whately?"

Megan Penworthy's tone was unduly sharp, but then she had meant it to be. It was also, along with the look she turned on him, filled with haughty disdain, as if she couldn't abide the fellow. That wasn't true at all. She actually liked the Honorable Tyler Whately.

He was pleasantly handsome, with light blond hair that needed only a minimum of Macassar oil to control it, a trim mustache, and whiskers that weren't so long that they hid the strength of his jaw. His dark green eyes were rather nice, too. And he was not excessively tall, so that a poor girl had to

1

crane her neck to look up at him. Nor was his body intimidating in its slimness, which was not to say he lacked strength. At twenty-seven, he was a young man with excellent prospects, not to mention a rather sizable estate inherited from his mother's side of the family.

Megan had no doubt whatsoever that Tyler would make a fine husband. She might even have set her own cap for him if her best friend, Tiffany Roberts, hadn't confessed soon after they'd met him, that *she* wanted him.

Those had been Tiffany's exact words. "I want him, Meg." The two girls had always spoken bluntly, at least to each other, and when no one else was around to be shocked by it. But Tiffany had been too excited that day to care if anyone else heard her. "This is truly *the* one. I've never felt so—so—when he smiled at me, well, the feeling was—damn, I can't describe it, but I swear I was going to faint."

"Probably your corset laced up too tight again," Megan had replied with a teasing grin. "You know you need at least a little room to breathe—"

"Oh, stop." Tiffany had laughed. "I'm perfectly serious. What do I do to win him, Meg?"

Just because Megan was the older by five months, she was supposed to have all the answers, but she knew next to nothing about that particular subject, though she was loath to admit it. After all, men fell all over themselves trying to get her attention. It was embarrassing, especially since she never did anything to attract them. But after two years of having every eligible male in the neighborhood come calling, she had finally concluded it was simply her looks, even though she had the most unfashionable hair color in the kingdom, an atrocious, gaudy, bright rusty-copper color, the one and only thing she had inherited from her father.

So Megan had drawn on common sense that day and said to her best friend, "Just smile and be yourself, and he won't have a chance."

And he didn't. Within two months of meeting her, the Right Honorable Tyler had been moved to propose to Tiffany. They were to be married on her eighteenth birthday, in a little less than three months. And no simple ceremony for this viscount's son. They would be doing it up grand right at the height of the London Season.

Considering how pleased Megan was for her friend, and what a fine fellow she thought Tyler to be, her churlish question to him should have surprised the affianced couple, whom she was chaperoning on the way to church this bright summer Sunday. It did, in fact, surprise Tyler, for her attitude toward him never ceased first to baffle him, then to irritate him, since he never did anything to cause it. It didn't surprise Tiffany in the least, but then she knew the reason for Megan's behavior.

Tiffany had appreciated it at first, when Megan had set out to make Tyler think she was the veriest bitch, for any young man

Tiffany had ever been the least bit interested in had understandably fallen in love with Megan instead. It wasn't that Tiffany wasn't pretty. She was quite pretty; her blond curls and deep blue eyes were in the height of fashion. But pretty didn't stand a chance next to the kind of mesmerizing beauty that Megan had been blessed with. So Megan had set out at the start to make sure that Tyler's interest didn't roam elsewhere, most especially in her direction.

But Megan's rather unorthodox strategy had been going on long enough, that Tyler no longer just flushed and stammered apologies for whatever it was the outspoken Megan had taken offense at. He now fought back, and he was getting rather good at it.

As he flipped the reins sharply at the high-stepping bay that was pulling the open carriage away from Tiffany's home, where he had picked up both girls, he remarked without looking at Megan again, "Why, I was staring at nothing at all, Miss Penworthy. Absolutely *nothing.*"

Tiffany stiffened. Tyler had never been quite that cruel in a comeback before. Megan, she saw, took his reply to heart, blushing furiously and turning away so he wouldn't see that his barb had hurt.

Tiffany couldn't blame Tyler. There was just so much nastiness a man could take without getting nasty in return. No, it was Tiffany's fault for not putting a stop to Megan's scheme long before now. The reason she hadn't was that small kernel of doubt she still harbored that if Tyler ever saw Megan as she really was, he would become just as smitten as all the other men who were treated to one of her smiles.

But enough was enough. She *was* sure that Tyler loved her. And if she couldn't hold him by now, then she didn't deserve him, or more to the point, he didn't deserve her. She would speak to Megan right after the vicar's sermon— or maybe before, at least before the hurt wore off and Megan got mad instead. That thought worried Tiffany, because when Megan got angry, which fortunately wasn't often, she could be utterly unpredictable.

Tiffany found her chance when they arrived at the parish church on the edge of Teadale Village. Tyler moved ahead of them to pay his respects to Lady Ophelia and her three daughters. As Countess of Wedgwood, Ophelia Thackeray was in possession of the most lofty title in the neighborhood, and she lorded that over the lesser gentry. Even Megan was not immune to Ophelia's consequence. She never missed an opportunity to put herself before the lady's notice, because the countess was the reigning hostess in the parish and her invitations were highly coveted. Megan would do just about anything to get one.

Tiffany had to pull Megan back from plowing after Tyler to greet the countess, so she could have a few words with her. Megan's impatient look didn't promise she'd be attentive to those words, however, and she was quick to try to forestall them.

"I hope you're not going to mention what happened in the carriage, Tiffany."

"I most certainly am," Tiffany replied, undaunted. "I know what you're doing, Megan, and I love you for it. I'm sure it even helped in the beginning. But I'd like to think I can hold Tyler on my own now, that the sight of those cavernous dimples of yours won't have him fainting at your feet."

Megan blinked, then gave a spontaneous, unladylike hoot of laughter before she hugged her friend. "You're right, I know. I think it's just become a habit, my picking on the dear man."

"So break the habit this very day."

Megan grinned. "Very well, but you don't suppose he'll think something is wrong with me, do you, if I start being nice to him?"

"I think he'll quit subtly suggesting that I stop seeing you."

Megan's midnight-blue eyes flared, then narrowed. "The devil he did! When?"

"More than once, but can you blame him when you only show him your very worst? It baffles him why we're such good friends, since it appears to him that we are so very different in temperament."

"Fat lot he knows," Megan snapped. "We're cut from the same cloth, right down to the ragged hem." But then she bit her lip, unable to hide her concern. "He wouldn't insist, would he, after you're married?"

"You know he's not the least bit high-handed," Tiffany said reassuringly. "And even if he did insist, it wouldn't make a jot of difference. I'm afraid you're stuck with this friend for life, Miss Penworthy."

Megan smiled the smile that released both dimples and gave her a different kind of beauty, a look that was warm, open—approachable. It even gave Tiffany pause, though she was gifted by that special smile quite often. It still made her feel privileged each time it was bestowed on her, and quite certain there wasn't anything in the world she wouldn't do for this dearest friend. It also made the gentlemen in the churchyard who had been covertly watching Megan stop their conversations in mid-sentence to stare openly. Several even took hope from it and determined to try their hand again at courting the incomparable beauty of the parish.

Having said her peace, Tiffany put her arm through Megan's and led her to the church door, where Tyler was still talking with the four Thackerays. She whispered aside with a grin, "I feel lucky today, Meg. That long-awaited invite is going to be ours at last, I just know it. And you look smashing in that new blue poplin. Old hatchet-face will most definitely be impressed."

"Do you really think so?" Megan asked hopefully.

Tiffany wished that damn invite wasn't so important to her friend, but it was. And it wasn't just that the countess seemed to know everyone in the whole of Devonshire, that people came from miles away to her parties, always guaranteeing new and interesting people to meet. That was only part of it, though a big part for a young girl with the same hopes as every other young girl, to find the man of her romantic dreams, since she hadn't found him in the gentlemen of her own acquaintance.

That still wasn't the main reason, for Megan would be having her London Season in a few months and would meet all the eligible men she could hope for then. No, the Countess of Wedgwood had worked hard over the years to make it an *achievement* to be invited to her home. To never end up on the guest list implied you weren't quite up to scratch, or worse, that there was actually something wrong with you, a family scandal perhaps, that just hadn't made the rounds yet. Then again, every other family of note in the parish had received its invite, even if only once, even Tiffany's family. Her parents had gone, but she had begged off with an illness out of loyalty to Megan, though that was one secret she had never told her friend, for it would only have made her more desperate for that invite, and she was already desperate enough.

They had been so sure, the two of them, that the countess was merely waiting until Megan turned eighteen. But two months had passed since then, and the squire and his daughter were still being ignored.

Tiffany squeezed Megan's arm in answer to her inquiry, praying she wasn't just getting her friend's hopes up, only to have them dashed again. But this was the first time in over a month that they would have the opportunity to speak with the countess, thanks to Tyler. Perhaps all Lady Ophelia needed was to be reminded that Megan Penworthy was her neighbor . . .

"Next Saturday, then, Mr. Whately," Lady Ophelia was saying when the two girls joined them. "Just a small gathering of forty or so. And do bring your lovely fiancée."

The countess smiled at Tiffany, stared at Megan for a moment, then turned and entered the church.

It was a direct cut, a deliberate cut. Alice Thackeray, the youngest daughter at seventeen, even giggled before she hurried after her mother. The other two girls, Agnes and Anne, merely looked spitefully pleased.

Tiffany was appalled for only a moment before she got angry. How dare they? Everyone knew that Megan and Tiffany were best friends, and that Megan accompanied Tiffany and Tyler almost everywhere because she was their chaperon. It was as if the Thackerays had planned this slight, timed it perfectly for the greatest effect, this subtle telling that Megan's coveted invitation wasn't going to be forthcoming, ever. Tiffany was afraid she knew why. Megan was just too lovely to have around when one had three less-than-pretty daughters to marry off.

Tyler cleared his throat, recalling them to the fact that they were just standing there. Tiffany finally glanced at Megan to see how badly she was taking the Thackerays' snubbing. Worse than Tiffany expected. Megan's face was as pale as the white ribbons on her bonnet, her large blue eyes awash with tears that were going to spill at any moment, though she was trying to hold them back. Tiffany's heart ached for her, and it made her even angrier that there wasn't anything she could do to help other than to offer her support.

She squeezed her friend's hand, drawing those bewildered blue eyes to her. "Why?" Megan whispered.

Tiffany was angry enough to be blunt. "You're too pretty, damn it. She's got those plain chicks of hers to marry off, but no man will even look at them if you're around."

"But that's so—so—"

"Selfish? Petty? Absolutely, Meg, but—"

"It's all right, Tiff, really—but I need to be alone right—"

She didn't finish, walking abruptly away. "Megan, wait," Tiffany called out, but she didn't. She was even running before she left the churchyard, because she could no longer hold back the tears. Mr. Pocock held out a handkerchief to her as she passed him, but she probably didn't even see him. He stared after her, too, watching her hurry down the lane, away from the church.

"I s'pose we'll have to hie after her, since it's over a mile to Sutton Manor," Tyler remarked.

"That's not why we're going after her," Tiffany replied absently, her attention still on Megan as she stumbled, stopped, dug into her reticule for a handkerchief, then went on without using it. "She and I have walked that distance before." But Tiffany finally glanced at him, and his expression had her hackles rising again. "Don't you dare look smug over this, Tyler Whately. She didn't deserve what that horrid woman did."

"Allow me to disagree—"

"No, I will not. You're going to notice a difference in her after today anyway, so I might as well tell you. The only reason she's treated you abominably was so you wouldn't like her. It was done for love of me, because she knows how much I—I want you, and she didn't want to see me hurt if your interest went to her instead."

"But I can barely tolerate the girl," he protested.

"You didn't feel that way when you first met her, did you?" Tiffany shot back.

"Well, no, but—d'you mean to say it was all *deliberate*?"

"Yes, and if you want to get angry about it, then get angry at me, because I could have stopped her before today, but I—I guess I was still a little worried about your finding out that she's really a very warm, caring person—"

"And spoiled, and willful—"

"Only a little spoiled, but that's to be expected with a father as kind and generous as the squire is. And I happen to be just as willful, Tyler."

"Yes, but in you I find it rather endearing."

"Thank you—I think. But can you understand Megan's dilemma? She *knows* how men see her, Tyler. The attitude she took with you is the only defense she has to keep men from falling hopelessly in love with her."

"But I wouldn't want a wife who looks like her, darling. Good God, no!" And he really did seem appalled at the notion. "That girl needs a man with a strong constitution, with little to no temper, and who doesn't even know the meaning of jealousy. I couldn't abide having every one of my acquaintances in love with my wife—one or two I might tolerate," he added with a smile. "But all of them, why, it would drive me to despondency."

"You make it sound hopeless for her. What man wouldn't get a little jealous where his wife is concerned?"

"Well, actually, the man's jealousy won't matter all that much, I suppose, if he's assured of her affections. But she'll have to make a constant effort to keep him assured."

Tiffany wasn't sure she liked the sound of that one-sided scenario. "What if she ends up getting jealous for one reason or another—will he have to do some assuring of his own?"

" 'Course not. He married her, didn't he?"

"Not yet he didn't," Tiffany grouched.

Tyler blinked as she whipped the train of her skirt out of the way to march stiffly toward the carriage. He almost leaped to catch up with her.

"I say, we didn't just switch subjects there, did we?" he asked uneasily.

"You tell me, Tyler. Did we?"

"Certainly not," he insisted. "Your friend's case is unique, Tiffany, because *she* is unique—which is not to say I don't find you unique as well, but you see what I mean. There is simply no comparison to ourselves."

"All right, Tyler, I forgive you."

"Thank you—I think."

Chapter 2

"You're eating *again?*" Tiffany asked as she sailed into the dining room unannounced.

The Penworthy butler, Krebs, appeared behind her merely to close the doors, a disgruntled look on his face. He never was quick enough to beat Tiffany to a door, a point he should have resigned himself to a long time ago, but he never had, despite the fact that protocol had been dispensed with where Tiffany was concerned soon after she and Megan had first met.

Surprising Krebs by always using a different entrance to the house when she arrived was a game to Tiffany, one she still enjoyed. If Krebs was lucky enough to see her arrive—and even in that she frequently circled the manor to come around directly to the stable behind it

14

so he wouldn't—he might dash for the kitchen entrance, but she'd choose the French doors off the drawing room. If he waited in the drawing room, he'd soon hear her teasing call, "Anyone home?" as she came from the back of the house to head right up the stairs. Once, when he knew she was expected, he'd left all three doors wide open and waited in the downstairs hall, where Tiffany would have to pass no matter which door she used. She'd come in through the dining room window that day. Krebs didn't speak to her for two weeks after that defeat.

Megan had hoped the Robertses' butler would accommodate her in the same game. But he was a sweet old dear who just smiled at her and wished her a good day when she would appear suddenly in his domain, which took the fun out of it.

She covered a yawn now with her napkin before tossing it onto the table. "This is my first meal of the day, actually, though I've had enough of it."

"Well, do finish your tea," Tiffany said as she sat down next to her. "I could use another cup myself, so I'll share it with you." And then nonchalantly, as if she hadn't been surprised by Megan's remark, she added, "Your first meal, you say? Do you know what time it is?"

Megan shrugged, adding tea to her cup and passing it to Tiffany, who proceeded to add nearly an equal amount of sugar to it. There

was no question of sharing after that, since
Megan took her tea without sugar, but then
they both knew that. There wasn't much of
anything that they didn't know about each other after eleven years of friendship. But Krebs
was able to anticipate *some* things, and had
gone to the kitchen to have Cora deliver another cup.

Cora was the cook's daughter, a pretty girl
who had trouble containing her voluptuous
curves in the formfitting current fashions, so
consequently she was always out of breath
because of a too tight corset. Her maid's
uniform was simplicity itself, even if it still
sported the bustle and long train that had
been the standard ever since the crinoline had
gone out of style so many years ago. It was
the bane of some ladies that their servants
wore the same styles as they did, though of a
much cheaper quality. Even charwomen went
to work with their skirts trailing, but they had
ingenious little ties that got the trains out of
the way until they finished their jobs, releasing
the trains again when they left work.

Megan waited until Cora had bobbed her
curtsy and left the room before she confessed,
"I overslept."

That *was* a confession, since Megan never
overslept and they both knew it. "What is that,
the second time in your life? I can understand
the first time, after we waited half the night for
Lord Beacon's ghost to appear in that ruined
manor house he's supposed to haunt. What

a disappointment—" She broke off before she got carried away reminiscing, and asked sympathetically, "A bad night?"

"An understatement," Megan admitted.

"Damn, I knew I should have stayed over last night. But I thought you were good and mad enough that you wouldn't start brooding again."

Megan grinned. "You think anger is conducive to a good night's sleep?"

"Well, better than brooding."

"I'm in a position to disagree, Tiffany, believe me," Megan replied.

"Oh, well, then," Tiffany said matter-of-factly. "I guess it got worse after I left?"

"A trifle."

Megan's tears had dried up by the time Tiffany had hopped out of the carriage yesterday to walk beside her along the country lane, leaving Tyler to follow discreetly at a distance so they could speak privately. Tiffany hadn't realized yet that Megan had already put her self-pity aside and was stewing with a healthy fury. To cheer her, Tiffany had suggested she go back and sock Lady O in the nose. Megan had actually considered it, then dismissed the idea as not a good enough retaliation. Since Tiffany hadn't been serious to begin with, she agreed that the countess wasn't worth the scandal that would follow that particular brand of revenge.

But she was pleased that Megan wasn't feeling sorry for herself, and was good and furious over what had happened instead. It was much more healthy. Only Megan was mostly angry at herself for all the time and energy she'd wasted on what had been a hopeless endeavor from the start. She felt like an utter fool. Tiffany felt like one, too, for not having seen it coming sooner. But old hatchet-face hadn't had to be so bloody spiteful in delivering the blow. That was uncalled-for.

"I *knew* I shouldn't have listened to you!" Tiffany exclaimed now. " 'Go home,' you said. 'I'm just fine,' you said. 'It's not as if I haven't been snubbed before,' you said."

Megan chuckled. "Well, that's true enough."

"I don't know how you can laugh about it."

To this day it still made Tiffany furious that the other friends they'd had when they were younger had stopped coming 'round, one by one, when Megan started to turn into a beauty. Quite simply, the other girls felt plain and unattractive next to Megan, and they couldn't abide that. But some of them had actually snubbed her later in public, and that was taking their pettiness too far. You'd think Megan's looks were something she had developed to spite them.

Megan wasn't sure how she could laugh about it either, when having friends turn on you was a kind of hurt that never really went away completely; it just lay beneath the surface waiting for a similar instance to bring it all back. And what the Countess of Wedgwood had done yesterday certainly brought it all back.

"Better to laugh than to cry again, don't you think?" Megan said as she stared at the left-over sausage she was using to make circles in a dollop of jam on her plate.

Tiffany started. "Good God, yes! Absolutely! Do you want to talk about it?"

They both knew the subject had switched to those past hurts now, not the present one. "No—except, when I think of all the fun we've had over the years, I almost feel sorry for those girls that they weren't around to share it."

"Now that you mention it, I guess I do, too. After all, they turned into such boring creatures after they deserted us. On second thought, I don't feel at all sorry for them."

Megan peeked up with a grin. "Neither do I, but it sounded like a nice thing to say."

They both laughed, when it was honestly a dreary subject. Tiffany was quick to change it. "I suppose this late meal means you haven't had your morning ride and are going to be in a rotten mood all day because of it."

Megan usually breakfasted bright and early with the squire, then spent half the morning riding her horse, Sir Ambrose, and the other half grooming it. No stableboy—though they only had one since they owned a mere four horses—was ever allowed near her pride and joy, other than to feed Sir Ambrose, and even that Megan liked to do. For anyone who knew about her tendency to haunt the stables, it wasn't hard to guess that Megan absolutely loved horses.

"Actually, I did have my ride." Staring again at her sausage, Megan added, "Last night."

"You didn't."

"Around two in the morning."

"You *didn't!*"

Megan glanced up to explain earnestly, "I had to, Tiffany, I swear I did. I was near to going crazy."

"Did you take one of the footmen with you?"

"I didn't have the heart to wake them."

"Megan!"

"Well, no one saw me," Megan said, defensive now, realizing belatedly how scandalous it was for a young lady to go out in the middle of the night by herself. "I stayed to the road for Sir Ambrose's sake, since it was so dark last night. And it worked. I went right to sleep when I got back." Tiffany just stared, so Megan added, "That ride did more than just let me get to sleep. On the third trip to the village and back—"

"Third?"

"I ran the route five times—well, I only had the bloody road to stick to, and Sir Ambrose was as game as I for a full-out gallop."

Tiffany rolled her eyes.

"*As* I was saying." Megan got back to the subject. "On the third run it came to me exactly what I could do to set Ophelia Thackeray on her ear in the grandest way possible, and that's exactly what I'm going to do."

Tiffany's expression turned instantly wary. "You didn't reconsider socking her, did you?"

"No," Megan said with a grin, then triumphantly added, "I'm going to build a mansion twice the size of hers and become the new reigning hostess of the area. *That* will show her."

"Uh, how do you propose to do that?"

"Very simply. I'm going to marry a duke."

"Oh, well, that will do it. Which duke did you have in mind?

"Wrothston, of course," Megan announced. "He's the only one we know."

Tiffany sat up, because putting a name to this duke took the whimsy out of Megan's idea, enough to make Tiffany worry that she might actually be serious. "We don't *know* him a'tall. If you'll recall, he wasn't at Sherring Cross when we took tea with his grandmother. The only reason we even got on his estate was that your father had some obscure acquaintance with the dowager duchess and took the chance of writing her for advice when he was looking for a horse to buy you for your twelfth birthday."

"And it was fate that she invited us to come choose one from the duke's stables."

"Fate? They had hundreds of horses. She was delighted to get rid of one."

Megan leaned forward to whisper that word ladies weren't supposed to know anything about. "They *breed* them at Sherring Cross, so of course she was glad to sell one." Then she sat back to add, "We already have something in common—horses."

"We? As in you and the duke? Good God, Meg, you aren't *really* serious about this, are you?"

"Absolutely." Megan grinned excitedly. "Just imagine, Tiff, a magnificent coach pulling up to the church, with the ducal arms of Wrothston emblazoned on it, while the countess with her still unmarried daughters is standing there agog. Then yours truly steps out of the coach, assisted by the most handsome man imaginable. I will, of course, be magnanimous and bid the countess a good day, and even introduce my husband, the duke. And I will kindly not notice that her mouth is hanging open in shock."

"And it would be, too." Tiffany laughed, caught up in the pleasant fantasy for a moment. "Oh, that would be the perfect comeuppance." Then she sighed dramatically. "If only it *were* possible."

"But it is," Megan replied quietly. "And I mean to see it happen."

Tiffany was appalled to see Megan's stubborn look appear. "Now, wait a minute. Let's at least be realistic about this. If you want to marry for a title, we'll find you a nice viscount. Maybe even an earl wouldn't be impossible. Yes, an earl, which will make you Lady O's equal—don't shake your head at me, damn it!"

"Tiffany, if I'm going to stoop to marrying for a title, it might as well be the big one."

"Then don't stoop."

"I've already decided to stoop. And the more I think about it, the more I like the idea of being a duchess."

Tiffany groaned. "Why do *I* have to be the bad guy here? All right, listen to the facts, Megan. You may have an earl somewhere in your background—"

"Four generations back, plus a baron or two."

"Whatever, you're still just a simple country squire's daughter. Dukes can marry royalty if they want. They do *not* marry squires' daughters."

"Wrothston will, and why not?" Megan replied tenaciously. "He's already rich beyond imagining. He's already got all the consequence he can manage, so he doesn't need to marry a title himself. He can marry for love if he wants, and a duke can bloody well do whatever he wants. My background *does* happen to make me acceptable. Certainly he can do better than a squire's daughter, but he's not going to care a jot for that because he's going to be in love with me, hopelessly in love, mind you. And you know why, don't you? Because of this cursed face of mine. It's given me nothing but grief till now, but now it's going to make up for that and win me a duke."

There was a lot of bitterness and hurt in those words, which made Tiffany cautious in asking her next question. "What about you?"

"What about me?"

"What if you don't love him?"

"Of course I will."

"What if you can't, Meg? What if he's horrible and mean and not lovable at all?"

"He wouldn't dare be. He's a duke."

Tiffany almost smiled at that ridiculous certainty. "But what if when you meet him you just know, deep down, that he won't do a'tall, that he'd only make you miserable? Would you still want him?"

After a long pause Megan said, "No."

Thank God for that, Tiffany said to herself with a sigh. She felt on firmer ground now and so plowed on. "He could be ugly, you know."

"Are you forgetting that parlormaid who whispered to us how handsome he was?"

"She was trying to impress us."

"We were already overawed. We didn't need to be impressed anymore that day."

"That's another matter. You can't *really* want to live in a place like that."

"Are you joking?" Megan gasped. "Sherring Cross is the most magnificent home imaginable."

"It's not a home, it's a bloody mausoleum spread out over a good six acres. The stable alone was bigger than this house, and this is no small house you have here."

"I know. It was all so grand," Megan said dreamily.

"Grand? People probably get lost in that house every day and die."

Their eyes met on that remark and they both suddenly burst into laughter.

"Die, Tiff?"

"Well, worry about it, at any rate." They laughed again; then Tiffany finally conceded the point. "All right, I guess it isn't beyond impossible to win a duke, not for someone who looks like you. Are you absolutely sure, Meg?"

"Yes. Ambrose St. James can start counting his bachelor days good-bye."

"Good God," Tiffany gasped. "I forgot you named your horse after him."

Megan blinked. "So did I."

Again they burst into laughter, but were interrupted this time as Krebs opened the doors to announce the Honorable Tyler Whately's arrival. Megan gave him a brilliant smile with the greeting, "Good morning, Tyler. My, don't you look dashing today. If you'll just give me a moment to run up and get my bonnet, we can leave."

She sailed past him without receiving a word of greeting from him, but the man was still dumbstruck by the smile she'd bestowed on him. Tiffany hid her own smile behind her teacup, pleasantly surprised that she wasn't the least bit jealous over his reaction to her dear friend.

She remarked blandly, "You'll have to do better than that, Tyler, if you don't want her to revert to being nasty to you again."

He snapped his mouth shut, shoved his hands in his pockets, and scowled. "God, I don't envy the man who wins her hand, indeed I don't."

"He's already been chosen, so let's hope he wins her heart along with her hand."

Tyler's brow rose questioningly. "Did I miss something between yesterday and today?"

"Nothing much—but did you ever think you would feel sorry for a duke?"

Chapter 3

"This is taking precaution too bloody far, Mr. Browne. Walking, by God. Freddy would laugh his arse off if he could see it."

Mortimer Browne gave the tall man at his side another disgusted look. All he'd heard were complaints of one kind or another since they'd left Kent. But he'd been warned to expect them.

"You wouldn't be walking if you'd brought another horse along as I suggested."

"D'you hear how he insults you, Caesar?" Devlin said to the horse of that name.

Mortimer gave the stallion Devlin was leading a killing look for snorting in agreement, but he pressed on with the bare facts. "Traveling at night as we been doing is one thing,

Mr. Jefferys, but during the day, you see a lot more and get seen a lot more, and it'd only make folks wonder what a bloke like you is doing riding a horse like that, wouldn't it, now? You're here to disappear, not to draw extra attention to yourself."

"And you're here to badger me to death, I suppose," Devlin replied. "But in case you haven't noticed, the village is no longer in sight, and there isn't another bloody soul on this road."

"There wasn't, but there is now, or are you blind as well as pigheaded?"

Devlin ignored the carriage that had just come over a rise. Instead he stopped short to give Mortimer one of his more intimidating looks. From that six-foot-three, well-filled-out frame, it most definitely did some intimidating. But Mortimer hadn't been chosen to accompany this young man because he was known to buckle under. Just the opposite. And besides, he had his orders straight from the one and only person Devlin wasn't quite up to defying, and that gave Mortimer the upper hand—some of the time.

"We was told the squire's holdings ain't that far down the road," Mortimer explained reasonably. "When we reach it will be soon enough for you to get back on that fine beast. Till then, kindly remember you're no more than a stableboy now—"

"Breeder, Mr. Browne," Devlin cut in succinctly. "A breeder of fine horseflesh *and* trainer of same. Yes, a trainer, too. That has a nice ring—"

"But you don't know the first thing—"

"That's what you're along for, to see I don't make a fool of myself."

"That's not why—"

"That's why *I* agreed to your obnoxious company. If I have to live in a stable, I'll bloody well have top say in that stable, or this harebrained idea ends right now."

Mortimer opened his mouth to argue, but he could see on *this* point it wouldn't do him a bit of good. So he nodded curtly, but went back to giving orders that had a better chance of being heeded.

"Since that *is* a carriage coming our way, and most likely carrying some of the local gentry, pull your hat down to conceal—"

"Oh, give over, Browne," Devlin bit out, obviously at the limit of his patience. "We're at the bloody end of the world here. If those country bumpkins recognize me, I'll eat these atrocious boots you dredged up for me to wear."

"Could you at least slouch a little?"

"No." And that "No" had a definite ring of finality to it. "I'm walking, *walking,* for God's sake, with a moth-eaten jacket dangling from my shoulder, scruffed boots unworthy of a charity box, and I'm sweating, Mr. Browne. *Sweating!* Not another bloody concession am I inclined to make. Not another one."

"Sweating in a bloody white lawn shirt,"

Mortimer mumbled beneath his breath. "The very mark of a gentle—"

"What was that?"

"Nothing, Mr. Jefferys, nothing at all," Mortimer said. "But if we fail in this endeavor, we know whose fault it will be, don't we?"

"Indeed we do."

That wasn't reassuring in the least.

It wasn't unusual to see folks walking along the road from Teadale, even leading horses behind them instead of riding them. What was unusual today was the quality of the horse-flesh on that road.

Megan noticed the black Thoroughbred long before Tyler was moved to remark, "By God, did you ever see such a fine-looking stud?"

Tiffany and Megan exchanged an amused look. The word "stud" wouldn't have slipped out if Tyler weren't so impressed that he could even forget there were ladies present. But they were closer, and the black stallion's elegant lines were unmistakable now. Indeed, none of them had ever seen such a magnificent animal.

With her love of horses, Megan was as impressed as Tyler, if not more so. She had prided herself on having the finest horse in the parish, in all of Devonshire for that matter, but this Thoroughbred put Sir Ambrose to shame, and she couldn't even begrudge him that. He was just too beautiful. She could imagine the ride he would give, the speed a skillful rider could get out of him. It wasn't fair that stallions were considered unsuitable mounts for ladies, for this was one horse Megan would dearly love to own. She wildly considered asking her father to buy him. He always gave her anything she wanted—within reason. But then she had to dismiss the idea, certain that the owner of that animal wouldn't part with him for any price. *She* certainly wouldn't if he were hers.

It barely registered on her that Tyler had stopped the carriage, except that the stallion was right there in front of her now for her to admire, and she couldn't take her eyes off him. She started to stand up, with every intention of getting even closer, but Tiffany's laugh and whispered "Behave" recalled her to the fact that a lady didn't just walk up and examine someone else's horse, not without the owner's permission, at any rate. She turned now to get that permission from the man who held the stallion's reins—and promptly forgot about the horse.

He stood there, sweaty and dusty, and she thought him the most handsome man she'd ever seen. Without considering the impropriety of it, she cast her eyes over him with the same avid intensity she had given the stallion. Tall, broad, divinely put together, and clean-shaven, revealing every arrogant line of those stunning, sun-gilded features. She even found beautiful the hand that rose so slowly to remove his hat, and even the wildly unkempt hair that was as black as pitch. And then she

ran into the most amazing turquoise eyes—
and suddenly realized they were staring right
back at her.

The jolt she received from those eyes caused
her to become aware of what she was doing,
and she immediately looked away, grateful
for the wide brim of her own hat that would
conceal from all concerned the hot color of her
mortification. She simply could not credit what
she had just done. The only excuse she could
think of was that she had been avidly admiring
the stallion, then to see an even more magnificent specimen, though of a different breed . . .
that *was* no excuse for the way she had stared
at a complete stranger. She had never stared
at men she did know the way she had looked
at this man.

And then the picture of him, still branded
in her mind, pointed out the poor quality of
his attire, the slowness of his manners, as if he
weren't used to them, the lack of even a neckcloth, which no gentleman would be without.
He wasn't gentry, then, and thank God for that;
at least she hoped he wasn't, so her unspeakable behavior wouldn't make the rounds of her
acquaintances. It might be mentioned in a few
taverns, but she could live with that—no, she
couldn't. God, *what* had possessed her?

But Tiffany hadn't noticed, thankfully, and
Tyler was still utterly engrossed in the stallion
and hearing about its bloodlines, in answer to
the question he'd just asked. What else had
been said, Megan couldn't imagine. She wanted

to be away from there. She never wanted to lay eyes on that fellow again with his secret knowledge of her wretched behavior.

" . . . as if I had the blunt to own him," that deep voice was saying in something of a churlish tone.

"Then who does?" Tyler wanted to know.

"Squire Penworthy's the proud new owner."

Megan's head whipped around, but again she was struck first by the handsomeness of the fellow, so much so, with his eyes meeting hers head on, that she almost, to her horror, forgot his incredible statement.

As it was, it took five long seconds for her to remember and let the words tumble out. "I don't believe it. My father would have said something to me."

"And who is your father that he would know anything about it?"

"Squire Penworthy, of course."

It was his turn to pause overlong, but then his full lower lip curled up the slightest bit. "Ah, well, I don't see that his decision to start up a stud farm would be any business of yours, now would it?"

That was perfectly true—in most cases. Not in hers, however, when her father knew she would take a keen interest in the acquisition of new horseflesh, for whatever the reason. He would just have found a more delicate way to mention it. Not like this fellow, who seemed to take an undue amount of pleasure in saying the word "stud" as he did, which was saying it rudely. Even Tyler moved uncomfortably upon hearing that "forbidden" word, forgetting he had said it himself only moments ago.

Those turquoise eyes were still on Megan, flustering her with their directness, and now that he had her attention again, they moved over her in the same slow manner that hers had done to him—deliberately, she didn't doubt, an exact tit for tat. And there wasn't anything she could say about it without his announcing to the world—or to their small group—that he was merely repaying the compliment. But what he was doing was no compliment. It was an insult of the worse kind, something no gentleman would do no matter the provocation, but then he was proving he wasn't of that stamp with every passing moment—unless he thought she welcomed his personal attention. Good God, he might think just that after what she'd done.

"Then you're only delivering the stallion?" Megan blurted out. "You'll be gone afterward?"

The hopeful note in her tone had Tiffany looking askance at her. The man on the ground didn't miss it either. He seemed confused for the briefest moment; then he smiled, a downright nasty-looking smile that made Megan brace herself, and with reason.

"I'm a horse breeder, miss, and I come with this one, 'cause no one else can handle him but me. You don't think his previous owner would let a horse like this go without assuring he has the proper care, do you? Not bloody likely. But I'm also a horse trainer, so I'm a right valuable chap to have around. I have a knack for it, you see, cause I treat them all like women—with a gentle hand for the most part, a firm one when needed, and a good slap to the hindquarters when they get too feisty."

Now why the devil had he said that, Devlin wondered. Just to see if her cheeks could get as bright as that god-awful titian hair? Redheads did not blush becomingly. This one did, damn her.

The gent was starting to sputter indignantly, however. Devlin would have been surprised if he didn't. But he gave the blond chap a look of innocent inquiry, and got a look back that said, What could one expect of a horse breeder but ill-bred manners?

But the squire's daughter was good and furious now and not trying to hide it. "Drive on, Tyler. I'll have him dismissed before he's settled in, I guarantee it."

Devlin heard the young man's answer as the reins snapped and the carriage pulled away. "I'm sure he didn't mean that as it sounded, or at least, not as an insult."

"The devil he didn't."

"She's right," Mortimer said beside Devlin as they both stared after the departing carriage.

"Found your tongue again, did you?"

Mortimer's cheeks exploded with color. "So

I lost it. I ain't never seen anything the likes of her before, but what's your excuse? You didn't lose your tongue, you lost your bloody wits. That was *the* squire's daughter, the same said squire that don't even know yet that we're going to be guests in his stable, *or* that he's bought himself a prime piece of horseflesh. What if she had had that bloke take her right home instead to complain to her father?"

Devlin scowled because that hadn't occurred to him, when it should have. But he dismissed it by saying, "So we would have had a little race to see who would get to the squire first. Need you wonder who would win?"

"Oh, that's a fine solution, guaranteed to get the little miss in a worse snit. Why'd you have to go and insult her in the first place?"

"I thought I was being crudely in character."

"Whose character, a breeder of fine horseflesh who by his very trade associates with the gentry enough to know better, or a guttersnipe who don't?"

Devlin suddenly laughed. "I think I will be safer if I assume the guttersnipe's manners, at least around that little gem."

"Safer?"

"Without question," Devlin replied. But since that hadn't answered Mortimer's confusion, he added, "I do believe you were right, Mr. Browne. My wits went a-begging, and they haven't come back yet."

"She *was* something to look at, wasn't she?"

"If you like brassy redheads."

Mortimer snorted. "And you don't, I suppose?"

"No, thank God. If I did, I'd prob'ly have been laid to waste. But you know, Mr. Browne, I'm inclined to think now that I just might enjoy our sojourn in this tail end of the world."

"I hope that doesn't mean you intend to amuse yourself with that little miss."

"Amuse? Certainly, or didn't you notice she and I just declared war?"

Chapter 4

Arnold Penworthy glanced up from the letter in his hand to give Devlin another long look, his third since he'd opened the letter, but then he went back to reading. He had warm, friendly brown eyes. Even disturbed as he was now about what he was being asked to do, his eyes were still friendly.

She was nothing like her father. Devlin had felt like a bloody giant when the squire had stood up from behind his desk to accept the letter Devlin had handed over. The squire was definitely on the short side, might even be an inch or two shorter than his daughter. And rotund as a stout barrel of ale, whereas Devlin knew corsets, from as many as he'd had the pleasure of removing, and would hazard a guess that Miss Penworthy's hadn't been cinched in all that tight to give her that slim, hourglass waistline.

Miss? He didn't know. She could be married. She certainly looked old enough to be married. That could even have been her husband with her today. Devlin wasn't going to ask.

"It doesn't say here why he wants me to hide you in my stable," the squire suddenly pointed out.

Devlin considered his answer carefully, but finally opted for bluntness in saying, "A friend of mine wants to blow my head off."

A bushy red brow shot up. "A friend, you say?"

Devlin nodded. "My best friend, actually. It's a misunderstanding that he's too hotheaded to try straightening out just yet. So it was thought best for all concerned if I disappeared for a while."

"I see," the squire said. He didn't, but he went back to reading.

Their hair was perhaps the only thing they had in common, father and daughter, though the squire's wasn't that bright copper-red that hers was, but was faded with age and liberally laced with gray. And he had freckles, a whole slew of them across his nose and cheeks. You'd think he might sport whiskers to hide some of them, but he didn't.

Devlin wondered if there were freckles anywhere on her body. There'd been none on those ivory, soft cheeks.

What the devil was her first name?

He wasn't going to ask.

The squire had to be reading the letter a second time through, it was taking him so long. Devlin couldn't care less, for his mind was back on that dusty road, trying to come up with an excuse for his asinine behavior.

He might not have pulled his hat down at the approach of that carriage, as Mortimer had told him to do, but he'd kept his eyes downcast, a most humble bearing to assume, he'd thought, rather pleased with himself for thinking of it. But now he had to admit it would have been infinitely preferable to have seen her from a distance first, rather than to just look up and have her right there before his eyes. One needed time to adjust to such radiance so that one did not make a bloody fool of oneself. At least she hadn't noticed his slack-jawed astonishment, nor had her companions. All three of them had been staring at Caesar, long enough for Devlin to get his mouth shut, though that first question asked of him had needed to be repeated once before he'd actually heard it.

Caesar usually did create something of a sensation, but then so did Devlin. It was the first time he'd been ignored *entirely* in favor of his horse, however, at least by females. And to actually feel annoyed by it, for God's sake. Only then she'd given him *too* much attention, looked him over as if he were the prime stud, with the same thoroughness that Caesar had gotten from her. On the one hand, he'd bloody well felt insulted to be examined like that, as if he were on an auction block with the bidding about to begin. On the other hand, he'd been hit with a jolt of pure lust.

That in itself was a rather rare experience for Devlin. A man of strong appetites he might be, but he saw to them with such ridiculous ease, on such a regular basis, that he was usually too well sated to get aroused to the point of lust. But then women young and old had been thrusting themselves beneath his notice for as long as he could remember. It spoiled a man, indeed it did, to be the object of so much prurient interest.

But the redhead's interest didn't strike him as being prurient, which didn't explain his reaction to it. He had been offended and aroused by it. Whatever she had intended, however, such behavior was beyond unseemly, and so he'd thought to teach her a lesson by giving her back the same bold perusal. But instead the sight of her well-shaped breasts and cinched-in waist had increased the heat in his loins and probably fried his wits along with it.

Was she spoken for?

Devlin was having some difficulty sitting still in the chair he'd been offered. Every noise he heard beyond the study door made him wonder if it was her returning. Would she just burst in on her father to demand Devlin's dismissal as she'd threatened? With that red hair, he imagined she did do things spontaneously, thoughtlessly, passionately . . .

Devlin stifled a groan. He could not stay here. One of the reasons he had agreed to rusticate in the country had been the fact that he needed a break in his routine, and he could look on this sojourn as a sort of vacation, a time to put worries and cares aside for simple peace and relaxation. But he could not envision any peace with someone like her around, and at the moment, he was a bundle of nerves just waiting for her to walk in, which was utterly absurd. He would simply have to find somewhere else to bury himself—and let her think she had run him off? Not bloody likely.

Those friendly brown eyes came back to Devlin again. Hers had been the darkest blue of midnight. And not the least bit friendly.

"This horse he mentions as an excuse for your being here sounds frightfully expensive. Do I actually have to buy it?" the squire asked.

Devlin sighed, grateful to have something else to think about. "No, sir, Caesar isn't for sale. You only have to say you bought him, for anyone who asks."

Penworthy frowned worriedly. "I'm not very good at that sort of thing. Tongue gets tripped up over the littlest falsehood."

Would that we all had that problem, Devlin thought with a touch of amusement. "There is no reason for you to be uncomfortable with this arrangement. I will merely grant you temporary ownership of Caesar in return for your hospitality, said ownership to be relinquished

upon my departure. A gentleman's agreement.
Is that satisfactory?"

"Then I would actually own the animal? I
wouldn't be lying if I said so?"

"You would be speaking the absolute truth,
sir."

The squire smiled in relief. "My, won't
Megan be surprised."

Devlin pounced. "Megan?"

"M'daughter," the squire replied. "She has
an uncommon appreciation for fine horseflesh—uncommon for a girl, that is. Her own
horse—"

"I feel I should warn you, sir, that I've already
had a run-in with your daughter, and she took
an instant dislike to me, though I can't for the
life of me figure why. I don't usually have that
effect on the ladies."

The squire chuckled as he took in Devlin's
features again. "No, I don't imagine you do."

"It might be necessary to point out to her
that I come with Caesar and so can't be dismissed."

"Took that much of a dislike to you, did
she?"

"That was my impression."

"Well, since you do come with the horse,
and I've just bought the animal, there's no
question of dismissal—not that I could dismiss
you, mind, since you don't actually work for
me." The squire frowned then, not quite sure
he had that right. Then he digressed. "I've
spoiled her, you know. First to admit it. Just

can't seem to say no to her. But I'll be firm in
this case. It's not every day I get asked a favor
by the likes of *him*," he ended, nodding at the
letter.

There had never been any doubt of the
answer, but Devlin asked out of courtesy,
"Then the arrangement is acceptable to you,
sir?"

"Absolutely, Mr. Jefferys." The squire
smiled. "Most happy to oblige."

"And I needn't point out that this must be
kept in strictest confidence? Not even your
family is to know my true reason for being
here."

"No need to worry about that. There's just
m'self and Megan."

"Then she isn't married?" Devlin could have
sworn he wasn't going to ask that question.
"What I mean is, do you have a son-in-law
who might question you about suddenly starting up a stud farm?"

"No, not yet I don't, though I expect it won't
be long now—stud farm, you say? Does that
mean I'll be buying more animals?"

"A few mares—what do you mean, it won't
be long now? Is she engaged?"

"Who?"

"Your daughter."

The squire's brow knit, showing his difficulty in keeping up with the double subjects.
"M'daughter ain't, last I heard—no, no, I'm
sure she ain't. She'd tell me if she was, don't
you think?"

Devlin *hoped* they were speaking of the same thing. "Yes, certainly."

"But you met her. Can't help but notice she's a pretty girl, can you? And she's having her come-out in London shortly. No, I expect it won't be long after that."

Megan Penworthy in London? Devlin's brows were knit now, though he didn't know it.

"The mares, sir," Devlin said somewhat curt-ly. "They will be yours for the duration of my stay here, just like Caesar. But you needn't con-cern yourself with the operation. It takes a while for a stud farm to get started, after all, much longer than I intend to be here. We will merely go through the motions for appearances, you understand. It may not even be necessary to do any actual breeding, but having the mares here will lend credence to the operation."

"A stud farm," the squire mused, shaking his head with a chuckle. "Never even consid-ered one, you know. Megan will certainly be surprised."

She'd already been surprised, Devlin re-called. She hadn't believed it, in fact, which was what seemed to have got her animosity up to begin with, though he had to admit he'd helped on that score at the end. Not that a stud farm, real or not, was any of her business. He'd told her that, too. So there was no reason for the squire's daughter to cross paths with the squire's new horse breeder again. And Devlin would go out of his way to make sure of that.

He stood up. "If you have no further questions, I will take my leave."

"You're welcome to stay in the main house."

"Appreciate it, sir, but that would defeat the purpose of my being here. I'm to keep out of the way, and I can't do that as a guest. That's just what my friend will expect and be looking for."

"Well, if you need anything, just tell Mr. Krebs. He's m'butler and will see to it—"

"Father, I—"

She didn't burst in as Devlin had imagined she would, but she did come in quietly without any warning. Obviously, she hadn't expected Devlin to still be there, for her mouth snapped shut when she noticed him, her body stiffened perceptibly, and the look she gave him was just short of withering. Devlin, to his horror, realized that the way she had looked him over before didn't have much to do with the lust he had experienced, for his body was reacting to her again without the least bit of encouragement on her part.

"You're back early, m'dear," the squire remarked. "I believe you have met Devlin Jefferys?"

"Yes—I did." The word "unfortunately" hung unspoken in the air. "I'm sorry to interrupt, Father, but I need to speak with you—privately."

"Certainly," the squire allowed. "Mr. Jefferys was just leaving."

"Leaving?" She glanced at Devlin. "As in back to where you came from?"

That hopeful note was in her voice again, and it rankled just as easily as it had before. "Not quite that far, Miss Penworthy. I was just going to get settled in."

"Then you might want to wait in the hall," she replied stiffly as she held the door open for him. "Because I am quite sure my father will wish to speak to you again in just a few minutes."

"I will?" the squire said.

Devlin gave her a slow smile as he walked toward her. "By all means." And then when he reached her, he said softly, so only she could hear, "I'll wait so you can show me the way to the stable yourself."

Her look said she'd show him the front door or nothing. Devlin would have laughed if the study door hadn't closed so quickly behind him. He was left in the not-quite-empty hall staring at the Penworthys' butler across the way, who stared back inquiringly.

"I'm to wait," Devlin announced, at which point the helpful servant indicated one of the two benches on either side of the front door at the end of the hall. But Devlin smiled confidently to himself. "No need, Mr. Krebs. I guarantee it won't be that long a wait." And he wasn't about to move and miss hearing any possibly raised voices on the other side of the study door if he could help it.

Chapter 5

Megan whirled around the second the door closed and leaned across her father's desk to demand, "A horse-breeding farm?"

"You don't like the idea?"

"It's a splendid idea, Father, but why didn't you mention it sooner?"

"A surprise?"

Megan missed the question in his answer. "It was a surprise, all right. I made a bloody fool of myself, it was such a surprise."

The squire never took Megan to task for her less-than-ladylike vocabulary, since she was careful not to use such colorful words in mixed company—and she had got them from him in the first place. It amazed him sometimes that this was his daughter. He wished his dear wife had lived long enough to see what an extraordinary girl they had produced, but she'd died not long after Megan's third year.

"And that stallion must have cost a fortune!" Megan continued, but recalling Caesar, she got sidetracked. "Is he really yours?"

"He is now."

"And you're really going to breed him?"

"That's what I got him for. But these things take time," he cautioned.

"Yes, I know, and you can't breed a stallion like that to just any old mare. We'll have to buy the very best—"

"Already got some. They'll be delivered soon, and believe me, I got them at a bargain price."

"Well, good for you. We'll also have to enlarge the stable, of course, but you've probably already made plans for that."

"Enlarge the stable?" the squire repeated weakly.

"And the horses will have to be exercised. I can help with that, especially with the stallion. Oh, I can't wait to ride him!"

"Now, Megan—"

"Now, Father," she cut off his admonishment. "You know you don't have to worry. I'll be careful, and I won't ride him where anyone will see me do it."

She went on with more assurances, while outside the door, Devlin was grinding his teeth. Ride Caesar? Her? Not bloody likely. And when was she going to get around to demanding his dismissal?

Inside the study, the squire finally interrupted his daughter to say, "You'll have to ask Jefferys."

"What?!"

"He knows the animal, knows his temperament. He may not be ridable. And that's not what I got him for, after all."

There was a long silence while Megan just stared at her father. Then she burst out, "Damn! Not ridable? But I wouldn't ask *him* anyway, and speaking of him, he's not the least bit suitable for such an important position, Father. You'll simply have to find another—"

"He said you took a dislike to him. Can't imagine why. Damned fine-looking fellow, if you ask me."

"Damned rude fellow is what he is."

"But he comes highly recommended, m'dear, *very* highly recommended."

"I don't care if the queen recommended him—"

"Damned close," the squire mumbled.

"—his arrogant manner is offensive. I want him dismissed."

"Can't do it."

"Of course you can. Just send him back where he came from. How difficult can it be to find a replacement? I'll see to it myself, if you'd rather not."

"You'll do no such thing, m'girl. And I won't dismiss the man, so leave it go."

"Father?" She used the cajoling tone that usually got her her way.

"Now, now, none of that. Mr. Jefferys comes with the horse, a condition of the sale. If he goes, so does the stallion."

"But that's absurd!"

The squire shrugged. "Can't be helped. The seller wanted to be certain the stallion would have the best care possible. He trusts Mr. Jefferys to see to it."

"Good God, no wonder he's so bloody arrogant. He *knows* he can't be dismissed."

"I found him most likable m'self. He knows horses, knows everything to know about horse breeding." But then the squire's tone turned concerned. "I wouldn't want to dismiss him, Megan, but if he's done something that is totally unacceptable—"

"No, no, it was nothing specific," she quickly assured him. "I just—took a dislike to him, as he said."

"He's not a guest," her father pointed out. "It's not as if you have to entertain the fellow in your parlor. You prob'ly won't see much of him a'tall."

"I suppose that's something of a consolation, since we're obviously stuck with him."

She came around the desk and kissed her father's cheek to show him she wasn't too disappointed. But she was. The very thought of having Devlin Jefferys around agitated her as much as he himself had earlier. *Why* did he have to be the condition to having that magnificent stallion? If the horse weren't such a prize . . .

Megan ran right into the man as she turned from closing the door to the study. She'd had him on her mind, but she had completely forgotten that she'd told him to wait in the hall.

Her hands came up automatically to brace against the soft white lawn of his shirt. She felt muscles leap under her fingers, and her cheeks scalded with the impropriety of touching him, however accidentally. She jumped back, only she did it too quickly, right onto the train of her skirt, which pulled the bustle down and nearly made her lose her balance completely. By the time she got her shoes untangled from her skirt, Devlin Jefferys was laughing.

"Women do occasionally fall prostrate at my feet, but not trying to escape me."

"No doubt they swoon from your vulgar insinuations," Megan retorted before she looked up at him.

She wished she hadn't. He was still too close for comfort, and still so handsome he stole her breath. And those eyes, good God, they were lovely, such a perfect blending of blue-green, and such a wicked combination with that jet-black hair.

Nearly a half minute passed before they both realized, at the same time, that they were simply staring at each other. Megan looked away first, her face hotter than ever, so she didn't see the flush that also came to Devlin's cheeks.

"They have been known to swoon, though not from vulgar insinuations, which I rarely make. I'm much more direct, Miss Penworthy, in getting right to the heart of the matter. Shall I demonstrate?"

"No!"

"Too bad. You do look so nice in pink."

He was referring to her blushes, the lout, which he took such a delight in causing. She dared to look up at him again, just to give him a fulsome glare. His expression was smug, if not downright triumphant, and when she realized why, she gave him another blush to gloat over.

"Ah, I see your lagging memory returns finally," he almost purred. "You lost. It's time now to pay up."

"Pay up?"

"Take me out and show me your stable. That's what I waited here for."

He made it sound somehow unsavory, sexually unsavory, as if he weren't talking about a building, but part of her anatomy. "Our stable isn't hidden out in the woods somewhere, it's behind the house. A fool could find it, so I suppose you can."

"I should have known you'd be a spoilsport."

"I wasn't aware we'd placed a wager," she replied stiffly.

"Weren't you? You would have been quick enough to show me the door if you had got your way. You threw down the challenge, I accepted—and won."

"In that case, I'd say you cheated with unfair knowledge of a certain ridiculous condition."

"And I'd say, since you're *obviously stuck with me,* you ought to accept defeat graciously."

Those words sounded suspiciously familiar, making Megan gasp. "You were listening at the door?"

He gave her a mocking bow. "Wouldn't have missed it for the world."

She hissed through her teeth, "Only what one can expect of someone with the manners of a pig!"

His brows shot up in surprise, which she didn't doubt was feigned since his lips were just short of actual grinning. "I'm trying to step down, but I don't believe I'm aspiring to that level."

She didn't try to make sense out of that remark. What she tried to do was walk past him, but he moved, and still filled the immediate path to escape.

"So a demonstration is in order after all?" he said, and his arms suddenly came up to brace against the wall at her back, caging her to the spot so she couldn't miss his husky whisper. "We're alone now. Would you like to examine me with your hands as thoroughly as you did with your eyes?"

She made a sound of screeching outrage that wasn't all that loud, just damned indicative of her feelings on the subject. Then she ducked beneath his right arm and ran toward the stairs at the end of the hall.

But she could hear his laughter behind her,

and the taunt, "Now *there* were the manners of a pig, Meg-O-m'dear. Did you notice the difference?"

She halted, feeling safe now with some distance between them, and turned to hiss, "Between this vulgarity and your earlier crudity? No difference a'tall."

"Well, then, speaking of manners, you may as well look as touch, Miss Penworthy. It has the same effect on a man—coming from you."

"Bastard!"

"Spoiled brat," he shot back, then dipped his head mockingly and sauntered out the front door.

And the man was whistling, as if he were supremely confident he had won that round, while Megan was so furious she felt like running after him to do physical violence. She barely restrained herself. But if he ever spoke to her again . . .

Chapter 6

"I want to ride you, you can't imagine how much. Will you let me?"

Devlin's eyes snapped open at the sound of those softly uttered words coming through the partially open door. The door had no lock, wouldn't even close properly. But the first order of business yesterday had been a new bed to replace the moldy, lumpy cot in the room he had allocated to himself. Fixing the door hadn't been a priority, not over his comfort. Now he wished it had been.

Just what he needed to wake up to, the sound of lovers trysting in *his* stable, especially when he had gone to sleep fantasizing a tryst of his own, more than a tryst actually, with the hot-tempered Miss Penworthy. Of course, in his fantasy she wasn't hot-tempered, just—hot.

She didn't speak at all, didn't even open her mouth, except for his kisses, and to make use of a velvety soft tongue . . .

Devlin groaned as heat filled his loins again, just as it had last night when he'd imagined that redhead adoring his body. He was definitely going to have to avoid such thoughts, at least until he found a willing female in the area to see to the raging need they aroused.

He made a quick review of his current options. There had been that pretty little innkeeper's daughter the other night who had flirted with Mortimer after Devlin had shown no interest. Mortimer had in fact gone back to spend another night at the inn last night. Devlin wondered if he'd staked a claim there. Common courtesy required that he ask first.

Then there'd been the housemaid who'd come with the clean bedding yesterday. What was her name? He couldn't remember, but her overly generous attributes had reminded him of his last mistress, and she'd fairly drooled as she looked Devlin over. An easy tumble, that. Could have had her yesterday without the least effort on his part. Should have. But he'd just as soon avoid any dalliance with the squire's house staff. Servants tended to gossip outrageously, and he preferred to keep his liaisons discreet.

He had little doubt he'd find someone suitable to his taste and needs who would be agreeable to a brief affair, only the present condition of his body demanded he do so rather quickly, preferably today. Damn Megan Penworthy. And those lovers on the other side of his door weren't helping one bloody bit. Servants from the manor, no doubt, who hadn't yet heard that the stable was now occupied by more than horses. And they were up damn early. A glance at the one small window in the room showed it was barely dawn.

"Sir Ambrose just might be jealous, but I don't care. I can ride you both."

A husky laugh accompanied those words drifting through his door. Devlin stifled another groan. He tried to remember what was outside the door in this back section of the stable. Two stalls, wasn't it? And with Caesar in one of them, he was surprised the stallion wasn't snorting in disapproval at the disturbance.

Devlin felt like doing more than snorting. In fact, he was getting damned angry that his sleep had been interrupted by the feminine voice that was beginning to sound familiar, though he couldn't quite place it. He was even more angry at the effect it was having on him, because it *did* sound so familiar.

"That tickles." A giggle. "So you like that, do you? I thought you might. Sir Ambrose loves it."

Devlin shot out of his bed, in the grip of an inexplicable rage now that a face had finally come to him to go with that softly purring voice. He yanked the already open door wide, but abruptly halted at that point. No lovers cavorting in the one empty stall. No man to beat to a bloody pulp. Just Megan, standing in a pool of lantern light, with Caesar nibbling sugar out of her cupped palm. She was dressed in a jade-green riding habit, her bright copper hair in a thick braid lying like a flame down the center of her back. She hadn't heard Devlin, her full attention lavished on the animal she'd been seducing with her soft words and edible enticements.

Even with her innocence before him, the rage didn't leave Devlin completely. It couldn't. It had been too hot to begin with. He wasn't even aware of its cause, since jealousy wasn't in his sphere of normal emotions. But he'd classed this female as virginal, which put her off limits for himself—and accounted for a good deal of his previous irritation with her. So that brief, damning conclusion he'd drawn when he finally recognized her voice, that she wasn't virginal after all, was in fact sharing her exquisite little body not just with the lucky fellow she was presently with, but also with the soon-to-be-jealous Sir Ambrose—that had sent him over the edge, especially since he'd been lying there with a full arousal caused by thoughts of the same female.

He realized that he'd made a mistake—a ridiculous one, to be truthful—but that didn't help to calm him either. He decided he'd had good reason to be annoyed—a mild word for what he'd felt—after he'd denied himself the pleasure of seducing her himself, only to think she was actually quite free with her favors. But she wasn't, he'd still have to deny himself, and, perversely, *that* was what was keeping his emotions on an upper level.

"What are you doing here, brat?" His sour tone matched his mood.

Megan didn't turn around, but her back straightened stiffly, telling him she recognized his voice. Her hand dropped slowly to carelessly wipe the remaining white crystals on her skirt. Caesar didn't appreciate that, his head coming completely out of the stall in search of more sugar.

"I will thank you to address me properly—"

"So don't thank me."

"—or not at all, preferably the latter."

She whirled around then, about to say more, but no words came out other than a silent "Oh" as her eyes took in the sight of Devlin wearing no more than his trousers, and those had been half unfastened for comfort, revealing a considerable amount of skin below his navel. Helplessly, curiously, almost compulsively, her eyes moved over all that bare, golden skin, skimming the wide shoulders, the long, muscle-defined arms, the broad width of chest that narrowed down in his hard leanness to a flat stomach, then hips that flared out only minimally from his waist. Black hair lay thickly over his upper chest, with only a few strands swirling about his nipples, none at all on his smooth middle, but just below the navel it grew again in a straight line that disappeared into his trousers. And below that—a thick bulge straining at the bit of material still fastened on his trousers.

Her eyes went no farther, stayed fixed with a bemused intensity on that most private area of his anatomy, and Devlin watched her breathlessly, felt his tumescence grow even more under her stimulating regard, and couldn't believe she was doing this to him again. He'd slept in his trousers for modesty's sake because the door wouldn't close. He'd be standing there bare-assed naked if he hadn't, for he'd had no thought whatsoever about clothes or lack of them when he'd bounded out of his bed to demolish her lover. Would she still be staring like that if he *was* completely naked? He had a feeling she would.

"If my door would've closed properly, you'd have more to see right now, since I usually sleep in the buff. I can still rectify that. Would you like me to take them off?"

Her eyes had snapped up to his with his first word, but they rounded now as his meaning sunk in, and before the hot color could come flooding into her cheeks, Megan bolted. But not quickly enough. The rage that had been simmering in Devlin was now joined by the passion she'd just stirred to life, unleashing a primitive impulse in him that wouldn't let her escape this time. He leaped after her, his long legs closing the distance in seconds, and before she could even think to scream, he swung her around, gathered her close, and kissed her.

She felt nothing but shock in those first moments, then fear, because of what he'd just said. Her feet weren't touching the ground, her braid was gripped at its base so she couldn't avoid the ravenous onslaught of his mouth, and her body was crushed to his, but she began to struggle anyway, pounding at his shoulders and arms, unable to reach his chest because she was pressed too hard to it.

She didn't like what he was doing to her. His mouth was hurting hers. The arm holding her up was going to crack one of her ribs, she was certain. She was losing a good many hairs at her nape because of her own struggles and his grip that wouldn't loosen the tiniest bit. And she couldn't breathe, had actual visions of expiring of suffocation. Fortunately, self-preservation forced air through her nose right when she was starting to see dots before her eyes, but that only solved one of her discomforts. So she continued to punch, to push, to yank at his hair, but he ignored all her efforts and continued to grind his mouth down on hers.

It took Devlin a long while to realize that the woman in his arms was actually fighting him, seriously fighting him, without the least bit of pretense about it. It was such a unique experience, but then so was his complete loss of control, which had kept him from even noticing that his unbridled passion wasn't being reciprocated. But he *had* noticed finally, and his head came up so he could look down at the object of his madness. No tears, but something more than wariness in those big blue eyes, more like fear.

"You hurt me," she said in a small, accusing voice.

Good God, had he really? What the bloody hell was this woman doing to him, that he could behave in a manner so alien to his own nature?

"I'm sorry." And he was, sincerely, at least for hurting her. "But I went to bed with you on my mind, woke up hearing your voice, and I'm afraid having you caress me with those lovely eyes of yours again destroyed my common sense."

That sounded like a complaint to her ears instead of an apology, and one that put her at fault for what he'd just done to her. But it took care of her fear, swiftly replacing it with rising fury.

She was about to blast him with that new emotion when he added, "How did I hurt you?"

Angry that he didn't know, her eyes flared but she was quick to enlighten him, especially since his hold on her still hadn't slackened. "You're breaking my back. You've probably pulled out most of my hair. And if my lips haven't been shredded on my own teeth, I'd be surprised."

To his own ears, those sounded suspiciously like the petty complaints of a sulking young miss who didn't know the first thing about passion. But a slap would have been preferable to a man known for his finesse in the bedroom. He was insulted. He was reminded of why he'd always avoided virgins like the plague. He was also reminded that she *was* an innocent young miss, but one begging to have that fact changed by her very brazen behavior. All told, he absolved himself of guilt as well as amends-making, which he no longer felt she deserved. He wished he could rid himself of his lust as easily, but it was still running rampant, and was partly responsible for the pique that wouldn't let him apologize again.

"Incidentals, certainly," he replied to her charges, though he did set her on her feet to adjust his hold on her, which he had no thought of relinquishing just yet. "This is what you get for eating me with your eyes."

"I didn't!" she gasped.

"You did. And it's what you'll get the next time you do it, and the next. If you keep it up, you might eventually learn how to kiss a man properly."

He wanted to hurt her at that point, because he was hurting so badly with wanting her. And he'd come to his senses already, so he knew he'd go on hurting, that he couldn't, *wouldn't*, do anything more than kiss her. The warning was also designed to make her stay the hell away from him, because he had no doubt whatsoever that he wouldn't be able to withstand a steady dose of Miss Penworthy's unusual brand of enticement.

Her response was a heated "I hate you!" which actually made Devlin grin.

"I'd be wounded, devastated," he told her, the grin still on his lips putting the lie to those words, "except you haven't asked me to let you go yet, have you, which you should have done—if you really hate me."

"Let me!—"

"Too late."

And his mouth came down on hers again, only there was a wealth of difference in this kiss. Cognizant of her innocence this time, keeping it firmly in mind, he brought his own experience to bear, coaxing, gently persuading, enticing her mouth to open, and, when it finally did, swooping in to claim the prize. Good God, she was exquisitely sweet.

He received only two more punches before her hands were clinging to his arms instead. Her stiffness relaxed, letting her soft curves melt into his hardness, a response he was more accustomed to. But it made him want to thrust his tongue deep, to tap her passion, only he was afraid it would have the opposite effect on a virgin—how should he know?—so he kept a tight rein on the urge, continually cautioning himself to go slowly, carefully. He was also ready for a quick retreat if she thought to clamp her teeth down on him, but that didn't occur to her, innocent that she was.

She wasn't even participating in the kiss, was just accepting what he was doing to her, but that was perfectly fine with Devlin, for the hold he had on his passion was so tenuous, he didn't think he could bear it if she tried to kiss him back—if she even knew how. He didn't care about that either; her inexperience was all he could handle now. Her lips were soft, only slightly swollen from his previous assault, her breath sweet, her bemused acquiescence sweeter still, and her warm, pliant body . . . *God, God, give me strength.*

But Devlin's had run out, the urge simply too great to be inside her, and he couldn't stop himself from grasping her hips and pressing her against the full magnitude of his need. Her gasp told him she'd never felt the like. His own body told him he was about to carry her to his bed. He needed her anger back and quickly. He needed his bloody face slapped.

He released her lips, standing there trembling, in an agony of lust, fighting to get his breath back, and his sanity. "Now you know," he said to get what he needed before he took what he really needed. "Let me know if you ever want to feel it without these clothes between us."

After a long moment of stunned silence, he got the slap he'd asked for, but it didn't have the desired effect. Instead it made him want to grab her back and kiss her again. So he switched tactics to a more direct insult.

"The proper thing for you to have done in the first place would have been to close your eyes immediately against my semi-nakedness and turn around so you wouldn't be further offended by it. But then you're not quite proper, are you, Miss Penworthy?"

Another slap, deserved or not, for he'd just spoken the bare-faced truth. And then she disappeared around the corner that would take her to the front of the stable.

Chapter 7

Megan ran all the way to the house and straight up to her room. She stood panting against her closed door, her eyes squeezed shut, her body still trembling in reaction. Finally she let out a low groan.

He'd been right, so right. She'd behaved with the utmost impropriety *again*. She should have closed her eyes the very second she realized he wasn't fully dressed. Instead she'd let that splendid male body mesmerize her into doing the unthinkable again, staring at him, "eating him with her eyes," as he'd so crudely put it. But that was just what she'd done, without thought, without a care that he was watching her do it.

It was no wonder he'd offered to take his trousers off for her. How could she blame him after she'd stared the longest at *that* part of him? All he'd done was read her mind, because she *had* wanted to see what was under those trousers.

His appendage of procreation had seemed so huge, and she'd felt it later, actually felt it right through the thickness of her skirt, pressed hard at the juncture of her thighs. The feeling it had caused at the touch of it there, fear, yes, but also the most exhilarating sensation, starting at the point he was touching and spreading, rushing, tingling to the far extremities of her body. That was something she wished she hadn't discovered, that, and that other feeling that had come in her belly the second time he kissed her.

Megan groaned again and pushed herself away from the door to pace the floor in her agitation. None of it should have happened. All she'd wanted to do was make friends with the stallion so she could eventually ride him. She'd had no desire to come across Devlin Jefferys, just the opposite, which was why she'd gone to the stable so early, hours before her usual time, because no one would be up to see her.

It had been a good plan, foiled only by a damned door latch that wouldn't close—and a light sleeper. She'd been whispering to the horse, for God's sake. That shouldn't have awakened Devlin, even with his door open. But he'd said the sound of her voice woke him. He'd also said he'd gone to bed thinking of her. Had he really? Likely not. He said so many outrageous things, after all, that half of them had to be lies just meant to shock her, for that man dearly loved to shock her.

She stopped pacing, drawn against her will to the window that overlooked the side yard—and the stable. It was set far back behind the house, but still to the side of it, so she could see the entrance clearly and anyone arriving or leaving. She heard a horse now, and expected to see Timmy, the stableboy, arriving on the old nag he rode to work each day. Instead the black stallion burst out of the stable with Devlin on his back.

She wished he were leaving for good, but knew he wasn't. The stallion wasn't even saddled, and Devlin wasn't wearing his boots. He had put on no more than a white shirt like the one he'd worn yesterday. She wished next that he would lose his perch, but she didn't get that wish either. Man and horse rode as if they were made for each other. In moments they were gone from sight, but not from her mind.

Damn him, if he weren't so devilishly handsome, she wouldn't keep making such a fool of herself. But she'd never known anyone who looked like him, who could make her so forget herself.

She *had* been unforgivably rude by staring at him again. But he'd been ruder still with that crack about dropping his trousers. He'd had no call to say that. He hadn't had to be vulgar every time he opened his mouth, either, but he had. And he certainly hadn't had to attack her.

She was *not* going to take the blame for that, too. But maybe she ought to.

Hadn't he told her that staring at him like that was just like touching him? No! Megan wouldn't believe that she had provoked him. Nor would she believe his threat about kissing her again if he caught her staring at him like that. He wouldn't dare—would he? A low, despicable rogue like that? Of course he would. She never would have believed he'd have the audacity to do it in the first place, but he had. And *why* couldn't she stop thinking about it?

If only he hadn't kissed her that second time, which had been so different from the first, and so incredibly nice. She'd felt so dizzy, her stomach such a swirl of sensation. To her shame, she hadn't wanted him to stop. But he had, and no wonder. He'd told her right out that she didn't know how to kiss.

She frowned, remembering that. It was true that she had no experience in that area. The one kiss she'd had previously had been stolen by one of her local suitors, a mere peck on the lips, so brief that it was over and done with before she could decide if she liked it or not.

But she was going to be married soon. Shouldn't she know a little more about it before she did any kissing with her duke? She didn't want him to find her as lacking as Devlin did. Only now that she knew whom she was going to marry, it wouldn't be fair to encourage any other suitors who might try to kiss her, so she'd lost the opportunity to learn how to go about it. And she hadn't even paid attention when Devlin was kissing her, too caught up in what she was feeling for the first time to take note of what he was doing to make her feel that way. Nor was she about to let *him* kiss her again. That was out of the question. A horse breeder! That he had dared . . .

She was still standing there at the window when he returned shortly thereafter, his hair wet, his shirt now clinging to his damp chest. He'd gone for a swim, then? Not to *her* pond, she hoped. The very thought of him in her own private swimming hole infuriated her. It was bad enough that he was living in her stable.

Bristling anew over the man's audacity, she realized a moment later that he'd noticed her. He had stopped the stallion far short of the stable, right below her window, in fact, and was staring up at her. She stared back despite his warning, deliberately, defiantly, knowing that in her room she was safe from him and his threats. She even smiled smugly to herself.

But he continued to stare also. Even as he dismounted and moved to stand at the front of the stallion, he didn't take his eyes off her window. She began to think he was going to make a damn contest out of it, until he suddenly reached down and pulled his shirt off.

Megan gasped and yanked her draperies closed, but she could hear his husky male laughter, which was worse than his whistle yesterday—telling her he'd won another round. This was utterly intolerable. *He* was utterly intolerable. She would have to speak to her father about him. The man had to be put in his place.

Chapter 8

Megan had the opportunity to speak to her father over breakfast later that morning. She even worked out in her mind exactly what she would say, partial truths mostly, but damaging enough to get Devlin Jefferys a blistering setdown without actually warranting a dismissal, which would lose them the stallion. All she had to do was insert her account of Devlin's behavior between talk of her upcoming trip to London and her plans for today. She chickened out. She was afraid, and rightly so considering his insolence, that he would have his own accounting to give, which would paint her as culpable as he was.

She decided instead to warn Devlin of her intention if it became necessary, which she hoped it wouldn't, since she hoped not to have to speak to him again on any matter. After all, he might be under the impression that she wouldn't say anything to her father, because she hadn't said anything when she'd first asked for his dismissal, and Devlin knew that, had been listening at the door. So if he thought she *would* speak out if he wouldn't leave her alone, then he'd bloody well leave her alone.

But despite her confidence in her conclusion, Megan was still nervous when she entered the stable at her usual time after breakfast. She relaxed, however, when she saw that no one was about, not even Timmy, who usually was. She could hear noise in the back of the stable that sounded like hammering, but she wasn't about to investigate. She went straight to Sir Ambrose's stall.

She always gave her horse a quick rubdown before her ride, then a more thorough grooming when they returned. She thought about skipping the rubdown today, however, wanting to be gone as quickly as possible while Devlin still wasn't around.

"G'mornin', Miss Megan."

She started, but only for a second. "Good morning to yourself, Timmy."

"He's somethin', that Caesar, ain't he?" Timmy said as he climbed up on the stall rail to sit next to her saddle draped there.

It was their customary routine, since she didn't require his help, that he'd sit there and keep her company while she saw to her horse. It was soothing, that normalcy, and almost made her decide not to break her own routine.

"You were given a job to do, Timmy. Get to it."

Megan groaned inwardly at the sound of *that* voice. Likely Timmy did, too, for the boy responded instantly to the command in that tone, scrambling down from the stall rail and actually running to the back of the stable.

"You had no business doing that," Megan said, turning to see Devlin filling the front of the stall. "Timmy was merely keeping me company."

"Not when I've given him a job to do. He happens to be under *my* orders now."

She started to disagree about who was Timmy's ultimate employer when she realized she was looking at him. She snapped her mouth shut and turned around.

"What? No argument?"

"Go away," was all Megan said, and that in a mumble.

"Don't think I will," Devlin replied, just to be disagreeable, Megan was sure. "I live here, after all. In fact, you could say this is my house for the time being."

His cheerful tone was irritating in the extreme, but Megan managed to refrain from commenting about him and stables going hand in hand. She wasn't going to say another word to him. She was going to simply ignore him until he went away.

She moved to get her side saddle, but Devlin was suddenly behind her, his chest crowding her back as he reached for it instead. Megan turned to yank the saddle out of his hands. She got it, only because he wasn't expecting her to try to take it, but she'd yanked too hard. Her pull, along with the weight of the saddle, sent her stumbling back, and, unable to catch herself with her hands full, she landed on her backside in a small pile of hay.

She let out a screech of indignation and slapped the hand away that came down to help her up. How many times was she going to make a fool of herself in front of this man? She'd already lost count.

"I was only trying to help," he said, "since I'd sent Timmy off."

She didn't detect any laughter in his tone, but his mouth was probably grinning from ear to ear. She still wouldn't look, but *when* was he going to take the hint?

She got to her feet and dusted the straw from her riding skirt before she reached down for the saddle. Silence greeted her while she prepared Sir Ambrose for riding. She wasn't even sure Devlin was there any longer, but she still wouldn't . . .

"All right, you haven't looked at me but once since I've been standing here." His tone had turned sharp with annoyance. "Have I suddenly grown horns?"

Megan couldn't keep her mouth shut on that one. "I believe you had them already."

"Look at me when you insult me!"

She didn't, but she took a moment to explain to the dense man, "You may have forgotten your warning, Mr. Jefferys, but I haven't. I have no intention of provoking you again by looking at you."

"You're provoking me right now," he growled, then added with slightly less heat, "There's looking, and then there's *looking*, and you know which bloody kind I meant. Besides, I was angry when I said it. Chances are, the next time you stare at me like that, nothing will happen. Care to try it?"

"No."

"Just as well. That bloody pond was colder than I cared for."

She looked at him then, with acerbity. "That 'bloody' pond, Mr. Jefferys, happens to be *my* pond. I'll thank you to stay out of it."

"Then don't get my body so heated that either it's a cold dunking or I carry you off to my bed."

Her face heating, she said in a tight voice, "You can use the pond."

"I thought you might say that."

She led Sir Ambrose out of the stall and over to the mounting block, seething over the smugness in his tone.

"Stubborn brat," she heard mumbled behind her, apparently not for her ears, because he then said loudly, "You were supposed to ask for my help with that saddle."

"Whatever for? I see to my own horse, for

both grooming and saddling."

"*Your* horse?"

Her eyes narrowed on his surprised expression. "You find something unusual in that?"

"Only to wonder how you came by a Thoroughbred like that."

"Sir Ambrose was a present for my twelfth birthday."

"*That's* Sir Ambrose?" He started to laugh.

Megan caught herself grinding her teeth together. "What the devil do you find so funny?"

"I hate to be the one to point this out to you, Miss Penworthy, but that horse is a female."

"I'm perfectly aware of that."

He lost his grin. "Then why the devil do you call her Sir Ambrose?"

"I named her after her previous owner, Ambrose St. James."

"Why?" he demanded sharply, frowning at her. "Had you met him? Did he look like a bloody horse?"

Megan was amazed at the sudden anger he was displaying. "No, I haven't met him yet, nor do I know what he looks like. But what difference does that make? And what business is it of yours what I call my horse?"

"None. Certainly," he replied stiffly, actually scowling at her. "Except that's a bloody stupid name to give a horse, particularly a *female* horse."

"If you ask me, Devlin's a stupid name to give a man, conjuring up images of devils and

the like. Then again, I guess it suits *you* rather
perfectly, doesn't it?"

His answer was to set his hands to her waist
and lift her until they were eye to eye. "Do you
remember what I told you I do to horses *and*
women who get too feisty?" he asked in a softly
menacing tone. Megan could only nod, words
failing her. "You're due, Miss Penworthy."

She landed on her saddle with a jarring
jolt for its being unexpected. The hard landing served to also jolt her out of that brief
moment of intimidation he'd made her feel.
But Devlin hadn't waited around for her to
recover her temper. So Megan merely stared
after the odious man as he sauntered back into
the stable, his latest threat making her seethe.

He wouldn't dare lay a hand on her hindquarters. He'd better *not* dare. She had a good
mind to follow after him and tell him so—
only that tone he'd used was still ringing in
her ears. Maybe she would tell him another
time. Yes, some other time, when she wasn't
so . . . mad.

Chapter 9

"Pink?" Devlin said as he stared at the drapery Mortimer had just hung over the single window in his new bedroom. "That was the best you could find? Pink?"

"I was lucky to find anything at all readymade in a village the size of Teadale. And I don't know what you're complaining about. This room needed a little brightening."

The room needed to be torched, in Devlin's disgruntled opinion. "Did you fix the door latch?"

"Right 'n' tight. Some rugs will be delivered later today."

"No carpeting available?"

"Not in Teadale."

Devlin sighed, feeling extremely put-upon.

It'll do you a world of good, Duchy had assured him. *Might even teach you some humility, which you're sadly lacking, dear boy.* Duchy hadn't seen the squire's stable, however, which had been uninhabited by human occupants for a goodly number of years. Even Timmy would rather go home each night to his mother's over crowded cottage than sleep in one of the two small rooms that had once been used by stable grooms, but were now used only for storage. Devlin had found it incredible that a man of the squire's consequence had no more than one stableboy, and only four horses.

"Some paint on these bare walls would be appreciated," Devlin said. "*Not* pink."

"You'll have to sleep with the smell," Mortimer warned.

"I'm sleeping in a bloody stable," Devlin replied pointedly.

Mortimer chuckled. "You're right. One more noxious odor won't make much difference."

Devlin saw nothing humorous about it. He had a mind to throw caution to the wind and abide at the inn with Mortimer, but Duchy's warning to stay out of public houses was still prominent in his mind. When the devil was he going to learn how to say no to Duchy?

"I will need more shirts," Devlin said, looking down in disgust at a white sleeve that was already stained. "At least a dozen."

"Didn't I warn you gentleman's white didn't belong in a stable?"

"Just send for them, Mr. Browne, and while

you're at it, find out if there are any available women in the area."

"Available for what?" Mortimer asked in all innocence, but at Devlin's pointed stare, he said, "Oh," then, "Now see here, I ain't no—"

"Spare me the dramatics, Mr. Browne, or I'll—"

"Have to suffer along with the rest of us."

Devlin cocked a brow. "Struck out, did you?"

"This is a nice, quiet neighborhood. If a bloke wants a tumble around here, he has to marry to get it."

"Not even a tavern wench?" Devlin asked incredulously.

"Not even a tavern other than the taproom at the inn," Mortimer was delighted to say.

"What do I have to do, ride to London?"

"You don't dare show yourself there unless you're ready for that duel." Devlin merely glowered, so Mortimer offered, keeping the grin from his lips, "I hear tell there's a nice pond near here."

"I'm already acquainted with that bloody pond," Devlin snapped.

But now an image of Megan mounted on her Sir Ambrose came potently to his mind, thanks to the mention of his morning dunking in icy water. Sir *Ambrose*, for God's sake.

His urge had been to ride after her to make sure she didn't get hurt on such a spirited animal, but common sense said if she'd had the animal as long as she'd claimed, then she could ride it well enough. Common sense had little to do with the urge to follow her, however.

"Add a case of brandy to my order," Devlin said now in disgruntlement, then asked, "Not even one fallen dove in the whole area?"

"Not a one."

"Make that two cases of brandy."

Megan almost avoided the high meadow today, considering her bad mood. It was where Tiffany would meet her several mornings a week, to join her for her morning ride. Tiffany wasn't as enthusiastic about riding as Megan was, though she was accomplished enough, and she didn't come out every morning.

The girls had no plans to meet today. Tiffany was spontaneous about when she would show up, so Megan always included, in her daily jaunt the high meadow that lay between their respective homes, just in case.

Tiffany was already there when Megan entered the meadow, which was unusual, since Megan was early herself, her own schedule having been moved up in her haste to vacate the stable.

"It must be cleaning day to get you out of the house this early of a morning," Megan said as she drew up alongside her friend. "Or is your mother in another one of her redecorating moods?"

"Neither. I just have news that I couldn't wait to share, but I'm also dying of curiosity."

"I suppose your curiosity has to come first?"

"Absolutely." Tiffany grinned. "Especially since you didn't even come back with the carriage yesterday, but sent a footman with it. I would have come over later in the day, but my mother had already got my promise to read at her Poets Society meeting, and last night we had Tyler and his parents to dinner."

"How did that go?"

"Very well, considering how nervous I was. Now tell me, did your father *really* buy that incredible horse?"

Megan grinned. "He really did, and some mares, too, though they haven't arrived yet."

"You must be thrilled to pieces. Tyler was, too. He couldn't stop talking about that stallion last evening. Told his father all about him. They've got a wager going that it's likely a retired racer, so I wouldn't be surprised if they both stop over for a closer look sometime this week. Did you ride it yet?"

"You know ladies don't ride stallions."

"That wouldn't stop you," Tiffany replied knowingly. "Then you haven't?"

"Not yet." Megan sighed.

"What about his handsome trainer? Did you get the fellow dismissed?"

"Do you think he's handsome?"

"Divinely handsome. Don't you?"

Megan shrugged. "He has a certain attraction, I suppose, if you can overlook his rudeness, which I can't. But no, I had no luck getting rid of him. When Devlin Jefferys said he comes with the horse, he meant it literally. The damned sales agreement stipulates that he can't be fired."

"How unusual."

"It's preposterous, is what it is," Megan replied, some of her anger returning just thinking about it. "You wouldn't believe the license it gives him—to be arrogant, rude, outrageous in his behavior."

"Did something else happen?"

"Yes, all of the above."

"How strange," Tiffany said thoughtfully. "Men don't usually act that way around you."

Megan stared at her friend for a moment before agreeing. "They don't, do they?"

"It sounds almost like how you behaved toward Tyler."

Megan stared a bit longer before agreeing again. "It does, doesn't it?"

"Well, Mr. Jefferys *is* a bit more handsome than most," Tiffany pointed out. "Do you think he has the same problem you do, of having every woman he meets fall in love with him?"

Megan said, straight-faced, "Not every woman I meet falls in love with me."

Tiffany burst out laughing. "You know what I meant."

"Yes, but the fact remains that Mr. Jefferys isn't the least bit lovable."

"Neither were you to Tyler. Just the opposite."

True, but Megan couldn't see a man making

use of the same ruse. Deliberate? All those insults deliberate? Even the kiss no more than a means to another insult?

Reminded of the kiss, Megan said, "I really don't want to discuss that horse breeder. It has occurred to me that I have somewhat of a problem that you might be able to help me with. I don't know the first thing about kissing."

"Kissing?" Tiffany said blankly.

"Yes, how to go about it. I think I should know before I meet my duke, don't you?"

"Not necessarily—now, wait a minute. You don't expect *me* to teach you, do you?"

"Don't be a goose. But you do happen to know more about it than I. Did Tyler teach you? Did it come naturally? Did it take practice?"

"Practice, yes. Tyler didn't know he was teaching me, but he was. And no, I wouldn't say it comes naturally, since I was too nervous to enjoy it the first few times, though now it does seem like I always knew how. But—Meg, we don't do any *serious* kissing, you know, just brief kisses good-bye and hello, and that only when no one is looking, as you well know."

Megan was the one who, as Tiffany and Tyler's chaperon, had turned her head away more than once so no one would be looking, so she was grinning when she asked, "But has he put his tongue in your mouth yet?"

"Megan! However did you learn about that?"

"Quite by accident, I assure you," Megan

replied evasively. "Well, has he?"

"No, but Tyler has mentioned it, to warn me, he said, so I wouldn't be alarmed if he ever got carried away and did it. He also said that after we're married, well, that that kind of kissing is part of—"

"That?" Megan whispered.

"Yes, *that*. But it sounds rather disgusting, if you ask me."

"It's not actually."

Tiffany's eyes rounded. "Megan Penworthy, who put his tongue in your mouth?"

"Did I say—?"

"You didn't have to."

"Oh, all right," Megan grumbled. "Devlin Jefferys did, and before you ask why I didn't mention it, it's because I get furious every time I think about it."

"The *horse breeder?*"

"I *told* you his behavior was outrageous. And he blamed it on me because I was staring at him."

"Were you? Staring at him?"

"Let me ask you this first. If a man appeared before you half naked, would you turn around immediately?"

"Are you joking?" Tiffany chuckled. "I'd probably look a bit before I turned around."

"Well, I forgot to turn around at all."

"You saw him naked!?"

"Half naked, and I can see I'm going to have to explain everything." It took a while, but when she'd finished, Megan said, "Maybe you're right, that he's doing it deliberately. Do you think I ought to tell him that he needn't worry, that my heart is soon to be spoken for?"

"I think you ought to tell your father instead."

"If I do, we're going to lose that stallion. Father will dismiss him instantly."

"Well, that's a coil, isn't it?" Tiffany said indignantly. "Damned if you do or don't. There has to be something that we can do to make him mind his manners."

"We?" Megan grinned.

"Well, now that you've told me—"

"You aren't to worry about it. I've decided to ignore him, and if that doesn't work, then I will tell him that I'm going to marry St. James. No one in their right mind would dare tempt the ire of an all-powerful duke, even an unprincipled rogue like Jefferys. For whatever reason they began, the insults will stop immediately with that disclosure, you mark my words."

"You're undoubtedly right. You might even get some groveling out of him in his haste to make amends to the future Duchess of Wrothston."

"Groveling isn't necessary. I'll settle for seeing his shocked expression along with Lady O's the day I return in the ducal coach."

Tiffany suddenly gasped. "I almost forgot my news—which, by the way, is going to get you closer to that day of reckoning. My mother received invites to a pre-Season masked ball

from her old friend Elizabeth Leighton. And
my father's *Times* that arrived yesterday had
a mention of the very same ball because of the
notables on the guest list, which includes—"

"Him?" Megan squealed in delight. "And
here I've been agonizing on *how* I would
manage to meet him. Your mother *is* going
to accept, isn't she?"

"I believe she can be persuaded."

"And I can go with you?"

"Would I go without you?"

"There, you see? Fate is pushing me in the
right direction. It's almost as if it weren't my
decision a'tall, but preordained. Where is it?
When?"

"The Leightons live in Hampshire, and the
ball is next week—now don't look so horrified,
Meg. That's plenty time to prepare—"

"Not for a new gown."

"You've plenty—"

"This one has to be special. I'm catching a
duke, Tiff, a *duke.*"

"You're right," Tiffany conceded. "There's
no point in taking chances with this preordained stuff. I'll race you to—"

"I'll meet you," Megan called over her shoulder as she took off. "I'm too anxious to hold Sir
Am—"

Tiffany couldn't hear the rest, but didn't need
to, just as she didn't need to have it clarified that
she would find Megan at Miss Whipple's shop,
their village seamstress. Mind reading was only
one of the benefits of having a very close friend.

Chapter 10

Having found a lovely green poult-de-soie silk along with white tulle to fashion a stunning new ball gown, Megan was in high spirits when she returned home late that afternoon. Understandably, she was loath to ruin her good mood with a trip to the stable, even to return Sir Ambrose. But grooming her horse was a joy to her that she wasn't going to give up either. So for the first time, she sent a servant around to the stable to collect Sir Ambrose's grooming apparatus, and proceeded to tend her horse right there in the front yard in the shade of a hickory tree.

Ten minutes after she began, Devlin Jefferys showed up. "Just what do you think you're doing?" he demanded without preamble.

His appearance wasn't as detrimental to Megan's good mood as she'd thought it would be. His own mood seemed to have soured with her presence, however, or had he been brooding all day? He certainly looked irritated at the moment. The thought brought a half smile to Megan's lips.

"Why, whatever does it look like I'm doing, Mr. Jefferys? Surely it's rather obvious, isn't it?"

Her half-condescending, half-effervescent tone had him gritting his teeth. "Timmy can do that."

"Certainly he can, but I enjoy doing it myself. Didn't I make that clear this morning?"

"Then why aren't you doing it where it should be done, instead of making a spectacle of yourself on your front lawn?"

"Spectacle? Without an audience? Come now, let's not exaggerate. And why I'm not in the stable should also be quite obvious. I was trying to avoid your very unpleasant company. So just what are you doing out here, ruining a perfectly good plan?"

He stared at her for a long moment before he shoved his hands in his pockets and said in a low mumble, "It was not my intention to run you out of your own stable."

That was an outright lie, but Devlin had spent the afternoon bored to tears; the only thing he'd had to look forward to was Megan's return. He hadn't thought she would try to avoid him entirely. He had counted on her

entrenching and fighting to the bitter end—
as anyone with that red hair would—and he
had bloody well been looking forward to it.

But now? "Perhaps I owe you an apology,"
he said, the words a mere whisper, sour on his
tongue.

"More than one, but who's counting?"

*Oh, she's asking for it. Give her an inch, and she
thinks she can walk all over me.*

"Very well, accept my apology in duplicate."

Megan managed to conceal her surprise over
this amazing about-face. Of course, he didn't
sound the least bit sincere in his apology,
sounded more like it was being forced out
of him at the point of some gruesome consequence. She took a moment to wonder what
he found so loathsome that an apology to her
was the lesser evil. And in that case, why even
bother?

But on the oft chance that he really was
offering her an olive branch and was merely being churlish about it, she said, "I'm not
sure a simple apology will suffice for what—"
She paused, noting the tensing of his body,
the drawing together of his black brows. *This
round to me, Mr. Jefferys,* she thought smugly to
herself before giving him a bright smile. "But
on the other hand, I am presently in much too
good a mood to hold grudges, so I accept your
apology—in duplicate."

Devlin barely heard her. He was still trying
to recover from the staggering effect of the

smile she'd just given him. Who would have thought two dimples could be such disarming weapons? He was bemused, his thoughts gone adrift, his tongue tied in knots. He felt as if he'd been knocked on his arse.

That girl ought to have freckles, he thought in pure disgruntlement. Why the devil didn't she? There ought to be *something* to counteract a smile like that, which made a man want to wrap his arms around her and protect her for the rest of his days.

Devlin shook himself mentally. At her expectant expression, he merely nodded, and curtly at that, annoyed now that he wasn't even sure if she'd accepted his apology or not. But he wasn't going to ask her to repeat what she'd said. He moved around her to lean against the tree trunk and watch her. If she'd refused his apology, she'd have more to say, wouldn't she? At the very least, she'd ask him to go away. She didn't. What she did was ignore the fact that he was still there.

The devil. Now that he'd got the temporary cease-fire that he hadn't really wanted—if he had got it—he didn't know what to say to the girl. The normal conversation he'd offer one of her class would sound ridiculous coming from a "horse breeder." Besides, he rather liked being the horse breeder with her. It gave him freedom in his speech that he ordinarily wouldn't have. A rare pleasure, that, not having to guard his tongue or his temper.

"I'm going to a ball this week in Hampshire, a masked ball."

Devlin's brows rose at that unsolicited statement. "Now, why are you telling *me* that?"

Megan shrugged. "I'm just excited about it. I felt like telling you."

"You mean you felt like rubbing my nose in it, since it's not something I'd be invited to."

"That, too." She peeked at him from beneath her lashes. "Is your nose especially sore?"

Devlin just managed to choke down a burst of laughter. "Not especially. I've been to a ball or two."

"What?" she scoffed. "Those public masked balls at Covent Garden?"

"How did you guess?" be replied dryly.

"That's not the same as rubbing shoulders with dukes and earls."

"You have me there, brat—now, don't get your hackles up, Miss Penworthy. That just slipped out."

She didn't comment. She went back to rubbing down the mare with a bit more vigor. Devlin grinned, watching her pointedly ignore him again. She sparkled when she was mad. Her cheeks bloomed, her eyes brightened. He imagined she would look just so in the heat of . . . The tightening in his loins forced him to squelch that thought.

"What's so special about this ball in Hampshire?" Devlin thought to ask. "I'd think you'd be more excited about your Season in London, which is shortly to occur."

Megan turned to give him her full attention. "How did you know I am to have a Season?"

"Doesn't every young girl your age hie herself off to London in search of a husband?"

"Not every one, no. I may not go myself if everything goes well in Hampshire—oh, except for Tiffany's wedding. I'll have to go for that, but—"

"If what goes well in Hampshire?" Devlin asked a bit more harshly than he realized. "Are you anticipating a proposal?"

"Good heavens, no." Megan laughed. "I'll only be meeting him for the first time. My hopes are high, but not *that* high."

"In other words, you've already picked him out, but he doesn't know it. Who is this poor sod you've set your cap for?"

"I'll thank you to keep a respectful tone when you speak of my future husband."

"So don't thank me," Devlin snapped, then: "You aren't joking, are you? You really intend to marry a man you haven't even met?"

"Yes," she replied stiffly. "So you can stop worrying, Mr. Jefferys. My heart will soon be spoken for."

"Oh, you intend to fall in love, too, with this faceless—*do* you know what he looks like?"

"Well, no, but—"

"Aha! You're after a bloody title, aren't you?"

"So what if I am? You think it's never been done before?"

"It's done all the time, but the titled gent usually gets something he wants out of the arrangement. What have you got to offer?"

She was mortified by his sneering tone. "Well, that was a short truce, wasn't it?" She turned away to lead Sir Ambrose to the stable.

Devlin stubbornly fell into step beside her. "I'm sorry. That was uncalled-for."

"What's one more insult to add to all your others? Maybe Tiffany was right and it's a habit with you, to keep women from 'falling at your feet.' But as I said, you needn't worry about me doing any 'falling,' Mr. Jefferys. It was a ridiculous assumption on your part that I would—if you made it. I'm not the least bit attracted to you."

Red flag—bright, bright red. "That statement can be easily disproved. Shall I show you how?"

"Are you thinking of causing a spectacle on my front lawn?"

"We've already reached the side lawn, if you haven't noticed, and yes, I'm bloody well thinking about it," he growled.

"Well, don't. My father, who will be sure to hear about it after I scream my head off, won't like it one bit. Neither will my future husband, and the Duke of Wrothston is no one to trifle—"

"Who?"

Megan looked back, because Devlin had stopped in his tracks. She was delighted by his shocked expression. "I thought that might give you pause," she said smugly.

"Did I hear you right?"

"You did. I will be married to Ambrose St. James, the present Duke of Wrothston, before the year is out. And you, Mr. Jefferys, will not be invited to the wedding."

"Why . . . *him?*"

"Why not? I happen to like his stable."

"You like his—"

He ended up sputtering, so Megan shrugged and went on without him. The little man Devlin had arrived with was at the front of the stable as she led Sir Ambrose to his stall.

"Good day to you, miss," he said respectfully, doffing his hat.

"Good day to yourself, Mr.—Browne, isn't it?"

"Yes, Miss."

"And how is our fine stallion today?"

"Caesar is in fine fettle, just fine."

She turned to Devlin, sensing his presence behind her. She decided to take advantage of the present regret and anxiety she was sure he was experiencing, now that he knew what a powerful man she would soon be married to.

"I want to ride the stallion."

"No."

"Just like that? No?"

"Your hearing is excellent."

So much for her assumption. "You're impossible!" she told him before she stalked out of the stable.

"I'm impossible?" Devlin said, glancing at Mortimer. "She's got her husband all picked

out, Mr. Browne. Hasn't met him yet, but she's got her cap set for him. Guess who it is."

"Someone you know?"

"Yes, I know him. I bloody well know him. She thinks she's going to marry the Duke of Wrothston."

"But—" Mortimer's eyes rounded. *"You* are the Duke of Wrothston."

"So I am."

Chapter 11

Ambrose Devlin St. James, fourth Duke of Wrothston and a slew of lesser titles, was at the moment immersed in physical labor of the menial sort. He was pitching hay, and doing it with a vengeance, but also with a mindless sort of detachment that made him unaware of the soreness developing in his hands or the sweat soaking into his fine lawn shirt.

He had begun the labor in an effort to keep from smashing his fist through a wall, which was what he'd had the urge to do after his latest encounter with Megan Penworthy—and her most startling revelations. Pitching hay, however, did not take his mind off the encounter as he'd assumed it would. Just the opposite. The exertion seemed to fuel his anger with every pitch.

So she was going to marry him, was she? Over his dead body. The nerve of that girl. The bloody audacity, to set her sights on him before she'd even met him. At least the other women who'd coveted his title, and he'd lost count of their number, had wanted him for himself just as much if not more. He ought to be used to it by now, but damned if he was. Besides, Megan's case was unique. He could be a wastrel or the veriest saint, and she wouldn't care, because it wasn't the man she was after to marry, it was the bloody title. Good God, she'd even admitted it, and without the least embarrassment over owning up to such a cold-blooded aspiration.

He had taken her for spoiled, willful, hot-tempered even, but not for opportunistic. And when he thought of what could have happened if not for Freddy's temper and his need to absent himself because of it . . .

He didn't recall accepting an invitation to a ball in Hampshire, but then he accepted a good many invites that he promptly forgot and needed his secretary to remind him of. So it wasn't unreasonable to assume that if he were home where he should be, instead of playing the coward at Duchy's insistence, he would have gone to that ball in Hampshire, met Megan there under entirely different circumstances, and just might have succumbed to that devastating smile of hers without the least suspicion that she was a conniving little adventuress out to snare his title.

The thought chilled him to the bone—and enraged him. He ought to show up at that damn ball and give Megan just what she deserved, a callous rake, a dissipated rogue, a cad of the first water to scare the very drawers off the girl. But if she thought he'd be there, then a rumor had to be making the rounds that he was expected, which meant Freddy would hear of it. And although Devlin's disappearance would lead Freddy to assume he wouldn't show up at such a public affair, Freddy wouldn't take any chances. He'd be there with his pistols primed just in case. Not enough time had passed for Devlin to hope otherwise.

But how much time *would* be enough? Two months, according to Duchy.

"The gel will be desperate by then, if she really has got herself with child. She'll be forced to give up the real father's name, or to accept whomever her brother finds to marry her. Can't see Sabrina Richardson doing *that*, as willful and vain as she is, but Freddy will insist. He won't let the matter go just because you can't be found. He'll have to marry her off, which will leave you with only the one problem, instead of two."

The second had been how to avoid the altar with Freddy's scheming little sister, Sabrina, while the first one remained how to avoid getting his head blown off by his best friend. But two months was a long time to rusticate. Devlin was hoping Freddy would use his head before then and remember that Devlin didn't even like his damn sister, so he certainly wouldn't have seduced the chit and got her with child as she claimed.

The irony suddenly struck him that he was here to avoid marriage with one scheming young miss, only to run smack into another. The one was using lies to get him to the altar, the other would use a devastating smile—or would she? Just how did Megan Penworthy think to win him? How far would she go to get him and his stable? His *stable*, for God's sake. That was the most infuriating and insulting thing of all, that she'd picked him because she liked his damn stable. Oh, and he mustn't forget that he, Devlin Jefferys, wouldn't be invited to the wedding. Well, he'd bloody well like to see her have it without him.

"Is there a purpose to what you're doing?"

Devlin glanced back to see Mortimer leaning against one of the horse stalls, calmly surveying his handiwork. Devlin looked around at the hay scattered everywhere—on the horses, in the water, on himself. But he raised a brow in his most haughty manner, and endeavored to ignore the stinging heat in his hands that he was finally aware of.

"There is always a purpose to what I do, Mr. Browne. This one just escapes me at the moment."

Mortimer gave a hoot of laughter. "She got to you, did she?"

"No, she did not," Devlin denied emphatically. "It's this idleness that is getting to me, if you must know. Something will have to be done, Mr. Browne."

"Like what?" Mortimer asked warily.

"We can begin by enlarging this stable."

"We?"

"Find us a master carpenter, but we will help."

"You didn't do too well with a pitchfork. What makes you think you can do better with a hammer?"

Devlin didn't deign to answer that. "And send word to my secretary to have my correspondence forwarded here. In fact, tell Mr. Pike to come himself. There's no reason I can't conduct my business from—"

"Your grandmother isn't going to like this one bit," Mortimer warned.

"Duchy means well, but she doesn't always know what's best for me. She felt I could use the rest. I agreed at the time, but I've bloody well changed my mind. Resting here is driving me nearly mad."

"It ain't rest that's driving you mad, it's that—"

"Don't contradict me, Mr. Browne. Just carry out my instructions."

"And how do you expect to explain Mr. Pike, who don't know how to be anything but condescending after working for you for so long?"

Mortimer had a point. Devlin's secretary was

as toplofty as any lord, and wouldn't know the first thing about dissembling.

"Very well, just the correspondence will do for now—and the carpenter. We'll start on the stable tomorrow."

"Don't you think you ought to get the squire's permission first?"

Devlin sighed. He wasn't used to obtaining permission from anybody for anything. For a moment there, he had forgotten the role he was playing. It had been pleasant to forget.

"I'll speak to the squire, but I don't foresee any problems, since I will be paying for any improvements myself."

"Unnecessary improvements," Mortimer grumbled, "Since you and the extra horses won't be here long enough to enjoy them."

"Incidentals, Mr. Browne. I need the work. I need to keep busy. See to it."

Chapter 12

The study door opened just as Megan reached the bottom of the stairs. She started to call out a greeting to her father, but it was Devlin who stepped out instead. She was on her way to the stable for her morning ride, but she hadn't quite prepared herself for another encounter with this man. And it definitely took some preparation.

Once again he was wearing gentleman's white in his shirt—her father must be paying him too much—tucked into unfashionably snug black trousers—bloody show-off. Didn't he know tight trousers had died with the renowned Beau Brummell? All he needed was the neckcloth to look like a gentleman, too much like a gentleman, for he already had the bearing—and the arrogance.

"Well, good morning, Miss Penworthy."

He was actually going to be civil? *Careful, Megan, don't faint.*

"Good morning to yourself, Mr. Jefferys."

"The mares should be arriving sometime today," he remarked offhandedly.

"I suppose I won't be allowed to ride them either?" she asked, trying to keep her resentment out of her tone, but not succeeding at all.

"I don't see why not."

His answer caught her off guard, taking some of the stiffness out of her stance. "Then why can't I ride Caesar?"

"He's not a lady's mount. If you want to ride him, you'll have to ride double with me."

"That's out of the . . . all right."

Changing her mind in mid-sentence managed to catch Devlin off guard this time. "You surprise me, Megan. You do realize, don't you, that riding double means you'll have to put your arms around me?"

She hadn't thought of that, but she wasn't about to admit it. "Yes, certainly."

"Are you sure you can bear to touch me?"

"You show me what that horse can do, and I won't even notice that I'm touching you."

"Well, I'll bloody well notice."

Megan stiffened at his sudden surliness. "If you can't bear it yourself, why did you make the offer?"

"Because I didn't think you'd accept."

He sounded so little-boy sulky, she couldn't resist grinning, or taunting, "You aren't going to be a spoilsport about this, are you? You made the offer. I accepted the offer. And I'll have that ride now, if you please."

He scowled after her as she sashayed past him and went out to the stable. He didn't please, not one little bit. But he'd give her her ride. He'd let Caesar take the bit and give her the ride of her life. And if he survived it, he'd bloody well keep his mouth shut from now on.

Caesar was in top form, and game to prove it. The countryside sped past, a blur of greens, browns, and the occasional bright splash of wildflowers. And Megan laughed. She laughed in delight and exhilaration, thrilling to the speed and grace of the powerful stallion beneath them.

Devlin had guessed the ride would be pure hell for himself, however, and it was. Her arms wrapped tight about his waist was bad enough, but he had prepared for that and endeavored to ignore it. Her breasts pressed into his back was worse, but he could withstand it, his blood only thrumming in slow pulsebeats that kept him just short of actual arousal. But the laughter was doing him in. Her enjoyment was an incredible aphrodisiac, a husky tremor that vibrated straight to his loins.

By the time he circled back and came to the secluded pond that Megan termed hers, he was in as much discomfort as he had been the previous morning when he had stumbled upon this swimming hole and made quick use of it. He stopped and dismounted now, abruptly moving off without helping Megan to do the same. He needed distance at the moment, and took it by rounding the small pond until he was on the opposite bank. There he shoved his hands in his pockets and stood facing the cluster of white oaks and elms that formed a three-quarter circle around the pond. He closed his eyes, making an effort to forget that he wasn't alone. His companion wouldn't let him.

"You're very brave to leave me sitting on this animal," Megan called out.

He didn't mistake her meaning. "That isn't a sidesaddle, Megan."

It annoyed her that he had twice now used her given name without permission, but she let it pass again. It annoyed her also that she was being rudely ignored, and that she didn't let pass.

"A little thing like that wouldn't stop me if I was of a mind to continue this ride without you."

That got him to turn and face her, and she found his scowl quite satisfying, until he said, "I'll wager your father has never laid a disciplinary hand on you, has he?"

She didn't mistake *his* meaning. "You wouldn't dare. You'd be dismissed instantly."

"I believe you know I would dare. Care to put it to the test?"

With the pond between them and the stallion beneath her, Megan raised her chin a notch. But she still wasn't up to calling him on that particular subject.

"Do you make an effort to be unpleasant, Mr. Jefferys, or does it come naturally?"

"The only effort I'm making right now, brat, is to keep my hands off you. So don't push it."

She thought he was referring to the last subject, until she caught the look in his eyes. He wanted her again. The knowledge should have offended her, but it didn't. It gave her a warm, tingling feeling instead, and brought on a boldness that she wasn't quite accustomed to.

"Perhaps you ought to have a swim," she suggested, remembering yesterday morning and the reason he had given for coming here.

"Perhaps I should." After a long pause he asked, "Will you watch?"

"Will you kiss me again if I do?"

"If you're that brazen, I'll do more than kiss you," he promised.

She was getting into the realm of the unknown now. Common sense insisted upon retreat. Yet when he slowly reached out to lift his shirt over his head, she didn't take her eyes off him. Would he really strip down to nothing right there in front of her? The impropriety of it was scandalous. *He* was scandalous—but so beautiful, like a piece of fine art. Were he a statue, she could admire him for hours upon hours. But he was real, and audacious, and

Megan knew instinctively that she was playing with fire each time she got near him.

She must have been mad to think she could test her wings and play the coquette with him. A gentleman knew his limitations. Devlin Jefferys had none. But it was so unfair that her curiosity couldn't be appeased this easily, that there had to be an unacceptable consequence for it. She wanted to keep watching Devlin, she really did. To be honest, she wanted to find out what he meant by "more" than a kiss, too. But she didn't dare do either. So when those long fingers of his started unfastening his trousers, Megan promptly turned her back on him.

"Coward," she heard softly whispered.

"Prudent," she countered. "And in the name of decency, put your clothes back on, Mr. Jefferys."

"I'm only taking your suggestion, Miss Prudence," he reminded her.

"I didn't mean for you to swim naked."

"I'm not partial to wet clothes," he retorted.

"Then don't swim."

"Are you suggesting the alternative, Megan? Because after you just caressed me with your eyes again, it's got to be one or the other."

These sexual innuendos were exciting, but far beyond Megan's limited experience. Fortunately, he couldn't see the color that stole into her cheeks, but it was still embarrassing that he could so easily fluster her.

"Swim if you must, then," she conceded, "but do be quick about it."

She heard a splash accompanied by a sharp hiss and smiled to herself. The water was usually icy in the early morning, which was why she never swam until the afternoon, when it had warmed up considerably.

"I could have told you it would be cold," she said.

"Don't sound so smug, brat. Cooling off is what I needed, remember?"

"Must everything you say allude to—to—?"

"The day will come when you're in the same condition as I, and when you are, you won't feel like discussing the weather, believe me."

"I believe I'll have more sense than to get myself in that condition," she said primly.

Devlin gave a hoot of laughter before he realized something. "Were you implying I don't have any sense?"

"Was it so obvious?"

"I've got news for you, Miss Innocence. Desire isn't selective of place, time, or the individual. If you think I *like* being aroused by you, think again. When it happens to you, and it will eventually, you won't have any more control over it than I do. You either make love or suffer with it."

Her curiosity about this subject got the better of her. "Does that mean I'll have to dunk myself in icy water?"

"Actually, I don't know if that would work for a woman. Never thought to ask. Would you like to conduct a little experiment to find out?"

"How?"

"I make you want me, then you find out if this pond can alleviate the problem."

"I'm not allowing you *can* make me want you, but in either case, I have more sense than to swim with you around, so no, thank you."

"Smart girl."

More splashing indicated that he might be leaving the pond. Megan continued to resist looking behind her, but it wasn't easy.

When the splashing ended, she asked, "You were just funning me, weren't you, Mr. Jefferys?"

" 'Fraid not."

She chose not to believe him. Her curiosity was piqued enough. She didn't need even more improper things to wonder about.

After a while she finally demanded impatiently, "Are you dressed yet?"

He said right behind her, "You mean you didn't peek even once?"

She turned to see that he hadn't submerged completely. His clothes were damp only from the waist down. But even in that briefest glance down his long frame, she noted that the bulge in his trousers hadn't diminished very much.

As usual, he caught the direction of her gaze.

"It didn't work." He stated the obvious. "But then how could it when all you could talk about was sex?"

She gasped at that accusation. "Me? *You* were the one. You even admitted it."

"Shows what a bloody fool I am," he said tersely as he mounted again in front of her and set off at an easy gait so she wouldn't have to hold on tight.

Megan didn't know why she had even attempted conversation with this man. They had nothing in common—well, nothing except horses, and that was a safe enough subject.

"Even though you have been typically outrageous, I still thank you for the ride. Caesar is magnificent, the finest, the fastest . . . where does he come from anyway?"

"Sherring Cross."

She stared at his back incredulously. "I should have known. There are no finer stables in the land."

"I grew up in those same stables you've got such praise for."

"You didn't," she scoffed.

"Very well, I didn't."

A full five minutes passed before she broke down to ask, "Do you know him, then?"

"Who?"

"You know very well who," she admonished impatiently. "The duke."

"I thought I did."

"What the devil does that mean?"

"It means the man has changed, Megan. He's become a bounder, a cad, a seducer of innocents."

She leaned away from him, affronted. "You're a liar, Mr. Jefferys. And I'll thank you to keep a respectful tone when you mention the duke."

"So don't thank me."

Chapter 13

That afternoon, Devlin was the only one in the front of the stable when a well-dressed young gentleman walked his horse in and tossed the reins to him.

"New, aren't you?" Devlin was asked.

"To my great misfortune," Devlin mumbled under his breath, but louder he said, "If you're here to see the squire—"

"Miss Penworthy, if it's all the same to you," the chap replied disdainfully on his way out.

Devlin stared at the reins in his hands, wondering if he looked like a bloody stableboy. "Timmy!" he bellowed.

So she was having callers, was she? That was nothing to him—except, what the devil was she doing receiving callers when she'd already decided to marry him—the duke? He

had a good mind to go over to the manor and
let that chap know that she was almost spoken
for . . . at least, in her mind she was.

He was standing at the entrance to the stable, staring up at her empty window when
another man rode up. This one was older, heavyset, but decked out in his Sunday
best, his hair slicked down with Macassar
oil. Again Devlin got tossed the reins to the
horse.

"The squire ain't here," he heard himself
saying quite churlishly.

"Ain't here to see the squire," was the fellow's amiable reply.

"You still might want to come back another
time. Miss Megan already has a caller."

"Not surprised," the man said. "She usually
does. But I come in handy. Had to break up
a fight once between two of her more jealous suitors. Also had to toss Aldrich Little
out when he started bawling after she turned
him down. Made quite a spectacle of himself.
Upset the poor girl for months."

"If you're still calling, then you haven't pro-
posed to her yourself?"

" 'Course I have. But I'm not easily dis-
suaded. I come 'round once every month to
ask her again. It could be just a matter of mood,
don't you know. Catch her at the right time and
I might get lucky."

The fellow was too likable to dislike, but
that didn't mean Devlin liked the situation one
little bit. A matter of mood? Was she playing

them all along? Did she thrive on the attention?

When he remembered that incredible, highly inflaming conversation he'd had with her at the pond this morning, he couldn't help wondering if she wasn't as provocative with all her suitors. Was even her innocence a ruse? *I believe I'll have more sense than to get myself in that condition,* she'd said. No, only an innocent could say something that ridiculous. And to be honest, he'd had a devil goading him this morning, because he hadn't affected her the way she had him. She'd merely enjoyed the ride, while he'd suffered acute discomfort from it. So maybe he had instigated the whole improper situation. After all, what other innocent young miss would he have stripped naked in front of, daring her to watch, hoping she would so he'd have an excuse to behave even more improperly?

Good God, had he really done that? He was twenty-nine years old and he'd never in his life behaved so irresponsibly. What was it about that girl that made him forget a lifetime of good breeding and turn into the cad, the bounder, the seducer of innocents that he'd accused himself of being—and to which she'd defended him? Bloody hell, she had actually defended him! 'Course, she had to, didn't she, after she'd claimed she was going to marry him? Matter of principle, that. Nothing personal. How could it be personal, anyway, when she didn't even know him?

"I say, are you there?"

Devlin turned to find another man had come into the stable leading his horse, only this one he recognized as the blond gent who had been with Megan the day he arrived. "Toss me those reins and I may deck you."

Tyler was taken aback, but after a moment he said hesitantly, "Well, then, I suppose I'll keep them. Woolgathering, were you?"

"Was I?"

"You seemed miles away when I came in."

"Not so far as that," Devlin grumbled.

He might have been preoccupied enough not to have noticed the gent's arrival, but that didn't account for his unreasonable anger. He actually still felt like decking the man; would jump on the first excuse to do so. This one Megan didn't just entertain in her parlor, she went *riding* with him. And what else did she do with him, he'd like to know?

"I suppose you're here to see the squire's daughter?"

"I'd just as soon not. See much too much of the girl as it is."

Devlin took a step forward, unaware that his fingers had curled into fists. "Just what does that mean?"

"She's my chaperon." When that remark got only a blank stare from Devlin, Tyler explained. "I'm marrying her best friend, Tiffany Roberts, so Megan accompanies us everywhere—to my great misfortune. But Tiffany's father is old-fashioned and insisted, so what's a chap to do? It was either Megan or Tiffany's mother. Thought I was getting the better bargain, but I would have preferred the mother, believe me, if I'd known what a shrew Megan could be."

"You mean I'm not the only one she's singled out for hostility?"

Tyler chuckled. "You too? Well, don't take it to heart. She put me through hell making me wonder what I'd done to offend her when I hadn't done anything. Could have sworn she despised me. And now to find out it was all deliberate." Tyler shook his head bemusedly.

Devlin held his breath, waiting to hear the rest. "Deliberate?" he finally had to prompt.

"Every bit of it, all the derision and contempt. That girl's got a way of making a man feel about three inches tall. Couldn't understand it, but Tiffany finally confessed that it's a defense Megan uses to keep men from falling in love with her. And they do, you know. I've seen it happen again and again. For myself, she did it for Tiffany's sake, though it wasn't necessary and she's finally figured that out and ended the hostilities. I'm amazed to say she's actually a sweet girl. Damned if I was aware of it before, but she is."

Devlin was damned if he agreed. But he no longer felt like clobbering the man. He did wonder, however, why the fellow had volunteered such personal information.

Tyler was suddenly wondering the same thing as he recalled the fact of just whom he'd been speaking to. The Penworthy horse breeder. And yet there was something about the man that made Tyler feel he was in the presence of an equal rather than a servant. Servants didn't usually threaten a lord, after all, as this one had done the moment Tyler entered the stable. They didn't usually wear fine lawn shirts of a better quality than his own, either. And for someone of the servant class, the fellow wasn't all that respectful, was more in the way of condescending. Strange behavior, to say the least, but possibly accountable for Tyler's nervous chatter.

"The squire ain't home, if he's the one you're here to see," Devlin said.

"Actually, I've come by to have a look at his new stallion."

"Caesar?" Devlin suddenly smiled, clapping Tyler on the back and leading him toward the rear of the stable. "You should have said so. He's right back here."

"He's a racer, isn't he? Or he was?"

"What makes you think so?"

"I've been to the track a time or two, and that stallion seems damned familiar."

"St. James may have raced him a few times."

"The Duke of Wrothston? Good God, he's *that* Caesar? But that horse is famous! Never defeated. How on earth did Penworthy end up with him?"

"A favor owed, I believe."

"Then you used to work for St. James?"

"You could say that."

Tyler decided that explained the man's haughtiness. The more toplofty the lord, the more toplofty the servants.

"Wasn't aware the squire even knew the duke." Devlin just shrugged, but Tyler didn't notice as they came upon Caesar's stall. He whistled in admiration. "Now that's a horse worth stealing. I hope he's well protected."

"I protect what's—" Devlin had started to say "mine," but amended it to "in my charge."

"Glad to hear it, because there just happens to be a thief newly come to the area."

"A horse thief?"

Tyler shook his head. "Highwayman. Two coaches were robbed just the other night—" He broke off to stare curiously at Devlin. "The night you arrived, actually."

Devlin grinned. "Are you implying—"

"Not at all, not at all," Tyler quickly assured him. "It's obviously no more than a coincidence. But speculation will be making the rounds, so you're sure to hear about it again. It's been years since we've had a highwayman in our parish, after all, so he's guaranteed to be the topic at every tea and gathering for a while."

Later, Devlin discussed the possibility of horse thieves with Mortimer. At Sherring Cross it wasn't a problem, since he employed nearly as many grooms as he had horses. But this was country, there were no grooms, and the squire's stable left much to be desired in the way of security. Short of sleeping at Caesar's feet, which he had no inclination to do, Devlin ordered a bolt installed on the stable doors. There was no point in taking chances with a thief in the area.

Bloody hell, it wasn't something he'd ever worried about before, not until Tyler Whately—the fellow had finally got around to introducing himself—had mentioned it. The rest of what Tyler had mentioned, about Megan at least, was worth a good laugh. Imagine that girl being deliberately offensive to keep a man from falling in love with her. She'd even accused him of the same thing— because she was familiar with the ploy? She *had* been antagonistic toward him from the very first. But he didn't think for a moment that she was pretending with him. He'd been too temper-provoking himself for her hostility to be anything but real.

Yet it made him wonder how she'd behave with a man she didn't want to ward off. How, for instance, would she act with a man she'd set her cap for?

Chapter 14

"They say he has a terrible temper."

"*Where* did you hear all this gossip, Tiff?" Megan asked while staring across the ballroom at the man Tiffany had pointed out. "We only just arrived here today."

"Yes, but while you were resting this afternoon, Lady Leighton's daughter was talking my ear off."

"But how do you know who is who?"

"Because Jane dragged me into her bedroom, which overlooks the front of the house, and I swear she had something to say about every single arrival."

"But people are still arriving."

"I didn't say I know something about *everyone*, just the early—"

"Was *he* an early arrival?"

"I'm sorry, Meg, but they're not even sure he's going to come."

Megan stopped her avid perusal of the crowd to give Tiffany her full attention. Even behind the domino mask she was wearing, her distress was obvious.

"But he *has* to come!" Megan insisted with more hope than conviction. "The *Times* said he would, and who can you believe if you can't believe the *Times*?"

"I know, and he did accept the invitation, but . . . apparently your duke is somewhat absentminded when it comes to his social calendar. He'll agree to go to one affair, then promptly forget about it. Then he'll accept another invite for the same day and forget that, too—then accept another. Are you getting the picture?"

"Too many places to go on any given day?"

"Exactly. And so he won't end up offending one hostess in favor of another, he usually just skips every affair and stays home."

"How would Jane know that?"

"Because of all the times her mother has invited him, and they've lost count of how many, he's only shown up twice. She says it's also a joke in the ton, not to count on St. James to make an appearance unless no one else is counting on him to do the same."

"I don't think I like the ton making jokes about my future husband," Megan said.

Tiffany noted the stiffness in that response

and quickly said, "Did I say joke? Joke is definitely not the correct word I wanted. It's simply a recognized fact, Meg, and one that even St. James acknowledges with good humor."

"Then he's not coming," Megan replied with acute disappointment.

"Now, how do we know that? This is a pre-Season ball, after all. How many invitations can be floating around?"

"It's all right, Tiffany. You don't have to bolster my spirits."

Tiffany was looking at a girl who might as well be at a funeral for all the joy in her expression. "Don't I?" she said in exasperation. "You aren't going to enjoy yourself now, are you?"

"Sure I will."

"Damn it, you won't. I know you. I'll wager you're already thinking up some excuse to retire, when we haven't even made our appearance yet."

Which was perfectly true. They had come downstairs, but had gone straight to the gallery that overlooked the ballroom, to spend a few moments observing everyone below without being observed in return. But it was still early. The orchestra that had been hired for the evening, and which was situated in the center of the gallery, was just starting its second set. And the room below contained only half the people that would be there later.

Megan smiled ruefully. "You do know me too well, don't you? But I can't help it, Tiff. The disappointment is crushing me."

"But why?" Tiffany asked, genuinely perplexed. "If you don't meet him here, you'll have another chance when you go to London for your Season."

"That's just it," Megan replied. "I was hoping to avoid that altogether."

"Avoid it?" Tiffany repeated incredulously. "You'd been looking forward to it!"

"I'd been looking forward to finding my own Tyler, which we both agreed could only be done in London. I wasn't looking forward to going to London, however."

"But why not?"

"Let's face it, Tiff, we're country girls who aren't the least bit sophisticated. I just know I'm going to make a fool of myself somehow. I've been so nervous about it and, well, I thought that since I'd made my choice, I wouldn't have to go through with that. I would meet Ambrose here and he would then come to Devonshire to court me."

"Of all the unrealistic—where, I ask you, would a man of his consequence stay in our small parish? With our reigning hostess?"

"He wouldn't dare," Megan said unreasonably.

"But that *would* be the only logical place for him," Tiffany said reasonably.

"There's the inn."

"You would put the Duke of Wrothston in Teadale's tiny inn?"

"He's going to be in love," Megan insisted. "He won't care where he stays."

"Don't count on it, Meg. He's used to the very best accommodations. Are you forgetting he lives in a bloody mausoleum? He probably has a bedroom as big as that ballroom down there."

"Don't exaggerate."

"Who's exaggerating?"

"You are. His bedroom is probably only half as big as the ballroom."

"Don't skip the point, Meg. If he does follow you home, he won't want to stay long at the inn, or in Devonshire, for that matter. You can't expect him to suspend the business of his everyday life for a complete courtship. He's got a dukedom to see to, after all. A week maybe, and that's if he comes, and that's not long enough—"

"Sure it is."

"Megan! You can't accept a proposal after only a week's acquaintance!"

"I can, too," Megan replied stubbornly.

"That would cause a bloody scandal, and you know it. Besides, *he* won't be that impetuous. He might fall in love with you instantly. That's a definite possibility. Tonight even. But he'll still take the requisite amount of time to consider marriage. And *that* means that he'll visit you every few weeks to continue the courtship, which is going to take a long time at that rate. Or you can go to London as planned, where he can see you more often and make up his mind the quicker. Either way, you end up going to London."

"Damn," Megan said in disgust. "I'd actually convinced myself it was no longer necessary."

"What exactly has you so nervous?" Tiffany
asked hesitantly.

Megan sighed. "More treatment like I had
from the Thackerays."

Tiffany frowned. "I should have known your
misgivings were only recent. You *were* excited
about London before old hatchet-face gave you
the snub. But that situation was unique, Meg.
It's not going to happen again."

Megan smiled bitterly. "You don't think
there will be mamas in London who won't
want me at the same parties their marriageable
daughters attend?"

"It won't matter once it's learned who's
courting you," Tiffany said with complete
confidence.

"I don't see what that will have to do with
it," Megan replied.

"Don't you? Mark my words, *he'll* make sure
you're invited to every place he is, and he's got
the power and influence to open any door in
London for you. You'll end up invited to places
that you wouldn't have been otherwise."

"I don't see why."

"Because your romance with the duke is
bound to be the sensation of the Season, that's
why. Everyone who is anyone will want a hand
in playing Cupid to further it along."

"That's ridiculous."

"That's human nature and it stands to reason. You're going to be the ton's new darling, because you will have attracted the interest of their most eligible bachelor."

"*If* I ever get to meet him."

Tiffany grinned. "Don't be so impatient. If he comes tonight, the romance begins or ends, depending on the impression he makes—and you're not to forget your promise."

"I know, I know. Only if I think I can love him."

"Good. Now, on the other hand, if he doesn't show up, then think of tonight as practice for all the balls you'll have to attend later. This is our first, after all, or had you forgotten that in your preoccupation with *Ambrose*?"

Megan laughed at the silly connotation Tiffany placed on the duke's first name. "I know it's a horrible name for a man, especially after we're used to applying it to a horse. I'm stuck with it, however."

"*He's* stuck with it. You can call him anything you like. 'Your Grace' for starters; 'darling' when the time's right. Feeling better?"

"Absolutely. Now, what were you saying about that fellow with the temper?"

Chapter 15

"Frederick Something-or-other is his name."

"Something-or-other?"

Tiffany made a face, saying defensively, "What do you want from me? I heard too many names to remember them all. This one's a marquis. I remember that only because Jane mentioned that he's a very good friend of— guess who?"

Megan's interest perked up. "No kidding? But that increases the odds on Ambrose showing up."

"Not necessarily. The marquis just happens to have an estate near here that he was visiting, but remember, Kent as well as London is a long way off."

"Ambrose could have an estate near here, too."

"That's true," Tiffany allowed. "But don't count on it. They would have arrived together if they both were in the area, don't you think?"

"Possibly—unless Ambrose was detained for some reason. But I could just end the suspense by going down and asking Lord Frederick if the duke is coming. Our hostess might not know, but he ought to."

"That might not be such a good idea."

"Why not?"

"Well, look at it from the broader picture. He meets you and falls in love."

Megan nodded. "Yes, we already agreed—"

"Frederick does."

"Him? But why should he?"

"For the same reason your duke is likely to. And remember that they're good friends. If the marquis saw you first and confesses to love you, won't his good friend the duke forsake his own feelings to preserve the friendship?"

Megan laughed. "That's getting much too complicated. And besides, I wouldn't give the marquis the least bit of encouragement. So what harm can a little conversation do? And I'd be asking about his friend, showing clearly in what direction my interest lay."

"Now, there's another thing. Are you sure you want St. James to know that you were *clearly* interested in him *before* you met him? Because what are good friends for if not to confide such things? So don't think Lord Frederick wouldn't mention it. And a man doesn't like to know that he's been singled out for pursuit. They like to do that sort of thing themselves, after all."

"I see your point. Asking about Ambrose might give the wrong impression—well, the right impression, but one I'd rather not give. Not that I won't confess all eventually."

"But *after* the wedding."

"Exactly." But then Megan frowned. "Or would that be considered too devious?"

Tiffany's brows shot up before she grinned. "So now you're devious?"

"Well, aren't I? The whole courtship thing is going to be a waste of time just for his benefit. If I were honest, I'd tell him right from the start that I'd like to marry him."

"You can't do that!"

"I *know* that, Tiff. But isn't omitting that the same thing as lying?"

"No, it's just standard romance protocol," Tiffany said with firm conviction. "It'd be nice if we women *could* be that honest, but if we were, we'd scare away half the men we end up married to, the half that insist that the idea of marriage be their idea exclusively. And don't be so hasty in calling your courtship a waste of time either. That's the only time you'll have to get to know your duke and figure out if you can love him or not, because I *hope* you're not thinking it's going to be as quick for you as it probably will be for him."

"You don't think that's possible?"

"Highly impossible, Meg. He's going to fall for your stunning face first, then your sweet self later. But then you're quite conceivably the most beautiful girl in the kingdom. He isn't likely to be the most handsome man, however." Then Tiffany snorted. "That horse breeder in your stable might have that distinction, but your duke won't."

The mere mention of Devlin brought him fully to Megan's mind. She wished he could have seen her in her lovely new ball gown. The green poult-de-soie hugged her figure where the scooped neckline and capped sleeves weren't revealing it. The added white tulle flounces in the underskirt were an extravagance. With her hair artfully coiffed and her mother's heirloom pearls at her throat, she felt she looked sophisticated, even if she wasn't, especially with the matching green domino adding a touch of mystery. Devlin would have been dazzled by such splendor—and for once kept his insults to himself.

"My duke *is* going to be handsome, Tiff."

"Absolutely," Tiffany agreed. "Just don't expect *incredibly* handsome, all right? That's asking for disappointment."

"I suppose." Megan sighed. "Very well, now that we've established that I must give Lord Frederick Something-or-other the cold shoulder, we have to figure out how I'm to recognize Ambrose if he shows up. Did Jane happen to describe him to you when she was doing all her chattering?"

"She did say he's very tall. Of course, she's very short, so tall to her could be anywhere from here to here," Tiffany said, raising her hand from the level of Megan's head to a good foot above it.

"What else?"

"Black hair, or dark brown—she wasn't sure on that. And eyes some shade of blue or green, unusual, she called them. And by the way, *she* thinks he's incredibly handsome. Those were her words. But then she also thinks Lord Fred down there is incredibly handsome, so you have to take her opinion as a bit exaggerated."

Megan glanced down again at Lord Frederick, noting that he was rather tall himself and also had black hair. She couldn't tell much more about him from that distance and with his domino mask in place, but his body was nicely put together, his evening clothes were impeccable, and the younger women who were present seemed to be fawning over him.

"Oh, I don't know." Megan grinned. "I'd say he's probably very handsome."

Tiffany instantly caught the drift of her thoughts. "That's to be expected, since he's the highest-ranked lord here at the moment, and a bachelor."

"Poor man," Megan said dryly. "He must have to put up with that kind of adoration all the time."

"No more than your duke does," Tiffany replied. "Sure you can tolerate that?"

"But it won't be like that after he's married."

"He's a duke, Meg. There will always be women who will want one thing or another from him—even for legitimate business."

"That's not funny."

Tiffany grinned cheekily. "I thought it was. Oh, don't frown. I was only joking—well, not quite. There *will* be women who will try to take him away from you just because of who he is."

"But tell me something. If he loves me, do you really think I ought to worry about it? And be honest instead of down-on-my-duke for a change."

Tiffany chuckled. "All right, I'll concede gracefully. If he loves you, you won't have a thing to worry about. He'll be the one to suffer the talons of jealousy, not you." After a moment she added sheepishly, "Was I really being 'down-on-your-duke'?"

"With every other breath."

"I'm sorry, Meg. I guess it's hard to be positive about a man we haven't even met yet. I can't very well say the Duke of Wrothston is wonderful and perfect for you when we don't know if he is or isn't. All he has in his favor at the moment is his title, which might put him at the top of your list, but doesn't recommend him to me. I just want you to have a man who is absolutely right for you, and I'm afraid that you're going to let this getting-even-with-Lady O thing cloud your judgment and convince you that he's right for you—and he very well might not be."

Megan leaned forward to give her friend a hug. "I love you for caring like that. And it's all right, you can continue to play the skeptic if it makes you happy. Chances are, I might not even be attracted to the man." *Like you are to Devlin?* Now where had that thought come from? "And that will be determined at our first meeting."

"And end it?"

Megan nodded firmly. "That quickly. But on the other hand—"

"I'll be the first one to point out his good qualities—once we know what they are."

"Fair enough."

Chapter 16

"Would it be all right if I spoke with your father about marriage?"

Megan missed a step. Her dancing partner didn't seem to notice.

He was an excellent dancer. There had been a half-dozen previous partners who weren't, so she'd noted that right off. This one had a pleasant face, and right now a very earnest expression on it. She'd guess he was somewhere in his early thirties.

If he were younger she could have laughed and made some silly reply to his question. But she was afraid he was serious. Only she didn't want to be serious herself just now. She'd been having too much fun this evening, just as Tiffany had predicted she would.

Every single dance had been promised, except the two she'd saved for the duke if he'd bothered to show up, which he hadn't. But even that didn't bother her so much now. She realized she'd been letting impatience rule her emotions, when there was plenty of time to meet St. James. And with half the people at the ball from London, she wasn't quite so nervous anymore about her Season there, having found out that these people weren't so intimidating after all.

"Now, this is what London is going to be like," Tiffany had whispered only moments ago, just before Megan's present partner had made his way through her ring of admirers to claim this dance. *"Are you sure you want to settle for a stodgy old duke?"*

Megan *was* still set on her duke, at least until such time as meeting him might change her mind. But in the meantime, she could see no reason not to enjoy her "success," as her popularity tonight could definitely be termed. A serious proposal of marriage from a stranger was not her idea of enjoyment, however. It was absurd, was what it was, and deserved a bit of absurdity in return.

"You may speak to my father, certainly," Megan told her partner—she couldn't remember his name. "But if your subject is marriage, I feel I must warn you that you may be shot."

He missed a step now. Megan noticed.

"I beg your pardon," he said after a moment of incredulity. "Did you say shot?"

"Indeed."

"But—but—"

"Oh, it's not as bad as it sounds, sir, and it's only if marriage is mentioned. He's been plagued too often with proposals of marriage, you see . . . the women just won't leave him alone."

He missed another step. Megan kept from laughing, but it wasn't easy.

"Women? But I meant—"

"And I'm afraid he swore, actually swore, that he if heard that word once more in the next three months—he was rational enough to put a limit on his temper—no matter who mentioned it, he would shoot them. Now, I don't know if he meant he would kill them. He might have just meant a wounding. Yes, that's possible. But in either case, I did feel you ought to be warned."

"Appreciate it, indeed I do."

She thought he just might. And the fellow didn't have much more to say for the rest of the dance. He left her rather abruptly once it was over, and for the first time that evening, Megan had a moment alone. But it was a brief moment.

"I believe the next dance is mine."

The voice gave her a start, coming from directly behind her, and was entirely unwelcome, since she had hoped for a few minutes to herself. She wondered if she could pretend not to have heard and simply walk away. No, that would be too rude, though walking away was still an option as long as it was accompanied with a good excuse, which she had, considering the man's presumption.

So to avoid being drawn into conversation, she turned only slightly so he'd know she was replying to him and said with a degree of curtness, "No, actually, I'm not partnered for the next dance, and I'm going to keep it that way. Excuse me, but I was just going to take some air."

"That was going to be my suggestion, so I'll join you, if you don't mind."

"The air is free for the taking, of course, but I'd prefer to take mine alone."

"How unromantic of you, Miss Penworthy."

She turned then out of simple curiosity. He was tall, very tall, and masked. "Have we been introduced?"

"I would have remembered that pleasure, so the answer must be no."

"Then how did you—?"

"I asked. But allow me." He bowed ever so slightly. "Ambrose St. James, at your service. Are you sure you won't reconsider?"

Was he kidding? She'd given him up as a no-show, yet here he was, and he was much more than she had been hoping for. What she could see of his face beneath the black domino was definitely handsome, and his body was as finely put together as Devlin's was—*stay out of my thoughts, horse breeder*—though she would certainly never see Devlin arrayed so splendidly in black evening clothes. His eyes were too shadowed by the domino he wore for her to distinguish their color, but his hair was black and slicked back without a single strand out of place. She was attracted, quite definitely attracted. And to think he might have left offended by her initial curtness.

But before she blurted out, "Of course I've changed my mind," she realized how fickle that would sound after her firmness in putting him off. So she gave him a tepid smile, pretending an indifference she was far from feeling.

"You're very persistent, aren't you?"

"When it matters," he replied.

His own smile was quite startling in its sensual appeal. Megan imagined that Devlin would smile like that if he ever bothered to— *you're doing it again.*

"Why should it mat—?"

He interrupted her impatiently. "Let's not chew it to bits until your next dance partner shows up. You've already changed your mind, dear girl, so come along."

How did he know? She wondered as he ushered her, rather quickly, out to the raised terrace. And she didn't care for the sudden abruptness that had come right after his lovely smile, when he'd looked beyond her, almost as if he were trying to avoid someone he'd seen approaching. So as he headed for the steps that led down to the formal gardens, Megan veered toward the terrace railing instead.

"The air is quite satisfactory right here, I believe," she said, tugging her elbow out of his hand.

"No stroll through moonlit gardens? *Very* unromantic, Miss Penworthy."

"Look who's talking," she mumbled.

He grinned engagingly. It was as startling as his smile, and no doubt designed to disarm her now noticeable pique.

"Don't be angry, dear girl. There are several people here that I'd rather not speak with, and one of them was bearing down on us— which means I won't have much time with you. That very thought is devastating me, and is accountable for my appalling lapse in manners."

His excuse was acceptable since she had guessed as much, but that last remark had her forgiving him completely. She even blushed slightly because she could disconcert him that much. The man was *definitely* interested, and wasn't that what she had been hoping for?

She was thrilled with the thought, which brought on a degree of shyness as well as regret as she pointed out, "The next dance is spoken for, so you won't have much time in either case."

"Then I must take advantage of what little time I do have," he said as he swept her into his arms for the current waltz.

Megan was caught off guard by the unexpectedness of it, so it took her a moment to realize she was being held much too closely.

When she did, she stiffened slightly, and was promptly treated to the sensation of his warm breath tickling her ear and sending gooseflesh down her neck and arms.

"The urge to hold you in my arms was simply too overwhelming. The urge to kiss you was even more overwhelming, so you see I am trying to behave."

With his arms around her causing exciting remembrances of another bold embrace, and with his seductive words cutting clean through her defenses, it was on the tip of her tongue to say, "Then kiss me," because the urge was there for her, too. But she recalled that she was sadly lacking where kissing was concerned, so she said nothing, wanting this first meeting of theirs to be as memorable for him as it surely was going to be for her.

She was delighted that she would be able to relieve Tiffany's worries, because Megan now had no doubt at all that it would take very little effort to fall in love with Ambrose St. James. She sighed happily and relaxed in his arms, for everything was going just as planned.

He heard her, felt her yielding, and stiffened, for nothing was going as he'd planned. But then he hadn't expected her to be so ravishing tonight, so incredibly lovely, that she'd made him forget what he was doing here. Yet what he'd just told her was perfectly true. There was nothing more he wanted to do just now than kiss her. And he had no doubt she'd let him kiss her, and probably more, because this was not the Megan he knew; this was the scheming little miss out to snare a duke, and by God, she'd think twice about it after tonight.

His intentions recalled, he maneuvered them back to the terrace railing and abruptly ended the dance. But there was definitely a moment of keen regret when he saw her dreamy expression turn to surprise as he let her go. Again all he wanted to do was kiss her. He squelched the urge with the reminder that another man wouldn't have stood a chance against this kind of temptation— *he* wouldn't have if he didn't know her game. She deserved the lesson he was about to give her, the lesson he'd risked a run-in with Freddy to give her. Maybe next time she'd be more careful in her choice of victims.

Megan felt awkward under his pensive stare. She wished she could see his eyes, but they were even more shadowed in the dimmer light on the terrace.

"You don't care for dancing after all, Your Grace?" was all she could think to say for the moment.

"Ah, so you *do* know?" he said in reference to her "Your Grace."

She shrugged, though silently she berated herself for having called him that without a formal introduction. "Doesn't everyone?"

"In London, yes, but not in the country." Then he sighed. "A pity, that. Spoils half my fun."

"Why would it?"

"People tend to behave differently than they ordinarily would when they know who I am. All they can see is the title, not the man who bears it."

Megan detected a large dose of bitterness in those words that made her feel distinctly uncomfortable. She was guilty of just that, seeing only the title—no, that wasn't quite true. The title had been her first consideration, yes, but everything else hinged on the man. If he didn't suit, then it wouldn't matter what title he bore, for she wouldn't have him.

"I'm sorry," she said, and meant it. "That can't be an easy thing to live with."

He shrugged. "One of the little drawbacks of being a duke."

"I hope there are some benefits to compensate."

The comment had him grinning again. "Oh, a few."

Now why did that "few" sound so very wicked? No, it was the grin. That grin was definitely not wholesome.

"One of those things wouldn't be getting away with being a trifle high-handed, would it?"

She meant it teasingly. He answered seriously.

"A trifle? I dragged you out here, dear girl. That was most assuredly high-handed of me."

"Yes, it was, and now that you mention it, I realize you haven't apologized for it."

"Another benefit. I rarely apologize. Who, after all, would dare bring me to account for my actions?"

She didn't like the sound of that. Were Tiffany there, she'd be pointing out that they hadn't come across many good qualities yet, and Megan would have to agree. What the devil had happened to the charming man who had only moments ago confessed to an overwhelming urge to kiss her?

"I believe I would have no difficulty in doing so, Your Grace."

He half sat, half leaned on the railing, crossed his arms, and gave every indication of being amused. "Would you indeed? Your own character is so exemplary, then, that you can cast stones?"

Neither the subdued lighting on the terrace nor the half mask she wore could hide her blush completely. "Absolutely . . . not. I don't claim to be anywhere near perfect, but then I don't represent such an exalted title."

"And if you did, would that make you any less spoiled or willful?"

Megan stiffened. "What, I would like to know, has led you to assume either of those things about me?"

"A good guess?"

Disappointment was welling up again, much worse than what she'd felt when she thought she might not meet the duke tonight. It was nearly choking her, and that made her furious. She didn't know what had gone wrong, but if she didn't leave now, she'd say something to end the possibility of any future encounter—*if* she decided to give him a chance to redeem his appalling behavior.

"I believe I've had too much air. Good evening, Your Grace."

"Not so fast, my dear."

Not only his words detained her. His arm had snaked out as she'd turned to leave, and she now found herself drawn nearly between his legs.

"I've made you angry again?" he ventured with galling good cheer.

Megan decided that he had to be an idiot to ask that question. "Absolutely, and it's increasing by the second. Let me—"

"That wasn't my intention."

She felt a spark of hope. Maybe he just wasn't himself tonight. Maybe he thought her more sophisticated than she was and she'd merely misunderstood his insults. "What *was* your intention?"

"I want to see a lot more of you."

Exactly what she had hoped to hear—before this abrupt change in him. Now she wasn't at all sure if she ever wanted to see him again.

"Why?" she asked boldly.

"I'm becoming bored with my current mistress. I think you might do to replace her."

"Your *mistress?*"

He went on blithely as if she hadn't almost screeched. "Yes, I think you might do nicely. Can't say for certain, though, until I try you out. Shall we find a secluded spot in the garden to—"

The crack of her palm against his cheek cut off his shocking suggestion. Megan pushed away from him. He didn't try to stop her this time. But she didn't leave. She wanted to do more than just slap him. She wanted to rail at him for being exactly what Devlin had said he was, a bounder, a rogue, a seducer of innocents, but she was too angry to get the words out.

She thought about ripping off his domino. After all, she didn't want to mistake this rake if she *did* ever see him again, which she sincerely hoped would never happen. To think she'd actually been disappointed earlier that she might not get to meet him tonight, and even more so only moments ago.

"Ah, there you are, Miss Penworthy. I believe this dance is mine."

She turned with a start, feeling almost guilty for being caught alone with such a wicked man as she now knew Ambrose St. James to be. But it was the duke's friend, Lord Frederick, to whom she had promised the next dance. Two of a kind? Possibly. More than likely, actually, so both were to be avoided henceforth.

"You, sir, keep detestable friends," she told the marquis in her most chilling tone. "That one in particular." And she pointed a stiff finger behind her.

"That one?" Lord Frederick asked.

His bewilderment made her frown, then turn to see why he hadn't understood her perfectly.

But the reason was quite clear. The previously occupied perch on the terrace railing was now empty.

The odious Duke of Wrothston was gone, vanished, with not even a bush stirring on the other side of the railing to mark his passage. Too bad he hadn't done so sooner, before she'd met him. No, it was better to know, and now she knew. As far as she was concerned, Ambrose St. James and his title could rot.

Chapter 17

"Why haven't you told me, 'I told you so'?"

They were on the last leg of the journey home, the Robertses' coach jostling along at a steady put-you-to-sleep pace. Tiffany's mother was in fact dozing on the opposite seat, so the girls had had no conversation for a while.

Tiffany had been about to fall asleep herself, but that softly uttered question brought her wide awake. "I thought you weren't brooding about that anymore."

Megan had done nothing else but brood about her colossal foolishness. She'd just kept it to herself after their earlier discussion, when she'd related the entire humiliating encounter with Ambrose St. James.

"Why haven't you?" Megan repeated. "I certainly deserve it."

"No, you don't," Tiffany said loyally. "And I wouldn't do that to you. Besides, it might not have seemed like it, but I was really hoping everything would work out just the way you wanted it to with St. James. So I guess I'm just as disappointed as you are that it didn't."

"I'm not disappointed," Megan assured her. "At least not anymore. What I am is furious with myself for pinning all my hopes on a man we knew absolutely nothing about—which you tried to point out numerous times. I still can't believe how stupid that was. But I'm also furious with him. I can't seem to help it. You'd think a duke would have more integrity than to be a bounder, wouldn't you?"

"Absolutely. The title probably corrupted in his case. It's been known to happen."

"There ought to be a law against it," Megan grumbled.

Tiffany said nothing. She waited. After a moment the expected laughter came.

"I don't believe I said that," Megan said, still softly chuckling.

"I don't either, though I happen to agree."

Megan burst into another round of laughter. "Stop, or I'll wake your mother."

Tiffany got serious again. "It's true, though. Great power and wealth do corrupt, and St. James has both in abundance. A pity. Maybe if he'd been an impoverished duke, he would have been a bit more honorable."

"And desperate for an heiress, which I'm not."

Tiffany sighed. "Well, it's water under the bridge now, so are you ready to do things in their proper order?"

"You mean meet the man first?"

"That, too, but more importantly, fall in love first. That really *is* the way it's being done these days, you know."

"I know," Megan replied. "That just doesn't guarantee me the title."

Tiffany wasn't that surprised to hear this. Megan could be exceedingly stubborn and single-minded at times—most times, actually.

"So you *do* still want the title?"

Megan shrugged, her expression dispirited. "I don't know—no, that's not true. I'd still like to set Lady O on her ear, and I can't very well do that without a titled husband, so I guess I would still prefer it. I'm just not going to count on it."

Tiffany clicked her tongue. "Sounds like you're giving up before the game begins."

"Just being realistic from now on."

"Realistic? You want to talk realistic? Are you forgetting that you actually did what you set out to do—well, at least half of it?"

Megan frowned. "What are you talking about?"

"The first part of your goal was to gain the amorous interest of the Duke of Wrothston. That you did, and then some. It's not *your*

fault that he turned out to be a lecherous rake
with immoral propositions on his mind, rather
than decent ones. You still caught his interest,
Meg."

"I did, didn't I?"

"So I wouldn't worry about that title. There
will be dozens more for you to choose from
when you get to London. But this time you
meet them first, *then* you decide which one
you're going to fall in love with and let it
happen—unless you fall in love first and that
decides it for you. There is always that possibility, you know, and frankly, I highly recommend it."

"You would, but then there aren't very many
men as wonderful as your Tyler."

"True, but you're forgetting I fell in love
with Tyler before I knew he was wonderful,
the very day I met him, as it happens. I was
just so fortunate that he *is* wonderful, but I
don't think it would have mattered very much
if he'd had a few bad qualities. We have to take
the good with the bad when the heart makes
the choice."

"That does *not* sound too encouraging, Tiff.
In fact, it only supports my previous contention that I'd do well to choose the man first,
then let love take its course."

"Suit yourself, as long as you meet him
first to determine that you won't be wasting
your time on another bounder—and as long
as you're in love before you agree to marry

him. You will agree to that at least, won't you?"

"Absolutely—only how long do you think it takes to fall in love my way?"

Tiffany rolled her eyes. "You're asking me, who did it instantly? How should I know?"

Chapter 18

Megan was surprised by how anxious she was to get home. And once she was home, she was frankly amazed that her urge was to go straight to the stable, rather than into the house to greet her father. She supposed she just missed her horse. She *had* missed her morning rides. But that shouldn't account for such a compelling impulse, especially when she'd been away only four days.

And she had been away from home before. There had been that trip to Kent for her twelfth-birthday present—*why* couldn't she have found out back then what an odious man the duke was?—and a few shopping expeditions to towns that offered more than Teadale. Her father had accompanied her those times—maybe that was the difference, but her conscience told her otherwise.

Why don't you be honest? You want to see that horse breeder.

Absolutely not. If anything, he's the last person I want to see.

Sure he is.

You're forgetting his knowledge of St. James. He probably knew exactly what would happen at the ball, or guessed it would happen, while I was arrogantly informing him that I would be marrying the man. How can I face him after that?

With your usual charm . . . and arrogance.

Very funny. But what if he asks what happened? Not what if; he will ask.

You can lie.

And when I don't happen to marry St. James within the year, then what? Devlin will be good at gloating, you know he will. He probably wrote the book on it. I could have taken it from Tiffany, but an I-told-you-so from him—I'd probably shoot the man.

You have to face him eventually, so admit it, you can't wait.

I can't wait to be humiliated? When did I become a glutton for punishment?

When you noticed how handsome that man is.

Very funny.

Somehow, Megan managed to go to bed that first night home without giving in to the urge to see—her horse. But she was up at the first tinges of dawn the next morning, and on her way to the stable before the sun actually made it over the horizon. She was bubbling with anticipation that she refused to acknowledge, so she was incredibly dumbfounded to find the stable doors not just closed for the night, but also locked. Locked? Since when and why?

Megan stood there for several minutes, prodded with impatience, disappointment, and a number of other unwelcome emotions. She wondered how much noise pounding on the doors would make. Too much, especially since only the horses slept in the front of the stable.

She was about to go back to the house to wait for her normal hour for riding when one of her emotions got the better of her, and she marched around to the back of the stable instead. Of the several windows at the back, only one was covered with curtains. She tapped lightly on it, then a bit harder when she got no immediate response. But then the curtains—she felt a moment's amusement upon noting that they were pink—were yanked apart, and the window was opened more than the crack it had been.

She had to be grateful—*or not*, her conscience put in—that it still wasn't light enough for her to see very clearly into his darkened room, because she could just barely discern that Devlin Jefferys was standing in front of his window quite naked. It was lighter where she stood, so he had less difficulty seeing who had disturbed his sleep.

"What the devil are you about, brat, at this ungodly hour?" he demanded with a great deal of sleepy irritation before she could get her mouth open.

Megan bristled at the uncomplimentary name he persisted in calling her, but didn't bring him to task for it. Her eyes were adjusting and getting a clearer image of him by the second, and, cognizant of his previous threats about staring, she felt it was more prudent to find something else to look at. So she turned slightly, facing the bare frame of the extension that was being added to the back of the stable—and suddenly realized there might have been another way in without having had to wake him.

That realization caused a certain amount of embarrassment, prompting her to apologize. "I'm sorry. I found the doors locked, but I've just noticed a back entrance. Go back to sleep, Mr.—"

"What back entrance?"

"Why, where the stable is being enlarged. Surely a door has been cut—"

"Why don't you go have a closer look before you make assumptions, Megan? You'll find that the extension is going up and will be nearly complete before an opening is cut to connect it. What's the point of barring the doors out front if a bloody hole is left in the back?"

She detected the amusement that had slipped into his tone with that explanation, and that got her back to bristling. "Then the stable *is* completely locked?"

"Isn't that what I just said?"

"How dare you lock me out of my own stable? By what right—did my father tell you to lock it?"

"I don't need your father's permission to protect the horses," he said with a degree of condescension. "That happens to be my responsibility."

"Protect them from what?" she scoffed. "Open the doors, Jefferys."

"Go back to bed, Megan. The doors will be opened at a decent hour."

"I don't choose to wait until a decent hour, I choose to go riding now. Open the bloody doors."

"You insist?"

"Isn't that what I just said?" She tossed his own words back at him.

"Very well, you asked for it."

She glanced cautiously up at the window to find him gone. She bit her lip, frowning. He wouldn't do what that "you asked for it" sounded like, would he?

He wouldn't dare—but just to be sure, she called in through the window, "Don't you dare open those doors with no clothes on, Devlin Jefferys. If you do, I'll bloody well scream; then you can make your excuses to the servants who come running, *and* my father."

With that warning, she marched to the front of the stable, confident that she had put a stop to what he had intended. And she must have, because he kept her waiting a good five minutes before the doors finally swung open.

But he hadn't taken her warning completely to heart. The wait had been to light a lantern, since the inside of the stable was still pitch-dark. For clothes, Devlin had put on only his trousers and boots.

Pink-cheeked that he had obeyed her only in part, Megan swept past him and went straight to Sir Ambrose's stall. It was too much to hope that Devlin would simply go back to bed now and leave her in peace. He didn't.

"Someone ought to teach you a little common decency, courtesy, *and* sense."

Reprimanded by a horse breeder. His gall was utterly astounding.

"What does common sense have to do with it?" she asked without turning to look at him, allowing that she might be a little out of line on the decency and courtesy parts. "I wanted to ride. You had no right to keep me from doing so."

"I still might keep you from doing so," he growled at her back. "You don't wake a man from a sound sleep and berate him for doing his job. Common sense would have told you that you won't get away with it unscathed."

She stilled in the process of reaching for Sir Ambrose's saddle blanket. Her heart, on the other hand, was off to the races.

"You'd better keep your distance from me, Devlin." They both realized, at the same moment, that she'd just used his first name for the first time. "I meant, Mr. Jefferys," she corrected herself quite properly.

"Formality is a bit misplaced by now, don't you think?" he asked, amusement present in his tone again.

Megan continued readying Sir Ambrose for her ride. "No, I don't."

There was a moment of silence before he said, "Even after I've stood naked in your sight?"

She gasped, swinging around to glare at him. "I didn't look!"

"You wanted to."

She didn't answer that, again going back to what she was doing. He chuckled at her silence and the blush that accompanied it.

"I'm sorry I had to disturb you, but you can return to your bed now."

It was the stiffness in her tone which put the disgruntlement back in his. "Which is where you ought to be—in your own bed, that is. You've got no business riding out this early."

"When I ride is none of *your* business, Mr. Jefferys," she pointed out.

"It is when you wake me to do it." And then he sighed. "If you're going to insist on this foolishness, I'll go with you."

That gave her pause and she glanced at him with raised brows. "Whatever for?"

"There's a highwayman working these parts, or has no one told you?"

"I'm not carrying a purse."

He grinned at that bit of lopsided logic. "You don't think he'd find something on you to take? I know I would."

She didn't like the sound of that insinuation. "The hour might be early, but the sun will be up by the time I ride out of here."

"Just barely."

She ignored that. "If I were taking one of my midnight rides, I might worry, but not in—"

"Midnight rides?" he cut in incredulously. "Good God, have you got no sense a'tall, to risk your neck like that, not to mention your bloody virtue?"

Megan was determined not to lose her temper, so she said calmly, "This is a very quiet parish."

"Don't I know it," he replied in disgust.

"It's perfectly safe for me to ride at night when the mood takes me, or it was, before this highwayman chose our area for his robberies. But I haven't ridden at night since he showed up, because, contrary to your belief, I'm not stupid—and why the devil am I explaining myself to you, anyway? You aren't my keeper, Mr. Jefferys."

"Thank God for that."

Her eyes narrowed. Keeping her temper around this man was next to impossible. She didn't know why she'd bothered to try.

"For all I know," she said scathingly, "*you* might be the highwayman. His arrival in this area does coincide with your own, after all."

"I was wondering when you'd get around to making that accusation."

"Well?"

"Well, what?" He suddenly laughed. "Are you expecting me to deny it?"

"If you're innocent, then yes, of course I expect you to deny it."

"And if I were guilty, I'd also deny it, so what's the point of my answering either way? Or were you hoping for a confession?"

His amusement was infuriating her. "I was hoping you'd go away," she bit out caustically. "Since you haven't, I will, *on* my horse, and without you along to further annoy me. *I do not need a keeper!*"

"Is that your final word on it?"

"Absolutely."

"Well, here's mine," he said, and his expression was now implacable. "I've decided not to give you a choice. A spoiled brat like you most definitely does need a keeper. So don't leave this stable until I return with Caesar, Megan. If you do, I'll ride after you, but you won't like what will happen when I catch up, I promise you."

Since he'd glanced down at the area of her derriere as he made that promise, Megan was left with a clear understanding of what it was he was promising to do to her. The last time he'd made that particular threat, he'd managed to intimidate her. Not this time. This time her temper didn't cool, it was brushed to full heat. In fact, she was so furious she was rendered speechless, so he managed to walk away without hearing what she thought of his "promise."

He was bluffing, of course. He was a servant. He might not act like one, but he was, and a servant wouldn't dare lay an abusive hand on his employer's daughter. She could have him arrested, for God's sake, if he so much as tried to spank her. The very idea.

Fortified with her bristling indignation, Megan made quick work of securing Sir Ambrose's saddle and led her horse over to the mounting block. Angrily she mounted and gathered the reins, and angrily she walked Sir Ambrose out of the stable. But, cautiously, she went no farther than to the side of the doors, so she couldn't be seen from inside. And a few minutes later when Devlin, on Caesar's back, came tearing out of the stable to give chase, she let out a trill of laughter that brought him up short and nearly unseated him when Caesar objected to such an abrupt halting.

Seeing that was much better than calling Devlin's bluff. Indeed it was, and Megan rode off grinning, despite the fact that Devlin was swearing a blue streak at her back—or because of it.

Chapter 19

As much as Megan would have loved to let Sir Ambrose gallop across the high meadows, she suspected Devlin would make a race of it, and she didn't care to have her beloved Sir Ambrose shown up by the magnificent Caesar. So, as the sun came up to brighten the dawn sky, she kept to a steady trot. At least, she did until Devlin would ride up beside her. Then she would shoot ahead or fall back, thereby making the point silently that she did *not* care for his company.

Getting rid of him altogether was a hopeless endeavor, so she didn't try. Besides, her mood was much improved after the trick she'd played on him. She still wanted to laugh each time she pictured Caesar rearing up and nearly unseating Devlin. Too bad he hadn't. A humbling experience wouldn't hurt that man one little bit.

As for Devlin's bluff, it could wait to be called the next time he made it—*if there was a next time. Though there shouldn't be.* She was fed up with his attempts to intimidate her, after all, and she'd proved that nicely, if subtly, with the little trick she'd pulled on him. But then she sighed to herself. Who was she kidding? The man was too full of himself to take note of subtle messages.

He's also got something on his mind, Megan, or he wouldn't be sticking to your tail now that the sun has come up.

I've already figured that out for myself, thank you.

But you also know what it is he's going to mention. So get rid of him before he does.

And just how am I to do that?

No answer, but she did finally give it a try, riding through the meadow where Tiffany would meet her, hoping against hope that her friend would be there so she'd have an excuse to send Devlin back to the manor. But she had known Tiffany wouldn't be there this early, probably wasn't even out of bed yet, and she was right.

At that point she headed home herself, and urged Sir Ambrose into a gallop after all. If Timmy had arrived by the time she got to the stable, she would simply turn Sir Ambrose over to him and run back to the manor—and Devlin could sit on his I-told-you-sos and choke some.

He had something to say about the new pace she had set, however. He actually shouted something at her, though she couldn't hear what—probably to stop. She didn't, urging her mare to even greater speed instead. But that only set him after her at a tearing pace. And she had known there would be no contest if it came to racing. He overtook her in a matter of moments, and to her incredible surprise, she found herself being yanked off her horse and onto Devlin's lap.

"Didn't you hear me?" he shouted at her as he brought Caesar under control, then stopped altogether.

Megan didn't answer for a moment. Her landing had been bone-jarring as well as breath-stealing, and she was still amazed that he had resorted to such a dangerous method to get her attention. Good God, he could have dropped her! She told him so.

"You could have dropped me, you dolt!"

"Not on your life, brat!" he replied just as heatedly. "Now answer me!"

She finally glanced at him to see how really angry he was and decided to lie. "No."

"No, you won't answer? Or no—"

"No, I didn't hear you."

"You're lying."

"Prove it," she said unwisely.

"By God!" he exploded. "If you aren't the most obstinate, willful, spoiled-rotten, foolish—"

She cut in resentfully, "As long as we're washing dirty laundry, let's wash some of yours. Arrogant, high-handed, insolent, rude, overbearing, insulting—has the wash water turned black yet?"

It took about five seconds of a totally incredulous look on Devlin's face before he burst out laughing. Megan, needless to say, did not appreciate his reaction.

"That was not meant to amuse you—and put me down," she demanded.

"Too late for that. Your horse has gone on without you—or did you want to walk?"

"Anything would be preferable to this proximity to you."

"Did I forget to mention stubborn?" he said, shaking his head.

"You had it covered with obstinate," she returned waspishly. "But I know I forgot *insufferable*. Now put me down, Jefferys."

"I don't think I will."

"What?!"

"Give over, Megan. It's more than a mile back. Besides, you like riding Caesar."

"Not at the moment I don't. Now, if you don't do as I say this second, I'll—I'll—"

He gave her a moment to finish her threat, but she couldn't come up with anything impressive enough to make him obey her, so he prompted, "You'll what? Scream, maybe?" And then he shook his head in what had to be mock regret. "Afraid it won't avail you much out here. No, that's not quite true. It'd probably annoy the hell out of me, and I would either kiss you to shut you up or . . ."

He didn't finish himself, leaving the rest to her imagination. And there was nothing wrong with Megan's imagination. But it wasn't the word "or" that decided her. *That* she was ready to call him on. It was the "kiss you" part that turned her to face forward.

Coward.

So what?

You liked his kissing.

Not that first kiss I didn't.

It was the second one that counted, or have you forgotten how enjoyable it was?

That's beside the point, and you know it. He's a bloody horse breeder.

A bloody handsome horse breeder who could teach you a thing or two if you'd let him. You ought to take advantage of his experience, at least in the matter of kissing. I can't believe you're passing up this opportunity. All you had to do was scream a little.

Let's not forget that he'd prefer to abuse my backside, so I'd as soon not tempt him either way— and where is Tiffany when I need her? You're no help a'tall.

Megan took her annoyance with herself out on Devlin, snapping, "Well, what are you waiting for, Jefferys? Take me home—or did you plan to stay out here and trade insults all morning?"

Having said it, she was a bit embarrassed at how shrewish she sounded. But more to the point, she should have recalled that Devlin had never let her get away with such behavior without retaliating in kind. He did that now.

"Someone ought to kiss your pants off, brat," he said outrageously as he started Caesar off at a mere walk. "Didn't your duke?"

His sneering tone was infuriating, but the subject made her groan inwardly. And she almost defended St. James, because it had become automatic for her to do so. But she caught herself in time, for she wasn't about to defend that wretched bounder anymore.

She had known this was coming. The only thing that amazed her was that Devlin hadn't mentioned the Duke of Wrothston sooner.

She wondered if she could drop the subject with a simple "No, he didn't." She tried it. She should have known better.

"Could it be you played the haughty little brat with him as you do with me?"

Was that how Devlin really saw her? She *had* been rather curt to Ambrose St. James to begin with. What if he had merely been paying her back for that, as Devlin so frequently did? And what difference did it make? Pay-back or normal behavior on the duke's part, either way she had been gravely insulted, which had ended her aspirations to be a duchess most effectively.

To Devlin, she said, "What happened is none of your business."

"Isn't it? After you shoved your duke down

my throat? You didn't even meet him, did you?"

"I met him," she bit out.

"Then he wasn't interested, was he? It's no wonder, with that god-awful hair of yours."

Megan stiffened. "There's nothing wrong with my hair, Devlin Jefferys!"

" 'Course there is. It's red."

"I haven't noticed that preventing *you* from desiring me," she retorted.

"I'm only an ignorant horse breeder, remember, so I don't count. But did you really think a duke, who is constantly in the public eye, would marry a woman with the most unfashionable hair in creation? His friends would never let him live it down, brat."

She said nothing to that. She said nothing more at all. And her stiff back didn't unbend even a little.

After nearly five minutes of silence, Devlin finally asked hesitantly, "Have I hurt your feelings?"

"Would it matter if you did?"

"It might." She merely snorted at that, so he added, "I wouldn't care to make you cry, Megan."

"You could have fooled me."

"Nonsense. You were good and mad. What happened to change that? Good God, you aren't really that sensitive about your bloody hair, are you? Or did your duke remark upon it, too? Is that why you're so touchy on—"

"I'm not touchy, and he didn't remark upon my hair. Only *you* are ill-mannered enough to do that."

"Definitely touchy, and also incorrect. My manners are impeccable."

"Your manners are atrocious."

"I'm keeping my hands off you, aren't I?" he replied in the most reasonable tone.

"Does that imply you wouldn't keep your hands to yourself if you were ill-mannered?"

"Exactly."

"Then let me point out all the times you haven't been so impeccable."

"Don't," he warned her, "or this might be one of those times. Now about your duke—"

"Good God, you're not going to quit until you hear it, are you? All right, Devlin, Ambrose St. James was exactly what you said he was, and I hope I never see him again. Are you happy now?"

"Never see him again?" he almost sputtered in his surprise. "Just because he was a bit of a bounder? What does that matter to you? It was the title you were after, not the man. And let's not forget his stable. You're bloody well in love with his stable."

Megan turned around again to stare at him incredulously. His tone had been chock-full with resentment, too, which made no sense.

"The title would have been nice," she said dispassionately. "But it wasn't as important as you're suggesting, not by any means. I intend to be in love with the man I marry, or at least extremely fond of him, and assured that love will grow from that."

"That isn't the impression you gave," he replied in a tone that was definitely accusatory.

She shrugged unconcernedly. "Whatever impressions I give you, Jefferys, are usually provoked. At any rate, St. James won't do. I've never met anyone as insulting as he was—aside from you."

His disgruntled expression prompted a grin, so Megan quickly turned back around so he wouldn't see it. Damned man should have left well enough alone. She hoped he was choking on his I-told-you-sos.

"So you don't think you could love him?" he had the audacity to ask next.

Why wouldn't he leave the subject go? "Absolutely not," she almost growled.

"Then who have you set your cap for now?"

"No one."

After a few silent moments he declared, "Bloody hell, you're upset about it, aren't you?"

Megan's eyes widened and she swung around again. "What, may I ask, has brought you to that conclusion?"

"You had your hopes set on St. James. You even saw yourself married to him by year's end. You can't be pleased that you're not getting what you wanted."

"Because I'm a spoiled brat?"

"Exactly."

"Why don't you go to hell, Devlin, and stay out of my business on the way?"

"And why don't you admit that you were disappointed?" he shot back.

"So you can gloat over it?"

"I wouldn't do that."

"Like hell you wouldn't. What the devil do you think you've *been* doing? And I wasn't disappointed. I might have been, but I was too furious to notice it."

"I'm glad to hear it."

"Why?" she asked warily.

He shrugged. "Can't abide melancholy females. They're always bursting into tears for no apparent reason. So you didn't enjoy your ball a'tall?"

"On the contrary, I had a wonderful time— aside from my brief encounter with St. James. I even received two new proposals of marriage."

"How many does that make now, or have you lost count?" he said derisively.

"Quite a few, though I would have to think about it to come up with an exact figure, since I *haven't* been counting. But it would seem that some men must find my hair attractive, wouldn't it?"

"It's your little body they find attractive, brat, not your hair."

"Are you going to be crude again?"

"Why not? It goes well with your bragging."

"So I'm a braggart now, too, when all I did

was answer your bloody question?"

"Why hasn't your father done something about that foul mouth of yours?"

"Because he's not a hypocrite like you are. And if you say another word to me, I think I *will* scream."

He must have taken her at her word, for he was silent after that, and his increasing Caesar's speed managed to bring them into the stable just a few minutes later. Sir Ambrose had returned on her own, but then Megan hadn't doubted she would. The mare knew every inch of the surrounding neighborhood, but especially the way home.

Megan, not waiting for Devlin to help her dismount, jumped to the ground with only a little difficulty. Timmy had seen to Sir Ambrose's unsaddling, which was fortunate, for all she wanted to do was get to her room to lick her wounds. Trading insults with Devlin was a hopeless endeavor. He went for blood every time, and she didn't have much more to lose.

But she couldn't resist a parting shot. "The next time you think to protect me from thieves, don't. I'd rather meet up with a highwayman than put up with your brand of abuse."

"And here I thought you adored me," Devlin replied sarcastically.

"As much as I adore snakes," she retorted and headed for the door. But her curiosity wouldn't let her leave without knowing what had caused this latest verbal skirmish. She stopped to demand, "What the devil did you drag me off my horse for back there?"

Devlin shrugged before dismounting and sending Caesar toward the back of the stable. "You set off like a house on fire. I thought your animal had been spooked."

"So you were *saving* me?"

"Something like that."

He looked so embarrassed over that admission, she couldn't help laughing. "I'll believe that like I will it's raining outside."

A crack of thunder chose that devil-damned moment to announce a storm coming in from the east. So it was that Megan's laughter was short-lived, while Devlin's followed her out the door.

Chapter 20

Devlin spent the remainder of the day ruining his section of the stable extension, much to his master carpenter's disgust, and Mortimer's undisguised amusement. But he couldn't concentrate on the correspondence that Mr. Pike had sent, and that left him little else to do with his time except interfere in the enlargement he had instigated. But he'd started it to keep himself busy, he reminded himself, so it didn't particularly matter if he was mucking up his own contribution to the project, as long as the project was doing as originally intended, which it was.

At least in part it was. He still couldn't turn off his thoughts. And as he'd found with the hay-pitching fiasco, monotonous activities let his mind drift down its own paths, and nearly all paths today led to Megan.

He was feeling a tad guilty where she was concerned. Well, perhaps a whole lot guilty.

So maybe she wasn't as greedy and heartless as he'd first thought. So maybe he ought to apologize to her for the dirty trick he'd played on her at the Leightons' ball. So maybe he ought to tell her who he really was. And have her hate him even more? There was no reason for her to know. He'd be gone from here soon enough. So would she, for that matter, to her London Season. Bloody hell, what was it about *that* that irritated the hell out of him?

For that matter, what was it about the girl herself that brought out such defenses in him? Was he unwittingly doing what she accused him of, but in the reverse, deliberately causing animosity to keep himself from falling under the spell of her unusual beauty?

How absurd. He was the Duke of Wrothston. He'd like to think he had a little more control over his actions than that. So he desired her. So what? He had only to recall all of her irritating qualities to know that he would not care to spend any more time with her than it would take to make love, for he had no doubt a'tall that once passion was expended, she'd drive him crazy—just as she was doing now.

Still, the attraction was powerful and undeniable, so much so that he hadn't given her a chance to use that devastating smile of hers on him at the Leightons' ball. Good God, but she had been exquisite that night in her green ball gown, with her matching domino adding a touch of mystery. He had been hard pressed to concentrate on what he was there to do, when all he'd wanted to do was take her in his arms and kiss her. Damn Freddy for showing up and preventing him from getting at least one kiss before Megan either exploded in her righteous fury or slapped him.

Just his luck that Freddy *would* have to be her next dance partner that night. Had they danced after he hastily left, or had she been too angry just then to dance with anyone? Freddy, of course, knew how to charm a lady out of a pique. And he had been known to set his scruples aside and seduce an innocent if she was pretty enough. Bloody hypocrite, to get so killing mad just because his lying little sister claimed she was carrying Devlin's child.

He recalled that god-awful day with crystal clarity. He had done no more than he usually did, stopping by Freddy's town house to collect him on the way to their club for dinner. It was typical of Freddy never to be ready on time, so Devlin had drifted into the study to wait. But in had come Sabrina Richardson, all of eighteen now and determined to try out her charms on him, or so he'd thought when she started flirting outrageously.

He had actually been amused. Freddy had been his closest friend for more than ten years, so he'd known Freddy's little sister since she'd been a child in pigtails. She and her many cohorts had been terrible pranksters in those days who had played one-too-many so-called jokes on Devlin for her to have endeared herself to him. Quite the opposite; he could barely tolerate the chit.

But he was a fair man. She was grown now, a young lady, a beautiful young lady at that. He gave her the benefit of the doubt in assuming she had to have outgrown the bad habits of her youth that had made him take pains to avoid her. In fact, he hadn't seen her for the several years that she had attended finishing school.

She was much changed since then, in appearance as well as in manner, demure instead of boisterously loud, flirtatious instead of rudely sticking her tongue out at him every chance she got. Her giggling was still the same, however. There wasn't much hope on improving giggling once a girl started making that irritating sound.

But that day she'd only giggled once, so he hadn't been irritated too much. He'd been more interested in wondering what she was about with her flirting.

Actually, when Sabrina was fourteen, she'd told him she was going to marry him. He'd snorted, not taking her declaration at all seriously, and told her he'd already be married by the time she was ready to be. And he should have been, would have been, if he hadn't caught his fiancée making love with her coachman, in her coach no less, but that was another story.

He didn't think Sabrina even remembered that childish declaration. But that day in Freddy's study, she slowly worked her way closer to him until, unexpectedly, she threw her arms around his neck and kissed him. It was a bloody attack, was what it was, but after he thought about it later, he realized that the whole thing must have been planned, that she'd only waited until she heard Freddy approaching down the hall to make her move.

Freddy got an eyeful of the kissing part when he entered the room. Sabrina, to give her her due, appeared embarrassed to be "caught"— for all of five seconds. Then she recalled her scheme and burst into tears.

Freddy, as much a sucker for tears as Devlin was, tried to reassure her that she was making a big to-do over nothing. What was a little kiss? He was only a little shocked, and that because of *whom* she'd been kissing.

At which point she clarified the reason for her tears, wailing, "He won't marry me!"

To give Freddy *his* due, his reaction to that was the same as Devlin's. "Well, why should he?" he asked reasonably, if quite dryly. "Young misses like you are not exactly to his taste."

"That's what you think!" she countered. "I was his type enough for him to get me pregnant, but now I'm not his *type* to marry? Is that what you're telling me?"

"Pregnant?" was about all Freddy could get out at that point.

Devlin, on the other hand, was more vocal. "The devil I did. Is this the level your pranks have risen to, Sabrina? Because this joke is in very bad taste."

She actually looked him right in the eye to reply, "How can you say it's a joke? You know it's not. You seduced me. You let me think you would marry me. And now you won't. Freddy, do something!"

Freddy did. He leapt across the space separating them and plowed his fist into Devlin's jaw. While Devlin was on the floor trying to recover from that, Freddy demanded furiously, "How could you? With my own sister!"

"I've never laid a hand on the girl."

"You were just kissing her!"

"She was doing the kissing, you ass, and obviously for your benefit. I don't even like the girl."

"You liked her well enough to seduce her. Well, now you can bloody well marry her!"

"The devil I will!"

"The devil you won't, or you'll hear from my seconds! I ought to call you out anyway, just on principle, family honor and all that."

"Oh, good God," Devlin said in exasperation. "The girl's lying. If she's pregnant at all, and I doubt even that, it's not mine."

"Is that your final word on it?"

At which point Devlin got angry enough to say, "Yes, by God, it is."

"Then expect my seconds. You leave me no alternative but to kill you."

Devlin would have laughed then, except Freddy was much too angry to appreciate the irony of his statement: they both knew he was a lousy shot, while Devlin was not. Devlin left instead, confident that Freddy would calm down, see the absurdity of Sabrina's accusation, and come around to apologize.

But Freddy didn't cool off, not one little bit. Sabrina had no doubt given him more details to reinforce her tale, and, hot-tempered as he was, he did in fact send his seconds over the very next day. Devlin, not about to agree to meet his best friend on the dueling field, was not "at home" to receive them, and hied himself off to Sherring Cross to give Freddy more time to come to his senses. But the bloody seconds followed him even there, and when he again wouldn't receive them, they managed to get in to see his grandmother instead, forcing Devlin to explain the whole ridiculous affair to her.

The Dowager Duchess of Wrothston didn't find it quite so ridiculous. "Well, you can't shoot the boy," she said in her no-nonsense way. "I'm rather fond of him myself."

"I *know* that, Duchy. But am I supposed to let it make the rounds that I'm a bloody coward who won't meet him? It will, you know, if those damned seconds of his find out that I'm actually here."

"So you won't be here. If you'll recall, I suggested you take some time off after you jilted Marianne, but you insisted you weren't broken up by the incident and saw no need to abandon your work just because she had abandoned faith with you."

"I still maintain—"

"Beside the point, dear boy," she cut in with a dismissive wave of her hand. "I happen to know she's letting it go the rounds that *she's* the injured party."

"I suppose she feels that a little thing like infidelity wasn't grounds to cancel the wedding."

"Don't care what she feels, she hasn't exactly been silent on the subject. And you haven't exactly been correcting the matter with the truth."

"And ruin her good name?"

"She did that herself, which is neither here nor there. The point is, she will probably stop defaming *your* good name if you aren't around to hear about it. And now with our dear Freddy hankering to put holes in your body, you no longer have an excuse to ignore my advice. The House of Lords can get along without you for a while. You, on the other hand, can't get along with your head blown off. So you're going to disappear, my boy. I insist upon it."

"I will *not* leave the country, Duchy, not for any reason. I'm not about to put up with seasickness again that feels like dying, just to avoid dying at Freddy's hand. I'll bloody well shoot him before I—"

"No, you won't, and no one suggested you leave the country. All you need is a place where no one knows you, a change in identity, and an occupation that won't draw notice to you. Give me an hour or so to think about it."

But that evening over dinner, when Duchy had announced the destination she felt would serve perfectly for him, Devlin had laughed his head off. "I thought I was to disappear, not bury myself."

"It won't hurt you to rusticate for a time. Do you good, actually, since you're due for a rest."

"A matter of opinion, that."

"So we're going by mine, not yours," she replied. "And it will only be for a few months. By then Marianne will have—hopefully—got over her grudge against you, and Freddy will have married off his sister—or found out that she was lying, not just about you, but also about carrying a child, which would be my guess."

"But a *stableboy*, Duchy?"

"When's the last time you actually noticed one?" she countered. "They're almost invisible, they're so taken for granted."

Devlin had gone along with everything but the occupation. Mucking out stables was just too much for his dignity to stomach for the sake of friendship. But he did allow that he wouldn't mind working with horses, as long as it was in a position of some authority.

Never could he have imagined, however, that his sojourn in the country would lead to such frustration and aggravation that had nothing to do with his being there. But then he never could have imagined a girl quite like Megan, either.

Chapter 21

Devlin had put Megan in the most horrid mood for the rest of the day. She hadn't enjoyed her morning ride, which she had so been looking forward to. She hadn't given back as good as she got in their verbal battle. She hadn't even been kissed. No doubt about it, that round went to Devlin hands down.

So you did want him to kiss you?

What do you think?

Then why'd you put up such a fuss about it?

If he's going to do it, I don't want to provoke him into doing it.

What do you think the first time was all about?

That was different. I didn't know I was provoking him then. But if I had screamed this morning, after he'd already told me what would happen, that would've been asking for it, wouldn't it? And

I certainly don't want him to know *I want him to kiss me.*

I don't see why not. That would be the quickest way to have it happen.

When the man probably stays up late at night thinking of new ways to insult me? I can just imagine what he'd do with the knowledge that I might want his kisses.

Not "might." You said you did.

Well, I'm starting to rethink the matter.

As usual lately, Megan's discussions with her conscience were more annoying than helpful. Ever since her curiosity had been aroused by Devlin and his sexual innuendos, her common sense started losing the battle. Now, her supposed-to-be cautious inner voice was being anything but cautious, and her curiosity was thrilled that she was going to let it have its way—at least in part.

She did want to experience again the pleasant feeling that had occurred while kissing Devlin, that and a whole lot more. The "more" was wrapped in vagueness, unknown, yet she was nothing if not daring—some of the time. Of course, common sense had not lost the battle completely. She knew where the kind of kissing she was contemplating could lead to. To lovemaking and the ruination of a girl. It was exasperating to know the beginning and the end of a thing, but nothing at all about the middle, and not that much, to tell the truth, about the end either. Still, she would have to place limits on what she was willing to learn from Devlin. Actually, she would have to stop him before she learned *too* much.

I think they have a name for that, and it's not a very nice name.

If they do, I don't know what it is.

You do; you're just ashamed to admit it.

Don't start changing your tune at this late date.

I'm not, but you're not exactly taking Devlin's feelings into account. You ought to be willing to explore every avenue that he has a mind to lead you down. Instead you're already deciding at what point to call a halt to it.

That's because I'm waiting until I'm married to be that adventurous, and that's final.

Megan was in that same divided state of mind when she went out to the stable that night. One part of her was still having second thoughts about the wisdom of having Devlin teach her more about kissing—and other things—while the other part was looking forward to it with much too much eagerness. The first part had dragged her feet, waiting until it was late enough that Devlin just might have locked the stable by now and gone to bed, thereby putting an end to her plan—at least for today. The other part was rushing now, hoping she wasn't too late. Neither part expected to see Devlin ride out of the stable on Caesar as soon as she got there.

Well, what the devil, she thought, staring after him because he hadn't stopped, apparently preoccupied enough not to have even noticed her. After the battle she'd had with her conscience just to get her there, it was utterly deflating for Megan to see her quarry disappear into the night. And where could he be going this late, anyway?

A number of answers came immediately to mind. He had an assignation with another woman. Megan had finally annoyed him enough so that he was sneaking off to find employment elsewhere. He was the highwayman on his way to rob more unsuspecting late-night travelers.

Megan pounced on the third answer simply because the first two didn't suit her a'tall. And it made sense. There really hadn't been any robberies until he'd arrived in the area. The hour was ideal right now for such illicit purposes. And for once he wasn't wearing one of those finely made white shirts that he favored and could ill afford—except through illicit means, obviously. And that white shirt could easily be seen at night. His present dark attire could not.

It took her only a few seconds to decide to go after him, a few more to realize that if she was going to catch up with him, she wouldn't have time to saddle Sir Ambrose. The thought of riding bareback was daunting and almost kept her there to confront Devlin when he returned instead. Of course, when he returned, there might not be any evidence of his criminal activities to confront him with, since he could and most likely would hide it elsewhere before returning. And that decided

her, since she would very much like to have
something like this to hold over that man's
head. The thought of it was too tempting by
half. She could demand anything of him, put
him in his place, make him squirm, make him
end his insults.

She ran to get Sir Ambrose without further
delay, grabbing only the tack necessary to
control the mare, since riding bareback was
one thing, but not being able to control a
Thoroughbred like Sir Ambrose was another.
The slight delay was costly, though. When she
reached the road, there was no sign of Devlin
anywhere, in any direction.

Megan wasn't about to give up at that point
just because there was barely any moonlight
and the countryside stretched out dark and
ominous around her. She headed in the direction that the robberies had occurred, near the
Thackeray estate. In fact, now that she thought
of it, the only people who had been robbed were
guests of the Thackerays, and each occurrence
had been when they were leaving one of Lady
Ophelia's parties.

She almost laughed, imagining what vexa-
tion the highwayman must be causing old
hatchet-face. She did smile. Lady O might
even be getting a few no-shows at her parties
because of it, at least until the thief was caught.
Too bad Megan hadn't thought of it herself.

Her instinct for direction paid off a few minutes later as she caught sight of a movement,

just a shadow, disappearing over the next rise in the road. She didn't speed up to catch up with it, however. Knowing the countryside as well as she did, she turned off the road and headed inland, circling around until she finally came upon the small clump of woods that the road passed through just before the Thackeray estate.

A highwayman couldn't ask for a more perfect setting to work in, she supposed. There would be ample concealment for him and his horse, numerous trails in the woods for a getaway that a coach couldn't follow—if the victims even thought to give chase.

Those many trails let Megan come in from the back door, as it were, and stay far enough back from the road so that she couldn't be seen by Devlin or his victims, but she could hear any carriages approaching. Not that she thought she might be lucky enough to have a robbery occur right there in front of her, even though she had chosen to wait in a spot more or less centered in the woods. She still fully expected that she would have to follow the victim for a ways before anything exciting happened, if it happened at all.

This was a weeknight, and Lady O threw her big parties on the weekends, unless she had guests staying over indefinitely. Then every night could be a big "something or other." She was the queen of entertaining, after all. For that matter, she still entertained during the week whether she had houseguests or not, just much smaller gatherings. But a highwayman needed only one or two victims for a profitable night's work.

She settled in to wait, tethering Sir Ambrose and moving a little closer to the road. With the nearly impenetrable darkness of the woods that she had traversed, what she could see of the road seemed much brighter now.

Megan didn't get bored when an hour or so had passed and still no one had come along. She was enjoying herself too much, anticipating catching Devlin and having something to hold over his handsome head.

She finally heard a noise and moved even closer to the road until she could just make out the light flickering from a carriage lantern. The driver of the carriage wasn't very motivated, or perhaps he had imbibed some while his master was being entertained. The vehicle took forever to reach Megan, giving her enough time to decide that she could follow it more easily and more quietly on foot and still keep to the trees.

She did just that, counting her steps so she would know where she had left her horse. But sooner than she expected, the end of the woods was sighted, and for the second time that evening, she was utterly deflated. The carriage would be on the safer open road in seconds. Bloody hell. Either Devlin was letting this one go, or . . .

"Stand and deliver!"

Megan's heart jumped into her throat. He

came out of the woods on her side of the road to block the carriage, not ten feet from her. Another few seconds and she might have walked right into him. And if she wasn't mistaken, he was brandishing a pistol to reinforce the order he'd shouted.

The carriage did stand still. The occupants were slower to deliver. Megan was much slower in getting her heart back under control after the fright she'd taken at the sound of that high-pitched voice. High-pitched?

That wretched man, he was disguising his voice. Well, she needed better proof than the sound of his voice, anyway. Actually, she was going to have to confront him the minute he finished. Only how? She wasn't about to unmask him in front of his victims. That wouldn't give her anything to hold over him. It would merely get him arrested, which, actually, was the last thing she wanted to see happen, and that was a surprising thought.

Of course, he still had things to teach her, which he couldn't do if he was carted off to gaol. But was that the only reason she didn't want him arrested? This was no time to probe her motives, however, especially when she hadn't figured out how she was going to stop him from riding off on Caesar as soon as he was through. She'd just have to get closer and be prepared.

Megan did just that, which enabled her to hear more clearly what was going on, too, though that wasn't much. Some low grumbling from the victims, and a nasty chuckle from Devlin, who really seemed to be enjoying the power he was wielding.

But after a few moments more he became impatient. "Toss it down and be quick about it; then you can be on your way. And you'll be quick about that, too, or I might decide I need some practice with this pistol."

"You won't get away with this."

" 'Course I will, you dolt, or were *you* planning to stop me?"

The answer to that was negative. Megan was getting really annoyed with Devlin for his taunting. It was bad enough he was robbing the poor fellow; he didn't have to make sport of him, too.

She was going to tell him that just as soon as they were alone. And since he'd ordered his bounty tossed out on the ground, and would have to dismount to get it, she didn't have to worry about him immediately riding off. She would have ample time to confront him when the carriage left, and it did that now.

They both waited until the carriage was a good distance away to make their moves. But the moment Devlin dismounted, Megan took a step forward—but so did someone else from the other side of the road.

She dropped back, her heart pounding fearfully again. Two of them? Was Devlin involving that nice Mr. Browne in his crimes? But the newcomer was too tall to be Mortimer Browne.

And when Devlin noticed him, he was as surprised as Megan.

"Good God, you gave me a fright."

"I'll do more than that, Sanderson, if you don't explain yourself to my satisfaction."

Megan's eyes popped wide open in surprise. *That* had been Devlin's voice, no doubt about it. What the devil? And now she looked more closely at the horse to find that it wasn't Caesar. Did it have to be so dark that she hadn't noticed that little detail sooner? Well, if she had, she wouldn't have stuck around long enough to learn that Devlin *did* know the highwayman, even if he wasn't the culprit himself.

That got proved by Sanderson's reply. "Devlin, is that you? Well, good God, man, what are *you* doing here?"

"I am *not* here," Devlin replied with some very definite annoyance. "I have never been here. You have not seen me here. Is that clear to you?"

"Oh, quite, quite," Sanderson quickly agreed, taking off the kerchief he'd had wrapped over his lower face and stuffing it in a pocket. "Hope you haven't seen me either."

"You, dear boy, aren't that lucky. Now explain yourself, if you can."

The highwayman shrugged, trying to make light of it. "I'm just having a bit of sport, Your—"

"Highway robbery is not sport, you ass. Try again."

"Well, actually, I've had a devilish run of bad luck. Truth is, I needed the blunt."

"It didn't occur to you to ask your father? The earl isn't known to be tight-fisted."

" 'Course it did, but he's a bloody long way from here, and I'm stuck here courting one of the Earl of Wedgwood's daughters. Father sent me here himself. Thinks it's time I settled down. So what was I to do? I sent a letter off to him, but he ain't replied yet. I'm staying with the Thackerays, and my damned hostess thinks she's got to entertain me every bloody day with 'London amusements,' and you know what that means. I lost what little money I came with the first weekend. And I can't bloody well tell Lady Ophelia I'm down and out when I'm here to win one of her daughters."

"You could have suggested other 'amusements' besides gambling, was what you could have done. I would advise you to do that very thing, because your stint as a highwayman comes to an end tonight."

"But I was actually having fun at it."

"You're not thinking of arguing with me, are you, dear boy?"

There was such underlying menace in that question, Megan couldn't blame Sanderson for quickly assuring Devlin, "No, no, I wouldn't think of it."

"You will also return everything you've stolen from these good people."

"But I *can't* do that."

"You can and will."

"But I don't have it all, you see. The trinkets, yes, but there was another game of hazard last night, and, well, my luck hasn't improved yet."

"How much?"

"Eighty pounds."

Devlin made a sound of disgust as he reached into his pocket and came up with a wad of bills that he thrust at Sanderson. The young man took it in good grace, while Megan was flabbergasted that a horse breeder would have that kind of money to just give away.

"You will take that and the rest to the magistrate's tonight. Drop it off with a note saying that you've seen the error of your ways. Do you foresee a problem with that?"

"No, no, tonight it will be."

"Good, because if I don't hear through the gossip mill that everything was returned, and I mean everything, I'll be paying your father a visit. I wouldn't care to do that, he wouldn't care to hear what I have to say, and you wouldn't care for the outcome. I trust we understand each other?"

"Indeed we do. Sorry to put you to the trouble. Won't do it again, I swear . . . I . . ."

His words trailed off because Devlin had slipped back into the woods as quietly as he'd appeared. Megan didn't wait around any longer either, making her way back to where she'd left Sir Ambrose. But she was frowning all the way. Why would an earl's son be so intimidated by a horse breeder?

Chapter 22

The exchange Megan had witnessed between Devlin and the young lord-turned-temporary-highwayman bothered her all the way home. Certainly, she had to allow that there were any number of ways that Lord Sanderson could know Devlin, the most obvious being from the Sherring Cross stables, where Devlin had come from. But just because Devlin had worked for the Duke of Wrothston didn't account for the deference paid him by an earl's son. Sanderson should have put Devlin in his place and done the threatening, not the other way around.

Of course, threatening to go to the boy's father had made an impression, but that hadn't come until later. She supposed, though, that Sanderson might think that Devlin still worked at Sherring Cross and might go to the duke with his tale. He *had* been surprised to see Devlin here in Devonshire, after all. Then, too, she had to allow that Devlin, horse breeder or not, had a presence about him that was definitely formidable and downright intimidating when he chose to portray it. She had been susceptible to it herself.

Regardless, there was still something about that exchange that bothered Megan, and it wasn't until she was nearly home that it came to her. Sanderson's deference had been there from the first, as had been Devlin's command of the situation—as if their circumstances were reversed, with Devlin being the lord and Sanderson the servant. Which made no sense. Working for a duke, no matter for how long, did not give a man prestige above his station, some arrogance maybe, but a servant still ought to know his place, especially next to a peer of the realm.

You're being snobbish again.

But I'm right.

What you are is irritated as hell because he didn't turn out to be the highwayman.

That was true enough. She really had been looking forward to holding that over him. Now, instead, she was probably in for another lecture about riding out at ungodly hours. Dratted man, why couldn't he act like normal servants and not question his betters?

You're doing it again.

I'm merely getting into the proper frame of mind to face a tyrant.

He's not a tyrant, and hasn't it occurred to you that lectures only come from concerned people, those concerned with your welfare and well-being?

Ha!

In either case, you'd better come up with a good excuse for where you've been, or will the truth do?

You know it won't. But maybe he's not back yet and I can sneak Sir Ambrose into her stall and get out of there before I'm noticed.

I wouldn't count on it.

She didn't, and he was—back, that is—and standing just inside the stable doors with his hands on his hips and one of the most stern expressions she'd ever seen on a man. Megan opted to brazen her way through what was coming.

"So you're back?" she said before he could. "I was going to ask you to accompany me tonight on my errand, but you couldn't be found."

"Accompany you where?"

"One of my father's tenants is doing poorly. I was supposed to visit the family this afternoon to see if they needed anything, only I was otherwise occupied and forgot—but better late than—"

"No sense, no bloody sense a'tall," he said as he hauled her off Sir Ambrose. "And without a saddle!" he added as he noticed the lack thereof. His eyes came back to her. "You actually rode this animal without a saddle?"

Megan groaned inwardly, having completely forgotten about that. But brazenness was working. At least he no longer looked so stern, so she continued in that line.

"You make it sound as if I've never done so before," she retorted. "It's not difficult, I assure you. But I don't know what you're making such a fuss about. The only reason I was going to have you escort me was to avoid this very thing, this bad habit you have of involving yourself in my affairs, but the fact is that I certainly didn't *need* your escort, since I didn't even leave our property. But as long as this seems to be the hour for interrogations, where did *you* go?"

"Out to catch a thief."

She hadn't expected him to admit it. "Did you have any luck?"

"No," he lied.

She knew he lied, but to say so would admit she had followed him. "Too bad. Once he is caught, maybe you'll stop interfering with what I do and when I do it."

"When you do it? I doubt it. Someone has to teach you some sense, and come to think of it, there's no time like the present."

He caught her hand and started dragging her to the mounting block. Megan's mouth dropped open, her eyes widened incredulously, and she was a little bit in shock, knowing exactly what the man intended doing.

"Wait a minute. Devlin, you can't really . . . I'll have you arrested. I'll have you—"

She landed hard across his knees the moment he sat down on the mounting block. She was about to scream her head off when he said, "Making a lot of noise won't stop me, brat. It'll just draw you an audience to watch."

That was perfectly true and out of the question. She clamped her lips shut. She wouldn't make a sound now if it killed her. But, by God, the man was going to regret this. If it was the last thing she did, she'd get even, somehow, and then . . .

The first smack was a revelation. It made a lot of noise when his hand connected with her bottom, though it didn't actually hurt. She'd forgotten that she'd worn one of her thickest riding skirts. Well, the joke was going to be on Devlin, but she'd never tell. Of course, that was only the first whack. By the time he finished, and that was quite a while later, repetition had made silk out of thick wool, and Megan didn't feel like laughing. She was furious that he could get away with doing that to her.

When he set her on her feet, she didn't give it prior thought, she simply swung at him with a closed fist—and missed. If that wasn't enough to make her explode, she noticed his lips curling the slightest bit. Clearly the man found her impotent rage amusing.

"You are the most horrible bastard I've ever met!" she all but screeched.

"And how many have you met?"

His dispassionate reply gave her pause, long enough to inquire with genuine curiosity, "Is there no insult that you won't shrug off?"

"Why should I be insulted?" he asked reasonably. "You're all hot air and brambles, brat—except when you're in my arms. Then you're just hot."

She couldn't believe he'd said that. "You are dismissed! Fired! Exterminated!"

He cocked a brow at the last one. "Is that wishful thinking?"

"You know what I meant."

"Indeed. Shall you be the one to tell your father, or shall I?"

She thought that over for a moment and knew the wretched man had won—again. She wasn't about to tell her father or anyone else about this humiliating experience.

"Why can't you just get out of my life?" she asked begrudgingly.

"What? Retreat under fire? Desert the war? Wouldn't think of it, dear girl."

That bit of absurdity had her looking around for something to throw at him. But her obvious intention brought him to his feet and his hands to her shoulders.

"I gave you fair warning this morning not to take such stupid risks with yourself," he told her, no longer amused. "That spanking was to reinforce the warning, but perhaps you also need to be shown what happens to reckless females who go traipsing about at indecent hours."

His intent was just as clear and had her drawing back as far as she could, appalled that he could think of kissing *now*. But little good that did her with his hands already gripping her. She was pulled forward, his head bent, and his mouth descended on her uncooperative lips before she could get a word out to stop him.

As soon as she realized that he was playing right into her hands because he thought he was teaching her a lesson but unbeknownst to him it was a lesson she wanted, Megan relaxed her stiffness and immediately experienced a swirl of giddy pleasure. He held her closer and the pleasure increased, as did her pulse, her breathing, and her sense of wonder. So nice, this contact with his body. Who would have thought? But this lesson wasn't over. She decided she'd like it never to end.

She thought he was finished when he stopped the kissing, but it was only to move his lips along her cheek to her ear. And there was another new sensation to savor, and goose bumps spreading down her back.

"Teach me," she said on a gasp as his lips started down her neck.

"What?"

"How to kiss."

Devlin groaned, dropping his head to her shoulder. "I don't think I want you to know how."

Well, that was bloody unfair of him, she thought indignantly. "Why not?"

"I'm having enough trouble as it is, controlling what you make me feel."

"Then let me go."

His head came up, his eyes fixing on hers with an intensity that made her shiver. "Not yet. This was a lesson in what can happen to girls who ride out alone at night, remember? I'm going to finish it if it kills me."

"I got the point."

"Not yet you haven't." And his hand came up to cup her breast.

Megan sucked in her breath, never imagining that such a simple touch could evoke such a wealth of feeling. Of course, she knew he shouldn't touch her there, that this was part of his lesson. But she also guessed that this was some of the "more" that she'd wanted to know about.

He probably thought he was shocking her, or hoped he was, and she wouldn't disabuse him of that notion or he might stop altogether. So she closed her eyes just in case he could see there what she was really feeling. But she wasn't shocked, she was amazed that each movement of his gently kneading palm was sending sensations to other areas besides her breasts, which were already tingling beneath his caress.

She was starting to get urges that she didn't understand. She wanted his mouth back on hers. She wanted to touch him as he was her. She wanted him doing this because he wanted to, not because of a damn lesson he felt she deserved.

And then his mouth was back, but with much more passion than before, and his hands gripped her hips to pull them in to his groin. She whimpered, half in startlement at the heat that shot into her own loins, and half in discomfort from the tight grip he had on her. But the sound took his hands away from her completely, and it took a moment for her to realize that she'd been released, lesson over.

"Megan, I'm going to burn to a cinder in a moment," he rasped out, and the man actually looked like he was in pain. "Get the hell out of here while you still can."

She didn't want to. She wanted his arms back around her, his lips—but prudence and that "while you still can" let her common sense take over for the moment. Only she gave him one last look that was so full of yearning, it made him groan and reach for her again. Megan, startled out of her bemusement, ran like hell.

Chapter 23

Not until the next day, and only after careful examination, did Megan admit to herself that she might have been a little reckless last night and deserving of a scolding—not a spanking, but a scolding. She had acted impulsively to follow Devlin and to make assumptions about where he was going. The fact was, if Devlin hadn't been after the thief himself, he wouldn't have shown himself right before she was about to, wouldn't even have been there. And she would have confronted a stranger who wouldn't have been the least bit intimidated by her as he was by Devlin. She would also have been quite alone with him, on a dark road, with darker woods on either side of them.

It was entirely possible that exactly what Devlin was predicting could happen *could* have happened. Just because the thief was an earl's son and supposedly a gentleman wouldn't have saved her. A lord acting as a highwayman left his principles at home, didn't he? Confessing who she was probably wouldn't have done any good either. After all, she was out late at night, and without an escort. Why should she be believed?

It was galling to admit that Devlin was right. She had behaved carelessly, recklessly, without a thought to the danger and risk she was taking. Just the idea of a stranger doing to her what Devlin had done made her skin crawl. Aside from that, good God, she could have been seriously hurt.

Maybe you ought to tell him you were wrong and won't do it again.

And feed his colossal arrogance? Besides, Devlin still had no right to abuse my backside. He should have brought my behavior to my father's attention, not seen to it himself. I wouldn't have liked it, but that would have been the proper thing to do.

So tell him that.

I think I will.

Devlin hadn't made an appearance this morning when she'd gone for her ride—at a perfectly decent hour. She'd even lingered over Sir Ambrose's grooming after she returned, but he still hadn't shown himself. Mortimer had, before she'd left the stable, and when asked, he'd informed her that Devlin was sleeping off a "powerful headache." That probably sounded worse than it was, though she'd still spent more time than she ought to today worrying about it.

She could always inquire about his headache if she lost her nerve about upbraiding him for last night. But when she entered the stable for the second time that day, he still wasn't around, but again Mortimer was. The older man was just bringing out one of the new mares for exercising.

Megan stopped to admire the horse, and to ask with what she hoped didn't sound like concern, "Is Mr. Jefferys still sleeping off that headache?"

The little man actually chuckled. "He's starting on another one, is what he's doing now."

Megan frowned. "Another one? How does one 'start' on a headache?"

"By hitting the bottle, miss—two or three bottles, actually."

She wasn't quite sure how to take that startling news. Devlin was getting foxed? And he'd begun the effort last night, obviously, to have had a powerful headache early this morning. And Mortimer's amused look when he'd said it implied it might be because of her. Because of her? That was a thrilling thought, that she could drive the man to drink. Did she really have that much of an effect on him?

Don't be so conceited. His drinking probably doesn't have anything to do with you.

I know, but it was nice to think so for a moment.

At any rate, you don't want to run into that particular man while he's foxed.

Don't I know it. He's nasty enough as it is when he's sober.

That, too, but I was referring to the lack of control intoxicated people have over their emotions. And since his emotions are usually volatile when you're around—

"I get the picture," Megan mumbled irritably beneath her breath.

"What was that, miss?"

"Nothing, Mr. Browne." Megan sighed. "I've just decided to visit my friend Tiffany. I'll take the mare, if it's all right with you."

"Certainly. Saves me putting her through her paces, and she's gentle enough. I'll just change the saddles for you."

Megan nodded, but while she waited, her eyes kept straying to the back of the stable.

Don't even think about it.

Megan flushed guiltily. *Well, aren't you curious about what kind of a drunk he makes?*

Probably an ornery one.

Or a silly one. That I'd love to witness.

You're asking for trouble to find out.

Now you're getting cautious? Must be because I'm going to visit Tiffany. She's always a good influence on you.

And on you. She'll tell you to stay away from inebriated men.

Good God, you don't think I'm going to tell Tiffany about any of this, do you?

You probably will.

Megan had no intention of doing so, not when her own feelings were so confused and, yes, shameful. But she hadn't been with Tiffany for more than ten minutes before this question popped out: "What would you think if I married beneath myself?"

Tiffany responded pragmatically. "How far beneath yourself are we talking about?"

"This is just suppose, now," Megan thought it prudent to point out. "I'm not actually contemplating doing anything so ridiculous—"

"How far?"

"Say he wasn't even a gentleman. Would you be shocked? Would it cause a great scandal, do you think?"

Tiffany stared at her for a long moment before she burst out, "Megan Penworthy, you haven't fallen in love with that horse breeder, have you?"

"Absolutely not," Megan scoffed, though her cheeks were beginning to heat up. "All he and I do is fight. Why, we don't even like each other."

"I'm glad to hear it."

Megan ignored that as she plopped down in a chair in Tiffany's newly redecorated room, then let out a long sigh. "But I have to allow—I find him so exciting, Tiff. When I'm around him I feel so, oh, I don't know, bubbly inside. I'm sure it's just because our fights are so stimulating, and they are, you know. I actually shout at him."

Tiffany was starting to grin. "You don't."

"Yes, I do," Megan assured her. "And he gets just as furious at me."

"With reason?"

"Usually. But I'm beginning to think I might enjoy fighting with him, though it certainly doesn't seem like it at the time."

"You're probably just bored, and he's a handsome man, an incredibly handsome man. Perfectly understandable. But does he have any good qualities?"

"Not a one—well, actually, he does seem to be overly concerned with my welfare. He gets positively livid when I do something he thinks might be a danger to me."

Tiffany's eyes widened. "Megan, what *have* you been doing since we got back?"

Megan shrugged and said offhandedly, "I merely thought Devlin might be our highwayman."

"But haven't you heard? The man's conscience got the better of him. He's returned everything he stole and then some, swearing he'll never succumb to wicked temptations again. It was all in a note he sent the magistrate."

"So he *did* do it."

Tiffany blinked. "What do you mean, he *did* do it? That sounds as if you knew—"

"I did."

"Megan!"

"Well, I can't help it if I happened to be there when he was being ordered to return everything. I *told* you I suspected it was Devlin."

"You mean it was?" Tiffany asked incredulously.

"No, more's the pity," Megan grumbled. "He was out to catch the thief himself and he did just that. I just happened to be following him."

"Hoping to catch him red-handed?"

"Something like that." And Megan briefly explained her late-night adventure, ending with, "He was positively furious when I returned, not that I told him where I'd really been. I can just imagine his reaction if he'd found that out."

"Megan, you have *got* to stop acting so impulsively. Do you have any idea what could have happened?"

She did now, but she couldn't bring herself to confess the rest of what had happened last night, even to her best friend. "I know, and I'm turning over a new leaf. I'll even have one of your footmen escort me home tonight, which will avoid another argument with Devlin, since my going about unescorted is one of the things he objects to."

"You might as well get used to it. In London we don't go *anywhere* without the proper escort. But guess what? Tyler's mother has offered to sponsor us. She's also offered to let us stay with her."

"But that's wonderful!" Megan exclaimed. "I know the major and his wife are dears, and they've known my father forever or they wouldn't have agreed to host us, but to be honest, they don't *know* anyone. But Lady Whately knows everyone, doesn't she?"

"Just about. I'd say we'll have you married before the end of the year after all."

"I hope so, because my curiosity has really been driving me crazy lately about lovemaking. I can't wait to get married and finally find out what's the big to-do about it."

"As long as you *do* plan on waiting for the one before the other."

"Absolutely. I might be thinking about it a lot lately"—an understatement—"but that's all I'm doing."

"Maybe you'd better stay away from your horse breeder altogether," Tiffany suggested cautiously.

Megan laughed. "Now *that's* the kind of advice I'm used to. But you needn't worry in this case. I'm not about to ruin my chances for an excellent match by dallying with a lowborn rogue, no matter how handsome he is."

"And exciting."

"No matter how exciting, either."

"And stimulating."

"You've made your point, Tiffany. I'll never go near him again."

Chapter 24

She'd said it, but Megan knew she'd never stick to it. Staying away from Devlin was an impossibility. Not that she couldn't arrange it. It would be a simple matter to avoid the stable altogether. She need only have her horse brought to her when she wanted to ride, and returned when she was through. Any one of the footmen would be happy to oblige her in that. That she had always done the fetching and grooming herself was actually an abnormal habit, though one she could break if necessary.

The impossibility was that she didn't want to stay away from Devlin.

'Bout time you admitted it.

But tell me why it's so?

Maybe you're falling in love with him after all.

Don't be absurd. There's not a thing about him worth loving.

What about his concern for you?

Not a good enough reason.

His kisses? You can't say you don't adore them.

He can't be the only good kisser around.

What about his unique charm?

What charm? He hasn't any. He's a damned grouch, is what he is.

That's just it. He's not a happy man. He needs a woman to soften him.

I'm not a reformer.

What about what he makes you feel?

I don't know what that is any more than you do. Now forget it. I am not falling in love with that man. Do you think I want to live in a stable the rest of my life?

With someone like him to share it, I doubt you'd mind all that much. What do you love more than horses anyway—besides his kisses?

That doesn't mean I want to live among horses. Good God, do you know what you're suggesting?

Yes.

Megan looked around almost guiltily, but the footman escorting her home wasn't paying the least attention to her, wouldn't know that she was having an argument with herself anyway.

I don't know why I still talk to you. Tiffany puts me in a good mood, and you put me right back into a rotten one. Just because I've agreed to let Devlin teach me how to kiss—

He didn't offer to.

But he will—doesn't mean I would consider marrying the man. I won't consider it. I'm going to marry an earl at the very least.

Stepping down already, are we?

Just being a little more realistic. There aren't that many dukes to chose from, at least not young ones.

Is that grand house to outdo Lady O's still all that important?

Yes.

Stubborn. He hit it on the nose. Too stubborn for your own good.

So now you're agreeing with him, too? I suppose you also think I'm spoiled.

Well, aren't you?

Megan didn't say another word, simmering silently the rest of the way home. When she reached the manor, she thanked her escort and waved him off before dismounting and walking Sir Ambrose back to the stable. Amazingly, considering the conversation she'd just had with herself, she wasn't thinking about Devlin or possibly encountering him.

But he was there, and he wasn't alone.

" . . . but my mum got worried when you didn't come for your dinner," Cora was saying, "so I brung you this basket. Big man like yourself has to eat, don't he?"

"So sweet of you, but food isn't what I need right now." Cora giggled at that, causing Devlin to exclaim, "Good God, when'd you start doing that?"

"What?"

"Never mind. C'mere."

Megan stood rooted to the spot just inside the doors. She couldn't see them, but she knew both voices well enough, and if she thought she'd been angry with herself earlier, that was nothing compared with what she felt right then, imagining Devlin kissing the kitchen maid.

"Cora Lamb," Megan intoned sternly, "just what do you think you're doing?"

There was a muffled shriek, then Cora came stumbling out from behind the hayrick, trying hastily to right her uniform as well as herself.

"Oh, it's you, miss," she said breathlessly. "I swear you sounded like me mum."

"Perhaps your mum ought to be apprised of what you're doing out here."

"No need to do that, Miss Megan. I only brung Mr. Jefferys a bite to eat, is all. And I'll be getting back to the house now."

"You do that, and next time remember that your duties don't extend to the stable. If Mr. Jefferys wants to eat, he can find his way to the kitchen. Don't let me catch you waiting on him again, Cora."

With a bob and a hasty "No, miss, I won't," Cora all but ran out of the stable.

"You shouldn't have done that," Devlin said at Megan's back.

She swung around to glare at him. "Is that so? I'm supposed to turn a blind eye while you seduce the servants? I don't think so."

"If they want to be seduced, it's none of your bloody business, is it?"

She finally noted the slight slur in his words, as well as his appalling condition. Hay clung to his clothes and hair. His white shirt was open to the waist and only half tucked into his trousers. He was minus his boots. And he couldn't seem to stand there without weaving a bit.

"You look disgraceful," she said scathingly.

"I was sleeping when that female started yoo-hooing me. I came out because I thought she was you."

"I don't yoo-hoo, you wretched man."

"You don't giggle either, thank God. All you do is drive a man to drink." He was distracted then by her horse wandering toward the back of the stable. "And what are you doing with that mare?"

Her chin rose defensively. "I was exercising her—with Mr. Browne's permission."

His head swiveled to the open doors to note the darkness outside. Megan could almost read his mind, especially when those blue-green eyes came back to her, narrowed and starting to fill with heat.

She forestalled him coldly. "I spent most of the day at Tiffany's, but I had an escort home, so don't start in on me. *I'm* not the guilty party here who was cavorting in the hay with the wrong woman."

It must have been the contempt in her tone that set him off, because suddenly he was quite furious. "The wrong woman? Let me assure you that I have reached such a state of need, thanks to you, that *any* woman will do!"

"You're blaming *me* for your licentious behavior?" she asked incredulously.

"You're damned right I am!"

Having said it, or more to the point, snarled it, he surprised Megan by turning away. But he must have moved too quickly because he swayed again, and it was no straight line that he walked to the stable entrance.

He's still foxed, Megan thought smugly. She almost smiled, wondering if she ought to tell him he was going in the wrong direction. But he stopped on his own, and her eyes widened as she watched him close the stable doors and drop the bolt into place.

Amusement fled, replaced by wariness as she remembered what had happened to her the last time he'd been this angry, just last night. There might not have been any lingering evidence this morning that she'd suffered his wrath, but she'd gone to bed with her bottom still smarting. And the man wasn't himself right now. He'd been drinking a good part of the day, if Mortimer could be believed. He couldn't be thinking clearly if he'd thought *she* was Cora. By God, if he spanked her for interrupting his lovemaking, she'd—she'd shoot him.

"What are you doing?" she demanded, backing up as he started in her direction again.

"You should have turned about and gone back to the house without interfering. Should have stayed away from me today altogether. But I suppose I should thank you, since I didn't really want her, and now that you've sent her off, you can bloody well take her place."

Megan backed into the hayrick, losing her balance against it. She was only lying back on it at a slightly slanted angle, but that allowed Devlin to lean over her, one hand placed on either side of her shoulders. She shook her head wordlessly. He smiled down at her.

"What, you no longer want a lesson in kissing?" he asked lazily. "Or did I dream that, your asking me to teach you how to do it?"

Was that all he was talking about? Suddenly there were new possibilities to this situation, and the mere thought of these sent a warm thrill straight to Megan's belly.

"You're willing to teach me now?"

"If you tell me why you want to learn."

"I don't want my future husband to be disappointed in me," she said truthfully.

She thought for a moment he was going to laugh. Instead he leaned closer until his lips were just a hairsbreadth away from hers. She could smell brandy, but mixed with the scent of hay and musk, it wasn't unpleasant.

"Open your mouth, brat."

For once she didn't mind the name he persisted in calling her, because he said it tenderly this time, giving it almost the sound of an endearment. And she really couldn't think about that now, when his lips were so close to touching hers.

"Do you want to start slow, or do you want to find out what a real kiss is like?"

He had to be teasing her. What had he been doing those other times if not really kissing her?

"I want to know all there is to know about it," she assured him.

"Remember you said that if this shocks you," he warned just before his tongue invaded her mouth.

Megan would have gasped if her breath weren't locked in her throat, not from shock, but from a deluge of unanticipated sensations converging on her all at once. It felt like her blood was soaring, her legs were melting, her insides were coming apart. This was that pleasant feeling she'd felt before, only now it was magnified a hundred times, and she didn't know if she could withstand so much feeling all at once. Then there was more.

His body pressed slowly into hers and liquid heat spread into her loins. He groaned deep in his throat and her breasts responded by tightening. His hand came to assuage the feeling there and her heart slammed against her chest.

"Don't hide your tongue from me," he said against her lips. "Give it to me, Megan. Taste me."

It seemed like she no longer had a will of her own, she obeyed him with such eagerness. But then she wanted to taste him. She simply hadn't known that she could until he ordered it. But if she could copy him in the kissing, could she also copy him in the touching? Because that was another overwhelming urge she had, and this time she didn't wait to be directed.

When her hand slipped between them as his had done, he moved slightly to the side to give her access, which gave him more access as well, which he took swift advantage of. Suddenly there was no cloth between his hand and her breasts. He'd somehow worked her blouse open and got beneath her camisole, and she discovered fire. Good God, his hand couldn't be that warm, but it was. His chest under her own palm couldn't be that hot either, but it was. He'd talked of burning to a cinder last night. Was it possible?

Megan didn't care at the moment, not one little bit. She felt as if she were falling, falling . . . Good God, they *were* falling!

Devlin tore his mouth away from hers to say, "Bloody hell, we're—" He landed with a grunt, mostly because Megan landed on top of him. "—Falling," he finished after the fact.

At which point he started to laugh, deep laughter of the like she'd never heard from him. It was infectious, especially in light of what had happened. This was not precisely the best time to slip off a hayrick. Fortunately, they'd fallen onto a bed of hay, the remainder of what had been pitched earlier in the day. Still, it wasn't how she would have imagined a lesson in kissing to end.

She was laughing as hard as he was, then harder when the shaking of his chest caused her to slip off him as well. She rolled onto her back, holding her belly until her humor finally wound down. But her eyes had watered, and she tried to find the pocket of her jacket to get a kerchief when she noticed one dangling in front of her.

She made quick use of it, then lowered it to see that Devlin had rolled onto his side and was leaning on one elbow, grinning at her.

"That fall was not part of the lesson."

She grinned back at him. "Thank you for telling me. I wasn't quite sure."

He chuckled, but then his eyes lit on her open blouse and they seemed to kindle with heat again instantly. "Actually," he said in the most sensuous tone, "we're in a much better position now for kissing. Do you want to learn more?"

"There's more?" she replied in wonder.

"Most definitely."

"Show me."

He bent toward her, but then he stopped and shook his head as if to clear it, and suddenly he was frowning. "No, I—good God, I must be mad. Go home, Megan, and do it now. This lesson is over."

Her disappointment was almost too keen to bear. "Why?" she whispered.

"Because I lost myself in that last kiss. I forgot for a moment that you're an innocent miss with too much curiosity for her own good."

"Are you saying you would have made love to me?" she ventured.

"Yes, damn it."

She hoped that was all that was bothering him. "But I wouldn't have let you. I would have stopped you. You *would* stop if I told you to, wouldn't you?"

"Certainly," he said indignantly.

"Then I don't see a problem."

"Don't you? I'm not exactly sober, you know," he said, as if she hadn't noticed.

"I don't mind." She leaned toward him then and implored softly, "Show me."

He groaned and gathered her close. "Give me your tongue again." She did, but this time he didn't let her explore with it, but gently sucked on it instead for a while, then said, "There are other places to do that."

"Where?"

He moved to draw her earlobe between his lips for the same tantalizing treatment. She shivered deliciously, gasping. "Where else?"

She tried to concentrate on the path his mouth was taking so she could anticipate his destination, but she was enjoying the sensations that he was evoking on the way too much. And then she sucked in her breath as one nipple was drawn deeply into the heat of his mouth. She was incredulous and a little shocked that this could be part of kissing, but she didn't stop him. God, no, she wasn't about to stop him— not yet.

When she later felt a coolness on her legs, it didn't register that her skirt was being raised. When she felt a tugging on her drawers, that didn't make much sense either, but she finally asked, "What are you doing now?"

His mouth came back to hers for a deeply stirring kiss before he said, "Showing you everything. Isn't that what you wanted? Or are you afraid now?"

"A little."

"You should be."

It was the wrong thing to say, or the right thing, challenging her stubbornness and curiosity at once. "Don't stop, Devlin, not yet."

He kissed her again, so that she barely noticed her drawers coming off completely. But she couldn't miss warm fingers slipping between her legs. She shrieked in surprise, but the sound was muffled by his mouth. Then she was moaning, and gripping him to her, and reveling in the most startling sensations yet. Her legs parted of their own accord, her body and its responses were taking over, and she didn't care.

"Is—is this part of kissing?" she gasped out when his mouth returned to her neck, then her breasts.

"Yes," he lied without the least qualm.

"Then I have to do that to you?"

"No," he croaked, knowing he'd never survive it.

"But I want to."

"I'm going to die."

She thought she was, too, especially when he moved on top of her, placing his hips between hers, and that hard part of his body was pressing into the place he'd heated with his fingers, giving her the same pleasure as before.

But then a sharp pain swiftly pierced her and there was nothing pleasurable in that. Her eyes flew open in shock. How? No, maybe not. Maybe that pain and fullness inside her now wasn't him, but still his fingers. Yet she could feel his hands, both hands, beneath her back, holding her tightly to him. She felt shock again. This wasn't supposed to happen.

"Tell me you aren't making love to me," she demanded in rising panic.

He became very still, suffering some shock of his own. "I'm afraid it's too late to tell you that."

"But you can't be!"

"I'm sorry, Megan, truly, but the damage is done."

Her shock turned rapidly to resentment as all the repercussions bombarded her. "I won't marry you."

That wasn't the wisest thing to say to a man who'd just broken every scruple he possessed. "I bloody well wasn't going to ask you to—"

"Good!"

"—but now I have to."

"Well, aren't you fortunate that you already have my answer," she retorted acidly. "Now get off me!"

His face dropped into the curve of her neck with a groan. "I can't, Megan."

She wasn't interested in his problem. "Of course you can. You said you would."

"That was when I could. Now—oh, God." He thrust once, twice, then was still again.

That hadn't hurt, but she was too furious to notice. "I'm getting hysterical, Devlin. If you don't want a crying, screaming woman on your hands, then—"

"In all fairness, I owe you a climax. You've come this far, you might as well—"

"I didn't mean to come this far and you know it!" she hissed.

He rose until he was leaning over her and she was able to see at last his own upset. Guilt was tearing into him much more sharply than her verbal abuse, and in his present inebriated state, he couldn't handle either too well.

"Then you should have left when I warned you to!"

"That's right," she bit out. "Absolve yourself of guilt, why don't you?"

"If I was doing that, I wouldn't have offered to marry you."

"You know very well I can't marry a horse breeder! My father would never allow it, either."

"On the contrary," he said with a full measure of his arrogance. "Once the circumstances are explained, your father will give his wholehearted approval, I do assure you, so don't use that as an excuse for refusing me."

"Don't you dare tell him what you did to me! Don't you dare tell anyone. This did not happen."

"Megan, you can't pretend—"

"I can do anything I please, and if I please to go on with my life as if this didn't happen, I damn well will."

"Fine! You do that!"

He rolled over and got to his feet without swaying. Megan scrambled to her feet just as quickly, then spent a few moments gasping over each proof of his crime that she could see—and feel. She had been made love to and she was still fully clothed—well, almost. She swiped up her drawers and marched to the doors, throwing back the bolt. Devlin she didn't spare a glance for, but he was watching her with brooding eyes.

"When you come to your senses, brat," he said to her back, "you know where I'll be."

"You'll be in hell before I come to you again for anything," was her final retort before she stomped out, still without looking back.

Devlin turned and, with a growl, smashed his fist through the nearest wall, then went back to his room and smashed his remaining stock of brandy.

Chapter 25

Megan stayed in her room for three days brooding, though the word went out in the household that she was merely under the weather. But there was only so much brooding someone of her exuberant nature could tolerate. So she'd made a mistake. It wasn't the end of the world, at least not yet. And the fates couldn't be so cruel as to visit upon her clear evidence of her one and only fall from grace. She believed that wholeheartedly—but she'd wait until she had actual proof of that before celebrating.

In the meantime, she got back to her daily routine, with one major exception. She gave up riding for a while, or anything else that would cause her to send to the stable for anything. That, of course, kept her housebound, and there was only so much of that that she could stomach, too.

Finally, she packed a trunk and went for an extended stay with Tiffany, giving her father the excuse that they had innumerable plans to make for the upcoming trip to London, and that could be done more easily if they were together—which was nothing out of the ordinary. They had frequently, through the years, spent weeks at a time at each other's houses. It was nothing to cause comment about, nor did it imply she was running away from something. Only an arrogant horse breeder might get the latter impression, and she wasn't the least bit concerned about what he thought.

At least she wasn't until he showed up at Tiffany's house her second day there, requesting to speak with her. Apparently her absence from the stable hadn't bothered him as long as she had been at home and accessible, but now that she'd left home, he had something to say about it.

Of course, she refused to see him. And he went away—what else could he do?—without leaving a message, which told her it couldn't have been anything serious that he wanted. But he came back the next day, and the next, and that told her something else. The man wasn't going to give up until he'd said his piece. But Megan was nothing if not stubborn. She wasn't going to hear it.

The trouble with that was that this new, uncommunicative war they were having couldn't be fought privately. Tiffany's servants were beginning to talk, Tiffany was dying of curiosity herself, and Tiffany's butler, male that he was, was taking sides and starting to give Megan reproving looks.

But she could withstand all that easily enough. Obstinacy had its uses, and she had plenty to spare. It was her own urges that she was having trouble dealing with, for ironically, despite what had happened, she was beginning to miss Devlin. She missed their fights. She missed the sight of him, which was always, no matter how angry she might be with him, a pleasure to her senses.

But she still wouldn't receive him at Tiffany's. And she wasn't going to go home, where he had access to her house and could search her out, until she could tell him, truthfully, that he had nothing to worry about, that there would be no unwelcome results from their indiscretion.

She didn't even blame him anymore for what had happened. She blamed her curiosity. She blamed her body for liking too much what he'd been doing to it. And she blamed that part of her that had talked her into letting him teach her about kissing, when her common sense had been against the idea from the start.

"Are you ever going to say why you're so mad at him?" Tiffany asked one day over lunch, after Megan had given the order, for the ninth time, to tell Devlin she wasn't available.

"Do I look mad?"

"Well, no—but you must be. Why else don't you want to talk to him?"

Megan tried to shrug the matter off. "You advised me to stay away from him, remember?"

"And how often do you follow my advice?" Tiffany countered. "Now come on, why are you hiding here?"

"I'm not hiding."

"This is your best friend you're talking to."

Megan sighed. She was amazed that Tiffany had held her tongue this long. But at least she had two shameful experiences to choose from for this confession, and the first was no longer as shocking as the second one.

"The man thinks he's my father."

"Oh, come now," Tiffany scoffed. "His interest in you *can't* be paternal."

"In this one instance it most definitely is," Megan insisted. "He claims I need a keeper, and he's backed up that contention by assuming the role, complete with disciplinary measures. He—he—"

"He what?" Tiffany prompted impatiently.

Megan looked down at her plate, her cheeks starting to scald. "He spanked me."

"He did *what*?!"

"He put me over his knees and—"

"I know how it's done! But he's a—he's only a—how could he dare?"

"Easily. Devlin doesn't behave like he ought to, nor has he ever done so. The fact is, there's not a subservient or deferential bone in his body. I suppose that's one reason he's so fascinating. He just doesn't fit into the standard order of things. He's a servant, but a servant who won't take orders, who can't be dismissed, who's got more arrogance than ten pompous lords."

"You're making excuses for him?"

Megan glanced up to see that Tiffany's shock was mounting. "Absolutely not," she assured her friend, then shrugged. "But you asked how he could dare. That's how."

"Then he must have been surprised when he got dismissed despite that ridiculous stipulation in the stallion's sales contract," Tiffany said, drawing the wrong conclusion. "Is that why he's trying to see you? To beg your forgiveness so he can get his job back?"

The thought of it was so preposterous, Megan couldn't help laughing. "Devlin beg? He wouldn't know how."

"He doesn't think he can force you to reinstate him, does he?"

Megan squirmed now, seeing no way to avoid admitting, "He wasn't—"

She was saved for the moment when the Robertses' butler knocked and opened the double doors to announce in an aggrieved tone, "He's back, Miss Megan. He says he won't leave this time until you see him."

Tiffany shot immediately to her feet. "Of all the—*I'll* see to this."

Megan rose, too. "Tiff, no—"

But Tiffany was already out the door, and Megan could hear her accosting Devlin in the hall. "Your gall is astounding, Mr. Jefferys. How you can dare come here after what you did is beyond comprehension. And even if Megan would agree to see you, I wouldn't permit it, so leave this house and don't come— now just a—you can't—"

Megan braced herself, expecting to see Devlin marching into the dining room, and he did, not stopping until he towered over her. Even though this was a situation she had tried to avoid, her senses still ate up the sight of him.

"You *told* her?"

She knew what he thought. "Not about *that*," she replied in a furious whisper. "About the other."

"What other?"

"That you abused my—my posterior."

"Oh," he said, the heat going out of his expression, to be replaced, incredibly, with genuine concern. "Are you all right, Megan?"

"Certainly," she said uncomfortably.

"We have to talk."

"No."

"You can't avoid me forever."

He said that with such confidence that Megan's stubbornness reared its ornery head. "Actually, I can—at least until I'm safely married—to someone else."

That answer wasn't to his liking; it made him so furious, in fact, that Megan cringed to see his reaction. But he made no reply to her.

He stalked out instead, though not before he growled at Tiffany's stiff figure in the doorway, "She deserved it."

"Well, I never!" Tiffany said huffily and slammed the door shut behind him. "Is that the kind of behavior you had to put up with?"

"Constantly."

"He should have been dismissed sooner, regardless of any stipulations."

Megan sat down, a strange kind of dejection coming over her that made her feel like bursting into tears. Dispassionately, she said, "He wasn't dismissed."

"You can't be serious! What *is* your father thinking of?"

"My father doesn't know anything about it. I never told him."

"Megan! What can *you* be thinking of? If that wasn't grounds for dismissal and worse—"

"Even if I did deserve it?"

"Yes, even so. It wasn't *his* place to correct you—Did you?"

"Sort of—yes. But I told you that he gets overly concerned about me, and he was furious that I'd put myself in danger that night."

"That night? This wasn't the night you followed him, was it?"

"The same."

"And you kept that to yourself when you told me about it?" Tiffany said reproachfully.

Megan was feeling worse and worse and finally gave in to the urge to cry. "I didn't want to mention it now, either," she said miserably.

"I'm not exactly proud of the fact that I was treated like a child."

"Oh, Meg, don't," Tiffany said contritely. "I shouldn't have pried."

"Don't be ridiculous," Megan retorted. "What are friends for if not to pry?"

It took a few seconds before they were both grinning at that bit of nonsense. Megan wiped at her tears before adding, "Devlin was just trying to open my eyes to the fact that the most horrible things can happen when you recklessly ignore good common sense."

So why didn't I pay closer attention? she asked herself bitterly. But her inner voice was conspicuously silent on that one, and a week later Megan couldn't ignore the truth any longer. The fates had been cruel after all.

Chapter 26

Devlin dove under the water, swimming the length of the pond twice before he surfaced for air. He had taken to coming here each morning for a swim because he couldn't stomach the stable at this time of day, since Megan had stopped showing up for her morning rides. He didn't like it that he'd driven her away from not only the stable but also her home. He didn't like the guilt she was making him feel, when he didn't have all that much to feel guilty about. And he certainly didn't like it that he could barely remember what had caused it all. If she hadn't clarified the matter that one time he was able to see her at her friend's house, he still might be convinced that he'd dreamed the whole thing.

But he hadn't dreamed it. He'd made love

to Megan Penworthy. And it had been unbe-lievably nice—up to the time of penetration when he'd realized what he was doing, and so had she. The shock of it had ruined it for them both. Even his climax, uncontrolled and unwanted at that point, had been the worst he'd ever experienced. Yet he knew instinc-tively that it could have been the best.

But it shouldn't have happened at all. He'd been fighting his emotions since he met her, and succeeding admirably, or so he thought. And if he hadn't put so much brandy into his system that day, he would bloody well have insisted she leave the stable, rather than just suggesting it. Of course, he wouldn't have tried to drown himself in drink if she hadn't driven him crazy with lust the night before.

And now she wouldn't even let him do the honorable thing. Not that he wanted to marry a temperamental, spoiled redhead. He certain-ly didn't. So why did it infuriate him that she'd refused him? Simple wounded pride that she'd prefer anyone but him? Probably.

He dove under again, pressing it for three lengths this time, but didn't quite make it, surfacing with burning lungs in the center of the pond. A toss of his head got the hair and most of the water out of his eyes, but the sight that greeted him left him doubting his vision. Megan, dismounting from Sir Ambrose and walking up to the edge of the pond— and right into it, clothes and all. Nor did she stop until she reached him, and the second she reached him, she cracked her palm against his cheek, then slammed both fists against his bare chest.

Devlin let her beat at him for a moment before he asked, quite reasonably under the circumstances, "What the devil do you think you're doing?"

She shouted her answer. "You bloody rotten bastard, if you weren't so tall, I'd drown you!"

"Why?"

"Because I want to murder you!" She hit him once more to stress her point, then said, "Why couldn't you just kiss me like I asked you to?"

"When?"

"You know when! Why did you have to ruin it by making love to me?"

He almost laughed at the absurdity of that question. Any other woman he had been kissing like he had been kissing Megan would have been furious if he *hadn't* finished by making love to her. Of course, none of those other women would have been virgins.

"The kind of kissing we were doing that night generally does lead to lovemaking, brat," he explained. "And why the sudden fireworks over it? You weren't this mad when it happened."

"I was, too," she insisted. "But I was still in shock then."

His brow rose at that sulky reply. "It's taken you three weeks to come out of shock?"

She hit him again. "It's taken this long to find out that you've ruined me! I'm going to be disgraced!" she wailed. "I'm going to be a scandal!"

The dramatics suddenly made sense to him. He'd been expecting it; she obviously hadn't. "Is this your pleasant way of informing me that you're enceinte?"

"Yes, you stupid—"

"How do I know you're telling the truth?" he asked reasonably.

She stared at him incredulously for a moment before she turned and walked away in disgust. But she couldn't do so very quickly in the water, and he had only to reach out an arm to grab her back, which he did.

"I'm sorry, Megan, but there have been other females who've made the claim that I'd fathered their babes, and I bloody well hadn't."

Her eyes narrowed. "Are you trying to say it's not possible that I could be carrying your child?"

"Not at all. If you are carrying a child, it most certainly is mine, and I'll take full responsibility for it. Only, are you sure?"

"No, I'm not sure!" she shouted up at him. "How can I be sure this soon? But I'm a week late for my—I'm late, and I'm never late!"

"There's no need to get hysterical. I offered to marry you whether there was a babe or not, if you'll recall." Then he frowned. "Didn't I?"

Megan started at the question, her eyes

rounding. "Don't you remember?"

"Until I saw you at the Robertses' house, I wasn't sure if I hadn't dreamed the whole thing. Apparently not, but I'm still not crystal clear on everything that happened."

"Well, don't expect me to remind you. I'm trying to forget it myself."

His other hand joined the one holding her to give her a little shake. "One thing I am certain of is that you refused to leave when I advised you to, because you were enjoying yourself too bloody much. The only thing you'd like to forget is the end, and frankly, so would I. But as that's not possible any longer, there's no point in bemoaning it further."

"I'll bemoan it if I—"

He shook her again. "Megan, don't provoke me. D'you think I want to marry a spoiled brat who doesn't care a damn about me? But I've got no choice and neither do you."

"But it's not fair!" she cried. "You can't give me the big house I wanted so I could impress Lady O. All you can offer me is my own stable. And you don't love me either. You probably just want to marry me because you think it will bring you a step up in the world. But it won't, you know. It's not going to make you a gentleman. That takes—"

"That's quite enough, brat," he interrupted coldly. "All that self-pity is turning my stomach. Did it occur to you even once that I might have had other plans for my life that didn't include you? Do you ever think of anyone but yourself and what *you* want?"

That was unfair and he knew it. What Tyler had told him about her proved she did occasionally consider other people's feelings. But her near hysteria over the possibility of marrying him was shredding his pride to bits. Of course, from her point of view, he had no prospects, was below even untitled gentry, and was therefore utterly unsuitable as husband material. And if he was who she thought he was, that would be perfectly true.

He knew he ought to tell her the truth, which would turn her distress into a cause for rejoicing—at least for her. Damned if he would. It was the horse breeder she'd come to to satisfy her sexual curiosity. It was the horse breeder she could bloody well marry.

She'd been glaring at him after his question and turning quite red in the face because he'd dared to criticize her. "Who says I'm going to marry you, anyway?" she demanded now. "Do you know how many gentlemen of this parish have asked me to marry them?"

"And you burned your bridges, turning down every one of them."

"Which doesn't mean I can't change my mind, does it? So you can get on with the great plans you have for your life. I have no intention of complicating them."

She looked like she just might mean it, which made Devlin angry enough to shake her again. "Self-sacrifice doesn't suit you one little bit, brat. And you aren't marrying anyone else while you're carrying *my* child. We're going to elope to Gretna Green."

"What?!"

"Your father will give his approval after I speak with him."

"No, he won't. You're mad!"

"It will give the marriage a romantic aspect. Otherwise the gossips will tear you apart, counting the days until you give birth."

"They're going to tear me apart, anyway, for marrying a horse breeder."

"Then you agree?"

"I didn't say that," she grumbled. "I won't live in a stable."

"You'll live where I live."

"I suppose we could share my room."

"I'm not moving into your father's house!" he said with clear finality.

She went on as if she hadn't heard a single word. "And it will be costly, but we can improve your wardrobe. And—oh, what's the point? No one is ever going to mistake you for a gentleman. For one thing, you're a damned bully. Have you been listening to yourself?"

"I was beginning to think I was the only one who was," he replied dryly.

"I'm trying to find a compromise here, but you're not letting me."

"No, what you're doing is what you have a bad habit of doing, thinking you can have everything your own way. I hate to be the one to break this to you, Megan." He didn't sound the least bit distressed. "But the wife does what the husband tells her, not the other way around."

"Which is a good reason why I can't marry you. If you loved me, you'd try to please me, but you don't love me, so you're going to make me miserable."

"I'm not going to make you miserable," he gritted out between clenched teeth. "I'm going to make you my wife. The two are *not* synonymous!"

"In your case they will be," she maintained with infuriating stubbornness.

Devlin took his hands off her before he *really* shook her. "Go home, Megan. Pack a bag. We will leave directly after I speak to your father."

"You're serious, aren't you?" she said with some surprise. "You really think you can get my father's permission to marry me? You're dreaming, Devlin. The only way he'd agree is if I tell him it's what I want. And the baby won't make a difference, if that's what you're thinking. He'll find me another husband."

"Then shall we leave the decision to him? If he agrees, you'll go along with it?"

Her eyes narrowed suspiciously. "You aren't planning to bully him like you do me, are you?"

"I don't bully you, damn it!" She snorted, as if his response merely proved her point, so he continued with a little less volume. "I have no intention of bullying your father. Do we have a deal?"

"Yes," she snapped with ill grace, only to add loftily, "But there's no point in my packing. You won't get his permission without my help, and I still don't think I want to marry you."

"But you will if he says so?" he demanded, wanting it clarified.

"I've already answered that."

"Good. Then consider yourself engaged." He picked her up and gave her a short, hard kiss before setting her back in the water, turning her, and giving her a little push toward the bank.

She went, but she was only halfway out of the water when she turned back to say something else, only to finally notice his condition. "Good God, Devlin, you're naked!"

Her surprised expression was priceless. To have been so angry with him that she hadn't noticed a body she'd previously been fascinated with—he started laughing and couldn't stop, not even to tell her, "And you're wading in a pond with your clothes on."

Just as well. She wouldn't have appreciated having that pointed out any more than she did his humor.

Chapter 27

It wasn't possible that she was on her way to Scotland to be married. Only how many times did Megan have to repeat that to herself before it became true? The countryside they passed through continued to change. The miles continued to fall behind them. They were traveling steadily north—to Scotland—to be married.

They'd brought a footman along to take the carriage back, because Devlin planned to rent a coach as soon as a decent one could be found. In Somerset he'd found better than decent; he'd left her at an inn and come back with the Earl of Sedgemeer's sumptuous private coach, complete with a coat of arms emblazoned on the doors, and the earl's own driver.

Megan had looked the vehicle over dubiously, prompting Devlin to explain, "I told the earl we'd been set upon by robbers, had all our money and clothes stolen, as well as our carriage."

"And out of the goodness of his heart, he hands over his own coach to you?" she scoffed.

"I also told him I was the Duke of Wrothston. The man couldn't do enough for me after that. Even threw in the driver. I do look like St. James, you know."

"I've met him, remember? And you don't look anything like him." Which should have told Devlin that if he said the sky was blue, Megan would insist it was green.

But the luxurious coach at least made the trip tolerable, if her traveling companion didn't. Having Caesar along also helped: it got Devlin out of the coach for long stretches at a time.

Megan had wanted to bring Sir Ambrose along, too, but Devlin had flatly denied her request. Bossing her around already, and not even married yet. The man was going to be impossible to live with. Traveling with him was just as bad. And it was a long trip, with more than three hundred miles to reach Scotland and the renowned Gretna Green, where eager-to-be-marrieds had been going for decades; couples too impatient to wait the three weeks for the posting of banns, or couples who didn't have parental blessing—which Megan did.

That parental blessing still confounded her. No, what confounded her was that her father had seemed so genuinely *happy* when he'd come out of his study with Devlin to congratulate her and say how delighted he was that she'd chosen such a "fine man" to be her husband. He'd gone on to say other things appropriate to the moment, but Megan got stuck on that "fine man" and looked at Devlin as if he were suddenly a devil capable of casting spells of enchantment. Too bad he hadn't cast one on her.

She was too upset to accept this monumental change in her life happily. She might have been contemplating that same change, but having it forced on her *and* Devlin wasn't the same. She intended to keep silent about it, however, because she knew her upset would come out negatively and that certainly wouldn't help.

The trouble with that decision was she couldn't stand the silence beyond the second day and waited only until Devlin was about to doze off in the afternoon to say, "I don't understand it. What could you possibly have said to my father to make him so happy about a union between us?"

He didn't bother to open his eyes to reply. "I told him I loved you, of course, and that my only wish is to make you deliriously happy."

The words caused a pang in her heart, because she knew they weren't true. "I see nothing funny in this situation."

"That's one of your problems, brat. You've got a rotten sense of humor."

"Well, you've had your little joke—tasteless, by the way. Now answer my question."

"I told him the truth, Megan."

"That you seduced me?"

"I believe it was the other way around."

"It was not," she retorted indignantly.

He opened one eye to say, "I asked you for kissing lessons, did I?"

"My point exactly," she pounced. "Kissing lessons I asked for, not lessons in that other thing you did."

He sighed. "I've accepted responsibility for my part. Obviously you're not going to do the same."

"Why should I when the fault is entirely yours?"

"Have it your way," he replied tiredly and closed both eyes again.

Megan brooded silently for several minutes before she said, "You still haven't answered my question."

"Perhaps because talking to you is too infuriating to continue for any length of time." When she didn't respond, he looked over to see her staring forlornly out the window. "Bloody hell," he swore. "What the devil do you think I told him? I confessed that I'd got you with child. He happens to be of the firm belief that a child belongs with both parents—both *real* parents—so my offer of marriage was readily accepted. He would have preferred the marriage to come first, naturally, but he understands how these things can happen."

"Did you have to tell him about the baby?"

"You're the one who said it wouldn't make any difference, that he'd merely find you another husband. Well, you were wrong, Megan. He'd prefer you have the father of your child. And yes, I had to tell him about the baby, to explain the reason for a hasty elopement."

"That doesn't really say why he was so *happy* about it," she grumbled.

Devlin shrugged. "Unlike some people whom I shall refrain from naming, the squire happens to like me. He's not displeased with your choice."

"*I* didn't choose you."

"I believe he sees it differently—considering your condition."

Megan made no response to that, but settled for simply glowering at him, which he chose to ignore by once again closing his eyes. It didn't take long for her to slump back into dejection again.

This was *not* how she had imagined her wedding all the times she had fantasized about it. Granted, the man of her dreams was sitting across from her, the most handsome man she'd ever encountered. That part was fine, better than even she could have imagined, actually. And he was determined to marry her. That part was all right, too. So why was she miserable instead of ecstatic?

Because he doesn't love me.

What's there to love about you lately?

Are you taking his side again?

Are you saying you haven't been the veriest bitch since he first showed up?

Possibly, but with a great deal of provocation, or are you forgetting all the times I've been insulted, offended, or otherwise goaded into losing my temper? Besides that's not the only reason. Am I supposed to be delighted that he's being forced to marry me?

I didn't hear him complaining about it until you started blaming him for everything. And I thought you weren't going to do that.

I wasn't when it was only my life that was going to be ruined. But I'm not about to take full responsibility for ruining his life, too.

Shouldn't he be a bit angrier than he's been if he really felt his life was being ruined by you?

You'd think so, wouldn't you? But when does he ever do anything that you might expect?

You haven't been doing much of the expected, either, lately. You won't even admit you're getting what you want—him.

Megan snorted without realizing it, then wondered why Devlin was suddenly looking at her with raised brows. "What?" she said disagreeably. "Haven't you anything better to do than stare at me?"

The unprovoked attack amused him for some reason. "I was trying to sleep, but you seem determined to see that I don't. Bored, Megan?"

"Certainly not. I've been having a perfectly stimulating conversation with myself."

"There's no need to be sarcastic."

"I wasn't. In fact, you may as well know that you're going to marry someone who frequently talks to herself. It's not too late to change your mind and take me home, you know."

"And miss my only chance to step up in the world?"

Megan frowned, sensing his sudden rage as if it touched her physically, yet his expression hadn't changed. And then his eyes closed once more, and she wasn't about to protest, a bit unnerved by his anger this time.

But she complained to herself, *Can't he ever do what's expected? I give him the perfect out, that I just might be crazy, and he gets angry.*

Don't look to me for answers this time. I'm as baffled as you are.

Chapter 28

They spent their last night of unmarried bliss in the town of Carlisle on the English side of the border. The next morning, Devlin, in one of the rare times he'd spoken to Megan voluntarily on this trip, said they'd be married before noon that very day, since Gretna Green was supposedly just over the border. Megan thought to wonder aloud if their Somerset driver could find the place—he'd already got them lost twice—but decided to keep her mouth shut this once.

With the intimidating moment so near to hand, she was feeling a bit subdued, at least in no mood to start an argument. She was afraid the mood wouldn't pass, either, but grow worse. It wasn't just prenuptial nerves, though she definitely had those, too. But she'd been thinking too much the past few days about the unbelievable amount of control Devlin was going to have over her life after today. With any other man, that wouldn't be a worry, but Devlin . . . he didn't even like her. He didn't want to marry her. And he was going to make her life a living hell.

"You aren't going to cry, are you?"

She glanced over to find those turquoise eyes intently studying her, and wondered how long he'd been doing so. "Certainly not."

"It looked like you were about to."

"I'm not, I tell you," she insisted, but her lower lip was trembling.

"Is the thought of marriage to me that horrible, Megan?" he asked gently.

"Yes!" she said, and burst into tears, hiding her face in her hands.

So she didn't see his pained expression, or the firm resolve that took its place. And it wasn't until she quieted down to sniffles that she heard, "I don't know what you're blubbering about. I can assure you ours will be a marriage in name only."

She glanced up in surprise to demand, "What does that mean?"

"It means that I found making love to you as unsatisfactory as you did, so we won't be repeating that mistake."

Megan stiffened, her cheeks suffusing with color. So she could now add no-longer-desired to her list of complaints against him?

"That suits me just fine."

"I thought it might."

Before either of them could add to that, the coach rolled over something that sent them nearly bouncing out of their seats, there was a yell of alarm from the driver, and then, incredibly, the coach seemed to be sliding sideways.

"What the—?" Devlin began, only to end in a shout to Megan. "Get down!"

"Get down where?"

"The floor!"

"Don't be—"

He didn't give her a chance to finish her protest, reaching over to yank her to the floor, where he joined her, on top of her actually, and that so surprised her, she had nothing more to say for the moment. But Devlin didn't stay there. The crazy sliding picked up speed; then suddenly the coach was tilting at an odd angle, and Devlin was thrown to the side, hard against the wood casing of the seat. Megan followed him, rolled over him and up onto the seat, an easier, cushioned landing, until she crumbled headfirst into the side panel as the coach settled and was finally still.

"Are you all right, Megan?"

She wasn't quite sure. It took her a moment to get her skirt out of the way so she could right herself, then another moment to ascertain that she'd merely lost her bonnet.

"I think so, yes," she replied. "And you? Was that your head I heard crack?"

"Very funny," Devlin snorted as he sat up himself. "I believe it was one of the wheels you heard. Stay put while I investigate."

The coach wasn't lying completely on its side, but almost. When Devlin opened the lower door, it hit the ground beneath it, leaving only about a foot to squeeze through, not enough room for a man of his size. The other door had to be thrown back and crawled out of, but he managed that easily enough. Megan had a less easy time of it just trying to stick her head out of the upper door to see what was going on. She wasn't tall enough to stand there and look out, but had to pull herself up to the opening.

The coach was sitting in a deep ditch off the side of the road, which ran down a small hill. Coming down the hill could have accounted for the sliding they'd experienced, only it wasn't that steep a hill. And looking toward the top of it now, Megan could see that something wet covered the surface. It was that wetness that Devlin and the driver were both presently investigating.

Megan looked further around. At least the horses were all right. Even Caesar was still standing up on the road, but only because his lead rope had been long enough not to drag him into the ditch with the coach. And apparently they'd have help in a moment, for she could see three men riding up the hill toward them.

Her arms gave out then and she slipped down to sit wedged in the lower corner again. She could hear their help arriving, and a pretty thick brogue. Scotsmen, then. She hadn't realized they'd crossed the border.

After a few moments more, she grew impatient waiting for Devlin to return and get her out of there. The lower-door opening had been too narrow for him, but it wasn't for her. She squeezed right out to the ground, coming out on the down side of the coach. Crawling out of the ditch was another matter, with skirts to hamper her.

"Pig's fat?" she heard with a laugh. "Can ye imagine that, Gilleonan?"

"Some farmer got careless taking his fat tae market, I dinna doubt. What d'ye think, Lachlan?"

"Oh, aye, there's that, tae be sure. There's also reavers bold enough tae set traps for the unwary in broad daylight these days."

"Reavers?" That from the coachman.

There was amusement in the voice that explained. "Robbers, mon. Where're you from that you havena heard of Scottish reavers? 'Tis a pleasant enough activity for laird and crofter alike, though usually enjoyed late of a night."

There was a bit more laughter that Megan frowned over. Scots humor was definitely beyond her, but then she wouldn't be in this country long enough to need to understand the oddities of its people.

"D'ye smell a trap, then, Lachlan?"

"Blast you, Ranald, dinna be in such a hurry. When I smell a trap, I'll be letting you know. Give these gentlemen a hand now."

"That won't be necessary."

Megan was dusting off her hands, having finally achieved the road, when she heard Devlin say that. She stood behind everyone, unnoticed. The Scotsmen had yet to dismount. All she could see of them was some very broad backs. Devlin, on the other hand, or at least his face, which was all she could see of him beyond the horses, was looking too serious by half—which didn't explain to her satisfaction why he was refusing the Scotsmen's help.

"And why not?" she asked, drawing his eyes to her, and turning three horses about.

"Bloody hell, can't you ever do what you're told, Megan?" Devlin demanded as he pushed his way through the horses to confront her.

She blinked at the amount of anger she detected in his tone. "Apparently not," she replied stiffly.

"Then try it now and get back in the coach," he hissed so only she might hear.

"After I just fought my way out of it, no thanks to you?"

"Megan—"

"No," she cut in. "You're being unreasonable as usual. The coach has to be righted, doesn't it? Do you expect me to be bounced around in it while it is?"

"I expect you to do as you're told."

"Well, we aren't married yet, Devlin Jefferys, so you can save your ordering—"

"Och, but those are pretty words. So you're no' a wife yet, darlin'?"

The question came as a horse unexpectedly
nosed its way between Devlin and Megan, so
smoothly done that Devlin was nudged out
of the way, the animal completely separating
them now. Megan looked up as a giant of a
man slipped from the horse to land next to her,
immediately reached for her hand, and bent
over it, just brushing the back of her knuckles
with his lips. Her instinct was to snatch her
hand back and upbraid the fellow, but when
he straightened, his sheer size gave her pause,
as well as his startling good looks.

He had light green eyes and the darkest
auburn hair that had mere hints of red glim-
mering in the sunlight. His well-tailored navy-
blue jacket fit snugly over shoulders likely
twice the width of her own, and a barrellike
chest, yet it seemed to be, amazingly, all lean
muscle. Legs like tree trunks were covered in
buff trousers and knee-high riding boots. An
old-fashioned frilly cravat lent an abundance
of lace to his throat. He was quite the second
most handsome man she had ever encountered,
and he was staring back at her as if transfixed
by what he saw.

"Faith and be—such flaming glory, and the
face of an angel tae be going with it," he said,
his eyes touching on her hair, then on every
inch of her face.

Megan automatically brought a hand up to
straighten a bonnet that wasn't there, was still
in the coach. She was flustered, but in a pleasant way, not accustomed to such boldness in

a man who obviously found her attractive—
including her red hair. The urge was strong
to glance at Devlin and say, "Did you hear
that? Flaming glory—ha!" but she managed to
restrain herself.

"Lachlan MacDuell, at your service," the
Scotsman was saying. "Can I be offering you
a ride tae—Gretna Green, would it be?"

"Why, yes—I mean, that is our destination."

He grinned widely, quite an engaging grin.
"They say a great many eloping couples dinna
make it tae Gretna Green because they'd ne'er
spent so much time together as they do getting
here, and by the time they're getting here, they
despise each other. Dare I hope that is your
case, darlin'?"

He was too perceptive by half, but Megan
wasn't about to air her grievances to a stranger. "You may not. And I'll thank you—"

"Are ye smelling that trap yet, Lachlan?"
one of his companions called out.

"Not *yet*, Gilleonan," Lachlan replied with
clear impatience. "Canna you see I'm courting
here?"

Megan blinked. Gilleonan shot back, "Nay,
it doesna look that way tae me."

At which point Lachlan dropped down to
one knee. "*Now* does it?"

"Oh, aye, now it does indeed. Will ye be
long at it, then?"

"As long as—"

"Not long a'tall," Devlin interjected as he
came around the Scotsman's horse.

Lachlan sighed, but other than that, he completely ignored Devlin's presence and continued to stare at Megan. She in turn was embarrassed, yet undeniably flattered.

"Do get up, Mr. MacDuell," she urged.

"I canna, no' until you ken you've stolen my heart, darlin'."

"I certainly didn't mean to."

He grinned at her. "Aye, I know you canna help it, but there it is, in your hands. So I'll be plighting my troth in the proper manner, and you'll be so impressed you'll be giving me the answer I'm hoping tae hear."

She couldn't help grinning back at the outrageous fellow. "I will?"

"Aye, that you will. But then look at your choices, darlin', a stuffy Englishmon or a bonny Scot who'll give you laughter, joy, and ne'er a dull moment."

Megan laughed. "You can't seriously be proposing marriage."

"I am," Lachlan assured her. "Is that no' what you're here for?"

"Well, yes, but—"

"Marry me. I swear you'll no' regret it."

Megan was loath to disappoint the charming fellow, but disappoint him she must. "I—"

"This absurdity has gone on long enough," Devlin cut in tersely. "The lady is marrying me, Mr. MacDuell, with her father's blessing."

Lachlan came slowly to his feet. Devlin was tall, but the Scot had a good four inches on him and a lot more brawn. And he likely thought

his sheer size ought to make Devlin back off.
It should have, but it didn't.

"That's Laird MacDuell tae you, English.
And what does the lass have tae say about
it?"

Megan jumped in before Devlin answered
that for her, too. "He's right, Lord MacDuell.
I struck a deal of sorts with him that is bind-
ing."

"But do you love him?"

"That, sir, is none of your business," Megan
retorted indignantly.

Lachlan laughed heartily. "But I'm making
it my business, darlin', and I'll interpret your
answer as I see fit. You're needing more time
tae rethink the matter, and that I can give
you."

Megan frowned. "I beg your pardon?"

"Nay, I'll be begging yours, I dinna doubt,
for stealing you away. *Now*, Gilleonan."

Chapter 29

Megan was so angry she could spit. They were thieves, highwaymen—Scottish reavers, as they termed themselves. What transpired after Lachlan MacDuell's startling statement proved it beyond a doubt. Pistols had been immediately drawn, and Devlin's purse had been demanded.

But Lachlan had surprised his companions in crime in the last instance. "Leave the rest," he'd ordered as he tossed a struggling Megan onto his mount. "I've found all the treasure I'm needing today."

"But what about the horse?" the one called Gilleonan had protested. "There's a fortune tae be made in selling an animal like this."

Lachlan had stared at Caesar for a long moment before he chuckled. "Leave him. I'm feeling generous today. But spread the sand, Ranald. I dinna want tae be disabling vehicles I'm no' here tae plunder."

Devlin had known what was going to happen, had tried to get Megan out of notice and harm's way before the reavers owned up to what they had come for. But she'd stood there and argued with him until it was too late, until she'd drawn the leader's amorous attention. Laird MacDuell indeed. A pretension, no doubt, and irrelevant under the circumstances. She'd been abducted. Devlin and the coachman had been bound hand and foot and rolled down the ditch.

Devlin's one bit of resistance, slamming a fist into young Gilleonan's face, hadn't got him shot, thank God, but it did get him a good-sized headache from Ranald's pistol butt cracking against the back of his head. A hard head, since the blow had merely dazed him, rather than rendering him senseless, and his shouted curses and promises of retribution could be heard as they rode away, again irrelevant, since he couldn't give chase any more than Megan could get loose of the thick arms locked about her waist.

She was indeed furious, abduction a new experience she could have done without. There was nothing romantic or exciting about it. The wild ride over rough terrain that did not include roads quickly became quite torturous, especially since Megan absolutely refused to relax against her abductor, and was also sitting at a twisted angle in front of him. When he'd make a sharp turn, the breath would be squeezed out of her—damned Scot didn't know his own strength—but she said nothing, saving up her complaints to let him have them with both barrels once they alighted—if they ever alighted.

She became quite cold after the sun set. The horses were merely plodding along now considering the speed they'd given throughout the afternoon. She was beginning to wonder if the Scots meant to run their animals to death when they finally stopped and dismounted by a small stream. In quick order a fire was started, some food was dug out of saddlebags, and blankets were tossed on the ground. Camp. They actually meant to sleep—outdoors.

Megan groaned as she was lifted off MacDuell's horse, the stiffness in her joints screaming to attention. But even though she could barely stand on her own, she immediately slapped away the hands that had helped her down. Lachlàn was amused by that and even chuckled. Megan stepped back so she could better scowl at him.

"You won't get away with this," she said.

"I already have," he replied cheerfully.

"Just where do you think you're taking me?"

"Home."

A lot that brief statement told her, so she tried a different tack, warning him, "I won't stay there, wherever it is."

"You're no' getting into the spirit of the thing," he complained. "I'm doing you a favor, giving you this opportunity tae devote a wee bit more thought tae your choice of husband."

"What you're doing is showing me that I prefer an uncouth Englishman, who isn't the least bit stuffy, by the way, to an uncouth Scotsman."

He clucked his tongue at her. "You're angry wi' me, I take it?"

"Absolutely."

"But you shouldna be, darlin'. How else can you make the right choice unless you get tae know me better?" She just stared at him, prompting him to add, "Dinna fash yourself, lass. You'll no' be hurt, I swear it."

"I already hurt all over. Do you Scots *always* run your horses to ground?"

He grinned at the direction in which her complaints had turned. "They're sturdy mounts, bred for endurance, no' like your fat English horses. It's sorry I am that you're a wee bit sore, but the speed was necessary."

"You don't really think you're going to be followed, do you?" she scoffed.

"For you, darlin', oh, aye, he'll come—at least he'll try tae find you. No mon in his right mind would give you up wi'out a fight. But I promise you he'll no' be having any luck. There isna a Scotsmon who can find me when I dinna want tae be found, much less an Englishmon."

Which made Megan want to sit down on the ground and cry. She was supposed to have been married by now. Granted, nothing would have changed with Devlin insisting they'd be married in name only, but still, she couldn't *not* marry with a baby on the way.

Lachlan was spreading a blanket on the ground for her. His two companions, neither as big as he was nor as finely turned out, were bemoaning the loss of Caesar loudly enough for Lachlan to hear—and disregard. He bowed, offering his hand to Megan to help her to sit. She pointedly ignored his hand and dropped stiffly to the blanket on her own.

"You're no more than a common thief, aren't you?" she asked boldly when he started to sit next to her.

He paused, but it was only a moment before he started laughing so hard he fell to his knees in front of her. "Common? Never, darlin'. There've been reavers in my family for generations gone by. So who am I tae deny such an honorable undertaking?"

There were hoots and snorts from his friends over that answer, which got them a scowl that lasted no longer than it took Lachlan to gaze at Megan again with another of his engaging grins.

"You actually see nothing wrong with stealing?" Megan ventured curiously.

"Och, now, I didnae say that. But you must know it's been many centuries that the Scots and the English have had the pleasure of raiding each other. I've merely started up the practice again."

"You're saying you only steal from the English?" she demanded, indignant on behalf of her countrymen.

He shrugged indifferently, pointing out, "We willna be reaching my home until tomorrow afternoon, so as you can see, I go out of my way tae make sure it's only English pockets I'm emptying."

"How patriotic of you," she sneered. "There are no English near where you're from?"

"A few. But can you no' see my dilemma in that? I'd have tae stop every carriage tae demand, 'Are you English, mon, or Scottish?' But Scotsmen dinna like tae be detained for silly reasons like that, you ken. So 'tis much easier tae go where I'm guaranteed a great many English will be roaming, and that's near the border."

"To my own misfortune."

"Nay, dinna say so, darlin'. You're upset, naturally. I'm confused and amazed myself at the feelings you provoke in me as well. But dinna think I make a habit of absconding with bonny lassies. You're the first."

"Lucky me."

He laughed at her continued sarcasm. "Nay, I'm the lucky one. You canna imagine how long I've been searching for a woman like you."

Since he didn't appear to be that old, no more than in his mid-twenties or thereabouts, it couldn't have been all that long, but Megan merely said, "You still haven't gotten lucky, MacDuell, since I'm already spoken for."

Which didn't daunt him in the least. "You canna really want that sour-faced Sassenach," he admonished with firm conviction.

"I most certainly can."

"But you dinna love him," he replied confidently. "That was as plain as—"

"Of course I love him. I love him so much I'm going to have his baby."

He smiled, humoring her. "A fine goal that, tae have a mon's bairn."

"You mistake me," she told him. "It's not something intended for the future—well, it is, but it's also an accomplished fact."

She said that without the embarrassment she'd expected to feel. And his expression of surprise was worth all the discomfort she'd experienced in that race across the wilds of Scotland. Only it didn't last long, and suddenly he was laughing uproariously. It took her a moment to realize the man didn't believe her.

Now what?

The devil if I know. I thought you were convincing, by the way.

Then why didn't he believe me?

Maybe because he doesn't want to.

Well, that's just dandy, isn't it? He didn't believe my lies either.

What lies?

Notice I'm not laughing.

But Megan was frowning at herself. Lachlan noticed and thought her displeasure was directed at him—which it would have been if she hadn't gotten distracted by her deluded inner voice.

"I'm sorry, darlin', but you must see how unlikely it is for a fine young lady like yourself tae be having a bairn afore you're wed, especially the bairn of a mon you dinna even like." Then suddenly he wasn't amused anymore, his expression turning dark with suspicion. "Unless he—"

Megan caught the drift his thoughts had taken and cut them off before they were completed. "He didn't, and I resent your even thinking it!"

"Och, now, there's nae need tae be losing your temper," he said with a degree of embarrassment.

"Losing it? I lost it this morning, you dense man. You had no right to steal me away from my fiancé. I was to be married today!"

Lachlan actually squirmed a bit, thinking she was getting near to tears, which he couldn't abide. "You still can be. I'm sure we can find a kirk around here somewhere."

"I won't marry you! In fact, I demand that you take me back right now!"

"Courtin's no' going tae well, Lachlan?" Gilleonan asked straight-faced, though it was obvious the man was fighting not to laugh.

"I could've told ye kidnapped brides are a passel o' trouble," Ranald added.

Megan joined her scowl to Lachlan's until both his friends turned back to face the fire. He then tried to smile at her, but she wasn't having any more of that.

"Charm has its place, but this isn't the place," she said shortly. "Now, I'm sure you're a nice man for a reaver. You might even make some girl a fine husband if you ever give up thieving. But it won't be me."

"Why dinna we sleep on it?" he said, as if her little speech wasn't to be taken seriously.

"Why don't you take me back instead?"

"Have a heart, lass. The horses couldna manage it even if I was of a mind tae let you go so soon."

"So soon? Just how long will it take you to understand I mean what I say?"

He did grin this time. "After you admit I'd make a fine husband, reaver or no'."

"Incorrigible," she said in exasperation. "Absolutely beyond redemption, too. And I thought Devlin was pigheaded," she added in a mumble for herself.

"What was that?"

"I'm not speaking to you anymore, so don't say another word to me."

"Then let me feed you and—"

"I won't eat your food either."

"Och, now, I willna let you starve, darlin'," he said quite firmly.

Megan's eyes narrowed, warning him clearly to forget whatever good intentions he had about forcing her to eat. "Just try and stop me."

"Faith, but you're a stubborn lass," he said with some exasperation of his own, but then he sighed. "Verra well, but when you get hungry, just tell me."

She snorted and turned her back on him to lie down, hitting the blanket as if it were a soft mattress, regretting that bit of temper instantly as her hand throbbed. Damn, damn, damn. This had to be Devlin's fault. If she gave it enough thought, she was sure she could find some way to blame him for her sorry plight, or at the very least, for not rescuing her. Never mind that he had been tied hand and foot. He should have been resourceful enough to get out of that and come after her.

Why don't you consider getting out of this one on your own?

How?

You aren't bound hand and foot. Once they're asleep, you can just walk away.

Are you under the mistaken impression that I know where the devil I am? I don't, you know. I could wander about lost indefinitely and really starve.

Or you could find help just around the corner.

What corner? I'm out in the middle of nowhere, if you haven't noticed.

You won't even consider it?

Certainly I will. I'll be stuck in Scotland forever if I wait for Devlin to rescue me. But if I get lost and starve, it'll be your fault.

I didn't just refuse food when my tummy was already growling.

That was a matter of principle.

What has principle got to do with escaping?

"MacDuell, I'm hungry."

Chapter 30

"Are you sleeping, lass?"

"Would it matter?" Megan grumbled, keeping her back to Lachlan, whose voice was coming unnervingly from directly behind her.

He ought to be sleeping. She'd been waiting patiently for what seemed like hours to hear some sign that he was. His two companions were snoring away. But Lachlan had been suspiciously quiet, and Megan wasn't taking anything for granted in her bid for freedom. She'd been determined to wait until she was positive he was asleep, so it was beyond aggravating to find him most definitely still awake.

"I've been thinking—"

"That's a bad habit you have, MacDuell," she cut in dryly. "You ought to give it up."

"And that's a bad habit *you* have, trying tae

277

provoke a mon's temper."

"Is it working?"

He didn't answer for a moment, tempting Megan to turn over and look at him. She resisted. And then she heard his soft chuckle. Was there nothing the man *wouldn't* find amusing? He was as bad as Devlin, not taking insults to heart, but worse, always being in such infuriating good cheer. It was almost impossible to stay mad at a man who was constantly grinning or laughing—almost.

"It's come tae me, lass, that you might be thinking I'm no' sincere in my desire tae wed you."

"Not at all. Being tossed up onto a horse is quite clarifying."

"I didnae toss you," he protested.

"My bottom disagrees."

There was a long pause, then: "I'd be happy tae massage the—"

"Don't . . . even . . . think . . . it!"

Another chuckle had Megan gritting her teeth. "Verra well, but you should know I wouldna make that offer tae just any lass."

"Is that supposed to tell me I'm special to you?" she scoffed. "After all of a few hours' acquaintance, you find me special?"

"After all of a few seconds. I warned you that you'd stolen my heart."

You'd better redirect his thoughts real quick. Hearing things like that is liable to turn your head.

My head isn't turnable, and stay out of this.

"I don't happen to believe in love at first

sight, MacDuell." Which was a lie, since Tiffany was proof that it was definitely possible. "Lust, now—"

"You're wounding me, darlin'."

"About time."

He burst into laughter. "I wish you could see as clearly as I do how well we'll deal together just as soon as your temper calms down."

"What makes you think my temper's up? It's not, you know. This is how I always am, perpetually disagreeable. It comes from being spoiled rotten, which I also am. Just ask Devlin—well, it's too late to ask him, but he would have told you it's true. He even calls me brat."

"Och, it's nae wonder you dinna like the mon," Lachlan replied in an I-just-figured-it-out tone.

"I *told* you," Megan bit out, rolling over in her frustration to castigate him royally, "I love—"

His mouth swooped down the moment she was on her back. She'd forgotten how close his voice had sounded, but he'd merely been biding his time, waiting to provoke her into facing him, in the perfect position to kiss her once she did.

Megan was shocked, not that he was kissing her—she wouldn't put anything past a damned thief—but that it was so nice, almost as nice as—no, not quite that nice. She didn't feel the surge of exciting sensations that she did when Devlin kissed her. Which wasn't to say she felt nothing, it just wasn't overwhelming.

"That'll be enough of that, MacDuell," she

said as she pushed the Scotsman back.

He was grinning down at her unrepentantly. Now why didn't that surprise her?

"You canna say you didnae like it."

"I can—but I won't," she allowed. "However, that's quite irrelevant. Or have you forgotten that I'm carrying another man's child?"

"I havena forgotten that you said so, but perhaps you're forgetting that I dinna believe it. Admit it, darlin', you're as innocent as they come."

"Naive, yes, but no longer innocent," she maintained staunchly. "Now, I know there are men who would overlook that to marry me anyway, despite the baby, but somehow I doubt you'd fall into that category. So give it up, MacDuell. My condition isn't going to go away, it's just going to get disgustingly— noticeable."

"Noticeable, but not disgusting, brat."

Megan gasped at the sound of that familiar voice. Lachlan's response was to swear quite ungentlemanly. And for a really large man, he moved incredibly fast in getting to his feet. But he had no more luck than Megan did, as she stood up more slowly, in trying to locate where Devlin was. It was just too dark beyond the immediate area of the fire to see anything but dense shadows.

"If you're waiting for an invitation tae join us, mon, it willna be forthcoming," Lachlan said. "I canna say I'm pleased at your arrival."

"What a shame," Devlin replied. "And here I was sure you were expecting me."

They swung around to find him coming slowly out of the shadows from the north, rather than from the south. Megan ate up the sight of him, overjoyed that he'd actually come for her. She wanted to run to him, throw her arms around him, shower him with kisses, but the cursory glance he gave her kept her where she was.

Lachlan was more interested in the pistol Devlin had pointed at him. "I dinna suppose you'd be considering this an unfortunate mistake?"

"Would you?"

Lachlan had the audacity to grin. "Nay, I'd no' be that stupid."

"Neither am I," Devlin said as he paused by Ranald to toss aside the gun the Scot had laid near to hand, then did the same with Gilleonan's weapon.

"Are you sure, mon?" Lachlan dared to taunt. "You seem tae have come alone."

Devlin shrugged. "A necessity, since no one else could keep up with Caesar."

"Ah, the stallion. So I made a mistake, after all, in leaving him behind."

"Generosity coming back to haunt you?"

"That it is."

Megan had heard quite enough. "Do you two think you might get beyond this idle chitchat? I'm cold, hungry, and I'd like a decent bed before I attempt sleep again."

"And here I thought I was keeping the wind off your back, darlin'."

"Is *that* what you were doing?" she asked, her tone thick with sarcasm. "I'd never have guessed."

The man *still* wasn't abashed. "She says you call her a brat," he said to Devlin. "I'm beginning tae see why. 'Course, it doesna matter a'tall when a mon looks at her," Lachlan ended with a dramatic sigh.

Megan snorted her lack of appreciation for his wit. Devlin gave her a warning look. She noticed then that Gilleonan and Ranald had been awakened by the sound of their voices, and both were eyeing Devlin with not a smidgen of the nonchalance Lachlan was displaying. Foolish of her to have forgotten that this was still a situation on the dangerous side, and she and Devlin had yet to make their escape from it.

"I won't kill a man for making a fool of himself over a pretty face," Devlin said now.

" 'Tis glad I am tae hear it."

"But daring to take what's mine deserves a black eye or two."

Megan hadn't heard that correctly. She couldn't have. Lachlan didn't doubt what he'd heard, though, and threw back his head with great guffaws. Gilleonan and Ranald were now smiling. Was she the only sane one there?

"Devlin, you don't want to do that," she pointed out in what she hoped was a perfectly calm tone.

"On the contrary, my dear," he said with an underlying determination that made her groan inwardly. "I can't think of anything I'd like to do more at the moment."

"But—"

"Do you know how to shoot a pistol?"

She blinked at the change of subject and started to retort, "Certainly," but that would have been prideful boasting, and this was no time for that. "No."

"Good," he surprised her by saying and handed his weapon over to her, but not before he had placed her finger on the trigger and aimed the gun in the direction of Lachlan's two cohorts. "You'll be more likely to shoot them if they even blink, won't you? And watch *them*, Megan, not the fight. Can you do that?"

She was too upset at that point to do more than nod. She'd never held a gun before, never shot a man before, never had a fiancé about to get pounded into the ground by a veritable giant. Watch the audience instead of the fight? She'd probably faint if she had to watch Devlin getting hurt. How was *this* going to get them out of there?

The first blow was heard, making Megan cringe. Despite Devlin's admonishment not to, and her own determination not to, she glanced swiftly toward the two combatants, then right back to the two she was supposed to keep from interfering. They didn't look the least bit inclined to interfere, hadn't even done more than sit up. And in that brief glance toward the fight, Megan hadn't been able to determine who'd been hit, though she assumed it was Devlin.

Another solid blow, another cringe, and another swift glance. But again she couldn't tell who was taking the punches, who was receiving them. All she saw was the two men circling each other, searching for openings. Not surprising was that Lachlan was grinning. Devlin wasn't. But Devlin's form, fists raised, one arm slightly extended, straight-as-a-board stance, *was* surprising.

Megan had witnessed two other out-to-really-hurt-you fights in her life, one at a fair between a local blacksmith and a traveling fighter who was there to take on all comers for the entertainment of the crowds, and another between two of her suitors who were minor lords with some small knowledge of the gentleman's art of college boxing. Devlin wasn't fighting like the blacksmith, as she would have expected. Lachlan was, but Devlin was fighting like a gentleman. Now where the devil had he learned how to do that?

She had to be mistaken. Her glances had been too brief for her to be certain. Three more fists-to-skin-and-bone sounds were heard. She resisted looking. But the two men she was watching were telling. Gilleonan winced at one point. Ranald just looked amazed.

Megan couldn't stand it anymore. She turned to watch the fight in earnest, and she hadn't been mistaken. Devlin was indeed fighting like a gentleman, with straightforward punches, lightning jabs, and not a single wild swing or wasted movement. He was also, incredibly, the one landing all the punches. His ducks and retreats were simply too fast for Lachlan. Of course, one punch from Lachlan would probably bring Devlin to his knees. The Scotsman just wasn't getting a chance to demonstrate that fact.

On the other hand, Devlin's unusual advantage didn't seem to be doing him much good. Lachlan was still grinning, for God's sake, and didn't seem to be feeling any of the damage Devlin was inflicting. And there was some visible damage now. One of Lachlan's eyes was most definitely going to turn black by tomorrow, was already red and starting to swell. His lower lip was a bit puffy. And was the left side of his jaw starting to swell, too?

Megan made her swift glances toward Gilleonan and Ranald now, continuing to watch the fight with distressed fascination. She ought to put a stop to it. Devlin had gotten what he had claimed to want, so why were they still going at it? And then it happened, what she'd feared would happen. Lachlan faked a left swing and connected with a right, squarely on Devlin's jaw. Amazingly, Devlin staggered back only two steps before he caught his balance. His form remained the same, both fists raised, which clearly said he was prepared to take more damage. Megan wasn't prepared to watch him do so.

"Enough!"

Lachlan glanced at her with an aggrieved look. "Have a heart, darlin'. I've only hit him once."

Megan stared at the Scot incredulously. By the look of him, you'd think she'd snatched a favored toy away from a little boy. Devlin didn't look too pleased either. Well, that was just too bad for both of them.

"You two might be having a great deal of fun, but I'm not having any. I'm about to have hysterics, actually, and I'll probably shoot someone by accident while I'm at it, but what do I care?"

Devlin's response to that was, "Can't you *ever* do as you're told?"

Since this was the second time in one day that she hadn't done as she'd been told by him, and the first time had put her in this predicament, she naturally turned defensive. "When you're my husband, Devlin Jefferys, you can give me orders to your heart's content, but until you make that a fact instead of an intention, don't expect me to obey you without a damn good reason."

"I *had* a good reason, brat, which you are amply demonstrating. But did you just promise to obey my every command once we're married?"

Megan opened her mouth for a quick denial, but snapped it shut, appalled that she might have done just that. "You can't hold someone accountable for what they say during hysterics," she pointed out reasonably.

Devlin snorted. "I didn't think so."

Lachlan was laughing by then. "I dinna think I'll be envying you after all, Jefferys. I could manage a week or two of her blathering, but no' much more'n that. Would you be swapping the horse for her?"

"How quickly your *sincerity* changes colors, MacDuell," Megan sneered. "And he doesn't own Caesar, he only borrowed him from my father."

"I dinna care who owns him, dar—"

"Call me darling once more and I'll shoot you!"

Since she'd turned the pistol toward him as she yelled her threat, Lachlan made no reply, and for once he wasn't grinning. But Devlin walked slowly toward her and took the weapon out of her hand.

Quietly, dryly, he said, "If you're going to shoot him, my dear, you'll have to take the safety off." This he did, then handed the pistol back to her with a smile. "Now you can shoot him."

She stared at the man she was supposed to marry and thought about shooting him instead. She didn't. She gave him a hurt look and dropped the gun at his feet, then turned and walked away from him.

"Bloody hell," he said behind her. "You didn't *want* to shoot anyone, Megan."

"That's not the point," she tossed back. "And see if I'll ever protect you again."

The Scotsmen were laughing again, all three of them this time. Megan didn't care. She'd entered the shadows beyond the camp to look for Caesar, and if she found him, she had every intention of leaving by herself.

Chapter 31

Megan's stiffness had lasted all of two minutes after Devlin had placed her on Caesar and mounted behind her. Then she'd relaxed against him and a few minutes later fallen fast asleep. She hadn't spoken to him, however. Her annoyance with him had been as plain as her red hair, but nothing new for him to worry over.

He supposed his rescue of her was not the romantic affair she might have been hoping for. She ought to be grateful he'd found her at all, for he'd had a devil of a time following their trail after the sun went down. Stumbling upon them had been pure luck, aside from the fact that the landscape provided very little in the way of obstruction to block his view of their campfire, which he'd seen from miles away.

Devlin flexed his jaw and winced. He supposed *he* ought to be grateful Megan had stopped that fight, which had been nothing but sheer folly on his part. He should have gotten her straight out of there instead of seeking revenge because his damned pride was a bit lacerated over losing her in the first place. But no, he'd thought he could take the man, despite his size. MacDuell had disabused him of that notion quickly enough. Damned Scot had a cast-iron jaw.

And the audacity of the fellow, to stand there grinning when he had had a gun pointed at him. If Devlin weren't still smarting over the whole affair, he would probably admire the chap.

MacDuell had even had the gall to ask Devlin before he left, "Do you and the lass ever get along, mon, or are you after arguing with her all the time?"

Devlin had shrugged. "I'm coming to the conclusion that she enjoys arguing. You didn't notice?"

"That I did, but do you enjoy it?"

"Not particularly."

"Then why do you want tae marry her?" Lachlan had asked baldly.

An excellent question. Devlin had merely smiled, answer enough for the Scotsman, as far as he was concerned. But the question had stayed with him as he'd gathered their horses to take with him—he was determined *not* to meet up with MacDuell again if he could help it—and gone to collect Megan. It had stayed with him after he'd found her and been given a dose of her silence, so complete that she hadn't even asked why she had to ride Caesar when he had the other horses. And she was asleep when he let the other mounts go several miles away, which would have answered the question she had stubbornly refused to ask.

But the Scot's question wouldn't go away. Why did he want to marry her, aside from it being the honorable thing to do? And he did want to. There was no denying that, after the fear and rage he'd felt when she was taken from him. He wanted her to be his wife. He wanted to have the authority over her that marriage would grant him. He wanted her in his house. He wanted her near at hand. He wanted to know where she was every minute of the day. He wanted her in his bed, though that was one thing he wouldn't insist on until she wanted it, too.

He wanted her to love him.

Good God, he'd fallen in love with Megan Penworthy!

How the devil had that happened? And no wonder his mood was so bloody rotten. Loving a girl like Megan was asking for nothing but heartache and an end to his sanity. She was beautiful, certainly. He'd give her that. But the only good thing he could say about her quirky temperament was that she didn't hold a grudge. The girl might explode frequently in anger, but her tantrums didn't last long. Although why should they, when she always had something new to get mad at the next time around.

He must be mad. On second thought, he must be trying to put a nice face on his lust. That was all. He still lusted after the girl. One visit to his mistress ought to take care of that; then he could start dealing with Megan a little more impartially. At the very least, he'd stop losing his temper, stop letting her emotions wring his guts, stop thinking about her constantly—stop wanting her so much.

'Course, he'd have to go to London to visit his mistress, but why not? He'd rusticated for nearly two months. Freddy's sister had to have married by now, or been found out for the little liar she was. And what would that matter anymore when he'd be coming back with a wife himself? Except Freddy still might want to blow his head off, but that could be dealt with when the time came.

It was nearing dawn when Devlin found the town he'd noticed on his race north. It wasn't Gretna Green, but it had a Scottish kirk, so it would serve.

The proper thing to do would be to register at the inn and get some much-needed sleep, then get married at a decent hour. But Devlin wasn't thinking of proper just then; he was thinking more in line with getting the thing done before anything else happened to prevent it.

The Scots clergyman didn't appreciate that. Neither did Megan. But a hefty donation to one, and a little bullying and prodding to the other, and Ambrose Devlin St. James, fourth Duke of Wrothston, had himself a new wife and duchess.

Megan woke to the sound of children shrieking in play and someone whistling a cheery tune. It took some time for her to realize the racket was coming from below an open window in the room where she'd finally gotten some undisturbed sleep—undisturbed until now.

She still didn't feel like getting up. She even thought about marching to the window and shouting down for some quiet. Some people had no consideration a'tall. But then she noticed the brightness in the room and decided it might be too late in the day for that kind of consideration.

How long had she slept? She had no idea, but she didn't exactly feel rested. There'd been too many interruptions—every time Caesar would slow to a trot, then when Devlin had dragged her into that church . . .

Good God, she was married! And her husband hadn't spent the night with her.

Megan looked over at the space beside her in the bed to make sure, but it was most definitely empty, the sheets still smooth. And then the memories starting returning with a vengeance: the fight, the dirty trick Devlin had played on her with the gun, the dirtier trick he'd played in marrying her while she was half asleep.

He'd asked for two rooms at this inn this morning, and had escorted her to hers, leaving her with a curt good-night and an admonishment to lock the door. She'd still been too exhausted to think anything was strange in that. Strange? No, he'd simply meant it, a marriage in name only.

Did you think he was joking?

Yes.

Well, I for one don't blame him. You never give the man any peace.

The man doesn't deserve any peace.

Then why are you crushed by his rejection?

I'm not.

You are.

Bitch.

Are you cursing yourself?

Megan turned over and hit her pillow.

Chapter 32

Megan had slept in half of her clothes. But after all the riding done yesterday, the rest were in as deplorable a condition as what she'd slept in. When she would be able to change she couldn't guess. She didn't even know if her trunk was still in that ditch with the coach, or if the coachman had managed to get the vehicle back on the road. Hopefully they would meet up with him today.

It was a splendid room that she'd been given, now that she was awake enough to notice. Scotland certainly outclassed England in the way of inns, and she'd stayed in enough this last week to know. She wondered if Devlin was throwing away good money again on account of it having been their wedding night, even though they hadn't shared it, or because this

was the only hostelry available in this town.
Probably the latter. But not for the first time,
she wondered how he came by so much money
to waste.

There was a vanity replete with perfumes,
cosmetics, and everything necessary to repair
her hair, but Megan was starting the day in a
peevish mood because of her embarrassment
over the rumpled state of her attire, especially
since the expensive furnishings in her room
declared the inn to be an elegant establishment
that only the rich could afford.

It didn't help her mood any to realize, when
she left her room, that she had no idea which
closed door along the corridor would lead her
to Devlin. And she couldn't just go knocking
on each one until she happened to find him.
The other guests certainly wouldn't appreciate that.

She was forced to go in search of someone who could direct her, but she slowed her
steps halfway down what was a grand staircase, amazed at the opulence below. So much
for thinking this was merely an inn. It had to
be a hotel, though she certainly hadn't noticed
the size of it last night. Of course, the lower
lobby had been dark when they'd arrived at
dawn, with only one light burning.

The more Megan looked around, the more
her reasoning faltered. It didn't really look like
a hotel; it looked like the foyer of someone's
home. In fact, the innkeeper who had admitted them could have been a butler. Admitted?

Devlin *had* knocked to gain entrance, now that she thought about it.

"Good afternoon, Your Grace. May I direct you to the dining room?"

It was the man who had let them in this morning, more fully dressed now, and definitely behaving like a butler. Your Grace? Megan groaned inwardly. Surely Devlin hadn't lied again about who he was.

"You may direct me to my husband, if you would," she replied.

"If you will follow me?"

She expected to be taken back upstairs, but instead he headed for a double set of doors at the end of the foyer. It turned out to be the dining room after all, a very large dining room, and Devlin was there, sitting at the head of a long table, being served lunch by not one but three uniformed maids who couldn't take their eyes off him, and were almost fighting for the honor of bringing him what he wanted.

Megan was struck by that same emotion she'd experienced when she found Devlin frolicking in the hay with Cora, and she didn't like it one bit. She waited for him to notice her. When he didn't, her temper snapped.

"Out! All of you," she said, looking straight at the maids. "There's more food before him than he can possibly eat, and the man knows how to serve himself."

The three servants weren't very quick to obey a stranger, especially one so rumpled-looking, but one look at the butler and they were gone.

"What would you like, Your Grace?" he asked Megan.

That damn title again made her wince. "Just some privacy, thank you." When he nodded but just stood there, she added, "And I'll seat myself."

The poor man seemed so appalled by that notion that Devlin stood up. "I'll seat her, Mr. Mears. But you can bring her an extra cup."

"Very good, Your Grace."

Megan waited until the butler was gone to say, "I'll seat myself," and marched down to the end of the table to do just that.

Devlin resumed his own seat. "Got up on the wrong side of the bed, did you?"

She gave him a disgruntled little smile. "You mean that splendidly comfortable bed that belongs in a bloody palace? That bed?"

Devlin sighed. "Very well, brat, get it off your chest. What are you in a snit about this time?"

Megan chose merely the most recent transgression. "You're telling that lie again, aren't you?"

He opened his mouth, closed it, then shrugged. "It seemed convenient at the time."

She frowned as she drew a basket of hot buttered muffins toward her. She could swear that wasn't what he'd been about to say.

Nonchalantly, though with some definite malice, she asked, "Can't you get arrested for impersonating a duke?"

"I should hope so."

Her frown increased. The dratted man wasn't making the least bit of sense this morning.

"Then why do you keep taking that risk?"

One of his brows rose slightly. "Are you thinking of turning me in, Your Grace?"

"Don't call me that, and yes, I ought to, and I *will* give it some thought."

He pushed a plate of ham and boiled sausages toward her. "When you do," he said as he went back to eating, "you might want to consider that you'd be turning yourself in, too, since you happen to be my wife now, and these people think you are my duchess."

Megan stared at him openmouthed for a moment before snapping, "You might have thought of that before involving me in your crime."

"Yes, I might have, but I was too bloody tired to think beyond finding us a place to sleep. The only lodgings this town boasted burned down last week."

"Oh," she said, fixing her eyes on the crumbs she was scattering from her muffin. "In that case, thank you for the comfortable bed."

Devlin put down his fork and did some staring of his own. Megan conceding a point? And actually *thanking* him for something?

"Did you get enough sleep?" he asked.

"Yes."

"Are you running a fever, then?"

She looked up, blushing slightly. "That isn't funny. You're making me out to be a monster."

"No, just a nag and a termagant, and, don't let us forget—a brat."

She gave him a furious glare. "You're not exactly per—" She had to stop as the butler returned with a cup for her. Her fingers drummed loudly on the table while the man made a production of pouring coffee and offering cream and sugar. But the second the door closed again, she said, "I'm beginning to think you're a worse bounder than that bounder you're impersonating, Devlin Jefferys."

"Good God, then there's no hope for me a'tall," he exclaimed.

He was actually smiling at her. Megan was getting angrier by the minute.

"Can you be serious for two seconds?" she demanded.

"I will if you will."

The man was impossible this morning. Megan almost got up and walked out, but her curiosity wouldn't let her. "Whose house is this, anyway?"

"It belongs to a Margaret MacGregor. She's an Englishwoman and a countess in her own right."

"Living in Scotland?"

"She married a Scot in her younger years. When he died, she elected to stay on."

Midnight-blue eyes narrowed in disapproval. "You've been gossiping with the servants, haven't you?"

"Servants don't gossip with dukes," he replied in a perfect imitation of a pompous nobleman, then spoiled it by grinning. "On the other hand, clergymen will gossip with anyone who will listen, and the one who married us happened to mention Lady MacGregor, and that she was putting up travelers until the inn is rebuilt."

But not in her best rooms, Megan didn't doubt, and with a passel of servants to wait on them. Unless, of course, they claimed to be the Duke and Duchess of Wrothston.

"You don't remember?" Devlin added.

That was another sore subject better left alone, but Megan wasn't inclined to. "No, I don't remember," she grumbled. "The one and only time I'm ever getting married, and all I have is vague memories of a ceremony in a dark church. When I'm finished being mad about it, I'll probably cry."

"The one and only time, Megan?"

She was too agitated to notice the softness of his tone. "The gentry don't divorce, Devlin Jefferys," she informed him haughtily. "If that was what you were hoping to do at a later date, you can just forget it. You're stuck with me until death do us part, and I don't intend to die so you can go about your merry way."

He laughed at that point. "Good God, the notions you get astound me sometimes. For your information, divorce isn't permissible in my family either, though why a woman who just got married should even think about—"

"I don't feel married," she interrupted him in a small, bitter voice.

Devlin became very still, not daring to even look at her. Keeping his glance on his plate, he asked carefully, "Do you want to feel married?"

Her head snapped up, but all she saw was his nonchalance. What else did she expect? He'd said that he hadn't enjoyed making love to her any more than she'd enjoyed it. Not exactly the words of a man eager to come to her bed, now that he could. But if he thought she'd ask him to after that crushing rejection— well, he could rot before she would.

"No," she said. "Whatever gave you that idea?"

His fork clattered loudly on his plate as he stood up abruptly. "A stupid question, wasn't it?" he said and headed for the doors.

"Wait a minute! Are we leaving?"

"We might as well," he replied curtly without looking back at her.

Chapter 33

Megan quickly swiped up a napkin to fill with the food she hadn't gotten a chance to eat. Wretched man. What had set him off all of a sudden? Could he possibly have wanted her to say yes? After he had rejected her? Not likely. And she wasn't about to leave herself open to another rejection. If he wanted her, he was going to have to say so.

Megan blushed furiously when the butler came in with a picnic basket full of food for them to take along, but like any good servant, he deigned not to notice. "Have a pleasant journey, Your Grace."

Her blush increased. She was really starting to hate that title that she'd once coveted.

She stuck her pilfered food into the basket as if she did such things every day and marched out into the foyer, where Devlin was waiting. As usual, he was a convenient target for her annoyance, this time over her embarrassment.

"You're going to drag me off before I even get a chance to thank our hostess?" she asked.

"Lady Margaret is visiting friends in Edinburgh and isn't expected back until tomorrow," he informed her rather stiffly. "Did you want to wait?"

"And risk the chance of her knowing the real duke?" she hissed in a whisper, since the butler was still there, though he had moved over to the front doors. "Certainly not. You can send for Caesar."

"I already have, as well as a carriage for your convenience."

"You found a carriage for rent?"

"I'm borrowing one of Lady Margaret's."

Megan groaned. "Not again." Then she added sternly, "I'm really going to have to insist that you not take advantage of this lady."

Devlin glanced down at her with a supercilious expression that would have done a duke proud. "How, pray tell, am I taking advantage?"

Megan leaned closer to whisper, "You know very well she'll think you-know-who has borrowed her carriage and not mind in the least, even be thrilled to oblige such an exalted personage when that isn't the case a'tall."

"Why deny her that gratification, then, since she's not here to miss the carriage anyway?"

That was a very good point, though entirely self-serving. "It still isn't right," she insisted.

"Then let it rest on my conscience, my dear, and be grateful you won't have to carry that cumbersome basket on your lap atop Caesar."

Another excellent point which she hadn't considered, so she said no more, though she made sure her expression told him she still wasn't happy about it.

After another moment when their transportation still hadn't shown up, she set the basket down and remarked, "That's the first time you've ever mentioned a family."

He gave her a wary glance, but she was staring across the way at the butler and didn't notice. "When did I mention family?"

"In the dining room, in reference to divorce. You can't have forgotten that quickly."

Devlin relaxed. "So?"

"So do you have family, brothers and sisters, that sort of thing?"

She appeared only mildly interested, but he knew her better than that by now. Her curiosity was more powerful than most people's. It had even led them indirectly to this state of marriage. And Devlin was sure that now that it was aroused, she'd find a hundred other ways to get that question answered if he tried to avoid it.

He should have come to that realization sooner, for there were several ways that he could use her curiosity to his own advantage. He'd have to give that more thought, but right now he said, "A grandmother, a great-aunt, and numerous distant cousins."

"No one closer than that?"

"Not for some time."

"Where is your family from?" she asked next.

"Kent."

"Near Sherring Cross?"

"Very near," he said dryly.

"I suppose that's how you ended up working in the duke's stable?"

"You could say that. Now, why are you suddenly so interested in my past?"

"It's something I ought to know about, don't you think, now that we're married?"

"I don't think. A wife doesn't need to know, nor should she know, everything about her husband."

Megan's mouth fell open. "Who says so?" she practically sputtered. "Men?"

He shrugged. "I suppose."

"And you agree with that nonsense?"

It was hard to keep from grinning, she was so incredulous.

"I believe I was a man last time I looked."

Her eyes narrowed suspiciously. "Are you teasing me, Devlin?"

"You finally noticed?"

It was his turn to be incredulous when she gave him a full smile, the one that brought out both dimples and made him want to grab her and kiss her. "That's all right, then," she told him. "I don't mind being teased." Since he was too speechless to reply, she added, "Now where were we? Oh, yes, your previously undiscussed past."

"No," he disagreed after a moment, "we were going to get to yours, or did you think this exchange of information would be one-sided?"

"But my life hasn't been all that interesting," she protested, then sighed. "Oh, very well, what would you like to know about?"

"Nothing for the moment."

Her eyes went back to narrowed. "I believe I'm going to develop a new habit—screaming. Consider yourself warned, you odious man."

Devlin burst into laughter. Megan opened her mouth to begin her new habit. But Mr. Mears opened the front doors first. The carriage had arrived. Only it wasn't their carriage, they found as they went outside. An elderly lady was being helped from it by two attendants who were quickly shooed away the moment she was firmly on the ground. And then she noticed Devlin, and a pair of faded turquoise eyes widened.

"I don't believe it," the woman said to herself. "After all these years—what the devil are you doing here, Devlin? I just had a letter from your grandmother last week, and she didn't mention you were coming."

"Because she didn't know. I didn't come for a visit, but to get married, which I've just done, and you have only to look at my bride to see why I was in such an all-fired hurry. She was planning a Season. I wasn't about to let the rest of the ton get a look at her before she was safely mine."

"How divinely romantic, Dev," Margaret exclaimed, "and so unlike you."

Megan was already blushing over his nonsense, meant to put everyone off from wondering about the real reason for such a hasty marriage. That this sweet-looking lady believed it was obvious by her answer, and Megan blushed the more. But worse and worse, the lady's eyesight must be nearly gone, for she actually thought Devlin was someone she knew. An odd coincidence, however, that both men were named Devlin. Or was it? Could the lady possibly know him somehow?

Megan was introduced. The old lady welcomed her into the "family" with a great deal of warmth and sincerity, which was making Megan feel simply horrible about the ruse Devlin was playing. But was it a ruse? Half the things Margaret MacGregor was saying didn't make a bit of sense. Then she was speaking to Devlin about people they supposedly both knew, and he was coming up with a satisfying answer for every question she asked.

Now that was just too damn coincidental as far as Megan was concerned. Something definitely wasn't right here. And Devlin kept giving Megan the most probing looks, which only increased her suspicions. But Margaret MacGregor was so genuinely pleased to see him, Megan didn't have the heart to ruin their "reunion" if she could help it. But she would have some answers the very second they were alone.

"What's this?" Margaret said now as the borrowed carriage and Caesar were finally brought up. "Don't tell me you're leaving?"

"I am."

"No, you're not."

"Yes, I am."

"You're not," Margaret insisted stubbornly. "After all these years of promising you'll visit—you're here, you'll visit a while."

"I'm not alone, Margaret," he reminded her pointedly. "And I have obligations. Duchy doesn't even know yet that I've married."

"Oh." She thought about that for a moment, then laughed. "You mean for once I actually know something about you before my sister does? She'll be furious with me for that." She laughed again, enjoying the prospect, then ended with a sigh. "Very well, it looks like I'll have to do the visiting as usual, but then I've got nothing better to do, whereas you never have enough time for anything. Don't know how you found the time to meet your bride, much less elope with her, but mind you, I expect to hear all about it when I come to Sherring Cross."

"Sherring Cross?" Megan said in a small voice that wasn't heard, since Margaret hadn't quite finished with her admonishments.

"Now that you have a wife," the old lady continued, "you can't spend *all* your time in the House of Lords, dear boy. I'll expect lots of great-great nephews and nieces to carry on in the St. James tradition—"

Margaret paused now because Devlin was suddenly groaning for no good reason. But before she could ask what was wrong, his beautiful young wife was calling him a nasty name and kicking him in the shin, quite viciously, Margaret noted with a sympathetic wince.

He yelped, and lifted his leg to squeeze the injured area. Hopping around on one foot for a moment, he didn't notice that his wife wasn't staying around to be reprimanded.

"I say, Devlin, should she be riding that animal?" Margaret asked.

"What animal?" He swung around only to see Megan setting Caesar into an immediate gallop. "Bloody hell. Megan, come back here!"

He didn't exactly expect her to obey him. She didn't.

Chapter 34

Since she wasn't paying any attention to where she was going, Megan came upon another town quite by accident. It was more a village, no bigger than Teadale, but the sight of its one eating establishment reminded her that she didn't have her purse or anything else that would buy her a meal. Like her bonnet, what little money she had brought with her had been left behind in the coach yesterday.

No money for food or lodgings. How was she supposed to get home? But the thought of returning to her husband was out of the question. She'd rather go hungry. And she had Caesar. With him she could reach home in half the time, only three days likely. She wouldn't starve in just three days, would she?

But what was the point? He'd only show up

a few days later, so she'd have gone hungry for no good purpose. Then she'd simply leave again, and be better prepared the next time.

The trouble with that plan was that he had the right to drag her back if he wanted to, as many times as he wished. He could even lock her up if he got tired of chasing her around the country. She'd given him that right by marrying him.

But she hadn't married *him*, she'd married Devlin the horse breeder . . . Maybe he hadn't put the right name on the marriage paper, so she might not be married to him after all. That was wishful thinking that she couldn't count on. He'd done the noble and responsible thing in his mind, after all, so he'd have made sure he'd done it right.

Only she didn't want to be married to him now. She hated him and meant it this time. He'd lied to her, deceived her, misrepresented himself, and who knew what else.

Shouldn't you be telling him all this?

Yes, by God!

Megan turned around and headed north again. And again she was too deep in angry thoughts to pay attention to where she was going. But Caesar stuck to what road there was, and it wasn't all that long before the carriage was there and was almost upon her before she even noticed it.

Megan stopped. Devlin did the same. She didn't dismount. He leaped out of the carriage and yanked her off Caesar, not giving

her an opportunity to leave again on the one
animal he'd have no chance of catching up
with. Megan, too intent on her fury, didn't
even notice his precaution.

"I have a number of things to say to you, *Your
Grace*," she began while in his arms—he was
carrying her from the horse to the carriage—
putting all the contempt she could muster into
his title.

"You can say them in the carriage," he began
calmly enough, then abruptly released some of
his own anger, growling, "Don't you *ever* take
off on my horse again, Megan, when I'm not
on him with you!"

"*Your* horse? He happens to be—"

"*My* horse."

"I see," she replied stiffly. "Another lie, and
one you even involved my father in."

"Actually, your father confessed he'd have
difficulty with subterfuge, so for the duration
of my stay, he did in fact own Caesar in what
you might call a short-term, cashless sale, to
terminate with my leaving—which I've done."

"I don't care how nicely you twisted it
around for my father's honest scruples. It was
still another lie, *Ambrose St. James!*"

"Ambrose *Devlin* St. James," he corrected
her, dumping her into the carriage none too
gently. "No one calls me Ambrose, brat, so
don't you start."

She had to yell after him, because he'd turned
to tie Caesar's reins to the back of the carriage.
"I don't care what everyone else calls you! I

have a few choice names that are more appropriate. Care to hear them?"

"No!"

That deflated her for a moment, long enough to notice that he was limping as he came back to get in the carriage. She looked pointedly at his leg and said, "If that's to make me regret kicking you, it's not working. I'm thinking of doing it aqain—in the same spot—only harder."

"Appreciate the warning, so I'll return the favor. Kick me again with those pointed little shoes of yours, and you will travel across England barefoot."

"You wouldn't dare!"

He cocked a brow at her. "I thought we had established the extent of my daring."

"You are exactly what you claimed you were—probably the only true words you ever said—a bounder, a cad, and I am not going to speak to you for the rest of my life!"

"Do you promise?"

Obviously not, for she wasn't done railing at him. "You are the most wretched man who ever breathed breath. The most despicable man in all of England—no, make that the world. And you're probably a terrible duke, too."

"You might want to reserve judgment on that, since you haven't actually met him yet."

"Met who?"

"His Grace, the Duke of Wrothston."

Her eyes flared. "Are you telling me I was mistaken in what I heard, that Margaret

MacGregor isn't your great-aunt, and she didn't say she was expecting some St. James nephews and nieces from—"

"Yes, yes, you heard exactly right," he cut in impatiently. "I *am* the fourth Duke of Wrothston. But kindly recall that I've been playing a role since we've met, which is what you're in such a snit about. Naturally, my behavior had to conform to that role, and that behavior was my interpretation—what I'm trying to say, Megan, is the way I've acted with you is completely different from how I normally am. I am usually quite circumspect, utterly proper, and I've even been called stuffy, though I can't imagine why."

But that wasn't the man she had fallen in—

I wasn't going to say that.

Yes, you were.

Stay out of this.

"Are you claiming you're not the least bit arrogant or bossy?" she asked.

He flushed slightly. "It's called leadership, not being bossy, and so a few of my own traits got mixed up in the role. I didn't say I'd got the horse breeder down perfect."

"Oh, I agree absolutely. If you had, you might not have been so provoking."

"Actually, I enjoyed our verbal skirmishes— some of the time, since I so rarely get to let go like that. Are you saying you didn't?"

She would be lying if she said no. "That's entirely beside the point," she answered primly. "The fact remains that you misrepresented yourself from day one. I did *not* marry a duke."

"But you wanted to," he reminded her with a good deal of smugness.

Megan's face went up in flames of mortification as she recalled the day she'd told him, *him*, that she was going to marry the Duke of Wrothston. How he must have laughed over her vain presumption and . . .

"My God," she said, appalled as the rest came back to her. "You rode all the way to Hampshire just to humiliate me with an improper proposition so I would no longer want to marry you. I didn't realize you despised me that much."

She was no longer angry, she was deeply hurt, and Devlin was horrified that he'd caused it. "Dammit, that is *not* why I went to Hampshire. I was merely annoyed because you were so bloody determined. I thought you were a scheming opportunist out to marry a title no matter how despicable the man holding that title might be. What I did was in the way of a lesson. I certainly didn't think it would work to put you off the idea altogether."

"How delighted you must have been to find out otherwise," Megan replied bitterly. "And appalled to end up caught anyway. I suppose you now think I got myself in my present condition on purpose."

"Don't be ridiculous," he snapped. "It takes two to get you in that condition."

"But you were foxed at the time, and I, of course, am a scheming opportunist who would have taken quick advantage of that."

"Bloody hell, weren't you listening to me? I said I thought that previously. I don't think it now."

"And you're a very good liar, Your Grace, proven once again."

"You don't believe me?" he asked incredulously.

"Of course I don't believe you. Or are you going to tell me you would have asked me to marry you if a baby weren't involved?"

She was infuriating him as usual. "How the bloody hell should I know what I would have done down the road, which is entirely irrelevant now. You *are* expecting. We *are* married. And you're being unreasonable."

"I'm not surprised *you'd* think so. Any time *I'm* right, I'm unreasonable."

"You're wrong, dammit!"

Her chin went up in the air as she looked away from him. "I don't care to discuss it anymore."

"Then I'll bloody well count my blessings."

Chapter 35

Megan didn't know the English countryside well enough to realize that the coach that had been retrieved in Scotland had changed directions midway through the return trip. She had assumed she was being taken home to Sutton Manor. By the time she noticed a few landmarks that seemed vaguely familiar, it didn't occur to her that she might have seen them years ago, rather than last week. But not long after that, she had no trouble in identifying the magnificence of Sherring Cross, which suddenly loomed on the horizon.

She was as spellbound as the first time she'd seen this ducal estate spread out across the land, but not for the same reason. It really was a grand edifice worthy of royalty. The trouble was that *her* husband owned it and she shouldn't be his wife.

Devlin was napping across from her—or pretending to. He'd been doing a lot of that lately, to avoid her sulky looks, she supposed. He'd given her his explanation of why he'd assumed the guise of a horse breeder. "Freddy" and "Sabrina" meant nothing to her, and so she hadn't been all that impressed that there had been a dire reason for his subterfuge.

But she had made a guess and said, "You told my father you were a duke, didn't you? That's why he was so pleased to have me marry you, isn't it?"

"I told him merely to expedite the matter."

"But you couldn't tell me?"

"When you were so enjoying your resentment over having to marry a horse breeder? Why spoil it for you?"

Answers like that had kept their conversation to a minimum, but Megan wasn't used to keeping her unhappiness bottled up, and she'd done so long enough. She leaned forward to wake Devlin, only to hesitate.

Not in your present mood, or are you going to start a fight with him only minutes away from being descended upon by his servants?

I don't suppose that would make a good impression, would it?

Definitely not. It's bad enough that you pity him for marrying you; at least let his servants be happy for him—until they get to know you.

Well, aren't you the bitch today. And he deserves to be pitied. I've ruined his life, remember?

What about your life? It's just as ruined.

But it was my fault—

Aha! 'Bout time you remembered that.

I hadn't forgotten. But before, I'd only ruined Devlin's life, which didn't have all that far to go to be ruined. And there was every chance that marriage to me would have improved his lot, despite his contrary opinion. But now I've ruined a duke's life, which is a whole different matter. It's no wonder he hates me.

You know, you ought to be finding some good in this mess, instead of nursing all the dreary aspects.

There isn't any good to find.

What about your getting just what you originally wanted—a duke?

The original plan included him loving me.

All right, scratch that. What about the fact that you're going to get to live at Sherring Cross?

I don't care anymore.

Liar, you fell in love with this house.

It's a bloody mausoleum like Tiffany said.

It's better than a stable.

That's true.

"You're awfully quiet." Devlin's voice came to her softly. "Nervous?"

She gave him only a brief glance before looking back out the window. "That's convenient timing you have, waking just as we arrive."

"What can I say? I have an excellent inner clock."

Megan snorted. "And no, I'm not nervous. Nor was I quiet. You forget, I talk to myself."

"You're right, I did forget. And anyone who

talks to herself never lacks for company, does she? You'll have to let me listen in on one of those conversations sometime. They must be fascinating."

She recognized humoring when she heard it, but decided that was better than the anger he'd displayed at the last mention of this subject. "I suppose you would find them fascinating, since they're usually about you. But I'm afraid I'll have to refuse your eavesdropping. My conversations are private—and quite silent."

"You mean you don't talk aloud to yourself?"

"Of course not."

He frowned sternly. "That's not the impression you gave me, Megan."

She shrugged, remembering that she'd encouraged him to think she might be a little crazy in order to give him an excuse to call off the wedding—and he'd been furious about it then. "It's not my fault if you misinterpret what I say."

"Isn't it?"

The coach stopped, saving Megan from answering that incriminating question. Devlin usually opened the door, but he wasn't quick enough for the bevy of footmen who appeared instantly. More started pouring out of the house as soon as it was realized that this wasn't a guest arriving, but the duke. And between the coach and the house, Megan heard more "Your Graces" than she ever hoped to hear again, and that was nothing compared with the commotion once they reached the mammoth entry hall, where it seemed every servant in the house wanted to welcome home the master. At some point Devlin got around to introducing his wife, and then the "Your Graces" started all over again.

Megan didn't know how she managed to get through it—it seemed the butler, John, and Mrs. Britten, the housekeeper, were determined to give her the name and duty of everyone present—but that they were all so genuinely welcoming quickly alleviated the nervousness she'd denied having.

Devlin had a moment to stand back and watch her interact with his people, and he was frankly dumbfounded to witness a Megan he'd never seen before. He'd done the unthinkable and brought a bride home without giving the household any warning to prepare for her, yet she was putting the frantic ones at ease by swearing she'd like to view the grounds first, then some of the house—which was undoubtedly true, since the *stables* were on the grounds—before she was shown to her rooms, giving them the time they needed to prepare those rooms.

He'd been too nervous when she'd met Margaret to notice her behavior or even what she'd said to his aunt. But this time he listened to her every word and watched her conduct herself graciously, like the perfect lady, and finally his amazement got the better of him and the words just tumbled out. "Good God, where did my brat go?"

He knew it was a mistake instantly. He saw Megan's back stiffen, watched her swing around to face him, felt the pain explode in his shin, then watched her eyes widen at the realization of what he'd provoked her into doing before his entire household. He wasn't surprised that she then burst into tears and ran out of the hall. He felt like doing the same.

He knew as well as anyone that first impressions were lasting impressions, and he'd thoughtlessly ruined Megan's introduction to his household, possibly undermining her authority. He had no excuse except that he'd been under the same strain as she this past week—and he hadn't been behaving normally since he met her.

Short of replacing the entire staff, which was displaying various degrees of shock and embarrassment, he offered an explanation. "We've been traveling continuously for two weeks. My wife, naturally is exhausted because of it, and so not quite herself."

"You surely must be exhausted as well," John said beside him, and it was thirty-some years in the household that made him bold enough to add, "Because I don't believe I've ever seen you do anything so stupid—Your Grace."

Devlin heard several murmurs of agreement, enough to realize that the blame was going where it belonged. He almost laughed in relief, but managed a serious "Quite right, John. Truth is, I haven't been at all myself since I met the young lady."

"That's love, sir, if you don't mind my saying so," Mrs. Britten volunteered.

"Is it? Then I'd better get used to it, hadn't I?"

The staff was back to smiling at that point, which was an excellent time for Devlin to take his leave to search for his furious wife. He owed her a thoroughly contrite apology this time, though he'd be lucky to get it out before she kicked him again. No doubt about it, he was definitely going to have to buy that girl some softer shoes.

Chapter 36

Megan was nowhere to be found in the stables. Devlin had hoped otherwise. He knew she adored horses. He had counted on the sight of so many Sherring Cross Thoroughbreds to charm her out of her current mad, or at least lessen it somewhat, so she'd listen to what he had to say.

One of the gardeners finally mentioned he'd seen her heading for the lake. Devlin had a moment of panic, considering the state of upset she'd been in, and treated the man to the unprecedented sight of the Duke of Wrothston racing hell-bent down a tree-lined path.

He saw her from a distance, sitting on the bank away from the boating dock. She looked like a veritable hoyden with her bonnet removed and her hair released from its constraints to form a bright red cloak down the dull gray of her traveling jacket. She had her skirt raised to her knees, and one foot dangled in the icy water.

Devlin could perhaps thank the icy water for dissuading her from jumping in, if she'd been of that mind, but now that he saw her, he knew how ridiculous that notion of his had been. Megan wasn't the type to hurt herself when she was upset. She was spoiled enough to prefer making her antagonists suffer right along with her. No, maybe not spoiled in that. It was human nature to retaliate. He'd caught himself doing it lately. She just did it with such a flair.

He approached her cautiously. She heard him and stiffened, but didn't turn around to see who was disturbing her peace. Was she still crying? God, he hoped not. He'd prefer her volatile temper anytime to her tears, for, like most men, he became a blithering idiot when faced with them.

With that in mind, he said the one thing guaranteed to provoke her. "Stubbed your foot, did you?"

Devlin groaned inwardly when all she said was a quiet "Yes."

He dropped down to his knees behind her in the soft mulch of the bank. His hands rose to draw her back against him, but he stopped himself, afraid she might tumble into the water in an effort to get away from him.

"I'm sorry, Megan."

"For what?"

"For putting my leg in the way of your foot."

She made him wait for a reply while she put her stocking and shoe back on, but finally she encouraged him with a surly tone. "You won't be forgiven for that."

"For my thoughtless words?"

"Nor for that."

"For being so surprised at your impeccable behavior?" he tried.

"Possibly for that."

Even though she couldn't see it, he kept his relieved grin to himself. "You were doing splendidly, by the by, and no one faults you for—for stubbing your foot. All censure has been directed where it belongs. In fact, my butler has assured me that I've never behaved so stupidly."

"I disagree. I can recall any number of—"

"One apology at a time, brat."

At that she stood up abruptly, so abruptly her derriere bumped into his chin. She swung around with a startled "Oh," but then remarked with what he could swear was a touch of humor, "Daring, weren't you, getting so close to me?"

"Not at all. Cold water isn't just good for cooling off lust. It also cools off tempers."

She amazed him by actually laughing. "You wouldn't throw me in."

"Possibly not. With that cumbersome train on your skirt, I'd probably have to jump in to save you, and I'd rather not, since I can assure you that my lake is much colder than your pond."

"I don't recall your even having a lake."

"Undoubtedly you couldn't tear yourself away from my stable to explore further."

She detected the ill humor in that statement, but chose to ignore it. "Actually, I saw a great deal of your house. One of your maids was having a fine time impressing Tiffany and me. Even showed us your private suite—well, only a peek."

"Were you impressed?"

"Oh, absolutely. Why do you think I wanted to marry the Duke of Wrothston?"

The taunt cut him to the quick. He should have realized she wouldn't let the matter of his embarrassing her go so easily, that she'd be getting even in some other way. And she'd chosen a truly sore spot to strike at.

"I recall your saying it was because of my stables," he replied with deceptive mildness.

"That, too," she said with a smile, then sauntered away, unaware of the black mood she was leaving him with.

He didn't attempt to follow her, too angry to trust what he might say. For a good hour he sat there brooding over his misfortune. And not once in that time did it occur to him that Megan might have been teasing him. The subject was too touchy for him, too painful, so he naturally assumed she must know that.

*   *   *

"I hear you made an ass of yourself upon your arrival," the Dowager Duchess of Wrothston said without preamble as she entered Devlin's office—also without knocking. "Sorry I missed it, but—good God, Devlin, what have you done to yourself? You look positively disgraceful—and have your valet cut that hair immediately."

Devlin leaned back in the chair behind his desk and twisted an overgrown lock around his finger. "You don't like it? This is what happens when one rusticates. Would you like to hear a few other things that can happen?"

"Am I getting the impression that you're annoyed with me, dear boy?"

"Quite possibly."

"Very well, we'll do this your way." And she sat down across from him to visibly brace herself. "Tell me what other things can happen."

"One could go insane."

"That hadn't occurred to me, but I suppose it's possible. What else?"

"One could get married."

"So John *wasn't* ribbing me? You actually came home with a bride?"

"There are a number of things I'd call her, but bride isn't necessarily one of them."

Lucinda St. James cocked a silver-white brow at him. "Trouble already?"

Devlin snorted. "Already? Never anything but."

"I believe I'll form my own opinion, since

you're in such a tetchy mood. Where is the gel?"

Devlin shrugged. "The stable would be as good a guess as any."

Duchy's brow shot a little higher, since it was after ten o'clock at night. "This late?"

"The time of day or night is never an issue when *she* wants in a stable."

She started to say something, then changed her mind. "I'm not going to touch that one."

"Don't blame you a'tall," Devlin retorted dryly.

"Very well, you've kept me dangling long enough. Who is she?"

"Squire Penworthy's daughter."

"Well, I'll be damned," Duchy said with a grin that told Devlin what he'd suspected.

"You ought to be. What maggoty reasoning gave you the notion that I would take to that redhead?"

"Now how could I possibly know that?" she asked with perfect innocence.

"But you hoped."

"I suppose I did."

"Care to tell me why?"

"I met her a number of years ago."

"So I've learned to my regret."

She gave him an annoyed look for that cryptic interruption. "Then you know her father brought her here to purchase one of our Thoroughbreds."

"And guess what she named that mare?"

"Something silly, no doubt. She was only a child, after all."

"I've always thought the name was ridiculously silly myself, which is why I never use it."

Both of Duchy's brows shot up. "You don't mean—not Ambrose?"

"*Sir* Ambrose, actually," he replied, at which point his grandmother burst into laughter. "I fail to see the humor in that."

"You wouldn't, dear boy, but then you're as stuffy as your grandfather was at seventy. Comes from too much work and little time for anything else, which I have been *trying* to break you of. You were under his wing too long, that's your problem. But I'm here to tell you he *wasn't* like that when I married him, and you're too damn young to be taking after him."

"I do *not* consider myself stuffy—nor does Megan, for that matter."

"Delighted to hear it, but then that's one of the reasons I'd 'hoped.' The gel makes a lasting impression—at least she did on me. I've found myself thinking about her quite often over the years."

"What'd the minx do, set fire to the furniture with her temper?"

Duchy chuckled. "Didn't notice any temper. But I did notice a great deal of enthusiasm and precocious charm. She was a delightful little chit, with an outspokenness that was quite amusing. It was also vividly apparent that she was going to be a great beauty. Is she?"

"Without equal," Devlin allowed grudgingly.

"Then where's the harm done? I certainly saw none in putting you where you could meet her and might be influenced by her vivaciousness."

"Playing Cupid doesn't become you, Duchy," he said disagreeably. "You'd met Megan Penworthy only once, six years ago when she was no more than a child, and on that one meeting you throw your only grandson to the wolves. I'm disappointed in you."

"So I gather. Wolves, Devlin?"

"Vixens, then."

"I take it you're trying in your ambiguous way to tell me she's not the girl I thought she was."

"Not at all. I'm sure that girl is still there and a great many people get to meet her quite frequently. I'm just not one of them."

Duchy sighed in exasperation. "Kindly remember that I didn't create the necessity for you to disappear for a while. I merely took advantage of it. The fact remains that you've gone through most of your adult life expecting to marry Marianne, so, quite correctly, you weren't looking around for anyone else. But that marriage did not take place as planned, and when it didn't, you should have immediately started a search for another bride. Did you? No, you did not. You were too set in your ways already, and too immersed in your work, even though you know full well that you have a responsibility to marry and produce a son for Wrothston."

"Why does this sound all too familiar to me?" he asked dryly.

"Because I have a duty to harp on it, and at least I know *my* duty."

"Haven't I seen to mine?"

Duchy lost patience with him. "You're pulling teeth, is what you're doing. If you don't like the gel, what'd you marry her for?"

"Who says I don't like her? No, actually, just now I *don't* like her, but what the hell's that got to do with it? It certainly doesn't stop me from lusting after her every time she comes near me, even when she's not near—bloody hell, any damn time of the day, for that matter!"

"I'm going to pretend you didn't say that."

"Beg pardon."

"As well you ought to," she retorted indignantly. "Now, before I expire of exasperation, what, exactly, is the problem, Devlin?"

"She doesn't love me."

Chapter 37

"He doesn't love me."

Lucinda St. James sat back, amazed to hear those familiar words in answer to her question. She had been expecting something else entirely, the hot temper Devlin had spoken of, possibly some haughty indifference. After all, the chit had far surpassed Lucinda's predictions in the way of beauty. She certainly hadn't expected to find the same dejection that her grandson had displayed—to the same question.

She had called on the new Duchess of Wrothston early this morning, and was received in the formal sitting room, a grand chamber where Devlin usually conducted his less official business. It divided his suite of

rooms from his wife's, a division that apparently was much wider than the thirty-foot length
of the room.

Megan had been reserved at first, understandably, but after they'd reminisced about
their first meeting, she'd relaxed enough to
show Lucinda glimpses of the vivacious child
the elderly woman remembered from six years
ago. But she could also see the unhappiness
Megan was trying to hide, which was what
had prompted her to ask the same question
she had put to Devlin last night. Getting the
exact same answer was a revelation.

Carefully, because the situation called for
delicacy—matters of the heart were so damned
touchy—Lucinda asked, "What makes you
think so?"

"If a man loves you, he'd tell you so,
wouldn't he?" Megan replied.

"He ought to do that, yes."

"Well, Devlin's told me that I've ruined his
life. He didn't want to marry me, you see. He
went to a great deal of trouble to put me off
the idea."

"The idea?" Lucinda said. "Then you'd
already decided to marry him?"

"The duke, not him."

"But, my dear, he *is* a duke."

"I know that now, but I didn't know it before
I married him."

"Then who did you think you were marrying?"

"A horse breeder. Didn't you know he'd been

masquerading as one?"

"He was supposed to be a stableboy, but that's neither here nor there. So weren't you the least bit pleased to end up with a duke instead of a horse breeder?"

"Pleased?" Megan exclaimed. "He deceived me. I was bloody well furious—oh! I beg your pardon, Your Grace."

"My dear, we're family now. I'll expect you to call me Duchy, and to feel free to speak your mind to me, good or bad." And then she leaned forward to confide in a whisper, "I've been known to swear a little myself on occasion. Not in public, mind you, nor where that stick-in-the-mud grandson of mine might hear me. He thinks I can do no wrong, which is as it should be. Can't very well chastise him for his swearing if he knows I do, now can I?"

Megan shook her head in agreement, grinning, and in that moment they became fast friends. "Wish I'd thought of that. But then Devlin takes such delight in complaining about my bad habits, it'd be selfish of me to mend my ways."

Lucinda burst out laughing. "You're just what that boy needs," she stated positively. "Someone to shake him out of his stuffed shirt."

"He doesn't think so," Megan replied with a return of her dejection.

"Are you still angry that he's a duke instead of a horse breeder?"

"Yes—no—I don't know," Megan ended with a sigh.

"He happens to think you're delighted with the title—and his stables."

Megan made a face. "Shows what a dense man he is. I'd told him I was going to marry Ambrose St. James merely to impress him into ending his antagonism and insults, which is all I'd been getting from him since he showed up. 'Course, he couldn't leave it at that and be impressed. He had to know why I'd decided on Wrothston. But I wasn't about to tell *him* the real reason. It was none of his business. So I mentioned that I liked the duke's stable, just to put him off the subject." Megan's eyes widened with the realization. "I can see now how that might have annoyed him, him being the duke in question."

"That wouldn't be the half of it, my dear," Lucinda said with a chuckle. "The boy's had women making fools of themselves over him for as long as I can remember. Same thing went on with his father, and my husband, for that matter. Damned St. James looks *are* extraordinary. It must have been a shock to the dear boy to find a woman who wasn't instantly enamored of him, and who might even prefer his stable to him. Good God, I wish I could have seen his expression when he heard that. 'Course, you weren't even aware that you were bending his nose out of joint."

"A shame, since that is one of my little pleasures," Megan said, straight-faced.

"Thought it might be." Lucinda grinned. "But what was the real reason you were after a duke, if you don't mind my asking?"

Megan shrugged. "It was a good reason, an excellent reason, though it would probably seem quite silly to you. I was snubbed, you see, cut to the quick, actually, by our reigning hostess, Lady Ophelia Thackeray. For two years I'd been waiting and hoping for one of her coveted invitations, but she finally made it quite clear that I'd never get one. Tiffany is sure that it was because of this damn face of mine—you remember Tiffany, don't you? My dearest friend, who was with me the day we bought Sir Ambrose?"

"Yes, but—"

"Now there's another thing Devlin got all huffy about, what I named my horse. I'd been paying the duke a compliment, because I thought there was no horse finer than mine, but Devlin didn't see it that way."

"He wouldn't," Lucinda said dryly.

"But anyway, Tiffany is sure that Lady O wouldn't have me at one of her parties because she's got three daughters she's trying to marry off. That's well and fine, but to never get one of her invitations, when the whole parish has got one at least once, implies there's something wrong with me. That's when I decided to marry a title more lofty than hers—she's Countess of Wedgwood—and bend *her* nose out of joint with it. That might sound petty and vengeful to you—it really does, doesn't it?—but I was angry and hurt at the time."

"But why Devlin?"

"He was the grandest lord I could think of, and I *do* happen to like his stable. But he was only a goal to work toward. I'd have to meet him first, and fall in love with him—that was a priority that Tiffany and my conscience weren't going to let me overlook, because I wasn't planning on ruining my life just to set Lady O on her ear. I wouldn't marry a man I didn't love, or wasn't sure that I could love, no matter how lofty his title. 'Course, I saw no reason to tell Devlin that. And he was determined to put me off the idea of *him* as my choice."

"How exactly did he do that without revealing to you who he was?"

"He told me the duke was a bounder, a cad, a seducer of innocents."

"He most certainly is not," Lucinda said with a good deal of huffiness.

"That's what I said. 'Course, I hadn't met the duke yet, so I was defending a man I didn't know. Well, Devlin then arranged to prove it to me. He showed up at a masked ball I attended as himself, the duke, and promptly propositioned me to be his mistress."

"He didn't!"

"He did."

"But that's so unlike him."

"I'm afraid I have to disagree. That was just one of many insults I've had from that man. At any rate, he then had the gall to be surprised when I returned and told him—the horse breeder—that I hoped I'd never see the duke again."

Lucinda sat back, nearly speechless. "How, might I ask, did you two ever manage to get through all that muck to an altar?"

"I'm entirely to blame for that, though I'm not about to admit it to him. But the truth is, I unknowingly *and* unintentionally instigated my own seduction. Damned curiosity of mine did it. And it was so nice, the kissing part, but I didn't care for what came after. He didn't either. He said so. In fact, he so disliked it, he said we'd have a marriage in name only."

Lucinda got over her embarrassment with this subject quickly enough upon hearing that last. "The devil he did," she said angrily. "He can't do that. He's got a responsibility to produce the next duke. He can't very well do that if he doesn't—well, if he doesn't."

"Actually, he can, if the child I'm carrying turns out to be male. Didn't he tell you I'm going to have a baby, and that's why we were forced to marry?"

"No, the damned boy must have forgotten to mention that little tidbit."

Chapter 38

It was two days before Megan visited the stables to discover that Devlin had arranged to have Sir Ambrose delivered to Sherring Cross for her. She was pleased to see her mare again, but she was actually even more pleased to have a reason to seek Devlin out, to thank him for his thoughtfulness. She shouldn't need a reason to speak with her husband, but she felt she did.

She had barely seen him since their arrival, much less talked to him. She had been led to the formal dining room to dine alone with him last night—Duchy was conspicuously absent—but eating at different ends of a twenty-foot-long table was not conducive to conversation.

She'd noted the change in him without comment, the elegant attire, the very correct posture and movements. He was every inch the duke now—well, not quite every inch. He hadn't cut his hair yet. Duchy had complained over breakfast this morning that he was leaving it long just to annoy her. Megan decided it was for her own benefit so she wouldn't forget that he was the man she'd married—as if she could.

She'd only had one remark for him last night before they parted to go to their separate bed-chambers, and that only because two hours of formal silence at that long table had gotten on her nerves, and she wasn't up to attacking his *new* self yet.

"It's patently clear now why you made such a lousy horse breeder. The next time you think to impersonate a member of the working class, leave your fine shirts at home, as well as your arrogance."

She'd gone to sleep regretting those sulky words, which hadn't even gotten a reply other than a condescending lifting of his brows, meant to exasperate her, no doubt. Then again, his grandmother possibly had the right of it. Megan had confided to her that the Devlin she knew was argumentative, disagreeable, and disrespectful, only to be told that simply wasn't Devlin St. James, that such behavior had to have been part of the role he'd been playing.

Megan sincerely hoped not, for the very proper, unflappable Devlin she'd dined with last night was a bore. Still, she was simply going to have to make an effort to get along with him, and to stop trying to provoke him into the same state of unhappy feelings she was in. Which was why she was glad of an excuse to speak with him now. She would be pleasant. She would offer an olive branch. He was her husband, for better or for worse. She was tired of the worse.

Megan entered the house by a side entrance, where the corridors were almost mazelike, though they eventually led to the main block where Devlin's office was located. She was nearly there when she heard a voice that was vaguely familiar raised in anger.

" . . . won't do you a bit of good to tell me he's not here when I bloody well know he is. I've had spies watching the house day and night to inform me exactly when he returned, so get out of my way, John!"

Megan came around a corner in time to see Devlin open the door to his office and ask mildly, "Were you looking for me, Freddy?"

"Come out of hiding at last, have you?" Frederick Richardson shot back in hot temper. "And where the devil did you go, Dev, that a hundred bloody runners couldn't find you? Clear to America?"

"You ought to know me better than that. I wouldn't put up with seasickness again for any reason—even to preserve your rotten hide."

"Preserve?" the Marquis of Hampden exclaimed with a good deal of indignation. "Let's not forget who intends to shoot whom."

"Have you brought your pistol with you, then?" Devlin was still showing a marked lack of interest, which was causing a marked excess of alarm for Megan.

"Yes, by God—I've got it here somewhere."

While Freddy was searching through several of his pockets, Devlin stepped forward and socked him one, catching him so off guard that the marquis was knocked off his feet. "I believe I owed you that," Devlin said, finally showing a bit of emotion, in this case satisfaction.

"The devil you did!"

"The devil I didn't, and I'm not referring to that blind punch you gave me. You cannot begin to know what your sister's false accusation and your pigheadedness have cost me. I never would have gone to the wilds of Devonshire if it weren't for your damned temper that needed time to cool off. It's *your* fault I'm so bloody miserable now, thank you very much!" And having displayed ample emotion at last, Devlin went back into his office, slamming the door shut behind him.

"Well, what the devil did he mean by that?" Freddy asked as he picked himself up off the floor.

"I couldn't say, my lord," John replied quite correctly, only to spoil it with an opinion. "Possibly he refers to the difficulty he is having adjusting to married life."

"Married life?" Freddy replied in shock. "Married! He didn't!"

"I assure you—"

Freddy didn't wait for the butler to finish, but barged uninvited into Devlin's office. Megan turned around to retreat unnoticed, heartsick to know that she didn't just have the ruination of Devlin's life on her conscience now. She was also making him miserable.

"How dare you marry someone else when my sister—?"

"Lied, Freddy," Devlin cut in curtly without pausing in the act of pouring himself a large snifter of brandy. "When are you going to get that through your thick head? Good God, it's been two months!" On second thought, he left the glass and brought the bottle back with him to his desk. "Didn't Sabrina own up to it yet?"

"Own up to it?" Freddy blustered. "She still maintains you seduced her."

"Why that little—Duchy tells me she's not married yet. If you tell me you were waiting for me to show up and do the honorable, I think I'll hit you again."

Freddy rubbed his jaw with a wince and dropped into one of the chairs across from Devlin's desk. "Rather you didn't, and no, I wasn't. Found her a groom, though. Carlton is knee-deep in debt and so is quite agreeable. They were to marry on the quiet next week."

"Were?"

"She lost the baby last week, so she's canceled the wedding."

"Lost it?" Devlin frowned. "Then she really was?—wait a minute," he said suspiciously. "Did you see her lose it, or did she just tell you about it after the fact?"

"Well, actually, she did tell me, but she was quite broken up about it."

"They're all experts at crying at the drop of a hat. Haven't you figured that out yet?"

"Well, that's damn cynical of you," Freddy protested. "I had no reason to doubt her, Dev."

"Except that I'm your best friend, and I *told* you I never touched her."

"She's my sister, dammit. What would you have done in my place?"

"I wouldn't have been so quick to believe a habitual practical joker, which you bloody well know Sabrina is. And I would have had a little more faith in my best friend, who doesn't go around seducing innocents—at least he didn't used to," Devlin ended in a mumble.

Freddy pounced. "I heard that. Who else have you been seducing?"

"I certainly wasn't talking about your damn sister, who, by the by, is going to get her neck wrung if I ever see her again. And you—I'm seriously thinking about sending *my* seconds round to pay *you* a visit."

"That's twice now you seem to be blaming me for I don't know what."

"Then let me enlighten you," Devlin offered. "Because of you, I was forced to bury myself in the country, where I met the most beautiful girl I've ever set eyes on, and my life has been hell ever since."

"I beg to differ," Freddy replied smugly. "*I've* recently met the most beautiful girl you're ever likely to set eyes on. Haven't been able to get her out of my mind. I don't mind telling you, I'm seriously contemplating returning to Hampshire to court her."

"Hampshire? She wouldn't happen to have red hair and blue-as-midnight eyes, would she?"

"How the devil did you know?"

"You can forget about courting her," Devlin said in a near growl. "And you will bloody well get her *out* of your mind. I've already married her."

"That isn't funny, Dev."

"Am I laughing?"

"Not Miss Penworthy?"

"The same."

"Well, I like that!" Freddy said huffily. "And you're *complaining*? You ought to be thanking me."

"When she despises everything about me, except my title—and my horses?"

"Well, at least she's got good taste. I like your horses myself." When Devlin just stared, he added, "Sorry, but it can't be all that bad."

"Can't it?" And Devlin proceeded to tell him just how bad it was.

Chapter 39

The situation was intolerable. Devlin was obviously avoiding her. That much Megan had figured out before she had been at Sherring Cross a full week. If she saw him at all, it was only in passing.

He never even made another appearance for dinner after that first night. And when Megan did see him, he was so disgustingly polite she wanted to hit him to find out if the old Devlin was still there, or if he really had been no more than a creation for a role he was playing. She didn't. The new Devlin was just too intimidating, and so bloody imperious that she couldn't even think of starting an argument with him without feeling utterly childish.

The situation was definitely intolerable. Megan was crying herself to sleep at night.

And for no good purpose, since Devlin didn't even know about it. But he was just as miserable as she was. She'd heard him say so. He was just making the same effort she was to conceal it.

The situation was *absolutely* intolerable, but Megan had finally figured out what she could do about it. Overhearing Devlin tell Duchy that Freddy's sister, Sabrina, was claiming to have lost her baby gave her the idea. She was going to tell Devlin the same thing, that she'd lost their baby. It wouldn't be an easy lie to tell, for the mere thought of something like that actually happening brought tears to her eyes. But it would solve both their problems by allowing him to get a quick annulment.

Even her conscience couldn't change her mind. And with the decision firmly made, there was no time to waste, what with Duchy planning a formal ball to officially announce the marriage. And Devlin's grandmother was determined to do that, since she'd complained of being denied the opportunity to arrange his wedding. So Megan had to act before those plans progressed to the invitation stage. The fewer people who knew about her, the quicker Devlin could get on with his life—and she could forget that she'd been foolish enough to fall in love with a man who wasn't real.

Megan waited nervously in the formal sitting room that night until she heard Devlin enter his chambers directly from the hallway. She paced, waiting for the sound of the door to close again, signaling the departure of his valet. Then she started crying—loudly. Within seconds the door connecting the two rooms slammed open and Devlin was rushing toward her.

"Why are you crying?"

"I—I'm not," Megan said, her mind going blank with him standing so close. "I—oh, never mind. Go away."

"Megan!"

"I don't know how to tell you," she cried into her hands. "I've been trying not to think about it, because every time I do, this happens. But I suppose you have to know."

"What?!"

"I lost the baby."

Utter silence greeted that statement, so Megan wailed louder. But she couldn't look at him. If he said one kind word to her, she'd be crying for real.

"I require proof," was what he finally said, quite *un*kindly. "Are you still bleeding?"

Megan blanched, never having imagined that he might actually doubt her. Fortunately, he couldn't see that, because her face was still buried in her hands.

But she quickly recovered, improvising. "It didn't just happen. It was on the return trip from Scotland. And I haven't told you sooner because—because I've been in shock. Are you so insensitive that you haven't even noticed?"

"You have been unusually . . . quiet."

A nice word to describe her present lack of temper, but uttered so dryly, she knew something wasn't going right. He either didn't believe her or—could he possibly think she had lied to begin with, that there had never been a baby, and so no reason to get married?

"Why are you badgering me?" she demanded. "Can't you see that I'm upset?"

"I would have thought you'd be relieved."

She gasped at what he was implying, her head coming up so she could glare at him. "I wanted that baby!"

"No, you didn't."

"Don't you tell me I didn't when I did!"

He sighed over her increasing dramatics. "Megan, there obviously wasn't a baby. It was a mistake."

"That's beside the point."

"We'll have others."

"No, we won't!" At which point she finally had something to really cry about, and her tears began in earnest.

His expression changed instantly from put upon to genuinely concerned. "Megan—"

"Don't touch me," she said as he reached for her and drew her unresisting against his chest.

"Megan, don't—please."

"I hate you," she cried into his neck, gripping fistfuls of his robe. "You don't know anything about what I want. I may not have wanted this baby before, but I do now." She didn't even realize she'd stopped using the past tense.

"Then I'm sorry. Tell me what I can do."

"Nothing. There's nothing you can—hold me, Devlin." Megan's eyes widened at the strength of his comforting, which went from awkward patting to a near death's grip. And she took advantage of it shamelessly, aware that he would probably never hold her again, for any reason, and desperately wanting those arms around her one last time.

When the soft nonsense he was murmuring in an effort to quiet her turned to kisses along her temples, her forehead, her wet cheeks, she knew she was really taking advantage now, but she didn't care. Just a little while more. She'd never ask for another thing.

But suddenly she was tasting her tears on his lips as his mouth brushed over hers by accident, only to come back once, twice, and when she didn't protest, to settle there for a gradually deepening kiss. She gripped his robe even harder, in case he thought to come to his senses and let go of her. He didn't. His tongue delved into her mouth with a deep groan, his, which drowned out her own.

The maelstrom of sensations that he so easily evoked with such kisses was there again, more overwhelming than ever after such a long absence. Megan forgot about her plan, forgot that she was supposed to be grievously upset. Concerns became nonexistent, thinking impossible, with such pleasure clamoring for notice.

Which was about all she noticed. Softness was suddenly beneath her. She had been fully clothed; now she was not. But she didn't become aware of these things until the heat of his skin covered her. And then it was only a vaguely curious awareness, because all the while, Devlin kept up those magical, drugging kisses that wouldn't let her think.

What had been previously offered as comfort became hot brands, his hands no longer soothing, but stirring new fires wherever they roamed. And they roamed all over, teasing, thrilling, causing shivers of delight on her neck, across her breasts, down her belly to what had become the center of her universe, that place aching for his touch.

She was not to be disappointed. Deeply his fingers caressed, bringing whimper, moan, gasp, whimper again, and need, burning, consuming need that was answered with remarkable astuteness. At the precise moment she was sure she could bear no more, she was filled with the thickness of his manhood thrusting to her depths, and the resulting explosion of relief nearly did her in, it was so electrifying. Nor did it end, delicious spasms of pleasure continuing with each additional thrust, until he reached his own shattering climax. Even then the aftermath kept her spellbound and so sensually languorous, there was no thought but to savor every last incredible sensation. If only the first time had been . . . The first time?

Megan's eyes flew open with the realization. "Dammit, Devlin, why did you make love to me?"

The question was so absurd, he could be forgiven the dryness of his tone as he leaned up to say, "I was comforting you in a very old, very reliable way."

"But you've ruined everything. You were supposed to get an annulment. Now you can't!"

He lifted himself off her with stiff, jerky movements that were indicative of anger. It wasn't until he'd yanked on his robe and turned to face her that she saw her guess was correct. He was definitely angry.

Megan reached for something to cover herself with, as if that could shield her from the fury in his eyes, but there was nothing. He'd made love to her on the sofa in the sitting room. Her own clothes were in a pile on the floor a goodly distance away.

"Is that what you were hankering for?" he demanded. "An annulment?"

"Certainly," she replied uneasily. "It's what *you* want, isn't it?"

"At this precise moment, it would be my fondest wish. But as you pointed out, it's too late now."

"Not—not if you forget this happened."

"Oh, no, my dear, I'm not *about* to forget this," he replied coldly. "Besides, you could well be with child again."

"That's not likely to happen twice in a row," she retorted, but she was groaning with another realization, that she was going to have to tell him she *was* still with child. Not tonight she wouldn't.

"Then let me put it this way, and this ought to sound familiar, brat. You're stuck with me until death do us part, and I'm not about to die to convenience you."

"Well, that's a fine attitude!" she shouted after him as he stalked from the room.

But he turned in the doorway for one last rejoinder. "You couldn't have taken the title of duchess with you if you'd got your bloody annulment."

"I know that, you stupid man," she replied, but he'd already slammed the door shut.

Chapter 40

Devlin left for London the next morning. Megan found out about it after he'd gone, when Duchy joined her for breakfast in her small sitting room, which was much more cozy than the formal one. The lavender shades in the wall coverings and furniture would have to go, however. She ought to consider changing it now that she was staying, but she wasn't in the mood to spend Devlin's money.

"You shan't be parted long, however," Duchy informed her, "since we're going to London, too."

"We are?"

"Yes. Told Devlin I was taking you shopping. He should have waited to escort us, but he got testy when I mentioned it. No matter.

We'll join him at the town house."

I run him off, but the poor man just can't get away from me.

You're assuming. He's been away from his work a long time. You know how men love their work.

And how that man despises me.

He didn't despise you last night.

So he liked me long enough to make love to me. It wasn't intentional. It just happened.

Then why don't you work on getting it to "just happen" again?

Because that won't solve anything.

It can't hurt either.

" . . . at least thirty dresses to start," Duchy was saying, "And, of course, the new ball gown."

Megan hoped she hadn't missed more than that, because that was too much. "I don't need a new wardrobe, Duchy. I've already sent home for the rest of my things, and my complete wardrobe is extensive."

Duchy waved a dismissive hand. "No wardrobe is *ever* large enough. And besides, after the official announcement at the ball, you'll be deluged with callers, and the Duchess of Wrothston has an image to uphold. Haven't you seen the size of your closet?"

Megan had wondered why that room was so large. "If you say so," she conceded grudgingly.

"I do." Then the dowager duchess frowned. "I'll be dropping you off for your selections and fittings. I find it too boring by half these days. I trust you know what colors suit you? I mean, you don't favor pink, do you?"

Duchy looked so worried, Megan assured her, "Pink gives me freckles."

The old lady's eyes widened. "Didn't know that was possible."

"It isn't."

"You minx." Duchy chuckled.

But now Megan was worried. "It's going to be a problem, isn't it—my hair? Devlin calls it god-awful red. He said once that the duke— he was talking about himself, though I didn't know it at the time—wouldn't be seen in public with a redhead. I believe his exact words were 'a woman with the most unfashionable hair in creation.' "

Duchy sighed. Love had turned her grandson into an utter ass, it seemed. "There is nothing wrong with your hair, child. I find it incredibly lovely, and I don't doubt for a second that Devlin does, too. If he said otherwise, he probably had some contrary reason for it. In fact, I'll wager that if I tell him you plan to dye it, he'll forbid you."

"That's not such a bad idea."

"Then I'll tell him."

"No, that I dye it."

"Don't you dare," Duchy scolded. "You'd be doing it for the wrong reason, and you know it."

Megan didn't try to deny it. "But *he'd* be happy, wouldn't he?"

"The only way that boy is going to be happy is if you tell him you love him."

"Do *what?*"

Duchy had promised herself she wouldn't interfere, so she shrugged. "It was just a thought."

But Megan's conscience had had the same thought. *So why don't you tell him?*

You know very well why. He'd laugh, and I'd never forgive him.

You know the old Devlin might laugh, but the new Devlin would . . .

Yes? He would what?

I don't know.

Neither do I, and I'm not going to embarrass myself to find out.

Well, something *has to be done. You could offer a truce in the bedroom for a start, and see where that leads.*

I'll think about it.

Why don't you not think about it for a change, and just do it?

That's easy for you to say. You're not the one facing possible rejection.

I'm not the coward either, but one of us sure as hell is. Or do you like the way things are?

Megan sighed. She really did hate it when her conscience was right.

Two days after arriving at the St. Jameses London mansion, Devlin barged into Megan's dressing room, where she was preparing for dinner. Her maid was so startled, the girl rushed out before she was dismissed.

Megan was just as startled, the more so when her husband said without preamble, in a don't-argue-with-me tone, "You may *not* dye your hair."

She had forgotten that Duchy had planned to tell him that. And it was apparently a good thing she hadn't accepted that wager. But this was the first time she'd seen Devlin since she'd come to London—he kept appalling hours when he was attending to ducal business— and her conscience wasn't going to let her back out of her newest decision, to bury her temper and charm the man into liking her.

So she gave him a smile, merely reminding him, "But you don't like my hair."

The smile threw him off, unexpected, and so suspect. "It's grown on me," he said grudgingly.

"But it's not fashionable."

That annoyed him, hearing his own words thrown back at him. "The Duchess of Wrothston makes her own fashion. She doesn't have to emulate it."

"But I wouldn't want to embarrass you in public. And besides, it clashes with the pink ball gown I've ordered."

"Oh, God."

She pretended not to hear that. "Black, I think. Yes, black. Blond is so common, after all, with everyone favoring it."

"If you dye one lock on that beautiful head of yours, I'll put you over my knee again, and you know bloody well that's not an idle threat!"

"If you say so, Devlin."

"I mean it, Megan," he warned, suspicious of her compliance.

"I know you do."

She confounded him with another smile. He had come anticipating a fight. After their last parting, he needed one. But she wasn't obliging him, and she wasn't behaving the least bit like the Megan he knew.

She must want something. Had she figured out another way to get out of their marriage?

Bloody hell, it infuriated him every time he thought of that damn annulment idea of hers. After making love to her, finally, as he'd dreamed of doing, and knowing that she had found it as incredibly satisfying as he had, Devlin realized that for her to tell him she wanted an annulment proved without a doubt how much she loathed him, so much so that she was even willing to give up the title she'd hankered after.

Then why hadn't she stopped him from ruining her goal? Her curiosity? He had wondered how he might use it against her. Had he done so without even knowing it? Or had she simply been so caught up in her own passion that her goal had temporarily been forgotten?

He ought to tell her that he wouldn't have given her an annulment even if they hadn't made love again. Maybe that would get him the fight he wanted.

He opened his mouth to do just that, but she turned her back toward him, revealing an only half-closed gown, and asking over her shoulder, "Since you're here and my maid isn't, would you fasten my gown for me?"

Devlin was appalled to hear himself say, "I'd rather unfasten it."

She swung back around in surprise. "Now?"

"Anytime."

"All right."

He couldn't have heard that correctly. "Liked it that much, did you, that even I will do?"

"*Only* you will do," she replied softly, her cheeks rosy with a blush.

Of course she had to say that. He was her husband. But he wasn't going to spite himself just because he couldn't comprehend what she was up to.

He made love to his wife right there in her dressing room, swiftly at first, because he was afraid she might change her mind, then with exquisitely slow thoroughness when he was sure she wouldn't.

But they were really going to have to try this in a bed sometime.

Chapter 41

It made a difference, their new relationship. By mutual agreement, silent though understood, a sort of truce was declared for lovemaking. It was an unusual concept, but it worked very well.

Devlin would come to her room at night, and without a word, Megan would move into his arms. She came to understand that despite what he might think of her as an individual, he absolutely adored her body. That she was still fascinated by his wasn't in doubt either. And although silence wasn't demanded or even encouraged, anything of a serious nature was expressly forbidden, for absolutely nothing was to disturb what was becoming a necessity for them both.

Outside the bedroom, it was like they were

meeting for the first time. He no longer deliberately avoided her. She no longer searched for ways to tweak his nose when something annoyed her. They spoke to each other with growing ease. They asked questions about their pasts and answered them without the least hesitancy.

His superior-than-thou attitude was also less noticeable, though not completely diminished. He was still the duke, after all, not her horse breeder. Accordingly, he never raised his voice to her anymore. And she continued to dazzle him with her smiles.

They were getting along.

It wasn't quite enough.

Megan still had to tell him that she'd lied about losing the baby, and hope she could make him understand that she'd done it for him. She still had to get up the nerve to tell him she loved him. And she knew she wouldn't be able to continue being pleasant indefinitely, at least not *all* the time, or keep watching her every word to avoid arguments. It simply wasn't her nature to be so guarded with her emotions.

And she still wanted her horse breeder back.

"I can't believe it worked out exactly as you planned it," Tiffany said on a happy sigh as she and Megan strolled through Hyde Park. She had arrived in London yesterday, for her own wedding was less than a week away. "You got your duke. You love him. And he adores you."

"Two out of three isn't bad, Tiff."

"What's that supposed to mean?"

"It means, what makes you think Devlin loves me back?"

"Of course he does," Tiffany insisted. "He must. He married you, didn't he?"

"Yes, but not because of any great affection, or any affection at all, for that matter." Megan looked off toward the lake before reluctantly adding, "There was a little something I didn't mention when I wrote to you, Tiff. I'm going to have a baby."

"But that's wonderful news!"

"I agree, now, but I didn't think so when I first found out—since I wasn't married at the time."

Tiffany stopped walking to exclaim, "But— good God, d'you mean to say you *had* to get married?"

Megan turned back to face her friend, but she still couldn't meet her eyes. "Yes."

"No wonder you doubt his affections. But certainly he's told you he loves you since then?"

"Not once."

"Then what does he say when you tell him that you do?"

"I don't."

"What do you mean, you don't? You just got through telling me that you do."

"No, I mean that I don't tell him."

"Megan! Whyever not?"

"As long as my letter was, I still didn't tell

you the half of it, Tiff." She did now, with little embellishment. It was still quite a while before she concluded, "So you can see why I've been reluctant to put him on the spot with a declaration, especially since—since I've so been enjoying our unusual truce, and don't want to do anything to ruin it."

Tiffany's cheeks were about as red as Megan's locks. "Is it really that nice?"

"Better than nice," Megan said as they continued strolling, nodding every once in a while when a gentleman would pass and tip his hat, ignoring those who simply stopped and stared. "Just don't expect to enjoy the first time, at least not all of it. Men do, which is bloody unfair, if you ask me. But it's our lot to not only face it in fear and ignorance, but to also have to deal with the pain of it."

"My maid says the pain is excruciating," Tiffany confided, her face a bit pale now.

Megan snorted. "The girl doesn't know what she's talking about. It was more annoying than terrible, and over before you know it. In my case, it merely brought me to my senses, which effectively ruined it for me. Actually, unlike me, you could go on to enjoy the rest."

"I can't tell you how relieved I am. I'd been getting more and more nervous as the day approaches."

Megan recalled her own panic the closer she'd got to Scotland, but for different reasons. Tiffany was assured of Tyler's love, and fully expected to be blissfully happy in their

marriage. Megan still wasn't assured of anything—except that Devlin liked making love
to her now.

"That's normal. They even have a name for
it, wedding jitters. I'm just as nervous about
this damn ball Duchy is giving, but they don't
have a name for that."

"Sure they do. Stark raving—"

"Stop." Megan laughed. "I'm not *that* nervous. And you are coming, aren't you, now that
you and Tyler have decided to postpone your
wedding trip until the spring?"

"Absolutely. I'll be the one organizing the
search parties—"

"Cut it out, Tiff." Megan laughed harder.
"Sherring Cross isn't *that* big."

"Maybe not, but at least you remember how
to laugh. I was beginning to wonder."

Megan sighed. "I'm sorry. I shouldn't have
said anything about my problems when your
big day is so close."

"Nonsense. And I wouldn't be surprised if
you're making problems where none exist. I
can't believe he doesn't love you, Meg. Every
man you meet—"

"Devlin isn't like them; he's unique himself.
His grandmother told me women have been
making fools of themselves over him for as
long as she can remember, and I don't doubt
it, because I've done the same thing. But all he
sees when he looks at me is a spoiled brat."

"You just get a little impatient sometimes."

Megan smiled. "Don't try and put a nice face

on it when we both know I'm spoiled rotten."

"Well, so what?" Tiffany huffed loyally. "I suppose he just shrugs it off when he doesn't get what he wants?"

Megan stopped, eyes widening. "Now that you mention it, he reacts a bit like I do."

"Aha, and it stands to reason. If anyone's bound to be spoiled, a bloody duke would be. He probably had ten nannies running after him as a child, and a host of other servants to see to his every need. You just had one nanny and a father who dotes on you, so if you ask me, he's probably more spoiled than you are."

"I'll be sure to mention that—if I ever get to fight with him again."

Chapter 42

It was a beautiful wedding, just what Megan had always envisioned for herself—well, hers wouldn't have been quite so grand as Tiffany's, or with so many guests, just friends and family in her small parish church. But she'd been denied that because her damned inner voice and curiosity had gotten together to conspire against her common sense.

She was miserable on the way home from the wedding, when she should have been only happy for her friend. Devlin was quiet, too, probably just as miserable, but for different reasons, and that only made her feel worse. He could have had that grand wedding, should have had it. Instead he'd been forced to elope to Scotland.

I ought to shoot you.

Me or him?

You. Better yet, you're retired. I never want to hear from you again.

Why is it you always get mad and need someone to blame when you feel rotten?

I'm not blaming someone else, I'm blaming you.

Good God, she was losing touch with reality. Her inner voice was *not* a separate individual. But it was right as usual. Megan really did have a difficult time accepting responsibility for her own misery. And maybe it was time she stopped doing that.

She returned to Sherring Cross the next day—alone. Well, not exactly alone, since she had five strapping servants plus her new maid to escort her. Duchy had gone back earlier in the week, confessing that at her age, she couldn't tolerate the bustle of London for very long, and she also had a thousand things to do in preparation for the ball.

Devlin was to have accompanied her. After all, the St. James ball was only another four days away. But he canceled at the last moment. Business, he said, that had to be seen to beforehand so that he could remain in Kent for a week or so after the ball.

In Megan's present mood, she had to wonder if that was true. Business was, after all, a convenient excuse to separate them. And Devlin's quiet mood yesterday after the wedding had continued for the rest of the day, to include his not coming to her room last night. After seeing how happy Tiffany and Tyler were, perhaps he'd realized that their own "half" marriage wasn't enough for him either.

The day of the ball began with a frigid storm that was nice enough to clear up before the guests started arriving. It was also the day Megan had picked to make her own announcement, albeit privately. She just hadn't decided yet whether to sit Devlin down and confess all to him before or after the ball. Either way, she was bound to ruin his day—*if* he showed up. He hadn't so far yet, and Duchy was starting to fret.

Megan kept to her rooms for most of the day. Tiffany found her there in the afternoon, the new bride of five days bubbling over with good cheer.

"Tyler went straight to the stables. He's decided to buy one of the St. James Thoroughbreds, but he's worried others will take advantage of their invite here to do the same, and the duke's entire stock will be sold before the end of the day. Just about everyone who is anyone is coming, you know. I've even heard the rumor that the queen intends to make an appearance. And you wouldn't believe the traffic on the roads and at the inns along the way. If Tyler didn't have acquaintances in the area, we would have arrived in the middle of the night, because I was *not* going to sleep in the coach."

Megan got her reply in quickly, while Tiffany paused for breath. "You should have come yesterday to avoid the crush, like my father did. You know very well you don't have to wait for an invitation to visit here now. In fact, I expect you to come for extended stays whenever you like."

"With the size of your guest list, we were afraid even Sherring Cross was going to run out of rooms. Honestly, Meg, I doubt there's a lord left in London today."

Megan laughed. "You more than anyone would never believe this house capable of running out of rooms. And besides, I had one prepared for your exclusive use before I went to London. Weren't you shown to it?"

"That miniature mausoleum down the hall? Yes, a maid is hanging up my gown even now. And where is yours? I can't wait to see what you decided on for an occasion of this magnitude."

Megan led the way to her dressing room, though she couldn't generate much enthusiasm for the stunning gown that Duchy had had a hand in creating because she'd guessed Megan wasn't accustomed to the kind of extravagance demanded for *this* ball. The result was a lavish though elegant gown of ivory-and-sapphire silk—not pink, as she had teasingly told Devlin—with a fortune in real pearls sewn along the deep bodice and dotting the train and the single wreath of white roses attached to the side of the gathered skirt.

"Good God, you're going to look like a princess," Tiffany exclaimed.

"No, just a duchess."

Tiffany raised a brow at her friend's dejected tone and accurately guessed the cause. "You still haven't told Devlin, have you?"

"Today I will."

"And you're making yourself sick over it," Tiffany concluded, again right on the mark.

Megan smiled weakly. "I guess I am."

"Then postpone it another day. You already have enough to be nervous about on this one."

"Postpone what?" Duchy asked as she sailed into the dressing room.

Megan made an effort to evade the question. "Has Devlin arrived yet?"

"Just, and the dear boy's quite annoyed with me, I don't mind telling you. I suppose I should have sent him a final copy of the guest list."

"Why? Did you invite someone he doesn't particularly like?"

"*That* was inevitable, but not the issue. No, he had to sleep in a stable last night."

"You're joking," Megan said incredulously.

"I told you," Tiffany told Megan.

Duchy just sighed. "He tried three different inns and not a room to be had in any of them. And he considered the hour too late to impose on anyone he knew. If he had left London at an earlier hour, there wouldn't have been a problem—or maybe there would have been. He simply wasn't expecting such a crowd, though I don't know why not. It may have been ten years since we've had a ball here, but he knows

very well that the St. Jameses have always
entertained in a grand manner—when we get
around to it."

Megan was reminded that she hadn't seen
the guest list either, final or otherwise. "Just
how many people did you invite?"

"About six hundred, but I expect every one
of them, plus a few I may have forgotten who
will show up to remind me that I forgot them."

There were ten seconds of amazed silence
before Tiffany said dryly, "It's a good thing
Sherring Cross has two connecting ballrooms."

"I'd wondered at that," Megan replied in a
horrified whisper. "Until now."

Duchy pretended not to notice the astonishment she'd caused. She just loved surprises,
which was why she hadn't included the reason for the ball in the invitations, nor had
she even told her intimate friends yet about
Devlin's marriage. Her sister, Margaret, knew,
of course, and she'd had to sit on top of her
to keep her quiet about it since her arrival, no
easy thing to do with that chatterbox.

"Here's another thing I forgot," she said
now, handing over the jewel box she carried.
"Devlin had to remind me to open the family
vault, though I can't imagine why he suggested
rubies to go with your gown."

Megan could, but she was laughing and so
didn't volunteer that he thought she would be
wearing pink. Duchy had too many things yet
to do to stay and question her strange humor,
though she did suggest, "You might want to

take a nap, my dear," before she turned to leave.

But Megan wasn't a total nervous wreck yet, just halfway there, and called after her before she was out of hearing range, "Is the queen really coming?"

"Certainly," floated back through the open door.

"Certainly." Megan groaned.

Chapter 43

"Make that bloody announcement already, Duchy, or you're going to witness the Duke of Wrothston causing a scandal."

Lucinda glanced incredulously at her grandson, then followed his gaze to where Megan was standing, but was barely seen, she had so many young lords surrounding her. "For heaven's sake, Dev, the ball has only just started. And you can get her away from that crowd by simply dancing with her. That *is* permissible, you know."

"That isn't going to do it," he growled, though he started toward Megan to do just that.

Duchy shook her head after him, unaware that he was going to make his own announcement. But she heard it, couldn't help hearing it, actually, as did everyone else, for the sheer volume he deliberately injected.

"Excuse me, gentlemen, but I would like to dance with my *wife*."

And anyone who hadn't heard that was quickly enlightened by his or her neighbor within minutes. Duchy sighed. So much for being the sole bearer of glad tidings. But then she chuckled to herself. If her surprise had to be ruined, she couldn't have asked for a better way. The dear boy was positively green with jealousy, and there wasn't a person there who couldn't see that.

Megan was the one exception. She had no reason to think that Devlin's appalling rudeness, as she saw it, stemmed from jealousy. She was too accustomed to male adoration to think anything was unusual about the excessive attention she'd been receiving from the moment she came downstairs. There were simply a great many men present, hence the large number wanting to meet her.

Even Devlin's pronounced use of the word "wife" didn't suggest jealousy to her. She'd been giving her name as Megan St. James. It wasn't her fault that it was being assumed she was a St. James relative rather than a wife, since she wasn't aware of the assumption.

No, rude was what he was, and she intended to find out why, saying the moment he pulled her into the current waltz, "If you're still put out because you had to sleep in a stable last night, I'll thank you not to take it out on me."

"So don't thank me."

Megan blinked. That sounded so much like her old Devlin that she was smiling without realizing it as she asked, "Brought back memories, did it, of your brief step-down to the servant class?"

Now that he had her in his arms, his jealousy was fast diminishing, soothed further by her smile, if not by her taunt. So he accepted the excuse she was offering for his appalling behavior—appalling now that he was aware of it.

"I had a perfectly good bed in your stable, Megan, fetched down from one of your guest rooms, hardly comparable with a stack of hay."

"A stack of hay?" she said in surprise. "I hadn't realized—" She broke off her sentence before she sounded too sympathetic, recalling that she hadn't finished scolding him yet. "All the same, it wasn't *my* fault, was it?"

"Quite right. I do beg your pardon."

"As you should. But as long as we're on the subject of complaints—"

"We're not—" he tried to cut in.

"Oh, yes, we are," Megan interrupted right back. "You don't see me for four days and you don't even seek me out to say hello when you finally return. That's not very husbandly of you, Devlin."

"If you knew the state of the typical ton

marriage, you'd know that's *very* husbandly of me. But in my case, Duchy told me you were napping."

"I wasn't. You should have found out for yourself."

She'd dropped her gaze to mutter that. Devlin bent sideways to see if her expression looked as sulky as her tone, but she turned her head aside. If she only knew that he'd tried a half-dozen times to get away from the guests who had pounced on him the moment he walked in the door—half his jealous anger had stemmed from *not* having a chance to see her before the ball commenced.

"Did you actually miss me, Megan?" he asked carefully now, unsure if he was getting the right impression from her complaint or not.

"Yes, actually, I believe I did."

"Would you, ah, like to slip away with me for a few moments so that I can make amends and greet you properly?"

"Yes, I believe I would."

He did *not* give her a chance to change her mind, immediately dragging her off the dance floor, her hand firmly in his, but her step hardly up to matching his. He didn't notice, too eager to find them a spot of privacy in a veritable sea of people. Duchy, standing near the doors he was determinedly heading for, with Frederick Richardson at her side, definitely noticed.

"Good God, he's going to make a scandal after all," she exclaimed. "Stop him, Freddy.

I'm sure you, of all people, can imagine what he's about to do."

"Indeed, and I'd rather not die tonight just to save him from a scandal, if you don't mind."

"He'll thank you once he comes to his senses."

"That, my dear Duchy, will be too late," Freddy replied and, against his better judgment, moved to block Devlin's exit from the room—just in time. "I say, old man, you aren't thinking of making an ass of yourself twice in one evening, are you?"

Devlin stopped, allowing Megan to move up to his side. "For a friend who hasn't been completely forgiven yet, you're pushing it, Richardson," he said in low tones.

Freddy relaxed at that point, even grinned. "I figured as much, but your grandmother was about to faint from the shock, so what could I do?"

Hearing that, Megan snatched her hand back. Having been dragged across the room, she understood perfectly well what the marquis was talking about, and improvised by offering him the hand she'd just retrieved.

"I believe my husband was rather eager to have us meet, Lord Richardson. If I had known it was you he was dragging me over to introduce to, I could have told him we'd already met in Hampshire at the Leighton ball. A pleasure, though, to see you again."

"Well said, Your Grace." Freddy beamed at her, then winked at Devlin. "And not to undo a brilliant rescue, I'll just steal her away for the next dance, if you don't mind."

"I do mind—"

"No, he doesn't," Duchy said as she joined them. "Run along, Freddy, but don't monopolize the duchess too long. She has to mingle with all her guests tonight, not just a select few." But after the marquis had whisked Megan away, she added to Devlin, "Which you, dear boy, apparently forgot," and then in exasperation, *"Have you lost your mind?"*

"Apparently."

"Are you blushing, Dev?"

"Apparently," he groaned. Then he pulled himself together to ask with all the starch and stuffiness she deplored, "Would you care to dance, Your Grace?"

"Go to the devil," she snorted, turning away from him, only to toss back, "And stay away from your wife tonight, unless you can manage to keep your hands to yourself."

It took more than half the evening, dinner the queen's visit and departure, the *official* announcement of his marriage, and a bottle and a half of champagne before Devlin felt he could safely approach his wife again without making a fool of himself for a third time that night.

But before he reached her, he spotted another female who had somehow managed to keep from his notice all evening—until now. He turned in her direction instead, coming up behind Sabrina Richardson to pull her rudely away from her group of friends and out onto the dance floor. "I told your brother that if I ever saw you again, I would wring your neck. Didn't he warn you?"

Sabrina stared up at him wide-eyed, but not quite frightened. "Yes, but—but I had to come, Devlin, to apologize. I owe you that."

"You owe me a lot more than that," he said coldly. "Why don't we start with the truth?"

"I just wanted to be a duchess, and you're the only duke around who isn't too old or married already."

"Bloody hell."

"Well, you asked for the truth," she said defensively. "I'm sorry it isn't more complicated than that."

"*Was* there a baby?"

"No," she answered, blushing profusely.

"Have you told Freddy that?"

Sabrina nodded. "When he told me you'd married someone else."

"I hope he blistered your hide."

The blush spread from her cheeks to encompass her entire face. "He did."

"Then I just might forgive him. You, on the other hand, I ought to toss out on your ear."

"Don't be a grouch, Devlin. It's worked out well enough in the end, hasn't it? Freddy said you never would have met your wife if it wasn't for us." Devlin hated to own up to the truth of that simple fact, so he didn't, but Sabrina was continuing. "I thought I'd dislike her, but I don't. Freddy's in love with her, you know."

"The devil he is!"

"He said he was."

"The devil he did!" Devlin looked over toward Megan to see if Freddy was in her group of admirers, and damned if he wasn't. "I knew I should have sent my seconds round to him when I first thought of it."

Chapter 44

Logic told Megan that after the official announcement of her marriage, she should have lost most of her admirers. Logic apparently had nothing to do with it, however, for she hadn't lost any, had actually gained some of the more disreputable kind: the lechers and charming though wicked rakes who considered her ripe for seduction now that she was a married woman.

She supposed she had been lucky not to have come across such men before—not counting her husband in disguise as himself. And although she received seventeen outrageous propositions of one kind or another, from amusing to really vulgar, she managed to keep her temper during each one and fend them off without causing a scene.

Aside from that, she was enjoying herself more than she thought she would, and that was because of Devlin's impetuous behavior earlier in the evening. She had no doubt now that he'd been taking her off to make love right in the middle of their ball. It would have caused a scandal of the worst magnitude and was so unlike her husband the duke—but so like Devlin the horse breeder.

Megan grinned to herself each time she thought of it, and she thought of it every time she looked for and found Devlin, and she did that all night long. It didn't even bother her that the same women kept showing up in his own groups as he circulated and mingled with his guests. It didn't bother her when she saw him dancing with other women and heard their girlish giggles as they flirted with him. She happened to know he abhorred giggling women. She also happened to know that it was her he wanted, not them, because she'd caught a number of *those* looks from him that told her so.

All things considered, she was nowhere as nervous as she had been about her confession, which was still on the agenda for tonight. She wasn't expecting Devlin to return her affections, at least not all at once, though that was now a more hopeful long-term expectation. But she didn't think he'd mind all that much now if she loved him.

"I suppose you've been accepting congratulations all evening."

Megan turned toward the lady who had spoken, a lovely blonde with light gray eyes who made Megan feel gauche next to her sophisticated flamboyance. "That does seem to be the order of the day," she replied.

"Then you're due for some condolences instead."

"I beg your pardon?"

The woman laughed, a brittle sound. "You don't know who I am, do you?"

"Should I?"

"Indeed yes. I'm Marianne Aitchison, the woman your husband jilted at the altar only a few months ago."

Megan just stared, dumbfounded, while one of the gentlemen present said, "I say, Countess, you never got to the altar, did you? Recall Wrothston breaking it off before it got as far as that."

"Then do you also recall that he kept me waiting for ten years?" Marianne almost snarled at the man. "Ten *wasted* years."

Megan was too appalled for words. The bitterness coming out of Marianne Aitchison was palpable. Ten years? Good God, Devlin had been engaged to this woman for *ten years*? Why had no one mentioned that to her before, when apparently it was common knowledge?

"You were amazingly lucky, my dear," Marianne remarked to Megan with less heat, but with no less bitterness. "To get him to the altar before his interest wore off. And it will, you know, quickly, abruptly. So don't expect his declarations of love to continue much longer."

What declarations of love? Megan wanted to know, but asked instead, "Why did you have such a long engagement?"

"Because he kept postponing the wedding, again and again, and when I finally refused to be put off any longer, he broke it off completely."

"But why?" Megan couldn't help asking.

"Why else, my dear? He simply didn't want a wife. But he liked being engaged. That kept all the aspiring mamas from targeting him for their sweet young daughters."

Megan felt sick to her stomach. She knew for a fact that Devlin didn't want a wife, at least not her, and obviously not Marianne Aitchison either. And Megan had no trouble seeing it from Marianne's bitter point of view, to wait ten long years to marry a man, receiving no other proposals because she was already engaged, or having to refuse those that she got anyway. And then to be left without a husband to show for her commendable patience.

The countess was no longer a young debutante, but quite positively on the shelf, as the saying went. She probably had no prospects now, no hope of finding another husband at her age, when there were so many eager young hopefuls on the marriage mart every year. Devlin had, in effect, condemned her to being a spinster.

She didn't know what to say to Marianne Aitchison. She understood her bitterness too well, but it would be trite and meaningless to say so. She felt sorry for her, and furious at Devlin for his callousness, and . . .

"Spreading your venom again, dear Marianne?" Freddy said, suddenly appearing at Megan's side.

"Just setting the record straight," the countess replied stiffly, though with a degree of uneasiness.

"Capital idea." The marquis smiled agreeably. "Shall we hear it from another perspective?"

"Stay out of it, Freddy," Devlin said, suddenly appearing at Megan's other side.

"But I feel the need to atone, old man—especially since you think I'm in love with your wife." Devlin had just cornered him to ask that question, snarled it more like, when they had noticed Marianne with Megan. "Which isn't to say I wouldn't have been in love with her in no time a'tall if you hadn't married her."

Devlin merely tossed his friend a look of disgust before taking Megan's arm and leading her away. She allowed it for all of three seconds before she jerked her arm back and hissed, "You, sir, are despicable!"

He didn't pretend not to know what she was up in arms about. "Condemned without trial, am I? But then our Marianne is very good at generating sympathy where none is deserved."

"What you did to that woman—"

"Give over, Megan," he interrupted impatiently. "I did nothing to her except come upon her at a most inconvenient time—by her reckoning—when she happened to be making love with another man."

Megan stopped cold, her eyes flaring wide. "Then you didn't break off with her because she wouldn't let you postpone the wedding again?"

"Again? We were to have wed eight years ago, and in all that time I set the date back only once, when my grandfather died. But I've lost count of the number of times Marianne came up with one excuse or another to postpone it."

"But that means—*she* didn't want to marry you."

"Not at all. I'm sure she had every intention of marrying me—eventually, despite the fact that we bore no love for each other. It was an arranged marriage after all, one of my grandfather's last outdated notions. She was simply having too much fun being a soon-to-be-duchess without the responsibilities of a wife, since engagement to me gave her the same prestige as if she were already my wife."

"And the fact that she had other lovers was no doubt another reason she was in no hurry to get married," Megan concluded.

"Quite possibly."

She didn't know why he wasn't angry with her. She was horrified herself at the appalling lack of faith and loyalty she had just displayed, and on the very eve that she was going to tell him she loved him. He'd certainly believe her now, wouldn't he.

Megan was furious at herself, but more so at Marianne Aitchison, and Marianne made a more convenient target, since Megan took blame only when all other possible culprits had been eliminated.

But first Devlin deserved one small admonishment for not speaking up *before* she had put her foot in it. "Why the devil didn't you defend yourself back there?"

"A good many people might believe her, but anyone who knows me doesn't," he replied.

Worse and worse, implying she should have been in the second category, which she should have been. "I'm sorry," she said wretchedly.

He sighed. "Megan, you *don't* know me well enough yet to defend me out of hand. I've given you enough reasons not to do so blindly, at any rate."

"Not good enough. I believed a complete stranger without even questioning you. And why does she blame you when she's the one—"

She didn't finish, her face exploding with color at the realization that she was describing her own spoiled tendency to pass the buck when it belonged in her own pocket.

Devlin astutely guessed her thoughts from her stricken expression. "Don't be a fool," he chastised sharply. "You're nothing like her.

You don't go around condemning me to anyone who will listen. When you place blame unfairly on someone, it goes no further than your target, and I know bloody well you don't mean half the things you say, that it's just your temper run amok."

That wasn't taken too kindly, effectively banishing all traces of self-condemnation and bringing her husband an I'll-remember-that look before she huffed, "I still say you should be defending yourself, and not just to me."

"When the truth would ruin her? As a gentleman, I can't do that."

"No, I suppose you can't," she replied, and before he could stop her or guess her intent, she whipped about and called out quite clearly through the crowd, "Lady Aitchison, you are a liar."

Devlin groaned beside her. A path was cleared instantly, so Marianne could see her accuser as well as hear her. Conversations abruptly stopped in the immediate area, the silence spreading rapidly beyond. A few couples on the dance floor crashed into others, bringing even the dancing to a temporary standstill, which so startled the orchestra that the music clanged to an end.

In the ensuing silence, Duchy's voice could be heard as far away as the other ballroom. "Good God, what now?"

A few twitters followed that, a few coughs, and a great deal of shuffling feet as the crowd moved closer to catch every word.

At that point, it would have made matters infinitely worse for Devlin to clap his hand over Megan's mouth and cart her out of there, as was his first and greatest inclination. Instead he placed a hand on her shoulder and said as softly as he could, "Don't do it."

She looked at him and amazed him by smiling, seeming totally unaware of the commotion she was causing. "You know I don't take insults lightly, Devlin," she said in the most reasonable tone. "And that I am very outspoken in rebuttal—one way or another. And for Lady Aitchison to slander your good name without cause *is* an insult to me. Had I known she was lying to me about you—well, you know my temper. There's no telling what I might have done."

Devlin had the most absurd urge to laugh. Amazingly, it seemed like she was talking only to him, for only his benefit, that she was completely unaware that every ear in the room was avidly listening. But he knew her better than that, and by deliberately—and he didn't doubt it was deliberate—making her warning—which was what it had been—so public, he had to wonder who else had insulted her tonight. He would bloody well find out and deal with that in his own way, but in the meantime, he simply couldn't resist grinning over the drama she was enacting, which wasn't nearly as damaging as he'd thought it would be. 'Course, it wasn't over yet, either.

"I think you've made your point, my dear."

"Not quite," she replied with just enough true anger to warn him that the scene for the assemblage wasn't over and she was going to say her piece anyway. "You might be too much the gentleman to stop her slander, but I'm not."

There were some outright chuckles over *that* statement, but nothing to stop her from facing a very mortified Marianne again and saying, "They say truth will prevail in the end, that it will even come back to haunt you. Would you care to discuss the *real* reason my husband ended his engagement to you, Countess—or were you leaving?"

It took Marianne a moment to realize she was being given an opportunity to escape complete ruination. She didn't answer. She took the out Megan offered and left abruptly, humiliated, labeled a liar, but no more than that.

"Are you finished?" Devlin asked at Megan's back.

She turned to give him a brilliant smile. "Yes, I believe so. What happened to the music?"

Chapter 45

Megan's comment about the music was like a signal for the resumption of conversation, which returned at full volume. And Devlin had only to glance toward the orchestra for a waltz to begin, offbeat at first, but the melody was corrected by the time he drew his wife onto the dance floor.

"I can't tell you how often I've wanted to do what you just did—or something to that effect," he admitted as other couples began twirling past them. "Thank you."

"It was my pleasure."

"I don't doubt it." He grinned. "It's going to drive the ton crazy, you know, wondering what that reason is that you hinted at."

"So?"

"So do you like causing such a furor?"

"No, but you asked me not to ruin her, so I didn't. If you hadn't asked, I would have done more than only embarrass her, Devlin. I hope you realize that."

"Indeed I do, as does everyone else. So don't be surprised if people get tongue-tied around you for a while. They'll be in dread of causing you the least little insult."

"I don't notice you having that problem."

"Nor will you. I thought we had established that I give as good as I get."

"I believe it was your daring that was established. Speaking of which, mine has been lacking of late."

"You can say that after what you just did?"

She shrugged that off. "That was temper, not daring. You see, I've been meaning to tell you something, but I've kept putting it off."

Devlin groaned inwardly, remembering the last time she'd put off telling him something. Emphatically, he said, "I don't want to hear it."

"You don't—?" she sputtered. "Well, you're *going* to. I'm having a baby."

That caught him off guard. "I thought you said it wasn't likely to happen twice in a row."

"I have no idea if that's so. But this is the baby I was having before."

That *really* caught him off guard, and slowed him to a stop on the edge of the dance floor. "Then—you lied?"

"Yes, but it was for a good cause."

"I recall your good cause, Megan," he replied coldly. "And what you're telling me is that you wanted me to get an annulment while you were still carrying my child. You would actually have left me while you *still carried my child.*"

She flinched at the fury in those words, for all their softness. "I wasn't looking at it from that viewpoint. All I knew was that I was making you miserable."

"Don't you mean that the other way around? No, don't answer that. One more word out of you, and the scandal we've been avoiding by the skin of our teeth will occur after all. I need a bloody drink."

He walked away from her. Ordinarily she wouldn't have stood still for that, would have shouted something to bring him back. But she couldn't do that now. A few people were already looking at her and probably wondering at her dumbfounded expression.

Well, she'd certainly handled that brilliantly. She supposed she should have first told him she loved him, then mentioned the baby after. But she hadn't expected him to get *that* angry about the baby.

She moved off to find her father and Tiffany, needing the bolstering they could supply, because the night wasn't over yet. She was still going to tell Devlin the rest of what she had to say, whether he wanted to hear it or not. But she'd let him cool off a bit first.

As it happened, however, she didn't see him again. He didn't even show up for the conclusion and the departure of his guests. At least half were leaving, those who lived in the area or only hours away, and those eager for an early start back to London. The rest would depart at their leisure the next day, with only a few dozen expected to remain as houseguests for a while.

It was nearly dawn before Megan was able to retire herself. She took the chance that Devlin might have done the same, only earlier, and checked his room before going to her own. It was necessary to enter his domain completely since he hadn't left a light burning, and leaving the door cracked open to give her a bit of light to see by actually made matters worse, creating an abundance of shadows.

She found him in his bed after all, a great lump with the covers pulled nearly over his head. She sat down next to him and drew the covers back enough to see that he was sleeping on his stomach, his head turned away from her, his arms circled around his pillow.

His back was bare. She had the urge to crawl under the covers with him and wait until a decent hour to tell him what else she had to say, but that would be putting it off again, and she'd done enough of that.

She shook his shoulder gently. "Devlin?" He mumbled. She shook harder. "Devlin?"

His head reared up, swung around to peer at her through slanted eyes, then dropped back on the pillow in his previous position. "What?"

"Are you awake?"

"No."

That sounded like his usual drollery, so she plunged on. "You didn't give me a chance to tell you the most important part of my confession. I know the other part made you angry, and I'm sorry, but I really did do it for you, you know."

Her nervousness returned at that point, lodging the other words in her throat. Her hand caressed his back for a moment, then moved up to lovingly push the hair back from the side of his face.

Incredibly, and to Duchy's keen disapproval, he hadn't cut it yet, not even for the ball, though he had at least clubbed it back for the evening, giving him a decidedly rakish appearance with his black formal wear.

She rather liked his hair long herself. It took some of the starch out of him—at least until he opened his mouth to speak.

Her mouth opened finally, the words rushing out. "I love you, Ambrose Devlin St. James." She waited breathlessly, but he said nothing, causing a sharpness to enter her voice. "Did you hear me?"

He jerked awake. "What?"

"I said, did you hear me?"

"Yes, yes, now leave me alone, Megan. I drank too much. Need to sleep it off."

She sat back, incredulous. Well, she hadn't been able to imagine what he might say when she finally told him. Now she knew.

Chapter 46

Megan walked out of the house with her small bag of clothes at approximately three o'clock the next afternoon, one hour after she awoke, and it would have been sooner, except she had to eat and pack first. She didn't call for a carriage. She marched down to the stable, but once there, she didn't call for her horse either.

She wasn't actually leaving, after all, though it certainly appeared that way to the servants she passed. No, she was making a statement, a very loud one that Devlin wouldn't be able to miss; nor did he, having been informed about it before she'd even reached the stable.

When she arrived, she ignored the grooms, who were hesitant to ask what she wanted, after getting a look at her expression—and her

399

bag. They still followed her from tack room to tack room as she searched for what she was looking for. But she was finally disappointed that she hadn't noticed before that there wasn't a room with a bed in it similar to the one Devlin had had in her stable. There being so many grooms here, they had their own quarters in a separate building, and of course it was out of the question to go there.

I noticed a nice pile of hay on the way in.

You think I won't make use of it? He did, so I can.

You won't, but I suppose it will serve your purpose. Do you really think this is going to work?

I retired you, remember? So I don't want to hear that I might be making a fool of myself.

She went back to inspect that pile of hay, dropping her bag in a corner, and kicking and tossing armfuls of hay about until she'd fashioned, to her eyes, an adequate bed in the center of it. She was still standing in the middle of her masterpiece when Devlin arrived, announcing his presence by barking at the gawking grooms to vacate the stable—completely.

Megan squared her shoulders, kicked the train of her cream dress out of the way, and turned to face her husband. She expected him to be in a powerful rage. He probably was, but he was wearing his ducal mien, so she couldn't really tell.

She opened her mouth, but he beat her to it. "What the hell do you think you're doing, Megan?"

Her chin went up at its most stubborn angle. "I'm moving into the stable."

He'd noted the bag in the corner, been told about it, but that wasn't what he'd rushed down here expecting to hear. "You're *what?*"

"You heard me. And I'm going to stay here until I have my horse breeder back."

She looked so mutinous, he didn't doubt she meant it. He just couldn't figure out *why* she meant it. But his frightened rage was receding. She wasn't leaving him. Not that he would have let her.

Bewildered for the moment, he said carefully, "Thought you couldn't stand him."

"You thought wrong," she retorted.

Even more carefully, he explained—just in case she didn't know it, "He doesn't exist."

"He does," she insisted. "You're just keeping him buried beneath all that ducal haughtiness. But I'm giving you warning, Your Grace. If I can't have your love, I at least want Devlin Jefferys back, and I'm staying here until I get him."

His breath escaped in a whoosh of surprise. "Are you telling me you *want* me to love you?"

"If that isn't the most stupid question," she replied, losing her temper over his denseness. "Do you think I've been agonizing for weeks about telling you I love you just because I like to agonize? Very well, so you weren't interested. I'll settle for having Devlin Jefferys back."

Getting blasted like that prodded his own temper. "The devil you will! And if you want to talk about agonizing—"

"I don't!"

"Then let's discuss your 'interested.' I would have been *very* interested if you had ever got around to telling me you loved me, so if you intended to, why didn't you?"

"I did."

"You didn't! I bloody well would have remembered hearing *that* if I'd heard it."

"You heard it, you wretch, last night in your bed. Don't try and tell me—"

"Megan," he cut in, striving for some patience, if even a minuscule amount. "I went to bed with a bottle last night, not you."

That gave her pause. "You really don't remember my coming into your room?"

"No. Did you?"

"Yes."

"Then would you mind repeating what it was you told me that I didn't hear?"

Her eyes narrowed suspiciously at his soft tone. "No, I don't think I will."

He swore a blue streak, striding about, kicking up more hay as he did. When he happened to notice his wife, it was to catch her wide-eyed look of feigned amazement. He stopped suddenly and burst out laughing.

"God, I love it when you provoke me, brat. It sets my blood on fire."

Her eyes got a little wider, especially since he'd started removing his jacket as he said it. "Does it?"

"Don't play the innocent. You do it deliberately, don't you?"

"Certainly not—Devlin, what *are* you doing?"

The white lawn shirt came off and was dropped to the floor. "What does it look like?"

She took a step back, though her eyes were caressing every inch of skin he was baring for her. "It's the middle of the day!" she protested.

"So?"

"So you can't mean to—"

"Can't I? I thought you wanted the duke on the shelf."

"I did, but—but—" She ended with a shriek as she went over backwards into the straw, her damn train tripping her up when she'd taken another step back.

"Falling at my feet again?" Devlin grinned. "I like that."

Megan shrieked and tried to get up, but he was there, on top of her, before she could. Then she was rolling about, making every effort to stop his fingers from stripping her own clothes off, along with the rest of his. Finally she was laughing, having failed utterly, and no longer able to contain her delight in getting the old Devlin back.

"We made love in my stable," she said, tantalizingly streaking her nails down his back and buttocks to feel his body arch into hers. "I guess it's only fair we try it in yours."

"Fair has nothing to do with it," he replied, his voice rough in his passion.

She sighed. "I love it when you put the duke on the shelf."

"What else do you love?"

"You," she gasped as his mouth fastened on her nipple and tugged gently. "Do you think you might ever love me back?"

His head rose to give her a dazzling smile. "What makes you think I don't?"

"Do you?"

"I'm thinking about it."

"I hate you!"

"No, you don't. You love me."

"And?"

"I'm still thinking about it."

She grinned, then chuckled. "You're a wretched tease, Devlin St. James. Are you going to make me say it for you?"

"No." He dipped down to graze her lips once, twice, then gave her a soul-stirring kiss before adding, "Knowing you, you'd say it all wrong."

"I'd simply say, I love you."

"But *I'd* say, I love you—brat."

Three weeks later they accompanied Megan's father home, because Devlin claimed to have business in the area, *and* claimed he wasn't about to be parted from Megan for more than a few days, so she had to come along. But he timed it so they arrived on Sunday morning, and when she realized his ducal coach was stopping in front of her parish church, Megan started to cry.

"This wasn't necessary," she said, throwing her arms around her husband's neck and squeezing tight.

"I know."

"You've already given me too much."

"Nothing can compare with what you've given me—your love. And I'm going to spoil you every bit as much as your father ever did. More, I don't doubt."

She leaned back to give him a watery smile that released both dimples and had the same effect on him that her smiles always did. "Can I spoil you as well?"

Devlin groaned. "You already do. Now let's go set your Lady O on her ear."

Someone had told him the tale, obviously. Megan looked out the window to see the stout figure of Ophelia Thackeray and all three of her daughters—and Frederick Richardson—*and* Tiffany and Tyler. Devlin had planned this well—for her.

"I can't do it. It's mean and spiteful, petty—*brattish*." She glanced back at Devlin. "I can see you went to a lot of trouble, but it just doesn't matter anymore. You're all that matters, Dev."

He put his hand to her cheek. "It was Tiffany's idea, my dear, a belated wedding gift."

"Oh." She grinned brilliantly at that point. "In that case, it'd be churlish of me not to do it, wouldn't it?"

The Duke of Wrothston burst out laughing. "Absolutely, brat."